Made in

Love, friendship, experiments with drugs, but above all India and Buddhism.

A novel by Emanuela Cooper

Published by Emanuela Cooper

First published in Italy as ebook 2013 by Emanuela Cooper
Original title: Made in Nirvana
Translation from Italian by Emanuela and Robyn Cooper
ISBN 978-1505489835
Copyright © Emanuela Cooper

All rights reserved

Cover: Many thanks to spacetelescope.org. for the cover picture. Credits: NASA, ESA, and S. Beckwith (STScI) and the HUDF Team. The image has been cropped and slightly stretched (and text added) by Richard Cooper.

Cover design and preparation for Publishing by Richard Cooper.

I dedicate this book to

Richard, to our daughter Robyn and to President Daisaku Ikeda.
In memory of my mother Mercedes Dal Fiore and of my dearest friend
Elide Chinellato, for all their support and encouragement!

Thank you!

To Tanya Myers, Stephen Lowe, David Gammons and Trudie Czuj, who encouraged me from day one. To Richard, my husband, who helped me find the time to write; to Robyn, my amazing daughter for her editing, ideas and clarity; to Austin Hardiman, Kate Young, Neo Oliver Watts, Tanzie Oliver and Jenny Oliver, Richard Lawson, Chrys Gardener and Cathy Pencak for their editing and encouragement; to Ariane Köhler, Alan McIntyre and Derek Andrews for their help and suggestions, to Dolly Kanwal for her advice and knowledge of India, to Salvador Gonzales Fajardo and Rosa Viñes Andres for their encouragement and inspiration. I also want to thank my Italian friends and family for their help with the Italian version: Grazie! to Laura Boato, Luca Giabardo, Santina Russo, Marilena Taboga, Roberta e Raffaele Tramma, Pasquale Giovannini, Elide Chinellato, Claudio Fabris and Silvano Calzavara, and all those friends who supported me along the way.

Little streams come together to form the great ocean, and tiny particles of dust accumulate to form Mount Sumeru. When I, Nichiren, first took faith in the Lotus Sutra, I was like a single drop of water or a single particle of dust in all the country of Japan. But later, when two people, three people, ten people, and eventually a hundred, a thousand, ten thousand, and a million people come to recite the Lotus Sutra and transmit it to others, then they will form a Mount Sumeru of perfect enlightenment, an ocean of great nirvana.

From: The Selection of the Time
(The Writings of Nichiren Daishonin, pages 579-80)
Written to Yui in 1275

Contents

PROLOGUE	1
1. Shanti, Madam, shanti	14
2. A red mark on the forehead	33
3. How many worlds are there?	44
4. Something 'incongruous'	65
5. Cheloh, cheloh! Here we go!	77
6. A moment of magic	90
7. Always carry your torch	103
8. The secret of happiness	116
9. The Valley of the Gods	134
10. Signed, Gautama Buddha	148
11. Are you God?	162
12. The expert touch of a massage	179
13. You are the Treasure Tower	193
14. We all die sooner or later	207
15. Opium	219
16. The Frenchman	236
17. The present is a gift	251
18. The temple of your life	265
19. The Princess of the stream	280
20. Allons enfants de la patrie	295
21. The weight of freedom	310
22. Turning poison into medicine	323
23. The impossible becomes possible	333
24. The list of gratitude	348
25. Back to the homeland	362
26. It starts again from now	378

27. Thank you Van Gogh	394
28. Believe in yourself	408
29. The stars and us	421
30. I wanted you to be happy	436
31. Life is beautiful!	451
32. Surprises	468
33. Together	480
About the Author	485

Emanuela Cooper

Made in Nirvana

PROLOGUE

Maria and... knit, purl, knit, purl, knit, purl.

It was a cold and wet evening in mid-November and her mother's birthday. Perhaps the baby had decided to come into the world that day to cheer her up? Gemma, her mother, had lost both her parents the year before, within just five days of each other. Her mother-in-law had not allowed her to go and assist them during their illness or their final days; she had *this* family to serve now. Gemma became ill with grief and lost the will to live. Had it not been for her two little girls she would have let herself go. While she was still in mourning, she discovered she was pregnant for the third time.

Being born was difficult. The baby was being pushed along the dark narrow canal when the pressure suddenly stopped, leaving her locked in a claustrophobic vice. Sitting upright in her chair, grandmother guarded the kitchen door, primly focused on her knitting. Knit, purl, knit, purl, knit, purl. At the same time, she kept a stern eye on the two little girls pretending to play in the corner, while they stretched their ears to catch the sounds oozing from the kitchen. Suddenly, the worrying muffled cries stopped and everything went quiet... too quiet. The children fell silent when auntie threw the door open.
"Call the midwife, mother!" she cried, flustered, her dark hair stuck to the sweaty skin of her sallow face. "She's fainted. She's not pushing any more. The baby's stuck!"

Through the doorway, the girls caught a glimpse of their mother. Lying on the mattress next to the burning stove her face was bathed in the red light of the fire, while the dancing shadows around her faded into thick darkness. She seemed to be asleep, her head turned to one side, a huge belly.

Grandmother's expression changed only slightly. She pursed her lips while the knitting needles moved faster and faster. Knit purl, knit purl, knit purl. She was an experienced knitter and didn't need to look at her work, but her eyes were fixed on the black wool wrapped tightly around her finger. Knit purl, knit purl, knit purl.

"Midwives cost a lot of money," she said dryly, "and *that one* is giving birth for the third time!"

Dressed as always in black, she wrapped her arms under her huge bosom, pushed it right up and let it settle heavily, engulfing her forearms. It was a clear sign that there was no use arguing. "Get a move on! Both of you!" she added, without taking her eyes off the black wool. Knit purl, knit purl, knit purl.

Fancy that, a midwife now! As if she, in her days, could have asked for a midwife. At least Gemma had a husband, her one and only son. Unlike her! Her husband had left her, and not for another woman, but for women in general. He liked them all, younger, older, rich, poor, educated, uneducated, clean, dirty, filthy! How could she compete with them? She was left alone with two children to raise and so much anger inside it hurt her heart. Her tight bun of thinning grey hair gave her a neat appearance, but her waxy complexion revealed that she never went outside. It wasn't that she didn't like the sun or the fresh air, quite the opposite, but she was too fat to walk; when she tried, after a few steps she couldn't get her breath. Moreover, she had no time, if she was to keep a firm and constant eye on her young daughter-in-law, lest history repeat itself! Her son was a lot like his father and it was up to his wife to ensure he wouldn't go astray. Who else, otherwise? Knit, purl, knit, purl, knit, purl. She knew they copulated every night, whether the young woman liked it or not. Regular pauses outside the door and glimpses through the keyhole confirmed that. She was jealous of their intimacy, but it was essential to keep him satisfied, and well fed. Men were so base, just like animals!

Auntie ran back into the kitchen, absent-mindedly pushing the door behind her. It remained ajar, but she was too worried to notice. "Gemma, Gemma," she shouted. "Wake up! Come back! You can't stop now, or the baby will die. You have to push!" She slapped her on both cheeks.

Gemma opened her eyes. "I'm so tired..." she whispered, her eyes unfocused, narrowly open for a second or two. She lowered her heavy eyelids once more as she slowly turned her head on the pillow.

"You can't do that!" cried auntie. "You have to push the baby out!" She ran her trembling fingers through her hair, again and again. With the back of her hand she wiped the sweat from her forehead and from her upper lip. "If you won't push, then I'll do it!" she said, desperate but determined.

With shaking hands, she rolled her sleeves up, lifted her skirt over her thighs and straddled her sister-in-law's swollen belly. She pinned her knees firmly on the bed and, with her feet either side of Gemma's head, she sat unceremoniously on her stomach. She began to push her whole body down and forward, following the instinct that drove her. "Come on, Gemma, if you want my ass out of your face, you better start pushing. Push hard!" she panted. She pressed firmly with her hands, down and forward, just above the belly, while with her muscular legs she clutched Gemma's sides. "Go for it girl, I know you can do it!" she encouraged her, unnerved by her own fear. "Push, push, come on! Yes, like this! Don't stop, come on, come on, and push! Let's get this baby out!"

Suddenly, like a wave, a surge of love for her little baby rushed over her. She wanted her baby to be born, safe and sound; she knew she could do it. Gemma began to push, trying to match the rhythm of her sister-in-law's riding. She pushed and pushed and pushed...

The baby felt the pressure squeezing and prodding her forward. This time the force was overwhelming. Her long wait in the dark, suffocating tunnel was ending and she found herself thrust forward, desperately gasping for air. Her auntie's hands, wet with her mother's warm blood, were ready to catch her and pulled her out completely.

She felt a pain in her chest when she drew her first breath and then the world toppled over. Grabbed by her ankles she was held upside down and slapped repeatedly. Finally she started to scream. She screamed and screamed and screamed, for fear of falling into the endless void, for the shock of her fearful dark journey, for the pain of being rejected by her mother's body.

"It's a girl, Gemma," said auntie, greatly relieved, looking at the baby. "Another girl."

"Can I hold her?" whispered mother, holding her arms out to her. "Thank you!" she said, shifting her grateful gaze from her sister-in-law's large brown eyes to the little tearful face. She kissed her wet cheeks. "I love you, even if you are a girl, my little Maria," she whispered lovingly, her eyes filled with tears.

Grandmother pushed the door open: "So, you've done it! See that I was right? You and your midwife!" She spat those words out, glancing briefly at the little screaming bundle, covered in blood. "And you've made another girl... as if two were not enough."

"It's not my fault," Gemma said weakly, clutching the baby to her chest.

"Do we have a new baby sister, mum?" The two little girls approached, full of curiosity. "Can we go and tell dad?"

"He'll be home soon," grandmother replied firmly. "There is no point in spoiling his English class. Had it been a boy..."

"Can we wait for him outside then?" begged the girls.

"Yes, you do that," auntie said, "while we tidy up the kitchen. But put your coats on; it's cold outside!"

They ran outside with neither coat nor hat and started to walk quickly toward the night school.

"Do you like the new baby?" the younger of the two enquired.

"No, I don't!"

"Why not?"

"Because she should have been a boy."

"But we're girls, too!"

"That's why, there are too many girls."

The younger one started to skip.

"Stop skipping," said the older, slapping her on the head.

"Why can't I skip?" asked the little one, keeping a safe distance. "Why can't I?"

"Because I say so!"

Their father appeared on his bicycle, pedalling down the road. They ran to meet him, racing to be the first one to break the news.

"Dad, mum had a baby girl!" panted the six year old, her braids stiff in the damp evening.

"She's screaming really loud," shouted the four year old, her ponytail swinging.

"A baby girl!" said the father. "Another girl!"

He slowed his pedalling as he reached his two daughters.

"Can I ride on your bike, daddy?"

"*I* want to. Can I ride with you, dad?"

"I asked first!"

"I don't care. I'm the oldest!"

He didn't answer. They skipped alongside his bicycle, but he was riding too fast. They began to run to keep up with him, but even so they were left far behind, blowing out warm breath into the cold November night, competing with each other to exhale the biggest clouds.

They saw him approach the house in his usual style, flinging his right leg over the bicycle bar and crossing it behind his left foot on the pedal. He covered the last few yards to their house, gliding elegantly toward it, like an ice skater on the ice rink.

Paul and the football match

When he was born it was cold too, but the end of winter was nearing and in the forest near the Major Oak the first timid buds were beginning to bloom. His mother was preparing the dough for a blackberry pie when the contractions started.

"I think we're near, love," she said to her husband, holding her bump with both hands. "It's starting, I'm pretty sure!"

"But it's Saturday, Jane!" Bill said with dismay. "The football match begins in less than... what... two hours?" His father looked worriedly at his wrist watch. "I've never missed a game! Are you sure it's started? Can it not wait till tonight?"

"It could be a false alarm, dear. The same happened with our Catherine," she conceded, rubbing her lower belly. "Why don't you get the midwife? Then you can go to the match. We'll be fine and I'm sure you'll be back in time."

And so his father set off in his shiny black car and came back with the midwife. She was a German woman who had lived in the Sherwood area for so many years she had lost count, but had maintained her strong native accent.

"Take my suitcase upstairs!" she ordered Bill. "Let's see how farrr ve are!"

When she saw Jane busying herself in the bedroom the midwife lost what little patience she had.

"You're not rrready yet, voman! Vhy did you call me so soon?" Before listening to the answer, she ordered: "Take the suitcase back down. It's too soon. You'll have to take me back home and I'll have to come back laterrr!" But, while Bill went obediently down the stairs with her suitcase, just to be on the safe side, she glanced at Jane's 'exit'. Without a word, she ran to the window, thrust it open and leaned out. Waving her arms she yelled at Bill who was already in the courtyard: "Come back on! Brrring the suitcase. It's not too soon. Baby's coming now!"

The baby was born quickly and in a way that was convenient for everyone; so quickly that his handsome father arrived at the game just in time to see it start.

Jane was holding the little bundle in her arms when Catherine appeared in the doorway. She stared at the picture on the bed, her mum with another baby; her big green eyes wide, full of muted concern.

"Come and see your little brother, Catherine." Jane held her hand out to her, but the little girl didn't move. She kept staring in silence.

"Go and see your new brrrother," ordered the midwife. Seeing that the child didn't move of her own accord, she took her by the hand and led her to the bed.

"You can touch him if you like," Jane said, looking at her with love.

Catherine couldn't tear her eyes from the baby's tiny red fingers. She stroked them shyly with her finger and gasped in surprise when the baby's hand tightened around it. Her eyes bright, she questioned her mother: "He's got hold of my finger and is squeezing it," she said, startled and amused.

"That's because he loves you already," Jane said, stroking her hair. "Come and sit on the bed."

"It is not hygienic!" scolded the midwife, whose name was Frida.

"Don't worry, Frida, we'll be careful. You have done an excellent job, thank you!"

Frida frowned, but she knew that her job was over and when to remain silent.

"What do you think we should call him?" Jane asked the little girl. Catherine stared at the baby, curious, confused, and didn't answer.

"Shall we call him Ernest?" the mother asked. The little girl shook her head, meaning no.

"Don't you like the name Ernest?" She shook her head again. "Do you like Paul? Shall we call him Paul?" The child studied her little brother for a long while and then she nodded.

"Can I give him a kiss?" she asked at last.

"Of course you can give him a kiss. He is your brother and when he grows up he will look after you."

She leaned against her mother and kissed the baby gently on the cheek. He opened his small toothless mouth and yawned. Mother and daughter laughed together, excited.

"He is funny," said Catherine smiling, settling more comfortably on the bed next to her mother. She offered her index finger to her brother's little hand and smiled happily when he squeezed it tight.

A few years later: Maria

She played alone with dolls while her sisters were at school; her favourite doll was black with short, curly hair. While her mother did the house work, she dressed and undressed them, changing their clothes a hundred times a day. Curious to know how they were made, tugging their arms and legs, she tried to look inside; the temptation to pull was irresistible, even though she knew the dolls were hollow. Sometimes the elastic band that held them together snapped, and arms and legs would fall off, defeated. At last she could put her finger through the holes and feel the smooth plastic.

"Oh, your sisters will be very upset when they come home from school and find the dolls broken!" Gemma would warn.

With a new elastic band she reattached arms and legs to bodies, a difficult skill she had refined, but they were never quite as taut as before. As a result all the dolls in the house had loose, dangling limbs and, when made to sit up, would fall forward in protest. Angry with her, whenever mother was not around, her sisters took the opportunity to get their own back and slapped her. But curiosity would always win and the day after Maria would pull the springy band again.

Grandmother sat in the kitchen all day, always on the same chair, knitting in stony silence. Knit, purl, knit, purl, knit, purl. From her chair she controlled everything, taking special care that mother didn't leave the house, except to buy fresh bread. She would scold her if she moved the curtain to look out. What was there to look at? Men?

"What are you making grandma? Is it for me?" asked Maria. She liked her grandmother, with her large comforting body, and would often sit on the chair next to hers, gazing at her knitting.

"No, it's not for you. This cardigan is for your older sister."
"And when you've finished that one, will you make one for me?"
"You'll have to wait. First I have to make one for your other sister."
"How long will that take you?"
"Two weeks, three if I'm not well. You'll have to wait."
"Will you make it pink?"
"We'll see!"

So she waited. They always reminded her that she was the third female, she knew she wasn't important. They told her she counted for next to nothing, that she was the runt of the litter! The three weeks would pass and grandmother would make her a sweater; Maria trusted her.

Her mother made all their clothes. She laid the fabric flat on the dining table and marked it with white tailor's chalk, which was smooth and didn't soil her hands; she cut the fabric with large scissors and tacked the parts with pins.

"Would you help me, Maria?" she'd ask the little girl sat watching her across the table. "If you thread the needles I can work much faster."

Maria was very good at threading needles and quicker than Gemma was at tacking. She licked her finger, made a knot and then smoothed the thread on the yellow tabletop, watching, waiting.

Gemma fell pregnant again when Maria was four. In the spring she had a big belly and the evenings were warm. After dinner the whole family sat in the garden overlooking the road and drank beer, because it encouraged the milk flow. It was true that they were not all going to breast-feed but they joined in the beer drinking nonetheless, children included. Maria hated the bitter taste but, since for once she was treated as an equal, she drank it too. After the beer they laughed and jumped on the beds, especially the evening when Gemma went into labour. As if he knew that this time it was going to be a boy, father took her to a clinic. Maria's brother was born ten minutes after they arrived; indeed, he was nearly dropped down the loo when Gemma went for a pee. Fortunately, she managed to hold onto him while she ran to the nearest bed. It would have been quite an undignified start for the heir of the Dal Fiore name! Within minutes he had come into this world and the next morning all were back home.

One day, an ambulance came and took grandmother away. Maria was on her way to the hospital with her aunt to visit her when they met father coming back on his bicycle. He paused, one foot on the ground and one on the pedal. Watching his sister, he shook his head. "Her heart..." he said. Maria and her auntie went back home.

She missed the presence of her grandmother, sitting on that chair knitting, but they hardly ever talked about her.

A month later father made them all go down into the courtyard and proudly showed them a large red car with a black roof, a second-hand FIAT that was as good as new. He had learned to drive in secret and passed his driving test, but for years to come they would wonder whether this was really true as he didn't drive very well. He was irritable and pushed in front of other cars as if to prove his superiority to all other drivers. Mother, sitting beside him, was always full of fear. She'd put her hand over her mouth and say: "Go slowly, Piero. Don't overtake now, there's a truck coming!" or: "The bend is tight. Why don't you slow down a little?"

But this irritated her father even more and, when he designed to answer, he would say: "If you don't like it Gemma, you can get out and walk!"

Sitting on the backseat with her sisters and brother, this sentence always made her laugh. Indeed, sometimes it would be the children themselves who'd say it, laughing out loud: "If you don't like it, Gemma, get out and walk!"

Most of the time mother kept her eyes squeezed shut in terror. When they arrived, father would say: "You had a nice nap, huh, Gemma! We're already here and you didn't even notice!"

A few years later: Paul

The older he grew the more he resembled his sister, with blond ringlets and big green eyes. They played together in the large garden where his mother grew beautiful flowers of all sizes, shapes and colours. There were flowers in spring, in summer and even in the autumn. He liked to look for 'creatures' in the ground, but Catherine ran away screaming whenever he tried to show her the worms he had found. Fortunately, their cousins often came to play, two girls and one boy of the same age as Paul. They dug the ground together, finding worms and all kinds of insects.

Jane grew vegetables in the garden, she baked bread and cakes in the oven, filling the house with wonderful aromas, and she also made wine. In autumn she sent the children to pick blackberries, handing them a big iron bucket. They returned home only when the bucket was completely full, so heavy they had to carry it between them. Jane was always very happy when she saw they had succeeded and with those blackberries she made wine and tarts. She told them they had done a good job and they would always find a slice of cake and a glass of milk on the table waiting for them, on a little plate with a napkin next to it.

His father was almost always in bed in the upstairs room overlooking the garden. Paul brought him the newspaper and Bill's face lit up with a smile. He took the paper with his lean, elegant hands. Despite the pallor and the illness Bill was very handsome and his eyes were full of kindness.

"Sit down here with me and I'll read you the news," he used to say, making room for Paul next to him, "unless you'd rather I told you a story!"

"Can you tell me the story of the little Buddha?" asked the young boy, hopefully.

"Again? But I've already told you that story many times. Are not you tired of it?"

But Paul was never tired of hearing it and his father always added new details. He sat cross-legged on the bed, next to Bill, ready to listen.

"I'll tell you the story of when he came face to face with a tiger. You like that one, right?"

Paul loved that story and nodded enthusiastically.

Bill began: "One day Siddhartha, that was the Buddha's name, went tiger hunting with his father, king Suddhoddana. It was the first time he was allowed to go hunting tigers because until the age of eleven children could not take part; it was too dangerous. But as Siddhartha had just turned eleven, after the huge party in his honour, with tables laden with sweets and fruit, his father decided that he was old enough and took him along with the men."

Paul was listening intently. "Was he not afraid?" he asked.

"Who, Siddhartha?" Bill looked at his son. The child nodded. "Oh no, Siddhartha was brave. Like many good people, he had a lot of courage! Shall I carry on?"

Paul nodded, smiling happily.

"They were riding the king's elephant; Siddhartha sat on his big soft neck, with the king seated behind him. Without realizing it, they were separated from the rest of the hunting party and suddenly the elephant stopped. He had heard a worrying noise from the bamboo grove and instinctively knew there was danger. The elephant bent his front legs, preparing to attack with his tusks any animal that threatened him!"

Paul lifted his face to look at his father, his eyes wide open, knowing what was going to happen. Bill winked at him, put his arm around him and continued: "Both Siddhartha and his father were holding on precariously to the elephant's neck and, when he made a sudden jerky movement, they were thrown to the ground. Suddenly, a huge tiger appeared from the bamboo thicket. The king put his hand on his son's shoulder and Siddhartha felt that his father was shaking. Without a second thought, he stood before the king to shield him."

The story never lost its charm and Paul was holding his breath. Bill patted him on his knee and continued: "Only king Suddhoddana had a sword, because Siddhartha was too young to be allowed a weapon. Nevertheless, the boy was not afraid. He was face to face with the tiger; she had thick and shiny hair... She was beautiful! He looked into her eyes; they were yellow, large, and full of fear. The tiger was staring at him, motionless. For a long moment they studied each other intently. 'Don't be afraid, I won't hurt you,' he wanted to say, but because words would not work, he tried to tell her with his eyes and with his whole being. He was sure she understood. The concern in the tiger's eyes slowly vanished and turned into curiosity. Siddhartha saw a kind of interest, perhaps even complicity."

Paul was leaning forward absorbed in the story and his father continued slowly: "So, to reassure her, he screwed his eyes to tell her that he respected and understood her. In response, the tiger imperceptibly lowered an eyelid. They had become friends and were able to communicate. The jungle was silent, as if all the animals were holding their breath. Siddhartha took a step toward the tiger; she didn't move. Slowly, he raised his hand, palm up, to tell her she could relax. The tiger bowed her head slightly, with a grunt she turned around and walked away slowly, swaying her hips, disappearing back into the bamboo grove."

Paul let out a long sigh of relief. His father concluded the story: "The king was very proud of his son. 'You beat the tiger,' he said. But Siddhartha had just spoken to her with his thoughts, sensing her fear. For her part, the tiger had felt his compassion, this thing so special within this child. She had trusted and understood him."

Paul smiled, trembling inside with emotion, as if he had heard the story for the first time: "Siddhartha was braver and stronger than the king, wasn't he dad?"

"Yes, much stronger. He was strong inside. He had a lot of compassion and this was his strength."

The little boy snuggled closer to his father, who held him tight to his side; he looked up at him and Bill kissed his fair head. They were silent in the warm bed together, for a long while.

When his father went to hospital, Jane went to visit him every day, while they went to play at their cousins'. One day Jane arrived at auntie's house with red and swollen eyes. She kept blowing her nose into a men's handkerchief, one of Bill's large white ones with blue piping. Once back home, she prepared three cups of hot milk and they sat around the kitchen table, sipping it in silence.

"Daddy is gone," she said to her children, "but I am here and will never leave you, so you mustn't be afraid."

"Where has dad gone?" asked Catherine, feeling the panic grip her heart.

"He has gone where there is no suffering," said Jane, looking at the children from one to the other. "But he will always love you. You must never forget it!"

"Has he gone to Nirvana?" Paul asked.

His mother looked at him with surprise and smiled sweetly. "It's not a place, my love, it's a state of peace and tranquillity... but yes, now daddy is in Nirvana," she said, stroking his head.

"Dad said it was a state!" he said confidently.

"Yes dear," replied his mother, with a sad smile.

Paul knew many things about Nirvana. Bill had told him that it was a state in which there was no suffering, rather it was just fine! Just like his mother said, there was peace and tranquillity and no fear. Paul thought it was probably a state where tigers were not afraid of people and children could play with them, maybe even ride them. And, probably, in Nirvana children had some good naps with their dads in warm, comfortable beds, and dads didn't have to leave, ever.

They started to go to auntie's every afternoon while Jane was at work. Auntie had another baby and let Paul hold her in his arms. The baby-girl had big blue eyes, she smiled at him and this made him happy. Every evening Jane came to pick them up and went home. She had bought chicks that grew and became chickens. Every morning Paul went looking for eggs and sometimes he found some that were still warm. Even though they were a bit dirty he brought them home wrapped in his sweater. Jane had also bought some rabbits that were kept in a box with a net in front. The children tore handfuls of grass and handed them to the animals through the net. The rabbits were delightful. They took the grass with their front paws and chewed it quickly with great enthusiasm, making them laugh with satisfaction. After a while, since none of them could or wanted to kill them or eat them, they let them free in the garden, where they multiplied and hopped happily, but one day they ate all the flowers and Jane gave them away.

TWENTY YEARS LATER - 22 June 1978

1. Shanti, Madam, shanti

When the Thai Airways flight landed in New Delhi at three o'clock in the morning, Maria and Franca were the first to the door, ready to get off, tired, but excited. They were anticipating their farewell greeting for the hostesses in silk saris: a slight bow with palms pressed together. They had planned it during the flight, seeing them perform this graceful movement every two minutes. As the plane door opened they were hit by a gust of hot moist air that took their breath away. Surprised by the sweltering heat Maria forgot her grand gesture, greeted the hostesses with a concerned nod of the head and descended the first few steps, holding on to the boiling hot handrail. From behind she heard Franca say: "I'm going back home on the next plane!"

She laughed, despite it being a choice between laughing and breathing, and wiped the dripping sweat from her forehead with the back of her arm. She closed her lips and started to inhale, sucking air through her teeth. If Indian people survived it meant that, in theory there was enough oxygen. She had taken a few steps, sinking on soft tar that appeared to be at the point of melting, when her problems, the ones she had brought from Italy, seemed much smaller than when she had boarded the plane.

"Try to breathe slowly through your teeth," she said, turning slightly toward Franca who was walking behind her. She laughed again, seeing her companion's eyes wide open. "This way, a bit of air comes in!"

Franca nodded, without a word. As soon as they walked through the airport doors the temperature changed dramatically thanks to the air conditioning and Maria turned around to wait for her friend: "It works, doesn't it? Breathing through your teeth."

"I knew this technique, actually, I just hadn't remembered to use it," she said, matter-of-factly.

At the luggage belt, Maria recognized a group of young Italian men who had travelled on the same plane, waiting for their bags. They seemed at ease, laughing and joking, which made her think this wasn't their first time in India. Leaning toward Franca, she said softly: "Look at those four.

They seem completely at home! Shouldn't we tag along to find a hotel somewhere?"

Franca grimaced; she was fiercely independent but, taking advantage of a brief moment of hesitation she saw in her face, Maria approached one of the boys and asked him if they knew of a hotel or a guesthouse for the night.

"We always go to the same place," replied the boy, surprised by the sudden approach.

"Can we come too?" asked Maria. "It's our first time in India and we don't know where to go." She saw Franca looking the other way, pretending not to know her, but she ignored it. "Maybe we can find a room there, too."

"Sure! Why not?" said the boy in a friendly manner.

Once they recovered their backpacks, they followed the four Italians. As soon as they were through the revolving doors the stifling heat hit them again. They walked to the taxi rank, where sturdy black cars with yellow roofs were waiting in line, the guys in front, Maria following closely behind and Franca keeping slightly further back. Maria observed with interest while they haggled on the rate, in their elementary English enriched by a strong Italian accent. The taxi driver held his own well, explaining that the price of petrol had increased and he had a family to support. The Indian accent turned out to be quite funny and, at the same time, easy to understand. After a long discussion they agreed on the price, the four young men put their bags in the trunk and got into the taxi.

"What about us?" asked Maria. "Where do we sit, on the roof?"

The taxi driver took the backpack from her hands and threw it on the roof rack, proceeding to do the same with Franca's. Worried about the precarious position of their luggage, Maria explained, in her rusty English, that he had to secure it, otherwise it could fall off. As he refused to listen, waving his hand to tell her not to worry, she felt compelled to insist, and followed him closely as he walked toward the driver's door. When she got hold of his arm, the man finally stopped; looking calmly at her, he said with a smile: "Shanti, Madam! Shanti!" and motioned for her to take a seat in the car.

She threw a worried look at Franca who, on the opposite side of the car, shrugged her shoulders. "Bah, everything will be fine! Shanti, Maria, shanti!" she teased, imitating the driver's accent.

Resigned, Maria looked at the three boys sitting on the back seat. "And where should I sit?" she asked.

"Here!" said the nearest one, slapping his thighs. She glanced at Franca, who was sat in the front seat, squeezed in with an Italian and their Indian chauffeur, tight and cosy.

"Oh, all right! Shanti, then," she said, trying to find a comfortable position on the boy's knees. "But now can someone tell me what it means?"

"Peace"

"Calm down!"

"Relax!"

And so she had learned her first expression in Hindi: 'Calm down Maria!'

She was very uncomfortable, her back was crooked and her head squashed against the roof. Hot and sticky air blew through the open window, lifting her hair and cooling the sweat that dripped down her neck. As the smell of fuel from the airport faded away, different odours wafted in, all new and none of them pleasant, a strange mix of rancid and sweet, intense and nauseating. She covered her nose and mouth with her hand, trying to breathe as little as possible. Lamp posts lit the road at regular intervals revealing hundreds of beds, all more or less in a row and, although it was night time, none of the occupants seemed to be asleep; most of them were chatting, many were smoking. Women in saris squatted on the ground, pumping smelly kerosene stoves on which they prepared food or tea. Maria guessed people took their beds outdoors because it was too hot in the house. It didn't cross her mind that for those people, the road was their home.

The taxi turned down a dark street and continued its speeding ride in the pitch black. Just when the pain in her back was becoming unbearable, the taxi driver began to slow down. With a flick of his thumb a cigarette butt flew out the window, and the black car stopped just outside a house.

The figure of a young man appeared through the large, illuminated window of the door. He was wearing white pyjama trousers and a long white shirt that came down to his knees, and seemed to be waiting for them. He smiled when he saw the first Italian boy get out the taxi, recognizing him immediately. He bowed with hands clasped in front of his chest as, one by one, they all descended from the cab.

The driver handed the backpacks to their respective owners and gave a particularly big smile to Maria as he gave her hers: "Here is your backpack, Madam," he said, tilting his head to one side, as if to say 'You see it's all in order? I told you.'

"That's good! Thank you!" she said with relief. Contained within was everything she needed for those three months, including irreplaceable medicine for any ailment from malaria to the most deadly diarrhoea. Shanti shanti! Easier said than done! She was definitely happier now that she had been reunited with her belongings. They walked in single file into the reception, taxi driver included.

An elderly man, dressed exactly like the younger one, greeted the newcomers as they came through the door, bowing with his palms pressed. The young Italians bowed in the same way, as did Franca. Maria felt embarrassingly self-conscious, she didn't find it natural to bow; besides, until she knew whether they had a room for the night she couldn't relax. She approached the older man, grabbed his rough, gnarled hand and shook it warmly. The old man looked at her in amazement. Everybody burst into loud laughter and eventually the old man laughed too, showing two upper teeth, three below and a completely red mouth inside! Blushing, Maria justified herself: "In Italy we introduce ourselves this way!" and then she laughed too, feeling even more stupid than if she had bowed. She peered at the old man's red mouth and noticed that the young man's mouth was just as red. What were they chewing... blood?

"They're chewing a leaf called 'betel'," the Italian boy who had hosted her on his knees explained earnestly, seeing her stunned expression.

"How weird! Are you sure it's not blood?" she asked.

"I'm sure," he replied, laughing. "It's a leaf that keeps them awake. It's a stimulant, a bit like coffee!"

"Thank God for that!"

She noticed that, once again, Franca pretended not to know her. The hotel had a room for them, but it cost more than expected. Delhi was expensive, said the boys, this place was one of the cheapest. The driver pocketed his commission for having brought them over and drove off. The younger of the two men, steadily sucking his 'betel', took a large bunch of keys and led the six Italians, with their luggage, up the stairs.

He stopped on the first floor landing and opened a door, the room for Maria and Franca. "Your room with bathroom," he said primly. He handed the key to Franca and continued up the stairs with the boys. How wonderful, a bedroom with a bathroom. At last! Maria sighed. She pressed the switch and a bare bulb gave out a white and trembling light, feebly illuminating the room with two beds... and nothing else. She rested her big red backpack, camera case, straw bag and duty-free carrier bag on the floor. What a relief to finally stop after such a long journey! More than twenty four hours had passed since she had left home. Franca went to the bathroom and turned on a dim light.

"Come and have a look!" she exclaimed.

The spartan version of a toilet: a hole in the floor accompanied a low tap, eight inches from the ground, with a red plastic jug close by, and a shower that hung from the ceiling, to make up the 'bathroom'. The walls and floor were bare grey concrete.

"Is this supposed to be the bathroom? It's dirty! Quite disgusting! I don't know if I want to wash myself in here," Maria said with dismay, "and no toilet paper!"

Franca laughed: "We are in India, Maria. You better to get used to it."

In the 'bedroom' the moths, who had been rudely awoken, started to fly around, slamming blindly against the bulb, while mosquitoes began to buzz in concentric circles, getting closer to the girls' heads, exploring the new odour. The room was permeated by the smell of an old, damp place that hadn't been aired for too long. There was a ceiling fan; Franca pressed a switch and got it started. Unfortunately, it barely moved and the warm moisture became more and more oppressive. Maria opened the window hoping to get a little air in, but despite being the coolest hours of the night, outside it was just as hot and humid. A dog began to bark and another answered from afar. Soon more dogs joined in the chorus, barking, yapping and howling from all directions. The combination of these unpleasant noises tore through the dark night and disturbed her mind, already on the verge of exhaustion. The mattresses were hard, dirty and had bumps everywhere, there were no sheets or even a pillow.

"How many stars does this hotel have?" Maria joked.

"None," laughed her friend. "In fact, minus one, and it's not even cheap!"

The mosquitoes seemed to prefer Franca and buzzed around her insistently. "They're eating me alive," she said irritably, following them with her eyes, trying to catch them and crush them between her hands. "We'll have to turn the light off or close the window."

"I have some mosquito coils in my backpack," said Maria.

"Great, get them out, otherwise we'll never be able to sleep. Close the window and I'll kill as many as I can." Stripped down to her underwear, she began to hunt them, threatening and hitting them with her jeans whenever she saw new ones: "You bastards, damn mosquitoes… Take that! Die! Look how fat this one is, got you! Say your last goodbyes… and another one!" Maria laughed as she emptied her backpack, the coils were buried somewhere deep within.

Meanwhile Franca was unleashing her inner assassin, with her jeans as a lethal weapon and letting a stream of thoughts flow freely: "If reincarnation really exists, you'll get another shot damn mosquito, but for now, you're done. Then, finally we may be able to get some sleep! Down and out!" With the window closed, it was unbearably hot and she was sweating profusely from all the exercise she was doing. At last Maria found the coils and lit a couple. They let out a strong smell, but it was a heartening stench, knowing they were going to decimate the mosquitoes.

There was a noise outside their room. Was that a knock at the door? The girls looked at each other. There was another sound; yes it was a knock, a little louder this time. At four-thirty in the morning?

"Who is it?" asked Maria, her ear next to the door.

"Hotel man, Madam," said a voice from the other side. "Can I speak to you? One moment only!"

"It's the hotel man, he wants to speak to us," she reported.

"What does he want?" asked Franca, irritated. The man knocked again.

"What do you want? It's four-thirty in the morning," asked Maria, speaking through the door.

"It's very important, Madam. One minute only!" insisted the voice.

"He says it's very important. Come on, put your jeans on and let's see what he wants! He's not going away by the sound of it," she said. While holding her hand on the doorknob she noticed a hole lower down, where once there had been a lock. "Look at this," she prompted Franca who, sweaty and out of sorts, was putting her jeans on. She opened the door a few inches, blocking it with her foot. The young man smiled with his red mouth, his left cheek swollen with a trusty ball of 'betel'.

"You have duty-free, Madam?" he asked, as if it were the most natural thing in the world. "You want to sell? I have money!"

Speechless, Maria turned to Franca.

"Tell him to come tomorrow morning! Is he crazy? It's the middle of the night!" her companion rebelled.

"Come back tomorrow. Not now!" Maria faithfully reported.

"Tomorrow is no good, Madam, police!" he insisted, showing her a nice big bunch of ten rupee notes. "Now is good time. Only two minutes, Madam. Look, I have money."

With her hand on the doorknob, Maria turned to Franca: "He says that tomorrow there will be police and that it only takes two minutes. He's waving hundreds of rupees under my nose. Come on Franca, let's do it now, so we get rid of those heavy bottles."

"What a pain-in-the-arse!" complained Franca, struggling to pull up her fly. Maria took her foot off the door and the man came in, looking around.

"It is very hot in here," he said. Yes, they knew it was very hot; they had sweat coming out of every pore! "You have whisky, gin, vodka?"

He sat gingerly on the bed and the bargaining began between him and Franca, who had already decided on the price, based on what 'everybody' had told her. Apparently, four hundred rupees a bottle, three times what they had paid for it, was the going price. The man wanted to pay less, she didn't budge from her price; things were dragging on. Maria suggested she accept three hundred and fifty, but Franca reproached her saying that, with her attitude 'she'd ruin the market' and to leave it to her.

They ended up agreeing on three hundred and seventy-five rupees, the man seemingly disappointed, Franca sweaty and irritated. He left, happily cuddling the two bottles of whisky in his arms. It was almost five o'clock in the morning. The girls peeled off the jeans that clung to their sweaty legs and stood in their underwear.

No sooner had Franca disappeared into the bathroom, she let out a scream.

"What's wrong?" Maria ran to join her, alarmed. A black cockroach was scuttling across the floor.

"It came out of the hole!" panted Franca, shocked and disgusted, in her underwear and untied trainers, "and I wasn't expecting it! I was going to have a pee, my legs spread, and this thing jumped out of the hole!"

Maria would have laughed if the cockroach hadn't been so ugly and she hadn't been so scared. "What do we do? Shall we kill him?" she asked, unsure.

"Who's going to catch it? Look how it runs!" Franca said with a shaky voice.

"Let's send him back into the hole, then, so we don't sully our hands with blood," suggested Maria.

"All right! Bring me a shoe," commanded her friend, without losing sight of her one-inch enemy with black and glossy armour.

Happy not to have to chase it, Maria ran to get one of her shoes and handed it to her friend.

Franca had a strategy of attack, banging her shoe on the ground, both from the right and the left, directing the speeding black beast toward the hole, always keeping at a good distance. She was a funny sight, in her underwear and trainers! Finally she succeeded and the odious insect disappeared back where it came from.

They took turns to pee, with the other keeping watch, ready to sound the alarm in case the horrible beast came out again.

Too tired to shower, they washed their hands with shampoo brought from home under the tap near the floor. Why on earth was the tap so low?

Given that it was almost daybreak, they turned the light out and opened the window to change the heavy mosquito-coil air. From outside came sounds of the night ending and the new day beginning. The noise of barking and howling dogs was now accompanied by honking of scooters and cars, by voices of people waking up and the loud clatter of road works. Maria leaned out the window to breathe a little air; far from being cool, it was nevertheless not as stifling as the air in the room.

The light of the rising dawn tinged with pink the figures sleeping below, on pieces of cardboard, in doorways and on the pavement.

She had the peculiar feeling there was something alive close by and looked up; a long, black swaying thing was dangling over her head! She stepped hurriedly back into the room: "Come and see Franca! What's that?"

Intrigued, her friend came over; she leaned out the window and looked up. She watched it for a while and then, turning to Maria, her eyes gleaming with excitement, said: "It's a monkey's tail!"

"A monkey?" Maria was tired of surprises, she just wanted to sleep. "That's the last thing we need! We can't leave the window open."

Franca closed the window, lay on her bed and put a scarf over her eyes. "Good night," she said, and promptly fell asleep.

Maria pushed her bed against the door; there were too many signs indicating the room had been broken into, and hung her jacket above the handle to block the old keyhole. She lay down on the dirty mattress at last; it was like lying on a hot radiator. She closed her eyes, too tired to think rationally, and wondered where Ugo was. Was he with another woman? She didn't care just now. What was she doing in this crazy place, anyway? Why had she decided to come to India? It had seemed a romantic adventure while they were in Venice, but now it no longer felt like such a good idea. She wiped the sweat from her forehead and fell asleep.

It was almost three in the afternoon when, with difficulty, she woke up. The heat and stuffiness of the room were unbearable while, from the outside, she could hear a cacophony of noises. Walking slowly, unsure of her balance, Maria went to the window and opened it. A gust of fiery air hit her face, flooding the room, filling it with scorching heat and blinding light, accompanied by a loud racket, a mixture of horns, banging and motors. With trembling legs, she stumbled back to her bed and threw herself on it. She was so hungry she could barely stand up and felt as though there was a hole in her stomach. Franca stirred; she moved the scarf from her forehead and opened one eye. She closed it immediately, offended by the strong light.

"Good morning! How are you?" Maria asked. "I'm bloody hot and so hungry my legs are shaking!"

"I'm sweating like a pig," said Franca from under the scarf. "I'm starving, I could eat an ox. I can't wait to go out. We're in India, Maria!" she said triumphantly, taking the blindfold off and lifting herself on one elbow. She looked at her with puffy tired eyes, but full of enthusiasm: "What time is it? Let's go and eat. Come on, get up! After breakfast we'll go to the Tourist Camp!"

"*Where* are we going? You don't expect me to repack all my things and move from here, I hope!" Maria asked, alarmed. But Franca explained that the Tourist Camp was much better, cheaper, you got to meet a lot of people and 'everybody' had told her that it was the place to stay. She was determined, and Maria didn't have the strength to argue; she resigned herself, suddenly feeling even more tired!

The shower gave only a slow trickle of warm water, but with patience she was able to wash. She finished rinsing her hair by filling the red plastic jug and pouring it over her head, far more effective! Feeling somewhat refreshed, she started to repack her things, putting jeans right at the bottom and placing t-shirts and summer skirts on top. Meanwhile Franca was chatting away, making plans in a loud voice from under the dribble of water. Maria was listening with one ear only. It was apparent that her friend had a lot of ideas already formed, unlike her; therefore it was much easier to rely on her wave of enthusiasm and programming. One of Franca's priorities was to buy and smoke some dope in a big chillum. She couldn't wait. "It's already two days since I last smoked anything and I'm ready to make up for all the lost time," she said from the bathroom. "I bet there is some amazing stuff here! We are in the land of Shiva Shankar! The country of my favourite pastime!"

They went down the steep stairs in search of breakfast, their ears ringing and their legs shaking from hunger. "I must have lost at least half a kilo since we left!" Maria mused. "I can't wait to get a cappuccino and three croissants!"

Her friend looked surprised, but didn't say anything. A stone's throw from their 'hotel' they found a place that served food. The 'restaurant', furnished with simple Formica tables and old chairs, was full of people, mainly men; everyone was talking loudly and suddenly paused to stare at them. Amid giggles and comments, they soon resumed their lunch, eating with their hands, deftly and casually stirring and turning a handful of white rice in the palm of their right hand, making it nice and round, dipping it in a little aluminium dish and shoving it in their mouths.

To Maria's dismay they had never heard of either cappuccino or croissants; they didn't even have bread, butter or jam. Franca declared that she would always eat the Indian way because it was cheap and she only had three hundred and fifty U.S. dollars; and anyway, there wasn't anything else! She ordered bhaji, samosas, chapatis and pakhora. And to drink? Chai, of course! She showed a familiarity with the Indian cuisine that surprised Maria, who instead hadn't the faintest idea. "Who told you what to eat in India? It's not as if there are Indian restaurants in Italy," she asked.

Franca explained that she had talked with friends who had returned from India, asking them about everything, every minute detail. She had been thinking about her first breakfast for weeks, she said.

The waiter, wearing a white vest and shorts, himself with a red mouth and sucking 'betel', wiped the table with a brownish cloth, which had once been white. It was hanging by a corner on his waistband and with it he cleaned everything; it was dirtier than Maria thought possible.

Eventually, he brought them two bowls filled with vegetables cooked in a red sauce: the bhaji, explained Franca pointing at them with her finger, and saucers filled with triangular samosas, fried pakhora and hot chapatis. He came back after a while with two steaming glasses of chai and left them to experience their first genuine Indian breakfast. Spicy. Very spicy! Hopeless! Franca tore pieces of chapatis, dipped them in bhaji, as she saw others do, stuffed them in her mouth and licked her fingers. Maria instead, her mouth burning, felt like crying. She had never been so hungry in her life and couldn't eat the food in front of her.

"Mmm, spicy!" Franca said, wiping her lips with the back of her hand. The bhaji was a nightmare, impossible to swallow and Maria dismissed it as 'out of question'. The samosas were just as hot, but at least she recognized potatoes inside. Despite that, she had to give up after the first bite. The pakhora was a bit better, thankfully, so she could eat it, accompanied by small bites of chapati, a flat dry bread that got stuck in her throat; and the chai was too sweet! Eventually, they paid two rupees each. Franca was dripping sweat from her forehead because of the chilli and Maria was still ravenous, but they got up, to go and collect their luggage for the move. Franca greeted the waiter with folded hands and Maria imitated her clumsily. They all did it and shaking hands was not an option, so...!

As soon as they left the 'restaurant' they were at the mercy of the sunshine; the afternoon heat was something they had never experienced before. While in Italy the sun was hot, here it was scorching. Within a few seconds brains overheated and throbbed inside skulls giving the unpleasant feeling of wanting to burst. Running, they covered the few metres that separated them from the shade of a house, where they began to walk again at a normal pace.

After preparing their backpacks they went downstairs to pay for the room. The man at reception wanted them to pay for two nights. "After midday you pay for next day, Madam," he said, as a matter of course. So, since it was past noon, they had to pay for another day.

"But we arrived at four o' clock in the morning! And now it's four in the afternoon!" objected Maria. An animated discussion began in which the two logics confronted each other. Given the ludicrous position taken by the employee, the girls claimed that, since only twelve hours had gone by, they had to pay for only half a day. It was a very original point of view, they knew, but at least they had their own ridiculous starting point to bargain with the absurdity of the man behind the counter. They started to enjoy themselves, too; it was like playing a game of ping pong, and they were two against one. The man didn't want to know, but when they began to list loudly their complaints: the hole in the door, the dirty mattresses, the lack of water from the shower, the cockroach from the hole, the mosquitoes, the moths, the monkey and its tail, and the duty-free hassle at half past four in the morning, the clerk accepted defeat. He lowered his voice and, despondently, waving his hand, said: "As you like Madam!"

Really? Wow! Victory! They paid the forty rupees for the night and departed, loaded with their luggage. Maria had her big red backpack, her camera pack with three key lenses: wide angle, telephoto and zoom, plus a straw bag, with her essential things. Franca was carrying a smaller and much more discreet backpack, of a greyish blue colour, and a shoulder bag. Maria would have liked a backpack like that, too.

Under the sun the heat was incredible. Thousands of people walked shoulder to shoulder. Among them, cars, bicycles, covered three-wheeled mopeds, rickshaws driven by thin men, bony cows, all pushed and shoved in the afternoon's hot steam. Over and within this chaos was again that all-pervading sweet and rancid stench they had noticed when they first arrived. It entered through the pores and attacked the senses, a mixture of urine, fresh flowers, animal dung, incense, spices and who knew what else... With the heat of the day it had become more intense and it was offensive, almost unbearable. Among the bulging crowd moving so closely together in the relentless rhythm of life, there reigned an atmosphere of calm endurance, of peacefully sharing the existing space, each person going about their own business, with no sense of superiority or entitlement from anyone.

The women, dressed in colourful green, red, yellow, orange saris, walked like queens, straight and elegant in their movements and posture.

Their neatly combed hair was partly covered by the end of their sari, which adorned their gentle, graceful faces. The little girls with tight and shiny pigtails were gracious and well behaved. The men all wore white pyjama trousers and long white shirts; some donned a colourful turban but most of them used brilliantine and didn't have a hair out of place. The smaller children were beautiful, their dark eyes ringed with lines of black kohl, which made them look even bigger and intense. They smiled easily and naturally, showing beautiful white teeth.

Suddenly a rickshaw braked sharply, stopping two millimetres from Franca's legs. She jumped in shock: "Are you out of your mind?" she yelled.

The man looked straight at them: "You want rickshaw, Madam?"

"No!" cried Franca. "Go away, stupid man! You almost killed me! Let's not take this one Maria, he's an idiot. You can tell from the way he drives!"

"This one or another is the same Franca, and I am melting beneath this sun!" she drooled.

The man, unperturbed by Franca's cries, said proudly: "I have the best rickshaw in Delhi!" Maria smiled amused and, while Franca calmed down, she began bargaining with the best rickshaw in Delhi. How much to go to the Tourist Camp? Why did they want to go there? He knew of a good hotel. No thanks, they wanted the Tourist Camp; did he know where it was? Yes, he did. How much then? Twelve rupees. No, that was too much. Despite not having the slightest idea of the distance, Maria knew that one had to haggle; she offered ten rupees. No, Madam, two people, a lot of baggage. Eleven rupees. Alright, eleven rupees then. The man motioned with his hand for them to sit down and suddenly seemed tired. The girls perched on the narrow seat lined with red plastic. Maria settled her backpack over her feet, the camera pack and the straw bag on her knees, while Franca, who was still recovering, got on sulkily without a word and adjusted her backpack with ease on her feet.

To their great relief, they found themselves sitting above the crowd, still a part of it, but at the same time separate from the mass of humanity on foot, with their own space where no one pushed or squeezed, and from there they could breathe better. The man wrapped a raw cotton scarf around his head, mounted on the bicycle pedal and pushed it forcefully down, beginning to ride slowly, looking for a way out of the crowd and into the chaos of the street; seeing the possibility of a slot, he accelerated suddenly. The girls held on tight to the seat while the man began to ride in the busy traffic flow. From their elevated position they could see something of the old city, the coloured roofs of the market stalls and a lot of heads that moved up and down, all close together, shoulder to shoulder, negotiating the next step. A light breeze made the experience enjoyable.

From under his shirt, which was wet with sweat in a matter of minutes, Maria could make out the bones of the pedalling man's back. His muscular skinny legs showed large veins throbbing from the stress and heat. As he pedalled with difficulty, she felt a sharp pang of discomfort, ashamed to be carried like that. Instinctively, she tried to lift her body from the seat, sitting less heavily to lighten the weight: "I feel terrible sitting here with our big luggage, being carried like this. Look at him! He's all skin and bones. It makes me feel so sad!"

Franca shrugged her shoulders. She kept one hand on her backpack that wobbled in rhythm with the rickshaw, and looked around. "It's a job. He's lucky to have a job, considering how stupid he is," she said.

Then, pointing her chin toward another rickshaw which was going in the opposite direction, she added: "Look at them! They don't seem to feel guilty, even though they weigh at least two hundred kilos between the three of them." She was indicating a family of father, mother and son, all big and fat. Their 'driver' pedalled hard. Seeing the look on Maria's face, Franca added in a more serious tone: "Stop looking at him like that and enjoy our first rickshaw ride. We're in India, remember, and this is how people travel. It's normal."

"Not for me!"

"No, but for them it is. That's the difference."

Maria nodded and shifted her gaze from their man's back to the sky in the distance. What at first looked like a black triangular cloud speeding through the sky revealed itself to be a busy, compacted flock of birds. Even they were moving by the thousands, just like the people. The rickshaw was going through a grey area where traders sat on the road side, on a blanket placed on the ground to mark their 'shop', selling used typewriters, second-hand pots and old objects of all kinds. There were bicycle menders, motorcycle mechanics and repair-all experts; with only a few essential tools and their imagination they repaired everything. Past that area began a colourful market selling fruits, vegetables, flour, rice, spices. Piles of coloured powder used for dyeing, intense patches of cheerful red, pink, yellow, blue, green were exhibited in the form of large cones on large round plates. Immediately after the market, her eyes rested on a small area of green grass, while on the left she could make out a park with statues and monuments. The rickshaw had picked up speed and a light breeze crept under her hair and lifted it, cooling her clammy neck. They were coming to a less populated area of Delhi, to a huge field used to dye fabrics. It was a real outdoors factory, with large metal bins on the far side of the road, where the fabrics were dyed. All around the fenced perimeter, hundreds and hundreds of yards of red cloth were hung out to dry; it was such an amazing sight, all that bright red silhouetted against the deep blue sky. A few minutes later the rickshaw slowed down and stopped in front of an iron gate. Their man put his foot on the ground and, using the scarf that had covered his head, wiped the sweat from his face.

"Tourist Camp?" asked Maria. The man nodded and got off his bicycle; stretching his back and arms, he wiped them with the same piece of cloth and pointed to a discreet sign saying 'Tourist Camp'. Franca got off quickly with her backpack, while Maria was slower with her bulky baggage. "You go ahead; I'll catch up straight away," she said. "I'll pay him, I have the money on hand." While Franca walked to the gate, Maria took out her purse and, checking that Franca wasn't looking, handed him a twenty rupee note. The man started to look for a lump on the cloth belt tied at the waist, where he kept his earnings, and made a brief pause before opening it. Maria made a gesture to stop him.

"It's okay," she said; she didn't want any change.

The man clasped his hands and bowed. "Thank you, Madam!" he said, looking calmly into her eyes, dignified. Maria nodded, returning his direct gaze. She walked toward the gate under the weight of her backpack and her large bags, feeling a little lighter inside. That overwhelming feeling she had felt when she climbed on the rickshaw was dissipating, being exhaled with a deep breath, and she felt freer to move forward. The man waved at her and was off again, pedalling slowly, looking around for customers. Looking once more in her direction, he touched his forehead and smiled.

The reception was just inside the gate. Sitting behind the desk was a man with an olive-green turban and a white beard, neatly contained by a net tied behind his neck. He was holding Franca's passport and copying her details into a large book open before him. He looked up when he heard Maria come in and smiled at her. His eyes were hazel green with golden flecks; he was handsome despite his advanced age, without any wrinkles on his smooth skin. And she had believed that all Indians had dark eyes. She realized how little she knew about these people. He smiled again when she handed him her passport and said: "Hello! Welcome!" Maria was almost moved, feeling that she had come to the right place.

"Italian," he said, writing her details on the line below Franca's. Was it the first time they were in India?

"Yes, first time in India, second day!" replied Franca in Italian, "and we're still alive, despite the heat, the mosquitoes and the rickshaws!"

Maria laughed, knowing that the receptionist hadn't understood anything. He smiled and explained that India was a big place; they had to take care of themselves. He shifted his gaze from Maria to Franca and warned: "Keep away from drugs. Drugs are not permitted in the Tourist Camp."

Imitating the paternal gaze with which the man had spoken, Franca looked at Maria and parroted: "Do not take drugs. Drugs are forbidden at the Tourist Camp!" and tried to hide a wry smile.

"Who? *Me?*" Maria burst out in surprise, pointing her finger at herself. "He's talking to you, darling! He's not stupid! He took one look at you and got you sussed."

Franca laughed, amused, and made them laugh, too. "No problem," she said, bowing with pressed palms to the receptionist, who smiled with the air of one who had seen plenty of young people and had already understood which type she belonged to.

They picked up their luggage for the final time and followed the man's instructions to the dormitory; it was cheaper than a private room, only six rupees a night per person. The heat was even more stifling. How much more could one stand, Maria thought, searching for a little bit of shade. It felt like being in an oven at fifty degrees and, under the sun, she wasn't far off the mark. Dark and swollen clouds were approaching fast, low on the horizon; the air was oppressive. Following a path made of stone and flanked by young trees, they crossed the bungalow area that extended on both sides, consisting of small rooms separated from each other by a concrete wall. The wall with the door didn't go as far as the ceiling, but stopped just below the roof, leaving a wide gap. One of the bungalows had the door open and Maria peered inside to see what it was like. The furniture consisted of two iron beds and a fan, nothing else; on the bed there was a thin cotton mattress, but no sheets or pillow. 'Basic' was the word that described them perfectly. Despite being so bare, they conveyed a certain intimacy, a kind of cosiness, and Maria regretted not staying there.

When they reached the dorm, they saw with pleasure that they were the only guests, at least for the moment. Of the six beds in a row, they chose the two furthest from the door, leaning their backpacks against them. Maria hid the bag with the camera under the bed and they went out to explore.

The toilet and shower block was close by. There too, the toilet was a hole in the floor, no toilet paper, and there was a red plastic jug under the low tap, just like at the hotel. The shower block had four doors, which later they would explore. A long-haired man came out from one of the showers and bowed his wet head in a silent greeting. Franca took the opportunity to ask him where they could find any toilet paper. He paused, visibly surprised by the question, hugging his towel and shampoo and, without the shadow of a smile, replied:

"You do not use toilet paper in India, only water!" He spoke with a strong northern European accent and seemed to reproach them for asking something so out of place. Oh... really? They didn't use toilet paper! And how did one clean one's bottom, then? With water. With water... but, *how*, exactly? This was a matter of huge importance and some urgency!

To apologize for such a specific question, Maria told him that they had arrived in India only the day before, for the first time. The long-haired guy relaxed and smiled, perhaps remembering his first day in India. Without any reluctance to talk about how to wipe his backside, he explained that one filled the jug with tap water and then poured it slowly down one's behind. Franca and Maria exchanged a puzzled look. With understanding and some complicity, he said: "I'll show you!" Good man, he was going to give them a demonstration. He crouched down, put his towel and shampoo on the ground and started to demonstrate the complicated process. He raised his arm holding a fake jug in his right hand, making sure they were following the mimicry; then he turned around and pretended to pour it down his behind, while with his left hand, he wiped. Noooo! With his hand? He stood up, ignoring the girls' expressions, a mixture of disbelief, disgust and concern, and pointed out that only tourists used toilet paper in India and that *that* was disgusting. "Then you must wash your hands with soap! You will learn," he said, encouragingly. "I did. We all do!" He smiled and, bowing his head, continued on his interrupted journey, tall, thin, straight, his blond hair almost dry in a matter of those few minutes they spent together.

The word 'tourist' had extremely negative connotations for Franca, who was fully persuaded by the man's explanation. Maria was still concerned, but for now she didn't need to... and she was hungry. "Well, we will learn, as he says. That sucks though... with your hands!"

"No problem! If they do it, we'll do it, too," said Franca, walking toward an area where they could see some people.

"Hadn't your friends explained how one cleans one's bottom in India?" Maria asked her, laughing.

"No. They must have got so used to it that they forgot to mention it!"

The restaurant was a low building raised by a few steps from the floor with large windows and a veranda, furnished with low tables, chairs and benches. It was crowded, mainly with young people. They found two chairs and began to study the simple menu that, happily, contained things like white rice, omelettes, boiled eggs; normal things basically. Maria ordered an omelette and rice, while Franca chose bhaji and chapatis; they were cheaper and it was genuine Indian food. While they waited, they observed the sky full of huge, heavy grey clouds that promised an awful lot of rain. The air was alive with electricity, the heat and humidity had reached an unpleasant level and there was a palpable tension, an unpleasant nervousness, in all people; it was difficult to think clearly or breathe fully. As the black clouds came menacingly closer, many people moved inside the restaurant. A few drops of rain started to fall, followed by more, stronger and stronger, heavier and heavier. Suddenly, lightning struck very close, followed a few seconds later by frightening thunder and then... the heavens opened with a big bang. The rain began to fall so strong, so furious, it hurt! Maria and Franca ran inside the restaurant and arrived just in time, but those people who were still outside found they were soaking within seconds.

While all the foreigners ran indoors, something quite extraordinary happened: Intrigued and encouraged by the cries of the waiters, the cooks and orderlies came out of the kitchen. The waiters laid their trays on the counter; the attendants took off their aprons, put down their brooms and mops; the cooks removed their hats and, one after the other, went outside, in the heavy rain. Under the deluge that fell in torrents they began to dance, laugh, collect the rain in the palm of their hands and drink it with delight. They raised their arms to the sky making signs for the rain to come down even harder. Smiling happily, facing up to the sky, they closed their eyes and gave themselves to the downpour with joy and enthusiasm, as if it were the most beautiful gift in the world. Wet and drunken with merriment they continued to dance and sing, unaware of the tourists watching them, stunned, from behind the steamed up glass of the restaurant windows, waiting for their chai, their rice with sabji, bhaji, pakhora, samosas, omelettes and boiled eggs, cola, fanta and lemonade. No one complained, no one tried to spoil such a spontaneous and overwhelming party. Respect! Great respect for the monsoon that had finally begun. It continued to rain for half an hour and, little by little, the waiters, cooks and attendants returned to resume their work. They were happy, relaxed, soaking wet and laughing like excited children. When the rain stopped, hot humidity rose from the ground, the flickering vapour clearly visible in the air. There was a pleasant smell of wet earth and a wonderful feeling of calm and relief. Everybody, tourists and Indians, felt a new, close solidarity.

Maria woke up with light streaming in through the gap between the wall and the ceiling. She felt a great heaviness and was still very tired.

The morning heat was becoming fierce as the sun rose in the sky. She peaked through her swollen eyelids at Franca who was fast asleep with a scarf covering her eyes. Maria found a cotton scarf and did the same. The heat and the stuffiness in the air lulled her into another deep sleep. When she woke up again she was dripping with sweat, had to pee and couldn't wait any longer. This meant she had to go to one of the dreaded toilets. Slowly, she sat up on the bed and put on her sandals. Halfway between the dormitory and the toilets there was a room with the door ajar, out of which came great bursts of laughter. She could hear the voices of a man and a woman; he said a few words and they were followed by an uproar of laughter. They spoke in English, just a few words between each laugh. Maria smiled at the sound. The woman laughed heartily, an infectious refreshing sound that came from the belly, free and strong. They were really having fun. The man had a deep voice and she could picture him smiling as he dropped a few more words. Room twenty-one.

The toilets were all occupied, so Maria took the opportunity to fill a plastic jug with water. This lack of toilet paper was a real challenge and it forced her to adapt to the local system. In her mind she went over the instructions the young man gave them the day before, in his crouching position. Somehow, she had to make do. Getting back from the complicated experience in the toilet, she walked past room twenty-one once more, slowing down before getting there, to have more time to observe. This time the sound that came out of the room was different, no more laughter but a steady flow of rhythmic sounds, of ups and downs; sometimes the voice came from deep down, other times it raised clear from that base, but the overall effect was of an engine working at full speed. The man's deep voice blended with that of the woman, which was higher but just as warm; it was a harmonic music but without any notes. Wave after wave, the uninterrupted sound went on rapidly, confident, without even a break to catch their breath; it was overwhelmingly comforting, inviting her to enter. But Maria didn't have the courage to do so, and stood there a little longer, pretending to be interested in the courtyard or looking for something under the trees, glued to that spot of land. When it became embarrassing to stop any longer, she walked away slowly, straining her ears to absorb a little more of such enjoyable vibrations. That sound kept reverberating through her body as she approached the dormitory.

Franca had woken up and was desperate for a cup of chai. The restaurant was full, but luckily there was one free table which they claimed enthusiastically. After an interminable wait the waiter stopped for them and took their order. They recognized him as one of those who had danced in the rain and smiled at him. Maria had just finished telling Franca about the outbursts of laughter and the peculiar sound she had heard, when she saw the couple from room twenty-one go past right in front of their table. She recognized them from their voices, but even if they had been silent, she would have known them. There was something familiar, as if they had already met. The woman looked at her, meeting Maria's eyes. "Hello!" she said with a friendly smile.

"Hello," answered Maria, a little surprised.

"Hi!" greeted the man, smiling and looking straight at her.

"Hi," said Maria, surprised, confused and excited. They were so handsome. The woman's black hair was loosely gathered and she looked like a flamenco dancer. She was wearing a long skirt down to her feet and her arms bore rows of bracelets. She walked with a long and lively stride and seemed to brim with life. He had green eyes, that kind of eyes that smile even when the mouth doesn't, was tall with dark blond hair and advanced in a relaxed way, as if walking on soft ground, swinging his arms without hurry.

Maria followed them with her eyes; she was glad they hadn't stopped, because just seeing them and exchanging that greeting had made such an intense impact that she needed to recover from the emotion vibrating within her chest. "That's them," she said, as soon as they were gone.

"Impressive!" agreed Franca. She too was taken by the couple who had just gone past and that, with their brief presence, had made everything around seem more vivid and intense. "Today we go to Old Delhi!" she announced, breaking a piece of chapati to dip in the spicy bhaji.

Maria, who was still thinking about the English couple, was caught by surprise. "When? Where are we going?" she asked, beginning to spread the melted butter on a slice of toast, casting her eyes on the jam and the boiled eggs, anticipating the pleasure of the first bite, and the second and the third.

"Don't you worry, you'll see!" replied Franca with confidence.

2. A red mark on the forehead

The heat was intense when they walked out of the Tourist Camp. They stopped at the edge of the wide two-lane road looking for a bus stop, but there were none. Perhaps a scooter-taxi would arrive, or a rickshaw. They saw a cart pulled by an ox approaching, led by a man dressed in white and wearing a white turban. Maria put out her hand to slow him down and as soon as he drew near, she asked him: "You go to Old Delhi?" The man pulled the ox's reins and stopped the cart. She asked him again if he went to Old Delhi. The man shook his head from right to left, rocking it as if he had a spring in his neck; the movement seemed to be saying no, but at the same time he was smiling at her.

Franca opened the map of Delhi and showed it to the man, who looked at it blankly, as if he didn't see it. He rocked his head again and motioned with his hand to sit on the cart. Strange! With his head he was saying no, but with the facial expression and his body language he seemed to be saying yes. It reminded her of one of those toy dogs that people put on the back shelf of their car and nod their heads with every movement.

Franca was exasperated: "Yeah, right! What the hell is he doing?" and started to walk away.

Since the man didn't move, Maria asked him again: "Old Delhi? Four rupees, okay?"

And yet again, there came the nodding and a calm smile. But this time, indicating toward the cart, the man also said three words: "Sit, Madam, sit!"

She jumped on the cart and the man made the ox move. Soon they caught up with Franca and Maria persuaded her to climb aboard: "Come on Franca! This guy is going to take us. He's understood we want to go to Old Delhi!"

Her companion jumped on the cart, complaining about the ignorance of this man who couldn't read a map, but with the slow and shaky pace of the cart, she gradually relaxed. With their legs dangling lazily they watched the traffic coming toward them and overtake them. They all seemed very surprised: scooter drivers, car drivers, even the rickshaws, turned around to look at them with an expression of disbelief. Meanwhile, they were enjoying themselves and greeted everybody by waving their hands.

The cart was advancing on a busy road with two lanes of traffic going in both directions. There was a constant loud coming and going of motorcars, scooters, rickshaws, bicycles, carts pulled by an ox like the one they were on, and of loose cows wandering aimlessly on their own. The fumes and the smell coming out of the exhaust pipes were unbearable. The central reservation, a strip of concrete about a metre wide, divided the lanes of traffic going in opposite directions, and on it people lived. Simple covered structures made from pieces of cloth and plastic, like rudimentary camping tents, had been erected and under these shelters people kept their few worldly possessions. Women cooked on the ground on kerosene stoves, pumping them every few minutes; young mothers breastfed their babies. Hundreds of people filled this small polluted space they had made their home. It was unbelievable! But even more amazing was the simple elegance with which they moved, the calm looks, the smiles that lit up their faces, their dignity. Maria felt a mixture of sorrow and respect, but could find no words to utter her feelings. Had it been in her power, she would have taken them all away and would have given them a clean place to live. Why, of all the places in the world, had they chosen to live there, where it was almost impossible to even breathe? At least clean air, at least that, for these people and their children!

At some point the cart stopped and the man turned toward them. Had they arrived in Old Delhi? Maria asked. No, Old Delhi 'idda, idda' he replied, pointing forward with his arm. He pointed his finger toward himself and indicated he couldn't. He was going to stop there! Surprised and puzzled, the girls got off the cart. Franca started to walk while Maria approached the man and showing him a five-rupee note made him understand, in words and gestures, that she wanted a rupee change. The man didn't take the money; instead he put his hands together and bowed.

Maria tried again: "Four rupees for you, one rupee for me," indicating the numbers with her fingers.

Again, he clasped his hands and bowed, and this time, touching his chest, the man said: "No one rupee, Madam," and then, as if to apologize, he pressed his palms together and bowed again. He didn't have a rupee.

Confused about what to do, Maria looked at him and then, embarrassed, handed him the five rupee note: "You five rupees! No problem," she said. The man smiled and took the money. She clasped her hands together and bowed, responding to his umpteenth bow.

She set off to join Franca, thinking about the exchange that had just occurred. He who had nothing wasn't going to take the money because he didn't have any change to give her. And she, who tried to barter, always ended up paying more than agreed. Well! Sooner or later she was going to understand, or learn, or who knows what. Indian people were having a much stronger impact on her than she had imagined, or been prepared for. What dignity these people had! Making her way through the thick crowd she reached Franca, who had stopped to wait for her. Following the man's instructions they carried on a little further and soon found themselves in the narrow, dusty streets of Old Delhi, resounding with the voices of children playing. A small stream flowed right in front of the doors of grey low houses, little more than huts. There were children urinating openly in the rivulet of water while women, dressed in their brightly coloured saris, squatted a little further down washing large pots, all of them dirty with a very black base. They rubbed them vigorously with their bare hands and a poultice made of earth and water. Other women washed their clothes, turning and stirring them, beating them with a flat stick that looked like a baseball bat, without any soap or detergent. Small children were carried on their mothers' backs, wrapped in large shawls tied at the front with a knot above their bosoms. Their small trousers were unstitched on the backside, leaving their bottoms in sight. They were funny and the logic was clear: always ready to poop and pee, they didn't need any nappies. The little girls wore earrings and plastic bracelets and even the smallest ones had at least one small bangle on their wrists. They were beautiful, with big brown eyes enhanced by black kohl.

Flies were everywhere, insistent, persistent, intrusive, irritating, and the heat was becoming more and more intense, approaching the midday peak. That sweet, sour and strong odour assaulted the senses with a thick gelatine-like consistency. Maria breathed through tight lips, trying to keep the smell out of her mouth but, looking around, she could see no litter. Thin cows were wandering slowly and, with their big tongues, picked up everything they found on the ground, from banana peels, to cabbage leaves to newspaper pages. Everything ended up inside their huge mouths and got chewed rhythmically, thoroughly. As they slowly waddled along they cleaned up the street of any waste; in return, they dropped big pats of dung behind them, which were immediately collected with great enthusiasm by women and little girls.

Maria watched a mother and daughter collecting a cow pat each. They walked over to a house with many similar shapes lined up to dry and, with a deft sweep of her arm, the mother threw hers against the wall. She fixed it more firmly, by patting her hand over it and leaving her print.

She then turned to the child who carefully handed her the warm dung she was holding. The mother repeated the same agile gesture and stuck the second cow pat to the wall. Having secured it well, she moved away and let the little girl make her small handprint next to hers, only slightly different in size. With a satisfied smile they admired the rows of dung cakes lined up. The mother wiped her hands thoroughly on her sari, imitated by her daughter who wiped hers in the same way on her dress. Then, one went back to washing her pots in the stream and the other to her games, both turning occasionally to look at the wall.

As they went around the corner the girls were hit by an explosion of colours and scents. They found themselves in a small square lined with stalls overflowing with fresh flower garlands. Mountains of red and yellow flowers of which they didn't know the name, white jasmine and orange marigolds saturated the atmosphere with their intense perfume. That's where the pleasant part of the cocktail of smells came from! They seemed to be made of velvet. Maria stopped to touch them to be sure they were real, absorbing the sweet heavenly scent. They were only one rupee each.

"I'll buy one for myself," she said dreamily. "Do you want one Franca? Come and smell this wonderful aroma!"

"There you go again! What do you want it for?"

"I'll put it around my neck, as a necklace. What else?"

"Not for me, thank you, I don't want to look like a Christmas tree!" said Franca, making her laugh.

"They are so cheap! They must have at least a hundred flowers each! They are connected by a small hole in the stem," said Maria, holding a garland on the palm of her hand and studying it closely. "Just think how much work it takes to make one."

"Yeah, okay. But don't always say that things are cheap!" Franca scolded her irritably. "It's like telling them to put the prices up."

"And this way I spoil the market."

"Of course! You're encouraging them, right?"

"Are you sure you don't want one?" asked Maria, her head buried in the thick of the hanging garlands, while she chose a white jasmine from the pile. "I bet they keep away the mosquitoes, too!"

"And not just them," said Franca, mooching some distance away from the stall.

The stall holder hastened to remove her garland and offered her an orange one, too. Maria couldn't resist and bought them both. She hung the orange one around her neck and rolled the white one around her wrist. The man smiled at her, surprised and amused, and nodded his head in that swinging manner; maybe it was a sign of approval, after all, because it certainly didn't mean 'no'. Maria thanked him with a smile and he bowed with folded hands. She bowed a little too, timidly, learning how to greet people without feeling ridiculous. She caught up with Franca, who looked at her garlands out of the corner of her eye.

"If you want, you can have one of these two," Maria offered. "You choose... the white or the orange one?"

"Not in this lifetime," said Franca, with an air that seemed to say 'I don't know this woman'. Shaking her head, she added: "You are just like my mother!"

Speaking of her mother... Maria had met her only once before they left Venice and she had begged her to keep an eye on her daughter. What, keep an eye on Franca? Impossible! Maria brought her wrist to her nose and smelt the jasmine with delight. Not a single fly had come near her so far.

After a pause, looking around, Franca said: "Can you see anyone else with a garland around their neck?"

Actually, no.

She went on insistently: "Are you a prime minister, or a famous film star who's just arrived at the airport and is greeted by a group of beautiful girls who put garlands around his neck?"

No, all right, so what? "Where do you think all the garlands go, then?" Maria asked curiously.

After a brief hesitation Franca said: "Maybe to the temple? Given that we're outside one!"

Maybe she was right. In any case, Maria was happy with her flower necklaces and no one looked at her with disapproval, except for Franca, and she was getting used to that. "Are we going inside? This way we can also see if they all end up in there!" It seemed the most natural thing to do.

Franca agreed, but decided they would enter in turn, so that they could keep an eye on their sandals, which had to be left outside, to prevent them from being pinched. Maria hadn't thought about the possibility that someone could steal her sandals, but with Franca it was easier not to argue and then, perhaps, she had a point. She went in first, leaving her sandals along with hundreds of others, made of leather, rubber, plastic, large, small, old, men's, women's, children's. As soon as she entered she was welcomed by a pleasant dim light and a cool inviting atmosphere.

The temple was lit by the flickering light of hundreds of candles and, right in the centre, there was a statue of a deity covered with flowers. Sure enough, the wreaths were all there! Women, men and children followed one another, laying a garland, touching the statue's forehead with something wet and lighting an incense stick. Then they stopped for a prayer, entrusting their desires, hopes, fears, joys, gratitude and dreams.

When they straightened up, the temple man, who had a flower necklace around his neck (*he* did have one!) and was wearing only a white sarong tied at the waist, made a mark with red powder on the women's forehead; they left a coin and bowed several times with folded hands before leaving the temple, serene, smiling.

Maria would have liked to stay a while longer and soak up the beautiful atmosphere of trust and enthusiasm she felt in there, but Franca was waiting outside. She removed her necklace of orange marigold and, walking barefoot on the cool stone floor, approached the statue of the deity. She placed the garland at the foot of the sculpture, as she had seen others do, and searched for a prayer inside herself. What did she want from this trip? The answer wasn't as simple and clear cut as when she had left Italy: The man of her life, she would have said until two days ago. But now she felt that her life was opening up at every moment, like a fan, and was much bigger than she had imagined. She stood there, pausing and reflecting, the future ahead of her, free to begin from this magical moment. Yes, she wanted to find love, but she was ready to accept everything that India was going to show her, teach her, offer her. She was willing to give whatever she could in return, although at that particular moment she didn't know what it was. She would begin to understand, day after day, bow after bow. She put her hands together and bowed her head, with the same ease she saw all around. When she lifted it the man was ready to place the red mark on her forehead. She hadn't expected it, she thought it was only for Indian women. He smiled at her and she leaned forward. With a flick of his thumb he made a vertical mark between her eyebrows with the red powder, and she put some money on the saucer, like the Indian women had.

She left the pleasant semi-dark, dreamy world of the temple and squinted when she got out into the bright day light. Franca was waiting impatiently. She looked at her, puzzled by the red mark on the forehead, the orange necklace gone.

"At last," she said, irritably removing her sandals. "I was dying from the heat! Is it nice inside?"

"Yes, you'll see!" Maria was glad to have a few minutes alone. "There is no hurry. I'll wait," she said to Franca, who looked at her once again, studying her briefly. She could see something was changing.

When her friend came out of the temple she was visibly calmer, looking thoughtful, absorbed and, for a while, didn't say much. They decided to stop for a drink in a nearby chai-shop. The piping hot chai smelled of cardamom and cloves and the glass was hot and sticky. Made by boiling together sugar, tea leaves, milk and spices, chai gave a lot of energy. It was strange how, in such hot a climate, people enjoyed a boiling hot drink. While sipping it slowly, they decided what to do next. Franca, who never ceased to amaze her, announced that they had to buy a sari.

"Why do you want to buy a sari?"

"So that we don't look like tourists," she replied, as if it were the most obvious thing in the world.

Maria laughed aloud. "But we travel with backpacks! On top of that I have my big camera bag; it's impossible not to look like tourists," she objected, amused and amazed at the same time. "In addition, we both have blue eyes and there aren't any Indians with blue eyes. They'll spot us a mile away!"

But all these minor details didn't matter, argued Franca. And anyway... a sari was always useful; five yards of cloth could come in handy for loads of things. True! And so they entered the market, which covered a huge area.

The well organized stalls sold fabrics, scarves, shawls, saris of all kinds and colours. Many traders had only a blanket on the ground where they displayed their goods: plastic bracelets, called 'bangles', by the thousands; plastic shoes and sandals, uncomfortable but cheap; pans, dishes and glassware, both new and second hand. Two places next to each other were selling the most original of things: the first one had a large selection of second hand spectacles, while his neighbour was a 'dentist'. Neatly aligned on the ground, next to the age-old tools, were grabs and grips for the extraction of teeth, dentures and teeth, all displayed in order of size, from the smallest to the largest. Looking closely, Maria realized that they were real teeth. How on earth were they going to be used? she wondered in amazement.

"You need dentist?" the old skinny man, sitting cross-legged on the blanket asked, lazily looking at them from behind his glasses with thick lenses. Franca and Maria shook their heads vigorously, laughing out loud. Thank heavens, no!

The noise around them was deafening, a mixture of voices that spoke loudly so as to be heard; bicycle bells ringing insistently to make their way through the dense crowd and the cries of vendors who offered their wares. The bright colours filled their eyes and pungent odours assaulted the senses, competing with each other to dominate. Tall, cone-shaped piles of colourful spices commanded the attention of sight and smell: chilli powder, turmeric, saffron, cumin and garam masala, browns of various shades, from red to rust to earth colour, teased their nostrils and entered through every pore.

Upon reaching the sari area, and persuaded to stop at his stall by a trader without customers, Franca asked to see the cheapest ones. Maria was happy to observe the exchange between them. With a deft flick of his wrist, the trader opened five metres of cloth and laid them on the bench, asking what colours they preferred and spreading them quickly one after another, aware of the danger of losing their attention. After a few minutes the stall was covered by a mountain of starched saris. Franca discarded the sixty rupee ones and concentrated on the ones for forty rupees. They wouldn't find less expensive saris, the man said with confidence.

"Are these for you, Madam?" he asked with curiosity, looking from one to the other. Sure, they were for them, replied her companion, without a shadow of hesitation. The man rocked his head from left to right and from right to left, looking impressed. Franca bargained with dexterity, taking a step back, threatening to leave, going back again when lured by the trader, offering sixty rupees to the eighty asked by him, gradually reaching a compromise of seventy-five rupees for two saris, one for her and one for Maria, who was still sceptical about the need to own one and even more unsure at the idea of wearing it. But, one day or another, she would experience going around dressed as an Indian woman.

With the package under their arms they pushed through the crowd of people and left the busy market. They were hungry and tired, but Franca insisted that they had to go and buy coach tickets for the trip to the Himalayan mountains; she wanted to leave the next day.

"I'm still tired from the journey," objected Maria. "I want to rest for at least another day, and I'd like to see a little more of Delhi!"

Her friend had thousands of reasons for wanting to leave immediately: In the mountains it was going to be cooler, the air cleaner, the place was beautiful and she could buy good stuff to smoke. Why did she want to stay in sultry hot Delhi? But Maria was too tired to argue or travel.

"If you want to smoke I'll help you find some dope at the Tourist Camp," she said, knowing that perhaps this idea would calm Franca's irrepressible enthusiasm and anxiety. "I saw some guys smoking a chillum yesterday. We'll call on them. I'm not leaving tomorrow!"

Enthralled at the idea of some good chillums, Franca was convinced and they took a scooter to return to the relative calm of the Tourist Camp. At reception, Maria stopped to talk with the Sikh receptionist, taking advantage of a lull without customers and asking the reason 'why' of a lot of things. Calmly he explained that cow dung was valuable for several reasons, such as fuel, because when it was dry it burned very well or, mixed with earth, it became a kind of plaster used on walls or to insulate a bare floor. When fresh it didn't have a strong smell, but once dry it didn't smell at all. In addition, the cow was sacred, so everything that came through her was valued and respected. When she told him how they had gone almost all the way to Old Delhi in a cart pulled by an ox, the receptionist looked at her open-mouthed.

"But that was a farmer who came from the suburbs!" he said, astonished. "He stopped to give you a lift and you took it?"

Maria told him how they signalled him, how he was bobbing his head, didn't 'see' the map, and had stopped the cart before arriving in Old Delhi. The receptionist explained that carts with oxen couldn't go beyond a certain point and that, as for the map, most likely the farmer could neither read nor write. He asked how the people passing by reacted to them.

"They all seemed very surprised and turned around to look at us," she replied.

He nodded vigorously; it all added up. The rocking motion of the head, he said finally, meant 'yes'. This was a very useful piece of information, Maria thought, still reluctant to accept that a movement that seemed to say 'no' was instead an affirmative gesture; she would have to get used to it. Just then a scooter pulled up with two new arrivals carrying backpacks. The receptionist looked at the red mark on her forehead.

"Have you been to the temple?" he asked.

She told him that inside the temple she had thought about her future. "I think I will learn a lot from India," she said.

He looked at her in silence for a moment and then, rocking his head, but just a little, he said: "We learn from everything and everyone, if we have an open heart. Take care of yourself; India is very different from your country." Without taking his eyes off hers, he added: "And take care of your friend. She's not like you."

Maria thanked him and took leave, while the two newcomers reached the front desk. Again, that slight rocking of his head. Now that she knew it meant 'yes', she reflected that it was a well thought-out 'yes', rather than a 'yes' with conviction, as in Italy where it was perhaps done too quickly, without thinking much before answering.

She walked back to the dorm, tired, her feet aching. Franca wasn't there. Maria took shampoo and a towel out of her backpack and headed for the showers, walking past room twenty-one. She could hear the man's and the woman's voices and felt happy that they hadn't left. Franca was in the shower and had almost finished. She came out with a towel wrapped around her head like a turban. Her light blue eyes were reddened and she gave Maria a big relaxed smile. "Have you been smoking?"

"Yes, I went past a room with an open door out of which came this wonderful scent. I put my head in and these French people offered me a chillum," she replied with a happy smile.

Great! Franca was settled, and the pressure to leave was gone, at least for a day. Maria went into the shower and started to relax whilst washing away the tiredness and the dust under the weak and irregular jet of water. She was beginning to get used to the rough cement floor and the grey walls. While shampooing her hair, she went through the thoughts and memories of that eventful day. Calm, shanti, rest, hunger. She was always hungry since she had arrived. It was hard to find something to eat, simple clean as it was at home, and that didn't light a fire in her mouth. As she went toward her room, she walked as close as possible to room twenty-one and, once again, the two voices in harmony produced that deep continuous sound that touched something inside and made her resonate with a hidden joy, new and familiar at the same time. Slowly she moved on.

"Did you hear the sound made by those in room twenty-one?" she asked Franca, when she arrived at the dorm.

"Yes, they were making it when I walked past. Strange sound, it made me think of a lot of wasps flying fast. Bioooob, biooooooob. Nice though."

"Yes, beautiful. I could feel it in the pit of my stomach, both times I heard it," said Maria. "I hope they'll be at the restaurant, maybe we can talk with them."

"Indeed! I'm curious about them," said Franca, lying on her bed with her hair still wet.

"Me too. Very!" agreed Maria.

At the restaurant they chose an empty table near the door that could accommodate both them and the pair of 'wasps'. It was late afternoon, and as the minutes went by, the tables were filling up. Two boys came and asked if the seats were free.

"No, they are taken, sorry, we're waiting for friends," Maria said quickly.

Then three more people came, two girls and a boy: "Are these seats free?"

"No! Taken! Sorry. Waiting for two friends," they said again, covering the empty chairs with their hands.

Finally, the couple appeared at the restaurant door and looked around for somewhere to sit. The woman swept the room with her eyes and, when she saw Maria, she recognized her and smiled. Maria waved vigorously, gesturing to come over. The couple approached, smiling.

"Hi! Is it all right if we sit with you? All the tables are taken," said the woman with a warm voice. You bet it was fine! They had defended those seats with tooth and nail.

"Yes, sure. Sit, please!" Franca said in her best English, smiling from ear to ear. They introduced themselves, she was called Sanya and he Colin, from Nottingham in England; they had arrived in India three days earlier, one day ahead of them. Sanya started to ask them questions: Where were they from? Did they travel by themselves? Were they going to stay long? She listened to their answers with great interest, glancing from Maria to Franca, nodding emphatically to reassure them she could understand their English, always smiling.

Colin listened and grinned as he read the menu, shifting his gaze from the girls to the list of foods. "We better order some food, love! Otherwise there won't be anything left," he said, with a radio presenter voice. His eyes were smiling with irony.

"Sure! Of course," she said with enthusiasm. She explained they were starving and that, once ordered, they could continue to talk. She spoke with emphasis and a certain complicity, which put them immediately at ease. While they studied the menu the girls observed them; she must have been about thirty while he was around forty, maybe a little younger. She was wearing a long skirt and a low-cut t-shirt, which showed a voluptuous bosom; her arms were covered with bracelets, she wore big earrings and her dark hair was held up by a large clip. He wore khaki trousers and a white shirt with short sleeves. They were a striking couple and stood out for their natural elegance and calm dignity as well as their beauty.

Maria and Franca rushed to ask all the questions they had on the tip of their tongues, using their best English. The couple nodded to confirm they had understood, or watched them wide-eyed, with an air of surprise if they hadn't understood what they meant. The girls discovered that she was an actress and he was a writer, they had a four-year old daughter who was at home with her grandmother and they were in India to do research on the 'shanty town', the Bombay ghettos, for a play he was going to write. They told them that Colin had been one of Sanya's teachers at Drama School, which is where they met and fell in love.

Maria was eating without chewing, swallowing the rice she had ordered, completely absorbed by the story and the concentration necessary to understand everything without missing a word. Finally, she came to the question she was waiting to ask.

3. How many worlds are there?

"I heard a sound walking past your room, something you were saying together. What was it?"

"Oh, I'm sorry," said Sanya, concerned that the noise had disturbed them.

No, no, not at all! Maria assured her; on the contrary, that sound had had a big impact here, in the stomach, and here, in her head! It had been on her mind since she had heard it in the morning, and she'd like to know what they were saying.

"It's a phrase we recite morning and evening, the words are Nam-myoho-renge-kyo," said Sanya, her hazel eyes lit by glowing specks of gold, and smiled: "We are Buddhists," she added.

Wow! That was exciting! Maria knew only a little about Buddhism and she liked it. Despite her limited knowledge, the Buddhist philosophy and the atmosphere that accompanied it had always fascinated her. She was dying to ask some questions, but didn't know where to start. Franca was quicker and asked why they repeated that phrase.

Sanya laughed: "That's a good question," she said.

Maria was relieved to know she didn't think it was a stupid question!

Colin nodded; it seemed good to him, too.

Sanya explained that when she recited that phrase her life state improved; if she was sad the chanting made her feel better, if she was confused, after the recitation her ideas were clearer.

Colin said that he always chanted before making a decision, whether big or small. He explained that the life state he was in at any one time determined the way he perceived reality and what action he would take. After chanting Nam-myoho-renge-kyo he didn't 'react' but 'responded' to the situations from a different life state.

This expression 'life state' wasn't so clear and Maria asked if there was more than one, what was the other one?

The couple looked at each other and laughed: "One simple question and ten different answers," said Sanya.

"Thank you, Maria!" said Colin, ironically, with his radio presenter voice. "Have you got half an hour?"

Yes, they had plenty of time and spending it with these two was a privilege.

"Okay, we'll explain briefly," said Sanya. Each of these ten states of life or 'worlds' had a positive and a negative side. She would explain one side and Colin the other.

"How many worlds are there? I thought there was only one! "Maria asked looking at Franca, but her friend silenced her with a quick shhhhhh and waved her hand to make her be quiet. They pricked up their ears. So, there were ten life states!

The first one is Hell, Sanya said.

"What? I didn't know there was hell in Buddhism," said Franca.

Hell in Buddhist philosophy, Sanya explained, was not a place but a state of mind. For example, when you felt down in the dumps, angry, desperate, that was the state of Hell. Depression, with its typical lack of vitality and hope, was another example; jealousy, the green-eyed monster that spoilt all enjoyment in life, that was Hell.

Maria understood perfectly, from the pit of her stomach. What was good about this life state? she asked.

Colin spoke this time, looking at them with those green eyes and smiling: "When you are suffering, because of jealousy, or depression, for the loss of a loved one, or for any other reason, you feel the pain physically as well as mentally, it's very real. Once you have *known* this, you can deeply understand another person's hurt. Besides, once you've experienced such misery, you never want to go through it again; it works as an antidote so, as soon as you recognize the symptoms, you can do something to combat it." He paused to let them absorb the meaning of what he was saying. Then, with great simplicity, he confessed that he suffered from depression and that, as soon as he felt it resurface, he'd take the necessary measures to block its advance. He took medication, herbal remedies, chanted 'daimoku', which was the Buddhist phrase Nam-myoho-renge-kyo, in order to increase his life force; he also did more physical exercise to increase endorphins, dedicated time to supporting others and worried less about himself. "Basically, I use my wisdom," he said. Both girls listened attentively. With the challenges of the language difficulty and the concepts themselves, this was a conversation that required energy! They ordered a coffee and while they were waiting for it, Maria wondered what came after Hell.

"After Hell is the world of Hunger," said Sanya. It was a state dominated by desires; once a desire was satisfied, it was only a short time before another one appeared. She gave a few examples: 'I'll be happy when I get a new car,' or 'I'll be happy when I get the bag I saw in the shop window,' or 'when I get the guy I fancy,' and so on; believing that happiness depended on the satisfaction of one desire after another. Since, however, this state of life was dominated by insatiability and greed, people always wanted something else: more things, more attention, more love, more distractions.

Maria and Franca nodded; they understood well. So, what was the positive side?

Colin explained that the positive side manifested itself in a desire to change things for the better. For example, people who emigrated to create a better future were driven by the desire to improve their life and the lives of their children; people who were committed to eliminating society's problems, such as poverty, disease, injustice, were motivated by Hunger, but in this case, for the benefit of all.

Glasses full of steaming coffee finally arrived. They were too hot to touch, and they had to leave them on the table, blowing on them from time to time to cool them down.

"The third life state is called Animality," Sanya began. "It is a state characterized by instinctive behaviour. We human beings are a type of animal and thus the urge to eat, sleep, have sex, the instincts that allow us to survive, are all natural and healthy. However, when one is in the *grips* of these instincts, with the pursuit of pleasure as their priority, they cannot control them and you can guess the results: eating without limits, getting drunk, having sex without thinking of the consequences, are some examples. In addition, this world can be described as being ruled by 'the law of the jungle'. He who is stronger mistreats the weaker one, but then, when faced with someone stronger than himself, behaves in a servile way, fearing him. Literally, think of the jungle and you've got the idea."

Maria nodded, eating or drinking too much, having sex without protection. Eating too much wasn't a problem for her, but the other two... Sanya had hit the mark, touché. She noticed that Franca was thinking. Her wild passion for getting 'out of it' in any way possible... Maybe she was thinking about that?

"The other side," Colin said, breaking the brief silence, "is that, in the world of Animality, one reacts instinctively to protect his or her loved ones. Think of a lactating lioness who is feeding her cubs and how she reacts if someone approaches them; she growls in a way that makes anyone think twice about getting near."

True, all true.

"The very fact of 'reacting' rather than 'responding' is a manifestation of the state of Animality," he added, to conclude. Interesting!

Sanya wanted to add something else: "With regard to the larger realm of a country or nation, when it is in the state of Animality natural resources are used in a reckless manner, as if they were infinite. People don't care for the environment, which becomes dirty and polluted, and in the end, they destroy everything around them. This gives rise to drought, famine, so-called 'natural' disasters that often originate from disrespectful exploitation of the environment," she said.

It was so true! Deforestation, toxic substances dumped in rivers, waste from chemical factories, such as those close to Venice, where they lived and whose fumes they breathed day in, day out; rubbish dropped on mountain trails, in the streets, in the squares. The girls exchanged a silent look. Franca raised an eyebrow, as if to say she'd got the idea and Maria nodded.

"The fourth life state is Anger," Sanya said, after checking with a look whether she could continue. Anger! Maria knew that one well, too. But no, it wasn't what she thought. Anger, went on Sanya, wasn't so much the feeling of rage, that was part of the world of Hell. A manifestation of Anger was the feeling of superiority toward others, or the desire to feel that way; it was a state of animosity. The amazing thing was that people in the state of Anger could behave amiably, but deep underneath this facade they were motivated by a sense of superiority. They often saw themselves as a benevolent person; however, if someone contradicted them, their anger manifested itself immediately. This emotion was poisoning people's blood and ruining their lives. Whole countries and nations were suffering from this poison, explained Sanya, and the result of Anger was war.

Maria nodded and she saw Franca do the same. Since Sanya had finished speaking, they turned to Colin.

"The other side of the coin is a sense of justice," he explained. "When we see injustice and we rise to confront it, we show the positive side of Anger. For example, if I see someone who mistreats an elderly or a defenceless person, I feel my blood boil. Buddhism teaches us to take responsibility so, rather than pretending nothing happened, which would be easier but cowardly, I do something to protect this person; I say something, I offer my help, it depends on the situation."

Everything they said was true and simple; nothing new, in a sense, but they had never heard it explained that way before. They took the glass of coffee almost all at the same time; it was very sweet, full of milk and still very hot, but they could just sip it. Maria looked at Sanya and saw that she was smiling; she was beautiful, there was an incredible warmth about her. She smiled at her, thinking that with such a person, she would like to keep in touch.

"Are you tired?" asked Sanya. "We can continue another time."

No, no, they weren't tired, both said at the same time; they wanted to know more, wondering what the other 'worlds' were. At this rate, they were going to learn a lot of interesting and useful things.

"These four life states are called the four evil paths and we go from one to the other hundreds of times during the day," continued Sanya. "Most people spend their entire lives at the mercy of these moods, reacting to what is happening in the environment around them."

The fifth life state was a surprise, it was called Tranquillity, or Humanity, Sanya said, as she pulled out tobacco and cigarette papers. She took a good swig of coffee and began to make a cigarette with tobacco. Franca looked with curiosity to see if she going to add some hashish, or better still 'charas', but Sanya licked the paper and lit a simple cigarette, inhaling with satisfaction.

"The State of Tranquillity," she explained, "is when you feel relaxed, content, at peace with yourself and the outside world. In this state of life, we can control our instincts, at least in part, we are able to have a clear understanding of things around us and try to live together in harmony; a beautiful world, in a nutshell."

"But," Colin intervened, "the down side is that this state of life is quite weak and has a tendency toward laziness, lack of initiative and, consequently, to stagnation. Even when all goes well, it doesn't last long and can easily be ruined by someone or something that happens and brings us to another state." After a brief pause, he began in a lighter tone: "For example, let's say that you are out and have just bought something you like. You decide to walk through the park, you're happy, enjoying your relaxed stroll, breathing deeply. Suddenly you are hit by a child on his bike; he falls off and hurts his leg. The kid's father complains, saying you weren't paying attention, and because of your lack of care his son was hurt. You explain that it was quite the opposite and that you have been hurt, too, but the father raises his voice and starts gesticulating like a madman. At this point, you get angry too; and so you went from the state of Tranquillity to the state of Hell!"

"Mmm," said Franca, thinking about what she had heard. "It takes very little to change one's mood, especially if we come into contact with aggressive people, or with injustice. What's the next world?" she asked, her pale blue eyes filled with interest.

"The sixth state," continued Sanya, between one puff and another, "is called Rapture."

"Rapture?" Franca repeated, to be sure she understood. Sanya nodded, while taking another puff. Exhaling the smoke, she replied:

"Indeed! Strange definition, I agree; it is also called 'relative happiness', which is a little clearer, in a way. Anyway, Rapture is a state of joy and happiness, perhaps the result of a wish come true, whether material, physical or spiritual, from having overcome, or avoided, a great difficulty, a disease, a problem that was creating suffering or stress." She paused and puffed a couple of times on the cigarette so that it stayed lit. "In this state of mind you feel elated, full of energy, life seems more beautiful and all sensations are more vivid," she added, looking from the girls to Colin.

"The problem," Colin began, "is that this 'world' is soon overwhelmed by the inevitable problems that life presents us. Also it is often confused for 'happiness' itself," he said, making the signs for inverted commas with his hands.

"But it *is* happiness, isn't it?" Maria interjected. "When a wish comes true, or when we recover from a serious illness. I know a lot of people who have started to live in a very different way, after overcoming cancer, for example. They appreciate life much more."

"Sure, it's true!" Sanya agreed, looking straight at her. "The happiness that comes from overcoming an illness is real and powerful. The perception of life changes after realizing you could have died. In a sense, you have a much more correct view of life after having stared death in the face."

"Buddhist philosophy speaks of two kinds of happiness," offered Colin, "relative happiness, as in the situations we have just mentioned, and absolute happiness, which we feel when we are in the state of Buddhahood. It is the tenth world and we'll talk about that soon."

Sanya asked if they wanted to continue. She relit the cigarette that had gone out after all, and took a good puff. Sure, they wanted to continue, it was becoming more and more interesting. She said that the six worlds just explained were called the six lower worlds and that, in our society, most people thought that life alternated only between the six states of mind.

"Well... yes," said Franca, in a thoughtful mood. "What else is there?"

"The seventh and eighth states are often seen together because they have strong similarities," Sanya replied. "They are called Learning and Realization. Learning is when you start to study, or do research on a subject that interests you. This could be anything, the study of economics, medicine, even life itself. Perhaps you feel a strong interest in discovering that there is something more to life, apart from living well and satisfying the various needs and desires. This is when you read, you ask and study the things that wise people have already figured out and, with their help, you grow spiritually."

"Doing yoga, for example?" asked Maria.

"Certainly," Colin nodded, "but also reading good books, attending courses, studying in general; it enriches the mind, the heart, and life in general."

Franca beckoned the waiter to get his attention: "I'm going to order some samosas; do you want some?" she asked.

"Yes, I want two," Maria said; she was beginning to like samosas, especially the less spicy ones they made at the Tourist Camp. Sanya raised her hand and asked for two, while Colin wanted four, he was hungry. Sensing the looks of four hungry people staring at him, the waiter turned around and motioned that he had seen them. They continued to look at him until he came over and took their order.

Sanya smiled at the girls and asked if they had had a good day. She showed a lot of interest when they told her they had bought a sari each and said she wanted one too, to take home.

Colin made them laugh by saying he wanted one too, he was sure he would look great, and they pictured him wearing a silk sari! They laughed again when Maria told them of the cart pulled by the ox and of how people looked at them in disbelief. They cracked up when Franca imitated the Indian woman who threw the dung pats against the wall of the house and how she wiped her hands on her sari, imitated by her little daughter. The first few days in India had been full of surprises, they all agreed on this. While they were waiting for the samosas, they went back to talking about the Ten Worlds. The restaurant was busy; speed was not a priority in India, this they had already learned.

"So, where were we?"

"Realization," said Maria, who had made a point of remembering.

"True! Okay, so, Realization is similar to Learning, in the way it enriches life," Sanya said, "with the difference that, instead of learning from others, one arrives at one's own conclusions. You get there yourself, perhaps during a reflection, or thinking about how to solve a problem. It often happens while we recite 'daimoku', you suddenly realize a new truth." Colin was distracted and had forgotten to do his part.

"Darling, it's your turn!" said Sanya.

"Darling," said Franca, giving him a nudge. They all looked at him.

"Come on darling!" Maria joined in. They laughed aloud at Colin's expression of surprise.

"Yes, the downside..." he began, as if they had just woken him from a nap. "This process of growth gives great personal satisfaction but it's often self-centred, an end in itself." He reached out and took Sanya's pouch of tobacco and her cigarette papers. Leaning back in his chair, he continued: "It carries with it the danger of a certain arrogance, a sense of superiority, especially in people who have studied for a long time; for example, the professor who feels superior to his students, or a doctor who treats his patients as if they were incapable of understanding." He opened the pouch, took a pinch of tobacco, sniffed it and then put it back.

"It's true! It happened at college with my teachers," said Maria, "not all of them, thankfully. There were some who were monsters of arrogance, but there was one, my Italian teacher, who was wonderful! Not only was she a talented teacher, but she was also a friend; Vania was her name. She was the first one to make us work in groups; she encouraged us to take the initiative and gave us freedom. I'll never forget her!"

"Yes, fortunately there are teachers like that," agreed Sanya, who finally put her cigarette out, after having lit it for the tenth time. She asked if they wanted to know the last two worlds. Despite the effort of listening in English, the girls were curious, especially now.

"Oh no, we are not tired," said Franca, her eyes bright with curiosity. Maria smiled at her enthusiasm.

"Okay, the ninth world, then," began Sanya, as if she were telling a fairy tale. "The ninth world is that of Bodhisattva."

Never heard that word before! She saw their blank faces and explained that the word Bodhisattva meant 'one who seeks enlightenment'. There was more fervour in her voice and she spoke with more emphasis: "It is a state of altruism, where you want to help others, as well as yourself, to become happy. It is a strong desire to alleviate suffering and replace it with happiness. The nursing profession is a good example. Often these people are seeking neither fame nor wealth, but are satisfied with their work, to which they devote themselves with passion."

"The negative side of the Bodhisattva," Colin interjected quickly, smiling ironically at Franca and protecting his side from another nudge, "is when these people don't take care of themselves, or when they devote their time and their energy, but begrudgingly. For example, people who tend to elderly relatives at home; if they resent doing so they lose all the benefits, in terms of satisfaction and joy, that they would feel if they did the same thing but with love."

"Yes, very true," said Maria, who, on hearing the word 'elderly' thought of her grandmother. In that case it was her grandmother who had had so much anger inside, one could see it in her eyes. She made nice things for them, but never felt any satisfaction. Knit purl, knit purl, knit purl; never a smile on that tense and pale face. She pushed aside the image of her grandmother and concentrated on Sanya who had begun to speak again.

"And the last of the Ten Worlds is Buddhahood," she said, her eyes shining with excitement. "It's a state of deep compassion and empathy for the suffering of others. In this life state wisdom permeates every thought and action, in fact it colours the perception of all reality. It is a state where we feel completely connected with each other and with the world around us. It's a feeling of being at one with nature." She sat more upright in her chair and continued, leaning imperceptibly toward them: "It is as if everyone were your brother or sister. You feel a deep connection with other human beings, with animals, insects, trees, everything. It is a state of absolute freedom," she said with emphasis. She paused, excited by the idea she had just explained, her cheeks burning with passion.

Colin had listened with a smile and, slowly, with his warm voice, added: "Buddhahood is the goodness we have inside." He paused, relaxed. "We all have it, without exception. There are those who manifest it and those who don't, here is the difference, but potentially we all have it." Then, to demonstrate something, he put his hands together, palm to palm: "Enlightenment could be described as the fusion of reality and wisdom," he said, holding up the palm of one hand with the word 'reality' and the other palm with the word 'wisdom'. "The reality is that we all possess Buddhahood, at times manifest, other times only as a potential, and the wisdom consists in perceiving that reality." He put the two palms together and shook them slowly for a moment, adding: "Enlightenment means to *firmly believe* in this potential that each of us has within, and to act accordingly," he concluded simply.

"It means striving to respect everyone. Not only tolerate, but respect!" said Sanya, "because we all have this potential to develop Buddhahood."

Just then the waiter arrived and put a plate of piping hot samosas on the table. They asked for chai, knowing it wouldn't come quickly. They were all so hungry they immediately concentrated on their samosas, blowing into them to cool them a little. "Do you have any questions?" Sanya asked, fanning her open mouth with her hand; the samosas were both hot and spicy.

"You said that you move from one state to another, is that right?" Maria began, timidly, her mind full of all the things she had heard.

"Oh, yes!" Sanya confirmed, "all the time. Our life state changes a thousand times a day, usually as a reaction to the external environment. This is why we chant Nam-myoho-renge-kyo!"

Maria looked at her quizzically.

Sanya nodded; reading Maria's perplexed expression, she concentrated on giving a clear explanation. "Regardless of the world in which I find myself at any precise moment, I can always 'extract' my

Buddhahood, even from the world of Hell!" she said, knowing she would cause even more perplexity.

"So, do you mean that you can go straight from Hell to Buddhahood?" Franca checked. "You don't need to do one step at a time; you can 'go' from any of the worlds straight to Buddhahood. Is that right?"

"Yes, you've understood perfectly. Well done!" said Colin. "If you want, I'll give you an example of how we constantly move from one world to another; but you'll notice that Buddhahood is the only world missing." Colin offered. He checked to see if they all agreed. They definitely did! Samosa in hand, the girls nodded enthusiastically.

"So, let's use a 'typical' day as an example: It's a cold winter's morning," he began, "you get up early and find the house is freezing because, in an effort to save money, you turned the heating off last night. You go into the kitchen wrapped up tightly in your dressing gown, to prepare a coffee. While waiting for the kettle to boil, you pour some water into the cat's bowl and he rubs against your legs, purring. You browse yesterday's paper and read that they have passed a new law, which will increase the price of gas, electricity, petrol, cigarettes and VAT. Concerned because it's already a struggle to make ends meet, you consider renting out a room in your home and the idea just doesn't appeal to you; you like living alone! You feel angry at those corrupt individuals in government who take advantage of people like you, who work day and night."

Chewing the hot samosas, the girls listened carefully, nodding. Colin continued: "You turn the page to see if there is anything interesting and come across an article on the benefits of honey, which you start to read carefully. You discover it has a lot of vitamins, minerals and provides a natural boost for the immune system; that's why it helps you beat a cold more quickly. Meanwhile, the coffee is ready and you sip it with pleasure, while the cat rubs up against your legs. You give him a pat, take him in your arms, so that he warms you a bit, and kiss him on the head. You love your cat!"

He took a samosa, but instead of biting it, he opened it to let the hot steam out and, since no one interrupted him, he continued: "Then you turn the page and read that your favourite musician is playing a gig in your town, and it's on your birthday. Fantastic! ... but the tickets cost a fortune, so you won't be able to go. You feel depressed and out of sorts. On your way to the bathroom you notice that there's a message on the answer phone; it's your colleague, the one you've fancied for ages. He says he has two tickets for the concert and invites you to go with him.

The surprise takes your breath away and you are bursting with excitement. With a smile that goes from here to here," he swept his right index finger from one ear to the other, "you get dressed quickly and prepare to go to work, no longer noticing the cold in your apartment." Maria saw that Franca was trying hard to understand what the message was.

"Lovely, darling!" Sanya said, smiling at Colin. Then turning to the girls she asked if they had understood.

"Mmmmmmm!" So so, indicated Maria, with her hand.

Laughing with complicity, Sanya explained: "When she gets up and feels the extreme cold, our 'friend' is in the world of Animality. When pouring water for the cat she is in the world of Bodhisattva. When she reads about the bills going up and worries about having to rent a room she falls into the world of Hell. Her thoughts toward 'those in government' lead her into the world of Anger. Then, while sipping her coffee with pleasure she moves into the world of Tranquillity, and while reading the properties of honey she is in the world of Learning and Realization." She paused to recall the scene illustrated by Colin then, remembering it, with a smile, she continued: "When she kisses and strokes the cat she is once more in the world of Tranquillity. Then she reads about the concert and moves into the world of Hunger and, when she realizes she can't afford it, she falls back into Hell. Then, when she hears the recorded message she feels in the state of Rapture, and in this state, she gets ready to go to work. She doesn't notice the cold in the house any more, but the temperature hasn't changed, it's just like before; the only thing that has changed is her life state," she concluded with a smile.

"Now I do understand," said Maria, pleased with herself.

"Elementary Watson!" added Franca, laughing. "So, going back to my earlier question, what difference does it make when you recite those words? Because, up to here, everything is clear, but what's the reason for repeating a phrase for any length of time?"

"Good question," said Colin.

"And like you said, the world of Buddhahood was missing from the story," added Maria.

Colin nodded, looking at her with a smile. He explained that, since you could move from one life state to another, depending on the changes in the external situation, so could you also change your life state at will. He said that when reciting Nam-myoho-renge-kyo you accessed the world of Buddhahood and placed yourself in rhythm with the universe; it was like attaching a rubber pipe to the tap of Buddhahood!

What an interesting image, Maria thought.

"Reciting the phrase awakens the Buddhahood that is *inherent* in us," Colin said, "this state of goodness that we already have; reciting this phrase simply awakens it. It is a state full of compassion, wisdom, courage and life force."

"Courage?" questioned Franca. "I wasn't expecting that. Compassion yes, wisdom I didn't know, I thought that you learn wisdom as you get older, but why courage? And why life force?"

Sanya looked at her with an amused smile: "The best way to find out is to try," she replied. "Do you like strawberries? Have you ever eaten some?" she asked.

Franca wasn't sure she had understood correctly.

"Yes, we like strawberries," Maria replied for both of them, but she was puzzled, too.

"Okay then!" continued Sanya, putting a hand on her arm. Maria looked at the dozen bracelets. "If you've never tasted a strawberry, I can explain to you that it is sweet and has a certain aroma, but this can't replace the experience of eating a strawberry and tasting it yourself." She removed her hand and leaned back against the back of her chair. Waving her arm, she continued: "I could try to explain for hours how you feel when you recite that phrase, but nothing can replace the experience of chanting it yourself. It's too much of a personal experience."

"Yes, I understand," said Franca with conviction. "Better to try!"

Maria thought the example was very clear and that she liked both Colin and Sanya very much, but the idea of reciting a phrase of which she didn't even know the meaning and, what's more, in a loud voice, seemed very strange; she felt as if her whole body was pulling back forcefully. "Uhh, I don't know," she said, blushing. "I would feel strange and also a bit stupid, to be honest. And then I don't even know what those words mean, Nam Myo what?" She felt her cheeks becoming hot with embarrassment.

"You decide, darling!" Sanya said, touching her hand, with a reassuring tone that meant 'no problem'. As for the meaning of Nam-myoho-renge-kyo, it would take an hour to explain it, she said. Very briefly, it was the title of the Lotus Sutra, the penultimate and most important teaching of the Buddha, his legacy and, in just a few words, it meant to dedicate one's life to live with respect for oneself and for others; profound respect, she said, for all people, animals, and even things. She smiled at her, looking into her eyes with affection; taking responsibility for our lives, for our happiness and the happiness of others, she concluded. She laughed again, with a joy that came from her belly, realizing how complex it might all sound.

"Yes I want to try it! What have we got to lose?" Franca said suddenly, turning to look at Maria with sparkling eyes. Then turning to

Colin and Sanya she said quickly: "Okay, I want to. When shall we chant?"

Maria felt confused. There was Franca, with her typical impetuosity, throwing herself headlong into this strange thing. Where did that leave her? What was she going to do? Was she going to be left out?

Sanya seemed to understand her thoughts. She said they had already chanted but, at about eight o'clock, they could do ten minutes together in their room, if they wanted to; they were leaving early the next morning. This was her only chance, Maria thought, hesitantly. Besides, she would have done anything to spend a little more time with them.

The waiter finally brought the chai. Sanya thanked him with a big smile and a warm "thank you." She asked him if she could take it to her room, promising to bring the glass back. The waiter paused for a moment in his running from table to table and smiled; he seemed transfixed by her and more than happy to let her do anything she liked. There was a real connection, made of warm humanity. Sanya could create that relationship with everyone. While Colin was going to get a bottle of water at the counter, Sanya began to put her cigarette papers and tobacco in order. After a long search inside her bag, she pulled out a piece of card, whilst with a hand still buried inside her bag, she continued to rummage through it. Finally she found a pen.

Maria took the opportunity to ask her where in India they were going to go next. Their first stop was Bombay for Colin's research, then to Goa for a week in the sun and then, on their way back, they wanted to visit Varanasi, also known as Benares, Hindu people's holy city. They hoped to have time to go to Bodhigaya, she added, where the Buddha had spent a lot of time meditating. They would leave for England from Delhi.

In the meantime, she wrote something on the piece of card; it was the sentence they recited. She wrote it twice, then folded it carefully and tore it in two pieces. She rose to leave, she had a lot of things to do, but before, she wanted to give them a hug. Maria was surprised by the long embrace that her new friend gave her with such pleasure. Again, Sanya laughed heartily as she held her by the shoulders and looked at her with affection. She gave her the card with both hands and a little bow: "This is for you, darling," she said. Then she turned to Franca and gave her the other piece, once again, as if it were a precious gift, delicate and special. "See you later!" she said cheerfully.

While Franca walked with a quick firm step in front of her on the way back to the dorm Maria walked slowly. They had an hour to spend before eight o' clock and she was reflecting. "Are you sure about trying this thing?" she asked timidly.

"What, chanting that sentence?" Franca said. "Sure, what's the problem? I like those two, they're really nice. Don't you like them?"

"Yes of course, I like them a lot. I don't mind talking about things, but saying out loud a sentence that I don't even understand is something else. It seems strange and I'd feel stupid."

"You're worrying about nothing," said Franca, taking her shirt off and putting a t-shirt on. "Just give it a try! What have you got to lose? There's no one here who knows you or can hear you, apart from me! And I won't say a word to anyone," she said glancing at her, puzzled. "And anyway, what do you care if you look stupid? I'm curious to try it. If it makes me as happy as they are and with that kind of energy, I'll definitely give it a go. I can't wait! Come on, you come too!" she spurred her.

"I'll think about it," Maria replied, defensively. In fact, she didn't think about anything else for the next hour. She put the piece of card in her pocket, after having read it once again, and kept repeating the phrase in her head. She remembered the sound coming out of room twenty-one and the effect it had had on her. She took a book and sat on the bed pretending to read it, whilst chanting in silence. When she had heard it, it had hit her so powerfully; it had moved something inside, in the pit of her stomach, which had awoken a feeling of tremulous joy and a certain anxiety at the same time.

They arrived at the door of room twenty-one, Maria shyly, Franca full of confidence. Sanya welcomed them with a happy smile. She was preparing their bags for the trip and Colin was still in the shower, she explained. She made room for them to sit on the bed, and asked what plans they had for their journey.

She continued to fold clothes, put things in her bags, moving from one side of the small room to the other, with her long flowing skirt and her jangling bracelets, listening carefully to their plans to go to the Himalayas, then to Varanasi, to Nepal and so on, and asking them questions to find out all the details. She prepared a tidy area around a little table upon which were two candles, a metal bowl, a little stick and a jar with green leaves. Colin returned from the shower and, since they had to go to bed early and it was already past eight o'clock, they prepared to chant. Encouraged by Sanya they each pulled out their card. Colin lit the candles and sat down next to his wife on the bed nearest the table, while the two girls sat on the other bed, further back.

Sanya picked up the little stick and hit the bowl three times; a clear sound rang and continued to vibrate in the air. Slowly they began to recite Nam-myoho-renge-kyo, following Colin's deep voice and Sanya's warm voice, in a slow and rhythmic way, increasing the speed little by little, until it became a fast and strong chant, intense and mesmerizing. Maria felt transported by a powerful wave, she wanted to keep her eyes closed, but she had to read the words so as not to get confused. She saw that Franca swayed back and forth, carried by the sound, while their new friends were sitting straight, hands clasped in front of their hearts, eyes open, focused and strong. They were a small choir made of different voices, each with its own unique tone; together they created a beautiful harmony. Maria continued to repeat that sentence, she learned it by heart and forgot herself.

When she heard the sound of the stick hitting the bowl three times she knew it was finishing, and she was sorry it was. The chanting came to an end, little by little, with three Nam-myoho-renge-kyo chanted slowly, and then silence. The sound seemed to continue in waves that widened like circles in water. Sanya turned around with shining eyes. She looked at Maria and Franca with a smile: "There you are!" she said. "That's how we chant."

Maria didn't know what to say, and at the same time wanted to learn more, at least what those sounds meant.
Franca was radiant; she seemed completely satisfied and kept saying 'beautiful, beautiful!'
Sanya looked at Maria and saw her hesitation; she asked her if she had any questions.
"Well, yes, I wanted to know more about the meaning of Nam-myoho-renge-kyo," she replied sheepishly, "but I know that tomorrow morning you're getting up at four o'clock and you have to go to bed early and…"
"No problem!" Sanya assured her. She understood why she wanted to know and they would explain briefly. She glanced at Colin, who nodded and began to speak with that captivating voice, looking at her. He seemed to have a smile behind his eyes.
"Nam comes from the word Namaste, we hear it in India a thousand times a day as a greeting; it is a Hindi word meaning 'devotion'. In our case, it means 'I devote my life to the law of cause and effect.'" He continued, explaining that Myoho had many meanings, but the most important were life and death, or rather 'manifested life' and 'latent life'. In Buddhism, life was believed to be eternal, a succession of manifested life, such as ours at this time, represented by Ho, and latent life, after one was dead and before they were born, expressed as Myo.
Sanya explained that she imagined it as a wave in the sea: when the wave rose, it was an image of the manifestation of life, and when it

overturned and went back into the sea it symbolized the latent state of life. The energy of the wave didn't disappear, she said, because energy was transformed, not extinguished.

To give another example, Colin explained that, in a painting 'Ho' was the physical part, the painting, the colours, the picture itself, while Myo was the spirit that the artists had infused in that picture when they painted it, or the emotion that we felt when we looked at it. Maria and Franca nodded, concentrating hard to understand everything without missing a word. Music was a good example, too; did they know the Ode of Joy by Beethoven? he asked.

Yes, she knew it, said Franca; it was the music used in Clockwork Orange, Kubrick's film.

Colin laughed and said that yes, that was exactly it! The notes written on a piece of paper by Beethoven were the physical manifestation, Ho, while the spirit that had inspired him to write those notes and that we could feel when we heard the music was Myo.

Sanya began to sing it with enthusiasm, making them laugh; la la la la la la la, la la la la la la la la! She was waving her arm full of bracelets, as if holding a conductor's baton.

Colin laughed and said: "Yes, just like she's singing it!" He continued, explaining that the music and the feelings of joy and emotion aroused in those who listened to it were Myo, something invisible but very real. Was he being clear?

Very clear! Franca confirmed, looking like she had drunk three coffees.

Maria nodded and smiled, fascinated by the concepts she was hearing.

"Can I explain Renge?" Sanya said, "I really like that part!" Of course no one objected. Renge meant Lotus Flower, she said, and was symbolic of two important things: "The first is that this beautiful flower, often used to signify purity, needs stagnant water and mud to grow well and become its most vibrant self. If we accept that life is full of problems and suffering, symbolized by the mud, we understand that problems are not just part of life, but *essential* to make us grow stronger and become happy. So, problems are our friends," she said, pausing to give them a chance to digest that concept which was, to say the least, original. She burst into a hearty laugh seeing their expression. "We *need* problems!" she confirmed, knowing that she was saying something new for them. Colin looked at her with that ironic expression, laughing to himself. "Yes, I know that you don't like them and would rather have no problems, but life is not like that," she reminded him. "That's a dream, not reality!"

"Yes dear," he replied, looking at her with mock seriousness.

"The second meaning of the lotus flower is that it blooms and produces seeds at the same time," Sanya continued, unabated, "and this is symbolic of the law of cause and effect." She leaned forward and, with a look of wonder in her eyes, as if she understood the concept for the first time, she enunciated: "With every thought, every word, every action we take, we create a cause, and to every cause there will be an effect. And that's for sure!" she said, emphasizing the last words with a movement of her hand, cutting straight through the air.

"What, even our thoughts?" asked Maria with a worried expression.

"Sure! Because, sooner or later, what you think becomes visible; either from an expression on your face, from something you say without thinking, or through a gesture. Not only that, but even if, at times, the effect seems to *manifest* a long time later, the *latent* effect is etched in our lives the very moment we create the cause."

"That sounds scary!" Maria said. "Does it mean that I have to be aware of everything I do, say and think, *all the time*?"

Sanya laughed and settled back on the bed: "It's like the law of gravity: it always works, whether one knows it or understands it, whether you agree with it or not! If you drop something from the window, it will fall to the ground; there are no exceptions. Buddhism tells us to look inside ourselves to find the cause; it encourages us to take responsibility for our lives."

"But sometimes it is not my responsibility!" Franca objected briskly. "Sometimes it is clearly someone else's fault." Maria couldn't agree more and Franca had taken the words out of her mouth. Sanya nodded vigorously at Franca's statement.

"Yes, we are responsible for our actions, thoughts and words, and not for those of others, this is true. Other people are responsible for *their* actions. The important thing to remember is that we can choose how to 'respond' in any situation we may find ourselves in; that's where we have a choice, as if we were at a crossroads." She paused, reflecting, then continued: "Often, it seems to me that a difficult situation in my life depends on, or is caused, by another person," she said with empathy, "but if I'm honest with myself and look back, I can often find a moment in which I have done or said something that caused a reaction in the other person; it could have been a sarcastic word, or I was annoyed when I responded to them, or a gesture of impatience. Sometimes it is very difficult to find this 'cause', which may seem small, but when I find it, then I hold the key to begin to clarify a particular situation!" she concluded.

"I don't understand," Maria said, and Franca nodded vigorously because she didn't follow either.

With her elbows on her knees, Sanya leaned toward them, her hazel eyes sparkling with golden flecks: "If you think that the fault, I prefer to call it responsibility, is the other person's, you feel a victim of the situation, don't you?"

True! Maria and Franca nodded. "I always feel bad when I think I'm a victim." Maria mused aloud.

"Absolutely, it's horrible!" agreed Sanya. "Besides, when you think that it is just the other person's responsibility, it is as if you were relinquishing all the power over your life to someone else, while you remain helpless, at their mercy. It's like handing over the wheel of your car! The moment you think: 'If he would change, if he were better, if he did as I say,' you feel that you can't change things, because the change depends on what the other person does, and thus you continue to suffer!" She made a sharp gesture with her head, as if to say 'What a shame'! With a smile, she relaxed her shoulders and leaned back on her elbow.

"I'm thinking about how I felt before I left for India, exactly like a victim," said Maria, her head crowded with all the things she had heard. "Now I have to rethink everything!"

Sanya smiled and said: "You can look at the old situation in this new light. It will help you see it from a different perspective, putting you at the helm. The important thing is what you do from now on. Buddhism tells us that the past is important so that we learn not to repeat the same mistakes, but what really matters is the present and the future; we always start from now!"

"Kyo is missing," said Franca, fully concentrated.

"Kyo means sound, sutra, teaching, speech, action," Colin said, smiling at her, amused by her complete absorption. "A lot of things, but it also means that we are all connected. Everything in life and in the environment is interconnected," he explained. "So, the pain or the joy of one person ripples out to many others. If one person in a family is sad or unhappy, the whole family suffers."

It was true. Maria thought, although some people showed it more than others. In the end though, every person in a family was important.

"There's much more," Colin said, "but to explain everything we'd need a lot more time!"

"Action, you said, is one of the meanings of Kyo," said Franca, full of enthusiasm. "I like it! But what does it mean? Doing a lot of things? Being active?"

Sanya smiled: "I'll give you an example. There was a time in my life," she began, "when I felt desperate because I had no money and no work; I was in the state of Hell. For years I had had a lot of theatre jobs, but those last few months, nothing had come up. I couldn't pay my rent and I had only enough money to eat beans and rice. One morning I was in bed, depressed and without energy. After a while, since there was nothing else to do, I decided to summon that bit of life force I needed to get up and chant 'daimoku'; that means to chant Nam-myoho-renge-kyo. I decided to carry on for an hour, even though it was difficult. At first I was crying, but after five minutes, I wiped my tears and began to feel some ideas surfacing, as well as a little confidence in myself, and some determination. My life state started to change and, as I carried on, my 'daimoku' became stronger and stronger; my voice, from being a mouse's little squeak became the roar of a lion."

The girls listened carefully, while Colin looked at her with a smile, recalling that period. She continued: "My profession was as an actress, however as there was no theatre or television work, I could, and had to, do something else. I remembered that, through my work, I wanted to create value and that it gave me great satisfaction to help others. I took pen and paper and began to write a letter in which I offered my services as a babysitter, assistant to the elderly, assistant teacher, or as a cleaner. I didn't have any problem in cleaning toilets, if needs be. Then, I made a list of schools, colleges and nursing homes in my area and I began to write the names on the envelopes, promising myself to correct the letter in the afternoon, make photocopies and find the complete addresses. Within an hour, from being in the world of Hell I had moved to a desire to work to help others, that is, the world of Bodhisattva. If you remember, when we chant 'daimoku' our Buddhahood surfaces in the form of wisdom, courage, compassion and life force. Colin said that Buddhahood is the fusion of reality and wisdom, do you remember?" she asked, bringing together her two palms.

Colin made a funny face, as if to say 'How good was I? I told you!' and made them laugh.

"And did you find work?" Maria asked.

"Yes. I was taken on as an orderly in a nursing home, but I would start work in ten days time," Sanya replied, "and I couldn't wait that long without earning. My financial situation was so critical that, after delivering the letters by hand, to avoid buying stamps, I made some cakes at home and took them to bars and shops in the area where I lived with the hope of selling them. On the first day, I met the owners of these places, and explained to them what I was doing and why. One of them told me that he needed someone to do the cleaning in his bar, including the toilets. I began that same evening, four hours a night, paid well and immediately. With the money I earned with the cakes and from the cleaning I managed to survive and pay the rent, and then I started at the nursing home."

Franca and Maria were absorbed by the story. Sanya continued to tell: "After four weeks of working as an orderly, which I really enjoyed, my agent called: there was an audition for the role of Florence Nightingale in a three-episode drama for one of the major television stations in England. The director was very impressed with my audition; he asked me if I had ever been a nurse by profession and offered me the part right there and then, on the spot. That period of work in the nursing home had been crucial in me giving an interpretation that was honest and heartfelt!"

"Did you ever return to the nursing home?" asked Maria.

Her friend smiled warmly: "Many times! I had made friends with the elderly patients and the other employees. I would have a job with them, they said, if I ever needed one!" Looking at Franca, she asked if her story had explained the meaning of 'action'. They had understood very well, and with an unforgettable example.

"Sanya transformed poison into medicine," said Colin, turning to the girls. "Without the courage to deal with the situation, as she did in the beginning, she wouldn't have had the part of Florence Nightingale."

"Yes, very true," she agreed. "Unfortunately we can't talk about everything in one evening!"

The girls realized that it was time to let them rest and stood up, ready to leave. Sanya said they could use the chanting of Nam-myoho-renge-kyo for whatever they desired.

"If you are afraid, chant to develop courage. If you are sad, chant to feel gratitude and become happier; whenever you want to feel at one with the universe; literally anything you want," she told Maria, hugging her and looking into her eyes.

"And if somebody makes you suffer..." Colin said, looking at Sanya; the result was a familiar giggle.

"Oh yes, this is the best! If someone makes you suffer," she said, grinning, "chant for their happiness!"

"*What*?" the girls burst out at the same time, provoking laughter from both Sanya and Colin.

"That may be very difficult," said Maria.

"Maybe I *don't want* him, or her, to be happy," said Franca at the same time.

"Yes, at first you may think so, and it *is* difficult to begin to chant for the happiness of those who hurt us. But, try and see for yourself," she said with confidence. And, as if that were not enough, she added: "And this happiness is genuine inner happiness, not what, in your view, should make that person happy!"

Preventing further protests from the girls, who strongly resisted this concept, Colin clarified, with his calm and deep voice: "When we chant for those who make us suffer, we start, imperceptibly, to see their point of view. Maybe we would act in a different way, but at least we begin to understand where their behaviour or attitude comes from." He paused and then speaking slowly, he added: "We always have a choice. It depends on us."

Maria thought of Ugo; could she really choose whether to suffer or not? Sanya was looking at her, then she looked at Franca, and said: "When we chant for the happiness of the other person we let go of our demands or expectations of them, we give him, or her, complete freedom!" She pushed her hands forward, palms outwards, as if to distance herself, or to give space. After a short pause she added: "At the same time, we give *ourselves* complete freedom."

They saw the girls' faces change with many different thoughts. Sanya and Colin looked at each other and smiled. Sanya embraced Franca, and Colin hugged Maria. Words couldn't express the intensity of that meeting, the enormity of the change they had put in motion and that the young women would continue to develop in their own way, each in her own time. It was amazing how so short a friendship could leave such a deep a mark, so sweet a feeling. They swapped partners and hugged again.

"Thank you for everything!" Maria said to Sanya, touched by this wonderful woman.

"Thank *you*," she replied, and added: "You're beautiful, inside and out!"

"You are both beautiful!" said Colin.

"Wait, I'll give you our address." Sanya hurried to find a piece of paper and carefully wrote their address and phone number. With care, she gave it to Maria, who quickly wrote her Venice address and gave it to her, inviting them to come and visit them. Franca joined her palms and bowed to them. They did the same, the Indian way, as in front of a mirror. They went back to the dorm in silence, smiling. Maria sat on the bed, while Franca was getting ready to go out.

"Where are you going?" Maria asked.

"To smoke a chillum with the French guys. Are you coming?"

"No, thank you; I'm stopping here. I'm fine like this."

4. Something 'incongruous'

When Maria awoke, she saw two other people had arrived. They had settled near the door, leaving an empty bed between theirs and Franca's. A boy and a girl, they were sleeping, barely covered by a sarong. Franca was fast asleep with a scarf over her eyes. It must have been around eight in the morning. Maria sat on the bed and put her sandals on. Immediately she thought of Sanya and Colin who would have already been travelling for hours; she was sorry they had left. Who knew if and when she would see them again? Nam-myoho-renge-kyo was her first thought, that sentence seemed to have imprinted in her mind, like an inscription engraved on stone. It was always there, behind, or rather, next to all the other thoughts, and she recited it silently. She got up to go to the bathroom; would she ever get used to this system without toilet paper? It was a challenge. She picked up her purse with money and passport before walking out in the sun, already hot. Gemma, her mum, had taught her since she was little that 'It's good to trust but not trusting is even better'.

Later, while sitting at a table in the restaurant drinking chai and waiting for warm chapatis, butter and jam, she chanted the phrase, 'daimoku' they called it, in her head. In which world was she right now? Tranquillity? She promised herself to write some notes before forgetting all the things she had heard. She saw Franca on her way to the bathroom and waving her arm in the air, caught her attention: did she want breakfast? Franca nodded firmly. Maria ordered chai, bhaji and chapatis; by now she knew what her friend wanted. Franca was still half asleep but delighted with the many chillums she had smoked the night before with the French guys.

"They had very good charas," she said wistfully, "and explained how to go to the Himalayas."

"We go tomorrow, right?"

"I think we could go today," said Franca, who had already decided to change their plans. "The bus leaves at six in the afternoon. If we go to buy our tickets now, then we can come back here, prepare our luggage, eat and go; all without rushing."

"Had we not decided to leave tomorrow?" Maria objected, without much conviction. "I wanted to see New Delhi."

"Yes, I know, but with the bus leaving at six, you'll have enough time to get a ride into New Delhi," said Franca. "Feel how hot it is already! And think how cool it is in the mountains. They said it's gorgeous!"

Maria wasn't entirely opposed to the idea.

Outside the Tourist Camp they stopped the first black and yellow three-wheel scooter that appeared. This form of transport, halfway between a motorcycle and a Fiat 500, had already become familiar; easy to stop, use and pay. No cart with oxen today, they decided. The man asked for ten rupees; with great satisfaction, they managed to lower to nine, and they were carried at full speed toward Kashmiri Gate Bus Station. The wind lifted Maria's long untied hair, while they both looked around, observing their surroundings with hungry curiosity. Franca had tied her hair in a braid, like Indian women did. They went from the relatively quiet area close to the Tourist Camp to a crowded and noisy part of the city, with their scooter opening a breach among bicycles, taxis and the ever-present ambling cows, driving only a few inches from them. Sucking 'betel' in his red mouth the scooter man drove in a jerky way, braking sharply, muttering to himself and advising others on how to conduct themselves. The girls had to hold on tight to avoid flying out at every sudden manoeuvre and to stop bumping into the driver's seat, but they were having a great time! They relinquished full responsibility for the drive; there was nothing they could do to persuade him to drive in any other way and they saw no traffic accidents, for the moment at least. Finally the scooter stopped outside the huge station from where buses departed to all destinations. Maria paid with a ten rupee note and motioned the driver to keep the change.

Legs wobbly from the shaky ride, hair dishevelled, faces covered with dust, they looked around and hesitantly entered the enormous grey, noisy and confusing station.

There were hundreds of counters, each one with a queue of dozens of people, women in saris, men dressed in white, some wearing a turban, others without. They had bags, backpacks, luggage of all types. The destinations were written in Hindi and English, but they couldn't find the one they were looking for.

"Where exactly are we going?" Maria asked, shouting to be heard.

"To Manali! Kulu Valley," yelled Franca back. They began to ask people here and there: "Kulu Manali?" But they all shook their heads. Everyone seemed preoccupied and only concerned with buying their own tickets. That place was stressful and they too shared the anxiety; buying a ticket for a coach trip looked like a big challenge. A man pointed them to a clerk in uniform who was holding a pad of paper and talking with a group of people. They approached him and he looked at them with curiosity. There were very few foreigners and they were the only two girls on their own.

They waited a little for their turn, but then, as he looked at them every so often while he dealt with the small crowd around him, Maria cried out: "Tickets for Manali, please?"

The man in uniform, ignoring those around him, flipped through the pages of his notebook and replied in a resounding voice: "Counter ninety eight, Madam!"

The girls thanked him loudly and he rocked his head, pleased with himself. Counter ninety-eight. Finally they found it: Kulu-Manali. The queue was long, but less than at the other counters, and they began to wait, happy to have arrived as far as they had.

"So, once we have our tickets, shall we go for a stroll in New Delhi?" asked Maria.

"You go Maria, I'm going back to the Tourist Camp."

"Why?"

"I'm going to meet up with the French guys."

"To smoke?"

"Yes, I like it!"

"I've understood that! But do you smoke even in the day? Afterwards you'll have no strength to do anything," objected Maria; the idea of going to Delhi alone frightened her.

"No, no, I'll have the strength to do everything," said Franca, laughing. "Actually, I do everything better, because I am happier and more relaxed. Why do you think I came to India?"

"Just to smoke? You could have done that in Venice. In fact, you did." Then, reflecting, she added: "From what Sanya and Colin told us, in which of the ten worlds would you be? Animality?"

"No, I'd be in the world of Hunger. I had already thought about it! The world of insatiable desire. Yep, that's me!" said Franca, putting her hand up. "Anyway, I didn't come to India *just* to smoke, obviously, but to enjoy it as much as possible, yes, for sure. You'll like going around Delhi on your own. It'll do you good and we'll become more independent."

Well! The decision had been made. Maria thought that perhaps she would go back to the Tourist Camp too, but she quickly dismissed the idea; she would be doing so only out of fear. Instead, she was going to go and see the shops. After all she had travelled quite a lot around Europe and North Africa, never alone, if truth be told, but Indian people seemed harmless, in fact they were very nice. As they approached the counter, her anxiety was turning to excitement. Finally, with the tickets for Kulu-Manali in their hands, they headed out of the station and caught two scooters in opposite directions.

"New Delhi, please!" Maria said to her driver. Where about in New Delhi did she want to go? She didn't know exactly, where there were shops. What kind of shops? Shops that sold all sorts of things, for tourists, basically. This driver was chewing 'betel' too, but as well as the typical red mouth he had also black teeth; he bobbed his head and took off like a rocket. Maria held on tightly to the scooter's frame as he accelerated, slowed abruptly, mumbled to himself, laughed and gave advice; they were once again dodging bicycles, cars, rickshaws and the thin cows with their protruding ribs. The dusty air infiltrated her eyes, ears, nose and ruffled her hair even more. She looked outside and smiled, amused, alone and with no fear. There she was in a scooter with an agitated driver, throngs of humanity out there, and felt just fine.

They came to a colossal roundabout, embraced by at least four lanes of traffic all around, with a park in the centre. Even there, among the relentless madness of the traffic, fast and neurotic, cows wandered lazily in the road. It was quite unbelievable! The vehicles dodged them, paying great attention not to touch them, while they, clearly used to the pandemonium, didn't seem to worry about a thing. They were skinny, large, loved and masters.

"Where are we?" she shouted to the driver.

"Connot Place, Madam."

She looked around and saw the name written on the colonnade surrounding the square's outer circle with its beautiful white, classic shape: Connaught Place. In the cool shade created by the row of columns, were hundreds of shops, cosy and relaxed side by side.

"Shall we stop here?" she shouted again.

"Here it's expensive, Madam," he cried; did she want expensive shops? No thanks, not expensive. The man bobbed his head, as if to say 'See? I had figured it out.' "I'll take you where there are cheap shops," he shouted, sucking his 'betel' behind his pink and black teeth. "Cheap is best!"

"Okay, thank you." Smiling, Maria leaned against the seat's back, lined with red plastic, and let the driver take her where he knew; it was clear that he had understood what she wanted. When they arrived at the beginning of a big boulevard, he snuck quickly into a clear space and, with an elegant S-shaped move, parked next to other scooters.

"Many shops here, Madam, and good prices," he said, satisfied with his work.

She got out and, as before her legs were shaking from the adventurous race. She paid him five rupees, the asking price, and after a moment to put her money away and get steady on her feet, she thanked him bowing with clasped hands. She could do the greeting well now, especially if she was alone. She walked on the pavement populated by dozens of shops, where people moved shoulder to shoulder.

The shopkeepers sat cross-legged on their shop floors, which were lined by a thin mattress covered with white cloth. The shops opened onto the pavement, without any doors or windows. The goods for sale were a feast for the eyes: silk saris, cotton fabrics, printed sarongs, dresses, skirts, shirts, all hanging from the ceiling and out in the open, they swayed to the passing of people. Fire red, pea green, sky blue, sunny yellow, candid white, bright orange; vivid colours commanded her attention and changed shade at every movement.

Further down the road, shops were selling statues and objects made of wood, bronze, brass that looked like gold, all beautiful, shiny and attractive. Statues of a god with its trunk and of another one with a flute, that was Krishna, she recognized him; there was a statue of the dancing Shiva within a circle, and many more. There were also, in the foreground, larger and smaller figurines... in the shape of a penis! Was she seeing properly, was it something else? Not wanting to stare openly, Maria glanced at them from time to time as she continued her stroll down the sidewalk, together with a mass of people, dragged by the steady crowd that, like a flowing river, seemed to fill every little space. Shopkeepers invited her to enter.

"Just look, Madam."

"Come and sit here Madam, good prices!"

"Chai Madam?" offered one of the shopkeepers, taking advantage of a break in the business.

"I'm just looking," she said.

"Okay, just look. I show, you look and we drink chai."

"But I don't want to buy anything."

"No problem, Madam." He invited her to sit. Still a little uncertain Maria sat down. The man clapped his hands and, to a boy who arrived running, he ordered: "Do chai"; then to Maria he said: "I wasn't doing anything, I'm glad to show you my goods, so maybe another customer comes in." He unfolded sarongs, cotton and silk shawls of many colours; meanwhile he wanted to know where she was staying, when she had arrived, whether she liked Delhi. He told her he had three children and didn't want any more; that work was a bit slow but he didn't worry: Bagwan (God) would give him what he needed. After the chai, he was pleased with the company and the attention received and Maria bought a white sarong of light cotton and stood up to leave, feeling enriched by their shared experience full of humanity. The merchant bowed and she returned the salutation.

She walked along the pavement, feeling at ease within the thick crowd that surrounded her. Eventually, the stores ended and a quieter area shaded by some trees and shrubs began. She strolled along until she came upon a big gate that opened onto a lengthy avenue lined with trees. The long path, bordered by a large swimming pool with sun beds and tables, led to the famous Imperial Hotel; barely visible it stood framed by tall palm trees at the end of the avenue. She had heard about it, apparently the pool was open to the public for a fee. Too shy to venture in, she peered through the gate. Behind her there were queues of taxis waiting for the wealthy clients.

A voice caught her attention. Her eyes fell on a beggar sitting on the ground; instead of hands he had two stumps, and beckoned her over. He pounded his belly with one of the stumps, taking it to his mouth, as if to say that his stomach was empty and he was hungry. A little further down, a few metres away, there was another beggar, without fingers; one more next to him without a leg, another still was without his feet. And so on, old, young, some little more than children, many with white empty eyes, blind... Maria was shocked, touched in her heart, her stomach, her throat. Everything inside her was twitching in a knot of pain, aversion, compassion, horror and embarrassment in the face of so much suffering. She couldn't turn away and leave, nor could she pretend not to see, because the man looked straight at her and his eyes were kind. Approaching, though it was hard, was the only thing she could do. She took a few rupees from her purse; then counted the beggars and took out fifty paisa coins. She handed one to the beggar without hands. He took it between his stumps, brought them to his forehead and then lowered his arms to touch her feet, to thank her. Looking at her again, he smiled, he had beautiful white teeth.

"What's your name?" he asked.

"Maria," she replied, surprised. He couldn't have been more than thirty years old, at most.

She gave a coin to all the other beggars. They each thanked her with a smile, touching their foreheads, gently touching her feet. With her face she smiled at them, but in her heart she wanted to cry, scream, run away. She glanced around, looking for a scooter; she wanted to go 'home', back to the Tourist Camp, away from the pain, and feel protected. There were taxis, but they were too expensive and to spend her money like that seemed an insult to those beggars. Besides, she had little more than a thousand rupees a month, about a hundred dollars, and had to be careful as to how she spent it. She hurriedly retraced her steps along the row of shops on Janpath Boulevard, she needed peace of mind, didn't want to think, or see. She moved to the curb and motioned to the scooters that flew by, until one stopped. While the wind comforted her and the jarring of the scooter kept her alert, Maria thought how those poor men were probably among the lucky ones, begging outside a luxury hotel.

Back at the Tourist Camp she entered the reception and, finding the receptionist there, asked him why those beggars were without fingers, hands, or worse. He listened, looking at her with those green eyes, his face calm, his white beard neatly retained by the net. He told her that some of them had lost their limbs because of leprosy.

"Leprosy? I thought it was a thing of the past. That it didn't exist anymore," she exclaimed, shocked.

"Unfortunately it isn't, Maria. There's less than there used to be, but it still exists. Those men are healed, but the damage to their limbs has been done." He looked at her intently in silence, as if wanting to add something else. She waited. "For others, what you saw is not caused by a disease," he added, with an effort.

"Isn't it? What it is caused by, then?"

"There are evil and ignorant people who cause those mutilations voluntarily. So they can collect more money," he said, partly embarrassed, partly disgusted.

"I can't believe it!" She didn't want to believe it.

"Many children are abducted, or are orphans, and are taken by bad people, who mutilate them and make them beg; like that they earn more," he said angrily.

"That's terrible!" she burst out.

"Yes, it is terrible. India is a big place and there are all sorts of things. There is poverty, a lot of ignorance, and people who take advantage of it. You come here from your country and don't realize what there is in India, the most beautiful and the ugliest. This is why I told you to be careful and take care of yourself." He looked at her intently to be sure she was listening. Maria nodded in silence. She thanked him for his attention and told him she would leave that afternoon, but would return every time they passed by Delhi. She was always welcome, he said, looking at her with the expression of a loving father.

The dormitory was empty, so Maria headed to the restaurant. She ordered a plate of rice with chicken and sat down to wait. She exchanged a few words with a group of young men from Israel. It was already two o'clock. After lunch she went back to the dorm; no sign of her friend. She went for a shower and saw Franca sitting outside one of the bungalows with the French guys. She looked at her, smiling, her blue eyes reddened, sat in a relaxed posture.

"What time do you want to set off?" asked Maria.

"Around four at the latest," she replied. "In a little while I'll prepare my rucksack."

After her shower, a towel twisted into a turban on her head, Maria returned to the dormitory, where two women were cleaning. She greeted them with a 'Namaste' and they replied the same way, cordially. Franca arrived shortly afterwards and began to prepare her luggage.

The two women watched, smiling. They had noticed the saris on the bed and, unable to restrain their curiosity, asked if they belonged to them. Yes, they are ours, confirmed Franca.

The two women conferred between themselves and then approached the girls. With gestures and a few words of English, they managed to explain that they wanted to show them how to wear a sari.

"Have we got time?" asked Maria.

"A little," replied her companion.

One of the women, miming something around her waist, wanted to know if they had a belt. The girls looked at each other and, no, they didn't have a belt.

"No problem," said the women, putting down the broom and mop. After some discussion, they lifted their own saris showing the skirts they were wearing underneath. From there, with some effort, they pulled out a strip of cotton fabric, which had been holding up their saris. They ignored the girls' protests and tied the belts around their waists; their saris would remain in place even without a belt, they reassured them. They motioned to the girls to take off their jeans and laughed like children when they saw them in their underwear. One dresser for Franca and one for Maria, they took hold of the new sari and began to drape it, the first piece neatly tucked inside the belt and then, fold after fold, gathering at the front. They looped the fabric around the middle of the back and then as the final touch, brought the last metre of sari diagonally across the front of the body and over the left shoulder. That was it! If necessary, they could use this last piece to cover their head, to shelter from the sun.

Maria looked at Franca, Franca looked at Maria. There were no mirrors, so they were each other's reflection; they laughed. The cleaners admired them; they were very happy and nodded approvingly, amused and proud at the same time. Four women from two different worlds, together playing a game, like little girls imitating their mothers. Although the sari was well draped and Franca looked almost elegant, there was something not quite right with that combination. Maria was not sure how to describe it, but it seemed somewhat absurd.

"How do I look?" asked Franca.

"Well, in a way you even look good, but there is something that doesn't add up. Perhaps that you're from Venice, you have blue eyes... I don't know. There is something 'incongruous'. And what do *I* look like?" asked Maria, expecting an equally honest answer.

"Mmm, it's between elegant and strange, I don't know; incongruent is a good definition. Well, let's change and go," she said, beginning to remove her sari.

Oh no, no, no! A chorus of loud protests started from the two women: "No, Madam, you are beautiful! Keep the sari!" But the belt, we give you your belts back, gestured the girls. "No, no! Keep the belt! You look just like Indian women."

The girls looked at each other. What were they going to do now? If they removed the sari they would upset the two women.

"All right, then, let's keep them on. Maybe it's cooler than travelling in jeans," Franca decided, putting her trusty jeans in her backpack and closing it tight.

"We would really upset them if we took it off," Maria mused, looking at the two women who were smiling proudly. "Okay. Let's keep it on. We have to go!" She squeezed her jeans in on top of everything else, pulled the strings to close her backpack and, with a snap, locked the plastic buckles of the flap that covered it.

She lifted it on her shoulders, picked up her camera bag and slung the purse with her documents across her front. With no time left to linger, they bowed to the Indian women who were watching them with folded hands, proudly admiring their masterpiece. They walked toward the exit of the Tourist Camp, trying not to stumble on the folds of the sari, which reached the ground. They said goodbyes left, right and centre, to people they had met, arousing a few surprised and perplexed looks. The reception office was empty, so, saris and backpacks, incongruent, 'like wearing a shoe and a clog', as they'd say in Venice, they went out into the street to wait for a scooter to come by.

"Can you tell me why you brought such a huge rucksack and one with a picture of the Canadian flag?" asked Franca, observing Maria.

"Is it the Canadian flag? I didn't know. I thought it was just a leaf; I had no idea!" replied Maria, surprised. "Do you think I look ridiculous?" she asked, looking at her feet.

"From the front it's not too bad." replied her friend, eyeing her from head to toe. "But from behind it's something else all together," she said, holding back a laugh.

"What do you mean?"

"Well, the red backpack with the Canadian flag covers you from your head almost down to your knees. Below that, I can see the last part of the sari and your feet." Franca laughed heartily this time.

"It's because you've been smoking that it seems so funny... I hope," said Maria. Then, on reflection, she added: "Well, it's done now. I hope we don't meet anyone we know!"

They arrived at Kashmiri Bus Station half an hour before the coach's departure. The huge station, grey and dusty, was in the throes of organized chaos; an atmosphere of 'every man for himself' reigned. People moved around with worried and anxious expressions and a lot of luggage. Many travelled with trunks made of grey iron, carried on the heads of men, protected by just a wrapped shawl. There were professionals porters, with red jackets and white turbans, almost all of them chewing 'betel' in their scarlet mouths, moving quickly and competently, carrying huge trunks, fully focused on the enormous effort required. They walked as if dancing, bouncing on their knees at every step to cushion the weight of their load.

Where was the platform with their coach?

They saw a man in uniform surrounded by a swarm of people, and approached him. Without any courtesy, Franca shouted: "What platform for Kulu-Manali?" The man looked annoyed and motioned with his hand to wait.

"Please! We're late," cried Maria.

The man gave her a serious look, but flipped through his notepad. "Seventy-nine" he replied at last.

"Thank you!"

Walking as fast as their saris would allow, they arrived at the platform. There was the bus with the word they were looking for, in both the Hindi alphabet and in their own: 'Manali'.

Maria noticed a blond man descending from the coach. He was wearing pyjama trousers of a burgundy colour and a white traditional Indian shirt embroidered with blue. His hair reached his shoulders... and he was the most handsome man she had ever seen in her life. He raised his green eyes and looked at her, briefly registering, with surprise, the sari she wore. He looked at her again, watching her a little better, winking a brief greeting. Maria felt herself blush to the tips of her fingers, her heart somersault and her legs begin to shake. She stood for a moment startled by the heat rising in her cheeks; she was not one to blush easily.

"Did you see that one?" she said to Franca, next to her.

"Yes, I've noticed him," she said irritably, focused on the task at hand. "Come on, we have to put our backpacks on the roof of the bus, and then find our seats," she added.

They hurried toward the back of the coach where the porters climbed the perpendicular ladder and loaded the passengers' baggage, carrying it on their heads, shoulders and arms. The luggage weighed tons, but they climbed like acrobats. People paid them one rupee per piece. Maria gave her backpack to a porter who loaded it on his shoulder and offered his other arm for Franca's. Instead she pushed him sharply to one side, pulled up her sari's skirt and, with her rucksack on her back, grabbed the ladder's rung and began to climb fast and agile as a monkey. The people stood watching her with a mixture of surprise and admiration. The porter followed her with the rest of his luggage and, when he met her on the roof, gave her a big smile, which Franca didn't reciprocate. She climbed down as fast as she'd gone up and, wiping her dirty hands on her sari, ignoring Indian people's stares, she hurried back to Maria, who was waiting just outside the crowd. "No way I'm paying one rupee every time I have to put up, and then take down, my rucksack," she said nonchalantly.

"I need to have a pee before we leave," said Maria. "No doubt there'll be some toilets."

"You'd better go now. I'll have a fag! Leave your camera here. You have ten minutes; run!"

She couldn't see any signs for 'Toilets', but she saw one that said 'Latrines'. And latrines they were! They were spread over a large area, in proportion to the size of the station, and the floor was covered by an inch of liquid; was that water? If it was water, it was dirty. Maria stopped at the door. What am I going to do? she wondered. Am I going to wade? If I don't do it here, *where* can I do it? Overcoming the disgust, she lifted her sari and waded through the 'water', taking great care not to slip; the last thing she needed was to fall in the urine of hundreds of people. The cubicle was even worse and the fetid odour was unbearable. Trying not to breathe, she had her pee, whose jet, when touching the ground, spattered back up on her legs; sprays of collective urine! Preferring not to think about it, she hurried outside as quickly as possible. At least now she didn't have a bursting bladder!

Back on the bus, ticket in hand, she looked for her numbered seat. Franca wasn't there yet, but she didn't worry, she would turn up. She found her place in a row of three. Sitting by the window, an elderly Indian woman with white hair was looking out. There was a bundle on Maria's seat.

"Excuse me! Excuse me," she said, but the old woman ignored her, as if she were deaf.

Maria took the bundle and put it on her legs. This time, the elderly lady looked at her; she was beautiful, petite, with regular features and smooth skin, her hair held in a long white braid. Maria smiled at her, showing her her ticket, but the woman turned back to look out the window. Just then, Franca got on and came to sit next to Maria.

"These seats are narrow, eh?" she said, trying to settle down, but she could hardly fit. "It's a good job that we are all slim!" she added.

Wearing almost identical saris, one pink, one red, with almost the same height and build, they could easily have been sisters. To keep her long hair tidy during the trip Maria, who was only slightly taller, had gathered it in a braid, like Franca, and this added even more to the illusion.

Behind them sat a pretty western girl with reddish hair and green eyes. She wore a long skirt and a beautiful hand embroidered waistcoat over a thin white shirt. Franca turned around and asked if she knew how long it would take to get to Manali.

"Seventeen hours, if all goes well. We'll arrive tomorrow morning at eleven o'clock... perhaps," replied the girl.

"*What*?" the girls exclaimed at the same time.

"I had no idea it was such a long journey! There is barely room for two people on this seat... I don't know how we're going to manage!" said Franca, visibly worried.

"And we have nothing to eat or drink. I thought we would arrive in three or four hours," said Maria.

"Me too! We didn't ask how long the journey took."

Maria felt the old woman begin to push imperceptibly but relentlessly to earn as much space as possible on the seat. The western girl, looking at the sari they were wearing, asked how long they had been in India.

"Three days," replied Maria. "And you?"

"Three years," she said. At that moment the blond man got on the bus and came to sit next to her.

"What's your name?" the girl asked.

"I'm Franca!"

"I am Maria."

"Italian?"

"Yes. And you?"

"We're English. I'm Karen and this is Paul," said the girl, holding out her hand. They shook hands. Maria felt Paul's warm palm joining hers and blushed again, unsettled.

5. Cheloh, cheloh! Here we go!

The driver opened his door and lifted himself on board. He folded his hands and said a prayer; then leaned his elbow on the horn and let it sound for a few deafening seconds.

'Cheloh, cheloh', they were shouting outside, while the bus started to manoeuvre in reverse, aided by a couple of people on the ground who made sure it wasn't going to hit anyone. They were off! The passengers were excited, talking loudly and laughing, in the knowledge that they could now sit back and be taken to their destination.

For over an hour the bus made its way through the dense traffic of Delhi. Eventually it left the big city behind and started on a long, straight road, where they drove for hours. The sky changed from a dusty blue to a dull grey, growing darker the further they travelled. Maria looked through the window, past 'granny's' pretty regular face. The elderly lady continued to ignore her and pushed at every opportunity to earn a few millimetres. At every jolt, she'd push that little bit, thinking it wouldn't be noticed; at every little push, Maria opposed with just as much resistance, pretending she didn't resist at all.

She would happily have spent her time looking out of the window if it weren't for the driver's crazy style. He hurtled down the middle of the road; whenever he saw a lorry or a bus coming in the opposite direction, also driving in the middle of the road, he held his ground, as did the other driver. So, every two minutes, they seemed on the verge of a head-on collision. At the very last moment both vehicles would swerve sharply and graze each other, only just avoiding a fatal accident. Neither of the two vehicles slowed down and no one seemed to care, except for Maria and Franca, who held on tight to the rail of the seat in front, trying not to faint from fear.

"Are they mad?"

"They're out of their mind!" Even Franca, who believed she was imperturbable, felt her hair stand on end.

"Didn't your friends tell you that they drive like madmen escaped from an asylum?"

"Yes, but I didn't realize it was like this," her friend replied, firmly holding on, staring at the road ahead.

Eventually, since no one else seemed to notice the danger of crashing every few minutes, they decided to relax. The road cut through the centre of the villages and was flanked by the everyday life that flowed outdoors. It was like watching a movie projected on a giant screen.

Carts clopped by, slowly pulled by white oxen with painted red horns. Children played with the wheels of old bicycles, pushing them with a stick to make them roll, and running alongside them, shouting and laughing. Women, in their colourful saris, crouched at the edge of a small stream that flowed along the road, rubbing dishes and pots made of brass with bare hands, using a mixture of earth and grass, until they glowed shiny and impeccably clean. They deftly scooped water with their hands and rinsed the dishes, all the while smiling and chatting with their neighbour. Some women did it all with a baby on their back, wrapped tightly in a large shawl, tied at the front just above the breast. They stood up, bent down, bowed, talked and laughed while the little one often slept soundly, secure in that intimate closeness. There was harmony in their calm movements, a slow rhythm that connected one person to another, every action to the next.

Maria pulled out a packet of duty-free Marlboro and turned around to offer one to the blond Englishman sitting behind her; it was just a pretext to look at him. When she met his magnetic gaze she felt her cheeks burning and a whirring vortex in her heart. He accepted the cigarette and smiled. He had perfect white teeth, a small straight nose and his hair, the colour of gold, rolled up into curls where it touched his shoulders. When he thanked her she was surprised by his deep voice; he said he would keep the cigarette for later, and put it in his shirt pocket. Maria turned around, once again sitting upright on her seat and blew out the emotion that swelled her chest.

"Are you okay?" asked Franca.

"Yes, yes, I'm fine. It's this guy behind us that has an overwhelming effect on me. How can anyone be so handsome?" she said, hoping the English couple didn't understand a word of Italian.

Franca laughed: "Why? Hasn't anything like this ever happened to you?"

"Not like this; at least not that I remember!"

After a continuous ride of at least two hours, the bus stopped midway between Delhi and Chandigarh. At the side of the road, surrounded by flat, parched countryside was a chai-shop. Maria asked Karen if she knew where the toilets were. The English girl laughed, amused by her question, and told her that there were no toilets; she had to find a private place and do it there. The problem was that all the passengers were walking around with the same intent. In the end, even though Maria had gone further than she wanted to, the place she found to pee was anything but discreet. Fortunately, everyone minded their own business and pretended not to see anyone else. When she returned to the chai-shop, Franca was eating lentils from a folded leaf.

"Is it hot?" asked Maria.

"Normal," replied Franca, with her mouth full.

'Normal' meant too spicy; this Indian food was a real problem. Maria ended up pointing at some fried things that cost two rupees; they were spicy and salty. She could have demolished a huge plate of spaghetti, happily leaving all the bhaji, sabji, pakhora and samosas to someone else! The long blaring sound of the bus horn informed them that it was time to climb aboard.

Once she reached her seat, 'granny' was already sitting by the window. This time, she had placed her bundle beside her, out of the girls' reach. She was leaning over it, trying to hide it, and occupying a seat and a half. This time Maria wasted no time asking for explanations; she leaned over the old lady, forcefully picked up her bundle, fighting against her passive but firm resistance, and put it on her knees with a look of reproach. "We have to fit the three of us on here; you cannot be so selfish," she said in Italian. The old woman turned her face toward the window so as not to look at her. Maria sat down and firmly pushed the woman's bottom to the point where her seat ended and Maria's began. Lesson number one: defend your space!

The sky was darkening as the bus began to climb the hilly road that preceded the mountain, bend after bend, jolt after jolt, advancing toward low clouds, swollen and threatening. The heat of the plains gave way to the fresh air of the hills, accompanied by an oppressive humidity. It began to rain, lightly at first, but with every passing minute, the rain intensified more and more until it became a downpour squeezing in streams of water through the gaps in the window. 'Granny', whose shoulder was squashed against the window pane, was beginning to get wet. Maria looked at her, for the first time since their dispute, and felt sorry for her.

"Franca, shall we swap places with 'granny'? She's getting soaked and I don't want her on my conscience."

Franca leaned forward to look at the elderly woman. She agreed: "Okay, but you'll have to make her understand. I don't think she trusts us." She was right. The old woman didn't trust that the exchange, explained with gestures, was entirely in her favour. Finally, after much insisting and already thoroughly wet, she agreed to move. Maria took her place and soon her right side was wet from the shoulder down. Meanwhile, outside it was growing dark as the bus began to climb up the mountain road itself. At every turn the passengers had to hold on to the bar of the seat in front, leaning against the passenger to their right, then to the left, depending on how the curves pushed them. The rain became more intense and was now accompanied by spectacular lightning and strong thunder. It went on like this into the night.

Suddenly the bus stopped in the middle of the road. The passengers looked at one another. The driver got out and lit his torch in the dark. There was an unusual silence among the people, interrupted only by uncertain whispers. After a few minutes he climbed back through his door. With a resigned posture, he stood in front of everyone and made an announcement in Hindi. Then he proceeded to sit in the driving seat, said a short prayer, crossed his arms on the steering wheel and rested his head on them. What was he doing? Was he taking a nap? Maria turned to Paul and asked him if he understood what was happening. In the twilight his eyes twinkled and she felt her stomach twitching with emotion. She tried to hide her feelings and focused on what he was saying; she found it hard to understand him because of his deep voice. "The road is blocked by a landslide," he said. "We will continue the journey in the morning. With the dark and in this weather there is nothing we can do until tomorrow."

"*What*?" exclaimed Franca, as if it were his fault. "You mean we're stuck here all night?"

Paul apologized, but that was indeed the truth. Everyone else had already accepted the situation and even seemed excited; they were joking and laughing. Within a few minutes an atmosphere of complicity had settled among the passengers and people were getting ready to spend those hours in the least uncomfortable way possible. They were blocked and isolated from everything; their coach was shaken by large chunks of earth that fell from the mountain and slid toward the road, stopping against its side, each time with a new jolt. The bus to Manali was a lonely firefly in the moonless night.

Maria realized she would need to venture outside. "I took my contact lenses out and didn't bring my glasses; how stupid! Are you coming along for a pee?" she asked Franca, hopefully.

"No, thank you. I am going to hold it as long as I can. It's coming down in buckets and I really don't want to go out." That was a shame! Should she take her torch? She decided to leave it in the bag; it would only make her movements more difficult. Stepping over feet, legs and bundles of luggage, she made it to the back door. No sooner had she opened it than she was hit by strong wind and driving rain. She went down the few steps and it was as if she were blind; the night was pitch black and from the bus came only a very dim light. She slipped on the mud and was afraid to slide even further. She lifted the sari's skirt and tucked it into her belt. Then, touching the side of the bus with her hand, she took a few timid steps; she couldn't see a thing and found nothing to hold on to. With great care, she squatted and peed in the mud, while the rain dripped down her neck and ran down her back, making her shiver. Paying as much attention again she went back, feeling the wet dirty metal of the bus with her hand. Greatly relieved, she climbed the steps and made her way back toward her seat, soaked to the bone. She stepped over the same legs and the same bundles and, just before she reached her seat, she saw that Paul was preparing a joint.

'Granny' was resting with her eyes closed. Franca was now sitting next to the window; it was her turn to get wet. After a few minutes she smelt the joint and Paul passed it to her, saying: "It's with charas that comes from the Himalayas and it's very strong; take care not to smoke too much." Maria took a puff and the strong smoke almost made her cough. She managed to control it and passed it to Franca, who drew deeply on it twice and passed it to Karen. The joint went around a few times, attracting the attention of all the passengers, who elbowed each other, laughing and saying 'charas, charas'. A spell of silence followed, while her thoughts were flying unchecked, free and rebellious, without any sense of direction, easy, undisciplined and inspired, happy, illogical, disconnected, colourful and light. She remembered something she had read in an alternative guidebook to the Himalayas and broke the silence, saying: "Shortly before leaving I read in a guidebook for 'hippies' that the Himalayan hashish is hilarious!"

"Hilarious? What a funny word," said Franca, to whom this word sounded peculiar. "Hilarious... ahhh, that's ridiculous!" She began to laugh, trying to repeat the word to hear it again, but this was becoming more and more difficult. "Hila... rious," she could barely pronounce it. "Hiii... laaraa... riii... ous!" She was doubled over and shook with laughter.

"Does it seem so ridiculous the word hi-la-ri-ous?" asked Maria, beginning to giggle too.

"Ahhhhh! Eeeeeee... yeees..." Franca could barely breathe. She nodded her head to say yes.

"The guidebook was right then," said Maria.

Her friend turned toward her and when Maria saw her, shaking uncontrollably, tears running down her cheeks, red and whooping, she was unable to contain herself. They tried to keep their voices down and hide from others, but that only made the situation worse. Bent in two, their heads resting on the arm holding the bar of the seat in front, they dissolved into laughter, and all attempts to stop, or at least to be less loud, were completely useless. Their shoulders and backs shook, while from under their arms came hysterical shrieks that took their breath away. Occasionally, one of them raised her head to catch her breath, like a swimmer pulls her head out of the water between one stroke and the next, and then hid again, in convulsions, tears flowing down their cheeks. They were becoming the centre of attention, and even if they tried, and they really were trying, they couldn't stop.

Soon, other passengers' smiles began to grow and crack, infected by their wild explosion of euphoria. At least a dozen had already joined them when those sat closest to them started to feel affected by the group in the throes of hilarity and began to chuckle. After a few minutes the whole bus was shaking uncontrollably, including 'granny', who was hiding her mouth with her hands, and had joined the collective howl; people laughed more and more, louder and louder.

"They are..." Maria tried to catch her breath to talk, "aaalll... lauuuu... ghii... iing!" she just managed to articulate, holding her aching stomach, before bursting into another fit of giggles filled with iiiiiiiiiiiiii.

Franca shook her head, unable to let out a sound that wasn't a eeeeeeeeeee... iiiiiiiiiiiiiiii. They couldn't look at each other lest they'd explode; and so they let themselves go with the pure pleasure of it all.

A little bit at a time, slowly, they began to calm down. Looking everywhere except at each other, they closed their eyes and slowed the pace, gradually lowering the volume, breathing deeply to recover from the exhaustion. They remained so, their eyes closed and a big smile on their lips, worn out, stoned. Time passed, Maria's mouth was dry; she felt tired and thirsty but had nothing to drink. She clung to the bar of the seat in front and leaned her head on her arm, trying to get some rest. It was ten o'clock and they had a long night ahead. The hours passed slowly, uncomfortably. Every now and then she leaned her head back and felt her hair touch Paul's hair, who was resting on the bar of her seat. This proximity gave her an intense, exciting feeling. She let herself be lulled by that new emotion, strong but harmless, just fine.

For the first time since she had left Italy she had time to think. Her thoughts went straight to Ugo. She remembered the moment, arriving home, keys in hand, when she saw him walk out the front door and toward his ex-girlfriend, who was waiting for him. He was carrying his guitar and his violin, in their black cases. She knew then that he was leaving, without a word. Their relationship had ended, after three intense and confusing years in which he had never really engaged because, in his heart, he had never ceased to love 'the other'. And Maria had always known. She loved him, wanted him, hated him, missed him immensely and couldn't shake off the physical and emotional dependency. Perhaps with this trip... At least she wasn't always thinking of him, there were moments when he wasn't forefront in her thoughts; she was making some progress, and she had time. India commanded so much of her energy. With her head, she knew that Ugo was part of the past; now she just had to wait for her heart to understand the same, immersing herself in the present, while the future promised to be exciting. She dozed off for a few hours and when she opened her eyes the darkness of the night was giving way to the grey light of a new day. The air was loaded with humidity and the sky still heavy with clouds the colour of lead.

She stood up and carefully made her way between legs, feet and luggage, trying not to wake anyone. When she opened the back door of the coach she found herself staring down a cliff that ended in a green, angry river, white foam exploding where the rushing water crashed against large boulders. Only a couple of metres separated the coach from the edge. There were no trees, no bushes, no parapet, the road simply ended and the empty void started; hundreds of metres and only a steep escarpment between her and the river. She remembered the night before in the darkness, she had crept close to the bus, feeling it with her hand, holding her balance with great difficulty on the slippery mud. A shiver of fear ran down her back. With great care she walked as far as it was possible and saw that the bus was blocked by a large mass of earth that had detached from the side of the mountain; it couldn't go any further and couldn't turn around. Just then, she saw a man approaching, holding a porcelain cup full of steaming liquid. She stared as if he were a mirage.

"Chai?" she asked incredulous.

He rocked his head: "Ahahan, chai!"

"Where?" she asked. He pointed 'out there' with his chin, 'idda, idda'. It had been hours since she had drunk anything. Short sighted and insecure, Maria advanced on the slippery mud in the direction indicated by the man, holding the folds of her raised sari. Just around the bend was a roughly made hut; inside a man was crouching on the floor, busy with a kerosene stove and a saucepan, where the chai was boiling. Incredible! Unable to believe it she asked: "Chai?"

The man bobbed his head from right to left and from left to right and said: "Ek chai?" One chai?

"Do chai!" she said and showed him "two" with her fingers.

He gave her a full glass of steaming tea that Maria sipped slowly. Too tired to think she watched the man, squatting on the ground busying himself, calm and focused, and she was moved. Although it wasn't so good, the chai was liquid, sweet and warm, and she felt comforted. With gestures she asked if she could take the full glass to the bus; she would bring it back later. The man swung his head to say it was fine. Slowly, without spilling a single drop, she arrived at the bus and woke Franca. "Look what I found!" she said triumphantly, and laughed happily when her friend's eyes widened.

"Where did you find that?" Franca asked sleepily, raising the glass to her dry lips and starting to drink in silence, in small sips.

"Over there!" Maria pointed with satisfaction. "When you have finished I'll take the glass back."

But it wasn't necessary. The chai had attracted a lot of attention and a tall, Indian man told her that he would take the glass back to the hut. Some people were moving and many had already got off the bus. Maria saw a group among which there were also Paul and Karen. She approached them and asked if they knew what the situation was like. They told her that on the other side of the landslide there were coaches, which were also blocked, and that the only way forward was to cross the landslide on foot. The word 'landslide' didn't describe adequately the mountain of dirt, mud and rocks that stood before them. Maria took advantage of the fact that she was speaking to Paul to have another good look at him; even after such a night he was still handsome. She regretted wearing a sari; she was sure she looked ridiculous.

"Do we have to walk through this?" she asked worriedly.

"There is no other way," he replied apologetically, looking at her with those amazing eyes. And there she was, blushing again! Not finding anything more to say, reluctantly she left and went to inform Franca. Her reaction at the idea of crossing the mountain of mud on foot surprised her.

"Great!" she said. "At least we can get a move on!"

"But… aren't you tired? I'm exhausted!"

"Don't think about it!" said her friend, preparing to make a start, full of energy.

People were mingling in groups. Everything was quiet for a while, until the driver said a few words in Hindi, including 'cheloh'. Maria understood it meant 'let's go' or 'we're off', and they all began to move. Paul and Karen started to walk, carrying their small rucksacks. He turned and told Maria to follow the guide and to not lose him. Behold, all of a sudden the people started to walk faster.

Their backpacks were still on the roof and this time she had to get it herself. Franca went up first, climbing with determination. Maria, who suffered from vertigo, plucked up some courage, lifted the edges of her sari and tucked them into the belt. The rungs of the perpendicular ladder were full of mud, but there was no choice other than to grab them and climb, carrying her camera bag over her shoulder. She reached the top and saw her backpack; it was the only red piece of luggage. She dragged it to the edge of the roof and, without looking down, loaded it on her shoulders, staggering under the weight. Looking straight ahead, she gripped the iron structure of the roof-rack, felt the top rung with her foot and, holding on firmly, began to descend. The weight of the backpack made her lose her balance, but she held on tight and reached the muddy ground in one piece. In the distance she could just see Franca walking steadily and tried to reach her.

She followed the line of people and saw that they all took off their sandals before sinking with their feet into the wet earth of the landslide. To save time Maria didn't remove hers but, as soon as she took the first step, she sank in the deep mud down to her ankles. With difficulty, she pulled out first one foot and then the other, but her sandals were left behind. She couldn't lose them. Without a second thought, she bent down and plunged her hands into the mud, feeling blindly and worriedly, till she managed to catch them, one at the time. Now her hands were covered in mud. She rubbed them on the sari but, to remove her hair from her eyes, she smeared her forehead and cheeks. Her luggage was heavy and she felt weak; she was exhausted and couldn't take any more. Everybody overtook her and she was afraid of being left behind. She couldn't breathe properly, her throat closed in spasms. She didn't want to cry, she knew it wouldn't help, but powerful sobs began to shake her from inside. Why wasn't anyone helping her? Overcome by discouragement and exhaustion, she started to cry aloud, weeping without tears and trembling inside, all the way from her knees up. Paul was already far away, but he heard her and stopped, looking at her, uncertain. She saw Franca turn around and climb back down.

A man who was walking behind her asked what the problem was.

"I can't go so fast! I'll do what I have to do, but I can't rush like this, I'm distressed!" sobbed Maria, "and I'm afraid of getting lost!"

"Don't worry! I'll walk with you! You won't get lost," he said gently in English, and then he added: "Shanti, shanti." Those words were all she needed.

She signalled Franca to move forward, that everything was fine. She rolled up even more of the sari into her belt so that it had now become a mini-skirt; ironic, to say the least, but no one seemed to notice.

They walked uphill in single file, slipping in the mud at every step, struggling and gaining ground with feet and hands, when necessary. She noticed that the women weren't carrying anything heavy. The men had taken all the loads, both luggage and children. She heard a light step behind her, turned around, and saw a young man who wasn't carrying anything. Without a word, she slid her backpack off her shoulders and, handing it to him, said: "Can you carry it for me, please?"

The boy, tall and thin, looked at her backpack with dislike and said: "I'll carry your camera!"

Maria insisted: "I am exhausted and I need your help. While we go uphill, you carry the backpack. When we'll go downhill, you'll carry my camera, okay?" With that, she thrust her rucksack on him. Unwillingly, the boy took it and loaded it on his shoulders. She smiled at him gratefully. Now she could climb better and faster. She felt protected and comforted by these two men who didn't know her but, walking one behind and the other in front, were taking care of her.

They climbed for over an hour, a long winding queue of men, women and children, advancing silently, sinking barefoot in the wet slippery mud; they were sweating, tired, thirsty, but no one complained. Finally, they reached the top of the landslide and from there they could see four coaches on the road below. Franca had already arrived and was in a group with the English couple and other people. The descent was not only easier, but the mood was much better, now that a way forward was in sight. The young man continued to carry her rucksack and also took her camera bag. At last, they reached the road.

There was a lot of confusion and no one seemed to know which coach was the one for their destination. Paul pointed to a bus and told them it was the right one. Feeling reassured, they climbed onto the roof with their rucksacks. Franca was fast and efficient, Maria was resigned, finding the required energy from an unknown reserve. Finally they settled on the last seats, close to Karen and Paul, but nothing was moving.

A man appeared at the front door of the bus and shouted something. They were on the wrong bus. Nooooo! Instead yes! They had to do it all the other way round, get off the bus, get on the roof, put the rucksacks on their shoulders and stagger down the perpendicular ladder. Fighting a dizziness that made her nauseous, Maria climbed down holding on tight.

So, which was the right coach? That one! A man said. Are you sure? Yes, sure! All right then, as long as this was the last time. Backpack loaded, up the perpendicular ladder, pulling herself up more by force of arms than with her tired legs, backpack placed on the roof, down again, carefully. Maria wiped her muddy hands on her mini-sari and, holding on to the door handles, climbed wearily on the new coach. This time they sat further away from the English couple, not wanting to seem too 'sticky'. Once again, they waited in silence, too tired to speak, but nothing was moving. A man appeared at the door of the bus and shouted something. They were on the wrong bus again!

Franca and Maria joined the loud chorus of protest, but it was no use complaining. They went down again, climbed on the roof, very big red backpack and much smaller grey backpack, careful not to slip down the muddy rungs, holding firmly with their hands where someone else's muddy feet had just stepped, and another small jump from the last rung that was far from the ground. Now what? They wanted the *right* coach! The one that was going to Manali! Someone pointed to the very first bus on which they had sat, but this time they didn't trust. Maria went to take two seats while Franca waited on the ground with their luggage. Finally, everyone agreed that this was their bus and the driver seemed sure of himself. With the last bit of energy, they climbed the ladder, threw their backpacks on the roof and descended carefully, slowly, with muddy feet, muddy hands, muddied faces. Sitting in silence on their seats, worn out, they saw a group of elderly people who had just completed the crossing of the landslide. Of course! Maria thought, *they* couldn't possibly walk quickly and she could have walked with that group, if she hadn't panicked. She saw 'granny' and waved energetically at her. The old lady returned her smile and greeted her from afar with her hand, a little embarrassed. Maria hurried to put her camera bag on a seat to save her a place and then went down to help her with her bundle. The old woman smiled weakly and allowed Maria to help her. 'Cheloh, cheloh!' they heard at last. The driver climbed on board through his door and, without sounding the horn to avoid further landslides, began to manoeuvre. Soon, they were on their way to Kulu-Manali.

Paul came up to them and said that the bus would go only as far as Mandi because, after that, the road was completely blocked. How far was Mandi? About six hours' drive. Was there a hotel? Yes, there was a guesthouse, they were going to go there, and so would a lot of other people, he said. If they walked fast and followed them, they would probably find a room.

"I want the most beautiful room," said Maria.

Franca didn't object, for once more interested in having a rest than saving money. "With a shower that works," she added.

"Yes, and then we eat!"

"Bhaji, chapatis and samosas."

"Rice with chicken, vegetables, potatoes, toast, and even a pudding, if they have some."

"I'm going to have a beer."

"Yeah, me too. What a good idea!"

"And a nice chillum with the Brits."

"Why not? Maybe that, too."

'Granny,' sitting next to them, was resting, her white head leaning against the window, her lips parted. Occasionally, the coach gave a jolt and she opened her eyes; when they rested on Maria and Franca she replied gently, fatigued, to their smile. With her bundle on her knees, her white braid just a little untidy, she was small and beautiful, dignified and vulnerable.

Karen and Paul sat in silence, not far away. The rain had stopped and gashes between the clouds let through a glimpse of deep blue sky. The bus trudged uphill, bend after bend, one hairpin turn after another. The driver drove more calmly and each time he passed another bus, the drivers stopped and exchanged information. They were in the hills now, getting closer and closer to the mountains that loomed tall and imposing.

Eight hours later they arrived in Mandi. It was almost sunset. The sky was striped with shades of pink, white and blue that changed continuously in a thousand different combinations. The air had the fresh and pure mountain scent. Maria breathed deeply and felt the oxygen fill her lungs. They hurried up to the roof to take their backpacks, while her eyes followed Paul and Karen, who had already started to walk. They followed them closely, walking uphill. The last part of the road leading to the hotel consisted of sixty tall, very steep, stone steps. They climbed with difficulty, one after the other, using their hands when their legs were no longer able to make the necessary effort. Finally they entered the hotel lobby, called Tourist Bungalow; it was empty, clean, and quiet.

A young receptionist with a dark blue turban came almost immediately and greeted them with a smile. Karen explained their adventure and he listened with great interest, nodding and saying that, with the monsoon, the road became very bad. He had two spare rooms, one for thirty rupees and the other one for forty. The English couple wanted the cheaper one, while they wanted the more expensive. They all agreed! With a charming smile, the young man offered the guests a chai, saying that they clearly needed it. They would bring it to their room, he added, and Maria thought she wanted to kiss him! Relieved to have finally arrived, they took leave of Paul and Karen.

They climbed the stairs holding on to the handrail. Their room was large, with a balcony facing the mountains. They rested the heavy luggage near the door to avoid dirtying the clean floor. Maria looked in the mirror and didn't recognize the person looking back; she looked like a street kid, dirty and muddy, her face swollen and hair caked with dried mud. "That's not me!" she exclaimed, half way between amused and shocked. Franca came to the mirror and stood next to her. She also looked like another person, just as dirty and muddy, her face unrecognizable.

They laughed and the mirror reflected back to them the image of two friends; the colour of mud made them look more alike, slender, small, exhausted but united. Together it had been an adventure and, thankfully, it was over. They had travelled for thirty hours, during which they had eaten a handful of lentils and had drunk two teas. There was a knock at the door. A smiling waiter handed them a tray with two porcelain cups full of piping hot tea. They sat on the bed to sip it slowly, completely exhausted; it was the best chai in the world.

They decided to take a shower and go straight to the restaurant. Maria uncoiled from the sari that had become heavy with all the mud it had absorbed and left in a corner those 'incongruent' five yards of cotton that had dressed her since Delhi. "This is the last time I wear a sari!" she stated. "From now on, I'm going to dress like a tourist!" They took it in turns to take two showers each, the first one to take off most of the mud, the second one to come out clean, body and hair. They wore their jeans and went down to the front desk. The young receptionist smiled warmly.

"You look very different from when you arrived," he said, observing them well.

Maria laughed and, as he was so kind, she wondered whether she could ask him some questions about India, maybe another day. "I realize that I know very little about your culture," she explained.

He was more than happy. That same evening there was a big wedding party in the hotel and he invited them to participate, so they could see in person an important part of their culture. She would have loved it, but they were too tired and, after dinner, they would go straight to bed. He understood; they looked very tired! He pointed to where the restaurant was and agreed to meet them the next day, at the end of his shift.

The potato and onion soup was hot and heartening and the scrambled eggs on toast were the most delicious they had ever eaten. That night they slept soundly and were not in the least disturbed by the noisy party with hundreds of guests talking loudly, dancing, singing and laughing.

6. A moment of magic

The next day, after breakfast at the hotel, they walked down to the town of Mandi where they had breakfast for the second time. They were three thousand feet above sea level and the air was cool and clear. The dust, heat and smell of Delhi were only vague memories, the sun was shining and the bad weather seemed to have passed. As they descended toward the town they saw a large green open space on the other side of the bridge where men, boys and children were playing cricket; some dressed in white, others barefoot wearing shorts and t-shirt, but all were running fast from one end of the field to the other, with the same passion.

Franca had another idea: this time she would have a waistcoat made, as tailors in India were cheap. They stopped at a fabric store and bought two pieces of red and black velvet material, each with slightly different patterns. As in Delhi, the shops consisted of three sides of a cube opening onto the street, without a door or front wall. In the evenings they were closed by putting up a removable wall made of wooden planks. The owner was sitting on a thin mattress covered with a white cloth that lined the raised floor; around him were shelves with pieces of cloth, all on hand, so that he needn't get up and could do everything from a sitting position.

A little further down the road in the tailor's shop the sewing machine was also placed on the padded floor and the tailor did all his work sitting cross-legged. Franca made a sketch of the waistcoat she wanted on an old piece of paper the tailor offered her. He rocked his head to let them know that there was no problem. She wanted lots of pockets inside the waistcoat. Did they have the fabric for the pockets? No. Wasn't the velvet they had bought enough for everything? No, it wasn't, but 'no problem', he would use scraps of fabric he had. He turned to Maria. And how did *she* want her waistcoat? Just the same as Franca, thank you. Very well! The tailor was satisfied and curious. Who are you? Where are you from? The road is blocked, eh? Yes, the monsoon is so, he said, bobbing his head in that familiar way. They could come back the next day to pick up their waistcoats; they would be ready by the afternoon. He watched them go, with an amused smile.

It was already cool when, late afternoon, they walked across the bridge to return to the Tourist Bungalow. The young receptionist greeted them with a smile and said his shift would be over within half an hour. Did they want to have a chat? Yes, perfect, they would come back downstairs in half an hour. Had the English couple left? Maria asked, looking around.

"No, Madam, the road is still closed, and they are still here too."

Good, maybe she would see them again; she was looking forward to that, especially to seeing Paul! She took a shower and decided to wear a dress she had bought at the Porta Portese market in Rome. It was long, down to her feet, white with small pink roses. She looked like a real tourist, she thought, smiling at herself in the mirror. She had lost weight and tanned a little. They had arrived in India only four days before, but it already seemed a lifetime ago.

The receptionist was waiting. He ordered something in Hindi from the waiter and then escorted them up the stairs. They arrived on the Tourist Bungalow's roof terrace complete with comfortable wicker chairs and tables. They sat and admired the landscape that lay before their eyes: mountains, mountains and mountains all around, with the town of Mandi down in the valley, the bridge over the wide light-green river, next to the pea-green cricket ground. He asked if they wanted to order dinner while they were there; someone would let them know when it was ready and, in the meantime, they could relax and talk. A few minutes later the waiter arrived carrying a tray with three glasses and three large bottles of beer, one each. The young man told him to come back with the menu. "So, what did you want to know, Madam?" asked the receptionist who must have been around the same age but treated her with an almost old-fashioned respect. Unlike the Italian language, in English there was no difference between the casual 'you' and the formal 'you' but Maria had the impression that he was using a courteous form, or even an older, traditional form of the language. But this was only her impression, due to the deference and politeness with which he addressed her.

"Well, I realized that we know next to nothing about the Indian culture," began Maria. "I'd like to know a little bit of everything, but what intrigues me the most are the women. I think you understand a lot about a culture by how women are treated."

The young man, who was tall, elegant and very attractive, today wore a light blue turban that suited him better than the dark blue he'd worn the day before. He looked at her smiling, his big dark eyes emphasized by long black lashes. "You're so right, Madam! As we all know, India is one of the few countries in the world that has a woman prime minister, Mrs.

Indira Gandhi," he said with pride. He turned to Franca, asking her if she had any questions. Franca said she didn't have any yet, but if she thought of something she would ask. The young man, whose name was Rup Singh, turned back to Maria and asked her if there was anything in particular she wanted to know.

You bet there was! She had a list a mile long. "How does it work when they want to marry? Who decides, they or their parents? Can they divorce? Do the men help in the home or with children? Do women work? Do they study? Do they go to college?" She laughed at asking a barrage of questions, but Rup Singh didn't seem to mind at all.

He opened the first bottle of beer and poured it into their glasses. They toasted merrily, to the three of them and to the landscape that was their setting. He began to answer one question after another, in a relaxed way, leaving time for them to ask for explanations if something wasn't clear. "Marriages are arranged by the families who consult an astrologer to see if the couple are compatible," he began, immediately arousing their interest. "Both, the girl and the boy can refuse the proposed partner, if they are not happy. However, in most cases they trust their parents' decision. They can influence the choice, of course, because as well as being ambitious and wanting a good match for their children, the parents also want their happiness." Could he go on? Yes, sure, carry on, Maria and Franca motioned, sipping their beer. The sun had begun a slow sunset, brushing with shades of pink, yellow and orange the fluffy clouds in the blue sky.

"Can they get divorced?" continued Rup, flattered by the attention he was receiving. "Yes, if they really want to, but divorce brings a certain shame to their family and parents put a lot of pressure to avoid getting to that point. However, things are changing and young people begin to have more freedom than in the past."

"In Italy divorce is allowed too, but only since a few years ago," said Maria. "Being a Catholic country it was forbidden, but they held a referendum and people voted yes with a big majority. My mother surprised me by how clear her views were at that time. Although she wouldn't have divorced my father, she liked to know that she had the possibility to choose."

"It's true!" agreed Franca. "It's amazing to think that divorce has only been legal in Italy for five years."

"In India it has been legal for much longer, but only recently people have started to take advantage of it," Rup said with a smile.

They all took a pause and drank a big swig of beer. Maria started to hiccup, as she always did when she drank it too quickly, and all three laughed.

"And the children?" she asked, interrupted by the hiccup. "Are they just the woman's responsibility?"

Rup looked at her and paused to observe her, it was clear that he liked her and she felt embarrassed. She could see Franca out of the corner of her eye and knew she had noticed, too.

"Are *you* married?" her friend asked provocatively. Rup didn't notice her tone, or perhaps he just pretended not to. He looked at her and told her that his parents had found a girl for him, whose family lived in Chandigarh.

"And do you like her?" prompted Franca. He didn't worry about this, he trusted his parents' choice, he said. He and his future bride had a positive horoscope and in India they thought that love would mature little by little. It started with mutual respect. Love would grow gradually, together with friendship and camaraderie through facing life together.

The sound of footsteps announced the arrival of the waiter who dictated the menu for the evening. Pleased and amused by such special attention, the girls ordered first course, second course and side dish. The man left and they went back to the beer that made them lightheaded and cheerful.

Rup returned to the answer that had been left pending: "With regard to the care of children, it depends on the man. If one wants to feel 'modern' he will help a little in the house, but the most important role is undoubtedly the mother's. Maybe you have already noticed that the children are almost spoiled."

Maria thought about it. She had noticed that the children were treated with great kindness, she said, but she had only seen a few examples of families in Old Delhi. Rup nodded, smiling, looking into her eyes, and holding her gaze for a while longer. "Regarding your question, if women work, the answer is all around you. You only have to look," he continued. "Most of them don't have a paid job, but they work at home, in the fields, everywhere! The Indian economy is mainly agricultural and people produce almost everything they need. They don't have any free time, except perhaps a little bit in the winter."

"Do they study?" asked Maria.

"Of course, both boys and girls. You'll see them go to school every morning with their satchel. Indian children study very seriously and with a lot of enthusiasm. Education is considered very important!"

It had been almost an hour since they had arrived on the terrace, the beer was almost finished and the sun had set behind the mountains. Thousands of shades were now fading quickly, giving way to a dark blue sky and cool moist air. The waiter came to let them know that their dinner was waiting for them. Reluctantly, they interrupted their conversation.

Franca followed the waiter straight away, Maria felt a little unstable. Rup supported her by the arm with great care as they descended the stairs. After that bottle of beer on an empty stomach she felt once again she could have kissed him, but thought that maybe it would be better to thank him by shaking his hand. Rup held her hand in his while he said what a pleasure it had been and that they could speak again tomorrow.

A little shaky on her legs and with sparkling eyes Maria reached Franca in the dining room. It was full of people and the waiter pointed to the table where Franca was already sitting, which had two welcoming bowls of steaming soup. The people in the restaurant looked at them with curiosity and Maria sat down, feeling like a queen.
"Look who's there! Mr Handsome," said Franca with a nod of her head. Karen and Paul were sitting at a table nearby and were looking at them. Maria waved and since they were not yet eating, motioned for them to come and sit at their table. They replied in turn with a greeting of their arms, inviting *them* to go and sit at theirs.
"We'd better go," said Franca, "since you're in love with him!" She mocked her, and with good reason, but it didn't matter; Maria had no hope or ambition toward Paul. She knew when someone was 'out of range' and he definitely was, too handsome and with a girlfriend. So, she relaxed and, paying great attention not to spill any soup, they moved to the English couple's table. It took very little to get the conversation going. The experience they had shared, helped by the beer, provided enough enthusiasm to start asking questions. Where were they from? She was from Liverpool. Like the Beatles said Franca, cheerfully! And he was from London. What had they been doing in India for three years? Were they working? Yes, he was a journalist who wrote travel articles for various magazines. Karen didn't have a job, but she made beautiful embroidered things, Paul said, looking at Maria and focusing on the roses of her dress. Was she imagining it or was he really looking at her more often than at Franca? She was dying to touch him; she felt her cheeks burning and hoped no one would notice. If they wanted to, after dinner they could go to see the things Karen made, he suggested. Perfect, said Franca and... that thing they had smoked on the bus was very good. Did he have a little to give her, or sell to her? He didn't have much, Paul said, but he could give her a little bit. Maria took advantage of every little opportunity to observe him, but sometimes the emotion she felt was too intense and made her blush. In those moments she looked away and focused on Karen, who seemed in a world of her own. She spoke quickly and in a small voice, making it very difficult to understand her and, try as she might, Maria could just make out a few key words, enough to get an idea of what she was saying. The other slightly odd thing about Karen

was that she was looking, but didn't seem to see. She smiled a lot and giggled to herself. She was strange, but likeable.

"So, see you in a bit in our bedroom. Room twenty-five," said Paul, with that deep voice.

Back in their room, Maria brushed her long brown hair in front of the mirror. The young woman looking back at her was not bad, the long dress suited her, it was discreet but sexy at the same time. She smiled at the mirror. The gorgeous Englishman might well be unattainable, but at least she looked good. Her cheeks were flushed and her eyes sparkling with anticipation.

Franca was counting her money. "If I can, I'll buy a lot of that charas from Paul," she said. "It's really good!"

"You said you have very little money," objected Maria, who knew that they had more or less the same amount, but Franca was much more concerned that hers may not be enough.

"I have little money for other things *because* I want to save it to buy something good to smoke," replied Franca. "It's cheap in India and if I don't smoke here, when will I smoke it, do you get my point?" Her logic was flawless, thought Maria, who was in a hurry to go to room twenty-five. She felt so excited, her heart was beating fast. And what for? She checked herself. She had no intention of trying to seduce him; he was out of reach, too good-looking and already taken, so, relax Maria, calm down. Shanti, Madam, shanti, she told herself.

Paul asked if they wanted to smoke a 'joint' or a chillum. Franca wanted a chillum, Maria had never tried it and didn't know what to do. Franca, however, couldn't wait and waved her hand, motioning to her not to worry. Paul prepared the chillum and gave it to Franca to light. She wrapped her hands around the pipe, which had to be held vertically, and he lit a match. Franca gave a great toke, then another and then, slowly, she let out an impressive amount of smoke. She shook her head, as if she had eaten very hot mustard, and passed the chillum to Paul. He wrapped his hands around the clay pipe in the same way and lowered his head to the side, taking a few confident tokes; then exhaled an even more ridiculous cloud of smoke. He passed the chillum to Karen, who did the same and who passed it to Maria. She had been watching closely, but had no idea of what to do. To her surprise, Paul came to sit on the bed next to her and put his hands around hers, to show her how to hold the chillum. He then brought Maria's hands, wrapped in his, near her mouth and told her to inhale. She was practically kissing his hands, and the way Paul was holding hers was very, very exciting. He was so close she felt his hair touch her face; his shoulder, his leg, his knee were also touching hers.

She managed to take a puff from the chillum; the smoke that rushed into her lungs was so strong it hit her like a fist.

"Exhale slowly," said Paul, looking closely at her, "otherwise it will make you cough!" Maria nodded with her mouth sealed, unable to speak. The pressure inside her chest was huge, but she managed to exhale slowly without coughing. Her eyes seemed to be about to pop out of their sockets. The chillum was passed around once again and, although she didn't wish to smoke, she didn't want to miss the chance of another 'lesson' with Paul. This time he helped her to place her hands around the pipe, then took his own away, and watched how she inhaled. He smiled when she was able to give a little puff and then went back to sit at the other end of the bed, where he was before. Within seconds, her ears were ringing and her head felt as if it were full of cotton wool.

Between him and Franca there was a transaction, and she saw a piece of black shiny charas pass from Paul's hand to Franca's greedy one. Immediately she began to prepare another chillum.

Karen stood up and came back with a bag, out of which she pulled some beautiful brightly coloured velvet things, embroidered with silk thread in stunning contrasting colours. There were purses, passport holders, soft bags for chillum and larger bags. Franca was impressed by a turquoise chillum holder. "How much is this one?" she asked. It cost twenty rupees. "I'll buy it for Gabriele," she said. It was the first time she mentioned her boyfriend.

Maria tried to imagine Franca having sex, but quickly chased the thought away. She focused on the embroidered velvet handicrafts, instead, and picked up an emerald green purse. She couldn't imagine what she must be like with Gabriele. She was very strong, even a bit masculine, while he was sweet and gentle, almost effeminate. Hard to imagine what they were like together. Bah! She glanced at her but, as the same scene insisted on popping up, she shifted her gaze to Karen who was looking at her embroidery work. She was bringing the objects close to her nose to look at them and Maria realized that she was very short-sighted. "Don't you wear glasses?" she asked her.

"No, I don't like to!"

"Do you wear contact lenses? I do."

"No, no, I don't use them."

"So how can you see clearly?"

Karen chuckled nervously and replied that she couldn't see well at all. That's why she had such a dreamy look, Maria realized. She decided to buy the emerald green purse, it was beautiful and she would either keep it for herself, or give it as a gift. She gave Karen twenty rupees and placed it in her bag.

The chillum that Franca had prepared was making the rounds, but this time Paul stayed in his place. Maria tried to smoke it, but couldn't draw anything. Just as well, she was already dizzy and her ears were muffled. Franca instead was doing great practice and inhaled with all the strength she could muster, not once but twice at every turn. She smoked the chillum as well as Paul and she was proud of it.

Maria asked him about their village in the mountains, but when he answered, with his low, deep voice, she could understand almost nothing. The sounds went in one ear and got all mixed up in her head, giving her the impression of having understood something but not knowing what it was. She so much wanted to sleep! She could have fallen asleep right there where she was.

Karen began to make a joint and soon afterwards passed it around. Maria gave a small puff, but her mouth was dry and she had no strength to speak, so she passed it to Paul and just sat there, leaning against the board at the foot of the bed. Karen was staring at the wall in front of her, smiling in silence. Franca was sitting on the floor, staring at the wall, too. Paul was lying on the bed with his eyes closed. There he was, a few inches away from her foot, she could have touched him, but she wouldn't. She actually didn't want to; the word 'respect' was spinning in her head, respect for him and his girlfriend, who was kind. Incredibly handsome and unattainable; forget about him, Maria.

Suddenly Franca stood up and, without even looking at her, said: "Goodnight, thank you," and staggered out of the room. Oh no! What was she going to do? She couldn't stand up. She couldn't even keep her eyes open; her eyelids were as heavy as lead. Sitting on Paul and Karen's bed, she had to leave, of course, but how could she go all the way to her room? She tried to get up but it was a struggle and standing was difficult. Paul opened his eyes and said something, out of which she understood the word 'address'. Maria walked over to him and quickly sat on the bed to avoid falling over.

"Are you okay? You look pale!" he said, watching her with concern.

Maria motioned 'so-so' with her hand and he made a space beside him. She had an address book in her bag, she groped for it and found it at the bottom. Paul had a pen in his hand and began to make a sketch on the last page, while he was telling her not to give their address to anyone; it was not to be shared, it was just for the two of them. While drawing the map, explaining how to get there, Maria felt their shoulders touch. She remained still, enjoying the unexpected closeness, which seemed to become stronger, as if Paul was pressing against her. She was imagining it, for sure. She tried to understand what he was saying, but she heard only the sound of his voice and felt the warmth of his body. They were breathing with the same rhythm, their arms touching and moving at the same time. She could have sat there for hours, to prolong that moment of magic, midway between dream and reality. Paul finished his sketch and gave the little book back to Maria, his fingers lingering on hers, or so it seemed. It was all in her head, surely. She thanked him, getting up from the bed with an effort. Now I'm going, she said, and Paul looked straight into her eyes with that intense look. "Come and visit us in the village," he invited her.

"Maybe we will; thank you. Are you leaving tomorrow?"

"If the road is open, yes," he replied.

"Have a good trip, and thank you."

Karen, who was sleeping with her eyes half closed, looked at her and smiled without seeing her. "You too. See you soon," she said.

Maria closed the door behind her, and immediately had to lean against the wall. If she didn't do something, she would fall to the floor. After measuring the distance between the wall and the staircase handrail, with two quick steps she managed to reach it and grab on. Her head spun and she knew she had to sit down lest she fell. Sitting on the top step, she took a few deep breaths, fighting the giddy desire to lie down and go to sleep. Instead, she began to go down on her bottom, one step at a time. Her feet went down first and then her bottom followed; down one step, and another one, slowly. The stone beneath her was cool and comforting. One more step, and another one. Fortunately there wasn't anyone in sight. She made it all the way down to the atrium; so far so good! There was a couch in front of her, she guessed the distance: two steps. She stood up, her head was spinning. The whole lobby swam around her; her ears were completely blocked and she felt like throwing up. She took the two steps blindly, reached the sofa and lay down, just in time, before passing out.

She heard a voice in the distance calling: "Madam, Madam!" She opened her eyes with difficulty and there, with his face above hers, a waiter was looking down, worriedly: "Are you all right, Madam?"

Her throat was dry, her mouth completely parched and she couldn't speak. She wanted water. The word 'water' was coming out all wrong: "Wa... er"

"What?" asked the waiter, nearing his ear.

"Wa... er"

"Sorry, Madam. What?" he repeated, concerned that he didn't understand.

"Ua... ter"

"You want water?" he asked, thoughtful.

"Yes…"

He disappeared and Maria closed her eyes. She woke up with the same waiter calling her, handing her a glass of water. She raised herself on one elbow and took a few sips. "Thank you," she whispered in a faint voice, her mouth less dry.

"Are you okay, Madam?" he asked again, watching her closely.

"Yes, a little better. I'm very tired," she said.

She saw his puzzled face but, after all, she was tired, as well as stoned! And while he was here she wasn't going to let go of him, she didn't trust herself to walk alone. As soon as she sat on the couch her head started spinning again. "Room twelve," she said.

"You want room twelve?" asked the waiter, looking at the stairs.

"No, not up the stairs. Outside in the garden."

"Room twelve is upstairs," he said kindly but confident.

Maria took a long pause… Suddenly she remembered that in the afternoon they had changed rooms because Franca had decided that a night in the most expensive one was enough. "Room six," she said, convinced.

The waiter looked at her carefully, confused. "Now you want room number six," he said. "You want number twelve or number six?"

"Number six is past the garden, right?" she was beginning to feel a little clearer.

"Room six is just after the garden," repeated the waiter, slowly, as if he were talking to an elderly deaf woman. "Are you sure that's your room?"

"Yes, yes! Can you take me there, please?" There was no way she was going to let him go until she reached her room, otherwise who knows where she would end up. She stood up, took a couple of steps and got out into the garden, but she felt dizzy again. The waiter was walking next to her and, to his surprise Maria grabbed hold of his arm, so as not to lose her balance completely.

Seated around a table a group of Indian men were drinking beer. She saw their curious and amused expression; she knew what they were thinking, but didn't care. The waiter was very embarrassed and tried to break free, but Maria held him tight, both with her arm and hand. If he lets go of me I'm going to fall, she thought. Room six was a stone's throw from the garden and the cool night air woke her up a little.

"Is this your room, Madam?" the waiter asked, studying her intently.

"Yes, thank you."

"Are you sure?"

"Yes, yes, there's also my friend inside, look!"

"No, no, thank you!" he said, alarmed. There was no way he was going to set foot in there, and Maria noticed his relief when she let go of his arm.

"Thank you," she said, a little ashamed to be so stoned, but happy to be near her bed.

"Good night," he said with a small bow and walked back toward the garden, turning a few times to look at her before disappearing.

Franca was moaning from her bed: "Ahh ahh! Is that you, Dal Fiore?" calling her by her last name, like they did at school.

"Yes, it's me. I fainted in the hotel lobby," she drawled, dropping onto her bed. She took a few deep breaths before speaking again: "Why did you leave so quickly? I didn't know how to get back here!"

"I felt sick," Franca said, speaking slowly. "I feel like throwing up right now." She got up from the bed and, supporting herself against the wall, went running to the 'bathroom'. Maria heard her vomit. Her head was spinning at the slightest movement, so she decided to stay completely still. Franca returned to her bed and threw herself over it, dramatically. From under the pillow made of her folded blue jeans, she pulled out a thermometer and put it under her arm. Fancy that! Maria thought. She had brought a thermometer from home! "Call a doctor, Dal Fiore...," she moaned, "... I'm dying!"

Maria didn't like to be called by her surname; she didn't like it at all.

"First of all, where do I find a doctor in this place, and at night? ... Second, I couldn't stand up if I tried...," she replied with great effort. "... Third, if that waiter sees me again he's going to die of a heart attack... and don't call me by my surname... if you don't mind, I feel like I am at school... Vianello!"

"I have a fever, look, almost one hundred..." whined Franca, waving the thermometer accusingly. "What kind of friend are you?"

"Oh stop it!" said Maria, with the last bit of energy she had left. "It's because of the beer and all you've smoked. Put away that thermometer and go to sleep." Keeping her eyes closed and her head completely still, she concluded: "You'll see how much better you'll feel in the morning."

She woke up the next day, the nausea from the night before had disappeared altogether. Paul was her first thought. She climbed out of her sleeping bag and, without putting her shoes on, went up to reception. The receptionist greeted her with a big smile.

"Everything okay?"

"Yes, thank you!"

"Did you sleep well?"

"Like a log!"

He looked surprised... "Like what?"

"Never mind. I slept very well, thank you. Is the road open?"

"Yes, at last."

"Have the English couple already left?"

"Yes, they left early this morning. Are you having breakfast?"

"Yes, in a moment, thanks." She went back to her room more slowly, enjoying the warm sun on her skin before returning to their damp room. Franca was awake and feeling better.

"I told you that it was the smoke and the beer."

"Yes, that charas was so good, I wonder if I can buy some more."

"No, they have already left. He gave me their address last night."

"Great, let's go and see them."

I don't know, Maria thought, curling up in her sleeping bag which was still warm. What would I do if we went to see them? She liked him too much, and he had a girlfriend. She would feel too shy, she knew herself well, and would find it embarrassing; besides it wouldn't be fair on Karen. What if someone did that to her? Indeed, someone *had* done it to her: Ugo and his ex; one night they had returned home together. She had heard them in the next room, but had pretended to be asleep. She had imagined them kissing, undressing, making love; he was still in love with her. She had felt terrible. No! Paul had already done so much for her. For the first time she had woken up and hadn't immediately thought of Ugo, but of him. She had felt an incredibly strong attraction toward him and this had shown her that there was life after Ugo. He had made her feel beautiful. She pictured him, handsome, sensual, amazing! She could fall in love with someone else, now she knew. For the moment, it was enough. "I don't know, Franca! I liked him too much! What would we do at their house?" she said, thoughtfully.

"Oh, don't start to get involved with men," Franca said, with complete confidence. "We've just arrived and have a lot of things to do. Can you believe we've only been in India five days? With all that's happened!"

No, she couldn't. It seemed like a lifetime, she thought, with her head inside the sleeping bag.

"We will find charas everywhere, no problem," continued Franca, pulling out her guidebook. "... although the one he had was very good, and maybe..."

"No! You'll get good charas from someone else," said Maria, who heard the temptation in Franca's voice.

"All right, then. Come on, let's make a plan. We can't stay here forever." She started to leaf through the book. The nightmarish bus journey, with the rain, the landslide and the primordial tiredness had traumatized her too, even though she was so tough, and the idea of setting off on the same road made her think twice about going to Kulu-Manali. "There is another interesting place in the mountains and the road is much better," said Franca, reading on. "Indeed, they are two places next to each other. One has a ridiculous Scottish name, Mcleodganj, and the other is called Dharamsala. It's the residence in exile of the Dalai Lama... and the rainiest place in all of India."

"Interesting," said Maria still snuggled inside her sleeping bag. "If it is damp here, who knows what it will be like over there."

"Let's go and see these two places first, so we recover from the experience of the landslide. Then we can go to Manali," suggested her friend.

"Deal!"

Franca jumped out of her sleeping bag: "I feel great! Come on, let's go and see what buses there are."

"Sure, but not before breakfast!"

7. Always carry your torch

When they arrived in Mcleodganj it was raining and, just like the guidebook said, the village was literally *in* the clouds. The bus trip from Mandi had taken five hours exactly, no landslides, no accidents, no changes. Climbing up the perpendicular ladder to put the backpack on the roof and once more to take it down. A little vertigo, a smattering of rain, a doddle! Franca had collected information from other western travellers and had been told of a place, indeed, *the* place to stay in Mcleodganj: a small group of bungalows called Rishi Bhavan, a name with spiritual connotations, as Rishi meant 'wise' or 'holy' and Bhavan she didn't know but it sounded a little like Bagwan, which meant 'god'. She would have to find out. From the square, which also served as a bus station, they walked uphill for about a mile, carrying their backpacks in the rain. The Rishi Bhavan compound was a rectangle of land bordered on all sides by charming bungalows, happily set on the hill top and surrounded by a pine forest. It was almost always hidden from the outside world by the thick grey clouds that covered it, like a hat that was too big, pushed all the way down on a head that was too small.

All the bungalows were full. The people who came here stayed for weeks, some even for months. There was only one spare room and it was their cheapest: four rupees a night. Per person? No, no, for the room. Did they want it? Well, yes, thank you. The girls looked at each other; it was great luck to find such a cheap room. They soon realized why. Calling it a room was a flight of fancy! In fact, it was an old barn, with walls and floor plastered with a mixture of earth and cow poop, brown colour, the natural shade. Inside the barn there were two 'charpoy' beds, the Indian type that consisted of a wooden frame with the surface made of braided twine that, over time and with use, sank in the middle, like a hammock. There were two old rickety chairs and nothing else. "It's depressing," said Maria, hesitating.

"It's dirt cheap, so it's great," decided Franca.

'Room' taken! It was very dim, because of the clouds outside and the forty watt light bulb, covered with dust and dead flies, inside the barn.

"There's no light," said Maria.

"You get used to it," said Franca.

You get used to anything, thought Maria, even being blind, deaf and dumb. She began to unpack her rucksack and settle down, when something on the opposite wall, in the darkest part of the shadows, caught her eye: it was the biggest spider she had ever seen in her life. She was barely able to hold back a scream. It's not that she was afraid of spiders, but there was a limit to everything. That one was horrible, black and huge! The body was as big as an orange with long, hairy legs. She watched it for a few seconds; it was completely immobile.

Trying to maintain a normal tone of voice, she asked Franca: "Do you like spiders?"

"Sure! I like them very much," she said boldly, her back to the monster. Maria would have bet money she was going to answer something like that. Well, thank goodness she liked them! "Why?" she asked.

"Look at that," said Maria, pointing to the 'creature'.

Franca turned and focused on the spider in the dark; then she let out a shriek of terror. "Oh my god! It's horrible! It's huge!" she cried, covering her mouth with her hands, her eyes wide open. Maria laughed heartily; for once she had caught her by surprise. They stared at the king of spiders, who wasn't moving.

Franca was shocked and unsure: "What shall we do, shall we kill it?"

"It's too big. How would you kill it? I couldn't," said Maria.

"Neither could I," admitted her friend.

"It's not moving."

"It doesn't look like it's going anywhere."

"It was here before we came."

"Yes, I agree, but all the same, we pay and it doesn't," remarked Franca.

They laughed for a while, reflecting on what to do. They decided to wait and see if anything changed. It could it be that it was dead and 'stuffed', or maybe it was in hibernation, suggested Maria.

"But it's summer and animals hibernate in the winter," objected Franca.

"It feels like winter here, maybe they get confused," Maria said.

"Maybe. Look, it hasn't moved an inch. Let's give it a name!" Franca suggested.

"Why? So it becomes part of the family?"

"No, so it feels less scary."

"Okay, what name do you like?" asked Maria.

"Don't know... Fred!"

"Fred? Yes, that's cute!"

They sat down on the step outside the barn, sheltered by a canopy. They watched the falling rain and the clouds that hid everything, isolating them from the world; it seemed as if there was no one else out there. For the first time, they had nothing to do.

"Did you know that the Dalai Lama was head of the Tibetans in exile?" Franca asked.

"Yes, vaguely. They are Buddhists, aren't they?"

"Yes, of course."

"In exile from whom?" asked Maria.

"From the Chinese, I think. We should find out."

"Speaking of Buddhism, do you remember the ten worlds Sanya and Colin were telling us about?"

"Yes, I thought a lot about that," replied Franca.

"For example, when we were in the middle of the landslide and that kind Indian man walked beside me to reassure me, he was in the world of Bodhisattva. And when we had to buy tickets and no one had time for us, that was the world of Animality, where everyone thinks only of himself," mused Maria.

"Well, to survive one must think of oneself."

"Do you think so? I think we can be kind even in stressful situations."

"Lucky you, I am more animal than you then," joked Franca.

"It's not like that; it's that when you are kind you are happier. How do you feel when you help someone?"

Her friend thought for a moment. Good, she answered.

"That's right! When you help another, who benefits more than anyone else is you."

"And in which of the worlds were you when you saw Paul?"

Maria laughed: "Between Animality and Hunger, I'm not sure. Animality is the world of instincts, and I instinctively would have had him!" They laughed aloud. "But the world of Hunger is the one where you want something and I definitely wanted him. I would say that I was in both worlds, if you can be in two worlds simultaneously. And you, with your smoking?"

"Easy," said Franca, I'm in the world of Hunger. But not only with smoking, I'm interested in anything that gets me high. It's fun! And now, what kind of world are we in?" They thought a little while, remembering the ten worlds.

"In Tranquillity? In Rapture?"

"Definitely not in the world of Rapture, don't go over the top."

"No, fair enough! But we are definitely in the fog. I'm hungry," said Maria.

"Me too. There are no shops up here, there's nothing. We must go down."

"Where?"

"Back to Maglo... whatever it's called. How do you get a Scottish name in the Himalayan mountains?" Franca wondered.

"Maybe it's because it rains all the time, like in Scotland. Come on, let's go and eat before it gets too dark."

"Close the barn. Has Fred moved?"

"No, not an inch."

They walked down the muddy path, sheltered by transparent plastic raincoats, the kind that tourists buy in Venice, with the hood over their heads. The sky was leaden. The rain gave no respite, and after a quarter of an hour downhill they arrived at the square of the village with a Scottish name. In its own way, despite the wet and the puddles, it was brimming with life. Before descending to the square level, Maria paused for a moment on the uphill path to take an overall look. Among all the people, one man in particular caught her attention, due to the height of his head; he had no legs and walked on his hands. A block of wood was tied by a strap to each hand and, by pushing on these blocks he lifted his body, moving with surprising lightness and speed; those pieces of wood were his legs. She followed him with her eyes and, as if sensing her presence, the man turned and looked at her. She came down the last part of the path and approached him, while he was coming toward her.

"Hello, my friend," he said. Did they need any help? Franca, who was already ahead, turned and watched the scene with surprise, approaching only a little. The man looked up at Maria and smiled. His cheeks were freshly shaved, his skin was smooth and tanned, he had an open look and wore a spotless white shirt. He was a handsome man with an intelligent face. He didn't look quite like an Indian, there was something almost European about him, because of the lighter colour of his hair and the hazel hue of his eyes.

"We're looking for somewhere to eat," she said, crouching down to look him in the eyes. "Do you know a cheap place where the food is good?"

"I know all the places in Mcleodganj," he said, laughing. "Don't go to the Tibetan chai-shop. They don't have the slightest idea about hygiene. You're better off eating at the restaurant where all the English people go." He gestured with his chin.

"We're not English," said Franca, who had approached. "We are Italian."

And he, to their great surprise, began to speak in Italian: "Come stai amico? Italia è un bellissimo paese. Io cucino indiano e Maria cucina italiano." How are you my friend, Italy is a beautiful country, I cook Indian and Maria cooks Italian, he said.

"How come you speak Italian?" Maria asked.

"I was in Italy with the British army during the war," he said, smiling; he had straight white teeth. Italian people were very kind, he said. He often went to eat at his friend Maria's house, she was a great cook. One day he cooked an Indian meal for her and her family, and they all liked it.

"My name is Maria, too! What part of Italy were you in?"

"South of Bologna. A beautiful place." He guessed the thought that went through her mind, and, looking down, where his legs used to be, he added: "It was a long time ago."

"Okay! We're going to eat where you suggested," said Maria, standing up. "Are you hungry?" she asked earnestly.

"No thank you, I'm not hungry. You go and I hope you'll enjoy it, even if it's not Italian food." He smiled, looking from one to the other, and the girls walked away.

"What an incredible man," said Maria, as soon as they had gone some distance. "At first I thought he was a beggar, but... what a surprise, huh?"

"Yes, he's a strange one," said Franca. "Who knows what he's doing here, where it rains so much. He would be better off where it's dry, considering that here he's always close to some puddles. Walking on his hands. That's crazy!"

"Maybe he was born here," Maria suggested.

"Why did you squat down to talk to him? It seemed patronizing." Franca asked, critically.

"Because I wanted to look at him in the eye," replied Maria, surprised. "It came natural."

"Mmm…" Franca disapproved. "I didn't like it!"

"I think he did," retorted Maria. "Shall we go to the restaurant he recommended? It's right here."

"You go. I'll go to the Tibetan chai-shop."

"But the man said it was dirty."

"And what do I care of what he thinks? It's cheap and I'm going there. See you later."

She walked off, leaving her standing there. Maria looked at her, confused, but Franca quickly reached the chai-shop and entered with confidence. Well, in that case, she would explore this one.

She pushed the restaurant's padded door and was immediately hit by the music, while a few playful notes sneaked out through the open crack and floated away, dispersing freely in the road's cool damp air. Maria stepped inside and closed the door behind her, returning the road to its previous peace. She found herself in a place that reminded her of a disco in the sixties, with red lights, a pop song blaring from the sporadically placed speakers, tables full of young western travellers who ate and spoke loudly to be heard over the music. She could make out different languages: English, German, French. She looked around, all the tables were occupied. When her eyes became accustomed to the dim light she noticed a table on the left with two girls. One had dark hair, she must have been around twenty, while the other one was younger and fair; she couldn't have been more than eighteen. Maria approached shyly and heard that they spoke Italian: "Excuse me, all the tables are full, could I sit here?"

The girls looked at her with surprise. They were engaged in an animated discussion and hadn't seen her.

"Yes, of course. Are you Italian? Where from?" The typical question among Italians; useful to start a conversation.

"I'm from Venice and you?"

"I'm from Verona," said the one with dark hair, "and she's from Padua," she added, looking at her young friend, with a touch of resentment.

"I'm Maria."

"Hi, I'm Barbara."

"And you?"

"Carla," the blonde girl said sulkily. It was obvious they were fighting, or at the brink of doing so. Maria sat down and told them she was starving. How could she attract the waiter's attention in this chaos?

"Baba," cried Carla, "Baba!" waving her arm toward the busy waiter, who was walking around carrying a tray full of cups and glasses. What did 'baba' mean? Maria asked. 'Man,' said the sulky girl. Did she speak Hindi? She was learning. The waiter came up quickly and bowed with folded hands. "Namaste Ji," he said to Carla with a friendly smile. Maria ordered soup, rice with chicken and a chai.

"She's in love with an Indian," declared Barbara, "and now she has to learn his language." Carla looked away.

"It's no problem having a fling with someone, that's fine, but now she no longer wants to return to Italy. She wants to marry him and stay here. Our visa expires in five weeks!" continued Barbara, flushed, looking at Carla, who refused to look at her and stared at the door. "Then he leaves you and you'll find yourself in trouble with the police!" Turning to Maria, she added: "She's only seventeen!"

Maria didn't know what to say. Barbara went on to explain that they had left Italy together, months before, and had come to India overland through Turkey, Iran, Afghanistan and Pakistan. "As soon as they see her, blond hair and blue-eyed, all the men want her. It was hard to keep them at bay. Sometimes we had to kick them away from the coach's steps, as some took advantage of that moment to touch her," she said earnestly. "And now this! What do I tell your mother?"

"This is *my* life!" Carla replied through clenched teeth, staring at Barbara with frustration. "*I* decide what I want to do. You don't tell me, or anyone else, is that clear? I don't give a damn about what others think. Period!" There was a moment of silence during which a Madonna song filled the air, cheerful and dynamic; it made Maria want to dance in spite of the situation she found herself in. To change the subject, Carla, who continued to look toward the door, turned to Maria and asked her if she was travelling alone.

"No, I am with a friend. She went to eat at the Tibetan chai-shop."

"And how come you're not together? Don't you get along?" she asked, her curiosity aroused. Maria explained that when they left Italy, they hardly knew each other and that the main reason for going to India together was that both were afraid to go there alone. They had made a pact that, if their partnership didn't work, each would go her own way, without a fuss. "And now have you had a fight?" the blonde girl asked.

"No, not quite... Franca is a bit unpredictable and very independent. She's decided to spend as little as possible so that she can invest her money to buy charas. She likes to smoke 'a lot'!"

The waiter arrived with the hot soup, the rice, the chicken and the chai, all at the same time. Maria was hungry and focused on the soup that smelled promising.

"I can help her find some good smoke," said Carla. "If you don't know where to go, you can end up buying some really cheap stuff, but I know how to find good Himalayan charas, the one she wants; I've already figured it out. Tell her to talk to me."

"Definitely! She'll be happy! Where are you staying?" Maria asked, blowing on the spoon full of steaming soup. They were also staying at Rishi Bhavan, except that Carla stopped in the village with her boyfriend, Rana was his name. In Italian it meant 'frog'.

When Maria laughed Carla looked at her condescendingly. It means 'king', she explained, as if her patience was about to run out: "It's so annoying! Every time I say his name, all the Italians burst out laughing."

"I'm sorry, it comes as a bit of a surprise," Maria apologized, trying to keep a straight face.

"Yes, and Rani means queen," said the young woman, to complete the explanation and shrug off the responsibility of such a ridiculous Indian name.

"Oh thank you; that's interesting!"

Barbara said she would like to go back to Rishi Bhavan with them. When Maria finished her dinner she decided to go and look for Franca, while the two girls stayed a little longer in the restaurant, where it was dry.

Outside, the rain had stopped, but the air was humid and there were puddles and mud everywhere. Maria walked toward the Tibetan chai-shop and almost immediately saw the man with no legs. He asked her if she had eaten well and she crouched down to talk to him. "Yes, thank you, very well." Now she was looking for her friend who had gone to the Tibetan chai-shop and who had the only key, and the only torch.

He told her that Franca was in the square, he'd seen her walk by. But why didn't she have a torch? He was amazed and clearly thought it was a very important thing.

"You must *always* carry your torch," he said, with a serious expression. "What happens if your friend decides to go somewhere else? Or if she wants to leave later? Or if she takes the wrong path? Or maybe you want to go in different directions." Seeing that Maria was taking what he said with laid back acceptance, he looked into her eyes with a sense of urgency: "You must take responsibility for your own life, Maria; you mustn't delegate it to someone else, never. You are responsible for where you go, for what direction you take!" Since Maria was beginning to listen to him, he continued eagerly: "You must always be able to see the road in front of you, with potholes, rocks, ditches, gullies maybe. Think about it! What if your friend's torch runs out of batteries? It may happen that, at some point, you're the only one who clearly sees the path ahead." Maria realised he wasn't just speaking literally. She was struck that the concept of 'taking responsibility' resurfaced again. But Franca was waiting in the square; she had no time to buy a torch now.

"When you understand something important, you have to put it into practice right away," the man insisted urgently. "You can't ignore it any longer and just continue as before. Your friend won't even notice if you get there a little later, she'll talk with people in the square. It will take two minutes."

All right, then, did he know where she could buy a torch? Of course, at that shop over there, he said, pointing to it with his arm. "Come on, let's go together!" he added firmly. Maria stood up and they set off. He walked raising his torso on the wooden blocks attached to his hands; she walked slowly by his side. She bought a yellow flashlight with good batteries and the shopkeeper gave her a discount thanks to her friend, whose name was Surinder. She was glad she had followed his advice; she felt more confident and independent now.

They went together to the square and she saw Franca who was saying goodbye to a couple of boys.

She turned to Maria, calmer than before: "There you are! Where've you been?" Maria told her about the torch and the two Italian girls. One of them wanted to return to Rishi Bhavan with them. Sure, no problem, said Franca, in fact she liked meeting new people.

"How was the food in the Tibetan chai-shop?" asked Maria.

"Good! And at the restaurant?"

It was good, but there was loud pop music and she had felt a sharp contrast between the outside world and the atmosphere inside the restaurant. Yeah, she knew, said Franca, that's why she had gone to the Tibetan chai-shop. How she could possibly have known was a mystery! As they approached the restaurant they saw Barbara waiting for them.

Maria took leave of Surinder and they headed for the hill that led to Rishi Bhavan, in the dim grey light of the late afternoon. Along the trail, the green of the trees and bushes was dark and flat, lacking the sunlight that made everything bright and cheerful. There was a depth in the humidity around them that calmed her spirit enough to prefer silence and reflection. But not for Franca, she had a lot of things to tell their new friend.

Walking uphill, panting, she told Barbara how she had asked the receptionist in Mandi lots of questions about their culture and how he had told her about women studying; about the families who asked for the horoscopes before deciding on their children's marriage; that they could get a divorce, and so on, one thing after another. She made it seem as if everything had been her initiative, as if Maria hadn't even been present. Maria was annoyed, but there was no way to get a word in edgeways. Barbara thought it would be interesting to see Carla and Rana's horoscope. She was concerned that Carla was so young and wanted to stay with him in India.

"Why don't you like him?" asked Franca.

"He uses and sells drugs," said Barbara, "and Carla has a tendency to go overboard with smoking charas. Who knows what else he's going to introduce her to. He is in trouble with the police, and doesn't have a good character, always angry, always against someone!"

"What does she see in him, then?"

"What do I know? He's good-looking, very handsome."

"Don't worry!" said Franca. "She'll change her mind, you'll see. I change my mind every two minutes." Maria smiled. "And then, even if she 'experiments' with drugs what's the harm? It's all experience, isn't it?" Maria glanced at Barbara and noticed that she wanted to disagree with this latest outburst; she wanted to say something, but Franca was in full flow. Was it him, by chance, who sold the good charas?

"Yes, of course, it's his job! Just talk to Carla, but..."

"Very well, very well," said Franca, rubbing her hands.

"I don't agree with your idea of 'experiencing' with any drugs," Maria objected, noting that Barbara shook her head in agreement. "There are drugs that are too dangerous, especially for someone so young."

"Bah! Everyone is free to do what they want, right?" asserted Franca, on the defensive. "And each of us has our own karma!"

"You may be right, Franca, but I feel responsible for Carla, and I love her. I couldn't forgive myself if something bad or irreparable happened," Barbara said, earnestly. "We got here together and I would like to go back home with her."

"You can't force her to think like you. In the end, she'll do what she wants!" objected Franca, belligerent.

"So what can I do to protect her?"

"Tell her that you love her and to use common sense," said Maria. "Even if she is young she's not stupid and she'll have some wisdom inside herself. She'll think about what her parents taught her and, maybe, she has some fears of her own, don't you think?"

They came to Rishi Bhavan that, as before, was covered by its disproportionate hat made of grey clouds. Barbara had a kerosene stove and was going to make tea. Franca went to get her piece of charas to make a chillum. In the dark stable, Fred hadn't moved at all, or so it seemed. He was probably dead as a doornail and simply stuck to the wall. One day or another it would fall to the ground!

They arrived at Barbara's bungalow where she rented one of the rooms. It was cosy, surrounded by a beautiful wooden veranda deck. During the day she spent a lot of time out there. With only a few red and yellow sarongs and a couple of straw mats she had turned the room into a warm and intimate den. The water in the saucepan was boiling and their new friend even had an aluminium teapot in which she made the tea. She pulled out a brown paper bag, stained with patches of grease, containing biscuits she had bought in the village and served them on a plate. Franca began to prepare the chillum, while talking nonstop. She told her of the landslide, the many changes of coaches, the people that crossed the mountain of mud, and about the English couple. "Maria has fallen in love, too," she joked, "with this English guy who looks like Jesus; a hunk, really handsome! It's him who gave me the charas we're about to smoke now. Can you believe that he gave us his address and Maria doesn't want to go and see him? Crazy or what! What do you think?"

Barbara looked at Maria, waiting for an answer.

"Franca forgot to say that he has a girlfriend, pretty and kind, and that the fact that I like him is not enough, is it? It takes two, minimum, to do something interesting."

"But he liked you a lot! You could it see a mile away."

"Who, me?"

"Yes, you! You must be blind."

Maria was silent for a while. She wasn't at all sure but, knowing herself, perhaps she didn't want to see; she always played it down, always on the safe side, so as not to suffer. Maybe he did like her a bit, but that didn't mean anything. She dismissed the idea once again, better to stick to the present and not get carried away by stories in her head. "Forget about it!" she said, making a hand gesture that concluded the speech. "Let's smoke the chillum and have a tea."

Barbara lit a match, taken from a box kept near the stove; it was the only good place, she said, as the air was so damp. She followed it with a 'Bom Shankar!' shouted with folded hands. She brought the flame near the chillum, full of tobacco and charas. Franca began to inhale, hands twisted around the vertical pipe, head at a ninety degree angle, her mouth pressed against the slot left open between her hands. She shook her head, her lungs filled and her mouth tightly closed, before exhaling a ridiculous amount of smoke that seemed like the locomotive of a steam train. She passed the chillum to Barbara, who did the same, and then it was Maria's turn. "I'm not able to smoke that thing!" she said with frustration. "I can't put my hands right."

"I'll help you," said Franca and, as Paul had done, she took Maria's hands between hers, and closed all the cracks. "Go on, smoke now!"

Maria inhaled and the huge intake of smoke nearly choked her. She remembered not to cough and, after a pause with her lungs full, she exhaled. She went quiet for a while and, on the second lap, she shook her head. She had had enough; it was very strong! Barbara put out the plate with biscuits.

"What was that thing you shouted?" asked Maria.

"Bom Shankar?"

"Yes."

"It's in honour of Shiva Shankar, the Hindu god of charas!" Barbara explained.

"Oh, I didn't know they even had a god of charas."

"Of course they do!" Franca butted in.

"Indian mythology says that he lives in the Himalayas and the Ganges River flows out from his head." Barbara explained.

"That's awesome! So we are protected by him?"

"Sure!" Franca confirmed.

"Charas is a sacred thing in this culture... I think," Barbara added.

"Fancy that! And I didn't know anything about it. What a place India is!" Maria mused.

They each bit on a biscuit, and finished them in two bites. A few sips of tea, another biscuit, and so on. Goood! Tomorrow they were going to buy some.

"Can I have another one?"

"Here you go! There are five each."

Unlike Franca, Barbara understood why Maria didn't want to go to the English couple's house. "I'd be the same," she said. "You can't build your own happiness on top of someone else's unhappiness." In addition, the law of cause and effect meant that what you did to a person, would then be done to you. 'What goes around comes around', she said. Was she a Buddhist? No, but she would have liked to be. She knew, however, the law of cause and effect. It didn't take much to understand it; it was obvious! Speaking of Manali then, if they didn't want to go by the English couple's house, they would find a guesthouse, she had been there already. She explained what Manali was like, which restaurants there were, how much they cost. And if she wanted to buy something to smoke? asked Franca. Just ask anyone, if that person didn't have any they would recommend someone else. It grew everywhere. Manali was surrounded by marijuana plants, Barbara said, laughing; even outside the police station was full. Franca was very happy! She began to prepare another chillum. Barbara had one last piece of information, and the best. She said there was a place above Manali, called Vashist, they *had* to go there, there were natural hot water springs and, by paying two rupees each, they'd get a room with a big tub to be filled with hot water. Two people could lie in it comfortably and they could finally wash "the way God commands!" This was an old, peculiar, Italian expression. It meant 'properly' but what a way of expressing it.

"Beautiful sentence, as God commands!... a bit absurd, though," reflected Maria, who felt the effect of the chillum: "And God commanded: Wash yourself you filthy old bag!" she said, with a Florentine accent... "Wash your feet, too, properly; look how dirty they are. You ought to be ashamed. Scrub them well!" They began to laugh.

"Don't forget under your armpits… if you raise one arm I'll pass out from the stench," said Franca.

"And while you are at it, you might as well wash your 'little rose'," continued Maria.

"What's that? That one?" Barbara asked, looking down.

"Yes… that one!"

"How do you call it?" Franca asked with curiosity.

"Little rose! That's what my mum always called it. Why? What's yours called?"

"Vagina," said Barbara

"Yeah, right! Surely you have a nickname for it in your house, don't you?" objected Maria. "Don't tell me that your mum tells you 'Wash your vagina, Barbara, otherwise it'll grow mushrooms'." They were laughing holding their bellies.

"No, my mum calls it 'little butterfly'," said Barbara.

"What a beautiful name! The philanderer butterfly. Is your mum's butterfly a philanderer?" Who knows why the Florentine accent came out so naturally.

"No, that's gross. My mum doesn't have sex!" replied Barbara, pretending to be shocked. "No, it's called butterfly because it is shaped like a butterfly, isn't it?"

"True, true, I never noticed. And in your house, Franca? How do you call it?"

"In my house it's named after a biscuit!"

"Seriously? Which one?"

"Puff! Cream puff!"

They laughed so hard that even Fred must have heard them from their stable.

"So, what does your mum say? Wash your cream puff, Franca!"

"Now she doesn't say anything, but when I was a child she used to say 'Don't forget your cream puff!"

Their stomachs hurt from laughing so hard, they almost vomited all the yummy food they had eaten.

When it was time to go back to the barn, it was pitch black outside and a gentle, but persistent rain had begun to fall. Franca had left her torch in the barn. For the first time, Maria used her new yellow flashlight and thought of Surinder with gratitude.

8. The secret of happiness

Maria woke in the middle of the night with an incredible desire to scratch her right arm, where she found a monstrously big insect bite. While scratching, she began to feel another bite on her leg, one on her foot, another on her head. She was twisting and turning but couldn't scratch every bite, and they were itching like crazy. Reluctantly she slipped out of her sleeping bag, turned on her torch and lit a few candles. She could see at least a dozen bites, red and inflamed. It was so cold that she quickly blew the candles out and fled back into her sleeping bag. She tried to rest and dozed off until the light filtered in from outside to tell her it was morning, at last. Franca opened her eyes and immediately began to scratch. She had also been eaten alive.

"We'll have to do something about these bites; I must have twenty or thirty!"

"So have I," said Franca, scratching.

"And now, if we want a cup of tea and something to eat, we have to go down to Mcleodganj?"

"Unless you want to buy a kerosene stove, pots, cups, and so on," replied Franca.

"I don't want to stay here very long, as much as I like this stable and Fred's company," Maria said, glancing at the spider. "Joke! It may not be as hot as Delhi, but there's mud everywhere. It doesn't even seem like India."

"So, let's explore what there is to explore and then we leave. The guidebook spoke of the Tibetans and the Dalai Lama," said Franca.

They wore the same wet jeans as the day before, the same wet socks and shoes. It wasn't raining, but it didn't make much difference, everywhere was soaked. The descent to Mcleodganj seemed much shorter than the day before; they slipped on the muddy trail and walked arm in arm to support each other. Seen from the top of the path in the grey light of morning the village consisted of a row of low huts, some houses, shops and restaurants, all encircling the tallest building, which had several pagoda roofs surmounted by a golden spire. Just outside the small town was a group of houses where the Tibetan refugees lived; poor shacks put together with pieces of metal and wood, and a few lucky bricks here and there. Each hut was brightened by pots of orange marigold hanging from the window sills or placed neatly outside the doors. The other thing that stood out were the many strips of colourful Tibetan flags hanging from tree to tree, their colours bleached by the sun, shimmering with every breath of wind, exuding a sense of peace, creating a solemn mystical atmosphere. Despite the poverty, the place communicated a feeling of contentment and cheerfulness.

In a few minutes they arrived at the chai-shop, a dark and damp structure with two rough wooden tables and a couple of benches. On the kerosene stove there stood a huge pot, boiling the chai with aromatic spices; cloves, cardamom and cinnamon gave out an exquisite aroma. The sweet tea cheered them up; even their damp shoes felt a little less cold. They ate two large biscuits and asked the chai-shop owner how to get to the Tibetan prayer area.

"Go down the road, this way," he said, coming up to the door and pointing to the left. Today was very important, he added: it was the Dalai Lama's birthday and the Tibetans came from all parts of the region. "Go where they go," he said simply.

In the distance, from the top of tall poles, the long strips of coloured flags reached diagonally down to the ground and waved cheerfully. Maria thought that each flag might symbolize a person, a vibrant life; maybe she was wrong, but the feeling awoke something inside and moved her. On reaching the road they joined a crowded queue of Tibetan people who advanced slowly. They looked very different from the Indians. They had high cheekbones, eyes that reminded her of the Mongolian race and skin that looked like weathered leather, darkened by generations of high mountain sun. The men's and women's hair were held in a long braid; the elders' braids were white and thin. Around their necks they wore stunning necklaces made of large chunks of turquoise stones and rough pieces of orange or red coral. The traditional dress was composed of a hand-woven woollen shirt and a long skirt; it looked like a blanket wrapped around the body, of earthy colours. An apron of woven wool in bright red, green and yellow brightened the greys and browns of the main gown. Around their waist was wound a woollen shawl, which served also as a purse and wallet. Where the skirt ended, a little above the feet, colourful boots could be glimpsed; they were made of cloth, lively and cheerful in combinations of red, turquoise, green, yellow and black. They gave the impression of a vibrant people, who liked to laugh and have fun, although the long procession was pervaded by a focused attitude. Almost everyone was holding a wooden rosary or a small metal cylinder supported by a stick, which they turned round and round, while murmuring their prayers.

Walking faster than the people in the queue, the girls soon arrived at the prayer area. In the centre of the square was a rectangular building. All around its perimeter were arranged rows of revolving hand-engraved silver cylinders, as big as buckets. People touched them with their fingertips and made them rotate, one by one, whilst walking around the entire rectangle, counting their rosary beads or turning the small prayer wheel in their hands. What at first seemed like silence, revealed itself to be a constant mutter, little more than a whisper; every Tibetan produced a sound that created a deep resonance and made the air vibrate. It was a ceremony of a beautiful simplicity. She couldn't understand what they murmured, but something within Maria answered, quietly but strong and determined, and tuned in with them. Nam-myoho-renge-kyo, she kept repeating in her head, motionless, absorbing the atmosphere of peace and strength, next to those people who didn't seem to notice her. Responding to a strong sensation, she turned and saw Surinder advancing, rising on the wooden blocks strapped to his hands.

Franca followed her gaze and said: "Look who's there!"

"Perfect! So we can ask him what to do about these insect bites."

Maria went to meet him and crouched down to speak to him. Surinder greeted her with a smile; he wanted to know if they had slept well and if she had used the torch. She had used it, indeed; without it she didn't know how they would have got back to their room, in the dark of night. She thanked him for having advised her to buy it. "Now we have another problem; look," she said, lifting the sleeve of her sweater and showing him three large bites, red and swollen, which almost covered her whole arm. He raised an eyebrow; they had to see a doctor, he said, studying the bites. Was there a doctor in Mcleodganj? There was a Tibetan doctor, who lived just a few yards away, right there, and pointed his finger at a small house within walking distance.

Glad to find a local doctor, Franca immediately started to walk in the direction of the house, while Maria walked more slowly to keep in step with Surinder.

He introduced them to a very old and small man, his white hair tied back in a braid and wearing large black-rimmed glasses. The Tibetan doctor was getting ready to go to the ceremony, but he would see them straight away. Franca lifted a sleeve and mimed the itching and scratching. The doctor looked carefully at the bites and then said something: flea bites, translated Surinder. *Fleas*? Yes, fleas. The doctor spoke again and told Surinder he would prepare a mixture of herbs to relieve the itching and discourage the fleas from biting again. What herbs were they? He didn't know the English name, but they grew in those mountains. They could trust him, he was an experienced doctor. Happy to trust, the girls sat down on an old weathered wooden bench to wait with Surinder, taking advantage of that time to ask him the questions they had on the tip of their tongues.

Why was it that the Tibetans were in Mcleodganj? They were Buddhists who fled the Chinese invasion. The Chinese army had destroyed their temples and killed thousands of monks and their students, as well as all those who were suspected to be against the invasion. They had stopped here, where they found refuge with the Dalai Lama, who was a very important figure, a mixture of father, holy man, spiritual leader and their political representative. And the flags, what did they symbolize? They were prayers, a statement of hope and faith.

"Are you a Buddhist?" asked Maria.

"I am a little bit of everything," replied Surinder. "I am a Hindu by birth, to an English father and an Indian mother. My mother was an untouchable, as you call them; 'harigen' Gandhi called them, which means God's children. So, I'm a 'harigen' too. In the Hindu religion you are born into a caste and there you stay for that lifetime. I'm not ashamed to be of the lowest caste, I am proud of my origins. I am different from others and I'm fine with that."

"If you want to, can you change religion?" Maria asked. "Could you become a Buddhist?"

"Of course! And I like the Buddhist religion, there are no castes and everyone is equal. What I like most about it is that it doesn't accept fate passively; it sees karma as a condition that changes constantly. It focuses on the present, so, every thought, or action that I make now, is a cause creating my future. It is a positive, dynamic, philosophy."

"So, why don't you change to it?" asked Franca.

"Because I am already free," replied Surinder. "I don't need anyone to tell me that I can live with pride, because I already do so. I *choose* to remain a 'harigen' to prove to the people of my caste that we too have great dignity. I want them to feel proud of who they are. My life is perfect as it is and I don't need to change anything," he concluded, as if it were the most obvious thing in the world.

Maria was curious to know how he had lost his legs, but she couldn't find the courage to ask him that question; besides, with what he had just said, that his life was perfect, he was telling her that the rest didn't matter. She asked him instead about the ceremony for the Dalai Lama's birthday. It took place at the Dalai Lama's residence, where there was a beautiful temple. Had they been already?

"No, but we'd like to go today. Do you think non-Buddhists can go?"

Surinder laughed, showing his beautiful white teeth: "Of course you can go. Everyone can. Be respectful, that's all!"

"How do we know what to do and what not to do?" asked Maria.

"Watch how others behave and don't do anything they don't do. It's simple!"

"Will you go?" asked Franca

"Of course! As soon as the sun comes out and the ground dries a little."

"Do you think the sun will come out?"

"For sure! It's always sunny on the Dalai Lama's birthday," he replied confidently.

The doctor had prepared two packets of brown paper. He told them not to scratch the bites, to take the content of one sachet dissolved in water every morning and every night for a week, and to eat less sweets. All together it was ten rupees: a dollar. Very little, Maria thought. She saw that Franca was staring at her and she understood she was being warned not to say anything that could spoil the market.

Hope to see you this afternoon, she said to Surinder. There will be a lot of people, he said, and it will be very interesting for you. If they didn't need anything else, he had to go. He said goodbye by touching his forehead with his fingers and moved away. Maria followed him with her eyes, as he raised his torso and walked with his hands.

"His life is perfect the way it is," she said, feeling sorry for him, but also a great deal of respect.

"If he says so, he doesn't need your pity," chided Franca, who could see it in her face.

"Easier said... Don't you feel sorry for him?"

"Not really. I protect myself from pain; otherwise it becomes too heavy here in India."

"And how do you protect yourself? Do you not feel anything?"

"I accept things as they are. I observe and register," she said, pointing her index finger to her temple and tapping it a couple of times.

While her friend went to explore the area around the square, Maria sat down to watch the crowds who kept arriving, fascinated by this new people, who came from a land so close to the sky. She allowed herself to absorb the atmosphere, while in the background that almost imperceptible sound that came from deep within every person awakened the chanting words which were so often in her mind but that she rarely pronounced. Barely moving her lips she said it without being noticed, whilst observing those around her. They wore the most incredible hats, some leaf-shaped, others seemed a giant visor that covered the head and protected their eyes from the sun, set with red coral, turquoise and amber stones. The children were carried on their mothers' or grandmothers' backs, wrapped in blankets that held them tight. They had red cheeks, dishevelled hair, dripping noses and looked sweet, puppies of man. Franca came back; if they wanted to go to the ceremony, it was better if they ate beforehand: "Let's go to the Tibetan chai-shop, come on. It's cheap!"

"I don't want to get diarrhoea. I already have thirty flea bites. That's enough for me!"

But Franca said they made a soup with pasta that looked like spaghetti. "If you eat only cooked things you don't risk anything, even if they are not very hygienic!" she assured her; in Italy she was a laboratory analyst and she knew these things. Well, the idea of spaghetti *was* very inviting.

The atmosphere inside the Tibetan chai-shop was of calm excitement, without a doubt because it was such a special day. They served a hot soup full of noodles, which looked indeed like thin spaghetti, and some parcels stuffed with fried vegetables, which were delicious.

"Do you like your job as an analyst?" asked Maria, who knew little about Franca's life. Yes, she liked it, but she didn't like living with her parents. Why not? Didn't she have a lot of freedom? She did, but every night when she went back home she had to answer the same old questions and felt she was being treated like a little girl. She longed to leave home, do what she wanted to do and be free. Maria understood; she had lived away from her parents since she was eighteen and it had been good. Her freedom meant that she had a lot of responsibility, though. In a sense, to be free *was* to be responsible; it seemed like a contradiction, but it wasn't at all. Freedom without responsibility was foolhardiness! She discovered that Franca was bored in her relationship with Gabriele and saw him as a friend. Until then she had believed that Franca had everything that *she* would have liked, and perhaps it was so, but she wanted something else.

The sky was beginning to clear, revealing slithers of blue where before there were only dense grey clouds. They set off toward the temple, joining large groups of people walking in the same direction. It seemed a procession, full of excitement. It was pervaded by an air of festivity and people moved at a fast pace, covering the path uphill with an enthusiasm that erased the tiredness accumulated over many miles. There were Indians, Europeans, but above all Tibetans. One could see who had come a long way by the coat of dust that covered their hair and clothes.

In the distance the golden spires of the temple stood out against the bright blue sky. The building was surrounded by green woods blending into a darker, thicker forest behind. For the first time since their arrival the sun was shining, beginning to dry their clothes and shoes. Maria lifted her face and, with her eyes closed, absorbed the heat of those warm and comforting rays. As they approached, the silhouette of the temple became more clearly outlined. It was a three storey golden building, with long and slender pinnacles connecting the earth to the sky. Along the outer walls rows of prayer cylinders stretched out, like in the Mcleodganj square, and people turned them, pushing them with their fingertips, each person waiting patiently for their turn in the queue. The large temple courtyard was crowded with hundreds of Tibetan monks wearing a sort of long burgundy skirt, a sleeveless yellow shirt and a burgundy shawl over the shirt. Sitting on the temple steps, they were enjoying the sun in small groups, talking in a low voice, going through the rosary beads.

Seeing that foreigners went up the stairs and entered the temple, the girls decided to do the same. They walked in, with some emotion, and were greeted by giant images of Buddha. Franca barely held a whistle of surprise. "They're huge," she said.

"Beautiful," said Maria, who couldn't find better words. In the background there was that deep sound again that made the air vibrate with a resonance almost imperceptible to the ear, but felt by the body. Impossible to decipher, it was discreet, calming, reassuring and at the same time, like a big clean wave, decisive, strong, unstoppable, invigorating for the heart. It vibrated, resonating, trembling, expanding, further and further, deeper and deeper, more and more profound. Maria focused again on the great images of the Buddha. It was very different from the images she had seen so far; this Buddha was thin, calm, serene. Was that the face of happiness?

Franca suggested they go for a walk in the surrounding forest before the ceremony began and Maria followed her willingly, wanting to feel the sun on her skin.

In the woods there was peace and a quiet solitude, the scent of resin was beginning to spread, released by the heat of the sun that finally touched the pine trees' trunks. They sat on a fallen tree and Franca began to prepare a chillum.

"Are you going to make it here? Now?" asked Maria. "Do you think you can?"

"Yes, of course! Charas is sacred, isn't it? And this is a sacred place. I'm sure they don't have a problem with this," she replied confidently.

Well, it didn't seem out of place. Franca leaned the chillum on her forehead, Maria prepared the lighter and Franca shouted 'Bom Shankar'; then she inhaled and released a powerful cloud toward the blue sky. Maria smoked very little and Franca finished it, having the lion's share, as she liked. They absorbed the peace of the forest, breathing deeply the smell of damp moss mixed with the pungent resin, appreciating the sun shining through the branches and warming their backs, heads and faces. It was a great feeling, after days and nights of dampness and wet. The sky was completely clear, deep blue, not a cloud in sight. Relaxed, they walked back to the temple and found a good place to stop, to one side in the shade, from where they had an overall view.

Hundreds of Buddhist monks, known as 'lamas', were now kneeling in long rows inside the temple and outside in the yard, flooding it with burgundy colour and shaved heads. To her surprise, Maria noticed some westerners among them, both men and women who were also wearing red robes and had shaved heads. Large trays of fruit were placed here and there. The recitation of a mantra, the deep sound uttered by the lamas, was now stronger, increasing in volume as the minutes passed and the people joined them. It radiated an irrepressible power, touching the conscience of anyone who perceived it, whether near or far away. Maria tuned in, motionless, absorbing it through the skin, until she could hear nothing but the waves of vibrations that awakened something inside her, from her belly, squeezing her stomach, filling her chest and taking her breath away. She moved like a leaf in the wind. She sat down under a tree, closed her eyes and let that unknown emotion take her wherever it wanted to. It was like a wave and she let it wash over her and submerge her, while from deep inside a different sound answered and joined the others, Nam-myoho-renge-kyo. She couldn't say how long the chanting continued. She felt fine, a sense of peace and joy lulled her from inside, hugged her and comforted her. When the sound stopped she had to make an effort to open her eyes. Franca was gone, but she didn't mind.

No one moved; the excitement pervaded the air around her. The lama who had led the prayer turned and smiled at the crowd. People whispered and Maria thought she might be in front of the Dalai Lama. Almost immediately he began to speak, slowly moving his eyes over the crowd, watching them, smiling: "It's so good to see you all here today. Thank you. Many of you have come from far away, by any means possible, many on foot, mile after mile. Thank you!" He was always smiling, and continued, sometimes in his language, sometimes in English, saying that he was glad they were there all together. He hoped they'd be feeling that deep happiness that flows from inside, that doesn't depend on anything or anyone, that can be felt regardless of where, how or with whom one was. He spoke of the happiness that came from appreciating the most precious things in life: parents, children, brothers, sisters, friends, and life itself. The way he smiled made him look like a carefree child, without any worries. People didn't move, even the children were silent and motionless in their parents' or grandparents' arms. He continued, speaking of the happiness that one feels at the sight of a rising dawn, the gratitude that fills one's heart with each sunset. This happiness was the strongest, the most real and didn't change depending on the circumstances. It was always at hand, within us, giving us courage and strength, whenever we needed it.

He took a long break, smiling, looking at the people, one by one. His voice was calm, but firm. Our people are going through one of the most difficult moments in our history, he said; many had been killed, many had lost loved ones, many had to flee and leave friends and family in the grips of fear and danger. But we haven't lost the most important things: our humanity, our strength, our limitless courage. On the contrary, we have become even stronger *thanks* to these difficulties. Our faith, wisdom, compassion, these are the qualities of the Buddha that each of us holds in that great casket of our heart. We are determined to make them grow day after day, never giving up. Let's show the world who we are, with kindness and strength. Let's wake up the world that is sleeping and doesn't realize that our ancient culture is in danger of being wiped out for good. It would be a terrible loss not only for us but for all humanity.

He paused again, looking at the people in front of him, nodding and waving his head as his eyes swept over the silent crowd, kindness shining through his eyes. Then, with a firm voice he continued: "How lucky we are!"

Maria listened carefully. Had he said 'lucky?' Yes, to be living in these difficult times, to withstand this storm of injustice. What an enormous challenge we face. Our role is to resist, endure and persist, without ever letting up. Persistence is the quality of the Buddha. The more difficult the challenge, the greater the reward. He smiled again, and went on calmly. Fortunately, we have many friends who help us and support us. He thanked India that had given them shelter, a place to live, where they could continue their existence, and their resistance. From here we can communicate with the world, find support and make many friends. We can educate our children in our wonderful culture of peace and respect and teach them our faith.

Be happy, he encouraged them, appreciate life, every day, every moment, the good and the bad things. Respect yourself and others. Respect life, nature, plants, flowers and birds, everything that surrounds us. The world is beautiful, life is precious. "Thank you," he said with his hands clasped in front of his heart, "thank you," bowing to the crowd; "Thank you, thank you, thank you." People cheered loudly, smiling, happy, comforted, calm, confident, feeling stronger.

As if she had just awoken from a dream, Maria stood up from the tree trunk on which she was sitting and looked around. She caught sight of

Franca and Barbara farther away, at the edge of the crowd, and slowly, carefully, she made her way through the people. Finally she reached them and together they walked toward the nearest chai-shop. They hadn't heard what the Dalai Lama had said and wanted to know it from her. "It all seemed very simple and clear," said Maria, "but now I couldn't repeat it."

"It will come to you," Barbara assured her, "while we drink a chai."

She remembered that he said they were lucky. This had really struck her, because they didn't seem lucky to her, given the situation but, the way he had said it, it seemed convincing. And then he had spoken about happiness that came from within, of feeling gratitude for the good things and for the bad ones; he had also said that the more difficult the situation the more someone grew.

"It seems to me like pretending that everything is fine even when it's not," said Franca, critically.

"I think it's more than that," mused Maria. "What you're saying means accepting things as they are, even if we don't like them; it's a passive attitude." She tried to recall the Dalai Lama's words. "He was talking of letting the world know about their situation and fight on, but still *being grateful* for the good things, and be happy within. It is an active, dynamic attitude."

"What you are saying seems right to me," assented Barbara.

"And then, I noticed there wasn't any hatred in what he said," Maria reflected. "Most people in exile would be full of anger, and loathing, toward the invader, while I didn't hear any of that in the way he spoke. He spoke of becoming strong inside, instead."

"He seemed happy. He was always smiling!" remarked Barbara, and then, reflecting, she added: "I like this concept of the happiness that comes from within and is not dependent on the external situation. I wouldn't mind having a bit of that."

"Let's smoke a chillum," said Franca, "and have a good laugh!"

"Yes, that too, but there's more and it comes from inside. I'm curious to see what else India is going to give me," said Barbara.

"How much longer are you stopping in Mcleodganj?" asked Maria.

"I don't know! It depends on Carla," she replied. "I feel really bad at the thought of leaving without her. What am I to do? Leave her and go? If I go back to Italy alone, what do I say to her mother? Your daughter has stayed in India with a drug addict and wants to marry him?"

"I think you worry too much," said Franca, who hadn't yet met Carla. "She'll do what she wants, anyway. And after all, we also learn from our mistakes!"

"Mmmm. And you, where will you go from here?" Barbara asked, unhappy. "To Manali?"

Yes, to Manali, confirmed Franca. She was expecting mail at the Post Office, and also Maria had given that address, she added quickly, to remove any doubts she might have about the next destination. From there, they would go to Varanasi.

Barbara was glad to change the subject and assured them that in Manali it wasn't as rainy as it was here and that it was beautiful; Indian couples went there on their honeymoon! And Paul was there, Franca said provocatively, who had such good charas. She wouldn't mind buying some, but Maria was hiding the address.

"Are you really sure you don't want to go and see him?" asked Barbara.

"Absolutely," said Maria, "no doubt whatsoever." The girls looked at her quizzically.

"I can't explain why I have such strong feelings about him. It's not just because he's so handsome. There was something else, much more."

"Perhaps you had already met him in another life," said Franca, teasing her.

"It's possible! In India strong things happen, very strong," added Barbara.

Maria shrugged. She didn't know what to think. "If I'm meant to meet him, maybe I'll bump into him, walking down the road. Like that it would be all right."

"Let's hope so!" said Franca laughing.

"I came to India to understand who I am," continued Maria, turning to Barbara. "I was lost. The story with Ugo messed me up, in a big way. I didn't know who I was any more; I felt like a complete failure. I drank too much, I was drunk every night and I did some stupid things. I was in the world of Hell, the Buddhists tell me, depressed, confused, very unhappy. When I left I closed that door."

"So, welcome to India and welcome Paul," said Barbara.

"Indeed! He made me realize that there is life after Ugo. But he is only a dream. I can enjoy a dream, because nothing and no one can ruin it. It's safe. Fireproof!"

She saw Franca shaking her head, the Indian way, and she did it just fine! She laughed.

"When have you been practicing the head bobbing?"

"I haven't. It comes naturally to me."

"You do it perfectly!"

Her friend continued to nod her head for a while, whilst taking out her chillum and the necessary paraphernalia. And where was *she* going? Maria asked Barbara.

"Eh! Good question! From here I'll go to Rajasthan for a couple of weeks and then back to Italy, with or without Carla," she replied. Did she really think Carla would want to remain in Mcleodganj? No, Rana was from Bombay and they wanted to travel around India, go to Goa. She was seriously thinking about getting married and taking Indian nationality.

"She's crazy! Crazy! At seventeen," said Franca. "Come on, let's light it!" she encouraged Barbara, giving her the lighter and resting her hands on her forehead. "Bom Shankar!" she shouted. She inhaled deeply, held the smoke for a while, looking at them with shining eyes, her mouth tightly closed, and then let off the locomotive steam. Maria dodged the cloud of smoke that came in her direction and declined the chillum she was offered. They ordered another chai.

She was thinking in silence. How many things had happened that day, the Dalai Lama, the Tibetan procession, those words about happiness; Ugo, of whom she thought less and less, she noted with satisfaction; Paul whom she remembered with a calm feeling of longing; Barbara whom she liked very much and their plans for the next few days. They decided to leave the day after tomorrow for Mandi and then spend the night back at the Tourist Bungalow. The next day, they'd catch a bus to Manali. It would take from six to ten hours, Barbara said, depending on the weather. Franca crossed herself and they laughed loudly. They were hungry. When the chai arrived, they ordered samosas and pakhora; that way dinner was sorted. Some more chai and biscuits, and then, despite the Tibetan doctor's advice, they decided to buy more biscuits to take to the barn and go on to Rishi Bhavan before it became dark. For the flea bites they would take the medicine in the sachets.

Carla was outside the restaurant with the pop music. She greeted them coldly, defensive; she was waiting for Rana. No, she wasn't going to sleep at 'home', she answered, annoyed. She was going to stay in the village with him. She said goodbye and went into the restaurant to avoid continuing the conversation, which had started to feel like a confrontation. Barbara was upset, almost in tears, but there was nothing she could do; Carla didn't even want to look at her. They walked up the dirt path that was dry for the first time. In twenty minutes they had reached Rishi Bhavan. Fred was still there, it didn't seem to have moved, they could never be completely sure.

The next day started with a drizzle. It was the last day and they decided to explore Mcleodganj and Dharamsala. Maria took her camera, determined to take pictures since it was her last chance. Around noon the rain intensified and they were immersed in lead-grey clouds. They took refuge in a Tibetan shop where Maria bought a pair of boots made of brightly coloured cloth, to take home. They bought the tickets for the bus to Mandi for the next day. On the one hand she was glad to get away from the incessant rain, but on the other she was sorry; there was something very special about this place, which held her back. Surinder was nowhere to be seen. It was raining heavily and he couldn't walk on his hands in that weather. They saw Barbara going into the Tibetan 'restaurant' and they ran to join her. The town was deserted; everyone was sheltering from the rain. They spent all afternoon in the chai-shop which was full of local and western people. Outside, the clouds had burst. The rain fell in showers on the tin roof making a deafening noise. They had no umbrellas and she had the camera to protect; they were stuck! It was full of smoke and humidity in there. They drank chai, smoked a chillum, ate biscuits. Later, they ate soup with noodles, fried dumplings stuffed with vegetables, more chai, another chillum and some cookies. Maria had already smoked too much.

More and more silent and withdrawn into herself, she was sinking into a thick fog, sounds and perception were muffled, thoughts kept coming one after another, like fast trains that suddenly dissolved into the mist, forgotten, confused, leaving her empty. What was she thinking about? Gone! Disappeared, she no longer remembered. Colours came out of nowhere, lively, overbearing. Voices became thundering noises, disturbing, annoying. And more of that pelting rain on the tin roof, deafening, intrusive, exhausting. She had to go for a pee but couldn't move. I can't, I'm not able, she thought. She was afraid to move, she was afraid of everything. She was caught in the eye of a cyclone and in there she was turning, twisting, pinched on all sides, unable to move. Time didn't exist. She felt the insecurity and the fear, unable to think or decide, anxious in that world in which she had entered and from which she couldn't get out. She couldn't speak, even if she tried. She couldn't find the words or the voice to utter them. She didn't have the desire, or the strength, to do anything, not even to exist. Thoughts vied with one another in a whirlwind of excitement and anxiety, appearing and disappearing, filling her head with confusion, with worry, and her belly was bursting. She had to get up and go into the filthy toilet that was outside the 'restaurant', which was a low tavern, to call it by its proper name. She stood up, and it wasn't as difficult as she had feared, but her perception was altered so that it all looked different.

"Are you okay?" Barbara asked, looking at her between the clouds of smoke that filled the room. "You look very pale!" No, she wasn't well, but she had to go and pee. "I'm coming with you," Barbara said, "I need a pee too. Franca, order some more chai, please; our friend needs one!"

Maria was grateful for the company and they went out together. "My blood pressure must be very low," she said, breathing the fresh air. "My head feels like it's full of cotton wool."

"You've smoked too much," Barbara said. "Let's stay here for a while, until you feel better."

The toilet was disgusting, but at least she felt liberated. They found shelter under the tin roof and Maria breathed deeply the moist clean air. "So much paranoia!" she said with a sigh. "I felt claustrophobic in there."

"Unfortunately, unless the rain abates, we're stuck," said Barbara. It seemed as if it had always rained and would continue forever. It was hard to imagine that, once they'd leave this valley, they'd find the sun again. Despite all this, however, she was sorry to leave.

That evening Maria and Franca prepared their backpacks and then walked to Barbara's bungalow. They had almost arrived when they heard raised voices. They climbed the few steps and entered. Carla and Barbara were facing each other, quarrelling.

"She's come to get her things," Barbara said, turning to them. "She's going to live with him and they've decided to get married! I don't know what to say!" She spread her arms with a sense of helplessness, frowning with concern.

"You're only seventeen, why on earth do you want to get married? You're going to get stuck without a visa," said Franca.

Carla turned toward her, her eyes blazing.

"And who the fuck *are you*? I've never even seen you! Everybody's giving me advice. Why don't you mind your own fucking business?" Turning to Barbara she raised her arm and, her palm wide open forward to prevent further objections, she continued quickly, exasperated: "I don't want to hear anything else! You don't give a damn whether I'm happy or not! You don't want to travel alone, that's what bothers you. I love Rana and he loves me, we're getting married, and that's it. I don't care what you, or anyone else, think!" she shouted, glancing briefly at Franca. Going back to look at Barbara, she added: "You are all against us. We love each other, is it a sin? We want to be together. You are envious, that's what it is! Because you don't have anyone who loves you." Focusing on Barbara, she added: "Instead of being happy for me. What a rubbish friend you are!" She picked up her bags and walked toward the door. She turned one last time and said: "Don't worry about my mum, I'll write to her myself! Happy? You no longer have any responsibility!"

"Carla, not like this," pleaded Barbara, on the verge of tears.

Carla went down the steps and walked in the fog, a thin rain falling. Maria ran out onto the front porch and called her, but Carla was walking fast and didn't stop. She chased her and caught up with her. Touching her arm she said: "Good luck!" Carla slowed down and, after a few steps, she stopped. She turned to Maria, her face full of tears, anger and sadness. "Good luck, Carla," repeated Maria, searching for the right words. She could only find: "I hope you'll be happy!" and instinctively hugged her.

Carla was tense and rigid, but something began to melt. She leaned briefly on her and wept. "I too am sorry to leave her! But she doesn't understand!" She would tell Barbara, Maria reassured her. She told her to take care of herself and to stay away from hard drugs, her life was precious. Carla let her hold her tight and nodded her head. Slowly she pulled away and looked at Maria, her cheeks streaked with tears, her eyes red, pain and loneliness in her beautiful face, a young woman, determined, alone, courageous. "Thank you," she said.

"See you soon, I hope," replied Maria, and watched her walk away with her bags hanging from her shoulders, until she disappeared, swallowed by the dense cloud.

She stood looking in that direction, oblivious to the rain that wet her. Would she have the courage to take such a decision if she had met a man she loved so much? Would she decide to stay in India? No more mum and dad, no more friends from her childhood, no security, only the future to create, in a difficult country, and so far from home. Even Rajiv Gandhi had married an Italian woman, Carla had said at one point. She didn't know this. Maybe it was *they* who had a limited view of life and were too afraid of change, rather than Carla. She felt tenderness for her, while retracing her steps. She climbed the stairs that led into Barbara's room. Franca was preparing a chillum.

"She was crying," she said, looking at Barbara, who was so stunned she seemed to have collided with a wall. "She said she is sorry to leave you."

"Great consolation!"

"She's crazy," said Franca.

"She's in love, she's romantic, and very brave," said Maria.

"And now what do I do?" Barbara said, forlornly.

"Why don't you come with us tomorrow? Let's go to Mandi together, after that you go south and we go north," suggested Franca. After a brief hesitation, Barbara said: "I'll do just that!" Rising to her feet, she picked up her backpack and began to gather her things quickly, her misery rapidly developing into anger.

"Maybe you get ready after this chillum, huh?" Franca said with irony. "Come on, you light it!" Barbara slumped heavily on the wooden floor and took the chillum with gratitude. 'Bom Shankar', Franca cried and lit the flame with a lighter.

When they left the bungalow it was pitch black and Franca had forgotten her torch again. Maria searched in her bag and, at the bottom, she found her yellow flashlight. With pride, she turned it on and pointed it forward, illuminating the dark and muddy trail. How right Surinder was! They covered their heads with their hoods, Franca took her arm to help steady them both and together they walked up to the barn. The backpacks were ready and, shivering, they slipped into their damp, cold sleeping bags. Fred was watching over them for the last night, as motionless as ever, hopefully!

"You like Barbara, eh?" said Franca.

"Yes, very much. You like her too, right?"

"Yes, of course. But you like her more than you like me, I think."

Maria was surprised: "You are very different. I like you both! Why do you say that?"

"Well, nothing, I just noticed... Good night."

"Good night, Franca." She closed her eyes, tired, stoned and fell asleep thinking about Carla.

It was raining as they arrived in Mcleodganj square, the bus was there waiting and many people had already taken their seats. One after another, they climbed up the vertical ladder and arranged their rucksacks on the roof. She would never get used to this part of the journey and would have happily paid a porter, if there had been one. Maria looked around, but couldn't see Surinder. She didn't want to leave without saying goodbye and they had twenty minutes before the bus was due to leave. She approached the market stalls along the road and asked the first Indian man if he had seen him. Surinder? Blank expression on his face. The one with the wooden blocks on his hands, no legs, she explained with gestures and words.

"Ahhh, *Srinder*!" he said. No, he wasn't there. Maria told him she was leaving on the coach. Did he know where he was? The man said no with his head but, when he saw Maria's disappointed expression, he was sorry. Suddenly, his eyes lit up. He motioned for her to sit there at the stall while he went looking for him. Franca leaned out of the bus door.

"What are you doing?"

"I'm looking after the stall, while the owner has gone to find Surinder."

"Who?"

"The man with no legs!"

"We're leaving soon."

"Yes I know. We have ten minutes."

After a short while she saw the stall owner approach, smiling. Surinder was alongside him, advancing as quickly as possible, lifting himself on the wooden blocks. Maria went to meet him and squatted down, happy to see him. He, too, was pleased.

"I wanted to say goodbye before leaving, and to say thank you."

"It is I who must thank you," he said.

"Why?"

"For wanting to see me before you left."

"I wanted to ask you a question," said Maria.

"What is it?"

"Are you happy?"

He looked at her straight in her eyes.

"Are you asking this because I have no legs?" Maria nodded. "Yes, I'm happy, because I appreciate what I have: my culture, my friends, the fact that I am alive. You people in the West think that happiness depends on what you have, but you are wrong; this is why so many people are unhappy." Maria listened to him, giving him her full attention: "Happiness depends upon us. There are two requirements to be happy."

"What are they?" she asked urgently.

"The first is that you must know that true happiness comes from within, not from what you find outside of yourself." The bus honked and nearly deafened her. Maria kept her gaze fixed on Surinder, who went on hastily: "The second is that to be happy you must help others to become happy and not think only about yourself. Be altruistic. Try it, and you'll understand immediately!"

Maria leaned over to him and gave him a kiss on the cheek, while the bus began to move. Franca called her from the door. Maria got up and ran, grabbing the hand that her friend was holding out to her. She stood on the steps and turned to look at Surinder with affection. He smiled at her showing his beautiful white teeth and waved his arm, with the block of wood strapped to his hand. The stall holder too was smiling and waving his arm.

The driver told her to close the door, he was already driving out of the square, but he said it gently, as if he were a part of that friendship: "You must close the door now, Madam."

Maria went to sit next to Barbara and thanked Franca, who was sitting behind, next to an Indian woman.

"If I hadn't run to tell the driver to wait, he would have left without you," she said, irritated. "What were you telling him, so important that you almost missed the bus?"

Maria thanked her again, while recovering from the run: "He gave me some advice to be happy!"

"Yeah? Tell us too," urged Barbara.

"Let's hope it's good," said Franca from behind, adding: "I don't like people who give unsolicited advice!"

"But I asked *him*, that's why he told me!"

"Go on then. What did he say?" she asked dryly.

"Did he tell you the secret of happiness?" asked Barbara.

"Yes, they are two secrets. Well, they are not secrets at all. The first is that true happiness doesn't come from outside but from within ourselves, so that is where we should be looking."

"Nothing new!" said Franca from behind.

"And the second?" urged Barbara.

"The second is to be selfless, to help others become happy. Don't just think of yourself, he said."

"Is that all?" retorted Franca.

"Well, if I know that, working on these two points, I can become happy, at least I know which direction to move in," said Maria.

"It's worth thinking about!" mused Barbara.

"Mmmm," grunted Franca.

There was a long silence, during which Maria looked out of the window and thought back over all the experiences she had had in Mcleodganj. The mountains were beautiful even in the rain. There was a great sense of peace, and she became lost in her thoughts.

9. The Valley of the Gods

On the journey down from Mcleodganj, Maria recognized the road they had covered just a few days before. At the chai-shop when they stopped for a break she ate the samosas that she remembered were not too spicy. Everything seemed much easier than the first time. It was nearly four o'clock when they arrived in Mandi. The bus station, the street stalls, even the cows that gobbled up whatever was lying on the ground, were the same as the week before. They bought their tickets for the next day, Maria and Franca for Manali, Barbara for Delhi. Then they walked up the hill, trudging up the steep steps that led to the Tourist Bungalow. It was like coming home. Unfortunately, their friend Rup Singh, the receptionist, was in Chandigarh for a few days. The waiter who had helped Maria when she had fainted came past at that very moment and his eyes lit up when he saw her. She greeted him as if he were an old friend and he bowed with his hands clasped in front of his chest and said 'Namaste Ji'! Only Paul was missing. Maria looked around, it was as if she could see him coming down the stairs, or walking through the door. Did they want a room or three beds in the dormitory? It was cheaper in the dorm. They signed the guest book and the receptionist went to get the key. Wondering what Paul's full name was, she turned the pages backwards; it was a week ago, approximately. There they were! Karen Shaw and Paul J Spencer.

"What are you doing?" said Franca from behind.

She gasped, feeling like a thief caught red handed, and blushed violently: "I found Paul and Karen's names. Look!"

"Here we go again with this Paul," said Franca, winking at Barbara.

"Dreaming doesn't hurt anyone," demurred Maria.

"No, no, of course! Are you sure you don't want to go and see them?"

"Very sure," she said, red in the face, "even more than before!"

The receptionist came back with the keys and showed them outside. The dormitory was in a separate building from the main hotel, just two minutes away. From there, they had a spectacular view of the mountains and, for the moment, they were the only guests. Of the six beds, they occupied three next to each other. They unpacked the bare minimum for the night and were putting their sleeping bags out when the waiter arrived with three glasses of steaming chai on a tray. "I thought you'd appreciate a cup of tea, after your journey," he said, smiling with pride at Maria, whilst placing the three glasses on the table.

"Wonderful, thank you!" she thanked him.

"One moment," Franca stopped him. "How much do you want for these chai?"

The waiter smiled kindly and said he didn't want anything; he had prepared them in his kitchen. "No paisa," he said. No pennies! They could leave the empty glasses on the table; he would pick them up the next morning. He walked away smiling happily.

"You were a bit abrupt with him," Maria said, feeling uncomfortable.

"Yes, of course. It seems strange that someone gives us things for free. They're not rich, are they?" She pulled out the bag with her toiletries and put it on her bed.

"The first time we came here, the receptionist offered us a bottle of beer each, and spent an hour talking with us," mused Maria on her bed, smoothing her wrinkled sweater. "And Surinder helped me spontaneously. Don't you ever do something for nothing?"

"Of course! But that's me. They're different!"

"Maybe they're less suspicious than we are," said Barbara. "Often it is the people who have the least who give the most," she mused, as she counted the money she kept inside her passport bag.

"They seem happier than we are, in our society, and certainly more relaxed," said Maria, sitting cross-legged on the bed. "It's exactly what Surinder said, isn't it? Be selfless, think of others as well as yourself and see how happy you feel!"

"I *am* selfless, I don't need him, or anyone else, to tell me," said Franca, still in a bad mood. "If you remember, I even stopped the bus that would have left without you!"

"I remember, yes. You did me a great favour. And how did you feel afterwards?"

"Irritated!" replied Franca, pulling out her chillum and her piece, which was now quite small. "I've almost finished the charas! Tomorrow I'll have to find some more in Manali. If only our friend here could be bothered to go and see the English guy..."

"You'll find loads. Don't worry," Barbara assured her, "and really good!"

Maria got up from the bed and walked to the window, there was no rain here, not even a cloud. The mountains silhouetted against the pink sky. It was a beautiful and peaceful sunset. She wanted to change the topic of conversation and asked Barbara how she felt about travelling alone. She wasn't worried, after so many months in India, she knew there was no problem. Compared to Iran, Afghanistan and Pakistan, India was a doddle! What worried her was the thought of having to speak to Carla's mother, but for now she wanted to forget about that. She'd go to Jaipur to buy semi-precious stones to take to Italy: turquoise, garnet, amethyst, tiger's eye, moonstone. They were cheap in Jaipur, where they were cut. She would sell them to friends who made silver jewellery.

"What a good idea," said Maria from the window. "Maybe I'll do something like that, too."

The colours in the sky were fading quickly and night was creeping in. She went back to her bed and lay down.

"You'd make a lot more money if you take back some charas," said Franca, turning to Barbara, as she finished preparing the chillum. "Don't tell me you're not taking even a little bit."

"No way! I'd be terrified. It's too dangerous."

"No, it's not! If you do it well, it's easy! Especially if you look innocent."

"*You* don't look innocent," said Maria.

"No, I don't, but you do!" said Franca, pointing her finger at Maria, and laughing. "You really look the part and you'd get away with it because of that."

"Maybe, but I wouldn't do it," said Maria, sitting up straight on the bed.

"I know! It's written all over your face, and it is precisely for this reason that they wouldn't catch you."

"Not a chance in hell!" declared Maria, lying on her bed again. She was shocked by Franca's new gimmick. She wouldn't put it past her at all. She could easily imagine her taking some. Maybe it wasn't such a good idea to travel back home together.

"Who's going to help me light the chillum?" asked Franca. Barbara stood up and lit the match while Franca shouted 'Bom Shankar'. She passed it around and after a while they all became quieter. Maria drank the last sip of her cold chai and slipped into her sleeping bag. It was early but they were tired and the next morning they would get up at dawn. It was cold. As the minutes passed life seemed to shrivel. In a foetal position, trying to warm up her feet, she realized that when she smoked, fear always crept in and her world seemed to shrink. Everything seemed difficult, worrying.

The bed was comfortable and Barbara turned the light out. Through the window Maria could see the moon shining in the black sky. She thought of Ugo, but soon her thoughts turned to Paul. She saw him before her, his golden hair, his profound green eyes that looked at her and made her blush. Her head was spinning. Once again she had smoked too much.

"Wow! That chillum was strong," she said. "I feel faint."

"Don't worry. Close your eyes and it will pass," advised Barbara.

"Yes. What an effort to speak!"

"Breathe deeply," suggested Barbara.

"Mm, mm, thank you!"

"It's good this charas, eh? I absolutely *love* the substance!" said Franca.

"Mmmmmmmmmmmmmmmm."

"Yes, it's good, but now I'm hungry," said Barbara.

"Hungry? Now that you mention it, I'm hungry too... for something good!" mused Franca.

"A 'tramezzino'," said Maria, thinking of those amazing soft sandwiches full of mayonnaise.

"Yes, with mushrooms and ham," chose Franca

"Mine with prawns and mayonnaise. And a beer," decided Barbara

"My mouth is watering just thinking about it. I want one so much! Why did you start talking about 'tramezzino'?" complained Franca.

With her eyes closed, Maria laughed. Her mouth was dry. She groped for her water bottle and took a long sip. She laid her head on her pillow, the dizziness was passing.

"I'll also have 'mozzarella in carrozza'," continued Barbara, dreaming of a special snack, 'mozzarella in a carriage', made of a cheese and anchovy sandwich, dipped in a batter and deep fried in oil.

"Do you remember the 'mozzarella in carrozza' they make in the grill in the square?" said Franca to Maria. "With the melted mozzarella that becomes half a metre long?"

"Yes, with the little anchovy inside. Mamma mia, how delicious!"

"Three mozzarella in carrozza," ordered Franca.

"Waiter! Here, thanks," and they began to giggle.

"What an elegant name 'mozzarella in carrozza'. What style, what grace!" mused Barbara. "Weird though!"

"Do you know why the mozzarella is riding in a carriage?" asked Maria. "Because it's an aristocratic cheese. Coachman, get the carriage ready!" She chuckled at the image of the aristocrat mozzarella giving orders to the coachman, who, with a plumed hat, drove a gilded carriage.

"I can picture it. Fat and white... and wobbling," Barbara said, "with skinny, toothpick-like arms and legs," she continued, tickled by the image forming in her mind.

"Yes, white, fat and NAKED," Franca shouted. Their laughter became louder.

Barbara elaborated: "And such an effort to get into the carriage... that the coachman has to get behind her, grab her arse and push her up with all his might!" Laughter spread from their chests through their bodies.

Maria visualized the scene. "And when she finally settles down in her seat, she pulls out a lace handkerchief... and wipes the sweat from her forehead!" The mirth became hysterical.

Barbara was able to add: "And while she's at it, she also wipes her armpits!" Her voice had become shrill, trying to talk and laugh at the same time. The beds were shaking with laughter.

Maria wiped her tears. "No more, no more, I can't breathe, my stomach hurts."

Barbara was holding her belly, and Franca was rolling on the bed.

"Oi oi oi! I am so hungry! I want pizza," she panted.

"No, don't say it! I can smell it already," pleaded Barbara.

"Have you noticed how all 'these words have a lot of Zed? Tramezzino, mozzarella, carrozza, pizza," remarked Maria.

"You really are an intellectual!" commented Barbara.

"No joke, she is. Good night everyone!" said Franca.

"Shall we sleep?"

"No, let's just take a nap!"

"Good night then!" Maria turned to one side, after glancing one more time at the moon, with an empty belly and a big smile resting on her lips.

Very early the next day they walked to the bus station. Maria bought bananas, apples, biscuits and samosas. She wanted to have more food than she could eat during the trip and was determined never again to set off on a journey disorganized or hungry. They drank chai all together and then embraced. Good luck Barbara! They waved goodbye, their arms raised, while their friend leaned out the window from the bus bound for Delhi. Would they ever see her again? Their bus to Kulu-Manali was leaving half an hour later.

Franca decided that, this time, they were going to travel separately. Why don't you want us to sit together? Maria asked. Because it was always the same, said Franca and we 'never get to know anyone new'. If we sit one here and one there we'd speak with different people and then, on arrival, we'd have things to tell each other. She had shown she was comfortable with new people, hadn't she? Maria sensed the sarcasm in Franca's last comment and remembered her question as to whether she preferred Barbara to her. She also remembered her critical comment, and the disapproving expression with which she looked at her when she crouched to speak with Surinder. What a contradiction this woman was, so free and independent but, underneath it all, she resented it if she didn't receive her full attention... unless there was something else, that Maria didn't understand. In any case, a break would do them good. "It's an interesting idea," she said, preparing to climb the vertical ladder on the back of the bus to place her backpack on the roof.

She got on board through the front door and went to sit behind the driver, next to a man about thirty years old, who smiled at her with enthusiasm. Franca went up through the back door and sat next to an Indian woman wearing a blue sari. From her seat Maria tried to meet her eyes, but Franca was busy and didn't look at her. After hooting twice and stunning everyone with the deafening noise, the bus began to move. From outside they could hear someone shouting 'cheloh, cheloh'. They were off! Soon, the bus was climbing the mountain road, bend after bend. The frequent rains had cleared the atmosphere, the sky was a deep blue and the sun began to warm the fresh and clean air. The colours were bright; the greens especially seemed unreal, varying from shades of pea green, emerald green, olive green, bottle green, to blue-green, and the darker, almost black, of the trees immersed in the shadow. In a certain way she was travelling alone. Was she afraid?

"Excuse me, Madam! Are you French?" asked the man sitting next to her.
"No, I'm Italian," she replied.
He looked at her, smiling: "I have a French friend. Is France close to Italy?"
Maria laughed to herself at the naivety of the question. Smiling, she explained that the two countries were neighbouring, but Italy was more south. "And where are you from?" she asked.
He was from Kulu, near Manali. He wanted to know whether she was going there. Maria confirmed that she and her friend were going right there, was it a nice place? 'Her friend' had she said? And where was this friend? He looked very surprised when Maria told him that she was sitting far away. In India, friends wanted to be together, he said, not one here and one there. In Italy it was the same, said Maria, but this friend was very independent and besides, as he could see, she was right; it was thanks to her idea that they were talking together. True, true, said the man, who introduced himself as Chaman Lal. He shook her hand, showing that he knew the western way to introduce himself. He wanted to take a look at this particular friend and stood up to find her, without trying to hide his curiosity. Maria looked out of the window and let him watch. Satisfied with having checked, he sat down again and continued with his answer: Manali was much more than a nice place, it was stunning. Did she know how the British called it when they ruled India? No, she didn't know. "The Valley of the Gods, they called it," he said with pride.

"What a beautiful name. It must be really a fine place!"

Yes it was, and the people were friendly and polite. The Indians had this belief that the Himalayas was the place where many gods lived, especially Shiva, the god of destruction for reconstruction, the destruction of the old for the creation of the new. Shiva lived in the Himalayas and from his hair the River Ganges flowed. He gestured with his hands as he spoke; he had fine hands, maybe he was a teacher or a musician. "This is Hindu mythology. Do you know Hindu mythology?" he asked.

"I know very little about Hindu religion and mythology," replied Maria, "but I'm very interested." Chaman Lal's eyes shone with enthusiasm and intelligence. "Can you tell me something about the Hindu Gods? We have many hours travel ahead of us."

He was more than happy! "We have many gods," he began, "but the main three are Brahma, god of creation, Shiva, god of destruction, and Vishnu, the god of preservation. There are very many gods, some are more popular than others. Ganesh, the one with the elephant head, is one of the most loved of all, because he brings good luck."

Yes, she had seen him on many posters. Why was he so popular? Did she want to know the legend of Ganesh? Maria nodded and smiled at him happily. He began to tell:

"Well then, Ganesh was Shiva's son. After marrying the goddess Parvati, Shiva retired to meditate on top of a mountain and didn't return home for several months. Tired of waiting, Parvati wore her most beautiful sari and went to look for him." He was full of enthusiasm and spoke with a clear and beautiful voice. "Though he was in deep meditation, Shiva became aware of Parvati's presence and looked at her with desire... and so they conceived their son. The goddess gave birth to Ganesh. One day, many years later, while Parvati was having a wash and Ganesh was guarding the door, Shiva returned home. Finding a strong and handsome young man blocking his entrance, the god Shiva became very angry and cut off his head."

Chaman Lal looked at Maria, who was visibly surprised, and continued, undaunted: "When Parvati realized what had happened, she was desperate and told her husband that he had killed their son. Shiva was so sorry that, in order to repair his terrible mistake, ran out to cut off the head of the first living creature that walked by, and put it on his son's body."

Maria was listening, smiling and looking at him in amazement.

"As you already guessed, the first creature that passed by was a small elephant and this is why Ganesh is like that," he concluded, as if it were the most natural thing in the world.

He wasn't offended that Maria was laughing; he obviously loved to talk about these things. He then continued, explaining that the Hindus turned to Ganesh whenever they began a new enterprise: they held a ceremony, made ritual offerings in his honour and sought his protection. It brought good luck to have a picture of Ganesh in the house. Did she know Shiva's story? When Maria said she didn't but would like to hear it, he began to tell.

Time passed quickly, and absorbed by the stories of the Hindu gods, Maria hadn't realized that several passengers had noticed her interest. They were also listening to Chaman Lal's stories, as if they had never heard them before. Some of them were curious to ask *her* some questions.

A man sitting behind touched Chaman Lal's shoulder and said something in Hindi, whilst looking at Maria, smiling. There was a brief exchange and then her companion said: "I told him that you are Italian and he wants to know if there are Indians who live in Italy and if there are many Indian restaurants."

Maria thought for a moment and then said, "I don't know of any Indian people who live in Venice, perhaps in other larger cities... And, from what I know, there are no Indian restaurants."

The answer was translated to the other passengers and an animated discussion began. Soon, all the attention was focused on Maria. "What do they say?" she asked her friend.

"They say that opening a restaurant is good business. People who have restaurants in Germany or England make a lot of money and, when they visit India, they are very generous. In Europe they become rich."

Another man, sitting a few rows behind him, asked another question, this time in English: "How much was the price of the airfare to India?"

Maria didn't need to think about that: "About three hundred dollars. One dollar is about eight or nine rupees," she said. The answer was received with great interest and launched a lively discussion, as people calculated the corresponding cost in rupees. When they agreed, exaggerating, that it corresponded to approximately three thousand rupees, great exclamations of surprise and various comments were heard coming from all over the bus. There was another man who had a pressing question. Chaman Lal translated: "This man wants to know if you are rich."

Maria laughed heartily: "Oh no. I work, and I saved for months and months. I couldn't spend such a sum very often." While answering she turned, trying to make eye contact with as many people as possible. After her answer was translated, people began to talk more animatedly. They were all involved, including the driver, who, from time to time, turned to ask his own question, something that worried her very much. "What are they saying?" she asked Chaman Lal.

"They say you must be rich. For many of these people it is impossible to save, even ten rupees."

"How much do they earn?" she asked.

"A salary of six hundred rupees a month is not bad, with a family to support."

Maria was shocked; that couldn't possibly be enough. She explained that in Europe prices were much higher than in India, so even if the wages were better people were not rich. After her sentence was assimilated, they began to ask how much a house cost, and a pair of shoes? And a car? Since they were all so interested, Maria stood up and turned to face all the passengers who looked at her smiling, their eyes alight with curiosity. It had become a conference. For every answer she gave, a loud discussion between the people followed; everyone had something to say. She saw Franca talking with the woman sitting next to her, but even her attention was drawn to Maria when a woman asked the next question in Hindi. Chaman Lal translated: "This woman wants to know how old you are and if you are married."

Everybody was waiting for her answer: "I am twenty-four and I'm not married."

A string of comments and giggles crossed the bus. A couple of women said something out loud and everyone started to laugh. What did they say? "They say you should already have children."

Maria laughed and everyone joined in her laughter. "Thanks, but not yet. In Italy, women get married later than in India, and also have children later," she explained.

A woman sitting at the back of the bus stood up and said in English: "We will pray that you have many children soon!"

Maria reacted instinctively and with her palms forward, feigning fright, said: "No, no, please, don't pray, not yet!" Everyone laughed aloud and the merriment continued for quite a while. She felt at home.

The questions kept coming. They wanted to know how engagements and weddings were. Did women have to have a dowry? Did parents ask the astrologer's opinion before deciding on their children's future husband or wife? Their surprise was immense when Maria said that a dowry wasn't necessary and that young people decided who to marry, without having to obtain their parents' approval. Since astrology was one of Maria's great passions, she asked her own question: Did people pay much attention to what the astrologer said? Chaman Lal explained that not only did they pay attention but that, if the possible partners didn't have a good chart, the marriage wouldn't go ahead. Maria asked if it was true that the couple could divorce in the Hindu religion. Yes, confirmed Chaman Lal, after five years of separation.

"It's the same in Italy, five years," said Maria.

This piece of information spread through the coach, passed from mouth to mouth, and was received with great enthusiasm. They had found a point in common between the two cultures and everyone was happy. Maria was beginning to feel nauseous from standing facing backwards. She apologized and sat in her seat, quietly. After a while someone passed her an orange, then came two biscuits. When the bus stopped for a break, the driver invited her to his table and insisted on offering her chai and biscuits. Franca was invited to join them, but tried to refuse. Nevertheless, they ordered a chai for her too, which she accepted reluctantly.

"You're the star of the bus!" she said with half a smile.

"I'm having fun and learning lots of things. They are very nice," said Maria.

"I can see that," said Franca, quieter than usual.

"You were right saying that by sitting separately we get to know new people," said Maria.

Franca gave a wry smile. "I'm always right," she said, half joking.

After the chai break, the bus began climbing again up the winding road. Out of the opposite window she could see the side of the mountain, while the view from hers was a sheer drop of hundreds of metres. Every time she looked out, Maria could see the raging green river rushing at the bottom of the slope, cutting the huge valley in two. The bus was driving dangerously close to the edge of the road. Maria was feeling dizzy and her stomach clenched with nausea as fear swept through her. She forced herself not to look down. After just over an hour the bus stopped again. There was a pink temple next to the road. Only the driver got out and entered the temple. Maria saw him pray. A man climbed aboard and began to distribute handfuls of puffed rice, placing it on the palms that people held out to him. In exchange for the rice the passengers gave him an offering of a few paisa. Maria took the rice and gave him a rupee. She turned to look at Franca and saw that she was giving her contribution, too. She had a serious expression.

"Why are we stopping here?" she asked her travelling companion.

"This is the last temple before Kulu, and after this point the road becomes dangerous. The driver is doing 'puja'. It's a prayer for our protection. The passengers too will now do 'puja'," he said simply.

"Do many accidents happen on this road?" she asked, trying to hide her anxiety.

"Sometimes," he replied, nodding his head from side to side. Maria looked at the driver who was climbing back up to his seat. He folded his hands and bowed on the steering wheel, remaining motionless for a moment. Then he started the engine and began to drive.

"And, sometimes, do coaches roll down the embankment?" she asked shyly. She wasn't sure she wanted to hear the answer. Once again he rocked his head.

"Sometimes," replied Chaman Lal, trying to reassure her; but then he added: "If you look down you'll see some. Sometimes it is difficult when two buses have to pass. In some places the road is not wide enough."

Maria couldn't hide her concern. "Aren't you scared?" she asked.

Chaman Lal thought for a while before answering: "In a way, yes, I am a little afraid, but that's why we pray for protection. On the other hand, we Hindus don't worry too much about dying. When it's our time to go, we go! In the meantime, we try to live well." He looked at her openly, and seeing the anxiety in her face, added: "The driver is very experienced."

Maria thought that at least it wasn't raining. God knows what the road must be like when it was wet and muddy. Just then their coach turned a corner and she saw a large, old bus coming from the opposite direction. She desperately hoped her coach would stay on the side of the mountain, but no! To her horror, she saw that it moved toward the edge of the escarpment. The two drivers nodded at each other and began to focus on the delicate manoeuvre of going through, side by side. They advanced inch by inch. Their driver checked all the time the side of the bus and the edge of the road. Maria looked out the window and saw that there was no road beneath her, only the green river, hundreds of metres below. She could feel her heart in her throat. She could barely whisper: "The coach is off the road," feeling on the verge of throwing up from fear.

"It seems that way, because of where you are sitting. But the wheels are still on the road... Well, at least three," said Chaman Lal in a low voice. "Don't worry. The driver is good."

On the bus there was absolute silence and the people prayed. Maybe it would be better if she prayed, too. She tried to remember the Ave Mary, but the words didn't come easily, she was too anxious, and quickly dismissed the idea. She decided to speak directly to God, wherever he or she was. Another look at the river below persuaded her to close her eyes. Protection, please. Don't let the bus fall over the edge. Do us this favour, God, please! Her life went by before her eyes: she loved her mother, her father, her sisters, her brother, her friends. She loved life and wanted to live for a long time. She even loved herself, the way she was now, with the Indians, and Franca. This prayer didn't make her feel any better. Why on earth couldn't the passengers get off while they did this manoeuvre? The nausea was mounting and she felt faint, her mouth was dry. She remembered Nam-myoho-renge-kyo. She had to transform her fear... into what? Courage, confidence? One of those two. Nam-myoho-renge-kyo, Nam-myoho-renge-kyo, Nam-myoho-renge-kyo, she muttered between her teeth. She felt a gentle touch on her arm and Chamam Lal said softly: "We're through. You can relax." She opened her eyes but didn't look at the road.

She looked at him instead, he looked calm. "You look very relaxed," she said.

"I have confidence in the driver, and in life. When you have confidence you don't worry so much. Trust fights fear." He was right. The road was still narrow but at least they were no longer on the edge of the abyss. Everyone on the bus remained silent. She turned back to the window, the scenery was amazing.

The mountains were imposing and their jagged shape was dramatic, so impressive. They resembled the Alps, except that they were much taller. Dense forests of fir trees lined the road and the valleys below, the sun was shining. The deep blue sky was completely clear. Two hours later they arrived in Kulu. Chaman Lal and many other passengers had reached their destination. Maria got out and waited while they unloaded their luggage from the roof. Many of them gave her their address, making her promise to come and visit them, and whatever she needed, she only had to ask. Maria sensed they really meant it and felt great affection for them. Franca was taking down the address of the woman she had sat with.

Back on the bus they sat next to each other. It would only take an hour to get to Manali. Let's hope we find a good hotel, said Maria, but Franca had other ideas. She wanted to find a house and stay with the locals. Her intention was to go to a bar or restaurant, get to know Italians who already lived there and tag along with them. It was easy, she said, so they wouldn't have to buy a kerosene stove, dishes and utensils. Maria was perplexed, but she didn't want to argue with Franca; there was already a distance between them. However, if it's not today, maybe they'd find somewhere tomorrow, she suggested. "We'll see!" responded Franca dryly; in any case, she liked Indian people's company, right? She had proven that during the trip. It was true, Maria thought and chose to be open to any possibility. The landscape was becoming even more spectacular. At every bend they drove closer and closer to the high mountains. Her heart swelled to see the beauty surrounding her. The air was cleaner, fresher.

Finally, the bus arrived in Manali's square, surrounded by a forest of tall pines. All around there were stalls selling blankets and colourful shawls, hand-woven rugs and mats, plastic toys and posters of Hindu gods. Maria recognized Ganesh, Kali and Laxmi, the goddess of wealth and prosperity. There were also a couple of chai-shops and stalls frying samosas and pakhora, creating a relaxed and welcoming atmosphere. As they climbed onto the roof to fetch their backpacks, Maria paused to feel the sun warming her back and the high mountain's cool air. The view in front of her took her breath away!

The sunny valley was bordered by a belt of green mountains while behind them stood the peaks of the Himalayas, covered with snow and ice, clearly silhouetted against the crisp blue sky. Instead of climbing down right away, they sat on the roof and looked around in silence. The Valley of the Gods, they called it, and she could see why. Filling her lungs with fresh, clean air, Maria felt a great sense of peace in her heart. Slowly, she slung her rucksack over her shoulders and went down the vertical ladder.

They went for an exploratory walk and, walking uphill on the main road they quickly arrived at the centre of the small town. They continued a little further, the towering mountains ahead dwarfing everything around them. She was beginning to understand why Paul and Karen wanted to live here. Who knew if she'd bump into them? She was both excited and anxious at the thought. She looked around, hoping to catch a glimpse of him.

On the road side there were several shops, a fruit and vegetable store, a grocery store, one that sold bread and biscuits, a pharmacy, and a little further down, the tourist office. Soon after that, the forest began again, thick with trees and plants. They walked slowly uphill, gasping for breath.

"I can't breathe easily and I feel so heavy! What altitude are we at?"

"About two thousand metres, six thousand feet, I think," said Franca panting. "Beautiful though, eh?"

In the Alps, at that height there were no more trees, while here it was all very lush. Once they reached the edge of the village, they retraced their steps and went downhill easily, returning to the centre of Manali. After the shops there were a couple of restaurants, and the first one was very inviting. Inside, they saw it was almost empty. They chose a table, suddenly hungry.

The menu was amazing! Maria ordered chicken Kiev, boiled vegetables and even a dessert, while Franca requested the Indian dish of bhaji and chapatis. They ate almost in silence and Maria enjoyed the best meal since leaving Italy. She felt much happier and stronger. There were some foreigners, German and English people, but no Italians. Maria looked at the door, half expecting to see Paul coming through at any moment. She wondered where their village was, Sarsai it was called, and if they often came into Manali.

"Do you expect to find any mail here?" Franca asked, shaking her from her daydream. No, it was too soon, Maria said, they had left only two weeks ago. And you? Maybe Gabriele, or some other friend. Tomorrow she would find out. The waiter brought the second chai; this had been prepared with ginger, whose strong spicy taste lingered for a long time. It was now late afternoon and there were no Italians in sight.

"Maybe it's better if we find a hotel for the night," suggested Maria.

Fortunately Franca agreed. "Yes, but only for tonight!"

They asked the waiter if he knew of a cheap but clean hotel. How much did they want to spend? Five rupees each was too little, he said, ten was better. They'd find a room just around the corner, on a small street parallel to the main road. Yes, the hotel was clean, he assured, no rats.

"Rats?" cried Maria, her eyes wide open.

"No, not at your hotel, Madam, don't worry," he replied, smiling charmingly. "Only mice. Nice little mice."

They laughed loudly, while the waiter smiled primly.

Following his instructions, they arrived at the hotel, a stone building only slightly larger than the surrounding houses. In the past the houses were made of wood, the waiter had explained but, a few years ago, a fire had destroyed almost the entire village, and after that, those who could afford it, had rebuilt their houses with stone. They saw no rodents but were so tired they could have slept through a raging party of 'nice little mice.'

10. Signed, Gautama Buddha

The sun came in through the cracks to wake them early and they went out straight away. Behind the hotel were many houses immersed in the woods, near the river that ran through the valley; it was an idyllic place. The people they met smiled easily. They were handsome, with regular features and white teeth. They dressed differently from the rest of the people in India, in a way that was more suited to mountain life. The men wore trousers made of a woollen fabric in natural colours, beige, light brown or pale grey and matching woolly jackets, just as warm. A touch of colour came from their caps, rimless flat caps of wool, with bright zigzag patterns woven at the front. The women wore a woolly blanket, down to the feet, wrapped around the body and over the shoulders; it was either light or dark grey, enlivened by geometric lines in pink or red and bordered with the same colour. At the front above the chest the upper flaps were held together by two long pins connected by a lengthy gold chain. On their heads they wore big scarves matching the colour of the blanket's edge; it covered part of the forehead and was tied at the nape, or simply wrapped around the neck in a natural, yet sophisticated, fashion. Long hair was gathered in a single braid down the back.

Almost by accident the girls found themselves in front of the post office and went in to check for any mail at the Poste Restante. Franca found a letter from Gabriele, but there was nothing for Maria. They sat down to read it in the sunshine. Life went on as usual in Venice. There was a reference to Ugo; it sounded as if he had a new girlfriend. A painful stab in her chest caught her by surprise, a big hairy hand was pinching her heart, it was rough, hard, cruel. She stood up and tried to breathe deeply; a lump in her throat was choking her. She took a couple of steps away, preferring not to know, while Franca continued to read. She forced herself to think of Paul, visualizing his twinkling eyes, his large and warm hands that embraced her smaller hands and touched her mouth. It was hot in the sun. Maria looked up and absorbed those rays, inhaling deeply that clean, fresh, new air. Franca folded the letter and slipped it back into the envelope before walking over to Maria.

"Shall we go for an explorative stroll? I need to walk," said Maria, wanting to run away. No, it was better to find this famous house, said

Franca, if they wanted to leave the hotel by noon. She was going to hunt for Italians. If Maria wanted to go for a stroll they would meet in the hotel before noon. They headed in opposite directions.

Walking downhill, she saw some huts. It was probably the Tibetan group, with the same orange marigolds hanging in the windows or placed in front of the doors, as in Mcleodganj. Continuing, the road was lined by big plants whose leaves were shaped like a five-point star and were much taller than she was. Maria stopped to touch them; they were beautiful, lush. She had already seen them somewhere but couldn't remember where. The tops of the large fir trees in the woods behind the tall plants were swaying lazily in the breeze. There was a large white sign with black lettering and she stopped to read it. "Forest Department: The forest is a peculiar organism of unlimited kindness and benevolence that makes no demand for its subsistence, extends generously the products of its life, and gives protection to all beings, offering shade even to the man with the axe who destroys it." Signed: Gautama Buddha.

What a surprise! The Buddha, as quoted by the forest department. She read the sign again, trying to memorize it. How solemn, and so much feeling in those words. She responded with folded hands, bowing. There wasn't anyone to see her, and even if there had been, they wouldn't have been surprised by that greeting of respect and oneness. She went into the woods, stroking the pine trees' rough trunks, treading lightly on the soft, fertile soil underfoot, making friends with the land that made her feel welcome and a part of it. She was completely alone. Crouching under a pine tree, she inhaled through her nostrils, smelling the scent of musk and resin.

It was all so similar to the Alps she knew well, the same earth, the same vegetation, even the scents were familiar. Leaning against a tree trunk she lifted her face and looked at the branches silhouetted against the blue sky. It didn't matter if she hadn't received any letters or even if Ugo had a new girl every day. It hurt, of course, from her heart all the way to her throat, and her stomach had contracted into a compact knot. She knew that pain well; it was a mixture of longing for his hands, his desire, his love. But was it love? If it was, he had hidden it well, maybe it just wasn't there, or maybe there had been some small bursts. He loved himself, this she knew. She recognized jealousy in her grief, that cruel primordial force that tore her heart to strips and muddied all her thoughts, uncontrollable, violent and forcefully self-centred. There was that feeling of being rejected, pushed aside and discarded, like a toy that has become a bore and a bother. Because of this she had drunk herself into a stupor.

Now she felt less pain, her head was clearer, there was a sense of freedom that she had never felt before and a detachment that allowed her to think more calmly. She took a deep breath and smiled at the tree tops swaying elegantly. It was strange but she felt almost happy, a feeling she wasn't used to. Just now she didn't need anything else. Nothing had changed on the outside, but a sense of joy was making its way into her heart, and it mounted inside, filling her up completely.

Slowly she stood up, stretched her legs, her back, her arms. Raising her palms toward the blue sky she stretched her fingers, trying to touch it. She remained still, absorbing the energy of the forest and letting it flow throughout her body, all the way down to the tips of the toes, in an incomparable feeling of being at one with the universe. She joined the palms of her hands, stroking life and the clean, new, innocent air. Slowly, she bowed to the universe and to herself. The breeze played with her long straight hair, making it flutter like the Tibetans flags, the sun warmed her shoulders. Everything was clean and she was clean too. Nam-myoho-renge-kyo. She was starting anew from now. Smiling, she walked back to the road, thinking 'Thank you trees, thank you sun, thank you breeze' and savouring the unfamiliar sweet feeling of peace and contentment. She forced herself to hasten the pace, panting uphill. She had been away longer than planned and Franca was certainly waiting for her. As she reached the hotel she saw her leaving, her rucksack on her shoulders, irritated.

"Finally," she said. "You were gone for ages. I'm off!"
Maria felt guilty. "Have you found a house?"
"Yes," she replied dryly.
"Where?"
"I'll tell you later. Get a move on!"
"Okay. Will you wait for me? It'll take me two minutes to get ready."
"I'll give you five minutes!"
"I'll see you at the restaurant." Maria ran upstairs, haphazardly threw into her rucksack the few things she had taken out, pushing them hard to close it and finally she slung it over her shoulder. She picked up her camera bag and ran down the stairs, with pieces of sleeves and socks waving out of the backpack's flap. Just as soon as they'd found their accommodation she would come out here again and take lots of photos.

Franca had ordered her a chai and had calmed down a little. She explained that she had met three Italians and they had smoked a chillum together. They were part of a group that had rented a house on the other side of the river; they came and went and, at the moment, there was space for them. Did they have an extra room? Maria asked. She didn't know, they hadn't specified and she hadn't asked; it wasn't a problem sharing the space with others, was it? Maria thought of the mountain huts in the Alps, where trekkers arrived, put their sleeping bags on one of the mattresses on the floor and slept all together. In any case, not having done anything to find the accommodation, she couldn't be fussy. She felt guilty and hated that feeling with all her guts. Guilt had the power to stifle the enthusiasm and the happiness she had felt earlier on. She chased it away, like one drives away a rabid dog. She could replace it with gratitude, instead and, after all, she had a choice: she could take the house that Franca had found, or leave it and go it alone. I'll take it! she thought. I might really enjoy it. She smiled. "Well done Franca!" she said, with genuine gratitude.

Her friend looked at her, her eyes red from the chillum, and bobbed her head, accepting the compliment and making her laugh. She always caught her by surprise with the Indian style head rocking; she did it really well, just like them! Her laughter swept away what was left of Franca's irritation.

They walked together, Franca slower than usual thanks to the chillum, Maria at ease at the same pace. With backpacks made heavier by the altitude they crossed the long rope-and-wood bridge that wobbled with every movement, even far away. It heaved, swayed and fell, making the crossing similar to those amusement park rides where the floor moves in every direction and you have to hold fast to the handrail. Below them, the deep green river flowed fast and cheerful, foaming whenever it came upon a polished boulder, colliding with the obstacle, boldly flowing over and around it, relentless in its course toward the valley, fluid, powerful and free. "I think it's that one," said Franca, indicating a two-story house overlooking the river. It was built like most of the local houses, with alternating layers of large stones and wooden beams, creating a pattern of horizontal stripes.

Soon they reached it. "Let's go and ask inside," she said. On the ground floor there was a barn and some hay. The rustic stairs were leading to the upper floor where a covered terrace encircled the entire house. They clung to the handrail to help them climb the steep and narrow stairs, resisting the weight of the backpacks that pulled them backwards. On the porch a pair of jeans was hung out to dry. Maria went closer, they were Fiorucci's. "I think we have arrived," she said with satisfaction.

A girl came out on the porch and recognized Franca. "Ah, you've made it," she said, without a smile. "And this must be your friend."

"Thank you for letting us stay," said Maria, holding her hand out to her. "Do you have a spare room?"

No, they hadn't a 'spare' room, said the girl, with a surly attitude. They could sleep inside if they wanted to, for a few nights.

"Okay, thanks. Do you mind if I have a look?"

"Feel free," she replied.

Maria took her backpack off and walked inside, lowering her head to avoid slamming it against the low door frame. Inside, floor and walls were lined with the typical brown plaster made of earth and cow poop. A low round iron stove dominated the centre of the room and, on the floor, over a couple of mats, there were piles of clothes and a couple of bags. Nothing else there. Then there was another small adjoining room, completely empty. In a corner on the ground was a square raised edge; a hole, about the size of an orange, cut through the wall of the house, and from there light came in and water could get out. No sign of beds or mattresses. Puzzled, Maria went out on the porch, where Franca was talking to the girl, who was preparing a chillum.

"Sorry, I don't even know your name," Maria said.

"Veronica," she replied, weary and detached.

"Hi, I'm Maria!"

"Ah, right."

Enthusiastic! Maria thought. Franca was telling her of their journey, the English couple they had met, the charas they had smoked, the incredible journey with the landslide, the Sikh receptionist who had explained (to her) a lot of interesting things. She was talking, talking, talking, while Veronica remained impassive, perhaps listening, perhaps daydreaming, it was hard to tell. Maria felt uncomfortable; this girl seemed to be doing them a big favour, albeit reluctantly. She asked her how long she had been in India. Veronica told her, with long breaks in mid-speech, always without smiling, that she had arrived four months before, with three other people from Rome, and had spent most of her time there, in the house in the mountains. "Usually I dress like them," she said drawling. Franca seemed very impressed by this detail. Maria swore to herself that this time she wouldn't fall for it. Her jeans were perfect! And where were the others? Maria dared to ask. They were travelling 'on business', and would be back in a couple of days. She didn't specify what kind of business and Maria, exchanging a puzzled look with Franca, decided not to pursue it any further lest she seemed nosy. But the lack of mattresses worried her.

"I saw that there are no beds," she said timidly, "but where do you keep the mattresses?"

Slowly Veronica raised her eyes from the ground and looked at her with exaggerated surprise: "Mattresses? Here you sleep on the floor, like the locals do."

"But... isn't it hard?" objected Maria, nervously.

Veronica took a long pause to show clearly that she was annoyed; then she deigned to add: "You put yourself inside your sleeping bag, and that's how it is. If you really want to, you go to Manali and buy yourself a mat. Otherwise you go to a hotel."

Maria felt herself blush. She looked at Franca, who avoided her gaze by looking at the floor. Veronica had filled the chillum with tobacco mixed with charas and motioned to Franca to light it. Franca was obedient, even servile, and Maria watched her in amazement; she had never seen her like this. She lit the match shouting 'Bom Shankar' and Veronica inhaled to fill her lungs.

Well, while she was at it, she would ask the second question, which was a pressing one. "And... sorry, one last question! Where is the bathroom?... I could really do with it." Maybe a little thing, a hole in the floor, somewhere down the stairs, but there would be some kind of toilet somewhere, right?

Veronica, her lungs full, opened her eyes wide while the smoke made her choke and started to cough, bringing up a lot of phlegm. She coughed for a long time and then, with red and moist eyes, she looked at Franca as if to ask where on earth she had found her. Franca smirked, as if to apologize and, once again, avoided looking at Maria, who was ashamed of having asked the question, but... she was bursting. She waited until Veronica's cough calmed down and she had recovered from the shock. Eventually, she pointed at the woods with her chin. "There are no 'bathrooms'," she said with a grunt. "People go in the forest, in the jungle, they say here."

"Every time they have to pee, as well as poo?" Maria *had* to find out. Some things had to be clear from the start.

This time Veronica didn't answer; she just shrugged. Then, addressing Franca, she said: "Hasn't 'this one' ever been to India?"

Franca seemed caught between a rock and a hard place, and hesitated. But Maria had had enough of Veronica's superiority.

"Yes, this is the first time I've come to India, and what's the problem? It is a sin? There's always a first time. How many times do you think Franca has been?" Out of the corner of her eye she saw Franca begging her to do, to say... what? "I'm sorry, but what's the problem?" she repeated, uncertainly. Franca breathed a sigh of relief, which Veronica didn't notice. There was something unclear in this situation, she was sure about it. She stood up.

"Alright, let's go to the public toilets. You need it too, *don't you?*" she said, looking at Franca, who was quiet.

"Yes, I'm coming," she said, standing up, with difficulty. They went down the stairs in silence and walked toward the 'jungle', in the direction indicated by Veronica. When Maria was sure she wasn't being heard, she let out all her frustration: "What a bitch that Veronica! She's treating me like a moron! Why did we come here, and what did you tell her?"

Franca nodded silently, looking guilty. "Okay, I met them, her and the other two, at the restaurant, right? And we smoked a chillum. Their charas is *amazing*!" She looked sidelong at Maria, to see if she was impressed.

"And so?" she asked, not at all affected.

"I told her that I wanted to buy some, and they said they sell, but only to trusted people, not to 'tourists'."

"And you told them that you're not a tourist."

"That's right! I told her that I was here two years ago, and now I'm back. If I hadn't said so they wouldn't have invited us to come and stay here."

"You've told her bullshit, basically! If you'd wear a sari you'd be even more convincing." Franca didn't say anything, she didn't need to. They stopped in the trees, Maria opened the zipper of her jeans and squatted to pee, her belly was bursting. Franca squatted down next to her to do the same. "I knew there was something! I'd got the one about India but I hadn't understood about the charas. So, how long are we staying here? Till tomorrow?"

"Hopefully..." Franca said, hesitantly. "Maybe the day after tomorrow, it depends when the guys come back."

"Ah, yes, those who have gone 'on business'," said Maria, standing up and pulling up the zipper. "Have you figured out what kind of 'business'?"

"No, but I can guess, living here!"

"Charas, you mean?"

"I think so," said Franca, focusing a long while on closing her jeans' zipper.

"Let's hope for the best!" concluded Maria.

They returned to the house and, before climbing the steep staircase, outside the barn they met a local woman. She wore the traditional blanket wrapped around her body, a red scarf on her head and was carefully leaning a scythe to the ground. She was beautiful and had clearly just returned from the fields. She greeted them with a big smile and, with a twist of her hand, as if screwing a light bulb on the ceiling, she said in English: "You here?" pointing her chin to the floor above.

"Only one or two days," replied Maria. She nodded happily and, looking at Franca, made the same hand movement. "Yes, Franca too," confirmed Maria. Franca greeted her with a nod of her head and climbed up the stairs. The young woman rocked her head, smiling. Then, pointing her index finger toward herself, said: "I go for 'lakri'." Not knowing the

English word, she mimicked tree branches falling to the ground and the action of collecting them. She was going to collect firewood. "You come?" she asked Maria, who thought for a moment and then nodded: "Sure, I'll come with you!"

The woman smiled and motioned for her to wait. She opened a small door near the barn and went in, bowing her head so as not to hit it against the jamb. She came back with two big cone-shaped baskets and handed one to Maria. She put her arms through the rope straps and was ready to go.

They walked along the trail, carrying the panniers on their backs.

"My name Maria," she said, pointing a finger at her chest. "And you?"

"Pushpa," the young woman replied, with a happy and ready smile. Then she asked: "Tum baccha?" mimicking a big pregnant belly.

"Me? No, no," said Maria, pretending to be scared, hoping her reaction would make her laugh. It did. Pointing her finger at Pushpa, she asked: "You?" and mimed a big belly.

Pushpa nodded vigorously, looking very happy. She was pregnant and already had a little boy, or a little girl, it wasn't clear. She said 'bacchee'.

"You already have a child? Boy?" Maria asked, speaking more loudly, hoping to be better understood. Pushpa kept saying 'bacchee'. Maria copied that hand gesture with her fingers upwards, as to fit a bulb which, from what she had understood, meant: how, when, why? Any question, basically. At that, Pushpa stopped in the middle of the path and looking at her, said with confidence: "Tum, bacchee!" and put her hand on Maria's vagina. She laughed heartily seeing her surprised expression. Then, mimicking a huge penis in front of her, she added: "This, baccha!"

They laughed with complicity, amused and excited by the straightforward boldness they shared. So, she had a baby girl, right?

"Yes, and this one," said Pushpa, pointing at her belly, "is baccha." She seemed to be sure about it, or maybe it was the strong hope that gave her that assurance.

They continued walking uphill. Maria was curious to know how old she was. She said: "I am twenty-four, and you?" Pushpa didn't understand. Maria took a stick and wrote the number twenty-four on the dust. And you? Pushpa said no with her head. What do you mean by 'no'? She spread her arms out as if to say she didn't know. She didn't know how old she was. Really? Maria asked, incredulous. Pushpa looked at her with an apologetic expression and said: "Sorry." Fancy that! She didn't know her age. It was a strange concept for Maria, but she could understand how this could happen in such a different society.

They came to the spot where she had come to pee with Franca and continued uphill, until they came to a round clearing. Pushpa motioned for her to put the basket down and sit on the grass. "Beto, beto," she said, tapping the ground with her hand. They rested a little while and then began to pick up the fallen branches putting them neatly into their panniers, in silence, smiling at each other every time their eyes met. When Pushpa's basket was full, she loaded it on her back and mimicked to Maria to put a few more branches inside, filling it completely. She discovered that the word 'bas' meant 'enough, no more'. "Bas?" she asked. "Or, or!" Pushpa replied, and that meant 'more'. Finally she said, 'bas', it was enough! Maria picked up her pannier, which was much emptier, and they began their descent toward the house. They met a few locals, men and women, walking steadily uphill, hands clasped behind their backs, without haste. They looked at Maria and smiled with approval, then said something to Pushpa and, laughing with her, they commented: "Tikeh, tikeh!" That meant 'very well'.

Once they reached the house they had to climb the steep stairs carrying the heavy and bulky baskets. Pushpa stopped outside her door, which was next to Veronica's, and put the basket down, rushing to help Maria remove hers. While they were out for 'lakri' the whole family had returned. Maria met the mother-in-law, thin and smiling; she had a few missing teeth but a big smile, and had just arrived carrying on her head a shiny brass container full of water. The father-in-law, serious and reserved, was smoking a water pipe sitting on the floor with his back against the wall; he wore the typical round cap with the colours on the front. Pushpa's husband, a handsome young man with green and smiling eyes called Telsin, was getting ready to go to the river for a wash after a day in the fields, and finally there was the little girl, 'bacchee'. She must have been two years old, beautiful, her eyes rimmed with kohl and many black curls, and was hiding shyly behind her grandmother's skirt. At first they were all surprised to see Maria with a pannier of 'lakri', but soon the surprise turned into a warm, amused welcome. Maria rubbed her aching shoulders and stuck her head inside Veronica's door. Once again, she was preparing a chillum. Did they smoke all the time? Franca looked at her as if to communicate something that the situation didn't allow her to say openly, and asked if she wanted to smoke.

"No thank you! I'll sit on the veranda for a while. I'm hungry instead. Shall we go to Manali to buy something at the store?" It was a long walk and she felt a little tired, but there was no choice. "Shall we go in a little while?" she asked Franca.

"Yes, after this chillum," she replied, with a note of apology. Maria had the impression that Franca was smoking too much, even by her own standards, and that she felt obliged to do so, in some way. She sat on the porch watching the scenery. The impressive tall mountains were holding the valley in an intimate embrace, protecting it. The setting sun was preparing a spectacular show, enriched by a few jagged clouds in the sky that would soon be painted in different colours. The river below was as green as jade. It rushed toward the valley, playing with white foam, amusing somersaults, cheerful and mischievous splashing.

Pushpa walked past and made the question sign with her hand, mimicking eating and drinking. Maria said 'Manali'. The young woman looked surprised. Again the gesture with her hand, why? Maria shrugged. She disappeared into the house and came back shortly with the little girl and a glass of steaming chai; she offered it to Maria with the happy smile of someone who finds great satisfaction in giving.

The child was very shy and remained stubbornly attached to her mother's dress, staring at Maria. Pushpa sat down cross-legged and placed the child in her lap; she unbuttoned two buttons of her shirt and offered her breast to her. She caressed her head gently, playing with the little curls, stroking with love her face, her forehead, her head. Meanwhile she explained to Maria, with words and gestures, that she didn't need to go to Manali, and that they would cook for her and her friends. It seemed too much to accept and Maria tried to refuse the offer. What right had they to scrounge dinner when they hadn't done anything toward it? The family had been working all day in the fields, while Franca and Veronica had smoked an endless number of chillums, lying down to rest every now and then, since they didn't even have the strength to stand. She preferred to go to the grocery store and eat what little dinner they could prepare. But the young woman wasn't going to take no for an answer and insisted.

The authoritative voice of her mother-in-law called Pushpa, who promptly stood up and, without a word, placed the little girl, Ritu, on Maria's lap. The child, who was as surprised as she was, tried to get up to follow her mother, but when Maria began to sing a children's song, she stopped and looked at her with those big eyes, enchanted by the sound of Maria's voice and her blue eyes. She reached out her little hand to touch them and Maria moved back instinctively, smiling and continuing to sing. She felt her relax over her crossed legs. The little girl smiled with those perfect white teeth and a dimple formed on both cheeks; she was irresistible.

Franca appeared on the balcony. "You've found a friend," she said.
"Isn't she beautiful?" said Maria.

"Very!" Franca's eyes were red from the smoke. She slumped next to her. "I smoked too much," she said.

"I didn't know the words 'smoked too much' were part of your vocabulary."

Franca smiled weakly. "True! Perhaps it's not too much, just a lot," she corrected herself.

Maria told her that the family was going to prepare food for them and, as Franca wanted to know how she had achieved that, she told her about the firewood and Pushpa. She explained how her local friend had shown her the difference between boys and girls, and they laughed together, for the first time in days. Speaking in a low voice, Franca said that the 'others' would be back in a couple of days. She could then buy the charas she wanted and, after that, they could leave. Maria nodded slowly and turned to look at the sky. The sun was disappearing behind the mountains and the sky was changing from blue to pale pink, yellow, orange and red. Even Ritu, who was quiet and relaxed lying on Maria's lap, turned her head to look at the sky.

Pushpa walked onto the porch carrying a stainless steel dish full of rice and two bowls, one filled with lentils and the other one with bhaji made with vegetables from the field: spinach, peas and beans. She placed them down in front of them with a smile, then looked toward Veronica's door and made that questioning gesture with her fingers upwards, as if to ask where she was. With an agile movement, she picked up her little daughter, put her astride on her hip and went back into the house, walking barefoot on the wooden porch.

They had no forks or spoons and Maria's hands were filthy, but she was also very hungry. She stood up and went to invite Veronica, who was dozing. When she heard the word food, she quickly got up and walked onto the balcony.

"Where can I find some water?" asked Maria.

"To drink or to wash?" Veronica asked, lazily.

"To wash my hands before I eat."

"Down the stream, a two minutes' walk, but by the time you go and come back the rice will be cold," she said, eyeing the full platter and crouching near. She dug her fingers into the rice and drew them out full of it. She began to work it into a ball, which she then dipped into the lentils bowl. Maria realized that the rice would not only be cold, but probably finished on her return, so there was no alternative but to eat with dirty hands; she would wash them later. She copied Veronica's system and they ate that good, warm and not too spicy dinner together, while the light was changing from the blue of the evening to the black of the night and the first stars started to shine, flooding with magic the roof of the universe. As for the mat, it was too late; she would somehow manage on the floor, she thought, licking her fingers.

Just then Pushpa came out again and stood near Maria, putting a big roll on the floor and saying: "For you!" She stood smiling with those beautiful perfect teeth. "For me?" asked Maria. Yes, for you. Waving her hand, she encouraged her to open it. Maria untied the rope that held the roll closed and, to her amazement, a large mattress made of woven straw unrolled before her eyes. What a surprise! But how did Pushpa know that she wanted a mattress? Certainly she couldn't have understood her words, so she could only have guessed. Franca and Veronica were equally impressed. Maria stood up and hugged Pushpa, kissing her affectionately. Her new friend laughed, delighted, and words, in any language, couldn't have added anything to what they were already expressing to each other. Shining her torch, Maria went down to the stream and washed the dishes on which they had eaten. She washed her hands and face and brushed her teeth.

Back at the house, Franca and Veronica were preparing yet another chillum and this time she shared it with them. "How I'd love to have a nice hot shower!" she said, whilst relaxing next to the round stove.
"There are baths in Vashist," said Veronica. True! She had almost forgotten about them. How did people get there? It was an uphill walk of less than two miles, but it was definitely worth it. You had to take your own towel, soap and shampoo. Shall we go tomorrow? Franca hesitated. "Tomorrow I wanted to go and make charas with Veronica, who said she'd take me to a plot of land she knows, right?" she said, looking at her friend, hopefully.
"It depends," Veronica replied, lying lazily on the mat. On what? On the weather. If it was even a little bit damp you couldn't do it. It had to be completely dry otherwise you didn't get anything from the plants, rather you'd ruin them. She did know how the charas was done, right? Franca had a moment's hesitation. Yeeeees... but not exactly, she hadn't had time to make any two years ago. Maria came to her aid, asking if Veronica could explain the *exact* process, since she had so much experience. Flattered, Veronica began to explain that she had to take the plant between the hands, starting from the bottom, holding it tight and rub it between the palms, moving up and rubbing at the same time; it required quite a lot of strength. The plant left a glossy and sticky resin that accumulated on the palms. As it built up, the colour turned black and shiny: that was pure charas.
"And then?" asked Maria, "You can't possibly smoke it as it is, can you?" No, of course not! You had to remove it with patience, rubbing the

palm with the thumb to form a little ball, until the hands were completely clean. She held up a piece in front of her and showed it as an example, saying: "Here it is!" Then, turning to Franca, she observed her, wondering whether she was bluffing, and added: "This is why it must be dry, with no moisture, otherwise you don't get a lot of resin, and the little bit you get goes mouldy." Then, laughing, she said that she never left the charas enough time to go mouldy. Maria asked if the plants died after receiving such treatment. No, said Veronica, the plants were very strong and, after a few days, they recovered and returned as good as new.

Were they by any chance, those plants with star shaped leaves? She had seen so many along the road. Veronica looked at her with genuine astonishment. "What a question! Don't tell me you don't know what marijuana plants look like!" she exclaimed. Ah, that's what they were... She knew she had seen them somewhere. Veronica laughed out loud at Maria's obvious naivety. Probably she had seen them on t-shirts, mugs, lighters, etcetera etcetera etcetera! Ahhh, true, true. That's where she had seen them! Now it all made sense, and... who planted them, there were so many? Veronica burst out laughing again and this time also Franca, genuinely amused, laughed heartily. Nobody planted them! They grew wild, everywhere. "The gods plant them," said Franca. Yes, especially those outside the police station. This made them laugh even more.

Veronica announced that she was 'knackered' and went to pee in the room next door. Ah well, it was official then, they could pee in that kind of sink; that was a relief! Veronica slipped into her sleeping bag, above the mat, with her Fiorucci jeans folded as a pillow, and goodnight! Franca made a pillow out of her sweater and jeans and, looking dubious, she slipped into her sleeping bag on a mat. Maria lay on top of the straw mattress which, despite being a little hard, wasn't too bad at all.

She closed her eyes and went over that day's images: the forest where she had gone to reflect after reading the Buddha's words which had touched her, the green river, smiling people, Pushpa with her demonstration of bacchee and baccha and baskets full of lakri, her happy smiles. The family that gave them accommodation, the food they had been offered, the chai, Ritu who listened spellbound while she sang the children's song, the mountains and the sunset. Veronica with her attitude and the hospitality she offered them, despite her superiority complex. And Ugo? Who was Ugo? A far away face, the beginning of a feeling of indifference; it didn't hurt so much any longer, it was another world! And Paul? Did he live in a house like this one? He was nearby but, at the same time, so far. Maria slipped into a deep sleep and dreamed of fast running water, of somersaults against the rocks, blue skies and a hot bath.

She woke up to the noises of the family who had risen, all busy preparing for breakfast and to start the new day. She opened the door to the porch and saw Ritu who was waiting for her, looking shyly in the direction of her door. Maria smiled at her and then she smiled at the mountains. The sun was still behind the peaks and the air still damp and cold. She fetched her toiletry bag and climbed down the steep stairs to go to the stream. How poetic to have a wash in the cold water of the brook. Crouched on the stones at the water's edge, Maria filled her hands with water, bringing them quickly to her face and washing with the few drops left.

Women and men passed by, heading for work in the fields, and greeted her with a smile. Other women filled buckets from the stream and asked, with that hand gesture with fingers up, who she was, was she staying at Pushpa's house? Yes, she replied, at Pushpa's, Ritu's. They bobbed their head, they had understood; they were pleased and amused. Baccha? No, I don't have children. Bacchee? No, not even little girls. And you? Yes, replied the woman in front of her, smiling openly. Had she eaten? No, she was going to Manali to eat. When, how, what? That hand gesture again! Now, she'd be going to Manali on foot. Maria bowed with folded hands, Namaste Ji! They smiled, Namaste Namaste, and with the full bucket resting on the hip, they walked carefully, so as not to spill a single drop.

Back at home, Franca and Veronica had awakened and were already preparing a chillum. Incredible! Do you smoke before you even get up? Don't you feel hungry? Let's go to Manali for breakfast, come on. Yes, yes, immediately after this chillum. Bah! They were getting on her nerves. She prepared her towel, soap and shampoo to go to Vashist and waited, sitting on the porch, for them to finish the chillum, while enjoying the first rays of sun that dried the moisture of the night.

They crossed the long wood-and-rope bridge that jerked and undulated beneath their feet and reached the restaurant where they ate breakfast. Franca was hoping to go and make charas, but Veronica was finding different objections, problems with the weather; she didn't quite have the right kind of energy to do it today, maybe tomorrow. It seemed as if she had no desire to take her there. The good places for this activity were a secret between experts... a lot of excuses. Franca was very disappointed, Maria wasn't. Shall we go to Vashist then? "Yes, let's do that," said Veronica. That's great. Thanks Veronica!

11. Are you God?

They walked briskly uphill for two miles on a paved road in the fresh, crystal clear air and came to Vashist public baths in just over half an hour. The reception was a bare room with rough concrete walls. It was four rupees for a deluxe bathroom for two people. Could the three of them go in together? Yes, no problem, six rupees, which they paid at the desk. But, before their bath, Franca and Veronica wanted to smoke another chillum to 'relax better' and went to sit on a fallen log at the edge of the forest that surrounded the spa. To pass the time, Maria lit a cigarette. Sitting on a wall in the sunshine, she watched the people who came and those who left, with wet hair and a rolled-up towel under their arm. In the distance, walking uphill, she noticed a couple.

That blond hair, the tall man was accompanied by a smaller woman with straight reddish hair wearing a brightly coloured waistcoat. She would have recognized him among a thousand people. Her heart did a somersault in her chest and her hand holding the cigarette began to sweat. He hadn't seen her yet, while Karen was so short-sighted she wouldn't recognize her until they were very close. Unable to stand up, her mind empty, Maria was lost for words, or thoughts. She looked at Paul, who was approaching with a long stride, rucksack on his back, engrossed. She knew that soon he would perceive her gaze and waited for that moment with her heart in turmoil, her cheeks burning hot. What would she do, or say? Paul raised his eyes and met Maria's. At first he didn't recognize her, but soon she saw the realization transform his absorbed expression in a flash of understanding. She smiled and stood up, waiting motionless, not knowing what to do. He smiled, without taking his eyes off her, and quickened his pace. He almost ran the last few steps and hugged her, lifting her off the ground, holding her close.

"I'm Maria," she said, assuming he had forgotten her name.

"And I'm Paul," he said, laughing. He held her tight, moving her away from him only enough to be able to look into her eyes, and kissed her on her lips. She laughed, surprised and thrilled.

"And this is Karen," she said quickly, suddenly embarrassed and freeing herself from his embrace that stirred her. Paul let her go but kept his hands around her waist for a few more seconds. Maria hurried to greet

Karen, who was still wondering where they had met before. "In Mandi," Maria said, answering her unspoken question. Karen lit up and kissed her on both cheeks. Ah, so the kiss on the mouth was not such an obvious thing, after all, if she had kissed her on her cheeks. What was she doing here? Karen asked. Waiting for Franca and another friend to go for a hot bath. Did they come here often? She asked both of them, glancing quickly at Paul, to look immediately back at Karen. She felt shy, troubled by her emotions and couldn't look at him for more than a few seconds. Karen began to talk, in her hurried fashion, speaking softly, looking at her without focusing. She told her they came to Vashist almost every week, before going to Manali for their shopping. The hot bath was a real treat with such huge tub. She was going to love it. What was their life like in the village? Maria asked. Always the same, normal, Karen said. Why didn't she come and see them? What was she doing here? Where was she staying? Was she going to stop long? Did she like it?

Maria began to tell them that she was living in a house with local people and had befriended the young mother, her child and her grandmother. She told them the first things that came to her, but her mind was in turmoil, her English was all wrong, mixed up with Italian. She explained how she had learned a few words in the local language, had gone to get 'lakri'; had sung a song in Italian to the little girl; the family had offered them dinner and the young mother had also given her a straw mattress. Everything came out confused, her cheeks burning and red with emotion. She felt Paul's gaze on her as she spoke, his intense presence, close, full of interest and warmth. Well, they were going to book a 'de luxe' bathroom, Karen said. Yes they had also booked the same; they allowed the three of them to go in together. Paul asked her what she was doing after the bath. They were going for lunch at a restaurant in Manali; why didn't she join them? It seemed a good idea. Which restaurant? The first? No, the second. Okay, she'll see them there, after their bath.

They disappeared into the reception and Maria sat down on the wall, sweaty, struck and shaking. Her dream had materialized, the impossible had come true. And now what? she asked herself. Now nothing, you silly, she rebuked herself. Now you'll go for a bath and then you'll have lunch with them, what's the big deal? The fact that she had met them again didn't change anything. He had a girlfriend and lived here with her, while she was a 'tourist' whom they had met for the second time. Calm down, Maria, re-dimension. It's all in your head. Shanti, Maria, shanti!

Just then Franca and Veronica reappeared. "Guess who has arrived," she whispered to Franca. When she told her of the English couple she knew at once from her expression what she was thinking: that excellent charas for which she was making so much effort, perhaps she would be able to buy it from them, freeing herself from that vague, somewhat uncomfortable, commitment with Veronica.

They entered a bare room with a big tiled tub. Veronica hastened to open the two taps to fill it with hot and cold water. The water that came out from the source was boiling hot, she said, and they had to be careful not to scald themselves. While they undressed the steam filled the room. They hung their clothes on a hook on the damp wall and entered the tub one at a time, naked and slender. They washed from top to bottom with a rich lather, lying lazily in the water that continued to gush out of the taps, playing with their feet in the fresh air, and then inside, in the warm water. Maria thought of Paul and Karen doing exactly the same thing with just a wall or two between them and she imagined him without any clothes on. She shook the thought off, and relaxed in the water that was getting deeper and deeper, enjoying such a pleasant moment, the present, the only reality that truly existed. She washed her hair with shampoo, rinsed it immersing herself in the hot water, hearing Franca's and Veronica's voices, not understanding what they were saying; her head was somewhere else, confused. What next? She would let herself flow with the moment, without asking too many questions. They'll eat together and then she would return 'home' to Pushpa and Ritu.

The descent from Vashist to Manali was the most exciting walk Maria had done since their arrival in India. She was in a hurry to get there, feeling a mixture of fear and anxiety swell in her heart. Calm down, Maria! She kept repeating to herself. Easier said than done. But she had to calm down or she wouldn't be able to say a word to Paul. He was a friend, she was going to behave as with any friend, and she owed respect to Karen, she was his girlfriend after all. She knew what it felt like when another woman wanted to take your man away. She had gone through that experience many times and she wasn't going to do it to someone else. Having taken this decision, she felt calmer and ready to push open the restaurant door. Franca was coming with her and this made it easier.

Paul saw them as soon as they entered and beckoned them over to their table. It was all simpler than she thought. While going through the menu, she asked him what they had ordered, what they normally ate, if at home they cooked on a kerosene stove. For each question, she looked at him and at every answer she could look at him again, making sure to share evenly her glances between him and Karen. Franca asked him if he had any charas to sell her, but he said that he was sorry, he had almost nothing. Franca vented the frustration she felt at not being able to go and make her own charas and complained that Veronica didn't seem to want to take her. To her amazement and delight, Paul knew a little plot of land nearby with some good wild plants and, if they wanted to, he would accompany them and show them how to make charas. He consulted with Karen, could they spare an hour for this activity? It was fine by her; she'd go shopping and meet them again in a couple of hours. Franca was ecstatic. Maria was thrilled to be able to spend some more time with him.

They walked uphill following a path that led to a small temple. It wasn't far away, Paul said, and it was beautiful, right in the middle of the forest. Maria filled her lungs with that clean air, still incredulous to be with him. The trees were very tall, their trunks so big they made her feel tiny. They continued to climb, steeper and steeper, around them only birds, squirrels and foxes, who observed them from a safe distance. She told him what they had done in Mcleodganj, about the man with no legs and the Dalai Lama's speech. He listened to her with a smile, keeping close, at times brushing her arm. Franca told him about Fred the spider and how much she had enjoyed the piece of charas he had given her. Finally, they came to a small wooden temple and sat on the steps to rest, listening to the birds singing, each one with its own different voice.

"Look around you. Can you see the plants?" said Paul, allowing their eyes to adjust and then to distinguish the marijuana plants among all the green. Franca saw them before they did.

"There they are!" she cried excitedly, heading straight toward a bunch of plants with star-shaped leaves. Paul laughed, amused by her enthusiasm and, looking at Maria sitting beside him, put his hand on her back, holding it there for a moment that seemed to last forever. She couldn't help but look at him and felt herself blush. Franca was very happy, she said, just to say something, she had always wanted to make her own charas, and he was doing her a great favour by taking her there.

"It's nice to make your own charas and then smoke it," Paul said, his hand still on her back; she could feel the heat passing through the fabric and onto her skin. "Do you want to see the temple inside?" he asked.

"Is it allowed? Can we go in?"

"Of course! Just take off your shoes and anything made of leather or metal."

They went in barefoot, Paul walking close behind her. There was a simple marble sculpture in the shape of a rounded cylinder, adorned with necklaces made of fresh flowers, orange, white and yellow, and wet by a substance similar to melted butter. At its feet there were more flowers of the same colours, a bowl of puffed rice, coconuts, apples and tangerines. He stood so close that he almost touched her; she could feel the warmth of his body. Paul explained that the rounded cylinder was a 'lingam', the image of the male penis. Maria blushed and, at the same time, was amused and surprised.

"I beg your pardon, did I hear that right?"

"You did, it is one of the images of god Shiva," he explained. "It symbolizes abundance, fertility and wealth." Suddenly, he hugged her from behind. It seemed the most natural thing in the world, after the first moment of surprise. Maria surrendered to his embrace and rested her head on his chest; she didn't turn around lest she couldn't control herself. She could hear his heart beating against her head and she listened, enraptured by that moment of intimacy stolen from their destiny. He spoke and his words created a resonance that went directly into her head, touched her heart and moved her. She closed her eyes. She didn't try to find the words, it didn't matter if she didn't know what to say; she didn't need to pretend. Franca's voice shook her from that moment, where time had stopped.

"I start from the bottom, right?" cried Franca. "And then I go up to the top. Like this, is this right?" They moved away and looked at each other, speechless. She felt herself blush violently. Without a word, they went out of the temple to join her friend. Paul looked at what she was doing and then, carefully, showed her how much pressure to put on the plant, much stronger than she had been doing. "But like this it's hard work, huh?" said Franca, who worked with all the strength in her arms. Paul laughed and confirmed that yes, it took a lot of strength and technique.

"Carry on like this," he reassured her. "Then it will get easier."

Turning to Maria he asked her whether she wanted to try. Sure, she'd love to. He looked for a good plant and told her to start with that, keeping close to check her technique. As she put too little force, he stood behind her and put his hands over hers, squeezing them and rubbing hard the sturdy leaves. "Like this," he said from behind her, "start from the bottom," and his head touched Maria's head, "then carry on rubbing, move up higher," his arms were around Maria's shoulders and she felt him breathe in her hair, "and then you go up to the top of the plant", she could feel the warmth exuding from him. It was hard to find the strength in her arms with him so close; she was losing all her energy and was melting inside. He spoke with that deep voice and her legs were trembling. She wanted to turn around, hug him and let him kiss her. Instead, she said she understood and that she would try it alone.

Paul took a plant close to hers and began to rub it in his hands. He looked at how Franca was doing and told her to keep working in the sunshine, so that the resin would be warm and come off more easily. He looked at Maria from time to time, did she need any help? Did it look right, the way she was doing? Stronger, he said, the plants are robust and won't get spoilt. Did she feel her palms become sticky? Carry on like this, he said and smiled at her, with those intense green eyes. They worked in silence for the rest of the time. After less than an hour Maria stopped, exhausted. She approached him with her palms of a yellow-golden colour, shiny and bright like honey in the sun, sticky as warm resin. Now what did she have to do? "Sit on the step," said Paul, "and rub your thumb against the palm of your hand. You'll see that the resin begins to come off and form a little ball that looks like chewing gum."

Franca was still very busy with her plants and reluctant to finish. Paul told her that soon they'd have to go down to the village and she ought to stop. Both of them came to sit next to Maria rubbing the palm of their hand with their thumb, as she was doing. Maria ended up with a tiny ball, black and shiny, Paul had one double her size and Franca had one halfway between the two. She was happy, but at the same time disappointed that she had made so little. He explained that she had to relax while rubbing the plants, that way she'd get much more, but both had done very well in making their first piece of charas. Did they want to smoke it? Maria offered her piece, but Franca insisted that they try hers; she was bursting with excitement. Paul prepared his chillum, from which Maria was able to inhale only a small mouthful. It was enough to lift her onto a different reality, a lighter, fairy tale dimension.

They went down toward Manali at a slow pace, with no hurry to get there. Maria wanted to prolong these moments for as long as possible; could she have stopped the time, she would have done so now. Paul invited them to drink a chai while waiting for Karen to get back. In the restaurant, seated side by side, her arm so close to Paul's she could feel the pulsing of his blood, Maria felt the passing of every second on her skin. She wanted to memorize every sensation of those precious moments. There was something about him that felt familiar, comfortable; she felt at ease and could fall asleep in his arms, as if she had always done so. The idea of parting was painful and, at the same time a relief, because his presence erased everything else, and if she wanted to continue her journey she had to be free from such a strong emotional embrace that could keep her here with him, willingly, readily, for a long time.

Karen came laden with packages and bags. Paul got up quickly and went to take the bags from her hands; then he returned to his seat next to Maria. Karen sat down, gasping and asking for a chai. She began to speak rapidly, softly, chuckling to herself as she recounted the episodes of those hours spent alone. Maria couldn't help but feel a strong sympathy for her; she seemed to live in the clouds, seeing the reality that surrounded her in a blurred way, choosing not to see properly because she preferred the free world of her imagination and vibrant creativity to reality as it was. She didn't remember how, but they began to talk about toilets. Franca asked if there was a toilet in the house. Oh no, it was considered a dirty thing to have a toilet in the house, they explained, and for quite a while they continued to talk about the difficulties caused by the lack of loos in the house and outside. Maria looked at Paul at every opportunity, finding that he responded immediately to her gaze, if he wasn't already looking at her. Meanwhile, Karen and Franca exchanged information about diarrhoea, amoeba, giardia, tips on how to avoid them and what medicines were available in India.

Where did they spend the winter? Maria asked, once they exhausted the subject of intestinal problems. In Goa, said Paul, and began to tell them of the long journey from the mountains, through Delhi, from there to Bombay and then down to Goa by ferry. It was beautiful, he said, they *had* to go: beaches, palm trees laden with coconuts, tamarind, tropical flowers. "People are different there," he explained. "They are half Indian and half Portuguese and it feels a little like going back to Europe." He told her the name of where they stopped, 'Vagator beach', and emphasised that it was definitely the best part of Goa. Once the chai was finished it was time to say goodbye.

Again, all words and thoughts deserted her mind, disappearing into a bottomless pit, leaving her stuck, unable to think of anything clever or funny to say and sad, very sad, lost for words. She nodded when Paul, and then Karen, invited them to go and see them. Franca filled the awkward silence with short phrases in her simple English. Karen kissed her on both cheek and then it was time to say goodbye to Paul. She looked at him, smiling, unable to utter a word, while he looked at her more seriously with his green, large, intense eyes. He held her by the shoulders and leaned down, kissing her on the lips. "See you soon," he said. Yes, see you soon. He took the bags and, before leaving the restaurant, turned to look at her one last time. Maria sat still, crestfallen, empty. She looked at Franca, who was watching her.

"He likes you a lot," she said.

"Do you think so? I wasn't sure… maybe a little."

"Even a blind man would see it," she said. Maria smiled, with her lips only.

Franca stopped in Manali with Veronica, Maria decided to go home and spend time with Pushpa and Ritu. She didn't want any more emotions that day. She wanted her heart to calm down, and to continue to feel Paul's presence. She went to a couple of shops and bought potatoes, eggs, cheese and apples. Walking without haste, she crossed the rope bridge, undulating and heaving at every movement, and slowly arrived home. She put her shopping down and sat on the porch to rest while watching the river below, always different, in his cheerful and foamy race. From her heart began a spontaneous chanting of Nam-myoho-renghe-kyo. She let it come out, freeing it through her lips, thinking about Paul. She chanted for his happiness and that of Karen; she let it fly, as free as a seagull. Ritu's little face appeared in the doorway, looking at Maria. When she called her, the little girl ran back into the house, only to reappear, showing her face and then, shyly, hiding again. Maria remembered that, in the bottom of her backpack she had Murano glass beads that she had brought with her for moments like this one, to make friends. She had to empty the whole rucksack to find the two little boxes, buried under everything else.

Back on the porch, she sat leaning against the wall and waited. When Ritu reappeared Maria shook the two boxes. The sound was enough to win the child's curiosity and cautiously she came forward. Maria asked her to choose which one she wanted, the one with the silver beads or the one with the golden ones? Without any hesitation Ritu pointed to the golden beads. Maria motioned for her to sit down and pulled out a spool of elastic thread with which she measured her wrist. Curious, the child settled at her side. Maria cut a piece to size and began to thread the golden beads, while the little girl leaned closer and closer. Within a few minutes the little bracelet was done and Maria slid it onto her arm. Ritu turned her wrist over and over, gently touching it with the tip of her index finger and then ran into the house. Maria could hear her talk to someone.

A few minutes later she came out again, followed by her grandmother. Maria took a better look at her this time: she wasn't so old, she must have been about fifty, but her legs were crooked and she walked with difficulty. Pointing to her knees she made her understand that they ached, and pointing to the fields she mimed back pain from too much work. She looked at the box of beads full of curiosity and made that gesture with her hand, as if to ask: what are they? What are you doing? Maria replied in Italian and pointed to her granddaughter's bracelet. Mataji touched it with her rough finger and then pointed to herself. She wanted a bracelet too? Maria asked. Yes, she replied with a bob of her head, her thin face lit up by a big smile, which, despite the missing teeth, was no less appealing. Maria was surprised and amused. And why not? Even grandmother liked original things. She motioned for her to sit down;

'beto, beto' she said, remembering the words spoken by Pushpa, and measured her wrist. Which ones did she want, the silver or the gold ones? No hesitation, the golden beads. Maria threaded one bead after the other, affected by the joy she saw in the woman's face, happy to have something to give her. She hadn't yet finished the bracelet, when three little girls' faces appeared at the top of the stairs. She didn't know how it was possible, but the news had already spread, and they handed their wrists for Maria to measure. She continued to make one bracelet after another, hoping to have enough beads for everyone and fortunately the box seem to contain a great quantity, never emptying. The three little girls left and she found herself alone, knowing that the peace wouldn't last long. Mataji came out and placed a hot chai on the floor next to her. Maria wanted to thank her, but she didn't know the word, so she clasped her hands before her chest and bowed. It seemed all right.

Just then Pushpa came from the fields. She spoke from under the porch and called to her even before seeing her. Her smiling face appeared at the top of the stairs and Maria got up to hug her. This greatly amused her local friend, who wasn't accustomed to this type of effusions, but understood the spirit. As soon as she saw the bracelets, she requested one, too. How simply these people knew how to ask; they gave and asked with equal ease. "Lakri?" she enquired. Pushpa nodded and Maria explained with gestures that she needed firewood for cooking. The young woman settled next to her, drinking the hot chai that her mother-in-law had brought her, taking a rest and observing with anticipation while Maria slipped one bead after another through the elasticised thread. When she slid the bracelet on her wrist Pushpa smiled with her open, innocent face and said: "Acchah!" turning her hand round and round, admiring it happily. 'Acchah' was a word they used a lot, and meant good, well done; 'bahut acchah' meant the same, but better. Had she been working hard? Maria asked with the few words she knew. Yes, very hard. Was she tired? No, not really; now lakri, and pani. 'Pani'? Yes, water. Maria, too, needed water to cook the potatoes.

They walked up the mountain carrying a pannier on their shoulders and came to the same clearing as the day before, but now they had to trek further up to find good wood. They stopped after a steep climb and Pushpa told her to rest. 'Beto, beto' she said, tapping the ground with her hand. They looked around, whilst getting their breath back. From her pocket Maria took out the piece of charas she had made and showed it to her friend. She took a good look at it and then asked: "Tum?" pointing her finger at Maria. "Yes, I made it," she replied, mimicking the rubbing of the plant. The young woman nodded; she smiled and said: "Bagwan!"

It was Maria's turn to raise her hand, fingers pointing upward, screwing and unscrewing the imaginary light bulb: "What does Bagwan mean?" "God," said Pushpa. Really? The charas was God? "Yes," nodded Pushpa and pointing to the sky, she said again: "Bagwan." Then she touched the grass on which they were sitting, Bagwan. Maria pointed to the trees, Bagwan? Yes. The birds flying in the sky, Bagwan? Yes, of course. Then, all of nature was God? Yes, everything.

Maria reflected. She liked the idea that nature was a manifestation of God, much more than the version she had been taught, of a being who lived up there, in the sky, who saw and knew everything. An idea crossed her mind. Looking at her friend she said:

"*Tum*, Bagwan?" Are *you* God? expecting her to laugh at her suggestion. Instead, her question seemed relevant and not at all ventured. "Maim acchah, maim Bagwan," Pushpa said, touching her chest with her forefinger. Then she elaborated: "Maim acchah naih, maim Bagwan naih."

She looked at Maria to see if she had understood. So, when she behaved well, when she was good, she was a manifestation of God, and when she misbehaved, she was not. It was an elementary concept and, at the same time, what a difference between the two cultures. In the religion she had been taught, she could never be equal to God, let alone a manifestation of God himself, while in Pushpa's the idea of God was not separate from life or from the people themselves. She liked this idea of human divinity. But people had to make an effort, acting like real human beings rather than animals. It seemed similar to the concept of Buddhahood, mentioned by Sanya. Wasn't that the highest expression of our humanity, that wonderful cocktail of compassion, wisdom and courage, embodied by Buddha? Maria felt relaxed and happy. She thought of Paul. Perhaps he had already arrived home. Who knew if she would ever see him again; but that embrace in the temple had revealed more than any words could, and in the depths of her heart, she felt that they hadn't had their final farewell. He was the most handsome man she had ever seen, and she knew he liked her, but what could such a meeting bring? She visualized Karen, the way she spoke, how she looked without seeing. She knew she couldn't build her happiness on someone else's suffering, and that there was nothing she could do to develop a bond with that beautiful man who had touched her heart. She could only wish him all the happiness in the world.

She filled her pannier to the brim, as did Pushpa, and they helped each other load it on their shoulders. Supporting the pointed bottom with their hands clasped behind their backs, they walked slowly downhill along the path. All the people they met recognized Maria. They arrived home much faster than the day before, emptied the baskets on the porch and then, without allowing her to stop, Pushpa said: "Pani." She didn't have a bucket for the water, said Maria. No problem! Her companion went into the house, lowering her head under the door jamb, came out with a large bowl of polished brass and offered it to Maria. It was very heavy even when empty. She showed her how to hold it, resting it against her hip and retaining its mouth in the curve of her arm.

At the fountain there was a queue and Pushpa replied to the questions asked by the women who watched Maria with curiosity, smiling. They asked her for beaded bracelets and she said yes to all of them. Carrying the containers full of water, they carefully walked back to the house.

She filled the tandoori stove with some of the thin sticks of wood she had gathered but lighting the fire was more difficult than she had imagined. Lying on the bare floor, she blew into the stove to encourage the flames, but with little success.

Pushpa appeared on the doorstep and laughed. She made a gesture to tell her to move out of the way and, crouching in front of the stove, she showed her how to adjust the influx of air by opening and closing a small vent on the door. The fire caught well and began to burn briskly. Maria placed a pot of water on the stove and took the potatoes out of the bag, joyfully anticipating Franca's and Veronica's surprise when they'd get back and find dinner ready. She liked to give; it made her happy, even happier than when she received.

Sitting on the porch, she started to peel potatoes, watching the green river that flowed fast, the blue sky, the huge, imposing mountains covered in trees. It was a beautiful day.

The hot bath had left her with a clean, soft skin, and there had been that unexpected encounter, so full of emotions. She wondered what Paul was doing at that very moment. Was he thinking of her? She felt a connection from her heart to his; at times she felt she could perceive his thoughts, his energy. Her skin still tingled at the memory of the touch of his hands; once more she felt him breathing in her hair. She leaned back, hoping to experience again his warm embrace, re-listening to his deep voice that spoke so close to her. All those feelings tied together to form a knot in her stomach and filled her heart. She entrusted them to the river, freeing herself from such powerful emotions that almost hurt her. Nam-myoho-renge-kyo, she whispered and let it blend with the water below. Paul had already done something good for her: he had made her feel desirable, charming, sensual, inviting her to like, accept and have confidence in herself, just as she was, something that she had long since lost. For this she was grateful. He had helped her to heal and appreciate herself. From here she could continue on her own. She smiled at the sky and at him. Good luck darling, and good luck Karen, enjoy your wonderful man! As for herself, she was free, she was flapping her wings and thinking that yes, she could fly again. Thank you Ugo, for pushing me this far, all the way to India. Without you I wouldn't be here. For now she was learning not to suffer and who knows what else she would learn; the journey had only just begun. "Nam-myoho-renge-kyo," she repeated softly, entrusting it to the unstoppable course of the river. That sound calmed her down and a smile rose from her heart.

She went back to the stove and put the chopped potatoes in the boiling water. The fire was in need of attention and she spent a few minutes adding wood and adjusting the oxygen flow, opening and closing the little vent. With great satisfaction, she saw the water beginning to boil again.

Back on the veranda the sun was a huge red ball, clearly defined and intense, like the flames she had just left. The clouds looked like candyfloss suspended in the pale blue sky. As soon as she sat down on the wooden floor, Ritu approached and, without a word, came to sit on her lap. Maria sat more comfortably and began to play with her locks, as she had seen Pushpa do. Then, remembering what Gemma, her mother, did when she was a child, she began to scratch her back. At first the little girl stiffened, but soon she began to enjoy the massage and relaxed on Maria's lap, watching the fire sunset with her.

The grandfather came out onto the terrace, wearing his grey woolly trousers, a jacket of a similar colour and the traditional hat with coloured zigzag stripes on the front. Noting the child with her, he smiled briefly at Maria. Pitaji, this was what the old man of the house was called, settled down with his back against the wall and lit a water pipe, which began to rumble at every puff. He watched the sunset in silence, sharing the sense of peace and calm. Telsin, Pushpa's husband, joined them, sitting next to his father. He smiled at Maria, who was holding his daughter with the same tenderness the family showed her, and pointed to the sky with his chin. She nodded; yes it was gorgeous. His father handed him the water pipe that rumbled a little louder. Without speaking, they relaxed, looking at the sky, waiting for the well deserved sunset. As the sun hid behind the mountains, she heard Franca's and Veronica's voices, as they climbed the steep staircase. They looked at her with surprise, seeing the harmonious scene with the locals, bathed in the golden light of the sunset. Maria smiled, struggling to find her voice, enjoying the silence.

"Are you hungry?" she asked.

"Yes, we're starving!" When they entered the house and saw the stove with the saucepan of boiling potatoes, they put their heads out: "Are you cooking?"

"Yes!"

"For all of us?"

"Of course!"

Maria lifted Ritu, who had fallen asleep, and laid her on Telsin's lap. He smiled, amused. She went indoors and announced the menu for the evening. Then, if they wanted to, they could smoke the charas she had made. Veronica wanted them to take her to the plot, so she could make some too. They would go tomorrow, if the weather was right, Franca said. Maria told them about the bracelets she had made that afternoon and of how many women had asked her for one. She felt happy to have filled that day with so many beautiful things. She explained what Pushpa had told her about the concept of God and asked Veronica for the word 'thank you' in the local language, because she realized she didn't know how to say it. Veronica thought, and thought some more, but she didn't know. She suggested 'acchah', but that meant 'good' and it wasn't the right word.

Maria served the simple dinner and the girls ate together, licking their fingers. "Good," said Franca. "Yes, good," said Veronica. Maria wondered whether they knew the word for 'thank you' in their own language, and the thought made her smile. The charas Franca wanted to buy had not yet arrived, so they had to wait at least another day, but then the friends would arrive, for sure. Maria was in no hurry to leave. She thanked Veronica for the hospitality, which allowed her to have this experience with the village people. Without her, she would never have known Pushpa's family and wouldn't have become part of this community. And wouldn't have gone to Vashist that morning.

They spent the evening around the tandoori stove smoking the charas made by Maria and the one made by Franca. Then they slipped into their sleeping bags. Veronica had decided that the weather was going to be perfect to go to the plot with 'Paul's plants' to make charas. They were going to organize a picnic, she said, so they could stay there all day.

Franca got up first, went to the river to have a wash and, on her return, woke them up. It was still early, it was cold and damp, but it didn't matter. "Come on, get up! It's time for a wash, then you'll want to have breakfast in Manali, then we need to shop for the picnic... Come on, hurry up!" She hadn't seen her so determined and full of energy for days.

They left together and crossed the rickety bridge, reaching Manali when the sun had begun to warm the air. They bought bread, cheese and fruit and walked toward the temple, with Franca leading, talking and explaining, enthusiastic and active.

Veronica was in as much of a hurry, and it was interesting to see them so motivated. They looked like different people from the stoned girls of the past few days. It was a pleasant morning and, for the first time, Maria felt that they had connected; three dissimilar women, with different expectations and desires, united by the Himalayan mountains. When they stopped to eat they had to remove the charas from the sticky and golden palms of their hands. Maria had made only a little piece, because she had been lying in the sun on the temple porch, sunbathing and dreaming. Franca and Veronica had a competition in progress, even if they hadn't openly admitted it. After lunch Maria decided to go to the grocery store to buy things for dinner and then home, while the girls were going to stay till sunset.

She arrived at the house with bags full and, knowing that the family were still out in the fields, she began to write a letter to her mother and one to Ester. She made bracelets for the women who had asked her until Pushpa arrived, who now expected Maria's kiss and embrace and had started to reciprocate. "Lakri?" Of course! They climbed the path and repeated their ritual of resting, sitting next to each other on the grass, talking little but enjoying the sisterhood that they clearly felt, growing each day. With full baskets on their backs they walked downhill toward the house, and Maria greeted the locals as if they had been friends forever. "Pani?" Yes, sure! With the brass container resting on the hip they went cheerfully down to the fountain, where Maria pulled the bracelets she had made out of her pocket, hoping they would be sufficient.

Surrounded by women who held out their arms, she slipped a bracelet on every wrist, receiving with each one a happy smile in return. Most of them were a similar age as she, but were already mothers of one or more children. In exchange for those Venetian beads she received their friendship, their warmth and even their god, that Bagwan that was everywhere, in the air, in the people, in gestures, in the small attentions they paid one another. They wanted to know everything about her and found it strange that she wasn't married. "You're beautiful," they told her, 'shubli'. She laughed and replied that *they* were beautiful, with their open and serene faces, those happy smiles, their big eyes. They found any pretext to touch her, wanting to feel her hair, her skin; it was so soft, they said; feel how rough mine is, and took her hand, rubbing it against their cheeks.

"You put cream?" she asked them.

"Yes, when there is a village festival they come here with stalls and sell the cream, but now it's finished."

"And when is the next festival?"

"In a month's time."

"A year?" she checked.

"No," they laughed, "a month, thirty days."

When her container was full of water, they helped her lift it and place it on her hip, checked her posture and finally let her go. Pushpa was waiting, amused and proud to be hosting her at her house.

The potatoes were cooking on the stove and the sun was disappearing behind the mountains; Ritu sat in Maria's lap; her grandfather behind her smoking the water pipe with Telsin. It was all just like the day before, in a precious and relaxed ritual. Franca's and Veronica's voices announced their arrival; they talked animatedly and she could feel the unity between them. "We leave tomorrow," said Franca, as soon as her head showed above the staircase.

Maria looked at her with dismay. Why tomorrow, so soon? Because Veronica's friends had returned and there were going to be too many people in the house. There were five of them, having dinner in Manali. "In an hour's time they'll all be here," said Franca. She had already bought the tickets for the bus leaving at one o'clock in the afternoon.

Maria hadn't expected this and didn't know how to tell Pushpa; she was going to miss her a lot! She would be going very far from where Paul lived and had to accept that separation. They ate around the tandoori, like the day before, talking about the bus trip to Delhi and then, from there, by train to Varanasi. Maria tried to muster some enthusiasm for the next part of her journey, but she was finding it hard to accept the idea. That evening she met Veronica's friends, all Italians.

They had enough charas to sell to Franca. Charas and money exchanged hands, while the boys' voices telling of their adventures filled the room where they sat, all in a bit of a tight squeeze. They smoked one chillum after another and Maria took advantage of the first moment of confusion to put her straw mattress in the corner, sneaked into her sleeping bag and closed her eyes, without anyone noticing.

She got up as soon as she heard the noise of the family waking and went to the stream to wash. Pushpa greeted her with a happy smile when she came back.

"Chai?" she asked.

"Yes, thank you, dhanyavad," said Maria, joining hands in front of her chest. It was cold on the porch and Pushpa invited her into her house to sit in front of the tandoori stove.

The whole family had gathered and was drinking chai. Mataji brought her a glass of tea and told her that she was going to have breakfast with them. Maria couldn't and didn't want to refuse. She sipped the sweet chai. She knew how expensive sugar was and that sweet hot drink told her how fond they were of her. Mataji brought her a plate overflowing with rice, lentils, bhaji and chapati. Sitting cross-legged on the mat next to Pitaji, she ate with her hands, making a ball with the rice in the palm of her hand and dipping it in the lentils. It was good, and they ate all together. They smiled at her in turn, and even the reserved Pitaji grinned at her openly. They brought a bowl of hot water to rinse the hand she had used to eat, Maria before anyone else, thus treating her as guest of honour. The bowl was then passed around to the other members of the family, in order of importance: Pitaji, Telsin, Mataji and then Pushpa all rinsed their hand. One by one, they stood up to go to work in the fields. It was time to say farewell.

Pushpa didn't understand what Maria was saying. Tomorrow, she meant, for sure. Aj no! Not today, why was she leaving today? Kal! Kal meant tomorrow. No, I'm sorry, 'aj', today. Why, why today? Because all the boys had arrived and there were too many people. She could stay at her house, Pushpa said, pointing at her door. But Franca had already bought their tickets! Franca could go, but she could stay, her friend replied promptly. She saw the tears filling Pushpa's big eyes and she felt like crying, too. She hugged her and held her close. "Vapas aana," the young woman said, wiping her eyes with the back of her hand. Come back! Yes, I will come back, she said before thinking. And why not? She could do whatever she wanted, she was free. "Yes, I will come back," she said, with more confidence. The rest of the family took their leave, surprised and sad to see her go so soon. They all said 'Vapas aana', come back, and Maria said that yes, she would return. She felt happy with this decision, even if she didn't know when she would return. One by one, they left the house to go to the fields. Maria began to prepare her rucksack with a lighter heart, now that she had determined to come back. At the bottom she placed the warmest clothes, which would no longer be needed, as they were returning to the heat of the plains: Delhi and then Varanasi, the sacred city of India. She began to feel some enthusiasm for this new journey, a new adventure. She kept out the two little boxes with beads for Pushpa, who loved them so much.

After a couple of farewell chillums Franca was ready and Veronica decided to accompany them to the bus station. With their backpacks on their shoulders, they went down the steep staircase and walked toward the bridge. The people they met greeted them; it seemed as if everyone already knew they were leaving. The women at the fountain stopped them and said to Maria 'Vapas aana'. Yes, she would come back, she said, more and more convinced that she really was going to do so. Walking in silence, for the last time they crossed the rope bridge that made them feel as if they were drunk, and soon arrived at the square, where the bus was already waiting. Franca climbed up the vertical ladder and Maria followed her. They laid their rucksacks on the roof rack and paused a while looking around. The valley was shining, the sun illuminated the deep green of the mountains covered in trees, the pea green of the rice paddies, the snow-covered peaks glistened in the bright light, revealing shades of pink and blue. The temple on one side; the hovels of the Tibetan people; the stalls selling posters of Hindu gods; mats and shawls; women with blankets wrapped around their bodies; men with those cheerful caps. In silence they took leave of that beautiful place and looked at each other.

"The Valley of the Gods," Maria said.

"It's really true," agreed Franca.

At the foot of the ladder Veronica was waiting. She looked at Franca and said: "You've never been here before, right?"

"True," she replied boldly. "Does it matter?"

"Not anymore," said Veronica. Then, turning to Maria, she said: "And you have made a lot of friends here! Everyone invites you to come back."

"It's true, I had a wonderful time and I will come back, although I don't know when!" She hugged her, thanking her, with real affection.

12. The expert touch of a massage

After hooting at full volume the bus departed and, by the time they reached the end of the road, the girls were holding tight to the bar of the seat in front. It drove downhill in twists and turns, once again toward the heat of the city. They sat together, after many days spent always with other people. The return trip seemed much easier than the one on the way there; the road was familiar and the mountains seemed even more beautiful. After a few hours they stopped at the small temple that preceded the most dangerous part of the journey. While the driver went in to say his prayer for protection, the same man who had come on board on their first trip came back to distribute the puffed rice, in return for which the passengers gave a few paisa. Maria exchanged seats with Franca, who hadn't had the privilege of seeing the cliffs over the river during the first leg and didn't want to miss the opportunity. Whenever she saw a jeep, a car or a bus at the bottom of the escarpment she'd say loudly: "Look, another one there!"

"Yes, thank you," Maria replied, who would rather not have known but, since she couldn't get her to shut up, she sent a thought to those poor people who had lost their lives in that terrifying way and joined the other passengers who were praying in silence for protection. Within half an hour the coach had passed the most dangerous part and stopped at the pink temple. This time, as well as the driver, some passengers went into the temple and Maria followed them. There, before the Hindu gods, she offered thanks for all the wonderful Indian friends she had met and who had welcomed her with affection into their lives. Then her thought went to Paul and his embrace, his mesmerizing eyes. In her heart she expressed the desire to find a love that was possible, someone special with whom she could share her joy, thrills, adventures and grow together. She wanted something beautiful, where no one had to suffer, or make someone else suffer. The passengers climbed back onto the bus and Maria felt a sense of confidence replace the anxiety she had felt before. She was going to trust her life and have faith in what India had in store for her. She relaxed and stopped being a passenger in the driver's seat; she gave up checking the traffic and decided to trust the driver, who had plenty of experience.

Franca was completely focussed on the future. She asked the other passengers how to get to Varanasi, how long the train took and where to buy tickets. They were happy to be of assistance, converting her questions into a general discussion where everyone had their say, gave advice and shared their experience. They were glad to know that the girls were going to the holy city, where many of them had not yet been. Maria was comfortable in silence. She was thinking about the week just gone by, letting the emotions settle in her heart and take the place they deserved. They spent the night on the road, sitting tight and uncomfortable, but this time they were prepared and adapted to the discomfort, sleeping when they could no longer keep their eyes open and swapping seats from time to time, so that they could take turns to relax against the window. As they approached the plain the temperature rose. Maria recognized the villages they had crossed on the way there.

Once again, the dust became part of the journey and their bus drove in the middle of the road, daring the vehicles coming from the opposite direction. Instead of the terror felt the first time, Maria and Franca were having fun, watching up to which point the two drivers played chicken; they'd suddenly swerve to the left, thus avoiding a crash that seemed inevitable, and then merrily continued their journey.

They arrived at Old Delhi bus station eighteen hours after leaving Manali, with only one hour delay. Tired but relieved, they climbed onto the roof to take their backpacks. Outside the station they confidently bargained the price of a scooter to the Tourist Camp. The hot air was making their hair flutter, the cheerful wobbly scooter drove along a familiar road; it felt like coming home!

Being still early in the morning the people who lived on the road side were rising. Some brushed their teeth with toothbrush and toothpaste; others used the old system of rubbing a stick carefully and repeatedly between their teeth. They were preparing chai on kerosene stoves, calling the children, having breakfast. The girls were watching the lives of the people whose home was the road.

At the Tourist Camp they asked for two beds in a dormitory, but the receptionist on duty said they were full. They only had a deluxe bungalow with 'bathroom', which cost ten rupees more than two beds in a dormitory. They were very tired and Maria decided to pay the difference; besides, she liked the idea of having a little privacy after so many days sharing their space with other people. There was an Italian girl, the receptionist informed them, who was travelling alone; they were bound to see her. The bungalow was basic, like the one that Sanya and Colin had, but this was one of the very few that had a shower and that hole in the ground which they called the 'bathroom'. As soon as Maria laid her head on her pillow of folded jeans, she fell asleep.

Franca woke her up with a glass of chai and introduced her to Patti, the young Italian woman she had just met at the restaurant. "You've slept three hours," she said. "It's better if you wake up now, otherwise you'll sleep until tonight and then spend the night awake." Addressing Patti, she introduced her, saying: "She's the one who makes friends with the locals." Maria nodded, unable to open her eyes from the extreme tiredness. She drank the chai with her eyes closed, her back leaning awkwardly against the wall, listening to the conversation between the two girls sitting outside the door.

Patti was back in India after a six-year interval, during which time she had had two children and her husband had died. She spoke calmly about it and seemed to have accepted what had happened. Maria pricked up her ears when Patti said that he had been found dead in a field. He was a junkie addicted to opium and someone had killed him, either because of debts, or to steal his opium, no one had ever found out. "Had it not been so, sooner or later he would have died of an overdose," she said. And she, did she use opium? Franca asked with interest. Sometimes, but she had to be careful, because she had become a junkie too, and getting out of it had been very difficult. Where could one buy some? Franca pressed. The best place was Jaipur in Rajasthan, where she was headed the next day; had they ever been? Why didn't they go, too? Maria remembered that Jaipur was the place where Barbara wanted to buy semi-precious stones to then sell in Italy. She had said it was 'real India', the traditional India. She wondered whether it was very far from Delhi.

"Is it far from Delhi?" asked Franca, as if having heard her thoughts. Five hours by bus, said Patti. A doddle, compared to the nineteen they had just done.

"Compared to the journey from Manali, it's a doddle," said Franca. "I'll ask Maria!" With her eyes still closed, Maria said yes, as long as they didn't have to get up early; she was very tired. There were 'de luxe' coaches said Patti, several a day, and they had air conditioning. She was going to find out and maybe they could leave at around two in the afternoon? It sounded good! So, a few days in Jaipur, then back to Delhi, and then to Varanasi. Maria lay down again; she felt a great weariness. Franca prepared a chillum with the charas she had made and they came to smoke it inside the room.

Patti went on to tell: she lived in Milan and, with two small children, she had separated, disillusioned by her husband who did nothing but smoke opium and sell it. Then, determined to break free from the addiction, she had 'locked' herself at home with the children and stopped using it. The first week had been hell, but she had resisted. The second week had been easier and, after about a month, she began to live a new life.

"Where are your kids now?" asked Maria. They were with her sister while she was coming to India to buy things to resell in Milan. She needed money and intended to buy clothes, jewellery and paintings on silk. She could make seven to ten times what she invested and had people ready to buy the things she would bring. Maria was waking up and was very interested.

"Could I go with you some time, so I learn where to go? I am very interested in this thing of buying here and selling in Italy." Of course she could, Patti said with enthusiasm, she would be very happy to go around with a friend.

They decided to continue talking at the restaurant. The stuffy atmosphere made it difficult to breathe and, where they could, they walked in the shade of the young trees. The waiter recognized them and greeted them cordially.

"Everything okay?"

"Yes, thanks, and you?"

"Bahut acchah, very well," he replied, rocking his head. "Where have you been?"

"In Manali."

"Oh, the Valley of the Gods," he said, with a certain deference. While waiting for the food they had ordered, Franca continued to ask questions about opium; she was very interested and Patti was glad to satisfy her curiosity. During this conversation they understood that, in addition to things to resell, she also intended to buy some opium to take back to Italy. Maria had a lot of objections. Wasn't she afraid of getting caught? No, she had a foolproof system. What would happen to her children if she did get caught? She wasn't going to get caught, she was sure. But if she had found it so difficult to get rid of the addiction, why was she going to sell it? It wasn't easy to get addicted, she said, you had to use it for a long time, and she knew people who used it only occasionally, once a month. Franca grew impatient at Maria's questions and cut her off: "I'm more interested in knowing what it's like, I've never tried it. How does it make you feel?"

"It makes you feel good," said Patti. "It relaxes you completely; you don't worry about anything. It makes you daydream. It's beautiful!"

"And how do you take? Do you smoke it?" One could smoke it or eat it. Did she have any here? Franca asked. Yes, a little. If they wanted to try it out, she'd give them a piece. "I do, for sure. And you, Maria? Come on, you try it too."

Maria was a little curious but didn't want to lose control. She didn't have to take it but, as it was happening right under her nose, the experience interested her. She wanted to be able to do the basic things, though, like standing up, preparing her backpack, going to buy her ticket, basically carry on with her life and her activities. Was it possible? Yeah sure, she'd take very little, only enough to get the idea. With some anxiety mixed with excitement, she said she would eat a little piece, but very little, a child's dose. "Not so little for me," Franca said, laughing, "make it a man's dose, a big man!" Patti had it in her room. It was better to take it on an empty stomach, she said, so that they needed less to feel the effect.

The waiter brought the chai and the girls sipped it slowly, blowing to cool it a little. They were excited about trying the opium and going to Jaipur; it was a golden opportunity, given that Patti knew how to get there, where to stay, the best shops and what to buy. She came back with two black pieces of shiny opium that she wrapped in a piece of cigarette paper. Maria's piece was very small, while Franca's was more than double. Feeling her palms sweating, Maria struggled to swallow hers. Franca instead, who couldn't wait, swallowed her piece cheerfully, with a sip of chai.

"And now?" asked Maria.

"Now nothing," Patti soothed her. "Keep doing your things, and eat because, in a little while, you won't feel hungry."

When the waiter brought their order they rushed to eat with enthusiasm; they were starving! Maria finished the rice, chicken, vegetables, and even the pudding and then ordered another chai; she hadn't eaten so well for days. They talked about the shops in Jaipur, the semi-precious stones, rings and earrings that Patti was going to order or purchase directly, if she found enough things she liked. The tailors were very good at copying anything. If she had a suit, or a jacket, made in Italy which she wanted them to copy, within a few hours they'd make a perfect match, or nearly so. You had to watch them closely, she added, otherwise they'd make mistakes. She explained about the paintings on silk she would buy, they were the best in India. She told them about the Hotel Evergreen with its beautiful garden and good restaurant. Jaipur was a very exciting city, she assured them. It would be a great shame to return to Italy without having seen it.

As the minutes passed Maria felt the tiredness resurface; her eyelids were getting heavier and her eyes wanted to close. She had to go to bed; after all they had travelled all night. Franca was also beginning to feel the exhaustion; she had only rested an hour and decided to follow her. In the room, Maria lay down on the bed, her shoulders, her back, her legs were aching. The heat was unbearable and she was sweaty, dirty, her hair full of dust. Sitting on the edge of the bed, she removed her trousers and the t-shirt that had stuck to her skin and closed her eyes, while Franca busied herself in the bathroom. She heard the water from the shower flowing and her friend speaking, but her words were covered by the sound of the water and she couldn't understand anything. Exhausted, lulled by the muffled sounds, she fell into a deep sleep. She dreamed that she was lying in the sun on the shore of a lake surrounded by green mountains, the sun warmed her and made her sweat. She woke up to go to the bathroom, feeling so heavy she could barely lift a hand. She turned her head on the 'pillow' and, with an effort, she opened one eye. Franca, sitting on her bed, was looking at her.

"I'm all sweaty… I fell asleep," said Maria. "I can't wake up. I'm so tired!"

"You slept like an angel," said Franca, looking serious, "… you were beautiful."

"Mmmmm. Thank you. You are not too bad yourself," Maria laughed, half asleep.

"No way. I'm not saying I am a monster, but I'm definitely not as beautiful as you."

Maria turned toward Franca; her eyelids were as heavy as lead shutters. "If I don't go to the bathroom I'll wee myself, but I can't move." She half-opened her eyes and saw that Franca was watching her in silence. She had showered and her long hair was still wet. Sitting naked cross-legged on the bed, she was making a joint, strange for her who preferred chillums. "Well, I can't go for you," she said. "While you are at it, take a shower; it will make you feel better."

Slowly Maria sat on the edge of the bed, trying to find the strength to get up. Supporting herself against the walls, she made it to the bathroom.

"Leave the door open," said Franca "otherwise you'll die of heat in there."

From the tap came a weak jet of warm water. She lathered without hurry and washed her hair with shampoo, letting the poor flow of the shower rinse her slowly. She came out dripping, without a towel; she had forgotten to take it out of her backpack. She was stunned by tiredness and maybe the opium was taking effect. She would dry in no time in that heat, Franca assured her, who had lit up her joint and was smoking it, her back against the wall, her legs crossed. She followed Maria with her eyes as she moved about the room.

"You want to smoke?"

"If I smoke I'll fall asleep."

"It's okay! Just have a toke. Come on, take it!"

Maria sat on the bed and took the joint that Franca offered her.

"You're so beautiful!" she said again, looking at her without smiling.

"Oh, come on, drop it!" Maria took a drag and gave the joint back to her. She adjusted the 'pillow' under her head and lay down, as she was, naked, with wet hair. She closed her eyes for a moment, and fell asleep again. This time she dreamed of being in a big tub of hot water, along with other people, men and women, whom she didn't know. They were washing her with bubble bath and massaging her legs and back. There was a strong good scent. She woke up to find Franca massaging her back: "How wonderful! What are you doing?"

"I'm putting coconut oil on your back. I've already done your legs but you didn't wake up." Maria lay motionless, receiving with delight the expert massage that Franca was giving her, sitting astride her legs and buttocks. "I didn't know you could give massage," she mumbled, her mouth on the pillow.

"Sure! I'm very good."

"Will you teach me?"

"Of course! Then you can give one to me."

Maria was lulled by the strong and experienced massage and fell asleep, while Franca was smoothing her back, shoulders, neck, arms, hands, head, and dreamed of Ugo. He touched her with love, and passion. But then his face faded and became Paul's face. She dreamed and didn't know whether she was awake or asleep, she was between the two states, tranquil. Hours later she opened her eyes and looked at Franca, who was fast asleep beside her, still naked. She leaned her head back and closed her eyes, content and relaxed.

They got up to go to the restaurant but didn't have much appetite. They ordered one chai after another, spoke little and slowly. They couldn't do anything in a hurry and it was fine. Patti told them of her life in Milan, a second baby quickly followed the first, and Rocco was arrested at the airport and sentenced to three years for smuggling drugs. He had got off lightly because he was a drug addict, a junkie and, as such, unable to make sensible decisions. In those three years alone she devoted herself to raising the children, consecrating her life to their happiness. After serving his sentence, Rocco begged her to take him back, but she knew he would never change and kept him at arm's length. One day the doorbell rang; she opened the door to a policeman with his cap in hand. Was she Rocco Malvolta's wife? It was over, that poor life of his, ruined, thrown away, like all those years spent 'using'. He had had happiness to hand, but hadn't been able to see it; instead he was looking for it in opium, deceived by the illusion of a life without problems. As if a life without problems ever existed. Only with his death they were over. What a price to pay! Patti's eyes grew moist with tears. It was such a shame, she said, blowing her nose, because Rocco was a good person, but weak, and had let himself be overwhelmed by drugs. What a wasted life! Did she miss him? No, she didn't miss him, but she was sorry, without a doubt. Things could have been so different if only he had had the strength to stop. He could have been a real father to their children. He would go to the park with them; take them to eat pizza; visit their grandmother; help them with their homework. Instead... She wiped her eyes and sat up straight. Well! Tomorrow, what time did they want to leave? At two o'clock there was a 'de luxe' bus which arrived in Jaipur at about seven. Was that okay? It was perfect!

It was nice to travel with someone who knew where to go. Between Franca and Patti they decided everything and Maria enjoyed being led. The bus ride was comfortable, even if they couldn't open the windows because of the air conditioning. She preferred by far the dust and the noise to that sense of claustrophobia, of separation from the people of the villages they crossed, barricaded behind the tinted glass, imprisoned by comfort and progress. The hours passed between a nap and a daydream. The effect of opium was still slightly noticeable. She felt less involved with the outside world, separate from reality, as if everything that was happening around her didn't matter. She had no desire or interest in talking to people; she just wanted to look out the window and let her thoughts wander.

The impact of Jaipur was very strong. What a place! What people! The massive Pink Fort greeted them from the main road. Hundreds of rickshaws flooded the streets and their coach was surrounded by them. Rajastani men wore huge turbans in brilliant colours, rolled above their heads and matched by the exaggerated moustache that gave them an almost savage appearance. Patti explained that they belonged to the caste of the Rajput warriors in the Hindu religion; they were proud people, courageous and cheerful at the same time. The women wore bright multicoloured skirts that stopped just above their ankles, embroidered with threads of contrasting colours and richly embellished with mirrors and beads. Their legs were adorned with large silver anklets that jingled at every step. The short blouses left their backs bare from the bottom of the shoulder blades down to the waist, while long and light cotton shawls of vivid colours covered their heads, fluttering with every movement and every breath of wind. The colours of the Rajastani clothes were very strong: bright pink, sparkling red, pea green, yellow with the intensity and warmth of the sun; close to each other they filled the eyes with a variety and strength of colour far surpassing those seen in Delhi.

A noble dignity accompanied the apparent poverty of these people, conveying an alchemy of courage and pride, friendliness and simplicity. The rickshaws were offering their services in a discreet way; at the first expression of denial, they continued on their way without insisting. Maria felt immediately at ease, fascinated by these people. It would have been relaxing to walk around Jaipur, had it not been for the heat which was more intense than in Delhi.

"How many degrees do you think it is?" asked Maria gasping.

"Around forty," Patti said. "We are close to the desert of Thar. It's much hotter here than in Delhi."

She was glad they had arrived in the late afternoon, when the fierce heat of the midday sun had begun to decline.

The hotel Evergreen consisted of a cosy rectangular courtyard, adorned by a lush garden and surrounded by a score of rooms on the ground floor; basic and cheap. Luxuriant flowering trees created large areas of fragrant shade on the long tables and benches in the courtyard, ready to welcome the visitors. On the far side was the restaurant counter, which took orders and communicated them to the kitchen. An atmosphere of relaxed familiarity pervaded the hotel and its garden. Patti asked if they had three beds in the dormitory: they had only one, which they could offer for four rupees, and a twin room for ten. Patti took the bed in the dormitory while Maria and Franca took the room with two beds. Maria put her luggage down, leaving Franca in the room to prepare the inevitable 'arrival' chillum.

She sat in the garden and looked around, trying to guess the nationality of the people sitting there. There was a group of Germans; that was easy to understand because she could hear them talk, and a couple of Nordic guys, either Danish, or Norwegian, or Swedish. She saw a beautiful girl who spoke with a couple of blond boys; she was more or less her age and a ravishing beauty. She had regular features and large eyes, smiled freely and laughed often. Maria couldn't take her eyes off her and tried to glance at her sideways, so as not to get caught staring. She would have liked to speak to her, but it didn't seem to be the right time. Shortly afterwards the two boys left and the girl remained alone.

Franca arrived just then with Patti and sat down next to Maria. The girl got up and disappeared into one of the rooms. They ordered something to eat and while they waited, Patti shared her programme for the next day. She would go on a tour of the shops in the afternoon, which both Maria and Franca were welcome to join. In the morning she would go looking for a friend whom she had met years back, hoping to find him.

If they wanted to, they could take advantage of the morning hours to visit Jaipur.

They relaxed and ate dinner, while the garden was filling with young people coming back after a long day around the city. There were visitors of all nationalities, French, British, Germans, Scandinavians, Italians, Israelis, and even Indians from South India who had come to visit the capital of one of the most traditional, cheerful and vibrant states of the Indian continent.

Maria noticed how Franca took advantage of every opportunity to be close to her, something she had never done before; she was polite, attentive to her every wish. "Do you want a chai?" she'd ask eagerly, or "Do you want to sit here? It's more comfortable." Yes, thank you, no thank you. She was surprised, almost embarrassed by Franca's attentions; it felt as if she was being courted, with these affectionate attentions, such a contrast to her behaviour up till now. As always, she'd make a chillum at every opportunity, but this time she offered it to her to light or passed it to her before passing it to someone else, a courtesy that Maria regularly refused. Nevertheless, she had the strong impression of being treated in a special and different way. Something had changed since the experience with opium. It was pleasant, but at the same time unexpected and she needed to get used to the new dynamic; it was as if Franca was driving and, all of a sudden, had changed gear.

Maria decided to go to sleep early, tired of the many hours travelling during those two days. She lay down in bed and closed her eyes, assuming that Franca would remain in the garden to smoke. Instead, shortly afterward she came into the room. She asked her whether she was all right and offered to give her a back massage. Who would refuse a massage? She let herself relax under Franca's expert hands, which stroked, kneaded and smoothed her tired aching shoulders, back and legs. Where had she learned? She had done a course. Underneath the expert touch, Maria felt affection and warmth made of caring, tenderness, even sensuality, of which she didn't think Franca was capable. She fell asleep with her friend caressing her.

When she woke up it was already morning and Franca was sleeping next to her, with a scarf over her eyes.

She went out into the almost deserted garden and ordered a chai. As she sat drinking it, she saw the beautiful girl from the day before, going out. She smiled at her and wished her a good morning. The girl replied in English: "Good morning!" with a cheerful tone and an open smile. She hesitated a moment, as if she wanted to stop and talk, but seemed to be in a hurry and thought better of it. She made a gesture with her hand, meaning 'see you later' and left, walking quickly, as if to an appointment.

Maria brought Franca a coffee, hoping to wake her up. "If we are going to see Jaipur we'd better go early, otherwise it gets too hot." Her friend nodded and smiled without opening her eyes, swollen with fatigue. She sipped the coffee with her eyes closed, fighting against sleep. Maria went into the garden and picked a half hidden corner; she sat down and began to recite the phrase of which she often thought, but hadn't pronounced for days. The sound and the vibrations made her feel good, aligning her mind and heart in perfect harmony. It seemed so natural and made her feel more peaceful, and stronger. It felt as if she were putting down deep roots that anchored her, wherever she was, and she had a feeling that the roots were in her life itself. After ten minutes she felt calm, alert and ready for a new day. Franca joined her and looked at her twice. "You look radiant!" she said. It was a good description of how she felt inside.

They took a rickshaw and along the way saw a beautiful building in the middle of a lake, which looked like a royal palace. The rickshaw guy said it was the Jal Mahal, the water palace; did they want to go there by boat? Maybe another time, now they wanted to go to the market. They went past two elephants with their trunks curled, carrying a tree trunk, advancing slowly, heavily, shifting the weight of their enormous tonnage from one foot to the other, without haste, their grey wrinkled and flabby skin close enough for them to stroke it.

The market came closer with an explosion of colours: fresh flowers, white, yellow, red, gave off a strong sweet scent. There were piles of neatly stacked oranges and tangerines. The pungent smells of spices, in cones of all colours and protruding from jute bags, tickled their nostrils. Cloths and fabrics of light cotton, hand-printed in geometric designs, shawls and scarves made of raw silk, all caught the reflections of the sun and changed with every little rustle of wind. Cups, bowls and earthen pots; statues of Hindu gods made of stone, copper, bronze and, everywhere, bullock carts, whose strong odours, both unpleasant and natural, mixed with the smell of sewage, cardamom, cloves and cinnamon: another world, other noises, different odours, another rhythm, chaotic and, at the same time, fascinating.

They felt the eyes of men and women on them, curious, interested. A snake charmer started playing as soon as he saw them from afar, and when they approached, he lifted the basket lid: an impressive king cobra with a flat diamond shaped head began to rise, swinging the royal head from side to side, while its forked tongue stuck out fast, withdrew and stuck out again to the sound of his master's flute. Maria had brought the camera with her. She took it out of its bag and began shooting, capturing the amazing images of such a different world. The snake charmer demanded money and she willingly gave him one rupee.

A young man approached them and asked if they wanted a guide, he knew where to take them to take good pictures. Franca didn't want him and tried to send him away, but Maria liked his honest face and thought his presence would be like a business card, an intermediary between them and the local people. She asked him what he usually did. He was a student and wanted to talk with them to learn something about their country, to exchange information on their two cultures, which were so different. He was called Rajiv and followed them discreetly. He explained that Jaipur was a great centre for dyeing and printing fabrics by hand and invited them to follow him into a small courtyard where the dyeing was being carried out at that precise moment.

Women at work looked at the girls, smiling and curious. With gestures, they invited them to sit close, while the word 'chai' went from mouth to mouth. At a request of Rajiv, the women started a new dyeing process, so that the girls could see it from beginning to end. They folded a cotton shawl in three, they wrought it, twisting it and wrapping it tightly; then they tied it with string in different places and began to dip it in buckets filled with liquids of different colours, a little black, a little yellow, a little red. Meanwhile, a boy came from the nearby restaurant carrying a tray with three 'masala' chai; it was the traditional chai of the neighbourhood, said Rajiv, prepared with a mixture of different spices. Maria offered to pay for it, but Rajiv refused: they were his guests. They sipped it slowly, while the dyeing process progressed, step by step. Once finished, they opened the fabric while still wet: it had become a shawl with geometric designs in three colours on a white background. They hung it up and, with a temperature of more than forty degrees, it would dry in a few minutes. Maria photographed it, including in the photo the women who had made it. Did they want to buy it? It cost five rupees. Sure, with pleasure.

A woman approached Rajiv and said something, smiling and looking at the girls. Did they want to eat with them? They were invited to lunch with the women. Maria and Franca joined hands in front of their chest, thanking them, but they didn't have time. The woman said something else and Rajiv asked if they would agree to eat some samosas, they would arrive soon. It was impossible to turn down such a kind invitation. The samosas arrived a few minutes later, accompanied by more glasses of chai. Again, they didn't let them pay. The women motioned that no, they were their guests. While they were eating, questions began to flock through the translation of Rajiv. How old were they? Were they married? No? How was it possible? No children? The women were repeating every reply so that all the workers became involved in the conversation. Did they have a boyfriend? Yes? The girls perceived that they wanted to know whether they had intimate relationships, but they didn't dare to ask. This unspoken question provoked waves of general giggles that crossed the courtyard. The women laughed and looked at the girls, and the girls laughed in turn, feeling the curiosity, the impertinence, the humour in that genuine communication between Rajastani women, belonging to a traditional culture, and two Italian, more modern, women; but at that time they were all simply, equally, women.

Maria asked to see other shawls and the older worker brought her ten. She chose three to buy. The women wanted her to choose another one, as a gift, and then insisted that Franca chose one, too. What a great people, what heart; Maria left a piece of hers there in the yard. She was learning what trust was, as well as unconditional friendship, endless generosity, and the joy that came from the simplicity of a life that, despite the shortage of money, had far more precious values.

Rajiv accompanied them to where they could catch a rickshaw to get back to the Evergreen. Maria tried to give him five rupees, but he only wanted their address, and to correspond with them in English. Knowing that she wouldn't do so, Maria insisted and slipped a five-rupee note in his shirt pocket, telling him that it was for his studies. Only in this way, the young dignified student accepted it.

Patti hadn't arrived yet. Franca sat on a bench and began to talk to some English people, while Maria took the opportunity to go for a rest. Her friend came into the room to get the chillum and her charas. Was she all right? she asked with concern. Did she want her to stay there? No no, thank you! What on earth was happening? Something had definitely changed; she didn't know what it was, but maybe she preferred the way Franca was before. When Patti arrived, Franca withdrew with her for almost an hour and it was five o'clock before they reappeared to go to the shops, most of which were in the vicinity of the Evergreen.

They visited a shop where they sold exquisite paintings on silk. Sitting cross-legged on the floor covered with soft white mattresses, they looked at one piece of art after another, unrolled before their eyes by the owner. Patti was experienced and she quickly chose what she wanted. In less than half an hour she decided to buy ten paintings. They were representations in Mogul style of ancient scenes of men and women, kings and queens, courtiers and warriors, skilfully painted on silk, beautifully elaborated in minute details. The owner carefully rolled them up and put them inside a rigid tube.

Then it was the jeweller's turn. Patti had her supplier, who recognized her as soon as she set foot in his shop, even though it had been many years since the last time, and welcomed her warmly. Seated on high stools, their arms crossed on the glass counter, bright lamps shining light over their heads, they admired tens, hundreds of rings, bracelets, earrings, necklaces, anklets and semi-precious stones such as white rounded moonstones, purple amethyst, dark red grenades, black stars, brown tiger eyes streaked with yellow, turquoise, dark blue lapis lazuli with gold flecks, opals in different colours and shades, and then emeralds, topaz, rubies. Patti decided to buy only semi-precious stones as synthetic versions of precious stones were virtually indistinguishable from the natural ones, and this made for a risky trade; it was more likely to get cheated than not, she explained.

Franca wanted to buy a silver anklet, but the shopkeeper insisted that she should wear two, not one. He strove to explain that women who wore only one were 'easy' women, women 'of the trade', but she didn't want to know about buying two and said that she didn't care what others thought. She bought a chunky one and wore it on her left ankle, defiant and confident. The shopkeeper looked at her, shaking his head, but Franca sent him light-heartedly to hell and left the store saying that she liked to go against the tide.

The evening at the Evergreen was interesting, with an infinite number of young foreigners who came and sat next to each other on the long benches, so that it was impossible not to make friends. Maria saw the beautiful girl arrive late, sit at a table farther away and exchange a few words with a couple. She seemed to be travelling alone. At each table people were smoking chillums and joints. There were those who smoked them all, like Franca, those who smoked just a little, like Maria, and some who didn't smoke at all, like the beautiful girl who passed them without smoking them. Maria went to bed early, exhausted after a busy day. After a while, Franca joined her, asking her if she needed anything, offering her a massage to relax. While savouring the expert touch of her massage, Maria knew that Franca's new behaviour didn't convince her and made her feel uncomfortable. She fell asleep while her friend's hands slid slowly from her shoulders down. Her doubts would wait until tomorrow.

13. You are the Treasure Tower

She got up early; it was hot even at night and sleeping was difficult. She decided to take advantage of the early hours of the morning when it was cooler and the garden of the Evergreen was still deserted. Franca was fast asleep with the faithful scarf over her eyes. Maria went out and closed the door, careful not to make a noise.

She looked around and noticed the beautiful girl from the day before; she was sitting in a quiet, partly hidden corner of the garden with her back to the courtyard, clearly wishing to be alone. She held her palms together in front of her and seemed to be meditating. Maria walked to the opposite side of the garden, carefully chose an equally quiet corner and, just like the girl, sat down with her back to the courtyard to create the illusion of being alone; she was going to meditate in silence, too. She closed her eyes and took a deep breath, trying to empty her mind, as she had learned from books. She breathed in deeply and began to feel a certain peace inside. It was short-lived. Her thoughts were thronging to get to the forefront, her head felt like Milan's railway station during rush hour, with trains departing and arriving, people coming and going, announcements from the speakers, and on and on! She was sinking into a world of resentment and unhappiness; negative thoughts had grabbed her by the hair and were pulling her back toward the past that had made her suffer, from which she had left.

She kicked against that unpleasant force; she wanted to stop the neurotic insane activity of her mind. Stop! Enough is enough. She stopped it like stopping a car in an emergency situation, slamming her foot on the brake. No more, stop! She wanted to feel good, now. She folded her palms in front of her diaphragm and began reciting in a low voice Nam-myoho-renge-kyo, Nam-myoho-renge-kyo, Nam-myoho-renge-kyo... for her happiness and for the happiness of others. Many faces appeared in front of her closed eyes: Franca, Patti, Barbara, Carla, Surinder, Ester, her mother, Ugo, Karen, Paul, the beautiful girl a few steps away from her, and out of her heart flowed a river full of desire for their happiness.

For every face she saw, she responded by sending them that sound, which was flying into the air and mingling with the breeze, wishing him or her to be happy; she was setting them free and becoming free herself. She felt strength rise inside and fill her chest; she became aware of a cheerful energy, a lightness, a clarity that was still new, but definitely real. She focused on chanting for her happiness, because this was more difficult; she forgot about it and had to consciously remind herself. But it worked, and soon a smile came to her lips and her heart opened up, naturally. Without realizing it, she was chanting with more energy and in a louder voice. After a few minutes she ended on a joyful note and bowed her head, her lips relaxed on her folded hands. She paused, sitting there, enjoying the clean and positive energy that filled her, smiling to herself, quiet, happy to be alive.

She turned to the garden and saw the beautiful girl coming toward her, who, even before reaching her stuck her hand out, smiling. "Hi, I'm Luna," she said cheerfully in Italian. "I heard you chant. Did you know that I was doing the same thing?"
"You're joking!" Maria laughed, surprised. "Are there are many people who practice this thing then?"
"No, not at all, we are very few. That's why it is so special to hear it from someone else!"
They sat together at a table under a leafy tree and ordered a coffee from the waiter, who had just arrived and was opening the restaurant.

Luna told her that she lived in London, her father was English and her mother Italian. She spoke the language with an interesting accent but just like a young Italian. She had five cousins in Italy, whom she had seen every year of her life. Through talking with them, she had transformed the Italian her mother had taught her into a more colloquial one. She had been practicing Buddhism for a couple of years and was very happy; in a way she had become more 'herself'. She was changing every day, she said, developing and improving herself, and was looking to the future with excitement, confidence and great enthusiasm.
Luna wanted to know about her and, without knowing how or why, Maria found herself talking to her about Ugo, their ambiguous relationship, full of pain, and how she had lost herself. Now she was trying to understand who she really was. Luna listened without interrupting and Maria continued to empty the heavy baggage she kept inside until she had told her everything. There was a long silence. Luna nodded to let her know she was thinking about what she had just heard. Eventually, she looked at her with a smile and asked: "Have you ever heard of the Treasure Tower?"
Maria shook her head: "No, never heard of it! What is it?"

Luna sat astride on the bench and Maria turned toward her, while the waiter placed two glasses of hot coffee on the table. "Dhanyavad!" she said with a smile, and he bowed, grinning. The Treasure Tower, she began, was an image that Shakyamuni Buddha had used to explain an important and beautiful concept. He had understood that within each person there was a huge potential for kindness, compassion, creativity and originality, but how could he explain it in a way that everyone could understand and remember? He spoke to people of all social strata, some were educated, but most of them were not and he wanted everyone to understand. So he told a parable in which he said that during an important event called the Ceremony in the Air, from the earth emerged a tower of enormous dimensions that rose up and was suspended in the air. This tower was encrusted with precious stones: diamonds, rubies, sapphires, lapis lazuli, turquoise, garnets... the people present at the meeting gasped in awe, admiring this wonderful tower. "It's a beautiful image, isn't it?" she said. "It sticks in your mind."

"Yes, it's very vivid. But what does it mean?"

Luna nodded, beaming. It expressed the infinite beauty that each of us has within. It is a potential that we can all develop, she added, from the moment we realize that we have this precious jewel inside. It is the life state of Buddhahood, our divinity. When we devote time to the quality of our lives, which is what we do when we chant, compassion, wisdom, courage and life force, qualities we already have inside, begin to emerge and manifest in a natural way; that's when we begin to behave differently, with more respect for life. She took another short break, smiling. Then pointing her finger to Maria she said: "You are the Treasure Tower; inside you, Maria, is the Treasure Tower. Your life is the Treasure Tower."

Maria felt moved by those words, spoken in that way. "But then you, too," she said, pointing her index finger toward Luna, "are the Treasure Tower!"

Her new friend laughed. "You have just completed the most important concept that lies at the foundation of all Buddhist philosophy," she said.

She explained that when we understand and accept that we really have this huge potential, we come to realize that everyone else has it, too. It is so simple, but it changes your life. She was getting more inspired. Leaning forward she pointed her finger toward herself and toward Maria, saying: "I am the Treasure Tower and you are the Treasure Tower. From the point of view of our humanity, there is no difference between me, you and every other human being. Every person has this tower inside, even if he or she doesn't know. This is why I respect you, I don't want to hurt you, I don't go to war with you, shoot you, kill you, or want to cause you any pain. On the contrary, I want you to be happy."

Maria nodded slowly, taking in the words and feeling the conviction behind them.

"Do you realize *how far* it takes us when we practice this philosophy of life?" Luna continued, her eyes sparkling. "It leads us to create world peace!"

Maria sighed. She was sorry to cool her enthusiasm, but things were not as simple as Luna made them sound. "Yes, I can believe in this beautiful ideal, and I can try to put it into practice, but if others continue to make war, to disrespect fellow human beings, there will always be war. It is utopian to think that we can change the world and create peace," she objected. "And anyway, if a potential is not developed, we remain very different people, some good, some bad."

"A utopia is an ideal that is not yet a reality, not an impossible ideal," said Luna, settling on the bench and taking a sip of the coffee they had almost forgotten about. "Good and evil are things that we all have inside; there are no 'goodies' on one side and 'baddies' on the other. It *would* be impossible to create peace, if we thought that only the '*others*' have to change, but Buddhism teaches that we cannot change other people. If we want to change a situation that we don't like, we have to start from here…" she said, pointing at her heart, "from ourselves." As Maria was taking a sip of coffee, she continued: "It may seem little, but it's not," she assured her. "Every time I make a small change in the way I think, this is reflected in my behaviour, in my words, and then in my environment. Consequently, as a response to my small change, the other person's behaviour will also change. There's a nice image, a story that was told centuries ago."

"I love ancient stories!" Maria said, taking a sip of her coffee.

Luna smiled and started: "There was a man who stood in front of the mirror and thought: If the mirror bows and shows me respect, I will bow myself and show *him* respect; this way we'll get along!" Maria smiled; she could guess how the story would end. Luna continued: "He stood in front of the mirror, but of course nothing happened. The longer he waited the more upset he became. 'Why on earth doesn't he bow?' He thought. 'It seems clear that he has no respect for me.' He even considered punching the mirror, to teach it a lesson in how to behave."

"Okay, I understand what you are trying to say," said Maria with impetus. "If I want to be respected, I must bow in front of the mirror. In this way, my reflection will answer me by bowing in response."

"Exactly!" confirmed Luna. "What happens in our environment is a reflection of our behaviour. Peace in the world starts from here," she said, pointing her finger at herself. "It is true that it's not easy, but if we try to change what is outside of us, without changing the values that exists *within* us, we will continue to repeat the same mistakes, because the tendency toward destruction is part of human nature, as much as Buddhahood is a real potential. Only when we perceive another person's suffering as if it were our own, then we will be able to put an end to wars."

Maria nodded. "Yes, but how do you change this destructive tendency," she asked. "If it's part of human nature, we will always have it, right?"

"True," agreed Luna. "But each one of us can transform our life, creating it every day! We are free to choose. What do I want to develop, my positive attitude, be happy and live in peace? Or shall I let my negativity win?" she said with conviction. "This is why we chant Nam-myoho-renge-kyo. When we recite this phrase, *with the desire to see the Buddha* that is within us, our anger turns into a strong desire for justice, ignorance becomes wisdom and greed turns into compassion. We take responsibility for our lives and transform poison into medicine."

Maria interrupted her, because a word she had said had struck her: "You said 'ignorance'. What a strange word to use!"

"In Buddhism it has a precise meaning," Luna replied. "It means that we don't recognize, or are not aware of, this huge potential we have, Buddhahood, this hidden jewel within ourselves and, consequently, in others. When we accept this concept, everything changes; we are on the path to enlightenment, and indeed, one might say that this *is* enlightenment." Maria nodded, she was reflecting. Luna asked: "How do you feel when you chant?"

"It makes me feel happier, it changes any feeling of unhappiness into a sense of... calm, I'd call it," replied Maria. Luna listened carefully. "Before, when I chanted, for example, at the beginning I was feeling sad, I was thinking about the past, as I told you. Then I realized that I was tired of living this way and I rebelled. So, I began to chant for my happiness and the happiness of others. Many people that I love came up, including Ugo, and *you!*" she added, suddenly remembering. "Little by little, I felt free, like a bird taking flight. To be precise, I felt happy. It's a big word! It feels almost strange to use such a word, because I don't think I've ever felt this kind of emotion before: it's a mixture of joy and freedom."

Luna nodded in silence. Maria waited for her to say something, but she took the coffee and sipped it in silence, so she continued, hesitating: "Since Sanya and Colin taught me, they are two friends I met in Delhi, do you know them?" Luna shook her head. "Since then, the times when I've chanted I've always felt different, kinder, I must say. But the interesting thing is what happens afterward..." As Luna showed no sign of stopping her, she carried on: "The first time I was in Delhi and, after ten minutes of 'daimoku', that's how it's called, right?" Her friend nodded, smiling, "I went to Janpath alone, to take a stroll. Instead of struggling to make my way among the people, pushing and dodging, as I had done before, I felt as if the 'others' were my brothers or my sisters. You know when you see this immense crowd walking and the heads bob up and down like a wave in the sea? Sometimes I feel overwhelmed by the multitude, all stuck to one another, but that day I felt great empathy with everyone; the man who walked next to me on my right; the woman with a red shawl that pushed me from the left; the other behind me carrying a bundle on his head; the one in front that slowed down or stopped when he couldn't move forward. They didn't bother the way the crowd bothered me other times, their closeness was almost... " she hesitated before finding the word that expressed her feeling, "... comforting!" Luna nodded. "I realized that we were many and that we could walk together, *cooperating*, instead of huffing, puffing and suffering. I became part of that wave of humanity and I was moving like the water of a wave moves, all together in the same direction, without resisting. When my eyes caught the other people's eyes, they smiled at me and I, of course, smiled at them." She paused and picked up her coffee. Luna nodded and only said 'Beautiful!' waiting for her to continue.

Encouraged, Maria, who was beginning to remember the rest of the day, went on: "When I went past a fabric shop where they sold beautiful sarongs, the shopkeeper called me, you know how they do, 'Madam, Madam, please come inside!' Normally I would have carried on, instead that day I thought, why not? I'll stop. I looked at him with new eyes. Instead of thinking he would put pressure on me to buy things I didn't want, and while it's also true that they do that, I saw a man who worked for a living, who did his best, and I relaxed, feeling that this man was 'my brother'. I didn't feel defensive, you know?"

"Yes, I know what you mean," Luna replied, looking at her with understanding.

"He ordered chai and showed me a lot of things. We talked about his life, his family, and then about my life, because he wanted to know everything, if I was married, why not, what I did, how much I earned, and on and on." They both laughed, because what Maria described was so true! "After half an hour, I bought a sarong and nothing else. As we continued to talk, he quietly folded the things he had opened for me, the mountain of silk saris, shimmering fabrics, hand embroidered shawls, and was no longer trying to sell me anything." She paused and took another sip of coffee. "We took leave from each other with affection. I felt there was friendship and mutual respect. It was a great experience and a joy to be in the centre of Delhi. What a difference!"

"And do you think this was because you had chanted before going out?" Luna asked.

"I'm sure it was! Because I felt completely different! I felt... at peace within, happy, enthusiastic; and... I felt a sense of trust that I had never experienced before."

"That's what we were saying earlier on, that the environment is a mirror of how we feel inside. When you bow to the mirror the reflected image bows back to you."

"That's true," confirmed Maria. "Before, you said that we must take responsibility for our lives. Sanya also said the same!"

Since Luna nodded, she continued: "Going back to my story, Ugo compared me to his previous girlfriend, he brought her to our house and they made love while I was in the room next door; he kissed other girls in front of me, didn't come home at night, and so on..." Luna was listening and seemed to know what Maria was going to say. "... In what way is it my responsibility? It was he who behaved like that, wasn't it? It seems to me that it was *his* responsibility, not mine. It was he who hurt me."

Luna tilted her head and took a deep breath, as if to say 'Well, yes and no, it depends.' She said: "He is responsible for his actions, there's no doubt about that, but you had a choice, did you not?" She looked straight into her eyes. "We always have a choice. You could have broken off the relationship with him. Why did you choose to continue?"

"Because I loved him. I wanted to be with him. When we were fine, it was beautiful. Unfortunately, the times when there were no conflicts were very few," replied Maria, remembering how she had suffered. "Many times I said 'That's enough, it's over' and walked away. But as soon as I began to make a new life for myself, found a bit of strength and balance, he came back to me. The relationship started again, until the next episode of infidelity."

"Taking responsibility in this case meant choosing to stay in the relationship, even if it made you suffer; because you were not a victim, you always had the option not to go back to him!" declared Luna. She looked at her for a moment, hesitating, and then decided to continue. "I also found myself in a similar situation."

"You? But you're beautiful!" exclaimed Maria. "How can any man possibly want to cheat on you?"

Luna laughed: "Thank you for the compliment, but it is quite possible. I was with my boyfriend, Mike, for four years, and things hadn't been going well for some time. He was kind, I liked his family, but he never took the initiative on anything. If I didn't organize a trip or an evening out, he'd stay at home with his friends watching football, drinking beer and smoking joints."

"How boring!" snapped Maria. "So, what did you do?"

"Well nothing, we carried on like this, until one day I discovered that he had telephone conversations, consistently, with another girl and that he had stopped the night at her place at least twice."

"No! And so?"

"I confronted him. At first he denied it, but I had gathered some information from a friend, and once his back was against the wall, he admitted that there was something between them."

"What an asshole!" burst out Maria. Luna smiled at the way she was getting involved.

"Exactly. The result of that 'something' was that the girl was pregnant and decided to keep the baby." She laughed, seeing Maria with her mouth open. "And so it was clear what I had to do. I closed the relationship, although he insisted that he loved me and that the story with the other girl consisted of a couple of episodes, when he'd had too much to drink. I suffered for a few months, but I'm fine now and I look forward to the future, because I have many things to do," she concluded with simplicity.

"When did this happen?" Maria asked, suspecting it was still a fresh thing.

"Two years ago," said Luna. "I was very depressed. But then I discovered Buddhism and everything began to change. I took responsibility for my decisions and I realized that I wasn't a victim. I continue to chant for my happiness and I know that, sooner or later, I'll meet the right person for me. In a sense, I am grateful to Mike because he pushed me to end a relationship that had been stale for a long time. "

"Then should I be grateful to Ugo?" asked Maria.

"Sure, why not? Look at it from this point of view: if it hadn't been for his loose behaviour, you'd still be in a situation where, in the end, you lacked respect for yourself, waiting every night to see if he chose to come home to you or go somewhere else. Instead you're here, you're experiencing the world, you're opening your eyes to life, and you're not wasting your time. I don't think you'll make the same mistakes again, right?"

Maria wasn't so sure. Luna explained that, when she felt a victim, she gave up all her power.

"It's like handing over to someone else the reins of your life, the steering wheel of your car," she said. "There, take, you drive!" She mimicked giving her some imaginary reins. "Instead, when you accept your responsibility, you take back those reins, that steering wheel." She paused. "Okay, I'm wrong, you say! I stayed in that relationship without respect: *my responsibility*. I could have left, but I didn't: *my responsibility*."

Maria nodded slowly, beginning to recognize the point of view that was being put to her. Luna leaned forward, her big green eyes sparkling with enthusiasm. "Start from now!" she said. "You can be grateful for all that you've learned!" Seeing the expression on Maria's face, she continued with conviction: "Think how much compassion you have developed. Through suffering we learn quickly and then we are able to understand another person who is experiencing a similar situation, as I understand you now."

"This is true, but being grateful, I don't know. It seems over the top!"

Luna laughed. "Would you have come to India if it hadn't been for him?" she asked, watching her.

"No, I'd still be there," replied Maria, confidently, "waiting to go on holiday with someone, *perhaps* with him, but maybe not."

"And then you wouldn't have seen these places; you wouldn't have met Indian people; you wouldn't be having the experiences you're having now. Don't you think India is changing your life?"

"Ah, without a doubt!" replied Maria.

Luna pressed on: "You wouldn't have met me or Sanya and Colin, or Nam-myoho-renge-kyo. You are opening your heart and your life!" She leaned toward her and, looking at her with affection, she said: "You will become happy, Maria, happier than you can imagine." She returned the look of hope she saw in Maria's eyes and continued: "Each of us has a mission in life; that's why we were born. Your mission is uniquely yours. No one else can do what you'll do, no one else can say what you'll say, to comfort, encourage, empower, and create happiness... and peace in the world." Maria looked at her, but couldn't speak. Luna continued: "Your mission is to become happy and make others happy Maria, in your own way, just as I do it in my way. You don't realize how much power you have, how beautiful you are inside, how unique and wonderful you really are."

Maria had never felt beautiful, nor unique or wonderful, but Luna was saying these things with such conviction that she could almost believe her. She let the sound of Luna's words fill her with wonder for a moment longer, before expressing her doubt: "But how can you be so sure that I will be happy? We've only just met and you know very little about me."

"True," said Luna, laughing. "I've just met you, and I tell you that you *can* become happy, happier than you can imagine. Because being happy is a choice we make. It depends on you!"

"Of course I want to be happy, but you say it depends on me. So tell me how it's done! Is there a secret? A technique?" Maria asked, laughing at the naivety of her question.

Luna surprised her with her answer: "Yes, there is indeed a technique, as you put it. It's not a secret. Have you ever heard of the law of cause and effect?"

"Well, yes. You reap what you sow, don't you? It makes sense," said Maria.

"Indeed, it makes sense! And it is a very simple 'technique'." Luna took the last sip of her coffee. The courtyard was filling up with people who were having breakfast, the heat was beginning to become noticeable and the shade in the girls' private corner was getting smaller. They moved the bench nearer the wall, disappearing almost completely under the tree's branches. They settled astride facing each other and signalled to the waiter to bring a bottle of water.

"We cannot know what the future will bring, right?" Luna began, looking into her eyes.

"No, I wish though!"

"But the law of cause and effect tells me that my present situation is the result of actions I have taken in the past." She paused to give her time to digest the concept. When Maria nodded, she continued: "Likewise, what happens in the future will be the result of the actions that I take now. This way I can get a good idea of the direction my life will move in."

"In a sense you are right, but not everything that happens in life depends on us," objected Maria. "Most of what happens depends on what *others* do!"

"Yes and no," replied Luna again. "Other people do what they do, but we can react, even better *respond*, as we think is right. We can choose, remember? In this sense, *we* create a new cause for the future."

"What's the difference between reacting and responding?"

"When we react, we do so instinctively, often without thinking. It's a bit like the reflex test: someone taps you on the knee and your leg goes up, you know?"

"Yes," Maria laughed, and Luna laughed too.

"Responding is different, because we think before reacting. In my case, I do 'daimoku' first and then decide. I *choose* how to respond, and it is usually a positive constructive response. There is a big difference!"

"It's worth thinking about it. And then, the effects on our future, when do we see them?"

"Sometimes they show immediately, other times we have to wait a long time, but they will come up, for sure," said Luna with great enthusiasm, cutting the air with her hand outstretched. "Do you want an example?"

"Yes, please."

"So, let's say one morning you come across a guy on the bus; it's the first time you've seen him!" She settled on the bench and waved her arm in the air to attract the waiter's attention, who had forgotten about them. "It's full of people and it's hot. The bus stops suddenly and he loses his balance, steps on your foot and hurts you, but then he apologizes." Maria was listening amused, engaged, and nodded. "What do you do? You either accept his apology in a good mood, because you realize that it's not his fault and tell him that it doesn't matter, it didn't hurt a lot, thankfully, and the bus is too full!" She caught her breath and continued: "or... you give him a dirty look, tell him that it really hurt and to hold on tight or keep further away, even though you know there is no room."

"Yes! I'm thinking that it depends on the mood I'm in. If I'm in a good mood, I react in the first way, if not I probably react in the second way."

Luna laughed. "Exactly! It depends on how you react," she said.

The waiter arrived with a bottle of cold water and put it on the table, but hadn't brought any clean glasses.

Maria looked at him annoyed and pointed at the dirty glasses. She was very thirsty and wanted a drink now, not in half an hour! Luna didn't seem to notice her reaction and thanked the waiter with a smile. She poured a bit of water in her dirty glass, rinsed it quickly and drank the watered-down coffee; then she filled it with cold water. Looking at the garden where the tables were all occupied, she said: "Everybody woke up at the same time and he is running around like a madman to serve everyone. If we wait for clean glasses we'll die of thirst, so it's better this way."

She offered the bottle to Maria and waited for her to rinse her glass, then she filled it to the brim with cold water. Bringing her glass next to Maria's she said: "Cheers!" They toasted and laughed, drinking it all in one go.

Carrying on from where she had left, Luna said: "So, the next day you catch the same bus and see the same man again. If yesterday you smiled at him, today you smile again and maybe you exchange a few words and find out that he is a waiter in an upmarket café. You have a feeling that this man is your friend, right?"

"Yes," said Maria, thinking of Luna rinsing her dirty coffee glass with a smile.

"If instead the day before you complained, when you see him again you look away. You ignore him during the journey and even when you get off, though you are both walking in the same direction, and you are left with the feeling that this man is somewhat an 'adversary'." Maria nodded silently, thinking of her reaction with the Indian waiter. Luna continued: "One day you go into a bar and who is at the counter? The man from the bus! In the first case, the man greets you as if you were old friends. He asks how you are, what you are doing in that area, makes you a coffee and offers it to you on the house. When you leave the café you feel happy and that feeling stays with you for the rest of the day!"

Maria could guess how the story carried on. She intervened and continued: "In the second case, when I see that the man at the counter is the one I snapped at on the bus, I regret having gone there but feel that I can't turn back and leave. I order a coffee and, to avoid having to look at him, pretend to be busy with a notebook, until I pay. I leave the bar, feeling uncomfortable. That discomfort remains with me all morning. Okay, I understand," concluded Maria. "But how could I be in a good mood when he stepped on my foot on the bus, if I was in a bad mood?" she asked.

Luna laughed: "Before leaving home, I always chant at least ten minutes, so I'm in a good mood."

"You always chant before leaving the house?"

"Yes, I try to do an hour, because often I am not in a very good mood in the morning," she chuckled. "But, if I don't have time, I chant ten minutes, with passion. As soon as I start, I feel grateful to be alive, and this puts me in a great state of mind. Gratitude is the most beautiful emotion you can feel, I guess. And then I pray for protection during the day." She paused, thoughtfully. "So, in your opinion, where are the cause and effect in the story on the bus," she asked.

"The cause is when the man stepped on my foot."

"Possibly..." hesitated Luna.

"When I react, then?"

"You can see it in both ways, but if you want to be at the helm of your life, if you take the famous responsibility we mentioned earlier, I would choose the second option, the one that depends on your reaction," Luna advised.

At that very moment Maria spotted Franca who was looking around in the garden. She called her to get her attention, waving her arm from under the leaves to get noticed. Franca smiled when she saw her and walked quickly in her direction, but her smile became fixed and tense when she saw Luna. "Ah... hello," she muttered, slowing down, while her smile died away. She looked at the new girl out of the corner of her eye.

"You were sleeping like a log when I got up. This is Luna, a new friend!"

Luna stood up and stuck her hand out to Franca with a warm smile: "Hi, nice to meet you!"

Franca shook her hand reluctantly. "I want a coffee. I'm still half asleep. I'm going to sit over there," she said, pointing at the courtyard with her head.

"Come and sit with us," Maria invited her. "We're having a great chat!"

"No thank you, I don't want to disturb your nice conversation."

"I'll have to go in a minute," Luna said, quickly. "I need to take a shower and then go into town."

Franca walked away. Maria looked at Luna, as if to apologize. "I don't know what's the matter; she has been acting a bit strange," she mused aloud.

"In what way?" her new friend asked. "Are you travelling together?"

"Yes, we set off together, knowing very little about each other. We are so different," she said, following Franca with her eyes. "At first she was very independent, and still is, but I noticed that if I get involved talking, or if I get along well, with someone else, her mood changes..." She paused, then, hesitantly, added: "In the past few days, she has become attentive, affectionate, gives me massage... and I feel a bit uncomfortable, I can hardly recognize her. Now she seemed almost... jealous?"

"She didn't seem happy to see me. But perhaps she got out the wrong side of the bed." Luna watched Franca. "Maybe she's insecure," she added.

"She's the least insecure person I know," replied Maria. "She is completely independent."

"Sometimes appearances can be deceptive and, behind the facade, there is much more!" She hesitated, but Maria could tell she was thinking. Timidly, Luna asked: "Is she gay?"

"What does that mean?"

"In England we use it to define homosexual men and women."

Maria reacted with astonishment: "Who? Franca? Nooo! She's had a boyfriend in Italy for years... so I guess it's impossible!" But then she paused.

Luna looked at her quizzically. "But…?" she asked, waiting for Maria to complete her sentence. There was a pause full of doubt, while Maria was thinking back.

"Sometimes she looks at me in a strange way... she stares at me... without speaking. Then this insistence with massage, and then she tells me that I'm beautiful... but in a peculiar way, it makes me feel uncomfortable."

"Having a boyfriend doesn't rule out that she may have fallen in love with you, or simply be infatuated. One thing doesn't necessarily rule the other out. And, if this were the case, she could have expectations, perhaps unconscious ones," Luna mused. "When our expectations are not met, we feel resentful." Then, to lighten the mood she said, laughing: "However it is true that you're beautiful!"

"Well, I don't think so. You, instead, are *really* beautiful!"

"Thank you! But you *are* beautiful, even if you don't realize it."

"Maybe," said Maria. "Well, thank you."

"You're welcome!"

They were still laughing when Franca approached with a cup of coffee in her hand. Luna got up to leave, but Maria wanted to spend more time with her and continue their conversation. What was she doing today? She was going to buy jewellery made with silver and semi-precious stones to take back to England. Did she mind if they went together? Quite the opposite, but what about Franca? Maria was almost certain that Franca would go out with Patti. In this case, she would be delighted; they'd be leaving in half an hour. Luna waited for Franca to arrive and said goodbye with a smile. Franca nodded stiffly. She sat down on the bench, her back against the wall. "Seems like you're getting on like a house on fire," she said, looking at the garden, avoiding looking directly at Maria.

"She's a Buddhist too, and does the same thing as Sanya. When I woke up, I felt like chanting and I sat over there. It turned out we were both doing 'daimoku' at the same time, in two opposite corners of the garden. It was her who noticed," said Maria, masking with enthusiasm the uneasiness she felt.

Franca glanced at her, and quickly returned her eyes to the garden. "What a coincidence," she said.

Maria asked what her plans were for the morning. She was going shopping with Patti and they were also going to shops selling charas and opium. Were there really *legal* shops that sold these things? Yes, and not only here in Rajasthan, said Franca. She was joining them, wasn't she? Maria told her she was going out with Luna for a tour of the market and other shops. Did she want her to buy the tickets to Delhi for the next day? No, said Franca, she and Patti would get them, and decide the departure time; did she have any objections? No, that was fine. "Well then," said Franca, coldly, and stood up, walking to the room.

14. We all die sooner or later

Luna was sitting in the garden when Maria joined her. A rickshaw accompanied them to the Johari Bazaar, a market specializing in silver and semi-precious stones where Luna wanted to buy some jewellery. The ambience, the colours, the sounds, the lights, the smells of the market were grabbing and fascinating, but most striking of all was the young woman she was with. Her presence conveyed joy. Luna seemed to illuminate the places she entered with her good mood, the attentive way she looked at the person she was speaking to, the consideration she showed toward those she came into contact with, even for a brief moment. When Maria pointed this out to her, Luna smiled and explained that, in everyone she met, she saw 'a potential Buddha' and felt great respect; she saw their Treasure Tower, she said, laughing. As a result, it came naturally to treat everyone like a precious human being, with the same consideration she would like for herself.

It was interesting to see how people reacted to her. They replied with warmth, friendliness and familiarity to her gaze full of enthusiasm and her warm voice. They followed her with their eyes and an expression of longing, fascinated, as if wishing she'd stay. After doing some shopping, they stopped at a chai-shop for some samosas.

While they were waiting, Maria told her about her encounter with Paul and Karen and the emotions she had experienced. She confided that she had felt something very special about him, as if she had already met him; everything seemed so natural. She described his embrace in the forest temple, how she had leaned her head on his chest and listened to his heartbeat, overcome with emotion, and the effort she had made to control herself. In the past, she admitted, she wouldn't have thought much of having an affair with a man she liked, and who clearly liked her, and almost certainly would have gone to his village to see him. On that occasion, however, she had wanted to act with respect for him and Karen. Luna listened with great interest and nodded. She reassured her that she had done the right thing by not going; she had behaved in a way to create positive causes for her future, to create a relationship based on respect. This thought pleased Maria. She had made a good investment, then. But how was it possible to feel such strong emotions for someone she barely knew? Her friend looked at her for a moment without speaking; then she said that perhaps she had *recognized* him. What did she mean, asked Maria, that she knew him in another life? It was possible, Luna said; if the emotion was so strong and it was reciprocated, there was 'something'. But then why had she let him go? Why hadn't she gone to his house, as he had invited her? Even without doing 'anything wrong' she could have spent more time with him and got to know him better. Because it wasn't the right time, Luna replied; she didn't need to worry. After all she had decided to go back to the Valley of the Gods, hadn't she? Yes, but who knew when! The best thing was to chant for his happiness whenever she thought of him, without worrying about the 'how' and 'when'.

With a giggle, Luna shared a thought: "Often I tell myself: I'm making loads of positive causes, so where are the positive effects? Why haven't I met someone special yet? Where are 'my effects'?" That's right, where were they? Maria asked. Luna laughed again and said she had asked for advice on this point. She was told that the positive effects would definitely appear. "In the meantime, said the woman I was speaking to, think only about taking positive actions, to create positive causes for your future. Instead of thinking 'cause and effect', think 'cause, cause, cause!" and laughed heartily.

She stated that she enjoyed taking 'positive actions', it was a nice way to live, and that this in itself gave her a lot of joy. Maria felt swept up in Luna's enthusiasm for life. She wanted to live like that, with total freedom of spirit, with no expectations for the 'effects', simply enjoying living in harmony with herself and with the rest of the world.

There was intensity, a joy in everything that Luna did and said, in the way she looked, listened, walked and moved. How could she be so, did it come naturally to her? She asked. Luna laughed aloud! No, it didn't come naturally; it was the result of constant work on herself: "I learned that if I want to be happy I have to appreciate what I have, express my gratitude and then encourage myself and others." She looked across the table at Maria and confessed: "You have no idea how many doubts I have about what I say and do, but, instead of wasting energy analyzing or criticizing myself, every day I decide to do my best, starting from now, and I reflect on the past only to learn from my mistakes. After that, I look to the future, enjoy the present and the people I have in front of me, at every particular moment." She smiled at Maria's face, who was taking in what she was saying.

"Right now you're with me. Does it mean that you are enjoying this moment?"

"Immensely! It couldn't be better."

"I think so too! And you said that you think about the future. Do you have any clear plans?"

"Yes, many," said Luna. "When I chant I ask my heart where I want to be in ten or twenty years' time and, based on the answer, I choose my path."

"And where does your path take you?"

"To work for world peace, in different ways, but all with the same goal."

"And is this the reason you're so... vibrant?"

"That's a beautiful word, thank you! Well, yes, that'll be the reason," she answered, smiling.

"I want to be like that, too!" said Maria.

"Then you will be," Luna said, looking at her and smiling encouragingly. "Everything starts with a desire."

They got back to the Evergreen tired, sweaty and dusty, but happy, and decided to meet in the garden after a shower and eat something together. Luna invited her to chant before dinner and Maria accepted happily.

At one of the tables she saw an Italian boy preparing a bowl of henna, a sort of paste made with a powder obtained from a plant that grew along rivers, mixed with water. Applied to the hair, it made it shiny with beautiful copper highlights. Maria had seen the result on other girls and had wanted to try it, but she had never seen a man using it.

"Are you putting henna on?" she asked with curiosity, walking by.

"Yes, and I've mixed much more than I need. Do you want some?" the boy answered.

"How tempting! How long would I keep it on for?"

"A couple of hours. If you put it on now, you can wash it off before going to bed."

"Do you think it would react well with the colour of my hair?"

The boy picked up a strand of her hair and studied it briefly. Then he confidently declared that it would look beautiful; she had the perfect colour, a mousy brown. She was persuaded! "Would you help me put it on?"

"Sure! Go and take a shower and then come back here with wet hair. Meanwhile, I'll do mine," he urged her. Maria took a shower and went back a few minutes later. The boy had his hands full of the mixture that looked like cow dung and had almost finished spreading it on his head of dark curls. "Sit down. I'll put it on you while I have my hands full!" Maria obeyed, and the boy began to smear the brown mixture with a particular smell, massaging it well onto her scalp and through her long hair, working quickly, with great skill. "That's it," he said, after ten minutes' hard work. "Now I'll cover it with a scarf. Keep it on for at least two hours, longer if you can."

"Thank you so much! What a great service, you're very good."

"It's my job, I'm a hairdresser," he said.

"Perfect! Hopefully the colour will be ok."

"It will be great," he assured her.

Franca and Patti arrived. They had smoked charas in the government shops and had bought tickets for the bus to Delhi the next day, leaving late in the afternoon. They were drinking chai, sitting on a bench, and Maria went to sit with them.

"Did you have fun, you and your friend?" enquired Franca, who added: "What have you got on your head? It looks like cow shit."

"It's henna, a guy had mixed more than he needed and convinced me to try it. He even put it on for me. In two hours I'll take it off. He said the colour will be fine," she explained hopefully. "And yes, Luna and I talked a lot. We thought we'd have dinner together in half an hour. She's taking a shower now."

"And am I invited too?" asked Franca.

"But of course! You don't need to be invited, neither you nor Patti. If you want, you can come and chant for ten minutes in her room before dinner," suggested Maria. "You can take a shower now and then..."

"*Don't* tell me what to do," interrupted Franca abruptly, moving backwards. "Take a shower, come to chant... *who do you think you are?*"

Patti looked at her, surprised, and said: "Shanti, Madam, shanti!" giving a puzzled look to Maria, to see how she reacted. Maria felt the blood rising to her face and realized she was blushing; it was as if Franca had slapped her in the face. She wanted to reply with equal unpleasantness but she remembered the concept of responding instead of reacting. She had no idea of how to put it into practice, though. She would think about it while she was alone.

"Do as you like! I'll see you for dinner," she said standing up, and walked toward her room, fuming with anger inside. She didn't understand Franca's reaction, but Luna's words rang in her head: 'Maybe she's in love with you!' She hoped not. It was much easier to think it was rudeness, and perhaps she did have a tendency to tell her what to do. She wasn't aware of it but from now on she would pay great attention. While she waited for the agreed chanting time, she began to make preparations for the next day's trip.

Luna greeted her with a cheerful smile, which turned into a quizzical expression when she saw her face. Maria told her what had happened. Luna said that when a person was angry, that person was suffering: "Think about how you feel when you get angry."

"I feel awful! I hate being angry, it hurts my heart, I get a knot in the pit of my stomach; sometimes I feel like throwing up," Maria replied.

Luna suggested they chant those ten minutes for her happiness and that of Franca, and laughed seeing Maria's perplexed expression. "Yes, that's right, for her happiness," she insisted. "You'll see how different you feel. Trust me!" she encouraged her. "What have you put on your head?" she asked, finally.

"Henna. It gives coppery highlights. Better than the mousy brown!"

Her friend smiled and, seeing Maria's unhappy face, she encouraged her once again to pray for Franca's happiness.

"Okay, I'll try," agreed Maria. At first it was hard, but as she chanted, little by little, she realized that Franca had a constant need for reassurance and to be at the centre of attention. Eventually she felt a certain empathy with her; she seemed so independent, but in the end Franca was as insecure and vulnerable as she was. Just like a pot of cooking beans stops boiling and grumbling when taken off the heat, her anger abated and Maria relaxed. She began to chant for her own happiness, grateful for having met Luna. She watched her out of the corner of her eye and smiled at the determination with which she repeated that phrase, fast, her back straight, focused, full of energy and passion. Her beauty was exquisite; she had regular features, big eyes, a perfect nose, full lips... and was incredibly kind.

During dinner, Luna paid particular attention to Franca, who began to feel at ease, flattered by the attention she was receiving. Maria remained quiet, observing the change in Franca, who laughed at the way Luna was telling the adventures of the day: the man sleeping on his rickshaw with his legs up, balanced on the three-wheeled bicycle and snoring with his mouth open. She described the motorbike that carried an entire family, father, mother, two sons and a goat. She told them of the things made of silver and semi-precious stones, bracelets, rings, anklets, that she had bought to sell back in England. Franca insisted on seeing everything.

Luna went to get the package and opened it on the table, showing the pieces they had bought together, one by one. Franca became engrossed and wanted to know the prices, in which shops they had gone, how to know if the silver and the stones were of good quality. Luna told her everything she knew and Franca seemed to have forgotten the antipathy she had felt for her. Maria watched them, noting Luna's grace and inner balance and comparing it to Franca's overwhelming and undisciplined enthusiasm and she saw that there was no friction between them; on the contrary, they complemented each other. While Luna re-packed her silver things, she said she'd like to see what they had bought. Looking at Patti,

Franca raised her chin, and this made Patti stand up and go to the dorm to fetch her purchases. They were fine things, different from Luna's but equally interesting. Maria asked if they had bought anything else and Franca laughed, glancing at her companion. Could she tell? Patti had bought something very special, she said. She had bought some, too, not so much, but good, and it came from the government's shop.

"The 'shop' is just a 'hole in a wall', a window open onto the road," she explained, full of enthusiasm. "Outside there was a queue of men, most of them quite old and skinny, with a fifty paisa coin in their hand. Now, that's so little! When their turn came, they put their coin on the windowsill, and the man from inside swapped it for a small lump of opium, or charas, all without a word!"

"What, just like that, openly?" Maria asked.

"Yeah! Just like that! Normal business. Amazing!" Franca was excited: "And then, it was our turn, and we asked for... well, quite a lot more!" She laughed out loud, glancing at Patti, who seemed reluctant to disclose the exact quantity.

"Some!" she said, with a reserved smile.

Franca was on a roll and quick to take over: "Well, they made us go inside a room and offered us a choice of two qualities of both opium and charas: 'standard' and 'superior'," she laughed aloud. "Needless to say we got the best one. It was so cheap!"

They talked a little longer and discovered that Luna was returning to Delhi the next day too, so they decided to travel together.

Maria went to take a shower and with a lot of patience, water and shampoo, washed the henna off. When she went back to her room her hair was still wet and seemed darker than before. "I hope it will be a beautiful colour," she said. "If not, it will wash off after a shower or two, right?"

Franca looked at her in surprise: "Henna is permanent, didn't you know? It doesn't go away."

Maria felt faint: "No, I didn't know. Poop!"

"It looked just like poop. Tomorrow we'll see the colour, maybe you'll be fine," said Franca. Now she could only wait and see. While preparing her backpack, Maria observed her companion: she was in good spirits, talking incessantly, about Luna and how nice she was, the trip to Delhi, the plans for next week; here was the Franca she knew well. Maria thought that there wasn't even a trace of resentment or anger. She relaxed and fell asleep with her hair still damp, hearing Franca's voice, talking, talking, talking... When she awoke she immediately ran to the bathroom and, to her great joy, her hair had become a little darker, but shiny and with coppery reflections. Luna, Patti, and even Franca, agreed that the new colour was great! Maria was changing from the outside, she thought, as well as from the inside.

The bus departed on time, full of people inside and luggage on the roof. They were sitting together, Franca next to Patti and Maria next to Luna. She was going to Delhi to welcome a friend who was coming from England, a fellow student who had studied drama with her, and was arriving with a South African guy she hadn't met.

She and Ted had finished University together, then she had left right away to travel around the world while Ted had a part in a theatre show in the West End. He was a talented actor and had already been noticed by the world of cinema. Was he her boyfriend? Maria asked. No, they had been good friends for years. Maybe they were such good friends that they couldn't become anything else; she loved him like a brother. Were they going to travel together? Yes, for a little while in India and then they were going to decide where to go.

"Were you not afraid of travelling alone?" asked Maria.

Luna laughed: "I am never alone, even if I try!" Then, smiling, she explained that she didn't like to be alone, she much preferred other people's company, but this time, as a challenge to herself, she had decided to try. "From the moment I left, I've never spent a moment alone, except for when I'm asleep or in the shower!" she said, laughing.

Franca wanted to know why she had decided to 'challenge' herself to be alone, if she didn't like it.

"I would have been scared," said Maria. "That's why Franca and I left together, although we hardly knew each other."

Luna explained that for her it was important to overcome her limitations and become more independent. She had been travelling alone for four weeks and now she knew there was nothing to fear. She explained that, by challenging herself to grow she was developing her potential. "Our potential is limitless," she said. "The only limits are the ones we set ourselves, usually because we are afraid of change or to take the first step into new territory." Even the profession she had chosen was difficult. She confided that her dream was to become a well known actress for two reasons, the first one was because she had always known her role would be on the stage, but the second reason had now become more important than her personal success: "I want to become well known because, in that way, I can have some influence on young people and communicate the values of this wonderful philosophy that I'm practising. A lot of people of my age don't have solid values to guide them to develop a useful life, not just for themselves but also for others. They no longer believe in the values of the past but they haven't replaced them with new ones."

Patti was listening carefully and nodded her head in silence.

"An altruistic life rather than a 'selfish' life," Maria said, making the 'quotation marks' signs with her fingers.

"Exactly! When we live only for ourselves, with our ambitions as our sole purpose, our life remains relatively small and our power equally limited," Luna continued. Even Franca was listening in silence. "But if our purpose is bigger than just ourselves and we plan to use our time on this earth for something that is of benefit to the whole of society, then our life expands, it becomes huge, and our power unlimited."

"Yeah, great," said Franca, quickly cutting in. "But not everyone wants to dedicate their life to society. Most people are only interested in themselves and their close circle of friends and family."

"True," agreed Luna. "But I think that's because they don't realize how happy they can become."

"In what way?" urged Franca. "It is *because* they want to be happy that they set their limits to their circle and don't want to get involved in things outside of it."

"My experience shows me that, as I have become less focussed on myself and more committed to the happiness of others, I am much happier," said Luna. "Let's say that I dedicate a lot of my time and energy to a cause 'bigger than myself' and I see clearly where I want to direct my life." After a short pause she continued, talking to Franca and glancing at Maria and Patti. "You know how we walk when we don't know where we're going, or when we're taking a stroll? We walk slowly, with our nose in the air, looking around, stopping here and there. To cover a mile it may take us as long as an hour."

Maria and Patti nodded, while Franca had crossed her arms and was listening with a critical expression. Luna went on: "Think instead of the way we walk when we know exactly where we're going, for example, to the station to catch a train." She raised her right hand and extended her arm with her hand outstretched, as if to cut the air in front of her nose. "We walk with purpose, fast, focused, with energy. We cover a mile in... what... ten minutes?"

"Mmmm," said Franca, without compromising herself.

"Well, I want to live with a sense of purpose, of mission," said Luna. "I don't want to waste my time hesitating. I want to use my life to the fullest and make a difference in the world. I want to create value, so that at the end I can say 'I'm proud of what I did. What a great journey! I've really enjoyed it!'"

"You talk of having a mission!" argued Franca. "Don't you think it's a big word? You think about when you'll die? Brrrr!" She pretended to feel a shiver down her spine, accompanied by an expression of disgust in her face. "I want to have *fun*, live, experience everything I can. I want to smoke, get drunk, take an acid, or two, travel with my mind as well as my body. I want to 'get out of it', why not? Maybe in a few years' time, I'll think about contributing to society, but for now, I want to get to know myself! Otherwise, what have I got to give to society? First I'll have to experience all sorts of things, right?" The liking she had felt for Luna the night before had completely disappeared and had been replaced by a seemingly unprovoked belligerence.

"Me too, Franca," Patti said, more quietly. "But what Luna says is interesting, and worth thinking about."

"For me, it resonates with what I want," said Maria. Turning to Luna, she said: "I understand when you say that it gives you joy to think of other people's happiness. After speaking with you yesterday I couldn't stop thinking about it. When you explained the Treasure Tower that everyone has within, and how precious we are, I started to look at people in a different way. I imagine that inside each person there is a cylinder, encrusted with precious stones and brimming with light. The cylinder is more or less the same for everyone, and around it there is the person's body, which is different for each of us. That's how I visualize it. So, if from the outside we are all different, on the inside we all have the Treasure Tower, and we are all equal, even if one is more intelligent and another is a bit 'thick'!" Luna was listening and smiling. Maria went on: "I feel like my own life is expanding." Then, turning to Franca, she said: "Your attitude worries me, Franca. It sounds like you're playing with fire. It's very important to respect ourselves, and if we use certain drugs we risk getting lost, seriously. It's the world of Animality, isn't it? The world of instincts; or the world of Hunger, with insatiable desires."

"*You* may be an animal!" snapped Franca, gesturing and openly aggressive. "Don't you worry about me. I know what I'm doing! Maybe you should explore *your* mind a little more; maybe you'd relax a bit!"

"Come on Franca, there is no need to talk like that. It's like you've been stung by a wasp," said Patti.

"We are all different and that's why life is so interesting," rejoined Luna, calmly. "What you were saying about the cylinder inside of us, with the Treasure Tower, is perfect, I really like it," she said, speaking to Maria. Then, looking at Franca and Patti in turn, she carried on: "There is a nice image that explains how the cherry, plum and peach tree are all beautiful, each one in its own way. It would be ridiculous if the plum tree was envious of the cherry tree's flowers and wanted to be like him. Imagine if he thought 'Look at my neighbour's beautiful flowers; he is so elegant and distinguished. That makes me so angry! I want flowers like that!' It wouldn't work, right? It's important to accept that each of us is unique, become aware of this diversity and appreciate it. From here mutual respect develops, and from that comes world peace."

Franca rolled her eyes in exasperation. Her voice was rising: "There you go again! All these Buddhists who are concerned about world peace," she snapped, waving her hand in the air. "Have a big spliff, guys! A nice fat line of coke! Relax! And have some fun! 'cause it won't be *you* who'll change the world!"

"And instead we will," Luna replied, with conviction. She didn't seem to be fazed by Franca's hostility. "The change begins with one person, every time we win over the negativity we have inside and transform it into positive thoughts, words and actions," she said. "It starts with one person and then they will become two, ten, a hundred, a thousand and one day we will be millions. It may seem like a slow change, but it is a long-lasting one, because it changes our consciousness; from heart to heart, from one friend to another, creating friendship, trust, and from there, peace. The more we are who make this commitment, each one in our own way, the quicker we will grow, like an upside-down pyramid."

"What exactly is this negativity you keep mentioning? I'm not sure I understand. Could you give me an example?" Patti said.

"Often it is another name for our ego. Buddhism calls it the 'smaller self', which is the voice within us that tells us that we are separate from each other, puts one against the other and creates suffering."

"If there is a 'small self', it means that there is also a 'big self'?" asked Patti.

"Indeed," confirmed Luna. "The 'greater self' is the opposite; it tells us that we are all interconnected and creates unity. When we help others become happy, we develop our 'greater self' and we are less obsessed with our 'small self'. This is how *we* become happy. It doesn't mean that we have a smile on our lips all the time, but that we *consistently* have a great life force, especially in difficult times." Realizing by her expression that Patti had expected a clearer example, she added: "Anger, for example, or feeling superior to others, are manifestations of the 'small self', unless it is directed toward fighting injustice. It has both a smaller and greater aspect." Since Patti nodded, looking satisfied, she looked at Franca and said: "You know what happens when you throw a stone into water!"

"It sinks," Franca replied dryly.

Luna laughed heartily: "Yes, it sinks; it also creates many circles in the water. In the same way, our actions, and also our thoughts and words, have consequences. Always! Like the law of gravity, the law of cause and effect works whether you understand it or not, whether you agree with it or not! If you jump out of the window you fall, this is the law of gravity. You hurt yourself, or worse. The law of cause and effect says that every thought, word or action is a cause that will result in an effect. There are no exceptions."

"Yes, but it's going to take forever before the world changes. And what can someone like you do? Nothing!" said Franca, enraged.

Patti looked at Maria and then at Franca, surprised; she didn't understand her provocative attitude. But Luna remained undeterred and kind. "Gandhi was one person. Martin Luther King was just a man! Nelson Mandela is only one," she said.

"Yes, indeed! And the first two were killed, while the third one is in prison," said Franca triumphantly. "Don't you see? Mandela tried to change apartheid and has been inside for the past twenty years! And there he'll stay until he dies, you'll see!" she concluded combatively.

"Yes, the first two are dead, but with his peaceful struggle Luther King changed the civil rights in America and Mahatma Gandhi, here in India, gained independence," Luna said. "As for dying, we all die sooner or later, don't we? We might as well use our lives in a way that creates value! Taking care of our life, of course, because every day of life is precious, but also using it to the fullest! And, as for as Nelson Mandela, I'm sure he will succeed in changing the system in South Africa, in a peaceful manner."

"Never! It's a utopia you're dreaming of! The whites will always oppose it!" Franca was raising her voice. People sitting all around had been straining to listen to their conversation, but as the voices became louder, their full attention was clearly on the girls.

"There are many whites who are against apartheid. I'm sure of it," Luna replied calmly, as if she hadn't noticed Franca's growing anger. "It's just a matter of time!"

"And how can you be so sure, can you tell us?"

"I don't know exactly how it will happen, but we are chanting all over the world for the end of apartheid in South Africa and the end of the conflict in Ireland."

"Oh, *come on*! They have been killing each other in the streets of Ireland for forty years!" Franca shouted, throwing her arms in the air. "It will never end. You are just idealists! Carry on chanting, and wasting your time! I've got better things to do with mine!"

"Your friend's friend who's arriving in Delhi is South African, isn't he?" Maria said, stepping in. Franca's attitude made her feel uncomfortable and, from what Luna had just described, it was her 'small self' that was shouting. "It will be interesting to hear what he thinks.

Where will you go when they arrive?" she asked out of interest, and to change the subject.

"I think we'll be going to Rishikesh, and later to Varanasi," said Luna. "But I'll see what plans they have; we'll decide together."

Maria told her about the Tourist Camp, which was a great place for when they stopped in Delhi. Luna made a note of it for the future, as this time they were staying at the house of some friends of Ted's, just outside the centre of the capital.

The bus had arrived in Delhi and it was time to part ways. She didn't know when she would see Luna again, but she would have liked to, very much. They hugged tight and Maria carefully stored her London address. She thanked her for all the things she had taught her, and was very sorry to leave her. Franca said goodbye with a forced smile and it was obvious she was glad to see her go. Maria's eyes followed the scooter that took her away until it disappeared into the sea of traffic. She missed her already. There was something unique and beautiful about Luna that she would never forget. Something told her that her life had changed through their meeting.

She turned to Franca and saw an expression of dissatisfaction printed all over her face. Maria had no desire to talk to her. They looked around for a taxi to share; she kept to herself and let Patti take the initiative. In her head she chanted for Luna's happiness. Little by little, the irritation she felt toward Franca faded. She glanced at her sideways. She was still upset and looked unhappy, and Maria felt a little bit sorry for her.

15. Opium

Patti was leaving for Italy two days later and they decided to leave for Varanasi on the same day, spending the last two days together. Franca had become very fond of her; she had found a friend who shared her passion for drugs but was a quiet person, leaving her plenty of space to express herself. This, of course, meant smoking a lot and after dinner at the restaurant, Maria decided to spend some time alone, to think and rest. On her way to the dorm she popped into the office where she found the receptionist with a white beard and leaf green turban which matched his eyes, Mr. Singh was his name. She told him of Manali and Jaipur, of the people she had met, while he listened, silent and attentive. With a worried expression, he asked how her friend was and whether they were still travelling together; he saw in Franca the potential to get into trouble. He told her in no uncertain terms that her friend didn't have enough sense and that she was to keep an eye on her. He had seen many Westerners ruin their lives by the careless use of drugs. How he understood the daredevil side of Franca she couldn't say, but he was sure; he had spotted it as soon as he had seen her. Maria tried to minimize his negative impression, but he wouldn't have it. He looked her straight in the eye and told her that he had a lot of experience, recognized what he saw, and was simply warning her. He said: "Your friend is one of those people who knows no limits and will stop only when, and because, she has to. Be careful you don't to get into trouble because of her."

The next morning, after a shower, she and Franca caught a scooter and went to get their tickets for Varanasi. The train station was huge and the queues very long. When at last they found the right queue, they waited patiently for over an hour; in the meantime they observed life in the station. There were whole families camped inside, maybe for a few hours, maybe for longer, cooking, sleeping, taking care of the children, as if they were at home. Maria noticed two western men in the same queue, a little ahead of them. They noticed the girls too, turning around a couple of times to smile at them. Once they got their tickets, they walked toward the exit and nodded at the girls.
"Nice guys," Maria said.
"Yeah, not bad," agreed Franca.

When they finally got to the counter, the female clerk, realizing they were two girls travelling alone, offered them two places in the ladies' compartment. Not knowing there were compartments just for women, they were taken by surprise and waivered. Yes, no, it didn't matter. "I give you two bunks near the ladies' compartment. If you change your mind, and if there are free berths, ask the ticket inspector to give them to you. They are very suitable for women travelling alone," she advised them. They thanked her and left the station, happy to have two bunks instead of just two seats. It was a long overnight journey and to be able to relax, maybe even sleep, was real luxury.

Franca was in a hurry to get back to the Tourist Camp where she had things to 'discuss' with Patti. Maria decided to take a trip into New Delhi. They caught different scooters and set off in opposite directions. They had become more independent and Maria felt safe being on her own. It was hot and stuffy and, even though it was monsoon season, it rained very little. She asked to be taken to Connaught Place where she could have a stroll in the shade under the arcades and go to the park which was right in the centre of a large roundabout. Not the ideal place in terms of clean air, but many of Delhi's residents went there and she wanted to explore it.

The warm wind blew in her face and lifted her long hair giving the illusion of a little fresh breeze. Every time the scooter went over a hole it gave her a big jolt, so Maria held on tight to its frame while watching the chaotic traffic. The inevitable, now familiar, lean cows were ambling here and there, without direction or purpose, carefully dodged by cars and bikes, undisturbed by the noise, respected by all. Men and women, in their thousands, filled the pavements; the men dressed in white while the women looked like queens in their colourful saris, patches of green, red, yellow, purple, turquoise, gold. Rich or poor, and the difference was noticeable, all the women wore dozens of bracelets, made of gold for the rich ones, made of plastic for the poor, but they all equally conveyed the same effect of femininity and coquetry. They advanced with an elegant bearing, the light cotton shawls framing their faces, the red mark from the temple on their forehead, anklets at their feet. She never tired of watching them.

Having got off in the square she began to walk under the arcades, looking in the shop windows, letting time go by, without hurry. The objects on display were expensive but beautiful, made of alabaster, green malachite, golden amber, turquoise. She stood at least ten minutes looking adoringly at a little statue: it was the figure of a young girl running with her arms raised, holding a fluttering shawl, finely carved out of a turquoise stone, only just bigger than her fist. She had never seen anything more beautiful and stood gazing at it, transfixed, for a long time. She walked past the offices of several airlines and of American Express; outside its doors there were at least twenty beggars sitting on the sidewalk. Among them were two westerners, skinny, dirty, their hands outstretched. Maria felt embarrassed just looking at them. Giving a coin to an Indian beggar was one thing, but to give a few paisa to a westerner seemed an absurdity. She didn't understand what could have led them to beg and, of course, couldn't ask. She looked away, shocked and confused.

She was ready to go to the park, but that meant crossing the four or five lanes of traffic. It was no mean feat, because there were no pedestrian crossings that worked and the traffic never stopped. Tired of waiting for the right moment, Maria took her first step and then a second, trusting that cars, scooters, bicycles and cows would shun her. Finally she arrived at the park entrance. Small stunted trees cast patches of shade just big enough for one person and, unsure as to what to do, she sat down by one of them on the few strands of dried grass.

She was approached straight away by a man carrying a wooden box: "Ear cleaning, Madam?"

Was he asking her if she wanted to get her ears cleaned? Surely she hadn't heard properly! "Pardon? You want to clean my ears?"

"Yes, Madam, very good for you!" he replied, confidently rocking his head.

"No thanks, I wash them every day," she answered, thinking with a slight sense of guilt that maybe sometimes she didn't wash them so well.

The man insisted: "Is very good, Madam, for wax and ishstones!"

To remove the wax and then what? She didn't understand the second word. Maria was annoyed; she was looking forward to spending a few minutes alone. "What is 'ishstone'?" she asked surlily. The man patiently explained that 'ishstone' was a small rock, a pebble. 'Ishstone', she understood at last, was the word 'stone', pronounced with the addition of a new sound. She stared at him wide-eyed: "Inside the ears? How do I get stones in my ears? I would be able to feel them, wouldn't I?"

"No, Madam," he answered patiently, a lot of people had stones in their ears without knowing, until he pulled them out. "Let me see," he said, turning on a flashlight and pointing it into her ear. "You have a big ishstone, I can see it," he said.

Maria was wavering between concern and disbelief: "And you can take it out?"

Yes, of course, but it would cost her ten rupees, it was a big 'ishstone'. He proceeded to open the wooden box, out of which he took two sharp tools, including a pair of long tweezers. "Neanche per sogno!" she said in Italian, standing up quickly; he could forget about that! "I'll keep the wax and the stone, too. I'll show it to my doctor when I go back to Italy, thank you and goodbye." He put his tools back in the box and stood up with resignation, peering around. Maria watched him from a safe distance and saw him approach an Indian man sitting in the shade and talk to him. The man asked a question and the stone expert shone his torch into the man's ear. The customer nodded and the expert went to work. The operation lasted a couple of minutes, but Maria was too far away to see whether he had extracted a stone. As much as the idea seemed absurd, she couldn't exclude it completely. Who knew, maybe there really were stones in her ears, but how would they get there? It was a mystery! She touched her ear, but couldn't feel anything.

She took a few steps and sat down under the small shadow of another tree. No more than two minutes had gone by before another man, a big man this time, approached her. He carried a wooden box, but this one had glass bottles on display. "Massage, Madam?" Ah well, this one offered a massage. As if she, a woman alone, would get a massage from a man! What kind of massage? Any kind you want, Madam, I have many different oils and they are all good. He knelt next to her and opened a bottle. "Check how nice they smell, sniff Madam," he said, sticking it under her nose. Smelling was free, he added with humour, and the fragrance was ideal for body and mind. The oil had a good scent of flowers. The man took advantage of her hesitation and said he could give her a head massage only. Only the head? He understood that her question meant a yes, and knelt behind her. He poured a little oil on his hands, spread it well on his palms, and then clapped loudly. The last thing Maria noticed was the amused smile of a group of Indian women who were watching the scene.

The big masseur's hands grabbed her head and pushed it forward, so that her chin was held against her chest. It felt as if it was being held in a vice or by a pair of pliers. The man began to rub her scalp with great enthusiasm and vigour. He rubbed, scratched, pulled, all with great physical strength, far too much for her small head. The word massage didn't express the action she was been subjected to; the spinning motion of a washing machine came to mind instead, and meanwhile he had already anointed and tousled her hair. Maria said 'softer' but the man had become deaf. Once again, he took her head between his two huge hands and tilted it strongly to the right, rubbing, scrubbing, smoothing, polishing. Slower, Please! Nah, deaf! He tilted her head to the left and away again, working with fervour. Between one movement and another he clapped his hands, giving himself a round of applause, Maria thought, noisy and dramatic. Then, as she had feared, he grabbed her hair, pulled her head back and began to rub her forehead, her temples, her scalp. He was almost hurting her, and since the words 'That's enough, thank you!' didn't get any result, she took advantage of another round of applause to lean forward and break free from the grip of the mad masseur.

She didn't want to seem ungrateful, but that was more than enough. "That will do," she said, and turned toward him, trying to get her head away from his clutches. He seemed pleased with his work. "Good massage, Madam?" he asked.

"Mmmm, very strong! I thought you were going to pull my head off!" He ignored her sarcasm.

"It's Bombay massage! Very good for you. Special massage!"

"Yes, yes, I have no doubt. How much do you want?"

"Give me what you want, Madam," he said, "maybe ten rupees." Maria gave him five rupees and the Bombay masseur stood up happily, telling her that if she returned the next day he would give her another massage. He was already looking around to find the next victim.

"Yes, sure, I'll come tomorrow, too," replied Maria. She tidied her hair as well as she could and slowly got to her feet. She could barely put one foot in front of the other. The massage had definitely done something; she felt more dead than alive. The masseur waved at her from afar, happy as a child.

Slowly she walked toward the park's exit and as soon as the first scooter stopped, she slumped on the back seat. She let the driver take her through the neurotic traffic, honking and shouting to the other drivers to get out of his way, dodging the cows. The wind, pleasant and warm, blew in her face. She closed her eyes, thinking about the stone and ear expert, and laughed. She thought of the crazy masseur, how he had grabbed her head and clapped his hands, and laughed again. When they arrived at the Tourist Camp she realized she could barely stand up and felt stiff all over. Walking slowly, she went up to the dormitory where she took shampoo and towel, before heading off to the showers. She had to laugh again when she saw her reflection in the old mirror: she looked like a witch with greasy and unkempt hair! However, after a shower, her skin was soft and her hair was shiny. Exhausted and unable to do any physical activity, she went to sit at the restaurant, watching people; she didn't even have the strength to speak. She had something to eat and drank a chai, wondering where Franca and Patti were; she hadn't seen them anywhere. She had heard there was a chai-shop outside the Tourist Camp, across the wide road. Slowly she walked in that direction, her legs as heavy as lead, and saw them before crossing the road.

Franca was lying on a charpoy bed, made of a wooden frame with a woven twine base. When she saw Maria she smiled softly and gently lifted an arm beckoning to join her. Patti was lying nearby on a similar bed and smiled sweetly. Maria noticed at once Franca's eyes. Normally they were a light blue colour but now were even lighter, piercing, like ice. She sat on the bed's frame and watched her; she had never seen her so relaxed. Looking at Patti she saw the same spaced-out expression, her eyes were lighter than normal, the pupils almost invisible dots. "Have you taken opium?" she asked. The girls looked at her with a stare, as if they didn't see her, a smile pasted on their faces, motionless. The answer took a long time to come. "A little," replied Franca, eventually. Not knowing what to say, she asked if they wanted a chai. Both girls shook their heads, but didn't speak. They were in a world of their own, each one by herself, alone.

"Do you want to know what I did today?" she asked, wanting to share the adventures of the park. After a long silent pause, with great effort, Franca nodded. Maria told them her stories, but she wasn't sure they were following because their expression stayed the same, immovable, a smile on their faces. "Have you eaten?" she asked. Both reflected a long time and, after an interminable pause, Franca shook her head weakly and Patti did the same, looking sick, pale in the face. "Do you want to eat? Are you hungry?" That was another difficult question.

Finally, Franca replied: "No, I'm feeling sick. No, thanks!"

Thanks? Franca had said thank you? Incredible, this was the first time she heard her utter that word. Maria looked at the chai-shop woman. She was lying lazily on a charpoy bed, smiling.

She asked her for a chai and the woman stood up slowly, with difficulty. There were no other customers. While she was waiting, Maria looked at the almost deserted wide road and thought of the next leg of their journey: Varanasi, the holy city where, if they could, Indian people went to die. She felt a little anxious. She looked at Franca, who instead couldn't have been less worried. She sipped her chai in silence. When were they going back to the Tourist Camp? Later, said Franca, now she couldn't. Did she want some help crossing the road? No, not now. In that case, Maria was going. She would come back in half an hour, she was getting bored there. Was that okay? "Yes, in one hour, please." Please? Franca had said please now! Maria was surprised and amused by these new developments. She stayed a little longer, unsure of what to do but, since nothing was changing, she paid for her chai and took leave from the woman by touching her forehead with her fingertips; she hadn't even thought about it, it had come naturally. That was the way Indian people took leave and their ways were becoming hers, too. Still feeling sore from the massage, she crossed the road and walked into the Tourist Camp.

Mr. Singh was standing outside his office and greeted her with a nod. "Everything all right?" he asked. She crossed the few yards and went over. She told him of the men she had met at the park in Delhi and he told her that the story of the stones inside the ears was for gullible people. She had done well not to let him touch her. As for the head massage, he concluded that the masseur hadn't the slightest clue on how to give massage and that if she felt so tired it hadn't been good for her. She had better rest now and become wiser in the future. Where was her friend? Maria, speaking candidly, in the hope of some advice, told him that Franca had taken opium and was lying on a charpoy bed, seemingly happy but unable to move. Mr. Singh's reaction struck her. He suddenly became very serious, and staring at her, asked what was she doing there then; why wasn't she with her friend? "You come to India and behave in such naive ways. You don't know this country and mess around with drugs!" He told her that Franca was vulnerable, that anyone could take advantage of her in that particular moment, and it was her duty to cross that road again, stay beside her friend and protect her. "Anyone could rob her of her money and passport. What would you do if something like that happened? Go back to her immediately and don't leave her until she's safe." Seeing Maria surprised by the strength of his reaction, he continued: "If I were to do my job seriously, I shouldn't let her back into the Tourist Camp, and I should also call the Police. And then what would happen? They could take her to the Police station and even arrest her. They aren't nice people in the Police force, you know? Many are corrupt and they could do anything to her." Maria nodded shyly, worried, ashamed of her naivety. She was also beginning to regret having told him the truth. "Do you know what Indian prisons are like?" insisted Mr. Singh.

"But I thought that opium and charas were not illegal, the government sell them in the shops in Jaipur! And charas is sacred, they told me, the god Shiva, Bagwan, god..."

Mr. Singh interrupted her sharply: "Jaipur is in Rajasthan, and that's another state with other laws! Here we are in Delhi, the law is different and drugs are prohibited."

"So, Indian people don't smoke charas? I thought that almost everyone smoked."

"You thought wrong! Normal people don't use charas or opium; only sadhus use them, but they are holy men, and they live outside of society."

"Who are these sadhus?"

Although irritated, the receptionist explained that sadhus were people who renounced the material side of life, everything they owned, including their family. "You must have seen them in the Himalayas! They wear a saffron or orange coloured robe and go around with only a small pot for water, usually made of brass. They don't possess anything, and whatever they need, people give it to them."

Maria remembered having seen one or two and she had wondered who they were: "Are they beggars?"

"No, absolutely not. Genuine sadhus are holy men. As a rule, they don't ask for anything, but people give them what they need, food, water, shelter at times, and in this way they earn merits."

"Why do they become sadhus?" she asked with interest. For various reasons, explained Mr Singh, who was beginning to relax and enjoyed Maria's undivided attention. Some were opportunists, who used that image to legitimize their begging, but most sadhus chose that way of life in order to be closer to god, and people saw them as an intermediary between them and god. He went on to explain that once they made that decision they couldn't go back, it was a final choice. The law regarded them as if they were dead and they lost all their civil rights, they couldn't even go back to their family. But why? asked Maria. Because if they went back they would become 'untouchables', the lowest caste, and their family, too. Looking at her and seeing her perplexed expression, he repeated: "If they need something, people will give it to them. They are holy men, everybody helps them!"

Just then two taxis pulled up with new guests and she knew their conversation was coming to its end. Mr. Singh surprised her by taking her aside, urging her in a low voice: "You must be responsible with your life, and also with that of your friend. You have to tell her what I have told you. Don't just think about yourselves. If she were to get into trouble, we would be in trouble too. And think about your parents, about the consequences of your actions. They must have taught you something good, right? They don't deserve worries or problems of this kind." He looked at her sternly and, seeing Maria's confused and ashamed face, he softened his voice: "People have arrived and I have to look after them. And you also have your work to do. Go back to your friend and stay with her until she is safe!"

Maria nodded seriously, and he went into his office, followed by the five new arrivals.

She felt mortified, but also grateful. He was right about their parents. She really didn't want to get into trouble, and Franca's mother had begged her to keep an eye on her daughter. Maria thought about all this while waiting for the right time to cross the road. She had come to India to understand herself and see this life-changing country, not to 'get out of it' with drugs. That side of India interested her next to nothing, compared to the spiritual discovery. Now she understood that she was also responsible for Franca.

She crossed the road with care and walked to the chai-shop, where the girls were still stretched out on the charpoy beds. She noticed that Franca was wearing the waistcoat with many pockets and even from that distance she could see her passport bag. She sat on the edge of the bed and looked at her friend. With an effort Franca opened her eyes and smiled weakly: she seemed to be on another planet. Her heavy head seemed to sink even deeper into the hammock-like base. The chai-shop lady was still lying on her charpoy and looked at her. Maria pointed her chin at Franca and Patti and said: "Opium."
The woman smiled and replied: "Shanti, shanti."
"Chai?" asked Maria. She needed energy if she was to cross the road with those two, who looked as heavy as potato sacks. The woman nodded and smiled, getting up from her charpoy bed very slowly, with difficulty. Maria wondered whether she too was under the influence of opium, or perhaps it was just that she was very fat and moving around in that heat was a real effort for her.

She looked at Patti who was lying with her eyes closed and an angelic expression on her face. She had two children waiting at home and she was going to take opium through customs twice. What madness! What a risk she was taking. She said she didn't have a problem and was not an addict. Maybe she was right, if she didn't use it often. Maria didn't know enough about it, but she worried about her. Was she responsible for Patti's life, too? She sipped her chai slowly and watched the traffic go by. She could hear the sound of the scooters way before she could see them, and that of the big Harley Davidson motorcycles which had been converted into taxis. Behind the bike the owners had added a two-wheel platform fitted with side panels and two benches facing each other, which could accommodate eight people. She loved that unique, beautiful motorcycle sound they produced. Every now and then a cart pulled by an ox went by, driven by a man with a white turban holding the reins. It was accompanied by the sound of hooves on the asphalt which covered the distance slowly, one step at a time, clop clop, clop clop, clop clop. Inevitably, Maria remembered the first day in India and the man with the cart who had stopped to give them a ride. She smiled at the memory of the two of them, legs dangling, waving at the passing drivers, who turned to stare in disbelief. They had already learned many things from the day they had arrived. Who knew how much more they had to learn?

"It's time to go back to the Tourist Camp," she said. She had to persuade them to cross the road so that she could tuck them safely into bed and then be free to do her own things. She was getting bored there, with nothing to do. There was no answer, as she had expected. She gave a few gentle bumps to Franca, then got up and did the same to Patti. She went back to Franca and tried with a dose of common sense: "Come on! It's time to get back to our little house. Wake up so that I can take you to bed and then you can sleep. I know it makes no sense to wake up to then go back to sleep, but I can't sit here all day and watch you dreaming." From the next bed, Patti opened one of her green eyes and looked at her with a surprised expression. "Come on Patti, you have to help me a little, I can't do this alone. Besides, I don't have much energy either after the torturer's massage. It's only a short walk. What do you see in this drug that just makes you sleep? Bah! I don't understand! Come on, let's start with you."

She sat on the bed and put her arm under her shoulder to encourage her to get up. With great effort Patti got into a sitting position. "Don't lie down again, stay sitting while I go and lift the other one!" She did the same with Franca, who finally managed to sit up. She then went back to Patti, helped her to stand and together they went to get Franca. One arm around each girl's waists, she led them to the road and patiently waited for the scarce traffic to clear. "When I say 'Go!' we cross, okay?" Taking advantage of the first gap without vehicles, she said 'Go!' and pushed them forward. With a few steps, they reached the other side. Fortunately, Mr. Singh was nowhere to been seen. Harnessing the power of inertia with which they moved, she continued to manoeuvre them up to the dormitory, and dropped each girl on her bed. Other people had arrived and had left their luggage on the spare beds; the dorm was now full.

Maria had neither the energy nor the desire to talk to new people so she sat on her bed and began to write a couple of letters, one to her parents and the other one to Ester. She was looking forward to going to Varanasi. She went out only to have something to eat. The girls didn't stir, not even to go to the bathroom, and slept until morning. When she woke up, Franca wasn't in her bed, while Patti was preparing her luggage, slowly. She looked at Maria and smiled warmly, her eyes still very green, but no longer as intense as the day before.

"Are you all right?" asked Maria.

"Yes, very well," she replied; then she paused and looked at her: "I have to thank you for yesterday. You helped us a lot. It was irresponsible of us to take opium together, without someone there to look after us. That's the one thing you should never do!" She said it with humility.

"No problem. I was told to stay close to you; otherwise I wouldn't have known it was important. You were very vulnerable. I thought about your children and I did what came naturally. How are you feeling today?"

"Very well, relaxed, rested. It's really high quality opium and I'm pleased with it."

"What time are you leaving?"

"Later tonight, but first I have to go to New Delhi for more shopping. I need to get perfumes, incense and other things. Why don't you come too? Your train leaves late, doesn't it?"

"At seven-thirty! Where's Franca?" She had gone for breakfast; she was starving, as they hadn't eaten anything the day before. Maria got dressed. She was looking forward to going to the market. She looked at Patti: "You'll be careful travelling with that stuff, won't you?"

Patti returned her gaze, serious: "Don't worry, I won't get caught!"

"I was thinking of your children, who are waiting for you."

"That's why I won't get caught!"

Maria hoped she was right; she liked this woman and hoped she knew what she was doing, as she claimed.

They spent the day at Paharganj market, noisy, smelly, full of dust and people, surrounded by hundreds, thousands of people, smelling one perfume essence after another and buying more than they had planned. Franca was in a good mood, relaxed and affectionate with Maria. She took advantage of every opportunity to touch her arm, stroke her, take her hand: the effect of opium, Maria thought, but she was relieved to see that she had lost the aggressiveness and antagonism of the day before. They returned to the Tourist Camp just in time to get ready to leave. Patti put a small lump in her hand: "So you understand what it's like."

"But I've already tried it," said Maria, looking at the piece of opium on her palm.

What she had taken the first time wasn't enough to get a good idea, explained Patti; this was the best opium in the world. If she didn't want to, she needn't ever take it again. Franca would take care of her. Maria was tempted; it was a unique opportunity and an experience she would never repeat. "It looks big to me, though. Are you sure it's not too much?" No, it wasn't too big. It would start to take effect once they were on the train and they had nothing to do all night; time would pass without her noticing. She was tempted, indeed, almost convinced. "I'll see you at the restaurant. I'll take it there," she decided.

She went looking for Franca, and found her having a shower. She asked her whether she would take responsibility to look after her if she took the opium. Franca said yes right away. Then she went to the reception office to take leave from Mr. Singh, but he wasn't there that day. Just as well, she felt quite embarrassed at the idea of looking at him with a lump of opium in her pocket. She went back to the dorm, took her backpack and her camera bag. In the restaurant, her friends were waiting for her and had ordered her a chai.

"Are you sure it's not too big?" she asked again.

"Positive! Swallow it with a sip of chai. You'll like the effect," Patti replied confidently.

"And you won't leave me, will you? Not even for a minute!"

"I won't, don't worry," confirmed Franca.

She put the lump of opium in her mouth, still suspecting it was too big, and swallowed it with the first sip of chai. She quickly drank the rest, trying to stop her hands from shaking. There! She had done it. She looked anxiously from Franca to Patti.

"I'm scared," she said. "I'm shaking, look!" She stretched out her trembling hand before them.

"You'll be okay," Patti reassured her again. "Franca will be with you all the time, and anyway, it's done now, so there is no point being afraid. It will be a good experience, you'll see!"

Maria thought that perhaps she was listening to the wrong person's advice; after all, she had been a junkie. But she had made the decision and now there was nothing to do but see what happened. Franca assured her that the effect would only last a few hours and, upon their arrival in Varanasi, it would hardly be noticeable. Her hands were sweaty and still shaking. "When will I start to feel the effect?" she asked nervously. It would take an hour or two and it was better if she didn't have anything to eat, she would just throw it up. In any case she wasn't going to be hungry. "But will I be able to travel? And to walk? And to carry my rucksack? It's heavy, you know? Shouldn't we get a move on? What time is it?" She couldn't relax. We leave in ten minutes, said Franca. "Let's leave now," said Maria, "so we have more time. Let's get a scooter, I don't want to be late, especially now!"

Patti and Franca exchanged a glance and smiled. "Okay, let's say goodbye now! It's not a good idea to leave too late, but don't forget that you have reserved seats," Patti reassured her, standing up. "I'll help you with the rucksack," she said, slinging Maria's backpack over her shoulder. Maria stood up, but her knees didn't support her and she panicked. "I can't stand, my legs won't hold me up," she said, with anguish.

Franca interjected firmly: "It's your fear that makes you feel like this. You can't already be feeling the effect, it's impossible. Don't panic, stand up and let's go. Forget about it. The sooner we get on that train, the better!"

Maria had the feeling that Franca was worried and forced herself to her feet. Her legs were still shaky, but she drew a long breath and, leaning on Patti, managed to get as far as the road, not looking in the direction of the office.

A scooter stopped at once. They embraced and wished each other good luck. Her friend patted her on the head, as would a mother with a frightened child. Once more Maria asked: "Are you sure it wasn't too big? That lump, I mean!"

"No, don't worry!" Patti confirmed one last time. She said goodbye to them, her arm outstretched, waving her hand in the air, while the scooter set off loudly.

It was still very hot but the temperature was falling slightly and the sun was low on the horizon. They didn't speak. Maria closed her eyes, savouring the air that blew in her face. They were about to begin another adventure and she felt it was going to be an important one. She smiled at herself, turned to look at Franca and smiled at her. Franca took her hand and held it in hers, caressing it. They sat in silence until they reached the station. Maria felt much calmer and let her friend deal with paying the driver.

In the station there were people and luggage everywhere. The official porters with red jackets and white turbans walked fast with their particular gait, bouncing on their knees to cushion the impact of the weight, carrying iron trunks on their heads, two or even three at a time. Franca took Maria's hand and started to walk behind one of them, taking advantage of the gap opened by the porter and following him closely. The train was leaving from platform six. Thousands of people were waiting, filling the platform with colour and luggage: men wearing turbans; women in their elegant saris; children kept under close supervision by their mothers and grandmothers; all in an atmosphere of excitement and anxiety. Maria wondered how it was possible that a train could carry all those people and all those bundles, but she pushed aside the insidious concern. She was confident that Franca knew how to deal with the situation.

A few minutes had gone past when they heard the whistle of the incoming train. Immediately all the people crouched on the ground stood up and began to stir, moving bundles, picking up children, lifting trunks on their heads. The train came puffing, spitting out clouds of steam, howling loudly. Even before it stopped, people began to run toward the carriages, pushing luggage through the open windows. They ran along the moving train, unconcerned about who could be in their way, pushing and bumping without restraint, shouting messages to the passengers on the train, every man for himself! Some of the passengers on the train were taking the luggage of those who ran and put it on their seats, thus reserving a place for them.

Without giving it a second thought, Franca launched herself in the middle of the crowd and Maria followed her. She didn't know where they were going, but didn't want to lose her friend. Surrounded by hundreds of agitated people, pushed and squeezed from all sides, they continued to follow the moving train. Finally it came to a halt, with a deafening screech of brakes; it recoiled slightly, accompanied by the wave of people who seemed glued to its sides, until it finally settled with a jolt. People became even more agitated, storming the openings that had neither windows nor bars, going in through those holes, pushed by relatives or friends on the platform, while the other passengers huddled at the doors, trying to climb in before the arriving passengers could get off. Maria watched the scene from within the bedlam and thought it was pure madness, the world of Animality in the extreme, where the strong overpowered the weak; or maybe it was the world of Hell; or Hunger, the world of insatiable desires; or all three simultaneously. She understood those people's anguish, but fortunately she didn't feel it. She was a detached spectator.

Pushed and pulled from all sides, she kept her eyes on Franca, even and especially when they were separated. They were now in the mouth of the funnel leading to the train door and, like her companion, she began to use the weight of her body and her backpack to make herself heavier and move forward, brainless like everyone else. She saw that Franca had one foot on the step of the train, her hands clinging to the sides of the door and was being pushed from below by the pressing crowd. Finally she managed to get on board. For fear of losing her, and being now close to the same door, Maria charged, head first like a goat. To her great surprise, she found herself on the train almost without her feet touching the steps, literally raised by the mass of people. Franca had saved her a seat, but they were not together. Maria thanked her and sat down. Then, shouting she asked: "Are these our seats?" knowing full well that they weren't the ones they had booked.

A look of surprise crossed Franca's face: "I don't know; probably not, but at least we're on the train! We'll find out later."

The wagon was filled by an enormous number of people and everyone settled as best as they could, carving out a small space on seats or on the floor, where they sat down with their luggage. The girls were some distance apart, but able to see and talk to each other, as long as they raised their voices. People had settled and quietened down when the ticket inspector came aboard. He wore a flawless white uniform, with epaulettes and golden buttons; it was very stylish, and he knew it. He noticed the two western girls and headed toward them, staring at Maria: "Can I see your ticket?"

Franca leaned over, tickets in hand. "Here they are," she said.

Reluctantly, the inspector took his eyes off Maria and checked the tickets: "You are in the wrong carriage. You have to go to your own, where you have reserved berths."

"But where is our carriage?" Maria asked in a stressed voice.

Pointing to the tickets, the inspector said: "Carriage F, berths ten and twelve. You must get off and walk along the train up to car F. Be quick, the train leaves in a few minutes."

Maria was overwhelmed by panic: "Oh no! With all this luggage. We struggled so hard to get on. Will we have time to change carriage?" She looked at him, unable to control her fear.

The inspector stared at her for a few seconds and then, to their surprise, he said: "I'll take you. Follow me, but be quick!"

Thanks to his authority he made his way through the people, followed by the girls with their luggage. Maria's red backpack, as well as being almost as big as she, seemed to weigh more than before, and her camera felt at least twice as heavy as during the previous trips. They followed him closely, until they reached a completely different section of the train. Here, the windows had bars and a glass pane and everything seemed much more civilized. They got on and the inspector found immediately berths ten and twelve. Unfortunately, young men had settled comfortably on their places. The inspector spoke sternly in Hindi, while the boys stared at Franca and Maria. At first it seemed as if a fight was going to break out, but then someone said something funny and everyone laughed. The boys shifted, leaving the girls' seats, who thanked the inspector profusely. Three people were sitting on one of the lower berths and three more on the one facing it. The top bunk was already in a horizontal position while the middle one was fixed to the wall until the evening, when people went to sleep. They had been assigned the two upper bunks. When the train moved everyone celebrated the departure with happy expressions and cheers. They had attracted a lot of attention and, after a few minutes, the men who had had to leave their places were back and sat down on the bunk forcing everyone to squeeze up so that now there were five people on each side. They were keen to talk with the girls, look at them, be as close to them as possible.

After observing her for a while, Franca said: "You look happy."

Maria was surprised. "I don't feel particularly happy," she said. "I don't feel anything at all. Why do you say that?"

"Because you look relaxed and beautiful," she said with admiration.

"I feel normal, if a little claustrophobic with all these guys so close. They're so excited... and they make so much noise. Why don't they go back to their seats?"

Instead they got out a harmonica and began to play, showing off their skills especially for them. Maria smiled politely, but soon the sound of their voices and the louder noise of the harmonica began to magnify in her head. The discomfort continued to grow and was becoming unbearable. She looked at Franca, who sensed her uneasiness.

"I'm going to climb on my bunk," she said. "At least I won't have them all so close. Why don't they leave?" She rose to her feet, but realized that moving was more difficult than she had thought. With great effort she stepped over the boys' legs, arousing their amused and excited comments. She had to concentrate hard to be able to climb, struggling to coordinate her arms with her legs and realized with dismay that she found it almost impossible to perform the most simple movements; but she had to get away from there.

At last, she managed to get on the wooden berth. She lay down and closed her eyes. The music and the boys' voices turned into a disconnected din, getting louder by the minute. She covered her ears with her hands, but it was uncomfortable. Meanwhile a sense of nausea began to climb from her stomach up to her throat. She took a few deep breaths trying to regain control, but the noise became louder and louder, deafening, and her body was shaking with the harmonica's vibrations, her stomach contracting into a tight knot. She felt bad and, even worse, she wanted to shout 'stop, please, stop', but she couldn't get any sound out of her mouth. She wanted to change position, but her body didn't respond; all she could do was lie there, motionless. Her hands refused to go back up to her ears to protect them from the noise. She could only breathe in a rushed, nervous fashion, her breathing had become short and laboured, made of sobs; she had lost control. She wanted to cry but she couldn't, she wanted to scream but couldn't. She no longer knew what she wanted, except for silence and some peace. Shanti, shanti, shanti, please!

She felt as though she was being shaken. She slowly lifted her heavy eyelids to see Franca in front of her, standing in between the berths, rocking her shoulder and pronouncing something inaudible. With great effort, she brought her head nearer to the bunk's edge and heard Franca say something about moving. "I don't want to move, I can't!" She thought she was shouting, and it was a huge effort. Franca was looking at her, still talking to her, but Maria felt only a great pain and couldn't concentrate on her friend's words. She only heard her repeat several times 'Ladies' compartment'.

"We can go there if you want!" She heard, at last.

"*If I want to!*" Maria said incredulously. "I don't know what I want. No. I don't want to move. I don't want anything. This noise, stop, stop, I can't stand it," she shouted.

Franca looked at her, surprised. "Are you crazy?" she asked.

"Yes! I'm crazy! I can't stand this noise. It's driving me mad!" she cried, beside herself, her throat tight. "I can't walk, my body doesn't respond! Where the hell is this compartment?"

"Maria, calm down! The compartment is right here, just a few steps from these berths. Come on down, I'll help you." Franca lifted herself a little to move closer. Slowly, Maria moved her legs, and then her arms. Getting down was much more difficult than going up, but she was doing it.

Greatly disappointed, the boys looked at the girls as they left. Franca held her firmly, pushing her down the aisle and, with a few steps, they reached the compartment for women: there were six berths, of which only two were occupied. It was dark and quiet and there was even a door that could be locked! Franca took her inside and quickly opened her sleeping bag on the lower bunk, where she lay down. The relief was indescribable. The rhythmic movement of the train running on the rails rocked her and Maria closed her eyes.

16. The Frenchman

Franca was shaking her: "Maria, wake up, we are in Varanasi, India's holy city!"

She opened her eyes but couldn't focus. Having her eyes open was a pleasant feeling, though; she didn't feel exhausted, quite the opposite, she felt well. She observed her body's sensations, her feet, hands, legs, arms, and herself inside; she sensed her internal organs, her stomach, heart, lungs, in their place, engaged in their work, their physical appearance. She perceived her body and her mind in a way much deeper than usual; it seemed as if they were two separate entities, observing and studying each other with interest, for the first time. She was waking up, but slowly, and although her body was responding to her mind, it was doing so in its own good time and her actions were delayed. Franca was busying herself with her luggage, but was also preparing Maria's backpack and her camera bag, while Maria looked at her calmly.

"You have to get up now. I don't know how long the train will stop. Come on Maria, get a move on, we have to go. I have all your stuff!" Franca hurried her. It was true; all the passengers had already left the train. With an effort, she sat up on the bunk.

Quickly, Franca crouched down and put her sandals on her feet. Then she pulled the sleeping bag out from under her bottom and slung it over her shoulder. Maria let her do so, focusing on the difficult task of standing up. Strangely, she didn't feel the need to pee. Franca was moving with a sense of urgency and helped her to load her rucksack. It weighed much more than before, and so did the camera bag. She felt herself being pushed out of the train door, down the steps and onto the platform, now virtually deserted. She walked beside her friend, slowly but relatively steady, leaning on her arm. They advanced in silence; it was still too difficult to talk.

As if in a dream, they found themselves outside the station and Franca was putting their luggage into a scooter. It was early morning, the air was fresh and the people of Varanasi were just beginning to wake up. They travelled for a while, the breeze in her face was pleasant and Maria observed the grey haze surrounding them, caressed by the gold shimmering rays of the sun, still low in the sky. "Where are we going?" she asked, touching Franca's hand with affection.

"To the Yogi Lodge, in the heart of Varanasi," her friend replied confidently.

Maria was satisfied and, with a smile, leaned back in her seat, watching the city wake up, little by little. The moisture penetrated deep into her bones and made her shiver.

The scooter stopped, Franca negotiated the price, and then knocked on the door of the Yogi Lodge, raised by a few steps from the old cobblestone street. There was no answer. She knocked again, louder and longer and, a short while later, they heard a rustle of feet. The door opened and a handsome young Indian man looked at them with a sleepy expression; he was wearing only a white sarong tied at the waist. The look in the young man's face changed when his eyes fell upon Maria, who was looking at him with a smile.

"Do you have a room, or beds in a dormitory?" asked Franca.

The boy continued to stare at Maria, and while moving to one side to let them enter, he replied slowly: "Yes, we have a room or beds in the dormitory, whatever you want."

He clapped his hands and a little boy appeared almost immediately, even more dishevelled and sleepy than he. 'Tin chai!' he said. Three chai. The boy nodded and promptly disappeared. The young man invited them to follow him up a few steps and they came to an open terrace, where there was a desk. He motioned with his hand for them to sit on a bench.

"Please sit down," he said politely. "I won't be long." He turned his back to them and put his palms together in front of a poster depicting the image of the god Ganesh, stuck to the wall with drawing pins. He lit a candle and a stick of incense before the image of the god with the trunk and began to pray in silence.

"How long do we have to wait?" asked Franca, betraying her impatience.

The young man turned slowly: "Chai is coming, and I have to say my prayer. Wait a few minutes, please." As he turned back toward the altar, his eyes met Maria's, who was watching him with a smile. He stopped to stare at her, and then, with effort, he completed the turn to continue his prayer. She clearly felt that he was sweating and thinking about her; the sensation was so strong it was palpable.

Finally the chai came. It was sweet and tasted of cinnamon and cardamom. It was too hot to drink and they had to blow on it for quite a while. Neither she nor Franca had drunk or eaten anything since they had left the Tourist Camp. She drank it in silence, enjoying all the nuances with every sip, while the young man concluded his prayer. As she finished her chai, she felt the tiredness surface. Finally, he turned around: "Do you prefer a room or the dorm?" he asked, looking at Maria.

"The dorm, if it is cheaper," replied Franca.

"The double room costs twelve rupees, a bed in the dorm four."

"The dorm then."

"If you want to leave your passports with me you can go straight away, the dormitory is right there. At this time people are still sleeping."

"I want my passport back now," said Franca.

"I'm going straight to bed, you can keep mine," said Maria, walking slowly toward the dormitory, dragging her backpack on the floor.

Rays of sunshine crept through the cracks in the window, illuminating the large dark room with bands of flickering golden light and dust. There were two empty beds next to each other. She put her backpack on the ground, with her foot she pushed the camera bag under the bed and lay down; but she felt cold and was shivering. With difficulty, she opened her sleeping bag, curled up inside it and closed her eyes.

She had no idea how long she had been sleeping when she heard male voices speaking close by. Unable to lift her heavy head, Maria opened her eyes. Just then the two westerners she had seen in the ticket queue at Delhi station were walking past right in front of her bed and looked at her. She had to close her eyes again, she was still too tired, but she heard their comments.

They spoke in French: "Est ce qu'elles sont toutes comme ça ici?" said one. "Je l'espère bien!" replied the other. 'Are they all like this, around here?' 'I hope so.' She knew they were talking about her and laughed inside the sleeping bag, flattered and happy. Being liked was a new sensation, one she was no longer used to, not since things with Ugo had started to go wrong, she began to drink too much and received nothing but criticism. But now he wasn't here while she was, happy and curled up, with the sun entering in beams, coming directly from heaven. She saw in a flash Luna's beautiful face while she was saying: "You are the Treasure Tower," pointing the finger at her, and smiled again.

When she woke up, Franca's bed was empty. She felt weak and remained lying in her bed, enjoying the flat surface, her stretched back, her head still heavy. She closed her eyes and fell back to sleep. She woke again in mid-afternoon having to go to the bathroom. She sat on the edge of the bed, feeling very weak. Slowly she stood up, with shaking knees. Walking toward the porch she supported herself wherever she could, along the wall, on the door frame, on the table. She had no idea where the toilet was and sniffed the air to find it, but there was no smell around. She saw the shower door, and the toilet was next to it. She crouched down and realized that she hadn't had a pee since they'd left Delhi; weird, it wasn't normal. The sinks were outside on the porch, but there was no soap. She rinsed her dirty hands and, lifting her eyes, she met the mirror. The image she saw astonished her; was that her face? Now she understood why people watched her 'like that'. The face looking at her had large blue eyes, with a depth of colour never seen before, full red lips, tanned skin, and even though it was dirty, it was beautiful. Was that really her? She smiled. From the depths of her mind came the memory of the lump of opium she had swallowed. It was definitely too big, she had no doubt about it now. It had had a very strong effect, which she still felt. Clinging to any support, she walked toward the stairs and descended carefully; her trembling legs were hardly able to hold her up and she could barely walk. She was ravenous! A waiter walked past. "Is there a restaurant here?" she asked him, staggering.

"The restaurant is closed until six o'clock, Madam," he replied, staring at her.

Maria sat heavily on the first available chair. She was so weak she could hardly speak. "I'm very hungry. I haven't eaten anything since yesterday. Look," she said, sticking her arm out and showing her shaking hand, unable to control it.

The man stared at her even more intensely, in silence, and after a long pause said: "I could make you some toast, if you want." With a growling stomach and a watering mouth, she asked for two slices of toast with butter and jam and two chai. The waiter bowed and disappeared. Maria remained sitting, too weak even to think, her hands trembling and her head spinning at the slightest movement.

After what seemed an eternity, the man returned, carrying a tray. She thanked him and began to devour the toast smeared with butter and jam, but suddenly she felt nauseous. She laid the bread on the plate and began to drink her chai in small sips. Then, one small bite at the time, she chewed the bread slowly, feeling enormous gratitude for the food, the chai and for being alive. After the breakfast she felt better, but still too tired to go out. She went back upstairs and, as there was no one around, she took a slow shower. She then sat on the terrace, letting her hair dry in the warm air, watching the people passing by in the street and those who entered the Yogi Lodge, enjoying the warmth of the late afternoon sun. Time didn't matter.

She recognized him by his head as he climbed the stairs with a firm step. Perhaps feeling someone watching him, the Frenchman from the station looked up and saw her. "Tu viens boire un thé?" he said without stopping, 'Are you coming to have a cup of tea?'

"Oui," she replied spontaneously. She walked toward the stairs, she would have run down, but couldn't do anything in a hurry. She felt attracted to this man, whose face she hadn't even seen properly. He was standing at the bottom of the stairs, waiting for her, with an amused smile full of admiration. He looked at her from head to toe and she felt conscious of wearing only a thin white sarong wrapped under her arms and reaching above her knees. Not much, she thought, but probably just enough not to scandalize, ultimately covering everything there was to cover. As she descended the last few steps she knew he was imagining her through the cloth, and she liked that feeling. She smiled at him: "Will you order the tea? I'll wait here!"

He bowed with a wry smile. "Bien sûr," he said, 'but of course'!

Maria sat in the open courtyard, looking at the sky and anticipating the pleasure of getting to know the Frenchman. He returned a few minutes later and sat down next to her, vibrating with vitality. "I've been all day along the 'ghats'. Have you been?" he asked, without taking his hazel eyes off her.

"Not yet. I just got here. Well... early this morning, but I slept all day, it seems," she replied, taking the opportunity to have a good look at him, trying to be discreet. He was balding a little, had round, almost woman-like, eyes, a carnival of hazel, green and gold flecks, highlighted by long, curled eyelashes. His mouth was hidden by a dark moustache, his uneven teeth indicating that he was a smoker. Settling comfortably in his chair, he pulled out a packet of Gauloise and lit a cigarette. Just then the chai arrived. The strong smell of his Gauloise reminded her of Paris and when she had worked there, living on campus. She had smoked them during those months, becoming accustomed to their strong taste. She associated the smell of dark tobacco with Paris itself and liked it very much.

"What's your name?" she asked.
"Jean-Claude, and you?"
"Maria"
"Easy!"
"Yes, woman's universal name!"

Smiling ironically Jean-Claude's gaze began at her feet and moved up her legs, knees, breasts, shoulders, face: "For the universal woman, *par excellence*," he said with open admiration.

Maria giggled; his closeness made her want to laugh. Was he travelling with someone else? Yes, with a friend from Paris, Michel, who was still out in Varanasi, exploring. And she? She was also with a friend, they were both from Venice, and had no idea as to where she was at the moment, probably out there, exploring, too.

She felt an irresistible urge to touch him, to let this man embrace her, to feel his hands on her body. She didn't move toward him, not even an inch, but she didn't want him to leave. They began to talk about India and of where they had been. Jean-Claude and his friend had been to Rajasthan, Agra, Jaipur, Udaipur and Jaisalmer, he said, caressing with his eyes her shoulders, her neck, her throat. They were incredible places, and the people were very kind, open and friendly. What about her? She told him about the rain, the landslide, their change of plans, and then about Mcleodganj and Manali, of the people in the village. She didn't mention Paul, it would have been like putting him between them, but her thoughts went to him. She remembered the emotions she felt with his embrace. Maybe that was just what she was longing for so much.

Jean-Claude was looking at her intently; Maria perceived clearly what he was thinking as his gaze went from her eyes, to her mouth, the dimples when she smiled, the line from her ear to her neck, her hair, her breast. He listened with a smile, pulling occasionally a puff of smoke from the Gauloise. He had beautiful hands, like a musician, or an artist.

"Aren't you hot with your jeans on?" she asked.

"Yes, indeed!" he replied, a bit surprised by her comment. "I knew it was hot in Varanasi, but I didn't expect this scorching heat. In a moment I'll take a cold shower. Will you still be here in a few minutes? It won't take me long."

"Yeah, sure, I'll be here." She hadn't noticed it was too hot, she was feeling just fine.

"I'll see you in a minute, then. We can have dinner together," he said confidently, already going toward the shower. He had a peculiar way of walking, lifting his heels and bouncing on the ball of his feet with a springy gait. She found it a little funny and could easily have imitated him. Maria laughed to herself; no one was perfect. She used the time to brush her hair and wash her sweaty face.

Suddenly, Franca's face appeared in the mirror behind her, tired and dusty, but sparkling with enthusiasm. "There you are! Did you sleep all day?" she asked. Maria was glad to see her.

"More or less, and now I was talking to one of the Frenchmen who were at Delhi station, do you remember them? They're staying here too."

Franca didn't remember them and, at this particular moment, she wasn't interested. "I've been around Varanasi throughout the day. What a place!" she exclaimed, dying to share with her what she had seen. "It's full of dead people's bodies! They carry them around on rickshaws! The city is full of rickshaws pedalling with these bodies hard as nails wrapped in a sheet, and they take them down to the 'ghats', which are the banks of the Ganges, where they cremate them. There must be hundreds of pyres, each one with a body burning on top. It's amazing, I swear. Then, to recover a bit from those scenes, I went to the market, to be in the midst of life; you need it after the ghats, I assure you. I ate there, a plate of local food for two rupees. Tomorrow you must go out; how are you feeling?"

With her mind still full of the images described by Franca, Maria replied that she was fine, although tired. She told her about Jean-Claude, that he would be back in a little while and they were going to have dinner together, probably with his friend Michel, too, who was still out in Varanasi.

Franca was in a hurry to take a shower and wash away the dust, the smells and the images of such an intense day under running cold water. She went to get towel and shampoo, while Maria sat on the table next to the showers, her legs dangling. She brushed her hair in the warm late afternoon sun. She could see her face in the mirror some distance away and she liked the image it sent back to her.

Jean-Claude came out of the shower room; a towel wrapped around his waist; his wavy hair wet, and went past her briskly. "Ciao bella!" he said, with an amused smile, walking toward the double room he and his friend had opted for. She followed him with her eyes: he had broad shoulders, narrow hips and slightly bowed legs, the way she liked them. Those two words, spoken in Italian, had touched something inside. Maybe she *was* beautiful, and perhaps the time had come to leave behind all her insecurities, the lack of self-confidence, a sense of inferiority and inadequacy that hammering criticism had persuaded her to accept as reality. It was time to look forward. She straightened up and threw back the hair that the breeze was pushing into her face. It was almost dinner time. She felt good in her skin, and very excited.

As soon as Franca was ready they went down to the restaurant. It was past six o'clock and they could order. Jean-Claude was waiting for her and went to sit by her side. He addressed Franca straight away. They began to exchange their impressions of Varanasi after the day's exploring and Franca accepted his presence without any problems. Jean-Claude turned slightly toward Maria and crossed his legs, so that his foot touched her leg. He looked at her all the time and she was beginning to get to know that new face, his sparkling eyes, his brown moustache, his high cheekbones, and felt at ease.

Michel arrived toward the end of their simple dinner of boiled potatoes and fried eggs. He was tall and athletic, with a tanned face and wavy hair. Soon they were all laughing together; both men were very pleasant and full of humour. "Let's go and have a joint in our room," they suggested.

Franca prepared a chillum with her charas, of which she was very proud, and explained how she had made it and how much effort it had taken. The men were impressed and shared the strong, aromatic chillum.

Michel was sitting at the bottom of the bed while Franca and Jean-Claude sat on cushions on the floor. Maria was sitting at the head of the bed and began to feel languid, both limp and sensual. She closed her eyes for a few minutes; she had no energy! When she opened them again, Michel and Franca were gone, while Jean-Claude was still sitting on his cushion on the floor. He was looking at her in silence, his expression serious now. Maria looked into his eyes and he held her gaze, motionless. She reached out and stroked his face with her hand; he hadn't shaved, and she liked that. With her finger she touched his lips. Jean-Claude took her hand, turned it palm up and kissed it. Slowly, Maria bent her arm and encouraged him toward her. He got up and sat on the edge of the bed. She touched his cheeks, his chin, his hair, filling her eyes with the image of his face. Jean-Claude leaned toward her and kissed her on the lips. He sat up and looked at her, serious, without speaking. Then he bent down and kissed her again. Maria looked at the door on the veranda which was still open. He understood, stood up, and locked it.

Afterwards, they held each other for a long time, her arms around his neck while she breathed deeply the scent of his skin. Jean-Claude was on top of her and, just to play, they tried to match all the parts of their bodies, from the shoulders, to their hips, down to their thighs, legs, and then down to their feet, one above the other, laughing out loud. Their bodies shook with mirth, making them laugh even more; they were in perfect harmony and she could have stayed like that forever. She closed her eyes and inhaled slowly and deeply. It had been so long since anyone had held her like that. Jean-Claude propped himself up on one elbow and looked at her. "Sei bellissima," he said in Italian, 'you are beautiful'. "Je ne peut pas le croire," 'I can't believe it', he added in French. He kissed her lips, the tip of her nose; he closed her eyes with his lips and kissed her eyelids, her forehead, her ears, until he saw her smile. He stroked her hair, her face and kissed her again, as if each kiss was naturally demanding the next. Maria opened her eyes and looked into his, floating in that sea of gold, green and hazel, surrounded by those curled eyelashes, and in that sea she saw love, surprise, worry, doubt, desire, sadness, wonder, tenderness, joy, and then love again. He smiled at her, with serious eyes, until Maria closed hers again and circled his neck with her arms. There was only the present, this perfect moment that she would never forget, even if everything else changed. No one could take away what she had now, and she felt her heart full, her eyes flooded with perfect joy. She was tired, very tired, and very, very happy.

She woke up with Jean-Claude caressing her face, looking at her closely. He was already dressed: "Wake up princess; I'm going to Varanasi to take photos. Are you coming with me?"

"What time is it?" she asked, halfway between wakefulness and sleep.

"Half past four in the morning. It's the best time to go along the Ganges; people begin to wake up now and they will soon immerse themselves in the river. Come on, get up," he encouraged her.

"It's too early. I'd love to... but I can't. I'll wait here... I want to sleep some more. Wake me up when you get back."

He laughed at her sleepy expression and kissed her all over her face: "As long as you wait for me in bed. Don't get up. I'll wake you up with a cup of tea! Okay, bella? Lock the door."

"Yeah, okay," she replied. She got up with her eyes closed, turned the key in the lock and went back to bed. Before falling asleep, she thought how much she liked this man, sweet and manly at the same time. Being with him was so easy. As soon as she closed her eyes, sleep carried her into the great palace of dreams, and she began to dream of Ugo.

They were in Venice, in Campo Santo Stefano, and he was surrounded by women. He went from one to the other, laughing and joking with everyone. Maria was sitting on the statue's steps and followed him with her eyes. Ugo watched her while, with his arm, he held the waist of the woman who stood closest to him. The girl looked at him in adoration, offering him her lips. Ugo looked at Maria and, with his eyes on her, bent down to kiss the woman he was embracing. She felt jealousy's knife slipping its long blade into the heart and twist it, twist it, twist it, and it hurt, it hurt horribly. She looked away, embarrassed, confused, screaming in silence with grief. Suddenly, she felt a hand touch her shoulder; she turned around and looked up. Jean-Claude was watching her with his smiling face; he took her hand and kissed it. He encouraged her to stand up, lifting her with his hand under her elbow. As soon as she stood up, he put his arms around her waist and kissed her. Smiling, he invited her to follow him, holding her by the hand. Ugo was watching them and had stopped smiling. Jean-Claude told her to walk with him and seemed to know exactly where to go. She wanted to ask him where he was taking her, but no sound came out of her mouth. They approached the canal where a couple of gondolas rocked softly in the breeze. There was a man sitting on the steps with his feet almost touching the water. The moon illuminated his blond hair which turned into curls where they touched his shoulders. Maria began to tremble, was that by any chance...? At that very moment, Paul turned and looked at her, calmly, as if he were waiting for her. He stood up, but didn't come forward; he waited. Jean-Claude reassured her, with an easy, amused smile. He took her hand and gently kissed it. Then they walked the few steps that separated them from the waiting man. He put her hand in Paul's hand, bowed and walked away. Maria looked at Paul, she wanted to ask him why he was in Venice, but she couldn't speak. Paul took both her hands in his and, looking into her eyes, tried to reassure her. With one arm he encircled her waist and they headed for the canal. With her eyes she asked him why, but Paul answered by kissing her on the lips and then, slowly, effortlessly, they walked together into the water of the lagoon.

Maria woke up and felt as if she were still floating. She tried to go back to sleep to resume the dream, but couldn't. The sun was high. Just then she heard Jean-Claude's voice; he was knocking at the door.

"Madame, your chai is ready, but if you want it you'll have to open up." Hurriedly she got out of bed and turned the key in the lock, opening the door.

Jean-Claude came in, placed a glass full of hot chai into her hands and began to busy himself with his camera and several films: "How are you? Have you slept some more?" Seeing that she nodded, he continued with enthusiasm: "You should have seen this morning, it was literally magical. There were lots of people making ablutions in the Ganges, and I was one of the first ones to arrive. I've taken some spectacular photos. Later we'll go out together. I'll take you down to the ghats. You've been here more than a day and you haven't been out yet. You'll see what a surprise! You've never seen a city like this, you can count on that!" His enthusiasm was contagious. He sat down on the bed and stroked her legs and hips. Maria had to get up. She was already beginning to sweat. "I have to go to the bathroom and take a shower," she said regretfully.

He laughed and slapped her behind as she went past in front of him. "Yes, go and take a shower and then you get up. You are not thinking of going back to bed, I hope," he said. Seeing her confused expression, he added: "I want to be with you in such a special city. We go out now and then we'll come back here during the hottest hours of the afternoon. What do you want for breakfast? I'm going to order it for you, so we get out sooner!"

"Another chai, toast with butter and jam, four slices."

"Okay, princess!" He blew her a kiss and walked toward the stairs.

Under the lukewarm shower Maria thought back to her dream. What did it mean? Jean-Claude took her to Paul and handed her to him. The shower water became colder and woke her up completely. She was famished. She wore a light blouse and wrapped her sarong around her

245

hips. She slipped her sandals on and, with her hair still wet, went down to breakfast.

The young Indian who had greeted them on their arrival was sitting at his desk and looked embarrassed, squeezing a faint smile. She realized that her night of passion had not gone unnoticed and she was sorry, but didn't feel guilty. She hadn't been so happy for ages. She asked Jean-Claude whether he had seen Franca. He hadn't, but Michel had seen her go out at about seven. "She's a sensible person like me! She knows what the best times in Varanasi are, and took advantage," he said with irony. Sipping the last drops of chai, Maria got ready for her first day in India's holy city.

It was only ten o'clock in the morning but it was already hot. Jean-Claude had decided they would go to the market first, because he hadn't been there yet and wanted to take photos. Then in the afternoon, they would go to the ghats on the banks of the Ganges river. Maria was happy to go along with his plans. The street outside the Yogi Lodge narrowed into an alleyway between two houses. There was one problem though: The alley was occupied by two large cows eating from a pile of hay filling it from wall to wall. "We can't go this way," she said. "These cows' huge horns take up the whole lane. This is their home, as you can see from the hay. If we try to get past they'll gore us!"

"No, they won't," laughed Jean-Claude. "I've already been here this morning; this is the way to go into town. Otherwise, the alternative is much longer, it means doing the same route as the scooters."

"You mean we have to go this way on the way there and back?"

"Exactly. Watch what I do and then do the same. You get hold of this horn, so you keep it still, and you go past. Voilà. Then take this beauty's horn here, you hold it nice and tight and voilà! Now it's your turn!"

"Not a chance! They'll get me, smash me against the wall and reduce me to a pulp!"

He laughed, but looked at her encouragingly and then, seriously, he said; "Come on Maria, you're the one who's in charge, not them. Do what I did!" He left her no choice.

She took the first cow's horn, it was big and pointed. She held it with both hands and slid in front of the animal. Quickly, she did the same with the second animal; she had never seen a cow so close up: its eyes were enormous, and were looking at her. She got through and found herself next to Jean-Claude.

"They are huge these cows! Did you say we have to come this way every time we leave the Yogi Lodge?"

"Yes, and when we return, too. Incidentally, they're not cows, they're bulls," he pointed out nonchalantly.

"But aren't bulls more dangerous than cows?" she asked, suspiciously.

"Not all. Those two, for example, aren't! Don't worry. I got used to it; you'll get used to it too," he concluded lightly.

The main street was full of people, scooters, bicycles and rickshaws. Maria saw a rickshaw carrying a dead man's body; it was wrapped from head to toe in a white sheet and was stiff. She stared at it for a long time. Although it was a new and very strange sensation, she had the impression of having already experienced something similar and wasn't completely surprised. What was new, instead, was the emotion she felt, a pain inside that touched her stomach, her heart, her throat. She couldn't utter a sound and had to look away. There, in the midst of everyday life, among the fruit and vegetables sellers, the women, the children, the skinny cows wandering aimlessly, Death was being carried under the scorching sun, sheltered only by a thin layer of cotton. It looked vulnerable; it could fall to the ground, for example, be run over by a car, or could bump into someone, a passer-by, a bicycle. She shivered just thinking about it, when she saw another rickshaw with another body, wrapped in a yellow sheet this time. And there was one more coming, at the end of the road, wrapped in white.

"How many dead people are there? I've already seen three in two minutes," she said, incredulous.

"This is the holiest city in all of India, Maria," replied Jean-Claude, "and Indian people come here to die, if they can. You'll see many more, and you'll get used to it."

"Seeing Death being carted under the hot sun? I don't think I'll get used to it. Besides, isn't it dangerous, health-wise?"

"It may well be, but this is Varanasi, you can't but accept it," he said wisely. "Let's go to the bazaar. You won't see any dead bodies there!"

From the main street they took a side road and, within a few yards, they found themselves inside a huge maze of shops, illuminated by bright lights. Although the sun was very strong the stores kept artificial lights on to enhance the fabrics for sale, hanging out on display. Maria had seen many fabric stores in Delhi, but no one had fabrics such as these. Heavy brocade woven with golden thread, in bright colours: red, green, turquoise, yellow, black. There were heavy silks, those too, woven with golden threads that twinkled regally under the bright lights. "I have never seen fabrics like these," she said, turning to Jean-Claude. "They seem to be interwoven with gold!"

A shopkeeper, who was standing outside his shop lovingly stroking his round belly, heard her words and interjected: "They are woven with gold, Madam, real gold. Feel the weight, try to lift it! These saris are for weddings."

"But how much do they cost? I thought people in India were poor," she said naively.

"There are a lot of rich people in India, Madam. Come inside and I'll show you some beautiful saris."

She glanced at Jean-Claude to consult with him and he nodded enthusiastically, opening his camera bag and preparing to take colourful pictures. Maria sat on a padded stool while the fan hanging from the ceiling moved the hot and muggy air around. Did she want chai? The man clapped his hands and, to the boy who came running, he ordered three chai, one for Jean-Claude, too.

He began to open all five meters of a sari made of blue brocade which he spread with mastery across the floor in front of her. It was beautiful! Then he opened a black and gold one, dramatic and impressive, and then, preceded by a pause to prepare her for the big shot, the shopkeeper opened a red sari woven with gold. It was the finest cloth she had ever seen! Pleased to see Maria's admiring expression, he encouraged her to touch it and feel its weight. How much did it cost? She asked out of curiosity. That was one of the most expensive saris, costing one thousand dollars but, if she wanted it, he could give her a discount. Thank you, very kind, but she was just looking, she reminded him. Who would spend so much? She enquired. The man explained that there were many very rich people in Varanasi. It was a city where people did a lot of business, with cremations and marriages in particular. Then, were cremations a business? she asked with surprise. He looked at her before answering; but certainly Madam, of course they were a 'business'. In her country didn't people make a lot of money out of funerals? She didn't know, she had never thought about it. Death was big 'business', the man assured her; she could take his word for it. But marriages were as good, of course, and when people got married, they spent a lot of money, and not just on clothes. This, for instance, was a wedding sari, he said pointing to the red one. So did women get married in red? Of course Madam, all brides wear a red sari, he replied, surprised by such an elementary question.

Jean-Claude kept taking pictures from every angle. He stopped only to drink the chai that the shopkeeper offered him, and soon was ready to leave. Maria thanked the trader, who seemed only slightly disappointed that he hadn't sold anything. He wasn't worried though, business was booming, as was apparent by his satisfied expression and his round stomach, which he began to caress through his striped shirt once he positioned himself again outside the store.

As they walked through the bazaar, Jean-Claude held her hand, sometimes he'd hold her by her waist, other times he bent over to kiss her, provoking nervous giggles from the bazaar people. Maria had the feeling that their behaviour was causing embarrassment and she felt judged. There was an atmosphere of modesty, of reserved chastity which reacted to their freedom with a certain bitterness.

After a long walk, they arrived at the section of the bazaar with jewellers shops. Maria, who was wearing a gold chain around her ankle, began to notice how jewellers moved their gaze from her face to her foot. While Jean-Claude was busy taking photos, a young jeweller convinced her to go into his shop, promising to show her diamonds, rubies and emeralds. She told him she had no intention of buying anything. It didn't matter, he said, it was a pleasure to show her his jewels; at least he'd be doing something.

They sat cross-legged on the padded floor covered by the white sheet, a little further inside the store, a few steps from the street, and the young jeweller opened the safe behind him. He pulled out a white envelope, carefully opened it and emptied its content on a tray covered by a white sheet of paper, dropping hundreds of diamonds. Maria's mouth opened of its own accord, while the young man smiled, pleased with her response. Once he had put the diamonds neatly away he brought out another envelope. This was full of bright pink rubies instead, by the hundreds. Maria asked if she could touch them. Yes, he said, but with some uneasiness, and while Maria let them slip through her fingers, laughing, he didn't take his eyes off her. Relieved, he put them back into the envelope and pulled out a third envelope, full of green emeralds, just as beautiful.

She noticed that the young man kept glancing at the chain she wore on her ankle. Finally, he asked if she wanted to sell it, was it twenty-four carat gold? No, it was eighteen carats, as was all the gold one could buy in Italy and, no thanks, she didn't want to sell it; it was her Christening chain. He offered her six hundred rupees. No, thank you, she didn't want to sell it. But why was she wearing it on her ankle? he asked seriously; gold was not to be worn so close to the ground. He'd give her seven hundred rupees. Maria didn't flinch; she knew that shopkeepers were insistent. She noted, though, that the jeweller was trying to make eye contact with Jean-Claude, who had finally stopped taking pictures and was watching them. At one point, the shopkeeper stood up and took him aside. They moved further away, talking.

After a few minutes, Jean-Claude went back to her and said: "Choose a pair of anklets, Maria. I'll buy them for you!" Surprised and happy, she looked at the many anklets that the jeweller showed her, until she saw a pair she liked very much. "These," she said, pointing at them with her finger. Jean-Claude smiled happily, with that wry and amused smile she knew well by now. She put her chain around her neck and the ankle bracelets around her ankles. As they left the store he took her by the waist and kissed her.

"He thought I was your husband, and told me that only married women wear anklets, and two, for your information. Instead, women who only wear one are 'loose women'. So, since I bought them for you, you're now my wife!" He kissed her again.

"We're attracting a lot of attention, I don't think they approve of all this kissing," she said, feeling uncomfortable.

"Then we'd better go back to the hotel. I'm ready for that nap and anyway it's getting too hot," he decided. It seemed as if a ray of sunshine lit his eyes. "Later we'll go out again and I'll take you to the ghats. Then you'll see something quite different."

The idea of being alone with him took her breath away and her heart started doing somersaults inside her chest.

"We'll take a scooter, it's faster and cooler," said Jean-Claude. "We've already walked enough this morning!"

He tried to stop several scooters, but no one seemed to notice him and continued their race, even if they were empty. Maria remembered the man who wanted to clean her ears and remove the stones, 'ishtones' he called them, instead of 'stones'. Raising her arm at the first approaching scooter she shouted: 'ishscooter' and this stopped suddenly, with a squeal of brakes, leaving Jean-Claude gaping and Maria laughing heartily. He wanted to know how she had managed to do so and, with the warm wind in her face, she revealed the secret of her success.

The scooter ran through the streets full of people and he squeezed her hand, hugged her, kissed her quickly. They arrived at the Yogi Lodge. There was no one around; it seemed as if everyone was resting during the hottest hours of the afternoon. They entered the room, and as soon as they locked the door they were in each other's arms. They made love with passion, gentleness, curiosity and wonder at this incredible attraction that had caught them by surprise and overwhelmed them. Then, they lay in silence, each one with their own thoughts, caressing, kissing tenderly. The heat was powerful and they closed their eyes.

17. The present is a gift

Maria woke up; she was sweaty, hungry, thirsty and immensely happy. Jean-Claude was still asleep, catching up from the pre-dawn rising of the morning. She looked at him in silence: his eyes closed, with thick curled eyelashes, his high cheekbones, wavy hair, strong shoulders; her heart was full of love. She tied the sarong under her arms and went downstairs to order chai and toast. On the veranda she crossed the young receptionist, who quickly looked away, avoiding meeting her eyes. She was sorry because she knew he liked her, but chased away the unease she felt. She was happy, for now. Happiness didn't last long and she wanted to savour it all, before it vanished. She went back upstairs with the chai that gave off the aroma of cardamom and a plate of toast with peanut butter and jam. She awoke Jean-Claude to the smell of chai: "Wake up! You said you'd take me down to the ghats."

With his eyes closed, he put his hand between her legs. She laughed, pushing it away.

"Come on, wake up. Can you smell the cardamom? I've got some food, too!" He was hungry and opened his eyes, surprising her with that glint of gold, leaf green, light and dark brown. He watched her in silence, smiling, but unable to hide a shadow of uneasiness that she had perceived. Sitting cross-legged on the bed, they ate the toast and drank the chai together.

"What's your last name?" asked Maria.

"Renard. Why?"

"Is there a Mrs Renard in your life?" she asked, awakening the ghost of an anxiety that lurked at the bottom of her stomach. She presumed there was, and she preferred to know now, before falling in love even more. He looked into her eyes, sadly.

"A Mrs Renard, no, there isn't. But there is a woman, we live together in Paris... it's been three years."

Maria nodded. She wasn't surprised, she expected it. Such a man was made to be together, to laugh, joke, enjoy life and build something beautiful. "And are you happy?" she asked with a certain lightness, blushing as she dared to brush past unhappiness.

Jean-Claude paused, he thought, and then looked at her seriously: "Yes, we are... we were... we *are* happy." He hesitated. "That's why what's happening with you is a surprise. I didn't think it could happen to me, not so soon. I left Paris only two weeks ago," he said, explaining to himself as he explained to her.

"Ah well, don't worry too much," she said casually, hiding the feeling that something in her heart was tearing. "I won't be around for long. After Varanasi we'll each go our own way!" They were together now, she thought, and that was what mattered. Better to know straight away, so she wouldn't get too involved and suffer when the time came to leave, at least not so much. The expressions on Maria's face changed, like moving clouds do, giving way to a clear sky, followed by other clouds. Jean-Claude looked at her; he was confused, unsure of what to say. Maria broke the silence: "I'm going to take a shower and then let's go to the ghats, okay?"

"Yes, okay. I'll take a shower too. I'll be ready in five minutes," he said, trying to shake off the sadness assailing him.

When they went out it was less hot, but the streets were full of people and traffic, just as they had been that morning, with one exception: "How come there are no dead bodies on rickshaws? There were dozens this morning!"

"I think they take them to the cremation ground early in the day. It takes many hours to cremate a body. That's where we're going now; maybe we'll find the answer."

She was keeping slightly away from him. He took her hand and pulled her toward him. She smiled at him, and when he encircled her waist, she let him, but something had changed, she didn't feel the same enthusiasm as before. It was inevitable, and she accepted the new feeling of calm distance. It was a shame, but that was the way it was! *You are the Treasure Tower, Maria*, echoed Luna's words. She smiled. He is also the Treasure Tower, she thought, looking at him from the corner of her eye, and as such she would respect him. She needed a little time to regain her balance, that was all. Jean-Claude perceived her gaze and returned her a confused look. When he felt her relax under his arm, he smiled with a hint of sadness, and held her tighter.

They turned into a narrow alley, away from the main road, the uneven ground paved with ancient stones. It was extremely crowded. Everybody was walking shoulder to shoulder and they had to wait patiently at times; other times they had to push instead, to advance between the tide of people going up and those coming down. Jean-Claude held her by the hand. They reached a big set of steps leading down to the banks of the Ganges, which stretched on as far as the eye could see.

"It's foggy here," said Maria.

"It's not fog, it's smoke. Now you will understand," replied Jean-Claude.

Hundreds of people were standing at the river bank and many others stood waist deep in the muddy brown water of the Ganges; some immersed themselves completely, others were drinking that dirty water, as part of the ritual they were performing. There were also many sadhus with long hair; she had never seen so many and so different. Some had their faces painted white, others had white marks on the forehead with a red circle in the middle, many wore an orange robe, but most wore only a small piece of cloth around their waist; others were completely naked, the long matted hair covered in ash, and seemed to walk aimlessly.

They descended more steps and turned a corner. There she saw the open space for the cremations, a large wide area that ran all along the river. The thick black smoke was coming from there. They stopped at the top of the steps to take in the vast view. At some distance from each other there were at least twenty pyres, huge piles of wood, over which she could distinguish the outline of a body. In spite of the height of the flames she could clearly see that the body was burning. People around the fire were busy adding and rearranging pieces of wood, tidying it up, taking care of the pyre with tenderness and love. The black smoke rose upwards in sudden regular gusts. Her voice died in her throat, she couldn't even move, stunned by what she was seeing; she could only watch.

Jean-Claude at her side opened his camera bag. Maria looked at him, shocked. How could he take pictures? But he didn't see her reaction and began shooting, moving naturally, click, click, click, taking pictures from every angle. No one seemed to notice. Maria turned back to look at the pyres. The relatives around them were serious and sad, they consoled each other. There was pain and sadness, but there wasn't despair. Belief in reincarnation didn't completely take away the pain of losing a loved one, and how could it? But perhaps it made it more bearable, less final. She had been wondering about that, and now she had her answer.

"Chai Madam?" The man who asked her was carrying a flask and a rudimentary wire structure that held ten glasses. "Chai and biscuits?" How could he? He sold chai and biscuits while people cremated their loved ones? Maria shook her head, unable to speak, and followed the man with her eyes. He turned to someone else, who instead bought both biscuits and chai. Sitting on the steps, she wondered whether someone had been cremated in the place where she was resting right now. She felt nausea borne out of compassion and shivered, despite the afternoon heat, and that of the fires. She lost track of time, absorbed by all that surrounded her, until Jean-Claude returned and sat beside her in silence. Her words came out in spurts: "Death is such an open thing here,

253

everything is done in the open air, while in our culture, when a person dies we don't see them anymore. We hide them inside a wooden box and bury them under layers and layers of earth. That moment is the most painful of all. I recall when my grandmother was buried. They lowered her coffin into a deep hole and then began to throw shovels of earth over it. I was just ten years old, but I remember that I wanted to scream; it was awful, as if they were killing her at that very moment." Jean-Claude didn't interrupt her; he lit a Gauloise and waited for her to continue. "Here, after someone has died, they still go around the city in a rickshaw, under the hot sun, protected by only a thin sheet. Those who have died are still among the living, while they busy themselves with all the things they need to attend to. And, even at this time, they are cremated under the blue sky, close to the people who loved them, who still love them." She paused, reflecting. Jean-Claude touched her arm with his, but didn't speak. He smoked in silence, looking at her from time to time, watching the Ganges and the people in the water. Maria continued: "I must admit that it is strange to see all these bodies that burn simultaneously, and it hurts, but I think it is a comfort to those who die, knowing that they won't be buried underground and instead will be cremated and freed into the air."

Jean-Claude put his arm around her shoulders and hugged her.

The chai seller was back: "Chai, Madam? Sir? Biscuits?"

She shook her head, but he asked for a tea. "How can you drink tea in such a place? It shows lack of respect," she scolded him.

"Because I'm thirsty. How much? Two rupees? That's expensive!" He tried to haggle on the price but the seller wasn't willing to lower it. He gave him two rupees and sipped the chai: "You know, this is the third time I have come here and I assure you that it makes a very different impression from the first time. You get used to it. And then, you said it yourself, the dead are still part of life. There's nothing wrong with selling and drinking tea. Many people here need it. Do you know how many hours it takes for a body to burn? As many as twenty four. If it weren't for the chai-wallah, where could they find something to drink? If you're grieving and cremating a loved one, a chai helps you, it gives you a bit of energy."

Despite the resistance she felt, Maria had to admit he had a point. "Why do you think so many people have shaved their heads?" she asked, looking around.

"Only the sons shave their heads as a sign of mourning when their father dies. Some will keep a tuft of hair at the top and from that you can see who has lost their father. And when the hair grows back, you can see who has suffered a loss recently." She nodded.

The sun was setting and she wanted to leave that place. They stood in silence and walked away. She had no idea how long they had spent in the cremation ground but it was almost evening by the time they left.

They arrived back on the main road where they were greeted once again by life, fast, loud, intense and beautiful. "Shall we go to a restaurant?" suggested Jean-Claude. No, she wanted to see Franca and Michel and hear what they had done during the day. It seemed a long time since she had seen them and had to remind herself that it was just the night before that she and Jean-Claude had been together for the first time. So many things had happened during those hours. He nodded.
"I'm sorry that you feel sad, now that you know I have a girlfriend. I love you very much and I feel very confused. I just know that I want to be with you."
Maria squeezed his hand. She understood and was grateful for his honesty. "Life is short, Jean-Claude. Let's enjoy what we have, without thinking too much about tomorrow. I'm glad I've met you." He hugged her and held her close.

The street lights all came on at the same time and the atmosphere changed. There were stalls on wheels that cooked and sold food. With their kerosene stoves at full throttle they were preparing sabji, bhaji and curry dishes that were served there and then with banana leaves for plates. People ate standing up and everywhere there was an air of celebration.
An old man was sitting on the floor with his back against the wall, rolling bidis. Maria smoked them sometimes; they were small but very strong. He used small pieces of dry leaves and inside them put a pinch of chopped tobacco; he then rolled them tight and tied them with a short piece of cotton. His hands were wrinkled, deformed by arthritis, and he moved them with difficulty. His face, furrowed by deep lines, seemed to be made of leather. He raised his eyes and looked at her with a straight face. "You want bidis?" he asked. Maria shook her head, smiling, no thanks. He didn't return her smile, lowered his eyes and continued to roll the narrow leaf, focused. He was visibly making a great effort with those crooked and gnarled fingers. He was so old, Maria thought with a pang, he shouldn't have to work. "Yes, a packet, please. How much?" she said.
"Three rupees," replied the old man, sounding tired. It was double the normal price. Maria gave him three rupees and thanked him, her hands clasped in front of her chest, bowing. He gave her a weak smile.

Music came from afar and spontaneously they walked toward it. Rather than music it was a cacophony of drums and trumpets. It seemed as if everyone was playing as they wanted, indifferent to the sound of the other instruments. It was madness put into music. For brief moments she could discern a certain harmony but this was soon interrupted by the intervention of an out-of-tune trumpet and everyone went back to beat their drums and blow into their wind instruments as they pleased.

"What kind of music is this?" she asked, covering her ears with her hands.

"I don't know, let's go and find out," said Jean-Claude, quickening his pace. Nothing could have prepared them for the spectacle that confronted them when they turned the corner!

A huge elephant marched slowly and heavily toward them, preceded by the out-of-tune band. Some of the members, elegantly dressed in white and red uniforms, blew into the shiny trumpets with all the strength they could muster, while others were energetically beating the drums, all without any apparent logic or a recognizable harmony to the western ear. Behind them, imposing and dignified, advanced the most colourful elephant she had ever seen.

Jean-Claude hurried to open his camera bag and started to take photographs. The procession was advancing noisily, without haste.

The elephant was covered in colourful drawings, painted with skill all over its head, ears and trunk. The huge head was adorned with golden chains, complete with a big pendant between its two large eyes, which sparkled under the bright street lights. Only then they saw that the first elephant was followed by two more, as big and colourful as the first one. On the second elephant's back was a canopy fitted with curtains partly sheltering the occupants, two young men. The one in front was wearing a strange hat made of gold stripes and a necklace of banknotes. The third elephant was slightly smaller and this, in turn, was followed by white bulls with red painted horns, pulling a cart occupied by beautiful people richly dressed. Some women wore red saris, the veil hiding most of the face, but allowing a glimpse of dark, beautiful eyes magnified and enhanced by kajal, intense and mysterious. Other women wore saris of different colours, green, yellow, blue, and the contrast between them, so close to each other, was a feast for the eyes. More people followed on foot, elegantly dressed in white uniforms, carrying large trays filled with gold and silver packets.

Jean-Claude was busy taking pictures and moved as best he could through the thick crowd that lined the road, watching the procession. Maria asked a man standing nearby if he knew what it was all about. It was a wedding procession, he explained, speaking of it with great deference. The man on the elephant was the groom and the one behind him was the best man. Was it a rich people's wedding? Oh yes, very rich, confirmed the man, with admiration. He added that she was going to see many marriages of that kind in Varanasi, it was wedding season. And what was that money necklace around his neck? That was symbolic of luck and abundance, and had she seen the men carrying trays? They were full of sweets covered in silver and gold, to wish good luck and abundance. Really? Could they be eaten, with gold and silver? Sure, he said, pleased at the interest that Maria was showing for his culture. And when was the marriage taking place, now? No, probably tomorrow, but the party continued for more than a week, with hundreds of guests. It was a very beautiful wedding, he said with sincere admiration, without a trace of envy or criticism. Maria thanked him and, with difficulty, made her way among the people to reach Jean-Claude. They stood back while the procession continued at a slow pace, followed by the crowd, and found each other again. His eyes were sparkling with enthusiasm: "I took some great pictures! It's a wedding, right?" Maria told him what the man had explained to her, as they walked toward their hotel. Thanks to the procession they had forgotten the sadness that had followed them like a grey cloud all afternoon. Jean-Claude hugged her and kissed her on the lips and Maria responded with freedom.

The air was losing the heat of the day and it was pleasant to walk with fewer people around. The street restaurants served tables full of patrons; rickshaw drivers pedalled in a relaxed fashion enjoying the breeze that began to blow, while others, empty ones, advanced idly, looking around in search of customers; men walked, holding hands with other men. How strange! There were so many, walking at ease, and it seemed perfectly normal to everyone. Were they all homosexual couples? Jean-Claude, who was better informed than she, explained that it was perfectly normal for male friends to walk hand in hand, while it wasn't for couples of men and women. But this didn't apply to them, he hastened to add, because they were westerners. He brought Maria's hand to his lips and kissed it, with his ironic smile.

When they reached the Yogi Lodge they were greeted by the porch lights that lit up the street. The bulls were gone, but in their place lurked a pack of skinny dogs, sickly and hostile, that began to growl with a guttural sound. Maria stopped abruptly, blocked by a primordial fear that prevented her from going any further. Jean-Claude stood a few steps in front of her, but the dogs were looking at her with eyes full of hatred. They felt her fear and, one by one, began to growl louder, more and more aggressive, until the first one burst into hysterical barking. Soon, the others joined in, staring at her with bloodshot eyes, full of madness. She could clearly see their sharp teeth that made them look like vampires.

Jean-Claude said: "Ignore them, Maria, they won't touch you." But there was some hesitation in his voice; he couldn't be sure.

"I can't! They are ready to pounce on me." She heard the panic in her voice, but the fear she felt inside was even stronger.

The dogs perceived it and, while completely ignoring Jean-Claude, they were preparing to attack her, howling, growling, barking and placing the weight of their bodies, all skin and bones, on their hind legs. They moved as a group and then, almost frightened by their own anger, retreated a few steps. They were too close to her and she was paralyzed by fear. Without taking his eyes off the pack, Jean-Claude bent down and quickly picked up some stones from the ground. Then he stepped back and positioned himself in front of her, protecting her with his body. He began to throw stones aiming at the dogs' heads while, step by step, gaining a bit of ground. Finally, the dogs drew back a little. It was enough to enable them to reach the Yogi Lodge. They went running in and shut the door quickly behind them.

Shaken by the experience, Maria was happy to be safe in the relaxed atmosphere of the guesthouse. The benches in the restaurant were all occupied. There were many new faces, but she couldn't see Franca. They went upstairs and found her in the dorm. She was sitting on the bed and was talking with Michel, who was sitting on the bed opposite, and stood up joyfully as soon as he saw them: "There you are! Where have you been all day?" He hugged Jean-Claude and Maria could see both the joy of seeing him and the shadow of confusion that crossed Michel's eyes. He was thinking of Jean-Claude's girlfriend, no doubt. Maria understood that brief moment of embarrassment, the unspoken question, but she didn't feel guilty. She was going to give him up but, for now, she would live in the present moment, with abandon. Was there anything else apart from the present? Present, gift, the two words meant the same. She went to kiss Franca, who greeted her with the same reserve, but full of curiosity.

"What did you do today?" Maria asked, to shift the centre of attention. They had explored separately, and had lots of interesting stories to tell. They ate together and Maria saw that Michel wanted to ask her something, but didn't know how. She encouraged him, with quiet self-assurance. It was not what she expected. He wanted to know why she had taken opium, what effect it had had on her, and whether it was worth it.

She had almost forgotten about it and had to think before answering his questions. She had taken it because it had been offered to her, pushed into her hand, literally, saying that it was the best and that she had to try it, and because she was a little curious to have the experience. What effect had it had on her? She had felt calm, at the beginning, which later became indifference. After that she had lost all emotions and the ability to move independently, to make decisions. It had cut her off from life. Had she liked it? What was there to like? she said, looking back dispassionately at her lack of strength, physical coordination, the loss of her most essential faculties. No, she couldn't say she had liked it. On the contrary, it had been a big waste of time; she had lost at least one whole day of her life sleeping like a log. While *they* were around Varanasi, she was in oblivion, losing all the experiences and emotions she would have had and felt, had she been herself. Would she take it again? Under normal conditions, she wouldn't, replied Maria, after a long reflection. But, had she been ill, with severe pain and no hope, had she wanted to erase all feelings from her physical and mental life, then it would probably be an appropriate drug. Otherwise, no. Opium had been for her the denial of life, a taste of death itself. There was only one thing though... What? all three of them asked. She thought she looked prettier when she was under the influence of opium, her eyes were lighter. "That's not true," said Jean-Claude, "you are more beautiful now, your face changes with a thousand expressions, it's vibrant with life, emotions, laughter, compassion."

"You looked a bit like a Martian," said Michel, "but, if you like Martians, then it's fine." They all laughed. Maria looked at Franca who had listened in silence. Feeling consulted, and after a moment's thought, she said, reluctantly: "You were strange, like an automaton, a doll made of flesh; you're better when you are you."

They smoked in the men's room and talked all evening, of cremations, the bazaar, ankle bracelets, the wedding procession, mad dogs. There were many dogs and monkeys with rabies, said Michel. They had to be alert not to get bitten; even a scratch would be dangerous. Maria shivered. So what can you do in a situation like the one they had found themselves in, especially if someone was alone, she asked. You mustn't be afraid, was the unanimous answer. Easier said than done! It was the only way, said Michel, he knew dogs well, they perceived the smell of fear, but for the same reason, they were also aware of the strength of those who didn't fear them. She had to show them who was boss. How? They obviously didn't understand words! No, but they understood the tone of voice. She had to shout louder than they, order them to be silent; they would back off. She had to turn fear into courage. Nam-myoho-renge-kyo, thought Maria, automatically. She said it aloud.

Both Michel and Jean-Claude were curious and wanted to know more, asking one question after another. They talked till late of the Ten Worlds, of life and death, the Treasure Tower, and they were fascinated. Maria and Franca tried to explain what they remembered, but it wasn't as clear as when Sanya and Colin, and then Luna, had explained it to them. At the end of the evening they recited it together, the male and female voices creating a small orchestra, a harmonious unison composed by the diversity and uniqueness of their voices and their lives. That chant had cleansed everything else; it had put the emotions of the day to rest, quietly and peacefully, and they felt free and light, relaxed and satisfied, with bright eyes and hearts overflowing with joy.

They spent six days together, inseparable. Maria got up at half past four with Jean-Claude and they went out, holding hands. The first time she took her camera, but it was a burden and didn't allow her to freely observe the life happening around her. She decided to leave it at home and immerse herself in the reality without any distractions. He instead never had enough, always found new things to photograph and she often showed him a new angle, a particular composition, looking through the eyes of a painter.

They went back along the ghats and she saw the cremations from the moment they began. The bodies were brought down by the river, along the steps. The family checked that the pyre was ready and well kitted out and then rested the body of the loved one over the woodpile. The eldest son lit the first wisp of straw, brought it close and, little by little, the flames were being fed, growing in volume and intensity until the pyre was burning strongly. There was no more hurry, just hours and hours spent to feed the fire, arranging and rearranging the pieces of wood, walking around the pyre, praying, wiping away the tears, saying goodbye to those who had gone, freeing them from the now useless body to let it merge with the larger universe, eternity and freedom. Until next time.

When the man arrived who sold the chai, she drank it, still feeling a little uncomfortable. The hot sweet drink comforted her, gave her strength and solace, as she watched Life in front of her turn into black smoke and go up in intense gusts toward the sky. Never, like in those moments, had she realized how precious the present was, she who had spent years thinking about the past and worrying about the future. Jean-Claude encircled her waist with his arm, took her hands in his, she felt his cheek stroking her hair, his warm breath on her neck. She would never forget those moments, and didn't ask for more. Sitting on the steps of the ghats, she unhurriedly watched life and death looking at each other, holding hands, mirroring one another like the moon in the water of the Ganges, and didn't ask herself any more questions.

Often, they took a boat that crossed the holy river to the opposite bank, the quiet side. From there they had an all-encompassing view of the activities in which they had been immersed for the first few days: the ghats, these people's faith, the trust in their existence, the slow pace of life that had time for prayer and gratitude. There were a multitude of palaces and temples on that bank and they took shelter from the heat of the midday sun, talking and kissing, sitting on the stone floors under the vaulted arches, in the cool shade, enjoying the breeze that blew through the temple, open to all who wanted to stop. They were quiet places and often almost deserted.

One day, despite the late morning heat, Jean-Claude left to take pictures. Maria stayed to shelter from the sun, watching the Ganges flow in front of her eyes. Sitting on the cool stone in their favourite temple, the crowded ghats on the opposite bank, she began to recite 'daimoku', as she often did when she was alone. She freed the sound of her voice, which bounced crystal clear between the stone columns. Leaning against one of the pillars she drifted with the vibrations of the chanting; it had become an engine fed by the energy of the universe. Unexpectedly, in front of her eyes, the image of her mother's face appeared, as if inside a cloud; it seemed so real she felt she could touch it. Surprised, she continued to chant. The image of her mother moved, as if it were the carriage of a passing train, giving way to the next car. Another picture showed, inside its own little cloud, it was her friend Ester's face. Even more surprised, she continued to chant, while the second image moved away. It was followed by the third and final image; in the third cloud, there was Jean-Claude's face, which slipped away, like the other two had done. What did it mean? She continued to chant, waiting for the answer that she felt to be close. She kept her back straight while the strength within her continued to grow, filling her heart and nourishing her body with energy.

What was the relationship between these three people? What did they have in common? Why them? Nam-myoho-renge-kyo. She had to relax, slow down her mind that was anxiously trying to understand. Finally, the answer made its way from her heart, clear and without any doubt. It was love that these three people had in common, the love they felt for her and the love she felt for them. She didn't stop; she continued chanting vigorously and, from the depths of her life, Maria knew they had met before, in a distant past, that her life had not begun when she was born, but before. She perceived on her skin, in every cell of her body, in every meander of her mind, with a warm and delicate shudder, that she had already lived. And if she had already lived before, she would live again in the future. This meant that her life was eternal. She gasped in surprise. As if a tap had suddenly opened, tears began to flow from her eyes, streaming down her cheeks, but she wasn't crying, her throat didn't close. On the contrary, she continued to chant faster, clearer, louder and, from the bottom of her stomach, indeed deeper from her navel, or even deeper still, from her belly and even further down... a giggle was freeing itself, making her tremble with joy. It rose up to her navel, continued to climb and made her stomach flutter with mirth. It rose higher still and her heart shook with laughter; it didn't stop, it reached her throat and she smiled, it rose even further and filled her mind. She was laughing, happy, while the flood of tears gave no sign of stopping. Total happiness, never felt before, filled her completely, while a calmness, a certainty, a solid confidence settled in her chest and led her, little by little, to calm the internal trembling that shook her physically.

The memory of it stayed, as clear as a photograph, a tangible feeling of a deep emotion, an overwhelming intense joy that permeated every one of her cells. She was in no hurry to wipe away the tears; a smile invaded her face, bliss filled her life, transcending her body and mind. She leaned against the temple's column and looked at the Ganges. She was happy, surprised, excited, quivering inside, vibrant, certain, grateful, full of energy and life.

Jean-Claude arrived and, seeing her like this, the words he was saying froze and died halfway in his throat. He looked at her twice, wondering: "What's happening? Have you been crying? Your face is full of light!"

Still happily shocked by the experience she told him what she had felt and perceived on her skin. Looking into his eyes, she told him she had realized that between them was love, true love, generous, selfless, unconditional, the one that wanted the other person's happiness, mystic. Jean-Claude, who had listened in silence, almost without breathing, nodded, moved. Even he knew that what they had was very special. He sat closer and hugged her, in silence. He kissed her hair, he closed her eyes, red from crying, with his lips, and kissed her smiling lips.

Those days they visited all the temples around Varanasi, they walked holding hands, laughing at the monkeys that, while jumping nimble and agile, watched everything from the top of the walls. They learned not to leave bananas inside the bags with their valuables, because the monkeys stole bags to get to the bananas and carried them away, jumping and laughing. Whenever they stopped to rest, they were surrounded by children with whom they played. They never spoke of their separation, until the last day. Both knew that everyone would continue their journey, the girls toward Nepal, the men travelling south.

"I don't know how I'm going to continue my journey without you," said Jean-Claude. "India will never be the same. I'll miss you too much."

Maria had thought about it a lot, and felt calm. "Instead you have to enjoy your trip," she said. "You came here with an idea in your head, and you must carry on with what you had set out to do. There is a woman in Paris who's waiting for you, and in a few weeks you'll return. What life has given us is beautiful, but for now, we'll go our own ways. Let's write to each other, and then just see what happens."

What a noble soul! But was she sure of what she was saying? She was sure. Jean-Claude had already done so much for her; he had cured her. Those two words "ciao bella!" had expressed everything. He loved her for what she was; he adored her, without any 'buts', 'ifs' or 'except for whens'... He had made her understand that she *could* be loved. Through his consistent love, he had helped her sweep away the insecurities and pain of the past, releasing her. Her new life had begun when he invited her to drink that first cup of tea. What else could someone ask, without causing suffering to another? She was free and light and felt a lot of gratitude for the present. But, at the thought of being separated from him, her heart grew heavy as lead, it felt like a bag full of wet sand inside her chest. She tried not to think about it, and when they spoke, they tried to convince each other that it was the best thing to do. They were friends, laughing, joking, playing, and if, when they looked at each other, the laughter died in their throat, they clung to each other, unable to speak.

The last night was full of giggles and grief. When she cried, Jean-Claude said something funny and they burst out laughing, mixing tears of sorrow with tears of hilarity, insecure kisses with hysterical howling. They had promised to give each other complete freedom, even if they would have gladly done without. They departed from the Yogi Lodge late in the afternoon, Maria and Jean-Claude on a rickshaw, Franca and Michel followed on another, which soon overtook them. Jean-Claude and Maria kissed, despite the looks from the people in the street. Their rickshaw man sped up the race and overtook Franca and Michel's, throwing their driver a defiant smile. Franca's rickshaw wallah began to pedal harder and soon overtook his colleague again, with a laugh of satisfaction. His lead didn't last long, because Maria's driver pedalled even faster in the evening's cool air and passed him again. Maria and Jean-Claude were rooting for their man and encouraged him to ride hard, while Michel and Franca spurred their own on to win the race. They arrived at the station with faces red with laughter, and paid double fare to the two fastest rickshaw drivers in Varanasi, for the fun they had given them.

Franca and Michel walked away to leave them a few minutes on their own on the platform. He held her close and whispered the sweetest things that came to mind, surprising her from time to time with a joke that made her giggle.

The train announced its arrival with a shrill whistle and the people stood up, with their bundles, luggage and children, to prepare for the assault. Jean-Claude gave her a small package and encouraged her to open it; inside was a beautiful silver enamel box, so that she wouldn't forget him, he said. Together with Michel they helped them find the right coach and their reserved seats, carried their backpacks and settled them in their places. Maria asked him to leave before the train departed, she couldn't bear to see him from the window as the train moved away. He understood, kissed her for the last time and got off the train, accompanied by Michel. He turned several times as he walked along the platform with his head low, waving his arm at Franca, who was waving goodbye through the open window. Maria remained sitting in her place, her heart suspended in limbo, refusing to think, unable to speak. Franca sat down and looked at her without saying anything. She heard the shrill whistle of the train conductor, start-up messages and 'cheloh, cheloh!' shouted by the railway workers, the doors being slammed, one by one, with a sharp bang and finally the train moved. At the first jolt, tears filled Maria's eyes, at the second they began to run down her cheeks. Her friend looked through her bag, pulled out a handkerchief and handed it to her. Then, she looked out the window and let her cry in peace.

18. The temple of your life

The train left Varanasi and soon it was running through the open countryside. Maria wiped her tears, her heart ached, full of all the love she had given and received and that had changed her. "How are you?" she asked Franca. They hadn't been alone for a long week.

"So so." What did 'so so' mean? Franca opened up, like a dam that can no longer withstand the pressure of the water. She had felt alone, and seeing the two of them so much in love had made her feel that something was missing. She liked Michel, but he hadn't noticed.

One day, while she was walking around Varanasi, she went past a door ajar onto the street. Something told her to stop and, looking through the gap, she saw a man sitting in the lotus position, dressed in orange, with hair down to his waist; he looked like a sadhu. While she watched him, he looked up and beckoned her to enter. He was an American who had been living in India for many years. He asked her who she was and, while she explained that she was Italian, he began to lift her shirt. She was a little surprised, but she liked this mysterious man, a quasi-sadhu, and let him continue. She told him that she had been in the Himalayas to make charas, and meanwhile he undid her pyjama trousers and pulled them down. She was still telling him about the landslide on the road, when he made her lie down on the mattress and then, without preamble, he penetrated her. With some unease, Franca pointed out to him that the door was still a little open onto the road. He pushed it with his foot... but it didn't close completely and, in any case, within minutes, it was all over. He lay on top of her for a moment longer and then rolled to the side, with a satisfied smile.

"If I hadn't told him to open his eyes, he wouldn't even have looked at me afterwards."

"And you? How did you feel?" Well, it wasn't the best sex she had ever had; from a physical point of view it had been a complete nothing, but sentimental soppy things didn't appeal to her, and this was certainly a different man, eccentric, original. So, it had been an interesting, new experience, such as those she sought.

"And after that? Did you see him again?"

"I tried, I wouldn't have minded," said Franca."But I went there a couple of times and the door was always closed. But it's fine!" she concluded, although Maria had a feeling she wasn't being completely honest with herself. Had she used any precautions, a condom? Franca shrugged! No, and the thought bothered her, she was a bit, but only a bit, worried. She had stopped taking the pill when she had left Italy, thinking that she wouldn't need it. In a few days' time she would know, because her cycle was almost due to start.

"And you? Did you take precautions?" Yes, Maria was on the pill and hadn't stopped it when she left Italy. "Well at least I had an interesting experience, and with a sadhu in India," she said, to console herself. Then, was he a sadhu? Well not quite, but almost. Maria preferred not to ask any more questions.

They looked out of the open window at the fields, the cows, the people who worked in the rice paddies. In the distance, villages lived at the familiar slow pace of life: carts pulled by oxen with long horns, dogs seeking food scraps. She saw three kids sharing a bicycle, one pedalling standing up, another sitting on the seat and the third balanced on the handlebars; they pedalled as fast as possible to keep up with the train, waving their arms to greet the passengers, hoping that someone would deign to answer. Maria returned their greeting and saw them smile, happy and excited. Before their eyes flowed the normal, slow life, made of acceptance and gratitude, typical of the Indian countryside; she couldn't be sure if it were really so, but this was the perception she had. Meanwhile, the warm wind lifted her long hair, drying it with the dust and the heat. Dusk arrived turning the pale blue sky into an intense blue background for the orange ball's descent, becoming fiery red as it neared the horizon.

Among the passengers of the 'second-class carriage with sleepers', normally noisy with endless conversations, crept a calm silence, while each one in their own way thanked the universe for another day that was about to end. As the sun sank below the horizon, the sky was painted with pink, red and orange hues in a cloudless sunset and, before long, it was night.

They bought a vegetarian dinner served on a stainless steel plate with compartments, prepared by the railway restaurant. It contained white rice, dal, two types of bhaji, some yogurt and a chapati. It was good and inexpensive. As soon as she could, Maria settled on her wooden berth and lay on top of her sleeping bag, while Franca climbed on the top bunk opposite. They closed their eyes, thinking of the past week, lulled by the rhythm of the train as it ran on the rails. She missed Jean-Claude so much! Had she given him up too easily? Could she have continued her journey with him and Michel? Without realizing it she slipped into a deep sleep, hugging his creased sarong that he had had given her, in exchange for hers.

They awoke to the sound of the other passengers' voices, who were freshening up with a little water from the toilets. As always, they were curious and would have gladly struck up a conversation, but the girls weren't in the mood to do so.

At the first station where the train stopped, Maria leaned out of the window, invited by the cries of the chai wallahs: Chai garam, chai garam! Hot chai. She caught a young boy's attention, who sold her two clay cups full of steaming hot chai, which they sipped slowly. The clay cups ought to be thrown out of the window, explained one of the passengers, but she kept hers.

The train arrived at Patna station during the cool early morning hours. Just outside they bought their tickets to Kathmandu and waited patiently for the coach to arrive. It didn't take long. The bus quickly filled with people who, in addition to their luggage, carried baskets containing chickens, lambs, sheep and goats. They were placed on the roof and carefully tied with ropes to the iron structure of the roof rack. The bus was completely full of Indians and Nepalese people. The latter looked very different from the Indians, with oriental traits and of a darker complexion, tanned by the strong sun of those living in mountainous areas. The girls had forgotten how uncomfortable normal buses were, but at least the journey would last only a few hours. They spent the time looking out the window, watching how the scenery changed as the plains grew into hills and the fields became green and more fertile.

A few hours later they reached the Indian border where everyone had to get off, taking their luggage with them. To cross the border they had to cover the last stretch on foot and then, in Nepalese territory, they would board another bus. They had learned to ask fewer questions and to adjust to whatever reality they found, so they got ready to walk a few hundred yards on the dirt road.

It was then that Maria realized that her friend was limping, trying not to put weight on one of her feet. She insisted that Franca lift the leg of her pyjama trousers and, with a shudder of disgust, she saw that her legs and feet were covered with huge infected purple boils filled with pus: "Mamma mia, Franca! I hadn't realized you had such serious infections."

"No!" said her companion," you were too involved with your Frenchman." But how had they become so large and so numerous? She had furiously scratched the flea bites and they had become infected. In addition, she had walked barefoot around Varanasi, to feel more 'sadhu'.

Fascinated by their free life style, she had adopted their most obvious customs.

"Why didn't you go and see a doctor?" asked Maria.

Franca shrugged. "You care so much now, but all week you haven't bothered with me in the least," she replied sullenly. If she had wanted to make her feel guilty, she had succeeded.

There was a group of rickshaws waiting for customers and Maria raised her arm to call one of them. Franca sat on its narrow red plastic seat. Maria loaded their backpacks and walked by its side, covering the few hundred yards that separated them from the actual border. The heat was unbearable. "We need to find a doctor as soon as possible, you can't possibly carry on with these infections, or hope to cure them by yourself," said Maria. For once Franca didn't object; even she found it upsetting to look at them. In a few minutes they reached the Indian border and were directed to the customs booth.

The guards watched Maria trying to help her friend get off the rickshaw, but the pain of the infections had reached her limit and, although she could stand up, she could no longer walk, let alone carry her rucksack. Maria looked in the direction of the guards and met a senior officer's gaze. She clasped her hands before her heart and bowed, her eyes asking him for help. The officer approached. Maria lifted a leg of Franca's pyjamas, and said: "My friend can't walk." At the sight of the infections the officer reacted with surprise. "Is there a doctor nearby?" she asked with little hope of a positive response. He nodded and told her to go inside the customs office and wait there.

Inside the booth, the girls sat on a bench along the wall. Two fans hanging from the ceiling were turning round and round, but they made little difference; it was hard to breathe in that heat. The young soldiers looked at them with curiosity. One of them came up: "Passports, please!" Maria gave him both passports and told him that her friend needed help, pointing to Franca's swollen feet. The soldier had a good look at their passports, slowly handed them back to Maria and motioned to sit there and wait. Franca looked angrily away, reacting with impatience and frustration to the pain and concern; she had lost control of the situation and she knew it. The officer returned before long, accompanied by a man carrying a wooden case.

He knelt on the ground; with a look at Franca he asked permission to raise her pyjama leg and glanced at the infections. Without a word, he opened his case and pulled out bandages, a bottle and a knife with a retractable blade. At the sight of the knife Maria was concerned: "Are you a doctor?" she asked. She was afraid to offend him but... a knife like that was quite worrying.

The man didn't answer her and instead looked at Franca, who was watching him with a downcast expression. In his elementary English he told her he had to cut the skin to let the pus out, before the infection poisoned her blood even more. "It's this big," he said, joining his index finger to his thumb: dangerous. He had seen a lot of infections like these and knew what to do. He didn't look directly at Maria, but he was answering her question. Franca nodded silently and held out her filthy dusty foot.

Maria met her brave gaze, knowing she had confidence in local doctors. The man let out the razor blade from the Stanley knife and warned her that it would hurt a little. Looking at the infection, she nodded silently and then looked away, focusing on the ceiling fan.

The tip of the blade cut easily through the swollen purple skin and a nasty mixture of blood and pus oozed from the infection, sliding along her foot. Maria had to look away and held her friend's hand, who squeezed it tight. The soldiers who were waiting to see Franca's reaction were impressed by her courage and soon lost interest. They turned to the passengers who were waiting in the queue to get through customs and began to check their documents. The doctor pushed the infected part with his thumb to bring out all the liquid, while Franca bit her lip to keep from screaming and clutched Maria's hand tighter. From the bottle he poured a yellow powder and dusted it carefully on the infection, now emptied and flattened. He quickly bandaged her foot and ankle and, without a word, moved to her other foot. He selected the largest infection, similar to the first one in size, throbbing, full of blood and pus. This time, when he cut her skin with the blade, Franca couldn't hold back her tears. Maria returned the handkerchief she had borrowed on the train and she buried her whole face in it.

The soldiers, who were waiting for this moment, stopped to watch and seeing Franca's tears, looked at each other, smiling as if to say: 'That's more like it!'

Franca soaked the handkerchief with tears, then blew her nose in it and said: "I want my mum!" and they both laughed. The doctor finished bandaging the second foot and then advised her to get some rest and buy a blood purifying syrup as soon as possible. "I cut the two worst boils, but your blood is no good, as a result of such bad infections. The syrup will purify it and this will help to heal the smaller infections, which I haven't treated now. Don't walk for a few days." He told her to do some foot baths with salt and hot water and let them dry in the sun, protecting the cuts from flies, and to wear shoes. "Why don't you wear something on your feet?" he scolded her. Surely she had the money to buy a pair of rubber flip-flops. Only the poorest people went around barefoot, they belonged to the lowest caste, didn't she know? And that was only because they were too poor to buy shoes. She had to take care of her body; it was the temple of her life. Franca nodded gratefully.

"How do you feel now?" Maria asked.

"It still hurts, but not like before," she said, pale and exhausted. "It's a different feeling, as if I've been beaten up." The man asked where they were headed. There was a very good doctor in Kathmandu, he said, called Dr. Mannah, a true authority in the field of natural medicine. He advised her to go and see him; he would certainly be able to help her, if she needed it. Maria paid him the five rupees he asked and thanked him.

The officer appeared in the doorway preceded by a boy carrying a metal frame containing six glasses of steaming chai. He went to the soldiers who, one by one, took their glass and then, with the last two, he approached the girls and offered the chai to them, with a smile full of curiosity. They were surprised and touched by the kindness, and thanked the officer with a nod of the head. They sipped the hot tea, blowing to cool it down. It was amazing how, with such searing temperatures, one could enjoy a drink that hot. The chai comforted them and gave them some strength, full as it was of spices and sugar. As soon as they had finished it, the officer waved them to come to the door. Their rickshaw was waiting outside. Maria, who was carrying all the luggage, set them up on one side of the seat and then helped Franca, who was limping with both her feet, to sit on the other side. All the soldiers went out to see them go. Maria clasped her hands in front of her heart and bowed: "Dhanyavad," she said, from the heart, and then she also said in English: "Thank you! Thank you very much!" Despite trying to keep a stern expression, the policemen smiled and returned a little bow of farewell.

Maria walked next to the rickshaw with a hand on the backpacks to keep them steady, slowly covering the short distance on the dirt path that separated them from the Nepalese border. She turned and raised her arm to wave to the officer, who was still watching them from the door. Just a hundred more yards and then they would leave India.

In a few minutes they reached the Nepalese customs. Maria walked into the office where she explained Franca's situation. A couple of soldiers came outside and checked their passports, leaving Franca on the rickshaw. They looked at her passport photo, then at the girl before them, they returned to look at the picture and then back to the girl. Maria could see from their expression that they found it hard to find a similarity between the clean, respectable face with make-up on in the photo and the dusty, thin, tanned and tired face they had in front of them. Finally, satisfied with the authenticity of the document, they returned the passports and the girls covered the last few yards to their coach, Maria walking with her hand on their luggage, Franca on the rickshaw.

The bus was waiting only for them. Maria climbed on the roof twice to place the rucksacks while Franca, unable to hide her pain, struggled to climb the coach's steps, and then limped slowly up to her seat. The passengers had seen the doctor taking care of her feet in the customs booth and looked at her with kindness. The passenger next to her squeezed into his seat to give her space for her bound feet. As soon as Maria climbed on board, the bus drove off.

"How are you?" she enquired.

"Pissed off!" replied her companion. "I hate depending on others, my feet and legs hurt like hell and I can't walk. What bothers me most about these infections is that I can't go anywhere, so they'll have to heal in record time. I'll begin immediately, as soon as we get to Kathmandu!"

"Excellent idea. Let's go to this Dr. Mannah, if he is as good as they say... he'll be a godsend, with a name like that!"

"We'll see," said Franca, curtly. Maria knew it was better to leave her alone, give her space and especially avoid giving her the impression of wanting to decide on her behalf. She took her hand, but her friend freed herself irritably, and surreptitiously wiped a tear.

They knew the trip would last several hours and turned to watch the scenery going past in front of their eyes. At first it wasn't very different from India, but soon it began to change. The terraced paddy fields were an amazing pea green. With few exceptions, the women working in them didn't wear a sari, but a long straight skirt, made by wrapping a piece of fabric around their waist. As a belt they wore a broad band of cloth of a slightly different colour, folded several times, so that within the folds they could keep the most essential things. As in India, in the rice paddies there were only women, mothers and grandmothers, most of them with a tight bundle on their backs. The babies were asleep, lulled by the constant movement of the women who bent down and stood up again, taking yet another rice seedling from the saturated ground, spending all day with wet feet. The rice fields ended and they travelled for hours without seeing anyone, in a much less populated landscape than India.

Finally they stopped at a chai-shop; the village consisted of a few huts around it. Maria ordered chai and samosas, while Franca came down from the bus slowly, with great care. She walked barefoot, but this time because she couldn't wear shoes and had no flip-flops; she had decided to buy a pair as soon as possible. Sipping their cup of tea, they observed the life around them.

These people seemed poorer than the Indians. The bright colours of the sari had given way to earthy colours, the more sober brown, grey, dark green. Like the Indian women, the Nepalese wore a long braid down to the waist, but instead of glossy hair treated with coconut oil, their braids were dusty and lacklustre. The natural elegance of Indian women was replaced by the Nepalese women's more robust and solid bearing; they looked as though they had a harder life. Around the neck they wore large coloured necklaces, perhaps made of plastic, but all the same, cheerful and bright.

She watched them squatting by the stream that ran along the road, washing pots with a handful of grass mixed with earth. They first washed the inside and then the outside, black as pitch because of the wood fire that soiled them relentlessly. They scratched and rubbed, turning the pot with automatic movements, without looking at it, scooping up some water and rinsing it occasionally, and then starting all over again with a handful of fresh grass and earth. Meanwhile, they spoke with other women crouched close to them, exchanging a comment and a chuckle. They stood up with a clean pot and stiff legs, straightening their bodies, rubbing the lower back with a mixture of fatigue and satisfaction. Here, too, the children's favourite game was to run pushing along a bicycle wheel with a stick. They ran back and forth, competing to see who came first to the finish line with the wheel still standing. She couldn't see any toys, but the children seemed happy.

There was a fountain a stone's throw from the chai-shop and the passengers took it in turns to pump the water, one raising and lowering the outer handle, while the other washed their hands under the small jet. The girls approached slowly, one limping and the other close to her. Franca began to pump while Maria washed her hands and face, covered in dust; then they exchanged roles, Maria pumped while Franca bent down, only that she cupped her hands and took a good swig.

"Don't drink this water!" Maria said, alarmed.

"And why not? If they drink it, I can drink it too!"

"But I haven't seen any of the passengers drink it!"

"The locals drink it for sure. And don't tell me what to do and not to do, you're not my mother!" said Franca, exasperated.

"Don't you think you have enough problems with your feet, without looking for more?"

She knew that Franca would get even more annoyed, but how could she pretend it was alright and let her hurt herself? She remembered the

Tourist Camp's receptionist, Mr. Singh, telling her she was responsible for her friend, too. But Franca stated clearly that her feet were her own business and that she would manage very well by herself. To put an end to the discussion, she started limping toward the bus. They spoke next to nothing the last few hours on the way to Kathmandu until, finally, there it was, the capital of Nepal.

Maria waited for the passengers to bring down their baskets of chickens, goats and lambs, their trunks and bundles, then climbed onto the roof and brought down one rucksack at a time. Franca could hardly walk; her feet and legs had swollen during the long hours sitting still on the coach. They found themselves surrounded by rickshaw drivers who offered their vehicle and shouted the names of hotels they knew. Franca already knew where to go; her Italian friends had given her the name of a small hotel in the hippy, or bohemian, quarter in the capital's centre, a short walk from Durbar Square, the old town's main square.

More impatient than usual because of the pain, Franca opened a breach in the crowd; walking with difficulty, dragging her backpack, she got out of the annoying and oppressive mob and stopped in front of a rickshaw driver who was waiting quietly. She instructed him as to where she wanted to go: Top View Hotel, and there was no arguing with that! She haggled on the price and tried to climb on alone, but her legs refused to obey her. Maria helped her to settle on the seat and the man promptly set off, pedalling hard.

They arrived at the historic part of the city; they left Durbar Square on their right and took a narrow street lined with shops selling clothes, bags, sweaters and silver jewellery. Between the different shops were many cafes; they each had a glass cabinet displaying huge and tasty slices of cake. They had never seen anything like that in India; the cakes were mouth-watering and Maria couldn't wait to get back there on foot. She glanced at Franca and was surprised by the expression of pain she saw on her face. She took her hand, and this time her friend let her, staring straight ahead.

Finally, the rickshaw stopped in front of the Top View Hotel. Maria wondered whether it really had the best view, as the name suggested. She tried to take charge of the backpacks, but Franca couldn't get down from the rickshaw by herself, or walk. Worry, pain and frustration were painted all over her face. Angry with the world, refusing the driver's help, she leaned on Maria's shoulder, while the man picked up their rucksacks with one hand, as if they were as light as feathers. They had a room available, large and comfortable, overlooking the narrow street full of shops, which had been nicknamed Freak Street. Maria loved both the guesthouse and the area. She couldn't wait to go for an exploratory walk, but Franca lay on the bed with her eyes closed, exhausted and worried.

"I'll help you with your feet, okay?" she said. Franca remained silent for a while and then nodded, without opening her eyes. "Do you want to take a foot bath with water and salt?"

"They're too dirty; I ought to wash them first. And how do I do the foot bath with warm water and salt? We have nothing," she replied with a choked voice that didn't sound like hers.

"Don't worry; I'm going to buy what we need. But as for washing them you'll have to go to the bathroom. You can wash them under the low tap; or you might as well take a shower, then you'll be all clean," she encouraged her, giving too many suggestions, she knew. Poor Franca; she had been very brave all day, but now she had had enough.

Maria went to consult with the clerk at reception, who advised her to buy a metal bowl and an electric element with which she could boil all the water she needed. He would have to charge them two extra rupees per day for the electricity. If she went to the trekkers' store, she'd find everything she needed.

Maria *had* to have at least a little look around the shops. There were some beautiful handmade sweaters with designs in black on a background of natural wool, thick and prickly, yak wool, said the Nepalese shopkeeper; colourful jackets, woven in the same bright colours she had seen in Mcleodganj's Tibetan shops, combinations of turquoise next to red, yellow near the green, interspersed with black and white. On display were trousers, kurta shirts, long skirts, all made by the tailor who worked in his shop's doorway. There were numerous shops selling silver jewels, set with turquoise and coral, the typical combination loved by Tibetan people. On trays covered with black velvet were rings of every shape with semi-precious stones, among which she recognized the white moonstones, black stars, blue lapis lazuli with flecks of gold, burgundy garnets, turquoise, coral. She noticed several restaurants, but the most compelling were the coffee shops with the slices of cake! Layers of sponge cake filled with different flavours and covered with a thick layer of cream. A note placed in front of each one revealed its flavour: Chocolate and cream, vanilla and coffee, banana and cream, strawberry and pistachio. Maria was starving! Despite the hurry, she stopped to buy a few slices to take back to the hotel and, whilst eating a banana and cream cake, she hastened to find the trekkers' store. In it there was everything one could need to go and walk in the mountains, or to climb the highest peaks of the Himalayas. Expeditions departed from Kathmandu for the Annapurna and Everest peaks. She bought the metal basin, the electric element and even found the salt. From the store entrance she could see the roofs of the many temples of Durbar Square.

The late afternoon was rapidly turning into evening, bringing with it the darkness and humidity of the mountains; they were at an altitude of over four thousand five hundred feet. She entered the square and walked toward a raised section, where street vendors exhibited their wares on hand-woven rugs. One by one they lit traditional fairy lights, small clay bowls with a wick in the middle filled with fat or oil, which burned like candles. With every passing minute the atmosphere was becoming more relaxed, a sense of intimacy and warm humanity pervaded the square, enriched and enlivened by the amazing sound of large conches, into which someone blew with all their strength; of trumpets playing a single note from the temples near and far; of bells and chants that performed the prayers of dusk; all joined in a mysterious and comforting atmosphere accompanying the setting sun.

She felt a hand touch her shoulder and she turned around, surprised. To her amazement, there was a girl from Venice who she recognized by the face, but couldn't quite place.
"You're Maria, aren't you?" asked the girl, with shining eyes.
"Yes, and you are...? I'm sorry but I don't remember your name!"
"Raffaella... Raffa! I am a friend of Franca's. Aren't you travelling together?"
"Yes, of course!" Maria explained the situation to Raffa, who she now remembered having seen many times in Campo Santo Stefano mingling with the group Franca belonged to. She invited her to come to their hotel. That was going to make Franca very happy, giving her some much needed encouragement.
As they walked together toward the Top View Hotel, Raffa explained that a group of Italians had rented a house outside Kathmandu and often hosted visiting friends. It was cheaper than staying in a hotel and it was great, just like being at home. The new girl was cheerful and Maria was digesting the idea of having met people from Venice in Kathmandu. On the one hand she liked it, but on the other it made her feel as if the adventure was somewhat diminished; after all, the reason she had left was to discover the world and herself. Raffa instead was very happy, apart from her in the house they were all males and she missed having a female friend. Now she had found two, she said, linking arms with her.

Maria knocked at the door to announce herself: "Close your eyes. I have a surprise!" Of course Franca kept her eyes wide open but, when she saw Raffa, her serious expression turned from irritation into surprise and then happiness. She uttered a cry of joy and opened her arms.

While Maria was preparing the bowl and warming the water with the electric element, the two friends were telling each other what they had done since the last time they had met. After ten minutes the water was boiling, Maria poured two handfuls of salt and dissolved them, stirring with a spoon. As soon as the water had cooled down sufficiently Franca put her feet in to soak and the conversation between her and Raffa focused on the various infections and diseases one could catch travelling in India and Nepal, such as diarrhoea. This way Maria discovered that Franca had diarrhoea that made her go to the toilet every half hour. Raffa invited them to move into the Italians' house, but Franca declined. For the time being she wanted to stay in the city centre, at least until her feet had healed, so she could go and sit in the square, soak up Kathmandu's atmosphere and take advantage of the shops and restaurants. The house was too far from the centre and she would be isolated. In addition, she had to be close to a toilet. But later on, yes, certainly, she would love to! The idea of not coming across as a tourist appealed to her immensely. Maria took out the slices of cake she had bought and divided them into three portions.

Raffa couldn't wait to go to Pokhara, a village at the foot of Mount Annapurna; it was beautiful, there was a large lake and the boys from the house went there often. She was waiting for the right opportunity, which never seemed to come, but since she was returning to Italy in a couple of weeks' time, and as it was also in the girls' plans, they decided to go together, just as soon as Franca's feet were healed.

During the following few days, Franca spent her time doing foot baths with water and salt, then limping the hundred yards to Durbar Square and sit in the sun with her feet in the air, while Maria and Raffa explored Kathmandu. The capital was quite a small city and, on the first day, they crossed the bridge leading to the temple area. The first excursion, virtually compulsory, was to the famous Swayambunath temple. They climbed the hundreds of steep steps leading to the temple where the Buddha's eyes, painted on the facade, watched thoughtfully over the Kathmandu valley. On top of the mountain, the golden tip of the temple shone gloriously, like an arrow silhouetted against the deep blue sky.

They liked being together; they understood each other without the need for words, so they often walked in silence. They had to stop several times during their ascent. With her slender body, Maria could climb without too much effort, but Raffa was more robust; she was out of shape and smoked a lot, and she was now panting with the effort of the steep climb. At each step, the Buddha's eyes became closer, and gradually they were pervaded by a profound feeling of reverence. The atmosphere was charged with a strong mystical vibration; the feeling of peace and respect grew as they went up and, in spite of becoming short of breath, they both hastened the pace. They reached the top and sat on the last step; from there they were so close they could have touched the Buddha's painted eyes. While the breeze cooled down their sweaty skin, their heartbeats gradually slowed down. They inhaled deeply the fresh mountain air, embracing with their eyes the valley that stretched out in front of them, filled with hundreds of smaller temples: they were built in different styles but all were made of white stone, seemingly feeding the main temple with their wealth of spirituality, peace and serenity. The sun warmed their backs, shoulders, heads, and they paused, in a silence that united them, feeling what they could not explain, accepting what they couldn't understand.

Maria confided in Raffa, telling her the concerns she had about Franca, how she treated her body and her attitude toward drugs. The new friend was pragmatic: "You can't live her life for her and she wouldn't let you. I've known her a lot longer than you. She's smart, but incredibly stubborn and thinks she knows everything. She will always do what she wants and doesn't listen to anyone, least of all to those who try too hard. If she thinks you want her to do something, you've already lost the battle. She can smell it, like an animal," she concluded with a laugh.

"But how can I stand there, watching without saying anything, if I see her doing things that harm her? Since we are travelling together we should take care of each other, right?"

Raffa snorted through her nose: "I don't think she's ever let anyone take care of her, not even her mother. She'll always do what she's decided to do, and no one can stop her. The best thing you can do is worry less."

"And if I see that she's killing herself, what do I do, look the other way?"

Raffa looked at her openly: "She won't kill herself, be sure! She likes to push things to the limits, and who are we to try and stop her? I told you, if you tell her not to do something she'll do it, on purpose!"

"Yeah, I noticed. I sometimes wonder how to get the desired result! What do you think, would it be a good idea to tell her to smoke all day, one chillum after another, and take opium every other day, to ensure that she gets bored with it?"

Raffa laughed heartily: "I don't think that would work! For Franca drugs are her field of exploration, her passion, like for a scientist is the study of science, or for a physicist the study of the universe."

"Or for an alcoholic to drink to oblivion, until he destroys himself!"

"The fact is that neither you, nor anyone else, will make her change her attitude. When she'll have had it up to here," she said, sweeping her hand over her head," she'll decide to change. She's much stronger than you think!"

Maria had her doubts, but Raffa's words and the conviction with which she said them, made her feel less responsible and confirmed what she already felt: she couldn't be Don Quixote tilting against the windmills. It was useless, even counterproductive.

They spent those days exploring the valley and the temples, all different, each with its unique beauty; many were deserted and unknown to most travellers, who were content to see just the biggest and most famous. In the evenings they returned to Durbar Square which was teeming with life; people sat in the square, or in one of the many cafes in Freak Street that served slices of cake. She went with Raffa to stores selling rice paper prints of dancing goddesses and more abstract drawings in black and white; they were cheap and they bought many to re-sell in Venice. There were statuettes made of bronze and copper in complicated tantric positions that made them laugh, proof of how the Tantric Buddhism practiced in Nepal saw sex as the most natural thing in the world. Maria bought two tankas, round mandalas of religious paintings in which hundreds of figures surrounded the Buddha's central figure. Raffa had a friendly way of dealing with the shopkeepers, as if she had known them forever. She bargained light heartedly, appreciating the goods but saying that she had little money and wasn't the king of Nepal's bank. Despite the reserved and taciturn nature of the Nepalese, she established a friendly rapport and at times even left with a discount.

Franca had met a lot of new people. Sitting around with her feet in the air all day, she had become the caretaker, the guardian of the square, who knew where to find this and that and was handing out information to anyone who would listen. Every couple of hours she'd limp back to the Top View Hotel, where she'd do one more foot bath, often accompanied by a new acquaintance with whom she smoked a chillum. More and more relaxed, her eyes every time more bloodshot, she returned to the streets, stopping for something to eat at the cheapest Nepalese restaurants, having a coffee in different chai-shops. The days passed pleasantly and her feet were healing. She had sent a message to the young Italians who lived with Raffa, instructing them to come and see her and, in groups of at least two at a time, they had begun to arrive. From what Maria had guessed, they used a lot of drugs and she understood why Franca felt so at ease with them. Raffa told her again that she couldn't hold her back, she would choose what to do, how and when: "Franca wants the buzz, the risks and dangers that make the adventure more exciting. But don't worry, she's strong, you'll see!"

19. The Princess of the stream

Finally the day came to go to Pokhara. Franca's feet were almost healed, but the diarrhoea was still a problem. She had taken opium to stop it, which had worked for a couple of days, but now it was back. She took another lump of opium for the trip, which would last from morning to evening. She knew it wasn't wise to take it day after day, that's how people became addicted, but she would use it only while she had diarrhoea as it acted as a medicine, then she would stop. They left Kathmandu by bus and travelled along the main road, flanking the hilly countryside dotted with rice paddies of a dazzling pea green, bright and clean. The landscape was lush, rich greens of every shade and hue, green with yellow, green with grey, green and blue. Along the way the rare villages were sparsely populated. They arrived in Pokhara shortly after five o'clock in the afternoon.

As they got off the bus, Raffa pointed her finger toward the summit, to her right: "If I'm not mistaken, that's Mount Annapurna, but we'd better ask, I've never seen it so closely!" Standing with her hands on her hips, she admired the mountains all around. "It was worth spending all those hours on a bus just for a view like this, don't you think?" A triumphant smile lit up her face and made them all forget their tiredness. The mountains were majestic. How could one describe a peak of over twenty four thousand feet, one of the highest mountains in the world, viewed from its slopes? And there was also the lake, famous for its beauty. And something else...

"Magic mushrooms from Pokhara," said Franca aloud. "They're famous! I'm going to try them. Are you?" Franca didn't even have her backpack yet, which Maria brought down for her, and she was already planning the next 'buzz'. She decided not to worry any more, as Raffa had advised her, who replied: "Well yes, you have to try them; they are mythical! I don't want to go back to Italy without having had the experience. And then, if they grow wild only here, there must be a reason, right? Can you imagine these mountains and the magic mushrooms together? What a trip!" Maria was listening, she had heard about Pokhara's mushrooms.

"And you, Maria? Are you going to try them?" both girls asked.

"I don't know, I have to think about it. I'm afraid! I don't want to repeat the opium experience; I was scared. I don't like losing control."

Franca was about to give her opinion, but Raffa was quicker: "Take a small dose then, just to get an idea, and then you'll be able to say you've tried them."

She was going to think about it.

They found a guesthouse nearby. A square courtyard, sheltered by a wooden structure covered in climbing plants, hosted tables and wooden benches and was surrounded by a few rooms; it was a simple place, with the bare minimum, but pleasant and cheap. They settled in a large room with three iron beds. As there were no curtains on the windows they hung their sarongs; with a couple of bricks and a wooden plank they made a shelf and quickly created a welcoming environment.

That evening they saw the first sunset from the feet of Mount Annapurna. Small clouds were dyed bright pink by the sun disappearing behind the majestic peaks; in a few minutes it was dusk and then, suddenly, it was dark. The temperature dropped considerably and, once in bed, the sleeping bag was just enough to shelter them from the cold.

Maria was the first one to wake up, happy and curious about the new place. She ventured outside, wearing her only sweater, rubbing her arms to warm them up, hoping to find a chai.

The sun was about to appear from behind the mountains; from a small room came the sound of bells and prayers; chickens and pigs moved in and out of the kitchen, rooting for something to eat.

She peeped inside the door. The cook was squatting in front of the tandoori stove, intently adding pieces of wood, heating a kettle of water. Maria walked in shyly and, with a smile, kneeled next to the stove to warm up, rubbing her hands. The woman returned her smile and began to prepare the chai, while Maria explained with gestures, and a few words of Hindi and English, that she had slept well, despite the cold. The cook offered her a glass of piping hot tea and they drank it together. She told her she had two children and her husband was the man they had seen the day before.

Raffa got up as the sun began to warm the morning air and dry up the humidity of the night. She stood admiring the scenery and then, while waiting for her chai, she began to do star jumps, to keep warm she explained, laughing. Then she went to talk about magic mushrooms with the cook, who said "No problem!" and called her husband to give him instructions. The man nodded and left, taking with him an old straw basket. The cook explained that she would prepare the mushrooms in an omelette; that was the way to eat them, she said calmly, as if they were part of the regular menu, and perhaps they were.

"Let's call Franca," said Raffa. "She'll be very impressed by the menu we have prepared for breakfast!" She went to wake her up with a glass of steaming tea. Franca had got up several times during the night because of her diarrhoea and was tired and fed up with being sick but, as soon as she knew what was awaiting her, she woke up completely; she was very excited and couldn't wait.

Maria was still confused; she had to make a decision. She could choose not to eat them and stay safe, but then she would miss the only chance to experience these famous hallucinogenic mushrooms. Or she could take them, but the idea scared her because she had no idea of what a hallucinogen was. Alternatively, she could take a small dose and go through with the experience. But what was a normal dose? She went to talk to the cook and, after several attempts, managed to explain her question. The woman replied assuredly that four or five mushrooms were a normal dose, depending on the size. Well, then she would take two! The husband returned just then, approached Raffa and lifted the cloth that covered the basket, showing its content.

"How many mushrooms are there?" she asked.

"Twelve rupees," he said. Raffa proceeded to count the mushrooms.

"There are twelve, they are quite big, a rupee each!" she announced, jubilant.

"I want an omelette with two mushrooms and one egg," said Maria, pushing her courage to the limit.

"I want one with four mushrooms and two eggs," Raffa decided.

"For me an omelette with two eggs and the rest of the mushrooms, that makes six, right?" declared Franca without hesitation and satisfied with the allocation.

The man, who had remained silent with a blank expression on his face, said: "Twelve rupees. You want?"

"Yes, yes, we want," Raffa said quickly, feeling in her pocket for the money.

Franca decided she was going to explain things properly. She sat upright to command the man's attention, looking into his eyes: "So, listen up!" He looked at her, absently.

Showing the numbers with her fingers, which seemed longer and leaner than usual, using both hands in a theatrical manner, she began to explain. "For her, Maria..." she said, pointing her finger, "an omelette with *two* mushrooms and *two* eggs!" She made the V sign for 'victory' with the right hand and then with the left, to say 'two and two'. No one could explain more clearly than that, even a chicken would have understood!

"Actually, I want it with *one* egg and two mushrooms," Maria pointed out; she had thought long and hard about it. "So it's easier on the digestion."

Franca ignored her and, pointing a finger at Raffa, continued: "For her, *four* eggs and *four* mushrooms. No, wrong, *two* eggs and *four* mushrooms, okay?" She was making a lot of confusion with fingers and numbers. The man looked at her, motionless. "For me... " she declared, pointing her index finger at her chest: "*Two* eggs and the rest of the mushrooms. Is that clear?" she shouted, convinced that the man would understand better if she spoke louder.

"Three omelettes?" he asked, with a flat expression.

"If I wasn't full of opium I would throttle you!" Franca said, mildly exasperated. "Don't you understand anything?"

Raffa intervened to explain things more clearly and made even more confusion. Two eggs and four mushrooms, six eggs and two mushrooms, no sorry the other way round, two eggs and six mushrooms, two eggs and two mushrooms. Why didn't they get it that she just wanted *one* egg? Maria thought, on the verge of exasperation! But no one paid her any attention.

"Got it?" asked Raffa. Yes, he said, without looking at them, and walked toward the kitchen with the basket in his hand, while Franca shouted: "And three chai and six slices of toast with butter and jam! Capish?" Yes, yes, he nodded.

While they were waiting, Maria started to have doubts. What if she lost control? How was she going feel? Would the mushrooms make her nauseous? How long did the effect last? Raffa interrupted her worried thoughts and reported that she had made enquiries before leaving Kathmandu, and the information had been confirmed by the cook: the lake was at the end of the main street and there were rowing boats for hire. Everybody took the boat across the lake because, on the other side, there were lovely beaches and a waterfall, somewhere. Three rupees per hour for a small boat. Was this fine with them? Yes! So, after *breakfast* they'd get a boat! Maria suggested they organize everything they needed to take with them *before* they ate the omelette, not knowing what the effect would be like. "Yes, good idea!" Raffa said with a smirk: "I'm going to wear a sarong and a head scarf to shelter from the sun, I don't need anything else." Did they have the money for the boat? Yes, all in order. Maria went to fetch the sarongs and the scarves and distributed them to the respective owners, feeling more organized. The breakfast started to arrive; first came the toast with butter and jam, six slices as ordered, brought by the cook. She was followed by her husband with three plates on which sat the omelettes; he placed them on the table and turned to leave. They were all the same! Franca shouted: "Hey, wait a minute, which omelette is which?"

The man turned around, shook his head and, with his usual blank expression, replied: "Three omelettes."

"Yes, right, but which is the one with six mushrooms? And the one with four?" Fortunately she was sedated by the opium, otherwise she would have pounced on him.

Again, Raffa took control of the situation and, speaking reasonably, she articulated: "Okay, don't worry. Do you know how many mushrooms there are in *this* omelette?" The man shook his head and turned to go back into the kitchen. "All right, we'll have to figure it out by ourselves!" she concluded light hearted.

"This is smaller," said Maria, sweating with anxiety.

"These two are more or less the same," said Raffa.

"This one is darker, so it has more mushrooms. I'll take it," said Franca.

"So this is mine," concluded Raffa cheerfully.

They took the first bite; the taste was strange, maybe they had forgotten to add any salt. The mushrooms had a slimy texture, not at all appetizing. Despite a knot seizing her throat, Maria swallowed the mouthfuls without chewing them, each followed quickly by a bite of toast and a sip of chai that the cook had brought just in time. The husband was not seen again. "I can't eat it all. It's horrible!" she said after a while, her stomach a little upset.

"Give it to me, I'll finish it!" said Franca, although she didn't like the taste either.

"Come on, let's pay and go get this boat," said Raffa, as soon as they swallowed the last bite.

They walked down toward the lake almost without speaking, excited, tense, not knowing what to expect. It was hot, but Maria felt cold sweats. Now she had them inside her body, those slimy mushrooms; who knew how many she had eaten. She felt like throwing up and fainting; mamma mia, how scary!

The boats were waiting and they didn't even have to haggle over the price; it was written on a piece of cardboard. Incredible! They pushed their boat into the shallow water of the shore and, one by one, climbed aboard awkwardly. Raffa took two oars and began to row. Maria took the other two and began to practice a little as she was a bit of a novice when it came to rowing. The sun was still climbing and pleasantly warmed the clear air. She looked around: the lake was very large, almost round, surrounded by dense lush vegetation and white beaches. The rays of the sun reached the shores, one at a time and, like a paintbrush loaded with light, transformed the colours of the trees from dark grey to a heart warming bright green.

When she looked up, the view took her breath away: at an altitude of almost nine thousand feet, the lake was surrounded by mountain ranges, the closest still shadowed by the higher mountains behind them which, lighter in colour, were already being touched by the sun. Behind the sunny mountains, and at least twice as tall as the highest peak, the imposing Annapurna group stood majestically; silhouetted against the clear blue sky, it sported numerous white peaks covered with snow and ice. That monumental image was mirrored in the waters of the lake; it seemed as if they were inside a painting with the real mountains and those reflected upside down in the water, clear, still, of an unreal beauty. The sun beat down while Raffa and Maria rowed slowly toward the centre of the lake.

Franca began to feel uncomfortable; irritably she complained: "Can't you paddle any faster? We're going at a snail's pace!"

"But it's so beautiful, don't you like it? Look around you," said Maria.

"It's too hot, I'm gonna dive," she snapped, standing up and taking off her sarong. She stood for a moment in her knickers and t-shirt and then dived into the lake, swimming skilfully with strokes full of frustration. She swam well and fast.

"Hey, wait a minute! You could paddle a bit too, right?" protested Maria.

"You do it! I'll see you later," Franca cried, swimming powerfully away from the boat. Maria watched her as she pushed toward the centre of the lake, one stroke after another, slicing the surface with energy, burying her head under the water and re-emerging again, with regular rhythm and controlled movements.

"So, now it's just you and me," said Maria, partly angry, partly concerned. "How crazy, jumping into the water immediately after a breakfast like that, with a stomach full of hallucinogenic mushrooms. I hope she won't get a stomach cramp!"

Raffa smiled, paddling quietly, admiring the scenery surrounding them: "She's fine, and we're fine too. Don't worry! Let's keep an eye on her until she gets to the other side."

Maria forced herself to relax. "Can you feel the mushrooms?" she asked with undisguised anxiety.

Raffa's laughter broke out loud and clear in the silence of the lake. "Without a doubt!" she replied, "and I also feel a bit sick, these mushrooms are big, but it will pass. Can you?"

"I feel slightly sick and also a bit weird. I want to get across the lake and put my feet on dry land as soon as possible."

Her friend perceived Maria's anxiety; she spoke in a calm and relaxed fashion: "If you worry too much you can have a bad 'trip' and become paranoid. Relax and enjoy the experience. If necessary, I can paddle alone. Breathe deeply, it'll pass."

Maria keenly followed her advice, looking around, watching Franca who had almost reached the opposite shore. There wasn't anyone else in the lake, it was getting hot and the scenery all around was amazing. Finally, Franca reached the beach and began to wave her arms, in her soaked pants and t-shirt, shouting: "I'm here!"

They laughed, relieved and amused. "There you are, see? She always manages in the end, our little Franca," Raffa said, and began to sing a mountain song: "Oh, up there on the Black mountain, there is a small tiny cave, with twelve outlaws by the light of a lantern."

Maria knew it well and began to sing with her: "Caramba let's drink whisky, iu hu, caramba let's drink some gin, some gin, and don't you listen to your heart, as everything comes and goes!"

They rowed in time with the song, laughing with excitement, singing with loud clear voices, fitting in a falsetto here and there, filling the air and the empty space with sound, blowing out all anguish and anxiety and letting a relaxed confidence settle in their hearts. Maria started to feel that everything was going to be fine; Raffa was with her and, before she knew it, the boat had almost reached the shore. She climbed out of it, into the lake where the water reached her thighs, her legs shaking a little. Without too much effort, she pushed the boat into the pebbles of the deserted and impeccably clean beach. They looked around to see where Franca was and saw her climbing up the hill, already far away from them, in her pants and t-shirt, bare feet. Raffa forestalled Maria's words: "She'll be fine, don't worry. She has nine lives like a cat, our little Franca! Let's go and see where this waterfall is."

Maria nodded, checking how she was feeling inside: definitely different; she had a stronger perception of images and sounds while her movements were becoming more awkward, time and space evanescent. She still felt nervous, but Raffa's calm and confident presence reassured her.

They walked uphill along the stream, partly under the sun, partly in the shade, in a perfect combination of warmth and coolness. The trees and thick bushes on both sides were a bright green of many different hues, enlivened by white and yellow blossoms and tiny red-purple flowers. "Can we stop here for a while?" asked Maria, fishing the words from the well of her memory. "I like this place, I feel comfortable. We can go to the waterfall in a little while." Raffa agreed, the place was idyllic, and she was happy to stop. Maria soon found *her* place: "I'll sit on that rock in the middle of the stream," she decided. It was just a couple of metres from the grass verge and the creek was not deep; she felt calmer. She removed her t-shirt and began to study it carefully. The weft was so complicated, infinite, strong; the pattern was sharp, full of lines and details, the colours had never been so bright, cheerful, piercing; and it had never been so soft or delicate. Maria rubbed it gently between her hands and stroked her face with the lightweight cotton. Carefully, she placed it on the rock and sat on it. The sarong was useful as a scarf and as a shawl to shelter her from the sun and she put it on her head. Raffa chose a rock nearby, on the shaded grassy verge, and so they sat, neither too close nor too far away. Maria hugged her knees and the time passed suspended, fluid. Gradually they stopped talking and let their minds wander, entrusted to the magic mushrooms.

The colours became more intense, the grass and the tree branches a more lively green, full of sap and moisture, and they were *breathing*. The bright yellow, pure white, deep red flowers radiated life, happiness, kindness. The water was not only running, it was alive in that movement: frothy, funny, full of bubbles, jumping and playing with the large and small rocks, flowing, running, living, safe in its course, unperturbed in the face of obstacles, too free to worry about what it would encounter, following its own way to touch the beach, and then merge with the water of the lake. Even the rocks next to her were breathing, she could see them in their details and as a whole; everything around her was pulsating with life, sweating, glowing and exuding energy. Maria stayed in the sun until it became too hot. She removed the sarong from her head, dipped it in the cool water of the brook, wrung it and wet her face, her dry lips, her hot cheeks; she closed her eyes and pressed the cool cloth onto her eyelids. She looked at Raffa and realized that she was plunging deeper and deeper into her fantasy world; she watched her smile, not focusing on anything in particular, she was looking into space and exuded a sense of peace. Maria perceived a certain strength coming from her heart and felt more courageous. If she wanted to move, all she had to do was decide where she wanted to go, visualize herself already there and tell her body to go, as and when she was ready. She concentrated on the task of moving into the shade. With her eyes she searched a good boulder to sit on and then, keeping hold on the nearby rocks, slipping on the stones covered with moss and lichens, she moved carefully along the stream bed, until she arrived at her new place and sat down in the shade, where it was cooler. Raffa smiled; her face looked different. If normally it was nice and sweet, now it was even more so; Maria wanted to hug her, but she was too far away. Only a few minutes had gone by, but it was already getting too cold in the shade. She didn't feel at ease among the darker colours, the grey light; she didn't feel safe and missed the comforting embrace of the sun on her skin. With great care she returned to her rock in the sunshine; there it was getting warmer and soon she felt curious enough to go and look for the waterfall of which she could hear the sound in the distance. "Do you want to go to the waterfall?" she asked.

Raffa looked at her in silence, thinking about the question, reflecting on the response. She hugged her knees and played with her feet in the water, carefully twiddling her toes, deep in thought: "There are fish in the stream, have you noticed?" She didn't expect an answer. "If you stay motionless, they come and nibble at your feet!" she added, deeply concentrated. Finally, as if awaking, she said: "Let's go and see the waterfall! How do you feel?"
"Good! I can move, but slowly. I wouldn't like to be alone, though, definitely not." Even if she knew that Raffa wouldn't leave her, she wanted to be completely sure. They walked uphill with their feet in the stream, keeping a distance from each other, giving and taking the space they needed. They slipped on the moss and the lichens and on the slimy substance that lived under water, laughing whenever they lost their balance. Their laughter sounded different, strange, it was the only human sound in the forest. Through their distorted perception, the short climb was turning into a huge adventure barefoot, full of dangers at every step, difficulties to confront, obstacles to overcome; they were walking uphill against the flow, the sun was hot and their tired legs struggled with the climb. The noise of the waterfall was clearly audible and the air was becoming more humid. They rounded the stream's last bend and there it was, white, impetuous, powerful and noisy. "How wonderful!" cried Maria, above the din of the outpouring. "It's so liberating, exciting, and… fun!"
"I'm going under the waterfall! Are you coming?" cried Raffa.
"I'm not sure... You go first! In a bit, maybe."

Her friend positioned herself close to the splashes, taking them in her hands and bathing her face. Then, with a bold step forward, she stood under the mantle of the cascade, which threw tons of water over her head and shoulders, with colossal force. She couldn't speak, but laughed happily. She then stepped back so that the wall of water was right in front of her, not touching her. Maria felt attracted to that power and approached slowly, feeling the weight of the water on her open palms; it pushed them down, it was phenomenally strong and heavy. She advanced one step further and closed her eyes, letting the fresh spray hit her face. Finally, with one more step forward she let the overwhelming amount of cold water fall over her. She uttered a cry, struggled to get her breath back and then cried again, first with shock, then with surprise, and then out of pure enjoyment.

They played a long time with the waterfall, enjoying its power, appreciating the incredible beauty of nature. The trees looked at them from the cliff above, silhouetted against the blue sky, protective, or perhaps hiding some inscrutable mystery. Around them were flying birds with gaily coloured feathers; butterflies of surprising hues moved fleetingly; and then small busy insects, perfectly efficient in their tiny movements; flying ants, delightful beetles, pea-green leaping grasshoppers, evanescent dragonflies and countless unknown insects, were dancing in rhythmic harmony. For the first time, she deeply appreciated their little lives, organized, varied, complex and so perfect!

When the noise of the waterfall became too intrusive and the lack of silence disturbing, they decided to leave. Slowly, they walked back downhill with their feet in the stream, and sat exactly where they were before, entering once again into their world of magic and discovery, imagination and deep respect.

Maria stared at the water that slipped over the boulders, avoiding them when it could, leaping over them when it had to, stumbling with sweeping enthusiasm, jumping and running, irrepressible. She lost the sense of her own self and body and identified with the water of the brook; she felt the rush, the pure unrestrained desire to accomplish its fate. She *understood* the water of the stream, completely, utterly, and like it, she felt fresh, clean, transparent and overflowing with the joy of living. She had become the water itself and like that mountain course, she felt the sun warm her life, illuminating her with a glowing golden splendour. She was a princess, the princess of the stream. Sitting solemnly on her rock, her heart bursting with jubilation, she felt grateful for her life, overwhelmed with happiness, full and satisfied.

Out of the corner of her eye, she noticed a black thing stuck to the sole of her foot; she didn't like it at all. She tried to shake it off but it didn't move. She took a stick and pushed it, but although the thing moved and twitched, it stayed there. A disturbing sensation got hold of her and she looked at Raffa, who was watching her.

Without a word, her friend got up, with care she picked a leaf and approached as fast as possible. She took hold of Maria's foot. "Stay still. I'll get rid of it but I'll have to use the leaf, otherwise it will stick to my fingers. There, it's gone!" she said, while vigorously rubbing the sole of her foot.

"It's horrible! What is it?" Maria asked, fighting the nausea.

"It was a leech."

A shiver of disgust ran through Maria, from her head, down her back, her legs and reached her toes. She wanted to leave that place, quickly: "Shall we go to the beach?"

"Yeah, no problem." Raffa understood without any need for explanation. They set off and within minutes had reached the pebble beach; it was much closer than she remembered. She felt as if she were emerging from a world of fairy tales, rich in experiences and adventures; it seemed as if days had gone by, rather than hours.

Large buffalos grazed the grass around the perimeter of the beach; they ignored the girls and the girls ignored them. Carefully they chose a sunny spot, covered in round pebbles. Neatly, they lay down their sarongs and sat, watching the lake flooded with light. It was a relief to see the horizon further away, the large and open space. They lay next to each other and closed their eyes. Their spontaneous and natural friendship was warming their hearts; it was made of affection, respect and, at that particular moment, a profound awareness of their uniqueness and preciousness. Little by little, the buffaloes approached, quietly browsing, taking advantage of their immobility to satisfy their curiosity. The horns, as big as an arm, were brushing the girls' heads while their huge mouths ruminated lazily; the large nostrils sniffed the trusting, relaxed young women until, satisfied with the intruders' harmlessness, they moved away, swaying heavily.

Raffa and Maria waded into the lake and swam close to the shore, enjoying the fresh water and its cooling effect on their bodies and minds. Gradually, they were coming to themselves, regaining normal perception of sight, hearing, touch, moving away from the lightness and heaviness of the magic, finding once again the ability to control their movements and a readiness of reactions. The effect of the mushrooms was waning and Maria welcomed the changes with a mixture of relief and gratitude. She wasn't hungry or thirsty; she felt safe, happy, at peace, and couldn't stop smiling.

Unexpectedly, breaking the stillness of the lake, from behind the side of the mountain appeared a rowboat. Franca, in her underwear, was standing in it while other people paddled; they were talking and laughing loudly. She greeted them waving her arms and shouted: "Do you want to come for a ride in the boat?"

Maria reacted with annoyance to Franca's shouting. She exchanged glances with Raffa and understood immediately: they were not in the mood to join a noisy group: "No thank you! In a little while we'll go back. See you at the guesthouse."

It was really time to go back. Slowly, ceremoniously, they took the boat; Raffa held the oars, while Maria pushed it into the lake, her legs in water up to her knees. She climbed on board and took her oars. They began to paddle, feeling as tired as if they had worked all day, but happy and bright. They paddled up to the middle of the lake where they stopped to wait for the sunset. They didn't have to wait long: the setting sun tinged the whole valley with a new light, bathing in golden pink the world's highest peaks, kissing Mount Annapurna's snows. The divine fireball began to hide behind the summits, taking the words out of their mouths, any thoughts from their minds. With the dimming light, they paddled to the lake's shore from where they had set off that morning. It seemed as if a whole lifetime had gone by.

It was already dark when Franca arrived, barefoot, still in her t-shirt and pants and wrapped in a sarong that one of the boys had lent her to protect herself from the evening dampness. None of them were hungry and they sat under the sheltered structure, talking about the day's experience, drinking chai and munching on a couple of biscuits. Franca had walked along the mountain side and, on a beach not far away, she had met a group of young Italians. She had spent the whole day with them, smoking chillums. Maria didn't feel like socializing and left Raffa and Franca talking together while she went to bed, to enjoy the solitude and the silence, reliving the strong emotions of that day. The next day they woke up late and famished and, after a hearty breakfast, they walked to the centre of Pokhara. Franca had arranged to meet one of the boys, but they had forgotten to arrange a time so she had to wait, hoping he'd arrive soon.

The centre of Pokhara consisted of a large tree, hundreds of years old, surrounded by a low stone wall on which they could sit in the shade of the generous boughs that extended widely, reaching all sides of the small square. The trunk was so big that the children could hide behind it playing hide and seek and the shadow of its branches provided shelter to entire groups of people and animals. Franca sat on the wall, chillum in hand, determined not to move until the boy arrived. She wasn't well, the diarrhoea had awakened her during the night and she had taken another lump of opium. While waiting for it to take effect, she had severe pain in her abdomen and often, leaving one of them on guard, she had to hurriedly go and squat in the woods, returning with an exhausted expression. They took it in turns to keep her company and, since Raffa was happy to stay there, Maria took the opportunity to go for an exploratory walk along the road.

The warm air smelled clean and fragrant, it had a light and ethereal feeling. A row of huts on both sides of the road formed the village of Pokhara. A little further down, the tailor's hut showcased some beautiful satin waistcoats, one in particular caught her eye and she fell in love with it: it was of a silver satin woven with purple flowers, lined in black. She looked at it for a long time, twenty rupees said the tailor. Nepalese rupees were worth less than the Indian rupees, however, all the same, it was a bit expensive; she thanked him and went on. Another shop was selling necklaces and bracelets with turquoise and coral, as well as loose stones and round beads of inlaid silver. She thought about getting some, after all her trip was already way into its second half and, within three weeks, she would be back in Italy. The idea of returning to Venice hit her, she wasn't ready, and drove the thought away, putting it off till later, much later. At the beginning of her trip the days were passing slowly, but now they were racing by one after the other, and she often failed to realize how quickly they were going; however, for now she was here and didn't want to think about anything else. She looked at every single thing, turning the stones in her hand, stroking the bracelets, leafing through the prints. She walked back at a leisurely pace toward the tree, admiring the huge snowy peaks that made her feel very small, but clean and fresh. Sitting under the tree the two girls were still waiting. Maria reported the results of her excursion and Raffa decided to go for a stroll and look at the shops.

Finally the Italian boy approached, skinny, walking without haste; he sat on the wall greeting Franca with a faint voice, completely ignoring Maria. He was holding a strange bamboo pipe and began to prepare something, awkwardly. Maria watched him with curiosity, she had never seen a pipe like that; it was the opposite of a pipe normally used for smoking grass.

"Are you leaving tomorrow then?" Franca asked.

The boy thought for a long time about the question, stopping what he was doing and, after an endless reflection, replied: "Yes, tomorrow." He looked at his pipe, as if to remember what he was supposed to do, and finally carried on with what he had interrupted.

"Then you're not taking the coke or the speed, are you?" urged Franca.

He paused again, unable to do and speak at the same time and, before answering, he finished filling his pipe with tobacco. "Yes... No... The others are finishing the coke... but we have too much speed... and more." It cost him a lot of effort to say all these things and he paused to recover from the effort. He looked at his pipe as if he couldn't see it. Absent-mindedly, he pulled a small package out of his pocket: "I've got this for you... speed, mushrooms... a bit of charas and a bit of grass... too bulky."

Franca took the packet and opened it as a child opens a Christmas present.

For the first time, the boy looked at Maria and, holding out his pipe, said: "Do you want to light it?"

The pipe was made up of a thick vertical bamboo tube and another smaller tube protruding out of the bigger one. Strange shape... Maria hesitated. She didn't like the energy of this boy; he never looked anyone in the eye. At the same time, however, she didn't want to seem grumpy. Assuming it was grass, she took it, while the boy was preparing to light a match. "What's inside?" she asked, just to be on the safe side. The boy struck the match, but hadn't understood her question; two things at a time, too hard.

"What's in the pipe?" repeated Maria. Waiting for his reply, that she knew wasn't going to come right away, she lowered the pipe. The match was still burning and the flame came to his finger tips, burning them. The boy suddenly jolted and Maria burst out laughing.

"Smack," he said.

"What is 'smack'?" she asked, looking from him to Franca.

After a long pause, the boy replied: "Heroin."

With anger she pushed the pipe away from her. "I don't want it!" she said, shocked. How could he offer it like that? She had almost lit it! She addressed him with dismay, scolding him: "And you shouldn't smoke it either. Are you crazy? Do you think you can handle it? Be stronger than this?" She wanted him to listen to her, with all her being but, from what she had learned about heroin, she knew she couldn't reach him. Indeed, the boy was expressionless and didn't answer, but she didn't expect to hear Franca's voice saying: "I'll light it!" The words hit her like a stone in the face. There she was, her arm outstretched, a light of excitement in her eyes.

"Are you crazy? Franca, don't! Don't light it! You know very well what can happen. You'll become a slave to it. You know how it ends up!" She spoke earnestly, desperately clashing against Franca's wild passion for the buzz; she searched for stronger, better words, but couldn't find any.

Franca's response was violent: "Get out of the way, Maria, that's bullshit! Why don't you mind your own fucking business? What do you care about me, huh? Move!" Franca pushed her aside, staring at her with anger. Then, unable to control herself, she let out what had obviously been festering for a long time: "You always find other friends who are better than me, of course! And now you've even stolen *my* friend. Don't tell me that you care about me! Watch me, *goody two-shoes*, while I smoke it all!"

At that very moment, something inside Maria died. She stepped back and walked away, with her body and her heart. Without a word, beaten, defeated, she watched as the boy lit the match. Franca inhaled strongly, filling her mouth with smoke, as she did with the chillums, keeping it in her lungs for as long as possible, and then exhaled. She saw her colour change; she turned red in the face, then white, then grey. Looking into the void she stood up and, holding on to the wall, she vomited.

Maria looked at the boy and shouted with anger: "Why did you come here? And with that stuff? Look at her now! Are you happy?"

He was taking small puffs on his pipe, but seemed disappointed that there was nothing left. He closed his eyes. "It's all right," he said, drawing out the words.

She felt like hitting him, but she knew that the responsibility was Franca's. It was she who had chosen to smoke heroin, just what she had feared from the start; as if she had always known it would end like this. Franca was still standing, leaning heavily on the wall, pale, unable to move, speak or open her eyes.

"Where *is* Raffa?" Maria cried softly, her heart full of pain and anguish. Now she was alone, truly alone.

20. Allons enfants de la patrie

One of Ugo's affairs had been with a girl who was addicted to heroin; her boyfriend was a junkie too, but Ugo liked her and decided to 'save' her. Unfortunately, after weeks of effort from him and other friends, she and her boyfriend robbed the hospital's pharmacy, were caught and ended up in prison. Maria knew that heroin addiction was strong and annihilated the user's will. From observing those who began to use it, she had learned that it meant the death of the person, as she knew them. No more conversations or exchanges between friends, no more laughter or making plans together. Heroin was tantamount to cheating, lies, death. Looking at Franca in that state she realized that, from here on, she was travelling alone. Seeing Raffa approach she hurried in her direction, telling her what had happened before she even reached her.

As always, her friend was philosophical: "Maybe she'll only use it this once," she said.

"Have *you* ever used it?" asked Maria, bewildered.

"No, but I know people who did. For the first few minutes they felt awful, then they felt great; this feeling great, however, only happens the first time. Some of them continue to use it, trying to match the experience, but it's never the same again."

"And how come you've never taken it?" Maria asked, still confused.

"Because I know how it works and I'm not stupid. You have to carry on using it simply to feel normal, otherwise you feel awful; it is absurd, nonsense; it's a scam. When they offered it to me I said no; I had decided beforehand, seeing what was happening to others." After a short pause she added: "I was tempted, but not much, and I had made up my mind."

"But you know what Franca is like. She won't use it only this time." Maria vented. She told her what Franca had shouted at her; would they split up? What could she do? Her friend told her she shouldn't feel responsible for Franca's decisions. Maybe she could help her by keeping close, as she had already done, ignoring her jealousy. When they reached the tree, the boy was gone while Franca was sitting on the wall, staring into space. Raffa told her to go back to the guesthouse and go to bed, or sit under the wooden shelter.

"Do you want us to take you there?" she offered. No, said Franca, without looking at them. Well, then they would go to the lake.

Addressing Maria she said: "Franca won't do anything else today. We can go for a swim and to sunbathe. I can't go home without a tan!"

"Are you sure she'll know how to get back to the guesthouse?"

"Yes, but it might take her half the morning. Relax! She'll manage very well on her own."

Maria tried to break free from the sense of responsibility she felt, but she couldn't, despite Franca's angry outburst toward her. If she had shouted those things, it meant she was suffering, didn't it? "I can't leave her on her own. I'll go with her to the guesthouse and then I'll catch up with you at the lake."

With patience, she encouraged her to walk and linked arms with her. Franca walked in silence, looking like a marionette, while an infinite sadness pervaded Maria's heart. What would happen now? She left her at the guesthouse, lying on her bed, glassy-eyed, far away, lost in a world where Maria didn't belong. She closed the door and walked toward the lake, confused and worried.

She sat down on the pebble beach next to Raffa and they talked about her upcoming return to Italy; she had only one week left. Her friend showed her the stones and two bracelets with turquoise and coral she had just bought. "I'm sure they'll be snapped up as soon as I show them around," she said, moving the stones on the palm of her hand. "And what fun to buy all these beautiful things! This way I'll get back some of the money I spent for the trip. I only regret not having brought more cash with me. Are you going to take home many things to resell?"

"Not many, only a few, but I should be able to make some money. My problem is that I like buying but not selling."

"I'll help you sell your stuff, don't worry," Raffa reassured her. "I know a lot of people who want to buy and I'm a born seller!" Maria could well believe that.

The last few days flew by, with the lake, the mountains, the sun and tanning. Franca didn't smoke any more heroin, but she was always irritable and tired. They had become accustomed to waking up to the view of Mount Annapurna and of the mountain next to it, which they discovered was called Macchapuchhare, and to watching the sunset, always beautiful and dramatic. Being so close to such high mountains made her feel miraculously alive, but delicate and transient, as if her life was borrowed, and one day she would have to give it back.

The day came to go back to Kathmandu and say goodbye to Raffa. They embraced in Durbar Square, where their friend took a rickshaw to the airport, reluctant to leave but in good spirits, as always. She was going to be greatly missed, but they too had only a couple of weeks before leaving. Only a few minutes after Raffa's departure Franca began to feel ill; she was weak, sick and looked terrible. Maria remembered about Doctor Mannah and advised her to go and see him; she would accompany her right away. Franca didn't object which, in itself, indicated how bad she felt. Like everyone else, the rickshaw man knew where the doctor lived and led them to his house, pedalling slowly in the warm afternoon.

The waiting room was outdoors, in a courtyard shaded by the branches of the trees that surrounded it, crowded with westerners and local people. After a long wait, their turn came.

Dr. Mannah was a distinguished man, short in stature, a little plump, with thick white hair and gold rimmed glasses; with his friendly manners he made them feel at ease. He checked Franca from head to toe, asked her a lot of questions, taking notes with clear and neat handwriting; he looked at her eyes several times, put pressure on her nails, made her roll her tongue and studied it carefully. When he sat down behind his desk he was serious. "Maybe you have amoebiasis, it's a gastrointestinal infection, but you definitely have all the symptoms of hepatitis," he said, as gently as possible. "Some call it jaundice. Your eyes are already turning yellow. They will become much more yellow than that; your skin will turn yellow, too."

Franca slumped in her chair and looked at the doctor without saying a word. Maria asked if he could treat these illnesses.

"Certainly," he replied. "I often see these conditions, especially in young people like you. I'll give her some herbal medicines that my assistant will prepare immediately; I will also give her a diet to follow." Looking at Franca, he added: "If you follow the diet, take the medicines and rest, you will get better and everything will be fine."

"How long will it take? In a week's time we'll have to go to Delhi," Maria said. She didn't expect the doctor's answer: It would take about four weeks.

"Four weeks? But we have flights to Italy long before that!" She looked at Franca, who wasn't saying a word; she sat there, limp, heavy, beaten by the illness.

"She can't go anywhere, if she wants to get better. Your friend needs to rest; she is very sick, but it could become much more serious. If she doesn't look after herself properly, she will end up in hospital... or worse!" He was polite but very grave. He told her that she could always come back to him for anything. They paid fifteen Nepalese rupees for the visit and the medicines and sat in the courtyard, waiting for the assistant to prepare the pills, one by one.

They had a lot of decisions to make: Franca couldn't return to Italy as planned, which meant that Maria would go back alone. But what would Franca do? Her answer was ready: she was going to stay at the Italians' house; they had already told her she could go.

"But when had you decided to go there?" Maria asked, startled. "And for how long? We only had a few days to stay in Kathmandu before leaving!"

"I had already decided not to return to Italy with you," said Franca, drawling. "The visa is valid for six more weeks... and I decided to stay."

"To stop here in Kathmandu?" Maria was shocked.

"For a while, yes, I wanted to... but now I have no choice... I'll go there tomorrow." She struggled to find the energy to talk.

Maria was too surprised to reply and, in any case, whatever she said wouldn't make the slightest difference. As of tomorrow she was going to be alone, and she didn't like the idea. The medicines were ready but Franca had no strength to walk. They took another rickshaw back to the centre of Kathmandu. As the minutes went by, the yellowing of her eyes and skin became more and more apparent; she noticed Franca's skinny wrists. Both of them had lost weight, but Franca had lost more, she was almost bony. That night, Maria started to come to terms with the idea of travelling alone and began to make plans. Perhaps she would go back to India a little earlier, or maybe not, all the possibilities were open. Maybe she would have time to visit Agra and the Taj Mahal; she would go back to the Tourist Camp in Delhi, where she'd see again people she felt were friends. A little bit at a time the worry she felt was turning into enthusiasm.

When Franca woke up she was even more yellow and weaker than the day before. Maria prepared her backpack while Franca watched her from her bed. How was she going to get through this alone? Maria thought she would go and see her every day and help her to follow Dr. Mannah's diet. This decision made her feel better; she wasn't going to abandon her now when she needed her help. She went to Durbar Square to get a rickshaw which took her back to the guesthouse. She carried her rucksack, while Franca came down the stairs slowly, holding on to the handrail, trembling. Maria pushed from below to help her get on the rickshaw and then, in silence, they let themselves be taken to the outskirts of Kathmandu. The man was riding slowly, the breeze was blowing and lifted their long hair. Maria looked with affection at the temples' roofs, the hills, the blue sky.

The Italians' house was a good distance from Kathmandu's main square, along a straight dirt road, which the rickshaw covered in ten minutes. Maria went through the open gate and took Franca's rucksack up to the door; then she went back to the rickshaw to help her get down and into the house. They were greeted by two Italians who had no idea she was going to move in; fortunately they didn't care and Maria placed Franca's things in the corner of one of the numerous rooms. The boys were a little distant but reasonably friendly, and explained that a lot of people came and went in that house, apart from Valerio, the only Italian who lived there regularly. Valerio, shortened to Vale, appeared a few minutes later, his hair and beard long and black and a holy-man look, his face sullen and unfriendly because he hadn't drunk his coffee yet. He prepared it with the coffee machine brought from Italy and Lavazza coffee powder, also from Italy. While the aroma of coffee wafted through the house, Maria sat with Franca on a rug, waiting to speak to him. Unfortunately, even after his coffee, Vale's mood didn't seem much better, but the boys offered to make a tea and Maria gratefully accepted, while explaining that Franca had hepatitis and perhaps even amoeba, and would need to be quiet and rest for a few weeks. They all seemed unperturbed; the boys looked at her yellow skin and eyes and laughed. With a sort of dismissive superiority Vale said: "I had it, too," as if that would make it a thing of minor importance. Then, with a little more understanding, he added: "It takes time!" When Maria explained that they had gone to see Dr. Mannah he nodded approvingly, without smiling, cuddling his cup of coffee in his hands.

It was time for her to leave; Maria wanted to go and buy the things that Franca needed for her diet and bring them that afternoon. They told her there was no need, she could wait until the next day, they had the right things in the house and Franca would eat very little, anyway. Maria knelt down and looked at her friend, noticing how she was more yellow than the day before. "I'll see you tomorrow then," she said, kissing her cheeks. Franca looked at her and smiled weakly, looking sad. Maria felt sad too, as she walked back to Kathmandu, reflecting, alone. Now she was on her own with the rest of the world but, instead of the fear she expected to feel, she experienced a sense of freedom. Now it was up to her to decide, judge, perceive. After all, she was no stranger to loneliness, she had felt alone for years during her relationship with Ugo; the only major difference was that, this time, she was on the other side of the world.

But the sun was shining, the sky was clear and, from a distance, just as she approached Durbar Square, she saw a procession coming toward her. On a canopy, carried on four men's shoulders, there was the 'defta', a statue of the local god. It was followed by dozens of people and accompanied by that strange kind of music that to her ears seemed out of tune. It reminded her of Sarsai village, in the mountains near Manali. They also carried the statue of their 'defta' in that way, playing that music without harmony, having a sacred ceremony and a big party for any special occasion. She wondered whether Pushpa had already had her baby; she would return there one day. Nothing was impossible, she just had to want to and take a decision.

From that moment Maria began to look more carefully, noticing details that until then had escaped her attention, she listened to and watched people with keener interest. Now that she was alone she didn't need to compromise on anything. She remembered she had her camera and that would become her travelling companion. She no longer had to experiment with drugs, which with Franca were a daily occurrence and had always made her feel uncomfortable. She didn't regret the experiences she'd had, but she remembered the fear, the anxiety, the time wasted with the opium, the lack of control over her life. She still had a little piece of the charas made with Paul, which she kept inside the silver box that Jean-Claude had bought for her, along with another small piece that Franca had given her. She reached Durbar Square and found the familiar relaxed atmosphere.

There was a tolerance of people's diversity, indeed it was a pleasure to see the variety of all those boys and girls, men and women, who had come there from all over the world. She noticed two boys and a girl whom she had seen before; they were looking at her and smiled. Maria approached them: they were French, Sylvan, Eve and Pierrot. They spent the whole afternoon together, visiting some of the temples she had already seen and others new to her. She photographed the architecture, the children, the women washing clothes in the river, the wild pigs running around, all over the place. Only the dogs were hostile; while they didn't seem to mind the locals, they stopped in their tracks whenever they saw a European approach and began to growl fiercely, crazy with hatred. In the evening they had dinner together at a restaurant and then they smoked a bit of Maria's charas. She returned to the Top View Hotel ready for a good sleep. While she lay in bed she realized that she had spent only a few minutes alone that day.

The next day was the same. As soon as she walked into a store someone would address her and if she sat down to drink a chai, someone would come and sit at her table. Shopkeepers, hippies or climbers, there was always someone who wanted to talk to her and she always found something interesting in them. She went to the grocery store to buy the things for Franca: rice, oil, fruits and vegetables for a light, low protein diet and, with a bag full, she walked to the Italians' house.

Franca was even more yellow than the day before, but the more disconcerting thing was the whites of her eyes that had turned a sickly yellow-brown with shades of green. She was sitting on a mat, her back against the wall, her arms limp and heavy.

"How are you today?" Maria asked, crouching down to kiss her, a knot in her stomach.

"Very weak," Franca replied, with a faint, yellow smile.

"Do they help you? Does someone look after you?"

"Every now and then they make me a cup of tea. I have no appetite," she said, speaking with difficulty. She had to pause to regain the strength to talk; she continued: "Two of them have had hepatitis... and they know what to do."

Maria tried to feel less concerned. "I've been shopping. Dr. Mannah said that if you follow the diet and take the medicines, you will recover in four weeks. Take care; make sure you follow his advice."

Franca smiled weakly and looked at her with a mixture of affection and gratitude. "I will. Hepatitis is like this," she said. Then she surprised her with an unexpected request: "Can I borrow your red rucksack?"

"Mine? The one you like so much? Why?"

"Vale has to take a lot of things to Pokhara... he needs a big rucksack. Yours is perfect."

Maria felt uncomfortable, the idea of lending it to Vale didn't appeal to her at all. "But I leave on Monday. I need my rucksack. And it's packed full of things."

"He only needs it for three days... he'll be back on Sunday... and you... don't need it while you are in Kathmandu..., do you?" she insisted, struggling to get the words out.

Maria didn't want to lend her rucksack, but she couldn't find an excuse to wriggle out of their request. After all Franca was a guest in Vale's house. But she knew how these things went: her backpack would come back dirty, ruined, perhaps even broken, while she had always treated it with the best possible care: "When do you want it?"

"Bring it tomorrow... so you come and see me again."

The following day Maria arrived in the late afternoon with her backpack, empty and light. Reluctantly, she laid it at Franca's feet.

Vale appeared almost immediately. "I need a big rucksack and Franca said that yours is perfect. It's true," he said, turning it over and over, studying it well. He thanked Maria, smiling for the first time and showing his teeth stained with tobacco, many were missing. As he walked away,

Maria glimpsed him digging his black nails under the white plastic plug at the end of the frame. She was left with an unhappy feeling, but Franca asked her what she had been doing that morning, what she was going to do later, and Maria talked to her about this and that, passing the time together. From the kitchen wafted the strong, pleasant aroma of cardamom and cinnamon and soon Vale reappeared with two chai and even two biscuits on a saucer, for Maria. Perhaps she had judged him too soon; this kindness didn't seem to be his style, but maybe she was prejudiced against him, she thought while she thanked him with a tight smile.

"If you come on Sunday evening I'll give it back to you. I only need it for three days," Vale reassured her. "If you want, I'll bring it to your hotel."

"No, no, I'll come over, so I can take the opportunity to say goodbye to Franca before I go," said Maria, hiding the discomfort that stubbornly refused to leave her.

"You're a real friend," said Vale, with a quick smile. Maria saw him glance at Franca and wink. Franca returned him a weak yellowish smile; the contrast between the yellow of the eyes and her pale blue pupils gave her a sinister look, Maria mused unhappily.

She left the house before dusk. It was a long walk to reach Kathmandu and she didn't want to be alone in the dark. She felt disappointed in herself; why couldn't she just say no? If Franca didn't want to do something, she'd refuse to do it, without any scruples, while she didn't have the courage. What a fool! This was something in her character that she would have to change.

She stayed at the Top View Hotel and spent those days exploring the town, accompanied by her three French friends and, when they left, by someone else she had met in the square. With a German boy, she climbed once more the endless steps leading to Swayambhunath temple, with its Buddha's eyes, populated by hundreds of monkeys. With an American girl, she wandered aimlessly through the poor neighbourhoods outside the city centre. With two French girls, she went to sit in the quiet part of the river where they could put their feet in the cool water and observe the stones on the bottom; women washing their clothes; bicycles gliding without haste. She took photographs and soaked in the reality of those moments, absorbing them completely. She spent the evenings eating in the restaurants around the square, meeting new people, exchanging a word here and there with other young travellers, or sitting on the stone steps of the square, talking Italian, French, sometimes English. Short conversations, small exchanges, but she felt lonely. It was a peculiar sensation, sometimes pleasant, at other times not so; on the one hand she had all the freedom to decide what to do and where to go, on the other she missed Franca's endless stream of words that had become so familiar. Maria imagined it in her head and so, although she wasn't physically present, it was as if she were: an imaginary friend! She went to see her every day. Things didn't seem to change much, the yellowish colour persisted and Franca was always sitting on a rug, her arms limp and heavy; she didn't do anything and could only find a small amount of energy to make a few comments about what Maria was telling her, what she had done, whom she had met.

It was her last day in Kathmandu and Maria, who had never ceased to think about her backpack, could finally go and pick it up. In Durbar Square she bumped into one of the Italians and they walked together to the house in the suburbs; it was already six o'clock in the afternoon. Maria would pick up her backpack and take her leave from Franca, then straight back to her hotel. "I don't want to be outside in the dark," she said. "So, I'll be quick! Tonight I'll have to prepare my luggage and the same things that were in it before never fit when you pack again, I've never understood why."

"I'll come back with you, don't worry!" promised the boy. "I want to return to the square for a couple of hours." They chatted away and the boy told her that Vale had been living in Nepal for almost three years; he went to India only when his visa expired and came back as soon as he could. Did he know why he lived there? Maria asked. Probably because he liked it, he replied, it was cheap and he did what he wanted. Or perhaps he wished to avoid doing military service, he had never asked him, he didn't feel at ease with him; Vale wasn't someone you'd make friends with, because he was superior and everyone else was inferior, he said with sarcasm. The world of Anger, Maria thought, surprising herself with this sudden association of ideas; it was the world in which people used others as a means to a goal, if she remembered well. She could imagine him in that role, bossing others around, with that heavy sense of superiority that he wore, like an old worn out suit. As soon as Maria arrived she immediately went to Franca.

"Is my rucksack back?" she asked, even before enquiring how she was.

"Yes... now Vale will bring it to you... He came back last night," she said, looking perhaps more yellow than the day before.

He arrived a few minutes later and, with another smile that showed his black and missing teeth, he handed Maria her backpack; his nails were rimmed in black, as if he had been working with soil. Maria was relieved to see that it wasn't in worse shape than when she had lent it to him. "It has been very useful, thank you," said Vale. "It's a good backpack, big, and I managed to fit in it all that I wanted. I put in a little present for you, to thank you for the favour."

Maria was surprised; she simply wasn't expecting a gift from Vale. She looked inside the backpack and pulled out a pair of traditional Nepalese hand-knitted socks, made of heavy, thick wool: "Thank you, Vale. How kind! You didn't need to, but..."

"Not at all! Your backpack has been very useful, perfect, really. Franca said that she wants to buy it off you once you're back in Italy, don't you?" he said, turning to Franca.

Maria was surprised: "How come? You've always hated it! You've never stopped pulling my leg about it. Don't tell me that you'd travel with this rucksack!"

Franca smiled weakly; it seemed as if her teeth had become yellow, too: "No, I want to keep it as a souvenir... and make sure you can't use it again."

Maria laughed, glad to have it back in her hands. Now she could go and prepare her luggage. But where was the boy who was going to walk back to Kathmandu with her? He had to wait another ten minutes, he said; he was waiting for a friend. Vale offered to prepare a cup of tea. Maria sat next to Franca to spend the last few minutes with her. She didn't feel good about leaving her alone, she was still so ill. "What can I do for you?" she asked. She had become really close to her in those two months. Despite all their differences and emotional problems, despite Franca's rebellious nature, or perhaps because of it, she had become fond of her.

"Don't worry Maria... there are a lot of people here. I'll be fine... Take care of yourself... write to me when you get to Italy... as soon as you get back."

"Sure! I'll come and pick you up at Rome airport, when you return." Time was passing, the ten minutes had turned into twenty, thirty, and it was beginning to get dark outside: "I can't wait any longer; it's almost night out there and the idea of walking in the dark worries me."

The boy showed no sign of leaving; unless his friend arrived, he said, he couldn't go. Maria was annoyed. If she had known from the start she wouldn't have waited so long. She stood up, put her backpack on her shoulders and decided to go it alone, the very thing she hadn't wanted to do. She crouched down to kiss Franca. "See you soon; take care of yourself!" she said with affection.

"You too," said Franca, feebly, unable to hold her gaze for long before looking at the floor.

When Maria reached the door, Franca said: "And remember… that rucksack is mine!"

Maria smiled: "If you insist!" she said, and blew her a kiss.

Before going out, she pressed the switch by the door to open the gate and closed the door behind her. She covered the few feet of the driveway; it was already dark. She went out and heard the click of the gate as it closed behind her.

The first dogs surrounded her within seconds, staring at her with red eyes. She tried to open the gate to go back inside, shook it a couple of times, but it was firmly closed and there was no bell. What was she to do now? She was stuck outside and surrounded by four, five, six dogs that began to make guttural sounds. Some showed their sharp teeth while others pushed each other to bark louder. Even if she screamed no one would have heard her; she was outside, alone, with no choice but to start walking. She looked around to see if there were any stones, but the dogs were too close to her legs for her to bend down. Meanwhile, the noises from deep in their throats became more audible, gradually turning into a growl and then into sharp barking. Attracted by the noise, other dogs approached running; they appeared out of the darkness and joined the pack, with their sharp teeth, their bloodshot eyes, growling and barking louder and louder.

Maria began to walk, her legs trembling violently, she was struggling to put one foot in front of the other and feared she would stumble. But she couldn't, they would tear her to pieces. One step after another, she remembered that Michel had told her not to be afraid because the dogs would smell her fear; but she was petrified. What had he said? You are in command, not them. Make sure they know you are the boss! That sort of thing. The dogs barked louder and louder and were getting closer. They jostled against each other, competing to see who got closest to her calves, on which she felt their warm breath.

Her heart was pounding so hard, she was sure they could see it through her clothes. I have to stop being afraid, she said to herself, but how can I? She thought of her mother, her father, her friends, Jean-Claude, Paul, Franca. Transform fear into courage. Nam-myoho-renge-kyo, she started to chant in her mind. In the distance she could see the light of a street lamp. 'I have to get out of this in one piece,' she told herself. Focusing on the light she quickened her pace; the dogs barked more and more hysterically, angrier and angrier, but none took the initiative to attack her.

With a trembling voice she began to sing the first thing that came to mind: "Allons enfants de la patrie-iii…" The French national anthem? Fancy that! she thought, surprised. At the sound of her voice, the dogs went crazy. Nope, singing was not a good idea. But now the song's marching rhythm had crept into her mind and made her march: "Le jour de gloire est arrivé..." she continued softly. She didn't remember the remaining words, but she kept marching, singing to herself: "Ta ta ta ta tatta tatta ta, ta tatta ta ta tatta tatta ta, na nanna na nanna na nanna na, la lalla la lalla la la! Pa pa... pa pa... pa pappa pa, pa pa pa pa... pa pa! Marchons, Marchons, la lalla la la tatta ta... ta ta ta ta! And then she started again: Allons enfants de la patrie-ii le jour de gloire est arrivé."

The courage was growing and her determination was becoming a powerful weapon. Nam-myoho-renge-kyo, Nam-myoho-renge-kyo, she continued. She quickened her pace and, while she felt more confident and resolute, she thought she could notice some hesitation in the pack of dogs, which imperceptibly began to let go of their siege. She took the opportunity to bend quickly and pick up a couple of stones. Immediately they slowed down, leaving a little space between them and her. Maria aimed at one of the dogs' heads and threw the first stone. Clonk! One down more to go, she thought, and laughed with a sense of victory. She reached down, picked up more rocks and continued to throw them, always aiming at the dogs' heads. There were at least fifteen of them, coming from in front, from the sides and from behind, still furious, but also a little bit uncertain.

She walked on, her pace more and more secure, stronger and stronger, until she finally reached the next lamppost. Once past it, she immediately fell back into another sea of darkness, but she knew that Kathmandu was not far away. Her panic was almost completely gone, replaced by a strong sense of defiance and courage born out of the knowledge that she had already won, because she had conquered her fear. "Get away from me, you bastards!" she shouted. And then she laughed, thinking that those dogs really were bastards, mongrels, as no one knew who had conceived them.

Finally, she saw the city lights and felt safe, even if the dogs were still surrounding her; she was too strong for them. She began to sing in a loud voice, shouting, marching forward and swinging her arms vigorously: "Allons enfants de la patrie-ii le jour de gloire est arrivé. Ta ta ta ta tatta tatta ta, ta tatta ta tatta tatta ta, na nanna na nanna na nanna na, la lalla la lalla la la! Pa pa... pa pa... pa pappa pa, pa pa pa pa... pa pa! Marchons, Marchons, la lalla la la tatta ta... ta ta ta ta!"

Jean-Claude and Michel, Sylvan, Eve and Pierrot, and all the French people she knew, would have been proud of her. At the end of the dirt road the darkness faded away blending into the lights of the city and the dogs stopped. They were still barking and growling, but they weren't moving forward any longer, the cowards who took advantage of the dark. She had won, she was safe!

The people spending the evening hours in Durbar Square had never seemed so warm and the relaxed atmosphere had never been so pleasant. She sat down on the steps, still shaken by the experience, and paused, absorbing the peace of the evening, giving time to her heartbeat to gradually slow down, watching the square as if she was seeing it for the first time. She smiled and congratulated herself, thinking that, perhaps, she was a brave woman after all. While walking back to the Top View Hotel she resolved to be much more careful from then on; if anything happened to her, there was no one to defend or help her: she was alone. At reception she paid for her stay and went up to her room where she began to pack. She set the alarm clock for half past seven and finally closed her eyes, exhausted. She had to be at the airport at nine.

She opened her eyes and looked at the time; it was a quarter to nine. How was that possible? The alarm hadn't gone off! She jumped out of bed, trembling with anxiety; was it a nightmare? No, it was reality, but it seemed a nightmare. She moved as quickly as possible and, without washing her face or brushing her hair, she ran downstairs with her heavy backpack and camera bag, looking around in search of a rickshaw. She shouted to call one and, as soon as it approached she jumped on, breathless, saying 'to the airport, *jaldi jaldi*,' quickly, quickly! The man understood and began to pedal fast. She prepared the extra rupees for him and, as soon as they reached the airport doors, she jumped off and ran with her bulky and heavy luggage, entering the terminal forty minutes late, distressed and panicking. She ran to the first policeman. "What do I do with my rucksack?" she shouted.

"Where do you go, Madam?" he questioned her, incredibly slow.

"To Patna, in India, where else? How many flights are there that leave at eleven?" she asked provocatively.

The policeman studied her. "The luggage goes here," he said, pointing to the moving belt, with a serious expression. "Then go through passport control," he ordered.

She knew she had to calm down, or at least control her temper. As soon as she arrived at passport control, she realized she was going to be searched.

A female police officer was waiting for her, while the policeman was watching from the entrance. She made her go behind a screen and frisked her everywhere, even under her hair. "Do you have knives?" she asked.

"No! No knives."

The police woman stared at her: "Are you sure you don't have knives?"

"I have no knives, I told you! If I tell you that I have no knives, it means that I don't have any. Is that clear?" Maria blurted out, unable to check her anguish. She shouldn't have spoken like that, she knew, but why did they make her even more late than she already was? Suddenly she remembered the silver box that Jean-Claude had given her, with charas inside, and her blood froze in her veins.

"I want to search your bag," said the police woman, feeling the content of the cloth bag hanging from Maria's shoulder, starting from the outside and then pushing her arm inside. She had to think quickly; she was trembling with shock and fear. At the same time, she was angry with the woman who pushed her, fondled, touched her. She wanted to scream.

Abruptly, she removed the bag from her shoulder, saying: "Let's do this, look!" and emptied the entire contents on the counter. Immediately she saw the silver box. She had to do something! Taking advantage of a moment's hesitation from the police woman, she began to throw the things back inside her bag, starting with the box. "See? No knives. I told you so!" she said. The cop let her continue without interfering.

Then, speaking more gently, Maria said: "I'm very late for my plane, can I go please?" She looked into her eyes, asking for understanding. The police officer pointed her chin forward, as if to say she could go. She walked quickly toward the plane, shaking even more than before. She was the last person to board, they were waiting only for her. She thanked the hostess and sat down. It seemed an eternity before they closed the plane doors, but her watch told her it had only been ten minutes. She tried to think calmly; she thought there were no problems about carrying a bit of charas with her, but she realized that it was not true, at least in Nepal it was officially illegal. While in India it was legal... But was it, really? She wasn't at all sure. She remembered what Mr. Singh had told her, it depended on the state, it was legal in some states, but not in others, and she had a lot of misconceptions about India.

This time she had got away with it, but she had to be much more careful, especially now that she was alone. Instead of feeling relieved, she felt sick at the thought of what could have happened. Although the authorities might have turned a blind eye for one gram of charas, her aggressive and provocative attitude would have caused her problems. She had behaved beyond the acceptable limits of respect and she knew it. As the plane climbed over the clouds she felt ill at ease with herself. The hostess went around offering boiled sweets while Maria was reflecting. It was a very short flight in an old airplane. After half an hour they had already started their descent. Her ears began to hurt and the discomfort continued, getting worse and worse as they got lower. She pressed her hands on her ears, hoping they'd land soon. It seemed as if her head would burst.

21. The weight of freedom

Finally they landed and, as soon as she stood up, she recognized a young man she had glimpsed a couple of times in Durbar Square. He nodded at her and, when she reached the bottom of the stairs, he approached her. "Have you bought any whisky to resell?" he asked casually. "Did you know that you can repay the cost of the flight with just one bottle?"

"I haven't had the time. I almost missed the plane. Have you?"

"I did! People wait outside the airport with money in their hands."

"How much can you sell it for?" she asked, out of curiosity.

"Three hundred and fifty rupees is easy to get. If you want more you have to haggle."

She had the uncomfortable feeling that there was something creepy about this boy and didn't stop to wait for him while he was bargaining over the price. However, a few minutes later he was by her side having sold his whisky for three hundred and sixty rupees, without a problem. "Where are you going?" he asked.

"To Delhi, and you?"

"Me too."

It seemed natural to share a rickshaw, it was cheaper, and how could she refuse? They queued at the station to buy their train tickets and, although both of them kept to themselves, they ended up booking berths near to each other. He spoke English well, but it wasn't his first language; she couldn't tell whether he was German, or perhaps Yugoslavian, she wasn't interested. He was kind, when their eyes met he smiled, he offered his help; he was discreet, almost shy. There was a train leaving Patna that evening and they had all day to wait. With too much baggage to go and explore the city, they stopped at a chai-shop where they ate samosas, bhaji, chapatis, almost in silence. The boy prepared a chillum and Maria took a small puff. She wasn't in the mood to ask any questions, he seemed to prefer it that way and they relaxed as the day passed.

She watched him while he wasn't aware: he had brown, clean wavy hair, a sweet triangular-shaped face, girl-like smooth skin; he couldn't have been more than twenty years old. She felt distant, and couldn't explain why.

Finally, the evening came and they walked to the station. They found the right coach and their wooden bunks in the corridor; she had the one above, while he had the one below. There were no closed compartments on this carriage and no privacy. It was already dark when the train left. Maria settled into her sleeping bag even though it was hot, keeping under her arm the pouch with her passport and her last one hundred rupee note. She would have to change her last travellers' cheque as soon as she arrived in Delhi. She felt more vulnerable travelling without Franca.

Maybe Raffa was right, and Franca was tougher than she believed; she thought about her with affection and knew that she would recover from the hepatitis and the amoeba. However, how far would she go with her experiments with drugs? Maria was glad she wasn't travelling on the same plane back to Italy; it seemed increasingly clear that Franca would try to carry something with her, maybe charas, or opium, or even worse! She had been mulling over something of the kind for a long time, Maria had no doubt about this.

The rhythm of the train rocked her, marked by the beat of a little jolt every time the wheel passed over a point. In a few days' time she would be back in Italy, and suddenly the idea surprised her. She was so used to travelling, going from one interesting place to another, talking with new people of all cultures and languages. While she, the character, remained the same, the stage of her life was constantly changing; she liked this life, composed of new and stimulating experiences. She wondered where Jean-Claude was just now; with Michel, of course, but where? Was he thinking of her? Yes, she knew he was, she could feel it. She missed his kisses, his passionate embraces, his smiling eyes full of irony, his unexpected jokes that always made her laugh; she had been happy with him during those six magical days. She would go to the Post Office in Delhi to see if he had written to her, as promised. And Paul? He must surely be in the mountains with his girlfriend, walking in the sun, in the clear and crystalline Himalayan air. She wished him all the happiness in the world. She remembered the warmth of his breath when he had embraced her in the temple, and felt a shiver down her spine. She shrugged, trying to feel once more that sensation of being protected.

She was going back to Italy, to Venice, to work as a life model at the Academy of Fine Arts. It seemed like a distant world. She thought of her apartment in Campo San Maurizio, above the gold-plating shop, the '*Dorador*', near the art gallery, which was waiting for her. In her mind she heard the sound of a bell that tolled the hours. A smile relaxed her face. She would have to find someone to share her flat and the rent. And Ugo? She felt no emotion when she repeated his name. She couldn't even visualize his face, or remember his voice. He was in the past and she had succeeded in leaving him behind.

She woke up in the middle of a carriage full of people, mostly men, who were talking and freshening up with a little water, before the prayer that everyone carried out discreetly. As always, they talked loudly, were cheerful and behaved as if they all knew one another. Maria didn't want to get involved in a conversation and kept her eyes low when she came down from her bunk to go to the toilet. She noticed a Japanese couple settled on two bunks nearby. They smiled warmly at her; apart from her and her new friend they were the only foreigners in the whole car. As she returned to her place she saw that the boy travelling with her was preparing a chillum. "Isn't it too early to smoke?" she asked.

He smiled: "The trip to Delhi is long; we'll be on this train all day with nothing to do and, with this, time passes more quickly." He was right about that; after smoking time lost any meaning.

Looking around, Maria saw that many people had noticed the chillum and were talking about it, commenting with each other, wearing a critical expression. She smiled but they didn't return her smile. Weird! In some parts of the country Indian people were quite amused, sometimes even impressed, when they saw westerners smoking a chillum. She felt confused, insecure, isolated. She had never before perceived such open disapproval. She tried to ignore it, but couldn't; she liked it when there was an atmosphere of camaraderie with the Indians. Was it just in her head or could she feel actual hostility in the air? She looked from one to another and saw a particularly serious group, in which the men, when they met her eyes, looked away.

The boy was ready to light it and handed her the box of matches. Pushing aside the discomfort she felt, Maria lit a match, he inhaled, and then let out a cloud of smoke into the air. He offered her the chillum. She wasn't sure. Oh, why not! She took only a small puff and gave it back to him. The young man offered it to the men around him, but not only did they reject it, they seemed offended by the advance. Maria didn't want any more and the boy finished it; it wasn't even ten o' clock in the morning. Nestled in her pleasant mental cloud, she sat on the lower bunk, which they now shared for the rest of the journey, and watched India go by before her eyes. The temperature was rising, the wind blew pleasantly in her face and when the train picked up speed it was almost cool. The green fields, the people who worked in them, the children who chased their bicycle wheels, the women with their princesses' saris; she loved the colours of India and was happy to be back. She observed, suspended in her timeless and unhurried bubble. The train began to slow down; it was approaching a big station. Excellent, she was craving a chai. Looking out of the window she saw the writing KANPUR.

With a deafening screech of brakes the train slowed down and stopped at the platform. Maria leaned out of the window, trying to attract the attention of the chai wallahs who were shouting 'chai' 'chai garam', warm chai. There were many of them but there were also many passengers who wanted a cup of tea. Finally, a young boy stood below her train window and she ordered a chai for herself and one for her travel companion. She took the two clay cups, paid the two rupees and sat down on the wooden berth, blowing on her hot tea; those clay cups again with the rough texture on her lips, ready to fly out of the windows once the owners had finished their tea. The chai didn't contain any spices, but it was comforting all the same. The train was not moving. Strange, it was stopping much longer than usual. Vendors came offering all sorts of wares: plastic sandals, fans made of straw...

She saw a group of policemen approaching the train and her heart jumped. There was nothing to worry about, she told herself, but she was breaking out in a cold sweat, a lump formed in her throat, she felt nauseous and her legs began to tremble. The policemen, about ten or twelve of them, got on at her carriage; she was paralyzed with fear. Now she had a strong feeling that there was a big problem and it concerned her. The leading policeman, with insignia on his shirt and followed by all the others, marched up to her bunk, where he stopped. Addressing the boy who was travelling with her, he ordered: "Come with us!"

The boy stood up, stoned by the recently smoked chillum and, unsteadily, went with four policemen. The others were with Maria. The officer studied her seriously. "Do you have any drugs? Give them to me," he ordered, sharp, but not too angry.

Maria was shaking from head to toes. Could they see it? With clammy hands, as cold as ice, she felt inside the cloth bag until she found the silver box that Jean-Claude had given her, and handed it to the policeman. He opened it, checked the contents and then put it in his pocket. There were only two small pieces of charas, maybe one gram. She looked around and saw that she was the centre of everybody's mute attention. The Japanese couple looked at her with sympathy, as did most of the Indian passengers, but when her eyes fell on the group of men who had appeared hostile, she saw they were laughing and had no doubt that they had called the police. No one spoke.

"Take your luggage. All of it!" ordered the officer.

Shaking like a leaf, Maria obeyed, unable to utter a sound. She saw the young man come back, accompanied by the four policemen. She was surprised; she didn't think she would see him again. He smiled weakly. The officer exchanged a few words with the policemen escorting him, and then returned his full attention onto Maria. "Come with us!" he ordered curtly.

A curtain of fear had fallen down around her. She felt the effect of that puff from the chillum and was still without contact lenses, feeling completely vulnerable. She loaded her backpack, carried the camera bag over one shoulder and walked with the officer, followed in turn by all the other cops. While passing through the aisle full of passengers who, like two wings of a crowd, were watching the scene, one of them, a distinguished-looking man, whispered: "Baksheesh."

"What?" she said, surprised, desperate, alone; she clung to that word like a drowning man to a wooden float. She had heard it, but didn't know what it meant.

"Baksheesh," he repeated, getting closer to whisper in her ear. Seeing that she didn't understand, he said in English: "Give them money!" She nodded and, surrounded by the khaki group of policemen, got off the train.

They walked onto the platform, Maria next to the policeman with the insignia, while the other eleven followed them. All the passengers were watching them from the train windows, many of them excited at seeing something interesting, others with a worried expression. Where were they taking her? She heard the officer's voice asking her: "You like?" What did he mean? Maria was concerned. What was she supposed to like? She looked at him as if to say she didn't understand. He repeated the same words: "You like?" Her blood froze in her veins. She was beginning to understand: she was alone and twelve policemen were taking her somewhere, asking if she 'liked'. She had to do something, take action, but what? She forced herself to shake off the panic that paralyzed her.

With her elbow she slightly touched the officer's arm, who reacted with surprise; improvising, she managed to get out a few trembling words. "Why are you giving me all these problems?" she said in a small voice.

"Because you have drugs," he said gruffly.

"But it's just a little piece; it doesn't hurt anyone," she argued, as politely as possible.

"It's no good, and it is against the law," replied the officer.

"You are right," she said, taking time, walking fast, her shaking legs barely holding her up, a stream of cops right on her heels. She felt cold, whilst walking under the scorching sun. "But it's only a small piece. There are people who have large quantities and that's no good... I only have a little charas. Charas is God, isn't it?… Bagwan?" She remembered Pushpa explaining that everything was Bagwan, including, and especially, the charas.

He almost tripped over his feet, visibly shocked to hear the word Bagwan; clearly, he didn't expect it. He stared at her while they walked alongside each other and again repeated: "You like?" Since Maria didn't understand and looked at him with concern, he said: "One hundred rupees, you like?"

Finally she understood. He wanted money! Could she believe her ears? "Yes, one hundred rupees, no problem," she replied immediately. She looked at him, full of hope. She wanted to hug him, but she wasn't out of it yet. They had walked a long way along the train, which still wasn't moving.

Suddenly, the police officer pointed to a wagon and ordered her to get on board. She obeyed, climbing onto the mail carriage, followed by all twelve uniformed men. It was completely empty. Pushed by their proximity, she sat on a wooden bench and suddenly she was gripped by fear. They were so many of them, and she was a woman, alone. The policeman spoke again and this time she listened with as much attention as possible. "Put one hundred rupees inside your passport and give it to me," he said.

They were the only rupees she had left, after that she didn't even have the money to buy a chai, but she willingly put the note inside her passport and handed it to him. However, it felt very uncomfortable to give him her passport: it was her identity, her freedom, the proof of her existence. If he kept it, she would be in even deeper trouble, but she had no choice. The officer took the banknote and then paused, looking at her passport. Maria reached over and looked into his eyes, saying: "My passport, please," as if he were a friend.

He hesitated a moment, then handed it back to her. "Stay here until the next station," he ordered, "then return to your carriage."

She nodded, full of gratitude, and the policemen began to move toward the door. She remembered Jean-Claude's silver box. "My little box, please," she asked politely.

The officer stopped in mid-stride, as if he couldn't believe his ears.

Maria repeated: "Can you give me back my little box, please?"

He seemed surprised, perhaps half amused. "A box is not important," he said, looking at her with curiosity.

"For me it is important," she insisted, feeling that she was blushing. Was she pushing her luck? "A friend gave it to me, *dosta*," she added, using another Hindi word she had learned from Pushpa; 'dosta' meant friend and friendship was important in India.

The officer stopped to ponder her request; he pulled out the small box from his pocket, turned it over and over, opened it, emptied the contents on his hand and eventually handed it to her, looking straight into her face. Flushed, her cheeks red hot, Maria replied to his look with a mixture of gratitude, relief, acknowledgement of his humanity, all the emotions mixed together. "Thank you," she said.

He bowed slightly and turned to get off the wagon, followed by all the other cops. She was still incredulous, she couldn't move, she didn't even dare to breathe too deeply. After a few minutes, the train moved. Gradually it picked up speed and finally left the platform and Kanpur station behind her.

She was incredibly relieved but still in shock and couldn't think. She felt tears running down her face, wetting her cheeks, and cried out of fear. She had come so close to a great danger and had gotten away with it for some mysterious protection. What if she hadn't had those hundred rupees? If he had kept her passport? If he had decided to rape her? And maybe all twelve of them? They could have taken her to the police station and, if they wanted to, made her disappear.

She was alone, no one knew who she was, nobody even knew her name. She felt nauseous from fear, on the verge of being sick. But she was free! She felt all the weight of her freedom, and of all the responsibility necessary to manage it. It was such a valuable thing and she had ignored it, taken it for granted, almost despised it, until she had come close to losing it altogether. Alone, in the mail carriage, lulled by the regular rhythm of the train shuddering at every point, she closed her eyes and let the wind lift her hair, caress her face, her forehead, her eyelids, her neck. She smiled through the tears. She was free and very grateful to be so.

The words Nam-myoho-renge-kyo came out by themselves and, full of gratitude, she continued to say them in rhythm with the train, giving thanks for her life.

Looking out of the window she let her disturbed mind calm down and merge with the green rice fields that lined both sides of the railway. Indian women were knee-deep in them, doubled over, many with a baby tightly held in a bundle on their backs, planting a seedling at a time. The villages passed, three children together speeding on a bike, racing with the train, waving to the passengers, smiling with joy because she was waving back to them.

Those black velvet eyes, those unreserved smiles, warm, innocent, full of life, had won her over. Women were walking along the road carrying on their heads golden brass containers filled with water; some supported it with one hand, others trusted their balance and walked upright, swinging their arms, swaying their hips like models on a catwalk.

It seemed as if their load was as light as a feather while Maria knew how heavy it was, because she had carried one, too. Their arms adorned with dozens of colourful plastic bracelets, fresh flowers in their hair, advancing like princesses in their red, yellow, green saris, they went to work in the fields looking as if they were going to a party, with that natural, unpretentious elegance. She felt her heart burst with love for these people.

She loved India, it was giving her so much. Once again tears began to slide down her cheeks, but this time they were tears of gratitude. And the train was running, free. It travelled at least one hour before slowing down, approaching another big station.

She leaned out of the window, letting the warm wind swell her hair and fill it with dust. The train finally stopped; the mail carriage was a long way away and there was no platform. Loaded with her luggage, she climbed down the steps and walked on the loose stones to reach the platform, hoping the train didn't leave too soon. She walked as fast as she could till she approached her carriage. A man in a white shirt was standing on the steps and leaning out, beckoning her with his arm; it was the man who had told her to give baksheesh to the policeman. When she reached the door he helped her on board and, studying her carefully, asked how she was. "Fine, thank you," she said, surprised by the concern he was showing, soon realizing that he wasn't the only one. The other passengers, too, wanted to know how she was; some were curious, no doubt, but they were also very worried about her. They had had time to think of what could have happened to her and all for a puff of a chillum. Since they wanted to know, Maria told the man what had happened, while everyone listened. "You were very lucky!" he said, serious. Many heads nodded. She knew they were right, and agreed with them, relieved. She sat on the wooden bench and the young man travelling with her smiled shyly at her. She returned his smile and, whispering, she asked him what had happened when they had taken him away. They had taken him into the toilet and 'searched', he said; trying not to be noticed by the other passengers, he added 'inside the body', raising his middle finger. Maria felt faint, realizing, if she still needed to, what could have happened to her and how much protection she had received.

The men who had denounced them stood on the platform and began to haggle with the vendors, pretending to be busy buying something, thus avoiding looking at her. She didn't feel angry with them; blaming someone else meant hiding from reality and postponed the important step of taking responsibility for the effects resulting from her actions: the law of cause and effect, Luna had called it, she remembered well. Who was responsible for what had happened? The boy who had made the chillum? The men who had grassed them up? Sure, they were responsible for their actions, but if she hadn't smoked it, if she hadn't had any charas in her bag, she probably wouldn't have been involved. So: 'It's up to you Maria! It's no use blaming other people. The sooner you understand this, the better for your own future,' she told herself.

The Japanese couple called her over, they had bought her a chai. She went to sit on their bench and took it with much gratitude, appreciating every sweet hot sip. They asked her if she had any money; she had the last one hundred-dollar travellers' cheque, but no rupees. They offered to pay for her scooter to go to the Tourist Camp and Maria thanked them for their offer, which she gratefully accepted; she felt embarrassed by the kindness and warmth that surrounded her. Every time she looked around, the passengers smiled at her, some bowed with folded hands, until she felt uncomfortable with all the attention she was receiving. She sat on her bench and looked out of the window, hoping they'd all forget about her. She spent the rest of the journey in silence.

They arrived in Delhi late in the afternoon and it was like coming home. She didn't tell the young man where she was headed; she said goodbye to him and wished him good luck, walking away before he could ask her any questions, never having known his name. She quickly bargained over the fare with the scooter driver and settled with her large luggage. The man drove off at full throttle; Maria had to hold on tight and couldn't help but laugh at the enthusiasm with which he was driving his vehicle. She relaxed, leaning back on the red plastic seat, and let Delhi's dusty air welcome her. She recognized the streets, the shops, even the shopkeepers who worked by the roadside. She couldn't wait to see the people who worked at the Tourist Camp.

Mr. Singh wore a dark blue turban. He recognized her at once, stood up with a smile and walked around his desk to go and shake her hand. Spontaneously Maria kissed him on the cheek, which surprised him and made him laugh. "Are you alone?" he asked.

"Yes, my friend has stayed in Kathmandu. She has hepatitis."

Mr. Singh shook his head, but smiled warmly. "You young people don't take enough care of yourselves." He looked at her up and down. "You're thinner, but you look well," he said with a father-like expression. He assigned her a bed in a dormitory for a week, her last week in India. All the people who worked there recognized her. They responded to her greetings with a warm smile, clasping their hands and bowing, as she had learned to do, and now came naturally. The cleaning lady, the one who had given her her belt and draped her first and last sari replied with a kiss to Maria's kiss and embrace. She could tell that she wasn't accustomed to this form of greeting, but was amused and accepted it with pleasure.

Maria realized how much she had changed since her arrival in India and that morning with the belt and the sari, when she was an insecure young woman with a great desire to be accepted and loved. And now here she was, relaxed, confident, having accepted and approved of herself, despite the mistakes she had made, assuming full responsibility for them, aware that it was up to her to turn them into victories. She had been loved for who she was, had found unconditional friendship, she had learned, understood and felt that happiness came from within and all this had changed her.

Life was rich and she was so lucky! She had understood the importance of staying healthy; she had seen people without limbs who seemed happy. She had enough money to do what she wanted and she remembered how the beggar to whom she had given half a rupee had blessed her by touching her feet. She was intelligent, well-educated and had seen so many bright, intelligent people, children and adults, who didn't have the chance to study as a result of extreme poverty, of the cruel inequality between those who had too much and ate sweets with gold and silver, and those who had nothing, not even a straw roof over their heads. Nevertheless, they had their dignity, an inner richness that made them masters of life for those who, like her, came from a materialistic western culture, so poor in spirituality. She went to the bathroom and stopped to look at the image that the old mirror sent back to her. Even her face had changed; in her eyes she could see the reflection of the compassion she had developed, the calmness from the love she had received. She had become wiser, had more respect for life and for the things she knew that she didn't yet know. She, who had been afraid to come to India, was there, smiling at herself and feeling beautiful.

During the last week in Delhi she met a lot of new people. Gianluca was a musician from Turin, who played the flute infusing his music with his whole life, classical, jazz, soul; as soon as he played the first note complete silence would form around him, hypnotizing them all with his magic. Then there was Siggi, a young Austrian with blond curly hair, an attractive oval face, green eyes that laughed or smiled whenever their gaze met. They ate together a few times and found out that they were travelling back on the same flight from Delhi to Rome.

The days passed quickly and, since she could do the round trip in one day, she decided to do an excursion to see the Taj Mahal. She booked a seat on a deluxe coach and at eight in the morning she left for Agra. It was still monsoon time and it had rained uninterruptedly throughout the night and all morning. Due to the torrential rain, the journey took much longer than expected, Agra was flooded and the roads were like rivers. The delay in arriving left little time for visiting the Taj Mahal but, after eight hours journey, Maria was determined to see it. Most tourists didn't dare get off the coach; they took pictures from their seats, from which they could see the building's imposing dome, preceded by the famous promenade along the straight, long pool. As soon as she got off the bus the rain whipped her face so hard it hurt. She saw that the water was still rising but, all the same, she ventured along the pool to the famous domed building. The water came up almost to her knees and, within seconds, she was soaking wet with rain. The air was hot and muggy and Maria kept her eyes on the Taj Mahal as she approached it.

 She knew that it had been built as a declaration of love from a Mogul emperor for his adored wife. She thought about how her idea of love had changed during this trip to India. While at first she identified it with the love between a man and a woman, now she saw it as something broader that pervaded all life and spread out among everyone and everything, impossible to contain, limit or describe. She felt that love could be expressed even without the existence of an object to give it to; it could be simply a love of life, a powerful joy that filled her heart, an emotion so strong that she had never felt before but was feeling now. Was that happiness?
 Surinder had said that happiness came from within us; Sanya had told her the same thing and had spoken of Buddhahood. Was that the way one felt in the state of enlightenment? The rain couldn't spoil the joy that swelled her heart; indeed, it allowed her to be alone and perceive it clearly.

 Finally, she reached the palace and went inside, soaked but happy. The beauty and purity, the space and the light stirred her. She stroked the white marble walls inlaid with flowers: petals made of blue lapis lazuli filled with specks of gold, stems of translucent green jade and transparent purple garnet flowers. She looked up at the dome and almost lost her balance, swaying in the infinite expanse. In the main room, behind an alabaster screen, the two 'cenotaphs' dedicated to the sultan and his beloved wife dominated the space.
 Maria bowed spontaneously in the Indian manner, as a sign of respect. Maybe one day she too would meet someone whom she could love completely without having to steal that happiness or obtain it at the expense of someone else's, and no one would have to pay a price for that love. She took the opportunity to walk around and observe, since she had

the good fortune to be alone in that huge space, undisturbed, and savoured the atmosphere full of magic and peace before going back to her coach, reluctantly retracing her steps.

The rain was even more furious on her return and the water level had risen, it now came up to her knees. She walked slowly, carefully feeling with her feet the ground that she couldn't see, dragging her steps. It took longer than she had imagined before reaching the coach, which was waiting for her. Drenched to the bone, she sat in the hot and humid bus; in silence, she looked out the window for the six hours it took them to return to Delhi. Finally she got off the bus and stretched her legs walking toward the exit, but had to stop to let a bus go round a tight corner; she looked through the windows, people were standing up to get ready to get off.

But… wasn't that Luna, the girl from Jaipur? It couldn't be! The vehicle was manoeuvring to enter the station and Maria didn't take her eyes off it, so as not to confuse it with others. She followed it closely, sometimes walking sometimes running, hoping not to have been mistaken. It would be wonderful if it were really Luna, she would come at the perfect time. With all the confusion and doubts she had in her heart for her upcoming journey back to Italy there was no one better to talk to. Standing next to the bus, she watched carefully to see if her hope became reality; at that precise moment, Luna looked at her. Her eyes widened in surprise and, after a brief hesitation, she waved enthusiastically at her. Maria replied, waving her arms, a smile all over her face and great joy filling her heart. People got off the bus, loaded with luggage, children and tiredness. The 'coolies' had already snapped into action, with their blue uniform and red turbans; they climbed with the speed of an athlete and unloaded the luggage carrying it on their heads and in their arms. Luna got down and hugged her for a long time, a warm genuine sister's hug. She noticed the two young men; they smiled at her and had positioned themselves at the foot of the ladder to retrieve their backpacks, leaving Luna free to greet her. They had arrived from Varanasi and were stopping in Delhi for a couple of days, before continuing toward the north. Luna had lost the note she had given her with the Tourist Camp's address on and had been racking her brain to remember it. How perfect that they had met at this very moment. What a coincidence! Maria said. There were no coincidences, Luna said, laughing happily. They shared a taxi and arrived at the Tourist Camp together.

Luna could no longer keep her eyes open; they had been up since four o'clock that morning. They agreed that they would meet the next day. Coming back from the shower, Maria walked past the restaurant and saw one of the two young men having a coffee; it was Harry, the South African man. She sat next to him. He told her that Ted had collapsed too and he suspected that they would sleep until the next morning. Harry was handsome, with regular features, and exuded a warmth that soon fascinated her.

22. Turning poison into medicine

Born in Johannesburg to white English parents, Harry had lived in Cape Town almost all his life, except for a few years spent in England. He explained how the blacks and other minorities were treated in the most unjust, cruel way by the whites, on the basis of the colour of their skin, and how much he hated the apartheid system. He was sure that one day he would see with his own eyes the end of that shameful discrimination and wanted to be part of the 'engine of change'. He had met Luna through his dear friend Ted, and spoke of her with great admiration; he was delighted to have discovered that she was a Buddhist, too. He had been practicing Buddhism for three years and was very happy with the change he saw in himself, day after day; he was learning to be more confident, to see his positives traits and transform his faults, instead of merely being self-critical. Buddhism was teaching him to have compassion and respect for others but also for himself, he said.

He spoke warmly, smiled a lot, his eyes expressed joy and enthusiasm; she felt immediately at ease with him. They talked about Rishikesh and Varanasi, of how deeply he was touched by the holy city. He wanted to know about her trip to Nepal and about Franca.

Almost without realizing it, Maria opened up and, little by little, she emptied the heavy load, with all her doubts and worries. She told him how Franca had stayed in Kathmandu, how they had been close and distant at the same time, about heroin and hepatitis.

He listened with so much interest that she even told him how uncomfortable she had felt about Franca's excessive interest toward her and of the resentment she had shown at the end. Harry understood, because the same thing had happened to him; these feelings of attraction 'muddied the waters of friendship', he said. He used a phrase that struck her immensely: 'We can turn poison into medicine.' Also Sanya and Colin had used that sentence but they hadn't had time to talk about it.

"What an interesting expression. What does it mean exactly?" she asked.

"It means that when we are in a difficult situation, or one that makes us suffer, we use it to become happier than we were before."

She wanted to know more, but they were too tired and decided to pick up their conversation again the next day.

She woke up late, feeling heavy with the tiredness of the previous day. She showered and, with her hair still wet, walked toward the restaurant. They were her last days in India and she had no specific plans on how to fill them. Harry was the first person she saw, sitting at a table, drinking coffee. Maria sat with him and ordered a chai. "I'm still thinking about the last thing you said last night. Is it too early to talk about it?" she asked, hesitantly.

"I've been awake for more than an hour," he replied with a smile, exuding an infectious vitality. He picked up the cup and sipped his coffee.

"Last night you said we can use any difficult situation in a positive way, by transforming it."

"That's right! When you think about it, life is beautiful but also full of suffering; have you noticed?" he asked.

"Yes..." replied Maria. This was already making her think; what he took for granted, she was turning over in her mind. These 'philosophical assumptions' gave her food for thought!

Without taking his eyes off her, he fumbled in his jacket pockets and pulled out a pouch of tobacco and cigarette papers, laying them on the table. Did it annoy her if he smoked? Not at all, quite the opposite. The waiter brought her chai. Harry ordered another coffee and leaned back in his chair.

"The important thing is how we respond to difficult situations," he continued. True! Respond rather than react, thought Maria. "The idea is to use them in order to grow and become a better person. Often we *need* to go through pain to find the motivation to change."

"Are you saying that we 'need' the suffering?" Maria asked, amused, enjoying the first sip of her chai.

He laughed: "I know it sounds strange, but it is through facing the hardest situations that we grow the most."

"This is something I've noticed too," she mused, "but changing poison into medicine is a big statement!"

Harry nodded: "Absolutely! I'm thinking of a friend who began to practice years ago. She was in a difficult relationship with a man who often hit her. They had been together for years, accustomed, addicted, to their dose of drama. Slapping, punching, verbal abuse, pushing, shouting; despite all this, she said he loved her. Every time after he beat her, he asked to be forgiven, she forgave him and so on, until the next time." Maria observed him and the way he gestured, a bit like an Italian. "I told her about respect and explained that this practice consists of learning to respect ourselves and others. One day, having reached the limit of her endurance, she asked me if we could chant. Of course, I agreed; I couldn't wait for her to wake up from that nightmarish relationship! We chanted together a couple of times and then she continued, even when she was alone. She read the Buddhist magazine and, during these small monthly discussion meetings, she listened to other people's experiences. One day, after a particularly violent episode, she realized that she had always looked 'outside herself', always believing that the relationship was sick because of his violence." Maria listened to him, caught up in the story. But why didn't she leave him? she thought; she could choose! "At that point she realized that *she* had wanted to remain in that relationship of mutual dependence and total lack of respect, masked by the word 'love'. She realized that, by continuing to do so she was not respecting herself, and as a result, he didn't respect her either. At that precise moment she knew that, if she wanted to, she could be free."

Oh, at last, thought Maria: "And did she leave him?"

"Yes, and in her case it wasn't even very difficult. The moment she decided to take responsibility for her life, the rest followed."

"Well done! And then what happened?"

"As she continued to chant, she realized that she wanted to devote her life to women who had suffered domestic violence. She studied for two years, she qualified, and began working in this field. She has a new life; she is happy, free, and devoted to her work."

"And he?"

"I don't know! I think he moved out of Cape Town. Everyone has their own path," he replied.

"I'm beginning to understand the principle of 'taking responsibility'," said Maria, thinking about her relationship with Ugo. "My ex didn't hit me, but he was unfaithful and I suffered a lot. I should have got rid of him as soon as I saw the way things were going, but it's not as simple as it seems. In the beginning we were so good together and I always hoped we could re-create the same exciting feeling. I was a bit 'addicted' to him, too. I didn't want him when he behaved 'like that', but I couldn't resist him."

"Has the experience been useful?" Harry asked, looking at her with his kind eyes.

"Oh yes, big way!" she replied. "I feel that I understand other women, and men, who go through such an experience, because I felt it on such a deep level. I recognize the depth of that confusion, the same excruciating pain that made me want to bang my head against a wall!"

He looked at her with sympathy: "If things had gone differently, would you be here now?" He didn't wait for her answer: "You know, we can always use what happens to us in order to grow. This is the concept of turning poison into medicine!" He paused briefly to reflect and then continued: "There are people who found themselves in situations of war and destruction so shocking that they decided to devote their lives to peace, so that no one else has to go through that kind of suffering. I know an old lady who was young when they dropped the atomic bomb on Hiroshima; she lost her entire family. Instead of being overwhelmed and destroyed by sadness, she fought to overcome her grief and dedicated her entire life to working for the abolition of nuclear weapons. She is the most active woman I know, even though she is almost seventy, and a deeply fulfilled person. She used her suffering to develop her life and inspire future generations."

"I can't imagine what it must have been like. Poor people!" reflected Maria.

Harry nodded and drank a long sip of his coffee. "Injustice gives rise to a great desire for justice. For me, apartheid in South Africa is the most unjust thing in the world!" he said with passion. "I'll do everything I can, with my Buddhist friends and cooperating with other organizations, for it to be abolished as soon as possible. What poison that is!" Maria sipped her chai slowly, waiting for him to continue. "Also when we become seriously ill; even then we have a choice. We can let ourselves be paralysed by fear, the poison, or we can use the illness to deepen our humanity, as we struggle with all our might to come out on top, the medicine. We fully accept what's happening and grow through it. It's a question of attitude," he said, putting a pinch of tobacco on the cigarette paper, wrapping it with care and licking the glue. "Transforming poison into medicine means that instead of complaining about the situation, we *use* it to deepen the knowledge of ourselves, our compassion and courage. We think, what can *I* do to change the way I feel? The more we do this the easier it gets... it's something you learn, you know?" he said with sparkling eyes. "And so, thanks to that particular challenge, we grow wiser, stronger, our lives expand and we become happier."

"Have you ever done it? Changing poison into medicine," asked Maria.

Harry laughed. "I do it constantly!" he replied.

At that moment she saw Luna approach, her long dark hair still wet from a shower. She had lost weight since she had seen her in Jaipur, had tanned and was even more beautiful. She wore a simple pink silk dress and had a light in her eyes emanating a unique intensity. Maria stood up and hugged her, took a chair from a nearby table and offered it to her. The waiter had noticed her, too and arrived straight away, as if attracted by a magnet. Luna asked him for a bottle of water and gave him a big smile.

"Rested?" Harry asked.

"Yes! I'm feeling almost human again!" she replied, beaming.

"Harry was talking about the concept of changing poison into medicine," said Maria, to bring her into the conversation.

"Ah, yes, it's a great topic, one of my favourites," she said with enthusiasm.

"Do you have other 'favourites'?" Maria encouraged her.

"Oh yes! Right now I'm thinking about the difference between criticizing and encouraging. It's something that Harry said..." she added, looking directly at him: "Do you remember? Yesterday afternoon you said: 'When someone does or says something that upsets me, I try to remember that this person needs encouragement, not my critical reaction, which would come so easily.'" He stared at Luna transfixed. She turned to Maria and continued brightly: "Harry was saying that when we criticize someone, this person becomes defensive, and no longer listens to what we're saying. But if we encourage them, they'll open up and become more receptive. Through this process, we both grow."

"How do you encourage rather than criticize?" asked Maria. "Maybe it's obvious to you, but I don't understand how it can work."

Harry stepped in: "Do you know the story of the wind and the sun? It's one of Aesop's fables." He glanced at Luna, and she smiled. With difficulty, he looked away from her pretty face.

"No, but I'd like to hear it," Maria replied, full of curiosity.

Returning his vibrant gaze to her, his eyes glowing, he began: "There was a competition between the wind and the sun, to see who could make a traveller remove his cloak!" Maria smiled and leaned back in her chair, while he continued: "The wind blew, stronger and stronger, but the traveller just pulled his cloak more tightly around him. After a while the wind gave up. Then the sun had a go; it came out from behind the clouds, began to shine and warmed the air. The traveller felt the heat on his shoulders and, quite naturally, took off his coat!" He smiled and took a sip of coffee.

"What a good story! The criticism is like the wind, while the words of encouragement are like the sun, right? The person opens up naturally!" Maria said, grinning. Then, suddenly aware of her empty stomach, she added: "I'm really hungry, aren't you?"

"I'm always hungry," replied Harry

"Me too," Luna said, her big green eyes lingering on his face.

"I want to talk more about poison into medicine," continued Maria. "How to apply it to different situations; so I can use it too. But before that, let's order!"

They looked around for the waiter to order omelettes with cheese, bread and chai. "Please, order for me and Ted, too," Luna said." I'll go and find him."

She got up and walked away, with her elegant, long stride. Both Harry and Maria followed her with their gaze, unable to peel their eyes away from her; then their eyes met and they laughed, aware of the effect she had on them both.

After placing their order, Harry explained: "Basically, any suffering, big or small, if we use it in this 'alternative' way, can become the springboard to transform our lives and the way we behave toward ourselves, other people and the environment. The possibilities are endless. We can always use it to become happier! From the Buddhist perspective all negative experiences have this tremendously positive potential. However..." he paused to light the cigarette that had been ready for a long time; he had a lighter with a marijuana leaf motif. He took a puff and continued: "... however, if we allow ourselves to be defeated by the situation, and the suffering is stronger than our effort to transform it, or if we react in a negative or destructive way, the poison doesn't turn into medicine, but remains poison. Basically, it all depends on us."

"I understand. And what about transforming criticism; how do you do that?" asked Maria.

Harry relit his cigarette: "I'll give you an example. For a while I lived with a friend who drank too much; he came home drunk every night. Not only was I worried about him, but I didn't like this way of life at all. I was judging him and I wanted to tell him that he was wasting his life, drinking wasn't good for him, and that he would have been better off chanting instead. I knew, however, that in this way I wouldn't achieve anything; in fact, he would probably have taken a step back, clutching his cloak around him, as the traveller did."

"I think you are right!" said Maria.

Harry smiled and nodded in agreement: "Instead, I began to chant for his happiness and I realized that he drank in that way to escape reality; he wasn't happy with his life and didn't believe he was able to change it. I chanted to believe in him, in his infinite potential, until I felt that I firmly did. At that point, from my heart came the right words to encourage him to have confidence in himself. I told him to believe in his unlimited power, in his Buddhahood, and that through this absolute certainty, he would definitely find the strength and the wisdom to create the life he wanted. I had no doubt that he would achieve it." He leaned toward Maria, one elbow on his knee, and continued: "The moment he began to trust he could do it, and started to fight against his negativity, he had already won. Sure, he had a long way to go, but it was just a matter of walking along a road, the destination was already clear. I encouraged him to chant to be firmly convinced that his life was much bigger than he imagined, that the power to create the future he wanted was already in his hands."

"That's great! Did he listen to you?"

"Yes, fortunately. I believe in him and continue to chant for him. He does too, regularly and has realized that he had a very negative opinion of himself. Day after day, he's changing a lot of things and doesn't drink like he did before. But this is the result of a much more profound change!"

"Well done Harry! What a good friend you are," she said, making him smile. "I used to drink a lot before coming to India; I was so unhappy, and lost! In fact I know a lot of people who drink too much or use drugs to excess, and I don't like it." After a short pause, she said: "I have one last question."

Harry smiled as he relit the cigarette that had gone out. He inhaled deeply, leaning back in his chair.

"I'm thinking of difficult situations, even extreme ones, such as infidelity, a serious illness, the death of a loved one; very tough situations. How do you *remember* to turn poison into medicine when they happen? I'm sure it wouldn't be so easy when you're overwhelmed by emotions," she asked.

"True! That's why we chant regularly, as we eat and drink to keep our strength up, as we sleep to regain energy from day to day. Similarly, if we nourish our spirit, this will be strong when we need it. The situations you're talking about are real. If we accept them as part of life and use them to grow, we can develop an understanding of ourselves, from which we'll receive a lot of happiness and a lot of benefits," he said, looking at her with a luminosity that shone from inside.

"Benefits?" asked Maria, with surprise.

"Of course! Huge ones! When we come to a deeper understanding of ourselves we realize that we have *infinite* potential. In practice, it manifests itself as ever-increasing inner strength, wisdom and compassion. You can feel it, you know? It's a state that fills your heart and makes you feel truly happy," he said with conviction. Maria looked at him, infected by his passion. "These qualities are within each of us; we just have to learn to draw them out. Buddha himself said many times that he was an ordinary human being like us, and that *anyone* could understand what he had understood. You just have to make a commitment to yourself!" He looked at the cigarette that had gone out again, smiled at Maria, and relit his cigarette stub.

"Anyone? But isn't it hard to achieve this state?" she asked.

Harry shook his head. "Anyone can experience this life condition, because it is part of who we are; it's *already* within us. It is just a matter of rediscovering it and putting it into practice," he replied with confidence. "It certainly takes a personal commitment, but all we need to do is start believing in, and working on, ourselves, a bit at a time." He paused, reflecting, and then continued, as if to himself: "Sometimes it's difficult, or it seems impossible, and I wonder whether we're dreamers. But we need dreams, because they help us expand our life. If we don't aim high, we'll never move forward. That's why we set goals and chant to realize them. Life is a constant struggle between negativity and positivity. The question is: which one wins? Our negativity, which negates this amazing potential, or our positivity, which tells us that we can become completely fulfilled, helping others do the same?" Maria was fascinated by his words. "That's why we practice together, to help each other when doubts assail us," he said. "And now let's eat!" he added, seeing the waiter coming to their table with steaming omelettes and toast.

Maria realized she was starving. Harry dropped his cigarette in the ashtray and picked up a knife and fork with great enthusiasm. They looked at each other and smiled, tired from the long conversation, but happy about their new friendship, and the omelettes looked delicious! He had already devoured his while she was still chewing on her second bite. She looked at his empty plate in surprise and laughed. Harry was looking for the waiter: "I'm still hungry," he said. "Do you want anything else?"

"Yeah, maybe one chapati with jam and butter. I'm hungry as a wolf."
Just then Luna reappeared, accompanied by Ted.

Ted was tall and slim, with a slightly dark complexion. He had a striking face and Maria, who watched him carefully while they greeted each other, thought that with his dimpled chin, velvety eyes and slightly long hair, he could easily have been a beautiful woman, as well as a handsome man. He had relaxed manners and was reserved, perhaps a little shy. She could tell he had a strong friendship with both Luna and Harry by the way they exchanged information through their body language, almost without need to talk. They were all ravenous and focused on their omelettes, already thinking about what else to order.

Once again, the waiter rushed over to their table. While all the other guests had to wait patiently to get his attention, for them it was easy, certainly easier than getting him to take his eyes off Luna who, with her big green eyes, had bewitched him. Ted and Harry joked that they had to check he hadn't mixed up the order and all three of them laughed, aware of the reaction she caused. Luna was the only one who didn't realize the overwhelming effect she had.

Ted was an actor and, while working on a West End show in London, he was 'discovered' by the world of film. He had just secured a major role in a trilogy for which, on his return from India, he would have to train in fencing, horse riding, wrestling and singing! In just one year's time, his unknown face would be on screens around the world, but for now he was just like them, happy to be 'normal'.

That day all three of them were busy, having to go to the British Embassy for Ted, who was waiting for news from his agent, then to the bank to see if the money Luna was waiting for had arrived, and then to book tickets for their trip to Srinagar in Kashmir, where they were going next. Maria would have gladly passed the hours with them, but these were her last days in India and she thought she ought to spend them in the most creative way possible.

She took a scooter to Janpath Boulevard and walked along the crowded pavement, making her way through the thick crowd, without haste, looking at the shops, walking almost unconsciously toward the Imperial Hotel to say goodbye to the beggars she remembered well. She bought a kilo of oranges from a street vendor and approached the luxurious hotel after having filled her pockets with fifty paisa coins. She wanted to thank them, in the only way she could, for what they had taught her. She saw them from a distance and felt as if they were old friends. She recognized many of them, realizing once again that these were the lucky ones, who had one of the best spots outside a luxury hotel. However, despite this awareness, as she drew nearer, they didn't seem lucky at all; without hands, or feet, some were blind, old, young and even children. Now that she knew what bad stories were behind some of those mutilations she felt even more indignant at the injustice of life.

She put down the first coin, clasping her hands in front of her heart, mirrored by the older beggar, the first in line, and then she gave him an orange. She continued like this, fifty paisa and an orange, looking into the eyes of the person in front of her, smiling at their 'Dhanyavad' and replying with the same word 'Dhanyavad', thank *you*, for what you are teaching me.

She heard a voice calling 'Maria'. Looking in that direction she recognized the young beggar who had asked her for her name, the first time around. She remembered him well, but the fact that he still remembered her name struck her. She approached and crouched down to talk with him. How was he? Well, thanks, and she? Had she had a nice trip? He showed genuine pleasure at seeing her again. She would leave in two days' time, she said. Would she come back?

Yes, she replied: 'Vapas aana'. He laughed out loud, with his beautiful white teeth and bowed, impressed by those words in his own language.

"When you come back, come and see me," he said. Sure, she would, she promised.

She gave him the last of the ten oranges and fifty paisa: "Good luck!" she said.

"You too!" he replied, and continued to look at her as she walked away.

She turned around a few times to wave at him and he responded, lifting his stump, beaming. A lump in her throat, touched deep in her heart by the affection she felt and what she had just received, Maria walked slowly, retracing her steps along the row of shops. She was bursting with emotion and walked as if in a dream. What a place, India!

The shopkeeper who had sold her the sarong weeks before recognized her and invited her to sit on the padded floor covered by a white sheet, to drink a chai. She was happy to stop. The man clapped his hands, and to the boy who came running, out of breath, he ordered 'do chai'. He also wanted to know how she was and how her journey had been. She told him she would be leaving soon, but that she would be back: "Vapas aana," she said again.

He answered with a warm smile: "Madam is learning our language. Very good! Bahut acchah!" and rocked his head. While waiting for the chai, Maria asked to see some scarves with threads of shining lurex; they were beautiful, cheap and weighed next to nothing. She bought ten all of different colours and then, after the chai, the many questions and answers, promising to return to greet him, she took leave of the merchant, as if he were an old friend. She returned to the Tourist Camp by scooter, feeling at home, recognizing the places and the people who lived by the roadside.

23. The impossible becomes possible

She took a quick shower to wash away the dust and smells of the day and then ran toward Luna's room, hoping she'd be there. As she approached she could hear Luna and Harry's voices, they were chanting. They welcomed her with a smile and Maria joined them for the last few minutes, palms together, their voices in unison, all different but in harmony. Nam-myoho-renge-kyo. Through the chanting she could lighten the load she was carrying inside, her heart full of emotions. She looked back on the day and went through many conflicting feelings, reflecting and letting go, releasing the intensity of the burden and the pity she had experienced. She felt calmer, lighter, freer.

As they walked to the restaurant, where Ted was waiting for them, she described in broad outline the experiences of her day. Once again, as soon as he saw Luna, the waiter dropped everything and rushed to take their order, looking at her, fascinated. This time she noticed it too and smiled warmly at him. They ate together, and while Luna and Harry were deep in conversation, Ted wanted to know all about her day.

They spoke with ease, he seemed interested in her stories, and soon she was also telling him how Varanasi had struck her, finding that Ted had very similar feelings; he too had been greatly impressed by it. She told him about Nepal and the magic mushrooms, about the mountains of Manali and the people of the Valley of the Gods, about the first few days in India and all the gaffes she had made. They were laughing, relaxed, when Maria heard the sound of Gianluca's flute.

They approached the group of young people sitting on the sparse dry grass of the Tourist Camp, among whom was Siggi and other people she knew by sight.

Ted put his sarong on the ground and invited her to share it with him. Harry quickly spread his own on the grass inviting Luna to sit down and settling next to her. Maria looked at them out of the corner of her eye, without being noticed. They were so beautiful together and they seemed to be in perfect rhythm with each other. At the same time though, she perceived a barrier between them, made of friendship and familiarity, of apparently detached, every-day gestures. She could tell there was something that didn't let them free to plunge into the sea of emotions, always close by, inviting and deep. Ted looked at them, first at one then at the other, and Harry looked at where Ted's eyes were pausing. Did his gaze rest a long time on Luna? The expression on his face changed from happy and relaxed when she turned to him with a comment or an affectionate gesture, to darkened and tense if she paid more attention to Ted than to him. Maria drew upon herself Ted's attention, to leave them free to relax and maybe get a little bit closer and win over the last resistance that stood between them. Ted began massaging her shoulders and she relaxed completely, forgot about everything else and flew with the music.

The next day she got up early and went to order the first chai with a breakfast of toast, peanut butter and jam. Harry was drinking coffee and smoking a cigarette. She had thought a lot about the things he had said to her. With the return to Venice just a few days away, she felt unsettled. She lacked a sense of direction and was in a state of limbo between travelling in India, which had become her life, constantly meeting new people and having new experiences, and the life that awaited her in Venice. The idea of catching that plane gave her the unpleasant feeling of being about to dive into an empty pool. "Is it too early to talk?" she asked him.

"It depends! What did you want to talk about?" he asked, smiling ironically, looking at her with those eyes full of light. There were very few people in the restaurant and the waiter came almost immediately with her order.

"Yesterday you said that when you do 'daimoku', you set yourself objectives and chant to achieve them. It seemed a bit weird when you said it, but now I realize that without a goal I feel lost. What kind of objectives are they? How does it work? And why?" she asked between one sip of chai and another.

Harry laughed and said: "These are three questions in one!"

"I know!" laughed Maria, "I feel like a petulant child who keeps asking why."

"It's all right! You want to understand and this is great! Chanting for our desires is a little like adding logs to a fire. Think of a bonfire or a fireplace..." Maria nodded with her mouth full of toast. "If you want the fire to burn well and strong, you have to add firewood, otherwise it'll go out."

"Of course," she said, convinced, whilst chewing.

Grinning, Harry continued: "So, our desires are like firewood. If you want something, anything, you chant to get it!"

Maria swallowed quickly, looking at him in amazement. She laid the slice of bread on the plate and said: "But isn't it selfish? Sorry to be so abrupt, but don't you chant for other people's happiness? Besides, I thought that Buddhism rejected desires, because they create suffering. I'm confused!" The toast was almost stuck in her throat.

Seeing her worried expression Harry laughed: "Okay then, one thing at a time. I chant for my own happiness and that of others, but it always starts from us. The relationship we have with ourselves determines the quality of the relationships we have with other people, don't you think? Our life state is reflected in our external environment." He paused to give her time to think. Since Maria nodded, he continued: "The idea of chanting only for others, and not for you, is not a Buddhist concept at all. I am no more important than anyone else, but not less important either, and to respect my life, and my potential, I have to start from myself. First I have to believe in my own Buddhahood and then I can see it in others. Not the other way round."

She nodded cautiously; she found it hard to accept the idea that she, as a person, was important. Years, generations of religious teachings, had drilled into her the concept of personal sacrifice for the good of others. The thought of her own happiness, as a natural and inalienable right, made her feel uncomfortable. Harry saw her resistance and understood her.

"There are different kinds of desires," he said to ease her mind, "and, in any case, Buddhism also tells me that desires lead me to enlightenment." Seeing Maria's face, which looked like a question mark, he continued: "I'll give you an example!"

"Yes, please!"

"Let's say that my desire is to find a job that I like. Okay?"

Maria tilted her head as if to say 'okay' and took her glass of chai, bringing it close to her lips. "Go on! I'm listening," she said.

"Then I chant to find the answer within myself. What kind of job do I want? My head tells me that I need to earn a minimum amount of money to pay the rent, the bills, and so on, okay?" He looked straight into her eyes with a light that showed the passion he felt for this philosophy.

"Yes, I'm following!"

"In the meantime, my heart tells me that I want to be an actor, it tells me loud and clear that I want to recite Shakespeare; I also feel a great desire to write a film about the injustice of apartheid." Harry was gesturing with his hands, just like an Italian.

"Yes, I'm with you."

"While I chant to understand in which direction I want to go work-wise, my life state changes; from being confused, and maybe a little depressed or worried, every day I become a little bit stronger. I find more and more clarity, I become wiser, and of course I chant also to solve the problems that life inevitably throws at me, day after day. If I have problems with people or friends, I chant for their happiness, and so on. Do you understand better now? It's a process of growth and discovery, sometimes slow, sometimes it is almost immediate."

"Yes, yes, explained like this it's much clearer," Maria said. "I thought that you meant to chant to buy a motorbike, or something like that."

"Even that would be fine. It's not important! At first maybe one chants to buy the bike." He laughed, seeing her eyes open wide. "Desires change, Maria. As we chant, our life state elevates, and desires become more altruistic."

"Mmmmm… But a bike! I think that's just materialistic." She was stiffening, leaning backward, distancing herself.

"It's not for me to decide what is acceptable for another person," Harry said gently but firmly. "Look, when I started to practice, one of the first things I was told is that, as Buddhists, we don't judge, don't criticize and don't complain, and I like this!" Maria relaxed a little. Don't judge, don't criticize and don't complain. Interesting! "I assure you! Desires change every time our life state changes. So, if I have no money or no work, I'll chant to find work and earn what I need. This doesn't mean that I stop chanting for other people's happiness, for world peace, for the end of apartheid. Maybe I'm not explaining myself properly!" he said with frustration.

"No, no, you're explaining things well, and I think I understand what you're saying," she assured him, "it just seemed a bit strange at first. Then, chanting for something that you want elevates your life state, right? You move from the world of Hunger to the world of Buddhahood?"

This time it was Harry who widened his eyes. "Yes, exactly! I didn't know you knew about the 'Ten Worlds'," he said in amazement.

Maria laughed, glad to have surprised him. "So, let's say I have a wish," she began, concentrating, "let's say to take a trip, to return to India, for example; or to find a job that I like, and I start to do 'daimoku' to realize this wish. While I chant to achieve my desire I start to feel stronger inside, wiser, and I have more compassion. And then what happens? I find the job, I do my trip? How does it work then?"

Harry laughed, amused by how practical she was: "It depends! I can tell you how it works for me. I always have pen and paper handy, because while I chant a lot of ideas come up. When you suspend rational thinking, you give more opportunities for your heart, and your subconscious, to express themselves. Meanwhile, I feel calmer and then, a little bit at a time, ideas begin to come up, sometimes they are quite disjointed. For example, it becomes clear that I don't want to work in an office, but I want to be in contact with people. Then maybe I feel that I would like to work with *young* people, to encourage them, for the exchange of energy that this entails. Not that we understand everything at once, hey? Sometimes it takes months but, for a decision that will affect the rest of my life I'm willing to keep going till I get it right; after all I want to be happy!" Maria nodded, pleased to find the explanation logical and understandable, with no more surprises. "Then, during another session of 'daimoku', I feel that I want to use my body and do work that involves movement, perhaps a sport. In addition, I want my work to fulfil three requirements."

"Three requirements?" asked Maria, with interest.

"Yes. It has to give me what I need to live on, I have to enjoy it and it ought to contribute to society. So, I came to understand that I want to work with young people, using my body, perhaps by teaching a sport, and that this work must be useful to society! Not forgetting that my true passion is to be an actor. So I need a job that has these features, but that is flexible, too."

"Forget it! It's impossible," Maria said decidedly. "You can't have everything."

Harry laughed. "Yes you can! And the impossible becomes possible. You must want it strongly enough, chant with determination, and then take action, working hard, until you get it," he said with confidence.

"And did you find anything?"

"I have several ideas. I might have to enrol on a course to get the necessary qualifications, but that's not a problem."

"And what are these ideas, if you don't mind me asking?" Maria was genuinely interested.

"No, not at all, quite the opposite, I like it!" he replied warmly. "For now I'm still chanting to understand. However, I think that my choice will be either specializing in one sport, or in some type of physical training. Then I would work as a freelance, offering my services to various organizations. This would give me the independence I need to work as an actor, and write my film against apartheid."

"And you understood all this through chanting?"

"Yes! If I want to be sure I'm listening to both my heart and my head, I do it through chanting," he replied, leaning forward. "Our problem is that we use always and only the head, but our mind changes every two minutes; one moment it tells you to go in one direction and the next it tells you to take the opposite path. The important thing is to work with both in harmony, the head and the heart. This I why I chant for what I want, so that I listen to my heart."

"And how do you know when you've found the right answer?" she asked. "Because you say that by chanting you find the right answer, don't you?"

Harry nodded his head with conviction. "What a good point!" he said with relish. "There comes a time when you think of a solution and your heart says yes! You feel this certainty, you are comfortable with the idea and start to feel excited. Then you check with your head if this solution meets all the criteria that are essential for you, and your mind tells you that it does. Then you check to see if all the people involved are going to gain out of it. In my case, for example, if I gain: I choose the job that I like and it gives me enough to live on; if young people gain: through my work they become happier, healthier, better people; and if society gains: it will have better citizens; then I've found the right job," he concluded with a smile.

"I like it! I understand," said Maria. Then, after a pause for reflection, she asked: "Does it work also if you're trying to find a partner?"

Harry laughed heartily, excited: "I think so! At least they told me it works!"

"And have you tried?" she asked, only half joking.

"Yeeeees..." he said, hesitating; her questioning was getting personal.

"And...? Did it work?"

"Maybe... I don't know for sure yet," said Harry, remaining vague.

She looked at him, a question was pressing insistently, but she thought she couldn't possibly ask. She looked away; then looked at him again.

"What are you thinking?" he encouraged her.

"Is it Luna?"

"You are curious, huh?"

"Yes, like all women. But am I right?"

"Maybe," he said. "I hope so."

"So, Ted is not her boyfriend, then?"

Harry told her that Ted and Luna had been friends for years, they were at university together and he had a girlfriend, who was in England for work. Ted and he had known each other for fifteen years; they had become friends when Harry's parents had returned to England and had lived there for seven years. The friendship had survived years of separation, when he had returned to South Africa with his family. A few years later, Ted had spent a whole summer with them and the friendship had become even stronger. Now, with the future all to be written, they had decided to take a trip to discover deeper values, and themselves. Ted had told him a lot about Luna, and Harry was not disappointed, on the contrary, she surprised him every day, with her warm personality, her beauty and the wisdom she showed. She was so young, he said, but so mature and so brave. He greatly admired her.

"And you two are not together?" she ventured.

He looked at her, unsure as to how much he could give himself away: "No. I broke up with my girlfriend recently... it was a painful separation." He paused. "I wouldn't like to get into another relationship straight away. I prefer it if we become friends, first of all, for a while at least."

Maria looked at him, perplexed.

Harry replied with an uncertain look.

Just then Luna and Ted approached; they were joking and smiling. Ted said something and Luna burst out laughing. Harry's face transformed, suddenly looking disturbed, worried. Maria took advantage of that last moment of confidence to whisper: "I wouldn't wait too long!"

He withdrew his gaze from the couple of friends and looked at her seriously. "Do you think so?" he asked, troubled.

"Definitely," she replied, confident.

As soon as she saw Maria, Luna smiled happily and ran toward her. She wore a white cotton dress cinched at the waist that enhanced her tan and her tall slender body; around her neck she wore a necklace of green jade that brought out the emerald of her eyes. Maria put down her glass and stood up, hurrying to meet her and hugging her with affection. Luna had kept the day free; her only plan was to spend it together with her. Maria was delighted. She wanted to go to New Delhi post office where she was waiting for a letter from Jean-Claude. Luna wanted to buy some perfume essences from Paharganj market and Maria, who had already bought some, wanted some more; they took little space in her luggage, were cheap and would make great gifts, or she could resell them for a good profit.

They chanted together in the room that the three friends shared; Luna and Maria sitting in front, while Harry kept a little back, blending his masculine voice and his energy, so strong and generous, to theirs. Luna's voice was clear and focused while Maria's was weaker and more insecure. As the chanting built up, it became stronger, more decisive and rhythmic, just like a galloping horse, which was how it was supposed to be, Luna said, or powerful enough to shake the earth, as Harry described it.

For my happiness, then, Maria thought. Nam-myoho-renge-kyo,Nam-myoho-renge-kyo,Nam-myoho-renge-kyo. Franca, Jean-Claude, the Taj Mahal, Paul, the coolies that climbed on the roof of coaches; Mr. Singh with the blue turban and serious eyes; the man who drove the cart pulled by oxen, who didn't take her five rupees because he didn't have a rupee change. The images followed each other, one after the other.

Pushpa who climbed the mountain with the empty basket, mimicking a big penis to make her understand the difference between boys and girls. Their laughter, the sisterhood that united them; her God that was everywhere, in the air, in the water, in human beings and even in the charas.

The policeman who had taken her down from the train and stumbled when she uttered the word Bagwan; the look in his eyes when he gave her back her little silver box, the way he bowed before getting off the train.

Raffa and her light-heartedness; under the waterfall in Pokhara; while she removed the leech from under her foot. The sun warming her shoulders and Maria feeling she was the princess of the stream, made of water, like the waterfall, like the lake. The two of them singing 'Caramba let's drink whisky'; paddling slowly in the lake, with the sun setting behind the highest peaks in the world.

'Granny' who pushed her to take up more space on the bus to Manali; the landslide, the rain, the mud; the sheer drop of hundreds of metres, where she had brushed shoulders with death.

The boy who dejectedly carried her backpack; the man who reassured her and walked by her side.

The chai in the china cup from the shack in the middle of the mountain.

Surinder and the wooden blocks on which he raised his body; his clean, honest face.

Paul's eyes, his smile, his embrace inside the temple, the feeling of his heart beating against her head; that moment of abandonment, surprise, and truth.

Franca with yellow skin and brown eyes, sitting on the floor, leaning against the wall, with no energy; who yelled that she always chose others over her, who pushed her away, who lit the heroin pipe. Franca who wasn't afraid of anything; giving her a massage straddling her; screaming in disgust at the sight of the spider in Mcleodganj's barn; standing on the boat in Pokhara lake; diving in her underwear and swimming to the other side, gesticulating and shouting 'I'm here!' Franca independent, fast, insatiable.

Jean-Claude and his wry smile, the passionate kisses, their sudden surprising love. The ghats of Varanasi and the pyres of the dead; the chai and the biscuits; the click-click-click of his camera, the boat trip to the other side of the Ganges. The temples' cool stone floors; the monkeys curiously eyeing the bananas inside the bag with their passports. The eternity of her life. His unshaven cheek on her hair, and the silver anklets with which he had 'married' her.

And now here, she, Luna, Harry, Ted, Siggi and Gianluca. This room, this sound, the present, her future. But her future would come. For the moment, back to the here and now, her happiness, her life that was pulsing and revealing itself, moment by moment, carrying her on the magic carpet that was her destiny, which she could transform at any moment. The sound of Nam-myoho-renge-kyo...

She took the magic carpet's helm, and the carpet became a white horse riding fast and free. She was holding its reins firmly in her hands and in front of her opened valleys and fields, mountains, meadows, clear skies, and the rest of her life; Nam-myoho-renge-kyo.

Thank you, they said to each other when they concluded the chanting, bowing, palms together, their faces transformed by the light they had lit inside.

Ted and Harry decided to go to Old Delhi, leaving them time to be alone. During breakfast, Luna wanted to know everything about her trip to Varanasi and Nepal, and enquired about Franca. Maria told her what she had shouted before lighting the dreaded pipe, of the jealousy she had hidden, but had obviously felt, of the complex feelings she must have had for her. Luna listened attentively when Maria told her how Franca had developed hepatitis. She was of the opinion that, if Franca's tendency was to get high at any cost, there was nothing else that Maria could have done. In her place, she would chant for Franca's happiness, trusting that her desire would reach her. Then she listened carefully when Maria told her about her story with Jean-Claude and asked her if she thought of seeing him again.

"I'd like to, but he has a girlfriend and lives with her. I can't go to Paris and stand between them, can I?" She was going to step back and never contact him again, she said; but Luna had a different opinion. She advised her to chant for her happiness and that of Jean-Claude, and to wait and see what he would do: "It may be that he decides he wants to be with you and will make the necessary changes for you to remain in his life."

"But I don't want my happiness to be at the expense his girlfriend's," Maria objected.

Luna said they didn't know what the future would bring, but they could get an idea from the causes they created in the present. "If our present is the result of the actions we have taken in the past, we know that the actions we take now will create our future," she said.

"Then it's better if I don't cause anyone else to suffer, surely."

"True! But he can choose, and decide which way to go. You don't know if they are happy. If indeed they were, this thing with you wouldn't have happened, don't you think? Wait and see!"

While sipping the chai, they made a plan for the morning: they would go to the Post Office in New Delhi and then to Paharganj market to buy perfumes. Maria told her about the long conversation she had had with Harry and that she liked him very much. Luna wanted to know word for word what they had talked about. She asked if he had mentioned his ex-girlfriend and Maria told her what she knew. "You seem made for each other," she added. "You have a lot in common, a philosophy of life, a great altruistic sense; you are perfectly suited. I'm sure he's in love with you. Don't you like him?"

Luna blushed and then looked at her without speaking, as if she found it hard to open up. Maria waited without saying anything. Finally she said: "I like him a lot, too much, even. But he said he just wants us to be friends, for now."

"That's better than nothing, isn't it?"

Her friend looked at her, her cheeks still flushed; she was both defiant and amused. "No. I told him that I don't want to be his friend," she replied, with a half smile.

Maria's eyes widened. "But why?" she asked in a loud voice. "I don't understand."

Luna giggled: "I told him that I like him too much. I don't want to become his friend and maybe watch as he starts a relationship with someone else. If he wants us to be together, that's fine, otherwise I don't want anything else."

Maria was astonished. Luna's determination and clarity left her speechless. She had never conceived that someone could react this way, or give an answer like that! "What did he say?" she asked, still in shock.

Luna laughed: "He didn't expect it! He tried to insist, but I'm really not interested."

"But how can you not be his friend? That's not easy while you are travelling together!"

"For me it's easy. I can travel with him and share experiences, that's not a problem. But I don't want to become his confidante, *that* kind of friend. Do you understand?" She looked at her straight in the eye: "The one to whom you confide your thoughts, your concerns, your hopes. I don't want to become emotionally involved, not with him, I don't want to suffer. I'll keep looking around." She paused; then continued: "In a way I understand him because, as you know, I was in a relationship that wasn't honest. But when I find someone I really like, I know it. And I really like him!" she asserted, blushing again.

"Do you think he could be the man you want to spend the rest of your life with?" Maria asked, looking at her dear friend, who nodded slowly, looking straight ahead. "How can you be so sure?" she asked, with real interest.

Luna hesitated before answering and Maria realized that she was a very private person when it came to talking about herself. She didn't insist for fear she might shut tight like a hedgehog and waited patiently. Luna opened her mouth to speak, but then changed her mind.

"If you don't want to talk about it, it doesn't matter," said Maria, pretending not to be curious.

"A few days after I arrived in Delhi," Luna began slowly, "... I received a letter from Mike, in which he said that he was getting married to the girl with whom he had betrayed me and who had his son." Maria held her breath, so as not to disturb the flow of words. "The whole letter was an accusation against me. He said I hadn't really loved him, that I had behaved selfishly, I believed I was superior to him, I was arrogant, a slew of criticism. Basically he said that I pushed him into the arms of the other woman and that he'd marry her, even if he still loved me."

"Is this man crazy? Who makes him marry another woman? Why not wait? And then this girl! I wouldn't like to be in her place!" Maria exploded.

Luna nodded slowly: "The truth is that he isn't a balanced person, but I loved him and his letter hurt me." Maria nodded in silence. "The afternoon of the letter the guys went out together and I went to 'rest', in reality to cry; I was sad and I had started to doubt myself. I cried as much as I needed to, then I chanted for an hour and I calmed down. When I heard they were back I put my sunglasses on so they wouldn't notice my red eyes." She smiled, her lips tight, then continued: "Ted didn't notice anything, but Harry knew at once. He came up to me and said that it looked like I needed a cuddle; then he hugged me in silence."

Maria imagined the scene. "It's the kind of thing a woman would do," she said. "Usually men are not so perceptive."

"That's what I liked about him, his sensitivity, his compassion," said Luna; then she laughed and added: "If we add those lovely eyes, and those muscles are not bad at all! Plus, his friendliness and energy... Well, I can't find anything wrong with him!" She laughed more freely and relaxed a little. "And even if I did find something wrong with him, I'd have him all the same; after all, perfection doesn't exist!"

"Harry explained that you can chant to get the things you want," said Maria. "Do you chant to get together with him?"

Her friend laughed and, without any hesitation, replied: "I chant for his happiness, for whatever it means *for him* to be happy, not for what I think would make him happy; and obviously I chant for my happiness. Naturally, as I think about him a lot, when I chant he is very much present. I trust life and I know that if it is right that we get together, it will happen. If it doesn't, I'll accept it. We'll see! I don't think further than that."

"And what other things do you chant for?" Maria asked.

"I chant for a lot of things," said Luna. "It's definitely important to have goals, otherwise you lose your sense of direction and chanting can become heavy, vague, without energy, and after a while you don't want to do it."

Maria remembered the super-concentrated way in which Luna did 'daimoku'. "But like what? Do you chant for your mother? For your sister? I don't know... Give me an example!"

"Yes, you're right," said Luna. "When I chant I normally think of many people, people I see in the street, people with whom I exchanged a few words, friends, relatives, people who are suffering in one way or another; I chant for their happiness. If I've done or said something that I'm not happy about, maybe I spoke unkindly, then I chant to develop more wisdom and compassion; if I was abrupt, I apologize."

"You seem very wise to me and you definitely have a lot of compassion," said Maria.

Luna looked at her and laughed: "You haven't seen me when I'm pissed off yet! I'm neither wise nor compassionate, or very pretty. Maybe one day you'll have the pleasure to witness it."

"Thank goodness," said Maria. "I'm glad to hear it. I thought you were perfect!"

"No, no, don't worry. I'll never be perfect, but I can try, that's for sure!" she assured her. Then she continued: "I'm also chanting to find a job that I like, to express my creativity, to create value ..."

Maria interrupted her: "Then I can chant for Franca, that she stops abusing herself?"

"Sure, but even without going into details, you can simply chant for her health and happiness, this includes everything."

"And should I chant for Jean-Claude, or is it better if I chant, in general, to find the man of my life? After all, I'm not entirely sure that Jean-Claude is the right one, and he's not free. Even the Englishman, Paul, made a huge impression on me, and he had a girlfriend by his side!"

Luna looked at her with an amused expression: "You decide. When you chant, your heart will tell you what it needs. Listen to it! If I were in your situation, I would chant for Jean-Claude's happiness, for Paul's *and* to find the right partner, so that you cover all the possibilities!"

They laughed heartily, happy to share the same desire to be loved, to find a man with whom to spend their lives and express all the love they had inside.

Maria mused aloud that this exciting Frenchman had restored the confidence in herself that she had lost during the years with Ugo. Luna pointed out that no one could give her confidence in herself. She said that Jean-Claude had simply loved her for who she was and she had seen herself in his eyes. He had been her 'mirror'. "That's what happens when someone appreciates us and shows it," she said. "It is the strength that comes from being encouraged, as opposed to what happens when we are criticized."

"That's what we were saying with Harry!"

"Yes, he is very good at encouraging others," confirmed Luna, "but he should also learn to encourage himself. Sometimes he is too hard, too critical and impatient toward himself." Encouraging ourselves was the hardest thing of all, Luna said. That is why she chanted for herself, for others, but also for world peace. This helped her to encourage herself, because she had a 'mission to fulfil'. Maria was perplexed! The idea seemed too vague, she couldn't see it.

"We'll talk later," Luna said, standing up. "Why don't we go to the post office? Aren't you excited to find Jean-Claude's letter?"

"It's not definite that there'll be one," said Maria cautiously, standing up in turn. "But if we want to go to Delhi too, we'd better get a move on."

They went out onto the main road and waited for the first available means of transport; it was an eight-seat Harley Davidson. The driver with the turban stopped with a nice S shaped manoeuvre to let them on, Luna in her white dress and Maria dressed in red. The five men who were already on board moved slightly to make room for them and never turned their gaze away, staring at them from head to toe until they arrived at Delhi city centre. The Central Post Office was an imposing building. The girls went straight to the Poste Restante section, attracting the attention of men and women, Indians and westerners. There were two letters for Maria, one from Italy, from her mother, and an aerogramme from Calcutta, from Jean-Claude. Maria put them in her pocket.

"Aren't you going to open it?" Luna urged her.

"Now?"

"But of course! I'm too curious," she said excitedly.

They sat on the Post Office steps and Maria carefully opened the aerogramme, studying Jean-Claude's handwriting, which she was seeing for the first time.

"It's in French," she said, looking at Luna.

"You'll have to translate it then," her friend said without preamble.

"Ma cherie, mon amour..." she glanced at Luna, who was listening thoughtfully. "How romantic the French language is! He says he misses me, they have travelled a lot, went to Bombay, then to Hampi; he tells me

345

of the temples in Hampi, about Kerala, he says it's beautiful, beautiful people, Christians and communists, an interesting mix. He talks about Bangalore, Madras, huge amazing temples, and then Calcutta, from where he writes; an incredible place." Luna listened in silence, but Maria could tell she was waiting for the romantic part. "He says that he misses me very much, that India is not the same without me, he dreams of me, he remembers our afternoons sheltering from the heat and our romantic nights... He says he is confused with regards to the relationship with his girlfriend and doesn't know how he will feel when he sees her again in Paris... He says I've changed his life, that he can't accept the idea that we won't be together any longer. He wants to see me again, but can't promise anything just now, because he wants to be honest and doesn't know what will happen... I love you, I want you, you have turned my life upside down, and I want you to continue doing so. It ends like that!" Maria kept the pale blue aerogramme open in her hand and looked at Luna.

"It is as I thought, what we were saying before," said her friend. "You need to have patience and give him time to figure out what he wants. How do you feel about him?"

"I like him a lot, I miss him, I get shivers down my spine when I think about how happy I was with him, but at the same time I'm glad that I have my freedom, to meet new people and have different experiences. For the moment it's fine as it is."

They spent the rest of the afternoon together. They went to New Delhi by rickshaw and meanwhile Maria told her about the adventures and the search at the airport, about the train with the twelve policemen. Luna shared her impressions of Varanasi and of Rishikesh, which she had liked very much, and about the ever-changing balance of travelling with two men.

Once at the Paharganj market, Maria wasn't able to find the same shop where she had bought the perfume essences before, there were many shops and they all looked the same. After searching for half an hour, tired of walking among carts pulled by oxen, of dodging rickshaws and making their way with difficulty among the people, they were persuaded by a kind shopkeeper to step into his cavern of fragrances. They smelled lovely essences of rose, jasmine, lily, frangipani, violet, orange blossom, lemon, peppermint, rosemary, and other more unusual scents such as myrrh, clove, camphor, cinnamon, saffron, sunflower, anise. Bombarded by one perfume after the other, all irresistible, genuine and convincing, they decided to buy two twelve-bottle boxes. They only cost three rupees a bottle and reminded them of Chanel and Christian Dior scents. The shopkeeper explained that those fragrances were indeed being used to make the most famous perfumes. Happy and inebriated, they stopped at one of Paharganj's chai-shops, where they ordered chai and Indian sweets, made from ghee, natural flavourings of pistachio and rose, and lots of sugar!

24. The list of gratitude

Spending time with Luna was pure joy. Whatever they did, Maria felt happy, alive, everything seemed full of meaning; there was always something important to discuss, apart from talking about love! They had left their conversation at the Tourist Camp with Luna having mentioned her sense of mission for world peace and Maria hadn't forgotten. They sat under the fan which hung from the ceiling and turned round and round.

"I'd like to go back to what you were saying earlier, about chanting for peace in the world," Maria said, as soon as they ordered the chai. "How does it work? I don't understand the concept! It seems a bit up in the air, still vague. In practice, how can it possibly work that you chant in a small room and the world becomes a better place?"

Luna nodded and settled on the bench, wiping the sweat from her forehead. There was an expression called 'kosen-rufu', she said, that meant that peace began from within ourselves. It taught us how to become absolutely happy, the equality of all human beings and respect for life. In practice, every small change in the way a person thought and acted had an effect on the people around them and on their environment. She gave her the example of the stone thrown into the water, making concentric, ever-wider circles, well after having sunk. They both remembered how Franca had replied with sarcasm that the stone sank, and laughed at the memory of it. Luna continued: As a result of her own change, for example transforming her tendency to anger quickly, into a tendency toward compassion, the relationships around her changed. "If I get angry with someone, that person definitely doesn't want to be near me, with the nasty vibrations I give out," she said, "and naturally I feel distant from her, thinking that she is separate from me and that we don't have anything in common; if something unpleasant happens to her, I don't feel involved. However, when I think in this way, I also feel lonely, detached, misunderstood, isolated from others, and this is when suffering creeps in." She looked at Maria. "Has it ever happened to you?"

Maria thought of all the times she'd felt lonely, left out, misunderstood and depressed.

"Yes, many times, and it makes me feel unhappy! I feel a sense of... void, of fear, almost," she said, thoughtfully. She was putting her emotions into words, for the first time.

Luna understood perfectly and went on to explain that instead, when she thought that everything was interconnected: people, situations, the environment and herself, that sense of separation vanished and she felt part of something much bigger, of the universe itself. Then the pain faded, compassion rose and she felt happy. At that point it became easy to reach out to someone who was suffering, because someone else's suffering, she said, was also her own. With every small change in herself, every new thing she understood and put into practice, she was doing her 'human revolution'.

"I like the word 'revolution'! It gives me a feeling of total change, of a thorough cleaning," Maria said. "But *human* revolution, what does that mean in practice? That you change *human beings?*"

Luna brought her feet up and sat cross-legged on the bench. "It means that you change *this* human being," she said, pointing the finger at herself, and settling a little better. "For example, whenever I notice negative trends in myself, such as anger, greed or stupidity, and maybe I do something driven by these feelings, I realize that my negativity has won; the clearest symptom is that I feel unhappy and begin to complain about something. That's when I chant to turn them into more... noble feelings!"

"You turn poison into medicine," said Maria.

Luna looked at her in surprise: "Is that what Harry told you?"

"Yes," laughed Maria. "But what are these 'more noble' feelings? In theory I like what you say, but in practice, what feelings are they? Sorry for the pedantic question!"

"Not at all! I like your questions, and when I explain things to you, I deepen my own understanding," Luna reassured her.

The waiter came, carrying a tray with two steaming chai and a saucer full of colourful sweets. He placed them on the table and looked from Maria to Luna, without any hurry to move away, curious, fascinated. Did they want anything else? No, thank you. Was the bench comfortable? Yes, thank you. Did they want any water? Yes, please, a bottle. Luna smiled at the waiter, who walked away happy, and then to Maria.

She continued: "Let's think of some examples: if I start to do 'daimoku' when I am angry at someone, little by little I begin to see the other person's point of view. By chanting for this person's happiness, my ego, my 'smaller self', reluctantly begins to step aside and I see things from a different perspective; gradually my anger becomes compassion, for me as well as for the other person." She shifted her position and leaned against the wall, then she continued: "If I am in the throes of insecurity and feel the need for approval, or admiration, which is again my 'smaller self', as it happens, after chanting for a while, I realize that I'm the one who doesn't approve of, or appreciate, myself. So, if I don't approve of myself, the one that comes from the outside is never enough; sometimes I won't even notice the approval that I *do* receive because, deep down, *I* am the one who lacks self-belief." She looked into Maria's eyes and, smiling, she said: "It's like having a bucket with holes in the bottom. You can continue to fill it, but unless you plug the holes, the water will flow out from the bottom... and your bucket will always be empty!"

"Whew! A bucket with holes. It must be mine," said Maria, reflecting. "I am very insecure and I always look for approval, a pat on the back from someone to tell me 'well done'! And what about stupidity? This word makes me laugh. I often am, stupid, I mean!"

"It makes me laugh, too; it seems such a common and 'modern' word, doesn't it? In Buddhism, stupidity is sometimes called 'ignorance' and it signifies not realizing, or not believing, that every person has this amazing potential that we call Buddhahood. It is hard to believe that we have it, but if we don't believe this, we can't see it in others. It always starts from us." She paused, thinking; then she said: "This ignorance is the cause of all the suffering, all the wars, all the conflicts among people. It is the most important concept of the entire Buddhist philosophy."

Maria looked at her for a moment in silence, amazed once again by this woman's way of thinking; they were the same age, but Luna seemed to have understood so much more. She was fascinating, to say the least, and Maria had a great deal of affection for her. She felt she could trust her; that Luna wanted her happiness, and she probably chanted for her. She thought again of the image of the circles made by the stone thrown in the water. However, if world peace, this 'kosen-rufu', as they called it, worked like that, it would take a million years to change the world!

"I understand what you're saying and the concept makes sense. But it is too slow, isn't it? From the moment you change something, maybe very small, in yourself, to changing the world. I don't know how it could possibly work," objected Maria. She would have loved to be in full agreement with her friend, but her doubts were too strong.

Luna agreed that it was a long process, but if they wanted a lasting peace, something had to change within human beings. If they tried to change only the external structures, the same problems would eventually present themselves again. They had to change *the values they had in their hearts*, she said, pointing with her index finger to her heart and her head. Each human being had the potential to be bright, wise, compassionate like the Buddha, or violent, cruel, a merciless torturer; there were no exceptions, the potential for good and for evil was inside each of us. Everything depended on which philosophy of life one chose, how one decided to respond when presented with difficult challenges and choices to make. This was exactly the essence of the human revolution and kosen-rufu; little by little, putting 'profound respect' into practice in every situation, at every cross-roads where we had to choose. "There isn't a land pure or impure in itself, explained a great sage called Nichiren," Luna said, "everything depends on the values that people have in their hearts! So, if you want to change your land, your environment, look at the values and principles that guide your actions."

Maria was listening carefully. Yes, but how long would this take? she asked again. Changing from within, she agreed, was perhaps the only way to really transform things, but it took too long.

"It's relative, like everything else, for that matter," replied Luna. "It depends on how many people commit to it! It's a great commitment to make because, apart from anything else, it improves *your* life; you're the one who gains! And then, of course it takes time, perhaps generations; the important thing is to begin. If we want a lasting peace, we have to work on ourselves, engage in dialogue with those around us, create friendships based on respect, getting to know the person in front of us, listening to them."

Maria had noticed that Luna always listened with her whole being, focusing on what she was hearing, as if not wanting to miss a word. "You listen with a lot of attention," she said with admiration.

"I try," said Luna. "I try to listen in order to understand not only the words but also the intentions behind the words." Seeing Maria's quizzical expression she clarified: "Sometimes it's hard to find the right words to express what you are feeling inside, especially when you're confused or if there is a lot of suffering. So, it's important that the listener makes that extra effort, to *perceive* what that person is trying to express. Behind angry words, for example, what is there? Probably a lot of suffering. If I can tune into the right wavelength, I will understand that the root of that anger is pain."

"It's hard when someone yells at you!"

"Yes, it's hard! Because someone's anger tends to awaken our own, but it gets easier with some practice and a lot of compassion," replied Luna. "Especially if we've been through the same. This is kosen-rufu hands on!" She took a short break, shuffling on the bench, while Maria absorbed the concepts. "Try to imagine what difference it would make if, instead of reacting defensively to someone's anger, as might feel natural, you can understand he's distressed and tell him you're sorry to see him so angry and to see him suffer!"

Maria tried to imagine the situation, putting herself in that person's shoes. She felt her anger melt away like a piece of ice in the sun. "If I were the angry one, and the other person told me so with compassion, I'd feel bewildered, for a start. Not finding myself in front of a wall of anger on which to bounce my wrath, the "ball" of my anger would fly away, if I may put it that way."

"What a beautiful image!" Luna said with enthusiasm.

"Thank you, yes, I like it too!"

"From this understanding attitude, friendship and trust can be established."

"True," said Maria slowly, reflecting on the concept. "Is this 'compassion'?"

"Compassion, in Buddhism, means that 'I care about you'! If you care about a person, you can be friends; you can talk 'heart to heart'. It doesn't even matter if you see little of each other, or if you are far away; you know this person is present. What matters is the heart," Luna said. "From this feeling comes the certainty that this person wouldn't do you any harm."

Maria thought of Franca. Did she trust her? She cared about her, but was the feeling mutual? There was something that bothered her, but she didn't want to think about it now. She pushed the uncomfortable feeling to the back of her mind, for the time being. "In the case of sincere friendship, yes, I can agree," she mused.

"If the friendship is not sincere, it's not friendship," Luna said simply, looking at her.

Maria went silent. That feeling resurfaced, obstinately, and wouldn't go away; it was a look, a wry smile, a feeling that had lasted only a second, something she had noticed but couldn't put her finger on. She drove the thought of Franca into the background; she'd think about it later. She nodded thoughtfully, encouraging Luna to continue.

"If there is trust between two people, most of the time there won't be any conflict," she continued. "If and when problems arise, they will resolve them through dialogue, because both of them care about each other."

"Like, for example, between you and me?" asked Maria, after a brief pause. "If we had problems, we'd talk about them and resolve them. We certainly wouldn't lose this friendship!"

"Thank you for considering me a friend," Luna said, pleasantly touched. "Yes, that's the way it is. From friendship to trust and from trust to peace. This is the process that leads to lasting peace."

"Okay, I understand but... I'm sorry if I keep asking one question after another!"

"Not at all, that's fine. What did want you ask?" Luna encouraged her.

"Two people can create friendship, trust and dialogue, but wars are between nations, so what can be done? It's not the same, is it? It's much more complicated."

While Luna answered her question, Maria took the opportunity to eat a sweet and take a sip of the chai that had now cooled a little.

"In a sense, the process is similar. It's very important that people from different countries establish links of friendship, if they don't already exist. We begin by talking about what we have in common; everyone likes sports, for example! We can organize exchanges based on sports, friendly matches. Who wouldn't like that? Then, everybody likes art, and all countries have good painters, sculptors, musicians, singers, dancers. We can organize exchanges of music, concerts, art exhibitions going from town to town."

"But don't we already do these things? Games, concerts, ballets, and so on," Maria asked, swallowing quickly and wiping the crumbs from her mouth.

"There are competitive matches, concerts to which few people can go, because they are too expensive! I'm thinking of more popular things, open to everyone. Later, as part of the dialogue process, we can talk about health, about love for children, respect for the elderly. These are all things that unite people, while differences may divide."

"And organize exchanges of young and older people?" asked Maria, with enthusiasm.

Luna looked at her, amused, and laughed. "Yes, but we don't leave them there. Only temporary exchanges, then everyone takes back their young and old people and brings them home!" They laughed at the funny image of swapping grandparents between one border and the other. "Exchanges in general, especially of young people, because they are the future, so it's important that they open their minds and have international experiences, but also adults, of course," Luna said.

"It would work, yes, I understand," nodded Maria. "When you spend a period of time in a foreign country, with the locals, you make friends. You eat like them, you live like they do and become part of the family. When you know the people and the customs of different countries, you stop thinking of them as "strangers" and see them just as people, like you and me." Luna nodded, smiled, and bit into one of the sweets. Maria continued with enthusiasm: "I remember an experience I had in Bulgaria a few years ago. Ugo and I were travelling to Greece by motorbike. The first week we rode through Yugoslavia and one afternoon we arrived at the border with Bulgaria, it was already late and was raining heavily. Bulgaria, as you know, is a very closed communist country. We stopped at the first bar, which was also a restaurant, but we hadn't changed any money, so we had no Bulgarian currency; the rain was terrible and it was too dangerous to continue, so we had no choice." Luna was listening with interest. She picked up her chai and sipped it, without taking her eyes off Maria, who was in full flow: "We sat at a table, arousing the curiosity of all the people in there. The waiter didn't speak a word of Italian, French, English or German, and we didn't speak Bulgarian. A boy from a nearby table, who spoke just a smattering of French, came to our rescue. I told him that we had no Bulgarian currency, so we couldn't order anything. This boy was with a group of young people and he translated what I told him to his friends who, waving their arms and with big smiles, invited us to their table. They brought coffee, tea, wine, water and plates full of meat, potatoes and vegetables." Luna listened, smiling. Maria was remembering and continued: "They encouraged us to eat, giving us affectionate pats on the shoulder and looking at us with such joy! They joked between them and laughed loudly. We toasted with red wine many times during this meeting where they spoke Bulgarian and we spoke Italian, and a bit of French!"

"That's wonderful! And then?" asked Luna, settling on the bench and straightening her back.

The waiter arrived with a bottle of cold water and two clean glasses and put them on the table, stopping to look from Maria to Luna and from Luna to Maria. They smiled at him, amused by how openly he showed his interest. Did they want anything else? No, thank you. Another chai? No thank you. More sweets? Very kind, but no thanks. Finally, reluctantly, he walked away.

Luna returned her gaze to Maria and asked her to continue where she'd left off: "And then?" she encouraged her.

"When it was time to pay, *they* paid, of course, and then they roughly explained that they were taking us somewhere to sleep, as the restaurant was about to close and the rain continued to pour! Tipsy as we were, we decided that Ugo would ride the bike and I would go in the car with the Bulgarian boys." Luna looked at her, worried.

Maria returned her a look of complicity and continued: "Once in the car, I sat behind with two guys, two others sat in the front and they began to drive at full speed. When I turned I could see the bike's headlights behind us, but Ugo was struggling to keep up. Sometimes his lights disappeared around a bend; the road was full of mud and I began to worry that he might slip. If he fell what would happen? I realized how vulnerable we were. Smiling, I kept motioning for them to slow down, I looked behind for the bike's headlights and they laughed loud. They'd slow down a bit and then accelerate again. We were all pretty drunk and they drove fast, so it seemed to me; maybe for them, who knew the road like the back of their hands, it was normal to drive like that."

"What a risk!" said Luna, involved in the story.

"Yes, and I was perfectly aware of it, but I continued to smile and laugh with them, I didn't want them to see my concern. Well, after some endless twenty minutes, maybe less, we arrived in the courtyard of a house in the countryside. The boys woke up the elderly couple who lived there, maybe they were the parents of one of them, and they welcomed us into the house, with big smiles, very protective. The young people said goodbye, they left and we never saw them again.

The elderly couple made us take off our wet jackets and trousers, they gave us a dry blanket and served us some strong liquor; all this without a common language, only gestures and words in Bulgarian from them, in Italian from us. Then they showed us a room with a very high bed. I remember that the bed was so high I had to climb on it," said Maria, laughing.

"What an adventure! And what beautiful people," Luna said.

"Yes, indeed! The next morning they woke us up early, I didn't know what time it was. The table was laden with a huge breakfast: fried eggs, homemade bread, butter, jam and plenty of coffee. They watched us eat, smiling, as if we were their children, keen to feed us, insisting that we take a little more. When they saw that we were getting ready to leave, they tried to make us stay, it was still raining; but it was difficult without a common language and we wanted to leave all the same.

So, they prepared a bag for us to take away, with bread, salami and cheese, apples, figs, all sorts of things. They were patting us on the shoulder as if to say, please, be careful. With gestures they told us we could come back if it was raining too much, and so we parted! Later we realized that we had woken up at five in the morning, just before dawn!"

Luna looked at her in silence for a moment and then, reflecting, she said: "That's the way it is, isn't it? Humanity. Listening to your story, I realized that I, too, in their place, would have done the same as the Bulgarian boys. You too, perhaps, would have done the same thing, wouldn't you? Helping people like you and Ugo, in that situation."

"Yes, I've done it many times with young people who were travelling in Italy."

"And what a satisfaction the two elders who took you in must have felt, to give you the big bed, to prepare you breakfast, the food-bag for the trip!" She paused, thinking to herself. "When we do something for another, in the end we do it for ourselves, too. We get a great deal of fulfilment from helping another human being," Luna mused.

"It's true! I have heard many stories of how people helped even the 'enemies' during the war; enemy soldiers who were lost, or who had deserted, hosted by peasants' families; persecuted Jews who were hidden by 'common' people, at the risk of their own lives and that of their families," said Maria.

Luna nodded and said: "There are stories like this in every country of the world. This tells me that humanity is the same everywhere, regardless of race, political or religious belief."

"You're right," Maria agreed. "If I think of how good I feel when I do something for another person, it's as good as the person receiving the favour, or kindness. At times it's a bigger pleasure to give than to receive."

"That's true, it's nourishment for that positive side that is in each of us," said Luna. "I find it's important to give wholeheartedly without hoping to be thanked. I prefer to give for the sake of giving and remain free of expectations."

"I have a question..." Maria said, pondering. "If I make a good action, I create a positive cause and then I'll get a positive effect, right?"

"That's right," Luna replied, laughing and expecting an interesting question.

"So, if I do something good just to get a positive effect, do I lose, how would I say, some of the benefits? In short, are my good deeds less effective if I *plan* them in order to achieve the positive effects?"

Luna laughed, amused, but she was also seriously considering Maria's question. After a moment's reflection she said: "If you do a good thing, knowing that you are planting the seeds for positive effects, I don't see why you should get 'watered down' effects. The fact that you are *aware* of the law of cause and effect doesn't change this law."

"Then I can create a future full of positive effects, just by taking positive actions! I really can plan a wonderful future?" asked Maria.

Luna thought about it for a moment and then replied: "Absolutely! Think about it, you are creating your future karma! In addition, with regard to the present, Buddhism tells me that the effects can be of two types, visible and invisible, or intangible. A visible benefit is to find a job that I like, for example, a partner with whom I can build a happy relationship, things like that, that you can see and touch. But there are also intangible benefits and those are perhaps the most important ones!" She poured some water into Maria's glass and then some into hers.

"And they are...?" asked Maria, intrigued.

"The way I feel, for starters, I'm happy, satisfied with what I have; and then the way I respond to the situations that life presents me. For example, let's say there are two people in the same situation: both have an office job, the same colleagues, a house and a cat. One of those people feels satisfied, happy and fulfilled, while the other feels unhappy, sad and lonely. For a long time I've wondered what the big difference between them is!"

"Maybe other things besides work, home and the cat?" suggested Maria.

"Sure! But above all, their state of mind. When we feel *grateful* for what we have, for our lives, we are happy, light, we shine like a star. If we complain, seeing the glass as half empty rather than half full," she said, looking at their glasses half full of water, "... even if we have the same things, we won't be able to appreciate them, and consequently we won't be as happy."

"Are you saying that it is as simple as feeling grateful for our lives, and then we are happy?" asked Maria, uncertain.

"Yes! Gratitude is the best recipe. Whenever I feel down, or I'm angry, I think to myself 'what's wrong, Luna?' and I realize that, inside, I'm complaining about something. There is nothing worse than complaint to make you feel like 'shit', if you excuse my French!"

Maria laughed, surprised. Luna didn't swear, her Italian was very correct, and then she came out with a phrase like that! They noticed that the waiter was laughing too, even though he hadn't understood a word; he hadn't taken his eyes off them, casting glances full of love, torn between one and the other.

"What do you usually complain about?" Maria asked, going back to looking at Luna.

"Oh, anything! Ted not getting up, the sun that's too hot, the bus that doesn't arrive, the bed that's too hard, lack of money, Harry who doesn't make up his mind to kiss me, and so on and so forth!"

"But these are real things! It's natural to complain about them," Maria pointed out.

"Yes and no. The fact is that it doesn't do me any good to complain, it drags me down even more," replied Luna.

"So, what do you do? Do you decide to be happy even if you're not?" asked Maria, drinking a sip of fresh water.

"More or less! When I realize that I'm complaining, I just accept that things are the way they are and, from there, I start to change my state of mind. I think: 'That's the way it is. Period! Now what do I do? Do I continue to be dissatisfied? No, thanks, I'm already tired of feeling like this.' That's when gratitude comes into play; I think of my list of gratitude, maybe I read it, and everything changes!"

"What list of gratitude?" Maria asked, intrigued.

"It's a list that I made a while ago, I have it here, look," Luna said, looking in her passport bag. She pulled out a piece of paper folded in four, opened it and began to read: "I am grateful for: One: being alive; two: being healthy; three: living in a country that enjoys peace; four: being smart; five: being educated; six: Having a family that loves me and supports me; seven: having a healthy mother and father; eight: having friends; nine: knowing and practicing Buddhism; ten: the sun rising every morning; eleven: the moon and the stars; twelve: the universe with its balance; thirteen: pasta with pesto, I love it; fourteen: tiramisu, it's my favourite dessert; fifteen: the snow; sixteen: the sea; seventeen: my cat, and so on. I have fifty points written down and I don't want to bore you, but you get an idea, don't you?"

"Whaw!" exclaimed Maria, "from the smallest things to things as vast as the universe. While I was listening I realized the effect of gratitude."

"Absolutely! Look, I felt good when I wrote the list, and every now and then I add things to it as they come to me. Then, every time I re-read it, it brings back this feeling of gratitude, and all complaints vanish," Luna said, folding her piece of paper and putting it back into her passport bag.

With the perfumes in their bags, happy with their dialogue and their friendship, they said goodbye to the love-struck waiter and took a rickshaw back to the Tourist Camp, making the most of those last moments together, on their own. For Maria this was perhaps the last time she would go through those parts of the capital before leaving India and everything she saw was coloured by the love she felt for this country and its people, as well as for the wonderful friends she had met; of all of them Luna was perhaps the most precious, showing her the clearest example with her life and helping her grow the most.

While the rickshaw man pedalled rhythmically with his skinny muscular legs, Maria looked around, saying goodbye in her heart to the people who lived by the side of the road; to the women who carried water in old tin containers balanced on their heads; to the men who mended scooters and bicycles with improvised tools; to the children running behind the bicycle wheels; to the little girls with their tidy braids helping their mothers; to the cows that hung lazily around in the afternoon traffic and to the noisy scooters, the proud Harley Davidson, the carts pulled by oxen, the chai-shops along the road.

They arrived at the Tourist Camp in silence, tired but satisfied.

They met up again to have dinner with Ted and Harry, who were delighted with the day they had spent together in Old Delhi. They talked about departures. The three of them were leaving the next day for Srinagar in Kashmir. Maria still had one more day in Delhi before leaving for Italy. After dinner, they chanted together for the last time and Maria thought about gratitude. During that 'daimoku' session, which lasted only ten minutes, her heart overflowed with the appreciation she felt for her life and for those two and a half incredible months that had transformed her so completely. She noticed that something had changed in Harry's attitude, too.

He seemed more confident and, instead of sitting further back, as he had done in the morning, he was sitting next to Luna, chanting with power and determination. At the end of the 'daimoku' Maria said she wanted to talk to Ted and went out looking for him, thus giving the two of them the opportunity to be alone. She saw them go out of the Tourist Camp, walking close to each other, talking. Ted was at the restaurant, having a beer with Siggi, and Maria joined them. Not far from them, Gianluca pulled out his flute and soon a small crowd gathered around him. Someone made a joint; someone else passed around a box of biscuits; there was a German boy with a king cobra as a pet which he kept inside a basket. The evening went by in an atmosphere of magic. Maria wanted to say goodbye to Luna and Harry, who would be leaving early in the morning, but she didn't dare disturb them. Ted told her it was better to leave them alone, something was going on; they both sensed it.

Around midnight, reluctantly, she said goodbye to everybody and went to her dormitory, accepting that she wouldn't be able to say her final farewell to Luna and Harry. To her great surprise, Ted arrived a few minutes later, asking if there was a spare bed. Yes, there was. She looked at him quizzically. "Are they back?" she asked.

"Yes!" replied Ted. "They need to be alone. At last!"

She felt a smile rise from her heart, slowly reaching her face: "Yes, finally!"

Ted lay down on the bed next to Maria's; he had nothing to cover himself with, all his belongings were in the room he shared with his friends.

"Do you need a sarong? To put over you."

"That would be lovely, thank you. It's hot but a sarong is always useful!"

Maria took one of the new sarongs out of her backpack, gave it to Ted and went back to bed. He partly covered himself with it and reached out to Maria; she held his hand in hers and so, from one bed to another, hand in hand, they shared the joy of knowing that 'those two' were finally together. If all went as hoped, the dam holding back the feelings they felt for each other would be broken and they could be happy together.

"They are made for each other," said Maria.

"They're perfect together," Ted agreed.

She closed her eyes and fell asleep with a smile on her lips and Ted's warm hand holding hers.

She felt a kiss on her lips. It was Ted, ready to go. "Luna will be here in a moment," he said.

With difficulty she opened her eyes, it wasn't yet five o'clock in the morning and the day was just beginning to dawn. "See you soon I hope," he said.

"Good luck, Ted. I'll see you at the cinema!"

"Come to London and we'll see each other for real," he replied.

Luna walked into the dorm, ready to leave, wearing a white t-shirt and Indian-style pyjama trousers. She sat on her bed and Maria saw the light she was hoping to see. "Everything all right?" she asked.

"More than all right, perfect," Luna replied, her face relaxed, her eyes full of love.

"I'm happy for you," Maria said, squeezing her hand.

"Thank you, we are happy too! Thanks for everything Maria. You are a precious friend."

"When will we see each other again? I know it's the heart that counts, but so does seeing each other, to celebrate your new beginning."

"We'll definitely meet up, let's keep in touch!" She gave her a piece of paper on which she had written her address. "Write to me, and we'll work something out. And let me know what happens with your life, and with the Frenchman!"

"You can count on that! Thank you for everything! Thanks for the Nam-myoho- renge-kyo."

"Thank *you!* Continue to use it to become happy."

Harry came in, relaxed, bubbling with joy as she had never seen him before. He sat on her bed and lowered himself to kiss her: "Thank you Maria, you have been instrumental!"

"Who? Me?"

"Yes, you. You gave me the push I needed. After what you told me, I asked myself if I was stupid or crazy to wait, or delay. Thank you!"

"The pleasure is all mine. You both deserve to be happy. Don't lose her!"

"Now she's mine, I caught her," said Harry, laughing and looking at Luna who was smiling. "If she tries to run away I'll scoop her up and carry her home!"

They laughed, delighted, and then the little procession of friends, who had whispered their happiness by her bed, walked out of the dormitory. Maria closed her eyes; a happy smile flooded her face and filled her heart. One day she would feel as happy, too, she was confident. She obliged herself to stay in bed, it was her last day and she didn't know how to spend it. She turned and tossed, and finally, with the sarong she had lent to Ted over her eyes, she fell asleep.

25. Back to the homeland

Maria began to prepare her backpack, but couldn't make all her things fit. Discouraged and dripping with sweat she went to the restaurant hoping that, on her return, she'd be able to find a better way. Unable to relax, she had something to eat, went to take a shower and then popped into Siggi's dormitory. She saw that his luggage was very big too and that was a consolation. He was making small parcels when she entered; he smiled and covered them with a sarong. "Are you ready?" he asked.

"No, the rucksack is too small!"

He laughed out loud: "But it's the biggest rucksack I've ever seen! It's bigger than you!"

"I know," she laughed. "I'm very anxious about travelling back to Italy; I feel as if two lifetimes have gone by since I left, rather than two and a half months. I'm sorry to leave India, are you?"

"Yes, I feel the same! Here it's too hot, everything is difficult, life is hard, but I don't want to leave. Next year I'll return, though. You'll come back too, won't you?" he asked.

Back to India? The idea kept coming up. There was nothing that prevented her from doing so. Her job gave her three months' paid holiday; life modelling didn't require much use of her brain but, from the point of view of free time, it was perfect. "I'm seriously thinking about it! What's under your sarong?" she asked, curiously.

"Oh... little presents for my friends," said Siggi with nonchalance.

She took her leave and returned to her luggage, repacking once again the content that stubbornly refused to fit. As if her things were not enough, Vale's socks were bulky and weighed a pound. She was extremely anxious and couldn't calm down. She went to the reception office, but Mr. Singh was not there yet; he began his shift in the afternoon. Gianluca had just left for the airport; he was going back to Italy, too. She saw the German boy with the cobra in a basket and stopped to talk to him: "How's the snake?"

"It's a king cobra, actually," he said primly. "Do you want to see it?"

"Yes, sure! Is it poisonous?"

"No, I had his fangs cut out, but after a while they grow back. He's not dangerous, look!" he said, removing the lid. The king cobra's diamond-shaped head moved slightly; it had been sleeping and they'd woken it up. It began to slide out of the basket and onto the grass.

"It's coming out!" cried Maria, alarmed, moving away from the area.

"He needs to eat grass, and there is not much grass in Delhi," said the boy, tenderly. He grabbed it with both hands and managed to put it back in the basket. "Do you want to stroke him?" he asked.

"Stroke it? But it's a snake!"

"Yes, I know. He won't harm you," he assured her. "Look, with me, even if I try to make him go around my neck, he won't. He knows he could hurt me and there's no way to persuade him. He's my friend, he loves me. I'll show you, so you believe me!" He pulled the snake out of the basket; it must have been very heavy by the strength it took to lift it. It was at least six feet long! He put it on his lap and made it climb over his body, all the way to his shoulder, which the snake, with its beautiful flat head, obediently did. It then slid behind the boy's head and over the other shoulder. When the boy tried wrapping it around his neck, like a scarf, the cobra refused. Forcefully it pulled its head back and pushed it toward his master's lap. The boy tried again, but the cobra wouldn't do it and pushed its head back down; it really seemed aware of what it was doing.

'I wonder if it has Buddhahood', Maria thought. She was very impressed: "Okay, I'll stroke it then." She touched it tentatively with a finger. "It feels like touching a snakeskin bag," she said stupidly.

"This is alive," the boy pointed out.

She touched it again, and this time she felt its life pulsing beneath the scaly skin, the force of that long body and the moisture seeping through it. She shivered; after all it was a snake, a king cobra, not the most obvious creature with which to make friends. She was glad she had introduced herself, though. With affection, the boy put it back in the basket and Maria thanked him for the experience.

She spent the afternoon fidgeting between a chai, a nap, a stroll around the Tourist Camp, another chai and, at last, it was finally getting dark. She went to say goodbye to Mr. Singh and thanked him for all the things he had taught her. Would she come back to India? Maria replied that, almost certainly, she would return. The idea of leaving seemed madness; India felt like home.

She went back to the dorm, and after a fight to the death with her backpack, she managed to push the last few things inside. She closed it for the last time, securing straps and buckles. Observing it, she couldn't believe that Franca wanted it; it was really ugly, now she could see that herself. It didn't have any charm at all, no elegance whatsoever, even the colour was over the top, and its shape was rough, there was nothing feminine about it. She would never again travel with this horror. The next time it was going to be a small rucksack, a blue-grey colour, like Franca's. For now, however, it would do its duty for the last time, carrying home all the beautiful things she had bought. The three boxes with the flower essences gave off some of their perfume and Maria could recognize the patchouli in particular, the smell of India 'par excellence'.

She loaded it on her shoulders: it was very heavy, but the weight was evenly distributed. She picked up her camera bag, which was also overly large and complex, and hung it over her shoulder. Next time she'd bring something much smaller. She had one last bag, her hand luggage containing the essential things for the trip and a few precious things she had bought: some rings, some bracelets, a couple of necklaces, a spare pair of pyjama trousers, a shirt and some toiletries.

She went over to Siggi's dormitory. He was nervous too, and had nothing left to do. They decided to leave earlier than scheduled, at least they were doing something; they could no longer sit around waiting.

With a mixture of sadness and anxiety, they walked out of the Tourist Camp's gate, stopped a scooter, settled in with their luggage over their feet and knees, and off they went, at full speed toward the airport. During the ride, the warm September evening air turned into a breeze that caressed them for the last time, impregnated with that mixture of sweet, intense, well known odours. She had to breathe deeply to control the strong emotion that filled her heart. She was about to leave India which she had come to know, appreciate and love, which had brought her friends, experiences, lessons, fears, understanding, love and, more important still, a new awareness of herself.

At the airport, the air was hot and muggy, lacking in oxygen, making it hard to breathe. Hundreds of passengers with huge amounts of luggage moved around nervously. Indian people, who were normally quite pragmatic and laid back, became easily agitated when travelling; they looked around, worried, apprehensive and unable to relax. Maria and Siggi found their flight on the screen: Delhi-Moscow with Aeroflot. They would change in Moscow, where they had a four hour wait before catching the connecting flight to Rome; too little time to go out and explore the city, which was apparently beautiful. They stood in line to deliver their luggage; it was a long and very slow queue. Two hours later they arrived at customs, where a young policeman checked Maria's hand luggage in great detail, slowly, carefully, before letting her through. Siggi was behind her. She waited for him in the lounge, where he reappeared, sighing: "He checked my whole luggage, every tiny corner of every single thing!"

Quite different from the outbound flight with Thai International, where the hostesses in their saris looked like queens and smiled like Miss World, the Aeroflot plane was grey, the hostesses were grey too, and Maria felt uneasy in their presence. She settled beside Siggi. It was comforting to have him near; it was like taking a little piece of India with her. The idea of going back to Italy, arriving within a few hours, was too strange and she decided not to think about it for now; she would focus on the present and postpone as much as possible the impact of her return home! Once in Moscow they didn't have to recover their luggage, it would be loaded automatically onto their next flight, so they spent the time as best they could in the transit hall, lying down on the benches for a while to rest their backs. It was almost dawn and they tried to sleep. Siggi looked ill; he was pale and often went to the bathroom.

"Are you okay?" Maria asked him.

"So-so," he said, smiling faintly.

"How are you feeling?"

"Weak," he replied.

He looked worried; he reminded her a little bit of Franca. Fortunately, in a few hours they'd be in Rome and, shortly after that, Siggi would be home. "Not long to go, you're almost there!" she encouraged him. He smiled with his beautiful green eyes, his oval face framed by blond curls.

They arrived at Rome airport at around eleven in the morning. They waited for their luggage and, while Siggi's came quickly, Maria's red backpack wasn't there. They continued to wait, watching the luggage belt gradually becoming empty. After a couple of rounds without anything on it, it stopped: nothing else was going to come out. Worried and tired, Maria turned to the first policeman she was able to stop.

"My rucksack is not there! It hasn't arrived. What am I to do?" she asked nervously.

The policeman wanted to know where they had come from and if they had changed flights. He advised her to go to the 'Lost Property' office to report the missing luggage. She didn't like the sound of the words 'Lost Property' in the least; they meant 'lost rucksack'! "But what's happened? Has it been stolen?" she asked. No, maybe not, replied the policeman. Sometimes luggage in transit ended up going on the wrong flight. She couldn't believe it! Her rucksack, with all the things she had bought in those two months. Shocked, tired, helpless, she went to the 'lost forever property' office. "What do you want to do?" she asked Siggi. "You can go if you want; I have to do this!" But he wanted to wait for her and she was grateful to him for that.

At the office they took all her details; she was asked to describe her luggage and sign a declaration. "And now? Am I going home without my rucksack?" They told her that it would probably be tracked down and she'd be notified. "And, if they find it, do I have to come back to Rome to fetch it? I live in Venice, it's an eight-hour train journey!" She felt so frustrated, at the mercy of others, confused and angry. No, no, they said, *if* it was traced, *if* it arrived in Rome, they would send it to her house. Yeah, sure! 'And pigs might fly!' she thought. She had learnt this expression from someone during her trip. She could just imagine it: her backpack arriving in Rome, all alone, and someone would lovingly welcome it, comfort it, and then they'd bring it home to her, four hundred miles away! And if it wasn't found? They would reimburse her at $5 per kilo. Five dollars a kilo? Ten kilos: fifty dollars! It was lost, stolen, she was never going to see it again, and she began to cry, out of frustration and sorrow. All her memories, all those things she had chosen, one by one, carried on her back, loaded on bus roofs, saved as precious witnesses of such an important journey. Lost! Disappeared, stolen by someone who would open her backpack and pull out, one by one, all her things; what would he do with them? He would sell them, give them away, to his girlfriend, his relatives, maybe keep them in his room, hang them on his walls. She was shocked, and sad: "And now? What do I do?" The clerk told her to go home; they would write to her. Deflated like a burst balloon, Maria walked toward the customs. Siggi tried to console her, but she could see that even he had no confidence they would find her big and full backpack.

His sickly appearance, as well as his extreme thinness, attracted the attention of two plain clothes policemen who asked to search his luggage and that of Maria. She was so depressed she didn't care; they could search all the hell they wanted. She *wished* she had a backpack to be searched! She looked at Siggi and saw a moment's hesitation; he was very pale. She remembered when she had entered his dormitory and had seen him cover the parcels with his sarong: the little gifts for his friends.
"Do you have anything to declare?" asked the older cop.
"I *wish!*" replied Maria with force. She was glad they had asked her that question; she hoped they'd say those words; at least she could vent some of her frustration.
The policeman looked at her quizzically: "What do you mean?" he asked.
"I said that I *wish* I had something to declare! Instead, they stole my rucksack in Moscow, with all my stuff inside and all the gifts I'd bought!"
"Maybe it's just lost in transit," said the older of the two.
"Yeah, of course! I won't see it anymore, I'm sure, I'm really angry and I feel like crying, again!"

The two cops shared an amused glance, trying not to laugh. "And what's in here?" he asked, pointing his finger to her hand luggage.

"Three rings, two bracelets, two necklaces, some clothes, what little I had brought by hand," she whimpered. The policeman took everything out, one thing at a time, while the other one began to empty Siggi's backpack. There was no one else besides the two of them; all the other passengers had already gone through while they were doing the declaration at the lost property office. The young policeman addressed him in Italian and, not understanding a word, Siggi looked back at him with a blank expression. The policeman turned to Maria and, pointing his chin toward her companion, asked: "Do you know him?"

"I met him on the plane," she lied.

"Ask him what else he's got, apart from these nice souvenirs."

Maria translated into English and then translated Siggi's response into Italian: "He asks what you mean."

"He knows perfectly well what I mean. Has he got any drugs? What do you call it... charas?" Addressing the other cop he added: "This one here is a junkie, look how skinny he is!"

"No, he's not a junkie," Maria interjected, surprising herself, as well as Siggi, who had understood the meaning of her sentence.

The cop looked at her, intrigued. "You said you met on the plane! So how do you know he's not a junkie?" he asked, all excited.

"Exactly! I met him on the plane and we talked," Maria replied with confidence. "He's told me that he has been sick for weeks, dysentery, amoeba and he's probably even incubating hepatitis, by the symptoms he has. He's hoping to get home as soon as possible, while he can still make it!"

To her surprise, the policemen began to put things back into their respective bags. After a while they grew tired and made a gesture as if to say 'you carry on with it', while they prepared to observe the passengers from another flight, who were beginning to filter through. Siggi began to put things inside his backpack, but now they didn't fit any longer and he had little strength. Maria complained loudly that before the search everything was nicely organized, she gave him a hand pushing his things in as well as she could, buckled his backpack up and helped him load it on his shoulders. As they headed toward the airport exit, she was sure she heard him let out a sigh of relief; she was certain he was carrying something. "Don't look so happy!" she hissed through clenched teeth.

Siggi smiled and softly said: "You helped me, didn't you?"

"Without meaning to," she replied.

The doors opened automatically and they walked out of the airport and into Rome's warm and sunny atmosphere. Maria paused to take a deep breath. The air was different from India's; it was cooler and cleaner, although it smelt of fuel, petrol and gas. She was back! Was she glad about it? She wasn't sure, but she was excited, despite her missing rucksack. Siggi had other surprises in store for her: two of his friends had come to pick him up.

"Are you telling me they've come all the way from Austria to fetch you?"

Yes, they had, and he spotted them almost immediately. They hugged tight, happy to see each other. Their original idea was to stop in Rome for the night, but the hotels were very expensive. Maria suggested they went to Venice, where they could all sleep at her house. It was going to take at least seven hours driving, sure, and they had already travelled all night but, in comparison to travelling twenty hours on an Indian bus, this seemed like a short trip: seven hours up the motorway, stopping to eat Italian food at a service station. The boys were tempted by the idea of going to Venice and sleeping there. "If we set off now, by eight o'clock this evening we'd be at home, and then you can sleep as long as you want!" she said with enthusiasm, managing to persuade them. Siggi was in a hurry to get away from the airport. As soon as they settled into the car she questioned him: "Did you take drugs through customs?"

"Yes. I'm sorry," he replied apologetically.

"Were they the 'little parcels for your friends'?"

Siggi nodded, smiling now with satisfaction. He had already told his friends in German and they were overjoyed.

"Where did you hide it?" she probed.

"Inside my body," he replied, with some hesitation.

"Is it charas?"

"Yes, of course!"

She was surprised, but not completely. Something had been bothering her, but she hadn't given it much thought. Well, it was done now and he had got away with it but, once again, she had brushed closely with danger. It would have been very different if the cops had discovered him. They wouldn't have believed her, even if she insisted she didn't know him. However, the concern for herself didn't last long.

They had only been in the car for an hour when Siggi began to feel ill and they had to stop on the hard shoulder because he couldn't control his bowels. One surprise after another! He climbed down the grassy bank and hid behind a bush. It took him quite a long time. His friend brought him plastic bags. Maria preferred not to know and, like the three little monkeys, she couldn't see, couldn't hear and couldn't speak. 'From the frying pan into the fire', she thought. When he got back to the car he looked very pale, emaciated. As they continued their journey, he got worse and they had to stop more and more often. In the end they couldn't drive more than twenty five miles without a break and, every time he came back to the car, he was even paler and weaker. What had she said to the police? Dysentery, a bit of amoeba and possibly hepatitis. Perhaps she was right!

Finally, nine hours after leaving Rome, they reached the outskirts of Venice. She began to recognize the roads, the signs with the names of familiar towns, the countryside, the buildings. It felt as if she were coming back from a trip to the moon, with a mixture of gratitude and detachment. Was she glad to be back? No, it felt strange but, fortunately, she had Siggi with her, a bridge between the past and the present, the witness who confirmed that it hadn't been a dream, that her trip to India had been real and that perhaps the dream was this reality.

The boy who was driving didn't need any help, he simply followed the directions, and she looked out the window. They drove onto the bridge that led straight to Venice, two miles between earth and sea, over the lagoon, with the water stroking the islets sprinkled with grass, and the first boats. At the far end, on her left were the lights of Venice with the sky line drawn by the roofs of houses, of taller churches and bell towers, and on her right were merchant ships, big boats and cranes silhouetted against the dark blue sky. As the daylight faded completely, the lights inside the houses were coming on and, like eyes opening, they looked at her returning, winking at her, unhurriedly waiting for her, while she approached. Strong emotions squeezed her heart until it almost hurt; her city, her beautiful Venice.

They parked near the station depot and got out of the car with stiff legs, sore backs and rigid necks. They took out their luggage, but Maria forbade them to take Siggi's stinky bags to her house. She recognized the smell of Venice, ever changing according to the wind, the tide and the weather. From there they could either take a boat or walk, but she didn't give them any choice: they would go home on foot. One of them shouldered Siggi's backpack so that he could walk lighter. Their eyes wide open, full of wonder, they were all happy to be there.

Maria needed to arrive slowly, one step after another, feeling the stones beneath her feet, touching the walls of houses, crossing the bridges one at a time, looking around, recognizing the eaves, the television antennas, the messy wires strung from one house to another, the doors of the inns, the larger doors of houses and churches, the squares and the shops: the tobacconist, the bakery, the grocer's, the printing house; the bar filled with smoke and people drinking wine as if it were water, talking loudly, commenting, judging, criticizing, planning, hoping, kidding, exaggerating, cursing.

They walked in silence through the deserted streets savouring the peace, listening to the sound of their footsteps and the faded noises that trickled through the houses' closed windows. The evening was cool and, while they walked deeper into the more intimate Venice, the traditional street lights were reflected in the water of the canals, as they had done for centuries: three lights at the top of each post, each one enclosed in its pink glass housing, the centre one tall and straight, the other two elegantly resting on arms of wrought iron, bent in the shape of a wave, a hug, a welcome greeting. She took a deep breath, absorbing the atmosphere of her beloved city, torn between contrasting feelings, strong and intense.

They arrived in the first square, Campo Santa Margherita, the pizza place was open and there were people outside drinking and talking. She didn't look that way, afraid she might see someone she knew. They reached Campo San Barnaba, which was almost deserted, apart from the bar on the right. They continued along the empty 'calle' and crossed the Ponte dei Pugni. It felt as if years had gone by; it was the same town she had left, but her life was no longer the way it used to be. They arrived in Campo of the Academy of Fine Arts, where she worked. She cast a brief glance at the institute's main door, but looked quickly away. And here was the Accademia Bridge; there was something friendly about it, with its wooden stairs which softened the step. And there was Campo Santo Stefano, which had seen the joys and sorrows of her life open like a fan: Niccolò Tommaseo's statue raised by the few steps where she had sat waiting for friends; the elegant buildings resting on classical columns; the white, majestic churches around her, full of beauty. On her right was the sidewalk along the canal which had appeared in the dream with Jean-Claude and Paul; she remembered it perfectly well, as if it had really happened. They took the lane on the right, crossed another bridge, went past the Galleria d'Arte and finally arrived in Campo San Maurizio.

She pulled from her pocket the keys she had ready and, with a confident gesture that hid the uneasiness she felt, she opened the front door to her house. The smell of damp in the entrance hall was exactly as she remembered it. They climbed the old worn out irregular stone steps up to the second floor. She opened her apartment door and turned the light on. Everything was as she had left it. One by one they entered and she closed the door behind them. She looked around; nothing had changed, except for her. She felt indifference, a sort of detachment for the objects that surrounded her and realized that, while her body had already arrived home, her mind and her heart were still in India. She needed more time to get there completely. She gathered some loose cushions and those from the couch, took clean sheets and blankets from the closet and prepared two beds on the floor for Siggi's friends. They were all tired, but they wanted to make a joint. Siggi settled on Maria's double bed, exhausted. They all shared a joint and then a second one, relaxing, joking and laughing. Within a few minutes the two boys were fast asleep.

Maria lay down next to her friend and fell asleep, but it was a light sleep. She was aware of Siggi getting up and going to the bathroom; she knew by the way he walked that, every time he came back, he was weaker. In the dim light, through half-closed eyes, she saw him sit on the edge of the bed and then, slowly, tiredly, lie down. She could make out the outlines of the curls that framed his oval, thin face and felt strong affection for him; in the semi-darkness she smiled at him. Siggi saw her white teeth, with difficulty he propped himself on his elbow and looked at her for a while. She wasn't surprised when he bent down and kissed her, a light kiss on her forehead, not to make her sick with his illness. He was very weak and stretched out again. It was her turn to prop herself up. She stroked his sweaty forehead, his hot temples, his sunken cheeks; she ran her fingers through his hair, trying to smooth away the pain, the tiredness, his illness. She felt him relax under her hands, drifting away into the sleep he needed so much; reluctantly she let him go, full of tenderness. For a while she lay there, staring at the ceiling, half way between wake and sleep, suspended in limbo! She turned to look at Siggi, her little piece of India.

She closed her eyes and her mind went back to the Tourist Camp, the German boy with the king cobra, Luna, Harry, Ted, Mister Singh with the green turban that matched his eyes, and his white beard, neatly held in place by a net. She saw the beggar without hands who touched her feet and thanked her with a smile; the three children riding the bicycle together and waving at her while she sat alone in the mail carriage. She found herself in Varanasi, down the ghats with Jean-Claude taking photos, kissing in the deserted temples on the opposite bank of the Ganges, and her stomach twitched with emotion. Then her mind went back even further and she blushed in the darkness at the memory of Paul embracing her in the temple; she felt the beating of his heart, her head resting on his chest. She saw him writing his address, sitting on his bed in Mandi's Tourist Bungalow, their shoulders touching, breathing in unison. Eventually she fell asleep.

She woke up hearing her name and, when she opened her eyes, saw Siggi's smiling face.

"It's nearly eleven o'clock," he said. "In a minute the bell tower out there will chime eleven times." He looked better than the day before, but had blue rings around his eyes. "We've been awake for quite a while and soon we'll have to leave. It's a long journey all the way to Vienna." Of course, he couldn't stay here forever! Maria got up and wore the same clothes she had been travelling in, because they still smelt of India. They went for breakfast at a café some distance from Campo Santo Stefano, in a 'calle' out of the way, and then they walked to the station depot, where their car was parked. She hugged Siggi, thin and vulnerable, rolling his blond curls around her fingers. He looked into her eyes and kissed her forehead, her closed eyes, her cheeks and the tip of her nose. They didn't know what to say. Would they ever meet again? "Thank you for everything," he said, holding her hands. Maria hugged him for the last time and then stood there, unable to move or think, waving her arm while they manoeuvred and drove away. The last piece of India had gone. She could see the back of the car that disappeared, with the brake lights winking at her.

She didn't do anything for a while, she didn't know where to go, what to do. She sat on a low wall, looking at the road ahead. When she saw a public boat approach she walked to the pier; she had no Italian money and smiled when she found some rupees in her pocket. She boarded without a ticket and sat outside. She had no idea where the 'vaporetto' boat was going and didn't care. She let it take her along the canals, sitting in the sun watching Venice from the water and, little by little, she was returning home.

She spent the first few days alone, she hadn't let anyone know she was back. She caught the boat and went to visit the islands of Murano, Burano and Torcello, where she didn't know anybody. She walked the lanes and along the canals, ate a sandwich sitting on the steps leading to the water, looking at Burano's colourful houses, which were different and more cheerful than those in Venice, and its gondolas which were painted in many different colours, while in Venice they were all black. The simplicity and peace of Torcello were a real surprise; there were very few people around and fields of green grass surrounded the church. Murano's shop windows, full of blown glass wares, were a feast for the eyes, and when they invited her to enter a 'fornasa' she was easily persuaded. There, working with a flame, an artist craftsman and his young assistant created a glass vase with dramatic colours and the lightness of a feather. The skill of those men filled her with admiration. As she left, the young assistant ran after her and gave her a small glass cat. She caught a boat across the lagoon and reached the Lido, Venice beach. She walked on the sand, along the sea, letting her thoughts come and go at will, engrossed in the present moment, gradually coming back to her roots.

Ester tracked her down at home and told her that Gabriele, Franca's boyfriend, wanted to see her; he was worried because he hadn't received any mail from Franca for weeks. Ugo had asked about her, too. "There are a lot of people who want to see you," she said. She wanted to know everything and, in the couple of hours they spent together, Maria began to put her memories into words, sharing them with her friend.

"Did you find the man of your life?" Ester asked her. It was something they had joked about before parting; Maria had said she was going to India in search of the man of her life, and had asked Ester if she'd go with her. But her friend had replied that she'd look for him in Venice.

"I don't know," replied Maria. "I found two men that I really liked, but they were already taken, of course. We'll see what happens. And you?"

Ester smirked.

"Are you serious?" Maria asked. "Did you find someone?"

"I did," replied Ester, "but he doesn't know yet!" They laughed loudly, as they always did when they were together. She told her about the lost rucksack and her friend agreed with her that she wasn't going to see it again. They decided to meet in Campo Santo Stefano that evening; Ester promised she would be there, and this gave Maria the support she needed to see everyone again.

She wore white pyjama trousers, her white embroidered kurta shirt and Pokhara's satin waistcoat. She fastened the silver anklets that Jean-Claude had given her, put some light make-up on, slipped on the silver bracelet with turquoise and coral that she had bought in Kathmandu and the turquoise earrings, bought from another jeweller on Freak Street. Her hair had grown and almost reached her waist, it shined with coppery reflections and she was happy with it. With some trepidation, she walked to Campo Santo Stefano. She sat on the statue's steps and lit a cigarette. Ester wasn't there yet.

The first person she saw was Gabriele. She raised her arm to greet him and he quickened his pace, coming to sit next to her and embracing her affectionately. She didn't know him well, but he was kind, pleasant, and worried. Maria explained things starting from the end, telling him how and where she had left Franca. He wasn't happy with the situation, much less about how Franca had thrown herself headlong into drugs. "I'm not like that," he made a point of saying, "and I don't understand this wild passion she has to try everything. Sooner or later she'll pay for it. I don't know if you've seen how she doesn't listen to anyone. She always does whatever she wants!" Maria laughed. Yes, she had noticed Franca's slightly anarchic tendencies. Gabriele spoke about her as if she were a friend rather than his girlfriend; he seemed interested but not involved. Now she understood the distance she had felt in Franca toward him, it was a real distance. Gabriele wanted to know more and after a while they were talking about her own experience of India and Nepal.

    While she was telling him about Pokhara, she saw Ugo coming. She expected her heart to skip a beat, but instead she simply acknowledged his presence. She observed him, while he hadn't seen her yet: that way of walking without haste, absorbed in his thoughts, those eyes that, because of the shape, looked sad but weren't so; it was just an impression to make women fall in love. Perhaps feeling he was being watched Ugo looked in her direction. She saw his eyes widen in surprise, changing expression from engrossed to shocked, and then excited. He quickened his pace and then started running toward her. She smiled, but didn't stand up. Ugo knelt in front of her and hugged her. He gave her a kiss on the cheek that Maria offered him, stroking her arms. He seemed really happy to see her. She let him touch her. She knew his hands well, that way of caressing her not only with his fingers, but with the palms of his hands, his wrists, his forearms. She recognized his touch; it was his friendship that seemed alien. Yes, she was fine, yes, a beautiful journey, yes, wonderful people, thank you. Her lack of emotion cooled his enthusiasm. "You look beautiful," he said, seeming surprised.

    "Thank you," she replied simply, thinking 'definitely not thanks to you!' She felt beautiful because she had changed inside and the opinion she had of herself didn't depend on him any longer.

    "Do you want to come to dinner at my house? I'll cook you something good," he offered.

    Two months ago she would have given anything for an invitation like that, to be chosen over the other girls. She would go to his house, hoping it could be a new beginning; trusting herself into his arms until the morning; keeping up the illusion into the afternoon; seeing it shattered around cocktail hour; disappointed and humiliated by dinner time. Now she didn't care. She observed her own reaction, surprised to feel such lack of interest, seeing herself from the outside, free at last, and saw the desire in his eyes. It wasn't the first time, she'd gone through detachment before, and freedom from Ugo's charm, who made her feel like a queen, only to end up being a drudge. She had fallen for it a few times and was aware she had to be careful, because he knew how to persist, woo and wait until he obtained what he wanted; then he'd look away and start a new game, addicted to conquest.

"Thank you, but I can't; I'm going out with friends," she said, using a reply he had given her many times. She knew she had hit the mark. But, apart from the small, petty satisfaction of getting rid of him, she felt a strength inside that she had never felt before.

Her small world had become big; the insecurity and lack of value she had felt inwardly had slipped away, thanks to the people she had met, the things she had learned about her potential, respect for herself and the uniqueness of her life. She was living the present with an eye toward the future and knew that her life was huge, that she had things to do, her unique mission to fulfil, a path that, although she still didn't know where it would lead her, would make her happy. She was going to find out, one step at a time!

Nam-myoho-renge-kyo, Nam-myoho-renge-kyo, Nam-myoho-renge-kyo, she chanted in her head, and it was like the drum of Red Indians who played the sacred ritual dance around the bonfire in preparation for the attack; it was like the notes of a piano weaving the plot of her new life, embroidering her future; it was a flute singing the freedom of a seagull flying high, the flap of his big wings strong and unstoppable. Ugo would no longer stop her, nor confuse her. Indeed, she was grateful for the way he behaved with her, grateful for the suffering that had spurred her to leave, to rebel against the smallness of her life, to go in search of happiness, of which she had found the source, with the help of her friends, inside herself. Never again would she allow herself to go through a relationship without respect.

"But thanks for the offer," she added, smiling with her lips, her eyes distant. She saw Ugo's hurt look. He knew her well and could see her calm anger. 'Why should I bear him a grudge?' she asked herself. He really had helped her, albeit unwittingly. The expression in her eyes changed, and with an honest smile, she said: "Thank you, really... but no thanks!"

Finally she saw Ester, who was accompanied by Enrico, a tall, attractive and cheerful man. They were laughing as they walked. It was clear that he was a man who didn't yet know that he had found the woman of his life. They spent an hour chatting in groups; Maria was the centre of attention, everyone wanted to know how her trip had been, and she patiently repeated the same things a few times. Ugo kept nearby, as he always did when she rejected him, as if a thread was tying him to her and, even when he'd moved away, he never let go of it. Maria observed Ester and Enrico: clearly at ease together, they had no need for words or statements, but were glued by an invisible bond that made their relationship natural and simple, but real and strong. That evening, after pizza and a beer in a pizzeria with the two of them, Maria wrote to Franca. The words flowed easily.

"*Dear Franca,*

I arrived in Venice three days ago and I'm still in the clouds! I didn't realize that 'landing' would be so hard. My body is here but my heart is still in India. In a sense, I have no desire to 'come back'. The pace of life seems hectic in comparison to India, everybody is in a hurry, they run to and fro, first to work, then shopping, then cooking and then to bed.

People seem superficial, with their talk of designer clothes, their beautiful hair styling, necklaces, make-up, all so pretty and tidy. They have everything but still it's not enough; it's never enough, because they try to fill the void they have inside by hoarding things on the outside.

Then I think of my friend with no legs who walked on wooden blocks tied to his hands, lifting his torso at every step. Do you remember him? Surinder, in Mcleodganj. His eyes shone as if he had a light inside and was always looking around to see if anyone needed his help. Generous and intelligent, he felt rich when he didn't even have his legs! What an extraordinary person; he taught me a lot. And then I remember the people of the village in the mountains. They were queuing to get their bead bracelets made and waited patiently for their turn. The joy and gratitude they showed for such a small thing! Both, children and adults with the same curiosity, the same enthusiasm. I remember them as a deeply happy people and what did they have? Very little! I say very little, because I think with the mentality of a westerner living in a capitalist country, let's face it. For them it is not 'little' because they have this clear sense of gratitude for what they have: a roof over their head, maize and semolina in the fields, apple trees and some cows that give the scarce milk, which is so precious; and the desire to smile, to dance, to sing, to learn everything they can from us who pass briefly through their lives. I miss them and I don't want to 'land', I'm not ready; my heart is still there with them.

I think of the beautiful people we've met, Sanya and Colin and their Ten Worlds, Luna and her friends whom I met in Delhi. I always think of that phrase and I often recite it in my head, or out loud if I am alone, to feel happier and more balanced within. I think of Jean-Claude and his girlfriend waiting for him in Paris, and also of Paul and his girlfriend; men who have shared my life, our lives, for a brief moment, and gave me a lot. Who knows whether I'll see them again? In a way, it's not even important whether I see them again. What people give you becomes yours forever and nobody can take it away, it's part of your life.

Coming to the present moment: tonight I 'faced' the square. I spoke with Gabriele, who wanted to know how you were and why he hasn't received any more letters from you. I told him how things went and he would love to hear from you. I hope that, when you receive this letter, the yellowish-brownish-green will be a thing of the past, that your eyes have gone back to being beautiful, and that your skin is the colour it should be, maybe a little tanned. I saw Ugo and I'm glad of the lack of effect he had on me, but I have to be on guard; I know him well and I'm aware that he has many ways of reattaching himself, slowly but surely! I decided to actively avoid him.

The return trip was interesting, to say the least. I travelled with a young Austrian man who had brought some 'stuff'. We went through customs together, because I hadn't sussed anything, but the cops had understood immediately. Luckily, he got away with it, partly also thanks to my (involuntary) help. Two friends of his came to fetch him at the airport all the way from Vienna, we came to Venice by car and we all slept here. A non-stop trip from Delhi to Venice, twenty four hours.

And now, the worst piece of news: my rucksack was lost during the return journey. You will be glad, with that love-hate relationship you had with my ugly red rucksack. Inside were all the things I had bought and carried on my shoulders with so much effort. They told me that, if they find it, they'll deliver it to me, here at home, but I think I have no hope of ever seeing it again. Can you imagine? Someone in Delhi, Moscow, or even Rome, will be enjoying my stuff. I haven't yet recovered from the shock! If I'm lucky I'll get 5 dollars a kilo, while in it there are things worth at least 500 dollars, which I wanted to sell to get back some of the money I spent on the trip. I'm very upset about this.

Well, now I'll say goodbye because I'm so tired and I'm working tomorrow. Take care of yourself and get completely better. Let me know when you're coming back and we'll come to pick you up at the airport!

Kisses Maria!"

26. It starts again from now

Maria got up early, she had a morning's work at the Academy of Fine Arts, which was the reason why she had come back from India in September. Just one morning's work but this year it was her turn to pose for the entrance exams for the faculty of sculpture. The institute's square courtyard, surrounded by ancient arches, housed the janitor's shed. Beppi greeted her warmly: How was she? She had lost weight, but looked beautiful. What had she done? A slimming diet? No, India. Ah, India, so how come she was wearing shoes? He thought everyone went barefoot in India. Maria joked with him, she asked him about his family, children, grandchild. They were all fine, he said, getting fatter by the day. He consulted his schedule: there were two students taking the exam.

She undressed behind a screen and put on her white and blue dressing gown. The students were already in their places, focused, a little nervous. She removed her robe and, naked, sat on the stool. She chose a simple position, one she could easily keep throughout the morning, in sessions of forty-five minutes: one foot on the stool rung, the other foot on the floor, one arm behind her back to keep upright, the other arm resting on the opposite leg, head turned slightly to the right, eyes focused on a point in front of her. The students began working with clay. Time passed slowly, nothing to do, time to think.

The first image was that of the mountains and Pushpa; she was sure the baby had been born, she felt a total certainty and also knew that the young mother was well and happy. She saw Mataji, Pushpa's mother-in-law, who pretended to breastfeed Ritu when Pushpa had yet to return from the fields; Grandma gave her breast and Ritu sucked, or pretended to suck, and calmed down. Pitaji, the grandfather, smoking the water pipe with his son, in silence, waiting for the sunset; Pushpa and herself going to collect firewood with baskets on their backs. Then came the image of Surinder on his blocks, accompanying her to buy a torch. She saw him waving goodbye when she was already on the bus leaving Mcleodganj, leaning out of the open door. She saw Delhi's children being carried on their mothers' back, with their trousers split on their bottom, ready to pee and pooh.

The voice of one of the students brought her back to reality; he seemed annoyed: "Can you keep your head still, please?" Maria apologized. It was her job and she wanted to do it well, but she didn't like his tone. The student was nervous; after all it was an exam.

She concentrated on keeping her head still while, with her mind, she returned to India. This time she saw Harry, smiling happily next to Luna in the Tourist Camp's dormitory; Luna looking at her with affection and giving her her address before leaving; Ted, polite and discreet, still incognito for a few more months. She would write to Luna today. She saw Colin and Sanya, relighting her cigarette going out after every two puffs, explaining the Ten Worlds; Sanya with dozens of bracelets and shining eyes, Colin with his charming look and radio presenter voice. She was going to write to them too, probably tomorrow.

She saw Jean-Claude about to enter the Yogi Lodge and asking her: 'Would you like a cup of tea?' She remembered how she felt at that moment, hurrying down the stairs, still dazed from the opium that had left her horizontal for twenty-four hours. She saw Paul, getting off the bus in Kashmiri Gate bus station and looking at her for the first time, his glance piercing as an arrow.

The same student's voice brought her back to earth with a jolt: "Can you keep your eyes still?" he said, clearly annoyed.

Maria turned toward him and took a deep breath before speaking: "I'm keeping my body completely still, and my head too, but not moving my eyes is much more difficult. You're doing a sketch for a statue, after all."

"And you're doing your job," he retorted. "So, can you keep your eyes still?"

She felt the blood rise to her face, her cheeks burning. She didn't answer right away, she knew she would react and be rude to him; in fact she could happily punch him on the nose. She had to respond, instead, but how did she do that? Nam-myoho-renge-kyo, Nam-myoho-renge-kyo. Chant for his happiness, Maria. Whose happiness, this asshole? Yes, and he's not an asshole. Nam-myoho-renge-kyo, Nam-myoho-renge-kyo. But he is incredibly rude and I feel like hitting him. Maybe you're right but he's taking an examination and he is nervous, perhaps his work is not coming on well. Nam-myoho-renge-kyo, Nam-myoho-renge-kyo. That means he's not a sculptor, maybe he ought to study household management. Think about it, for him these few hours are crucial. Okay, I understand, I see your point of view, but he's rude. He might well be rude, but don't be swayed, behave with respect, even if *he* has too little. Respect yourself. Okay, you've won, Nam-myoho-renge-kyo. She felt calmer, more in control, amused by her inner dialogue, although she was still boiling with the rage that had submerged her like a sudden wave.

She sat motionless and, at that very moment she took a drastic decision, a life-changing one. She would leave this job and go back to India as soon as possible. How long for? Six months, the maximum period allowed by a visa. Little by little her anger disappeared as she began to ponder the idea. Leave such a comfortable job? And how was she going to earn the money to travel? She could paint; indeed she could *continue* to paint. In those four years as a model she had learned a lot just by listening to the advice that teachers gave to students and looking at their work. At home she liked to draw and had done many paintings. Before going to India she had considered them mediocre and hid them from others; she judged her paintings just like she judged herself. However, since getting back, she had looked at them again and had to admit that they weren't at all bad. With all the tourists coming to Venice, she could sell enough paintings to earn what she needed to quit her job and start travelling again. It wasn't by chance, she thought, that she lived a stone's throw from an art gallery. She would show her paintings to the couple who ran it and maybe they'd help her sell a few. And how was she going to pay the rent? She could rent her house for six months. Ester knew a lot of people and would help her find the right person.

She started to feel some enthusiasm for the idea. She imagined a set of scales, with one of the plates holding the 'safe' option to stay in Venice, carry on as she was doing and maybe go back to India next summer, and the other plate with the 'crazy' option, which was surfacing with strength, to drop everything and leave again, as soon as she could. She decided to consult her heart. In her head she chanted Nam-myoho-renge-kyo to stay in Venice, and her heart told her it was a safe choice, but not exciting; then she chanted Nam-myoho-renge-kyo to return to India as soon as possible and her heart leapt and did a somersault, it started to skip and dance for joy, savouring the freedom; and she wanted to run, jump, laugh and cheer. She was breathing with some anxiety, realizing that anything she wanted to do was possible. The anger the student had provoked forgotten, Maria was struggling to hold back the smile that was pushing from inside and trying to break onto her face. She peered at him and sent him a virtual kiss. 'If you knew the effect you had on me!' she said to herself. 'You have changed my life.' Even if the details were still to be decided, she knew without a doubt that her heart had chosen: she would leave after the Christmas holidays, having sold the paintings she had already finished and those she would paint. And who would she go with? She didn't know. Would she have the courage to go alone? The answer came clear and simple: yes. She wouldn't be often alone, this she already knew, and anyway, between now and January there were still three months and many things could happen.

At the end of the morning, full of excitement, Maria got dressed and took leave from the two boys, wishing both of them good luck. She was about to go out of the door when the nervous student approached her. "I'm sorry I spoke to you like that, earlier," he said.

She was surprised, but pleased, that he should apologize. "No problem," she said. "If you knew the effect you had on me, you wouldn't believe it!"

The student looked at her questioningly.

"It's a long story," said Maria. "Maybe, next time, try to be more polite, but really, just now there is no problem!" She stepped into the Academy's courtyard in the midday sun and saw one of the tutors walking under the arches. "Good morning Sir!" she shouted cheerfully.

He recognized her at once: "Hello Maria, I'm in a hurry. I'll see you in October."

"I don't think so, Sir! I'm not coming back!" she cried, unable to control her euphoria.

"Wait a minute!" Professor De Filippo crossed the yard, shook her hand and bent down to kiss her cheeks. "What's this thing that you are not coming back? You look beautiful, by the way, what have you done?"

"I've been to India for two and a half months and I've decided to go back. So I'm leaving my job!"

The tutor looked at her in amazement." Have you thought this through?" he asked.

Maria laughed, thinking about the way she had taken such an important decision. "I'd say I have. I'm happy with my choice," she said, full of enthusiasm.

"If you're sure! It's important to follow your heart, especially when you are young. Good luck! Come back every now and then, if you can spare the time."

"Thank you Sir!" She crossed the bridge running, unable to contain her enthusiasm.

The Galleria d'Arte was still open and Maria went in, smiling: "Would you be interested in seeing the work of a beginner? I learned to paint while working as a model at the Academy."

The owner recognized her: "Looking doesn't cost anything. You live here in the square, don't you?"

"Yes, above the 'Guilder'."

"I'll pop in when I close for lunch, in ten minutes' time."

"Second floor. Dal Fiore on the doorbell."

The owner looked at Maria's paintings with an expert eye: "They are not at all bad, some are very nice. You have a good hand, your own style, and this is important." She told her that, if she didn't ask too much, she would certainly sell them. She put five paintings aside, could she take them to the shop in the afternoon? Maria felt happy and encouraged, even though she was sorry to give them away; she had poured her life into them, but she had to get used to letting them go. The owner, a painter herself, understood her dilemma and told her that paintings were like children, they were ours because we made them, but they no longer belonged to us, they were free. "When they grow up you have to let them go," she said with a smile. "You'll make more paintings!"

She was preparing some lunch when she heard the doorbell. Wiping her hands on her apron she hurried toward the intercom. She didn't quite understand who it was, but she thought he mentioned a parcel. "I'm coming," she said, searching the room with her eyes for the keys. As usual, she had misplaced her handbag. She looked everywhere and finally found it under her jacket. She ran down the stairs; in the entrance hall a man in uniform was waiting for her, with a huge parcel.

"Maria Dal Fiore, is that you?"

"Yes, it's me!"

"Sign here," he said, handing her a signature pad, looking at her with interest.

"Is this for me?" she asked, peering at the large grey package.

"If you are Maria Dal Fiore!"

"Yes, yes, it's me," she replied, surprised, excited, hoping the impossible would indeed be possible.

The man placed the signature pad back into the satchel he carried over his shoulder and took his leave. Maria was left with the large bundle next to her, reaching almost up to her waist. Was it, by any chance...? No, it couldn't be! But what else *could* it be? With an effort she picked it up, it must have weighed at least thirty pounds. She tried to rip the grey cover that was wrapping it, but it was plasticized and wouldn't tear. She was almost certain of what it was, although she couldn't quite believe it. She climbed the stairs dragging it, a smile on her lips. She reached her apartment, panting, her heart pounding from the effort. With her foot she pushed the door closed behind her. Leaving the package in the hall she ran to the kitchen to look for scissors, but couldn't find them. She took the first sharp knife that came to hand and went back to it. No sooner had she cut into the grey plastic than the red colour of her backpack peeped out from inside. Her ridiculous red rucksack with the huge Canadian flag was here, with her! If someone had told her that a friend she believed to be dead had been found alive, Maria would have felt the way she felt now: amazed, surprised, and over the moon. She laughed out loud and cried Hurrah! She danced and skipped for joy. She dragged the bundle into her room and, with many cuts of the knife she freed it from the tight plastic. It was dirty, spoiled, a little broken here and there, but here was her huge and loyal companion.

Full of excitement, she started to undo the straps; it seemed as if no-one had opened or inspected it. The things she had packed, and almost forgotten, began to appear, one by one. First ten different coloured sarongs wrapped in clear plastic bags, then a few metres of raw silk, neatly folded. There was a strong smell from everything she pulled out; it was the smell of India she remembered so well, a blend of sandalwood, patchouli, spices, moisture and dust. She sniffed the things with a mixture of wonder and nostalgia. She was going to have to air everything and, eventually, wash it, but for the moment she opened the window and went back to her backpack, full of treasures.

She emptied it slowly, with deep emotion, pausing on every single thing. Each one reminded her of the place where she had bought it, the person who had sold it to her, the exchange of humanity between them. The boots made of bright coloured felt that she had bought in the Tibetan store in Mcleodganj; she took them out of the paper bag and put them on the floor, next to the pile of sarongs and the silk cloth. The brass bowls in three different sizes, bought from another Tibetan store and used as measures for flour: a quarter kilo, half a kilo and a kilo, respectively, hand-crafted with rounded designs. She stacked them, one above the other, from the largest to the smallest, and gazed at them with affection; they shone as if made of gold.

She then found a piece of wood for which she had paid a lot of money, but it was so special she had had to buy it; on each side of the block the image of a person had been crudely dug. There was a note written in her own handwriting, which she read as if she had never seen it before: it was the healing block, said the description. Tibetans used the carved images as a mould. When a person was sick, they filled the mould with a batter of flour and water; once dry, the four "dolls" they had obtained were hung outdoors in the four directions of north, south, east and west, as an offering to birds and animals. Through feeding on the dolls, they took away the disease, thus helping the sick person's healing process. Maria put the healing block next to the brass bowls and pulled out the next treasure from the rucksack.

It was a bag with ten cotton and lurex skirts, bought in Delhi. She opened them, one at a time. Looking in the mirror she briefly held them in front of her and turned from side to side; they were truly beautiful, glistening in the sunlight, and they were a novelty. The colours were gorgeous: strong red, bright pink, turquoise, green, yellow, white, grey, black, each one better than the last, and would sell easily. She folded them into a neat pile and laid them on the floor near the other things.

She pulled out the shawls bought in a shop of Kashmiri handicrafts, remembering how much she had to haggle on the price, but they were striking, skilfully embroidered on a soft and warm fabric, a blend of wool and cotton.

Then she found a large package with the two Tibetan tanka paintings and one hundred prints on rice paper, bought with Raffa in Kathmandu. They were very cheap and she was going to sell them quickly. At the bottom of the rucksack there was a small copper statue of the dancing Shiva, a silver-plated one of Krishna playing the flute, and one of sitting Ganesh with the little mouse at his feet. Underneath the figurines were the Tibetan woolly socks that Vale had given her as a thank you for having lent him her backpack. And at the very bottom were the boxes with the perfume essences, bought with Luna in Delhi a couple of days before leaving; they gave out an intense scent, even while closed.

Out of one of the side pockets came the lurex scarves bought on her last day in Janpath Boulevard. In the opposite side pocket she found five beautiful batik bought at Paharganj market. She set aside a bag with medicines she had carried throughout her adventures, the toiletry bag with soap and ayurvedic toothpaste, some lingerie, clothes and a few personal items brought from Italy.

She sat on the bed, looking at the piles of things lined up on the floor, inhaling deeply the smell of India, and strong emotions filled her chest: a mixture of happiness, nostalgia and memories. Suddenly she felt a great weariness. The sum of all the feelings that were competing for a place in her heart could be summed up in one word: gratitude.

She lay down on the bed, exhausted from all the excitement of the morning. She was grateful to all the people she had met, for the things they had taught her, and to India itself which had changed her life, because it had changed the values that nourished her soul. What seemed top priority before her journey now seemed secondary. The important thing was respect for life, for herself and for others. Luna's face appeared before her eyes explaining that she, Maria, was the Treasure Tower. She visualized a bright tower, encrusted with precious stones, rising from the earth and radiating compassion, strength and light. Nam-myoho-renge-kyo, she said slowly, in a low voice. She wiped the tears that ran down her cheeks and into her ears. She smiled to herself; she wasn't crying, they were tears of happiness.

She wanted to see Ester; they had many things to talk about. She thought of their easy but deep friendship. She felt great affection and unconditional trust in her. Ester was always satisfied with her life, she had no need to assert herself, she *was* herself, without hesitation, inferiority complexes, insecurities; she appreciated what she had and was cheerful, generous and, of course, full of friends. For Maria, who had few real friends, she was a breath of fresh air, larger than life itself. Behind an elegant look, her beautifully styled hair and manicured nails, lurked Ester's rebellious and nonconformist side: she always surprised Maria with her strength, irrepressible energy and her loud contagious laughter.

She arrived in Campo Santo Stefano at about seven o'clock, the time when everybody started to converge; she sat down on the statue's steps and lit a cigarette, looking around. She had just stubbed out the butt when she saw Ester walking from the Accademia bridge with her relaxed pace. Maria stood up and ran to her; she was bursting to tell her everything, but didn't know where to start. Strolling together back toward the statue, she told her about the backpack that had been delivered that afternoon, intact, with all its contents. Ester wanted to see what had arrived, she'd probably buy some of the things herself, and then she'd help her sell what was left; between herself and Raffa, who at the time was in the Marche region, they'd sell the lot. Enrico arrived too and, suddenly, Maria remembered that Franca had made her promise to sell her the backpack. "It's weird, you know?" she said, looking from one to the other. "She criticized it from the first moment she saw it. She always told me it was ridiculous with that Canadian flag, it was so big it dwarfed me, and was too red. But, when she needed a big rucksack, she wanted to borrow it." Ester was only half listening to her, the other half was for Enrico. They looked at each other every two seconds and stood very close. It was obvious there was a strong attraction and they seemed completely at ease together. "In fact, it wasn't even Franca who needed it, but Vale. And then she tells me that she wants to buy it, as a souvenir of the trip, and to make sure that I never use it again." She saw Ester staring at her, suddenly struck. "Why are you looking at me like that?" Maria asked her.

"Did you say that Vale borrowed your rucksack? When, how and why?" her friend asked.

"Why? Is there a problem with Vale?"

"And with Franca, when she is with him," replied Ester, looking at Enrico. Then she turned back to Maria: "Tell me what happened."

Maria explained the whole story. Ester was listening with a serious expression, exchanging glances of increasing concern with Enrico. "Are you thinking what I'm thinking?" she asked him.

"I think so," he replied. They looked at her with the same expression.

"What is it? What are you thinking?" Maria asked, alarmed.

"I want to see the rucksack! There's something strange going on," replied Ester. "However, you have nothing to worry about; you've arrived safe and sound."

"Why? What do you think they did with it?"

"If they borrowed it for three days, Vale gave you a gift to say thank you, most unlike him, and then Franca wants to buy it, it makes me think that there is something very interesting for them inside," mused Ester. "What do you think?" she asked Enrico.

"Without a doubt! Knowing them!"

"Let's go to your place now, I'm bursting with curiosity," pressed Ester, setting off in the direction of Maria's house who, thinking back over how things had gone, was beginning to see them in a different light. They wouldn't have put drugs inside her backpack, would they? And where? No sooner had she asked herself the question than the answer appeared obvious; she had just emptied it and there was nothing left inside, so it could only be on the outside. But… how could Franca do such a thing? On the way to her house, they spoke in low voices, wondering what they would find and especially where; by now they all had the same suspicion. Maria mentioned her decision to return to India, but it wasn't the right time to talk about it; they were all too agitated by what was in store. Maria pushed the door closed behind her, Ester strode to her room, picked up her backpack and hefted it, looking at her questioningly: "Does it weigh more than normal?"

"I don't know, let me try." Maria weighed it up carefully. "Maybe. It's hard to tell." She looked from Ester to Enrico. "Do you think they put drugs in it?"

"Yes," they answered in unison and, looking at each other, burst out laughing.

"But where?"

"That's obvious," Enrico said, picking up her backpack, inspecting it. "Have you got a knife?"

Seeing her shocked expression, Ester gave her an excited smile. "We'll find a surprise, you'll see. Better than an Easter egg!" she said, laughing loudly, infecting them with her excitement. Maria came back with a knife; Enrico pushed the blade between the frame and the white plastic cap but the cap wasn't moving. He tried several times, applying more and more force, but neither of the caps budged. "They've been glued with superglue," he said. "Do you have a saw?" Since Maria shook her head, he said firmly: "Let's take it to my house; we'll open it with my hacksaw."

They walked all the way between the two houses almost without speaking, slowing down after the bridges only enough to catch their breath. Ester and Enrico walked close together, inseparable, the red backpack between them, to shelter it. Maria didn't want to touch it. "They will have put it in the top part of the structure," suggested Ester. He had his house key ready well before getting there and, as soon as he opened the door, he went immediately to the toolbox. He came back holding a hacksaw and, without a word, started to saw the backpack's frame energetically until he cut it in two. It hurt to see her faithful friend being destroyed like that, but Maria didn't say a word. Pushing down with strength, he bent the metal in two and separated the two parts, allowing him to inspect the interior. "It seems to be blocked by something," he said. He took a pencil and inserted it into the tube. "There's something!"

Incredulous, Maria stared at the backpack she had carried from Nepal to India, from India to Moscow, in communist Russia, and finally should have collected at Rome airport. She remembered the two plainclothes police officers as they searched Siggi's baggage. Her legs were shaking and her heart was beginning to fill with fear; she felt sick. Enrico, completely absorbed in his task, confidently sawed the opposite end of the frame. "We need a longer stick. The pencil is not enough!" he said. Ester looked around, went to the kitchen and came back with a long handled wooden spoon. Enrico inserted it into the tube and tried to push the contents toward the opening; nothing was moving, things had been glued. He placed one end of the wooden spoon on the floor and, clutching the tube with both hands, lifted it and beat it repeatedly. "Something's coming, get ready girls!" he said.

"Bring out the bubbly Maria," said Ester, laughing.

A small parcel wrapped in a condom appeared at the mouth of the pipe. By continuing to hit the spoon, the parcel came out just enough to allow him to pull it out with his hands. "Open it, Ester," he said, as he continued to hit the wooden tool on the floor, dislodging other little parcels.

With a knife, scissors and her teeth, Ester opened it in less than two minutes. She smiled from ear to ear. "Look what I found!" she said triumphantly, holding up a black shiny 'finger', as long as her index finger, including the fingernail, and of the same thickness. She sniffed it with delight, her eyes half-closed with pleasure: "Pure Himalayan charas, if I'm not mistaken!"

"You're never mistaken," said Enrico, laughing, as he continued to push the spoon into the pipe. Maria was watching the scene, dumbfounded. Enrico glanced at her: "Cheer up Maria! You'll make enough money to go back to India."

"I don't want anything to do with it. If things had gone wrong, I'd be sweating in an Indian prison, or maybe in a Nepalese one; or I might be in a cool Moscow jail instead, or behind the bars of a cell in Rome's Regina Coeli, explaining to the guards that I didn't know anything about this charas. When I see Franca I'll kill her!"

Ester laughed heartily: "When Franca comes back, we'll think of how to welcome her. Meanwhile, what we find is yours, Maria. You've carried it, and at great risk. Come on, keep pushing Enrico, I can see another parcel," she encouraged him.

"I'm going to need a longer stick in a while! Maria, see what you can find in the kitchen."

In the end, ten packets of charas and another ten of a darker colour and softer consistency, identified by Ester as opium, were lying on the floor.

"If I had been caught with opium, I would have risked *years* in prison," murmured Maria, with a lump in her throat and severe nausea, her stomach churning in knots. She couldn't share her friends' excitement as she watched the black fingers of charas and opium that Ester had neatly lined up; she was now holding one in her hand, weighing it up: "There will be ten grams of charas here." She put it back on the floor and picked up a finger of opium. She weighed it up in the same way and gave her verdict: "There will be fifteen grams of opium in each, minimum, maybe twenty."

Maria had been carrying one hundred grams of charas and one hundred and fifty, maybe two hundred grams of opium which, eventually, she would have given to Franca, who would have given her... what? A gift, in exchange for her old backpack? And what if she had been caught? She felt a cold sweat cover her, strong anger and a sense of deep disappointment fill her heart. How could Franca have put her in a situation so full of risk? Didn't she care about her at all? Had she held a grudge all that time? Maria remembered how weak she was at Vale's house, almost unable to speak, perhaps even to think, while Vale took advantage of the situation to plant drugs in her backpack. He had organized the whole scam, but Franca was aware of it, she had no doubt about this. Maria remembered how she had averted her gaze to stare at the floor; the look and the wink that Vale had given her. And then she had made her promise to sell her the backpack. Franca knew everything and had cooperated, if only for lack of strength. Maria had been used by them, heedless of any possible consequences. She was shocked; she felt as if she had hit a wall head on. "And now what do we do? I don't want anything to do with these drugs," she said to Ester who, with her eyes on the fingers lined up on the floor, was doing multiplications in her mind, guessing the overall weight of the bounty.

"I'll handle this, if that's okay," she said. They decided that they would leave it at Enrico's house, for now, except for a couple of grams that Ester was going to try as 'quality control'. Maria wouldn't have to hear anything more about it.

"What will we do about Franca? In my letter I told her that the rucksack had been lost!"

"Perfect," said Enrico. "Don't tell her anything else and pretend it never arrived."

"We'll think of what to do about Franca, and Vale. For now, don't you worry! Thankfully nothing happened, but what they did is criminal," said Ester. Then, unable to control her excitement any longer, she added: "Let's hide the loot and then, boys and girls, we celebrate! Champagne for everyone!"

They went out together, heading for Ester's house. On the way, they wanted to know from Maria, word for word, how they had persuaded her to lend them her backpack, trying to understand why they had used her in such a way. In their opinion it wasn't a typical behaviour from Franca. Maria explained that Franca had ambivalent feelings toward her and was very fickle, that she had smoked heroin, developed hepatitis and moved into Vale's house; at that point he had clearly taken advantage. They didn't know him well, but they knew he was a 'sinister character', said Ester laughing, who used everything he could get his hands on: heroin, cocaine, speed, and so on and so forth! He was a dealer and a junkie and would do anything to satisfy his insatiable need for money and drugs. He lived mostly in Nepal, occasionally in India, but couldn't return to Italy because he would be arrested.

"When they get your letter, they'll think that the rucksack was intercepted, or that you are lying to keep the drugs," said Enrico.

"Let's talk about this over a drink." said Ester, buzzing.

She took charge of everything. She took home the skirts, the prints, the shawls, the sarongs and the scarves and, once a week, Ester gave her the proceeds of the things she had sold.

Maria began to paint full-time, taking advantage of the last days of warm sunshine, going out with pastel colours and painting Venice as she saw it. She'd sit on a step overlooking the water, or on the threshold of a church, or at a bar. Without exception, people would stop, watching every gesture she made, every sign she traced. At first she found it intimidating, but soon she realized that this curiosity was the best way to sell her work.

She could tell if someone was interested in her picture from a little comment they made. The picture would be ready in half an hour, she'd say, she'd do it especially for them; did they want a particular colour in *their* picture? The client suggested a colour, a shade, Maria introduced their idea and then carried on as she liked: a touch of yellow here to enhance the purple, some green and a contrasting red to make it more vibrant. Invariably, the customers stopped until the picture was finished, seeing it develop and grow. She sprayed the completed work with a fixative and, while it dried, the client paid the reasonable price she asked. Soon, she'd find herself at the centre of another small crowd watching a new picture she'd be drawing.

It was a delightful time of her life. She was seeing Venice with new eyes: that detail, that view, the light of the sunset suffused with magic by the mist. When the weather changed and autumn advanced, Maria began to paint at home with brushes and easel, oil paints and watercolours, accompanied by the music of Keith Jarrett on the piano, or Bob Dylan's new album, which she learned by heart.

One day the doorbell rang: it was Ugo, his visit a complete surprise. She tried to calm the emotions that agitated her; the two of them alone in the house was too dangerous, and she didn't trust him. She continued to paint while Ugo was making coffee.

"When did you change the curtains?" she could hear him say from the kitchen. "Where's the sugar? Have you moved it?" Little sentences like that, to remind her that it had been his home too, for three years. He brought the coffee to the bedroom and sat on the bed, watching her while she painted near the window. She was beautiful, did she know? Her hair was much nicer with those coppery reflections. He wanted to take some photographs, with the light coming in through the window, on the one side, and the darker atmosphere of the room, on the other; unfortunately, he didn't have the camera with him but he would come back the next day. He began to walk around her, studying the light on her face, pushing her hair behind her ear.

"You're disturbing me! I can't paint like this," she complained, beginning to feel her resistance fading. He lowered the zipper on the side of her dress, just for fun. She slapped his hand, pushing it away from her body. She knew what he was thinking and wasn't willing to succumb to his momentary whim, or her weakness. If she could believe he wanted a relationship like the one they had the first few months, and to build something together, she would have taken him straight away, she would have been his, without hesitation; but she knew him well and trusting him would be suicidal. It was in Ugo's nature to be unfaithful. Who knew, maybe one day he'd find a woman he loved, and would change, but Maria doubted very much that she could be that woman. "Keep your hands off!" she said putting the paintbrush down. "Let's get out of here. I don't want to go backwards!" She left the brushes soaking in water and, hurriedly, put her jacket on. "Come on, get out. I don't trust you!"

He looked at her with a smile of admiration in his eyes: "When you get angry you're even more beautiful."

"And you're an asshole! Let's go for a walk." But it wasn't a walk that Ugo wanted, nor to talk to her about her experiences, her dreams. He took his leave in Campo Santo Stefano; he had masses of things to do, he said.

The next day he returned with his camera and insisted on taking pictures while she painted, and while she was sitting in the wicker rocking chair, her hair covering half of her face. He moved a strand of her hair, you're beautiful like this, now put your leg over the armrest, lower the strap of your dress just a touch; now with all your hair to one side, wait, I'll move it, it looks good so. He kissed her on the neck and moved away again. He had won and Maria knew it. Ugo didn't insist, he didn't impose himself; he threw a small invitation and then pulled back. She waited for the next move that didn't come, waited a little bit longer, ready to send him away, but he wouldn't do anything until, when the tension was at bursting point, he would touch her lightly, then touched her again, and then kissed her. Maria's defences vanished little by little; they crumbled by themselves, a little gesture at a time, the wait for the next one, until she wanted him. They made love as they had done hundreds of times before; she felt like the most sensual woman in the world, forgot all the others and believed she was *his* woman, the only one he loved. The illusion lasted only a short time. He got dressed; he had three hundred thousand things to do and was out the door, out of her life, for now, until when? Tomorrow? The day after tomorrow? Next week? The see-saw started again.

That evening she saw him again in the square. He came over, kissed her on the lips in front of everyone and invited her to go to the cinema. She cancelled the commitment she had with Ester to be with him. Sitting in the back row they held hands and kissed in the dark as if they had just met, and touched each other as if they were fifteen years old. Ugo walked back home with her. "Are you coming upstairs?" she asked. There was no need to ask, he had started to undress her while she was still looking for her keys. He kissed her as soon as they entered, leaning against the door, unbuttoning her shirt, lifting her skirt.

The next morning they had breakfast in bed, prepared by him, who loved making cappuccino with foam, like they did in the bars. It was a romance. He kept close to her, as if he needed her presence, caring, loving, funny, loyal. For two days. At the end of the second day Maria arrived at the Campo and sat on the statue's steps with Gabriele, smoking a cigarette. At about eight o'clock she saw Ugo coming from St. Mark's direction, accompanied by a friend.

At least, she was a friend until today, because now she seemed to be something more.

He greeted her from afar, with a nod and an elusive smile. Maria's heart gave a thump and fell from where it had been until then to the pits of her stomach, heavy as a stone.

Nausea made of pain, a mixture of well-known suffering, humiliation and anger, came over her, but it wasn't a surprise. History was repeating itself and she, stupid, had fallen for it once again. He looked very busy, going over and talking to his friends, then returning to his lady-friend, who looked at him with desire. Occasionally he glimpsed at Maria, who was glancing at him out of the corner of her eye. He didn't approach her.

Hurt and embarrassed, she dared not go near him. She couldn't bear any more hypocrisy. When he left the Campo in the direction he had come from, holding his friend by the hand, her heart sank. How could she have fallen for it again? Why had she believed he had changed? Stupid, stupid, stupid! She had to take responsibility for her life. After all, India had meant something, right? 'You're the Treasure Tower', she told herself, 'Respect yourself. Okay, he has taken you in again, so what? It starts from now, a new life, a new beginning. Thank you Ugo, I obviously needed this test, again!' She would start from now, and without drowning her misery in alcohol, as she had before going to India. This time she didn't need it.

She returned home and began to chant for her happiness, focusing on a dot on the white wall. She didn't chant for his happiness, he seemed quite capable of taking care of it himself. 'For now I'll chant for my own happiness, I need it', she thought: Nam-myoho-renge-kyo, Nam-myoho-renge-kyo, Nam-myoho-renge-kyo. She shook off the shame, the humiliation, the embarrassment, the longing, the pain she felt in her heart, the desire, the selective memories. She looked to the future: a wide road was open, full of light and of things to create, travels to go on, colours and pictures to paint, stories to write, new friends to meet, old friends to see again, a cheerful future, lively, bright, clean and new. She was surprised to feel that her heart desired Ugo's happiness too, and she let it; why not? May he be happy, in whichever way he wanted. She went to bed feeling calm, dignified and proud of herself. She concentrated on deep breathing and fell asleep easily. Goodbye Ugo, welcome back Maria!

The next day a letter arrived from Jean-Claude. He had returned to Paris, was back at work and was very busy. He had printed the photos taken in India and she was in many of those taken in Varanasi. He missed her a lot and wanted to see her. Was she thinking of him? What was she doing? Instead of replying right away, Maria wrote to the three French friends she had met in Kathmandu and who had invited her over, asking if they could host her for a week or two. She had worked in Paris two years before and knew a lot of people; it would be a good opportunity to see old friends.

Jean-Claude had his girlfriend, she knew, but he also had Maria. Luna had told her to give him time to think, to not give up without letting him have a chance to look inside himself. She would do just that. She would go to Paris, but be independent of him, leaving him free to do as he wanted, with no pressure.

She filled those days painting as much as possible, building her future, stroke after stroke, yellow after red, green after blue, black next to purple. She painted one picture after another, without a break, admiring her work, stretching her tired back, studying the next project while resting in the rocking chair. Keith Jarrett with his piano, Bob Dylan blaring and Maria singing along full blast. She had no time to waste, especially if she was going away for two weeks. The reply from Eve came quickly. She was welcome, it said, and she could stop as long as she wanted, the house was big and everyone was looking forward to welcoming her; Sylvan and Pierrot sent her a hug. She replied to Jean-Claude's letter. She would go to Paris and would call him from her friends' house.

27. Thank you Van Gogh

The train arrived at the Gare de Lyon as the sun was setting. As she walked slowly toward the exit Maria looked around the crowd, and finally recognized Sylvan, with his shoulder-length blond curly hair, standing next to Eve, waving her arm in the air. They embraced tightly, memories of the days spent together in Kathmandu vivid as if it were yesterday. Outside the large station a rather beaten-up pale blue 'deux chevaux' was waiting for them; the driver was their father. About forty years old, Didier was a nuclear physicist who, despite such a serious profession, was friendly, open and fun.

Shortly before nine o'clock the car stopped in front of a house in the suburbs of Paris, surrounded by a beautiful garden full of fruit trees: they had arrived. 'You must be hungry, are you tired?' they asked with concern. Pierrot came out to meet them, happy to see her, and introduced her to the six or seven friends in the house. Maria discovered that the house was often full of young people, with Didier always inventing something interesting to do. Sylvan who, with his seventeen years of age was the youngest of all, showed her to her room, overlooking the garden and with its own bathroom. She could stay as long as she wanted, he said, and invited her to come downstairs straight away, dinner was ready. They all ate together and then did a treasure hunt which had been organized in the afternoon, partly in the house and partly in the garden. She was tired from the journey, but Didier insisted that she join in. She had a great time and, at the end of the game, felt as if she had known them all for years.

The next day they showed her where to find the breakfast things and explained how to get to Paris: she had to catch a bus to the train station and, from there, the underground to the city centre. She could use the phone, do whatever she wanted. She asked if she could bring a friend. But of course, anything at all. Then they all disappeared, one to work, the others to the library of the college where they studied, and Maria found herself alone in the house. She had Jean-Claude's telephone number but, all of a sudden, she felt paralysed by uncertainty. It was Saturday; maybe he would be at home. With the note in her hand, sweating from the tension, she couldn't make up her mind to dial the number.

She went into the garden, explored it well all around the house, looked at the fruit trees, the green shrubs, the colourful flowers; it was a well-kept garden, but, though she was looking at it, she couldn't see anything. She forced herself to calm down: she'd stop here for a few days, visit Paris, the art galleries would give her a lot of inspiration for her paintings, and she'd see the friends from the Petit Gavroche, the bistro where she often went for dinner. With a pounding heart, sweaty palms and her stomach in a knot, she went back into the house and picked up the phone; it slipped from her hands and she had to dry them on her shirt. And what if Céline answered? Maria decided that, if she couldn't handle it, she could always hang up. Nam-myoho-renge-kyo, Nam-myoho-renge-kyo; she took a deep breath: I came here for him, go for it! She pressed the numbers one by one. It rang a few times, perhaps there wasn't anyone in; she was so nervous she thought she might faint.

"Oui?" said a woman's voice.

"Est ce que Jean-Claude il est là?" she said, asking if he was at home.

"Oui, un moment," said the woman's voice and then asked who was on the phone.

"Maria," she said, with dry lips.

She heard the woman's voice call him: "Jean-Claude? It's for you, Marià," she cried, putting the accent on the last letter of her name. She could hang up now if she wanted to, she couldn't think straight, her mind and heart were in turmoil. Nam-myoho-renge-kyo, Nam-myoho-renge-kyo. An Italian saying came to mind: 'You've stepped onto the dance floor, you might as well dance, Maria!'

"Oui?" said Jean-Claude's voice; she could tell he was holding his breath. It was the first time she heard his voice over the phone.

"Hello Jean-Claude, it's Maria!" Her cheeks were burning, she felt hot all over and her hands were shaking.

"Hello, how are you? Where are you?" he said. She heard his surprise, the confusion sweeping over him.

"I'm fine. I'm in Paris." The silence at the other end seemed to last an eternity. She sat down on the stool, her legs trembling, her heart in her throat.

"Are you free this afternoon?" he asked. Her heart did a somersault and her stomach unknotted.

"Sure! Shall we meet?"

"Of course! Where is best for you?"

"At Notre Dame, is that possible? It's my favourite place!"

"That's fine, at what time? About four o'clock?"

"Yes, four is fine."

"Wait for me if I'm late, it's difficult to park around there, I'll come by bike."

"I'll wait, don't worry," she said, with a big smile.

There was another long pause and then Jean-Claude said: "What a surprise!"

And she laughed, happy.

She took a bath and chanted 'daimoku' to calm down and transform the insecurity she felt into calm certainty. She had time and chanted for one hour, watching the branches of the trees in the garden. She felt part of it, made of the same substance as those trees, the birds, the air she was breathing and, at the end of that hour, she felt better, relaxed, confident that it was going to be a beautiful day. Now that she knew Jean-Claude was happy to see her again, she asked herself how *she* felt about seeing him again. Would she feel the same attraction for him as when she was in India? Was she going to like him now as much as she liked him then? Had he changed? Had she changed? Life changed people, but so did places, and Paris was not Varanasi. If she thought of him as a friend, would she have any doubts, any worries, any anxiety? No, absolutely none. And so she would wait for him as a friend, trusting that things would develop naturally.

She caught the bus to the station and boarded the train to Paris. Then, by metro, she came to Boulevard Saint Michel shortly after three o'clock; it was an area she knew well. She walked along the boulevard, but the clothes and shoe stores didn't interest her. She took a road that led to a small square where there was the gothic church of Saint Séverin, which had been her refuge on many occasions during the months she had lived in Paris. It was deserted and Maria sat down on one of the dark wooden benches near the main door.

The sunlight streamed in through the stained glass windows, carrying different hues on multicoloured bands that danced in the clouds of dust and played on the stone walls. When she had come here in the past there had often been an organist who played, doing his practice throughout the late afternoon hours, filling the church with a dreamy atmosphere. Today, instead, there was silence and it was beautiful even so. She looked around, at the ceiling, to her right, to her left, she recited 'daimoku' in her head, to fill it with good vibrations and keep it free from the negative thoughts that competed with one another: Ugo, Céline, she who was not welcome. No! Transform this insecurity! She chanted to enjoy the present moment and the beautiful church she was in, to savour the atmosphere of Paris, to enjoy what was in store for her, whatever it was; she trusted her life.

More confident, but still nervous, she left the church and returned briefly to the boulevard, full of traffic and people, and headed toward the

Seine. She crossed the road; there, over the tall parapet, was the big green river running fast and strong, cutting in two the wonderful city she loved. Notre Dame was on her right, imposing, proud, solid and stunningly beautiful on the outside, moving on the inside; it was waiting for her. She considered it an old friend and knew it would welcome her with poise and grandeur. The booksellers' stalls along the Seine's parapets sold the same books and the same prints as two years before; nothing had changed. Maria looked at them superficially; there was nothing that could attract her attention, her mind was elsewhere. She went over to the parapet and watched the boats that sailed, some fast, loaded with goods, others slow, full of tourists who had the pleasure of seeing Paris from the 'bateau mouche', on the green water. She walked slowly, admiring 'her' cathedral approaching at every step, and soon arrived in the large square.

She still had ten minutes to wait and took the opportunity to enter, stopping just inside the main door, absorbing that grey, bare and clean immensity. She looked up, ready to feel the dizziness that the height of the cathedral always provoked in her and that, as expected, she experienced. She sat on one of the pews and looked around, breathing in the atmosphere and that special smell she remembered.

At four she went out onto the cathedral square; she looked around, but couldn't see him. She sat on a low wall, trying not to get her white jeans dirty, and observed the tourists who took pictures of the cathedral and of themselves. Couples on their honeymoon, families with teenage children, kids running around chasing pigeons, young people with sleeping bags and backpacks, pensioners arriving on organized coaches, a variety of people, of humanity, was filling only part of the huge square. She took out her small mirror and checked her makeup; she added a little gloss to her lips, and then quickly put it back in her bag. It was quarter past four and still no sign of Jean-Claude. She smoothed her long hair, checked her unvarnished fingernails, brushed the dust motes off her sandals and smoothed her trousers from the knee down. She lit a cigarette and smoked it without enjoying it, looking around. She adjusted the sleeves of the embroidered white silk shirt bought in Delhi, straightened the satin waistcoat from Pokhara, but still no Jean-Claude. It was already half past four. From her bag she pulled out some mints and put one in her mouth; she counted the silver bracelets, six of them; adjusted her anklets, and waved her toes, looking down at her toenails, painted pink. Why wasn't he coming? The certainty and calm she had previously felt were being besieged by the long wait, the empty minutes passing inexorably slowly. Nam-myoho-renge-kyo. He would come, she banished her doubt.

And finally she saw him. He wore blue jeans and a black leather jacket; in his hand he held a motorcycle helmet. He hadn't seen her yet. His hair was longer than when they were in Varanasi and he walked in that particular way, as if he had springs under his feet. He was approaching quickly toward the cathedral's main entrance, looking left and right. Maria stood up and he saw her. She felt herself blush with excitement and saw a wave of emotion sweep across Jean-Claude's face, who hastened toward her. She approached quickly through the crowd of passers-by and tourists who occupied the square and soon she found herself in his arms. Jean-Claude held her close and kissed her hair; then he moved slightly away, holding her by the shoulders, looking fully into her eyes, at her mouth, her cheeks, her forehead. He held her hands and bent down to kiss her on the lips. "What a surprise!" he said.

She laughed. "Are you happy to see me?" she asked.

He pulled her close to him again: "Very happy... And a little surprised, I didn't know when you'd arrive."

Maria looked at him. "Was it Céline who answered the phone?"

"Yes."

"Does she know about me?"

"No," he replied, without hesitation.

"And do you want to be with me?"

"Why do you think I'm here?" He hugged her again and held her close, looking into her eyes. "These blue eyes," he said, moved, serious, and kissed her again, this time a longer kiss.

She wanted to fill her eyes with the image of his face, but there was no hurry, they had time. She was happy. Despite being in a different country, despite the autumn clothes and the months that had passed, they were finding each other again.

"What shall we do?" he asked. "Shall we walk?" He put his arm around her shoulders and kissed her again. How was Michel? He was fine and how was Franca? Ah, that was a long story. She told him what had happened, how things had gone, and Jean-Claude listened more and more serious, worried, and finally angry. "But how could she do something like that? I didn't think she was such a person, even though I saw little of her," he said. "I tremble at the thought of what you risked, Maria. If you had been caught...! I can't even think of where you would be now, instead of being here with me!" He stopped and, looking into her eyes, held her by the shoulders. "Do you realize how important you are to me?" he asked.

No, she didn't realize, she didn't know how much he cared about her. She always played it down, preferring to think she wasn't important; in this way she protected herself from pain and disappointment, even if Luna had insisted that she *was* important. This was something that was going to take some time before she could believe it, it wasn't easy. She told him about the changes in her life, her decision to leave work, paint and return to India. He was surprised, but didn't try to make her change her mind.

"And you? Let's talk about you now! How did India affect you? Has it changed your life in any way?" she asked.

He spoke with irony: "Has it changed my life? And who is this beautiful, sensual, irresistible woman who came from Venice?" He pulled her close to his side. "It has changed my life and has brought me you." He looked at her with those hazel eyes with shades of green and gold flecks, and that ironic, smiling expression she had learned to love and trust.

They walked for a long time, talking of their travels and adventures in India, of what they did after they left each other at Varanasi station. The memory of the days and nights spent together brought them closer, moment after moment, but they were no longer in India and the atmosphere of Paris was light-years away from that of Varanasi. Jean-Claude was not free, he lived with his girlfriend. Maria sensed that he was glad to see her, but also very confused, and she understood why.

They went for dinner at the Petit Gavroche, 'her' bistro in the heart of the Marais district, where she had made many friends two years before. The bistro had long wooden tables and benches, and those who chose to order the fixed price menu sat wherever there was an empty place; it was a foolproof way to meet new people and she used to go there almost every night. When they entered, the bartender broke into a smile and walked around the bar to greet her, kissing her four times, the Parisian way. While waiting for their dinner, some of her old friends came in; one after another they recognized her and came to their table, to tell her the latest news, as if she had left just the week before. Jean-Claude was impressed by how many people she knew. Maria wanted him to know that, even if she had come to Paris for him, she was not alone. She wished him to feel free to do whatever he wanted, without any pressure; if he wanted to see her, he would do so out of choice, not out of obligation.

After dinner they walked in the cool early October evening. One step after the next, she remembered why he had struck her so deeply: he was kind and made her laugh; he was light-hearted, ironic and funny. They went down the steps leading to the deserted sidewalks along the Seine, where the river lapped the stone banks. They walked hand in hand up to the extreme point of the island of Saint Louis, they talked and hugged, and found once again the taste of their kisses. Jean-Claude warmed her hands inside his, blowing his warm breath on her cold fingers, rubbing them between his palms. He took her back to the village on his motorbike. Maria clung to him, her cheek resting on his back.

Didier's extended family welcomed them warmly, showing only a slight surprise in seeing her with a boyfriend who, until then, they didn't know existed. Jean-Claude endeared himself with his simple, friendly ways and, as soon as they could, they withdrew. Maria closed her bedroom door, Jean-Claude kissed her and made her sit on the bed; he removed her waistcoat, unbuttoned her shirt. She embraced him... but something was wrong. Beneath the kisses she felt his confusion, the inner battle, the lack of freedom. A strong feeling of uneasiness made her open her eyes; Jean-Claude was on top of her, they hadn't made love. She looked into his eyes, so beautiful, so close. "You'd better go now. It's late," she whispered.

He raised himself on one arm, looking at her. "Est ce que tu comprends?" he asked. 'Do you understand?'

Maria nodded in silence. "Yes," she said, quietly.

Jean-Claude stood up and began to dress. She followed him with her eyes as he buttoned his shirt, slipped his jeans on. He did his shoes up, pushed his shirt into his trousers. She felt heavy as a stone. He leaned down and kissed her on the lips. He walked to the door; with his hand on the door handle he turned to her and, in the dim light, he said: "Je t'aime, je le sais." 'I love you, I know it.' In his eyes was the same sadness she felt within herself, unable to move or speak. She nodded slightly. The door closed gently. She heard the sound of the motorbike and closed her eyes. She listened to it fading and, in the silence of the night, followed it for a long time, while he went..., back home.

She didn't contact him again, she couldn't. Now only he could make that move; if and when was up to him to decide. She spent most of that week in the centre of Paris, going to all the art galleries, of which there were many, looking at contemporary artists' paintings, perceiving their inspiration, studying their techniques, their choice of colours and subjects, learning from every one of them, absorbing like a sponge. She strolled around flea markets and returned to dine at the Petit Gavroche. Often she spent the night at some friends' house in the neighbourhood, phoning home to let her friends know she wasn't coming back. Didier insisted that she did so; he wanted to be sure she was well and safe. She spent the weekend with him and his extended 'family' in the countryside, where he had organized a sack race, team games that made them run to exhaustion, a chocolate eggs hunt. They were a group of about a dozen, with a big picnic and determined to have a lot of fun.

It had been almost a week when Jean-Claude rang. "When can we meet?" he asked.

"Why do you want to meet?" she said. She felt distant; her mechanism of self-protection from pain had been working efficiently.

"What do you mean?" he asked, shocked by the tone of her voice. "I have all the photos of Varanasi and you're in many. I want to show them to you... and I want to see you."

"I didn't know whether you'd ever phone… and I started to think that maybe it hadn't been such a good idea to come to Paris."

"I had to work, I have many things to do and... I had to think. It's not easy for me," he said, more honestly. She knew it wasn't easy, and she understood; and after all she had come to Paris to see him. "Okay. I want to see you too."

She sat on a bench in the sunshine in the Parc du Luxembourg, waiting for him. She watched fathers playing football with their children, a boy and a girl sitting on a bench, kissing and fondling, creating a vacuum around them. An old man with a full head of white hair came up with a bag in his hand, limping; he was followed by dozens of ducks and geese who clearly recognized him and waddled, clinging to his legs. The old man sat down on a bench next to Maria's and, from the bag he pulled out chunks of dry bread, which the ducks took from his hand, crowding around him, speaking their own language, kwa-kwa-kwa. The old gentleman called each bird by a different name: Brigitte, Marlene, Sofià, Anità, all famous actresses' names. Maria couldn't help but laugh! There were also male names: Frederick, Ingemar, Rossellinì, Chaplìn! Of course! Charlie Chaplin couldn't be missing, they all walked like him! Baudelaire, Hugo, and even Rousseau, they all received their piece of bread.

Jean-Claude caught her by surprise; she hadn't heard him arrive. He sat down beside her and hugged her. He was happy, full of things to show her, glad that she had come. He pulled out envelopes full of photographs taken in Varanasi. There were those taken at four in the morning, when she couldn't get up to accompany him; they were extraordinary. He had captured a special energy, the moving atmosphere of the pyres while they were being prepared and then lit in the dim light of dawn, suffused with the mist rising from the sacred river.

There were those he had taken on the boat while crossing the Ganges, others taken in the deserted temples on the opposite shore, of Maria and the surrounding architecture. There were photos taken at the Yogi Lodge in which she recognized the young manager, Michel, Franca, and herself of course, with that white sarong wrapped around her body which left little to the imagination. She looked at Jean-Claude and their eyes hooked for a moment.

"Show me the others," she said quickly, blushing, her cheeks red hot. As she looked at the other photos she remembered with how much freedom she had invited him to kiss her, the overwhelming passion between them during that week, when they were completely immersed in the present moment, becoming friends, lovers, and travel companions. She knew he had his girlfriend, she just wanted to be happy and for him to be happy, while it lasted. It had been a magical week with a man who adored her. Even if she was never to see him again, what he had given her was immeasurable. And now they were together again, and this was more than she had thought possible. These moments with him were a gift, a present she hadn't even dreamt of while they were in Varanasi. She turned to look at him while he was describing the photos.

She was grateful for what she had received and wasn't going to ask for anything more than he could give; she wasn't going to let arbitrary expectations spoil these precious moments. She kissed him unexpectedly, surprising him, letting him know she loved him and was happy to be here with him. Jean-Claude turned toward her and stopped talking. He looked longingly at her, kissed her, and then kissed her again. He stroked her breast and Maria pushed his hand away; they were like the kids on the other bench. They got up and, holding hands, walked in silence to his motorbike. He drove toward the village and she kept close to him, her head resting on his back, sheltering from the wind, on another sunny October afternoon.

There was nobody in the house. Jean-Claude picked her up and carried her into her room, laughing, playing, happy in that magical moment, alone and undisturbed. They found each other again at last, and let their hands, their bodies, kisses, smiles, laughter talk for them. They let the passion that had swept them off their feet in Varanasi come over them once more, in that room overlooking the garden, with trees swaying gently in the breeze, birds flying from one branch to another, and nature welcoming them with calm and simplicity, just as they were. They rested, hugging each other, her head on his chest, his arm holding her close, his hand caressing her. She had no questions, no unresolved doubt, nothing else to ask for. She knew that he loved her, in whatever way he could, and she was happy to love this man. He spent the whole evening with her and her French friends, blending easily into that special, motherless family, with Didier being the father, the mother, everybody's friend, generous, and more youthful than his children. Jean-Claude stayed the night and woke up early the next morning: "It's sunny outside. Let's go for breakfast at the café in the square!" They ordered 'café au lait' and croissants and sat at a table in the sunshine, grateful for this late autumn sun.

Almost another week went by before he called her again. Her money was dwindling and she had to return to Venice to work. Jean-Claude was shocked to hear she was soon to leave and arrived the same evening. They went for dinner at a bistro near the village and then he stayed the night. They were finding each other, every time a little more, every time it was easier.

The following night she dreamed of Céline; it was a very simple dream.

Jean-Claude was in front of a woman who was leaning against the wall outside one of Paris' cafes, her hands behind her back. He was leaning with his elbow against the wall and looking at her with love. Holding his face close to hers, he spoke with confidence and familiarity. Her face was lined, but pretty. Maria liked this woman's face, but she could see that she was suffering; she felt her anguish, and a feeling of nausea blocked her throat. She knew that the time had come to leave. She left, unnoticed. Later she was told that Jean-Claude was looking for her everywhere, but couldn't find her.

She woke up covered in sweat; it was a relief to be awake. The face of the woman in the dream stayed with her throughout the day, as if she had really seen her, and so did the anxiety and the nausea. She sensed that Céline knew about her. It was time to go back home. She told Didier of her intention to leave the next morning and he told her decisively to keep herself free for the rest of the day; he was going to take her somewhere special. Maria packed her bag with the few things she had brought from Italy and then made the call.

"Oui?" said Céline. Jean-Claude was not at home.

"It's Maria," she said, as if she had known her all along. "I'd like to leave a message for him. I'm leaving immediately for Italy. Can you please let him know?"

"Yes, I'll tell him!"

"Thank you, goodbye."

"Goodbye," said Céline, without anger.

The phone rang a few minutes later, it was Jean-Claude; she couldn't leave just like that, he protested, he wanted to see her.

But in her heart, Maria had already left, feeling she was doing the right thing. "I've been here three weeks and we've seen each other three times," she replied; he had had many opportunities to see her, she thought. "It was beautiful, but now I have to go."

He had to work, protested Jean-Claude, if she didn't understand that she couldn't understand him; she was a hard woman, he said. He had understood exactly what Maria had not expressed in words.

"That's not true," replied Maria. "I care about you."

"Je t'aime," he said, 'I love you'.

"I love you too," she said before saying goodbye, and it was the truth.

The bag for her trip was ready, laid on the bed in her room, the zipper closed. She turned to Didier who was waiting for her: "Where are we going?"

"It's a surprise. You'll like it. Let's get in the car!" He had taken a day off work to spend it with her.

In Didier's pale blue 'deux chevaux' they took the road to Paris. While Maria filled her eyes with the historical sites, Didier took care of the traffic and parked near Place de la Concorde. He took her by the arm and led her to a stone building that Maria knew well: Jeu de Paume, it contained the masterpieces of the Impressionists, the giants of French and European painting.

"How did you know that this was my favourite museum?" she asked.

"Because I'm smart!" he replied. "Come on, Maria, for a painter this place is crucial. You'll go home with your eyes full of colours, your head full of ideas and your heart full of inspiration; you won't be able to stop your hands from painting. I wanted to give you a gift before you left, and this is my gift."

They went from room to room, admiring Matisse, Monet, standing speechless in front of Gauguin, Van Gogh, Pissarro, Renoir; all the paintings she loved were there, close at hand. Each one was a work that the painter had done with his own hands, had studied with care and passion, into which he had poured his whole life. In front of the Van Gogh painting of the peasants resting in the shade of a haystack, Maria imagined the young Vincent standing in front of the easel, with paintbrush and colours, his jacket and trousers worn out and dusty, his mind wandering, but always brought back by him to the subject. From his eyes to his shoulder, from the shoulder to his arm, and then down to his hand, his life flowed into and through the paintbrush, on the very canvas that was now in front of her. For many people this was one of Van Gogh's most famous paintings, worth a priceless figure, but for Maria it was the young Vincent's life itself. That canvas had absorbed, for hours on end, his fight against the demons that fluttered in his head; it was the expression of the life force that had supported him, and of the emotions that had pushed and tormented him, throughout his short life, urging him to paint in such a unique, personal, touching way. In the works of Van Gogh, she felt his cry of pain, the confusion of his mind's incessant clamour, but also the joy of being alive, quivering with the colours that fed the creation of such beauty. Maria felt like talking to him: 'Thank you Vincent, for what you gave us. What a life, your life. It was short but you gave so much. I wonder if you knew at the time. If you didn't, I'm telling you now: I feel your emotions and they make me feel rich. Our lives, yours, one hundred years ago and mine now, are connected by this thread, the energy of the universe itself, that you've been able to paint in a way that touches my heart. Nam-myoho-renge-kyo is my thank you, a 'kiss' that I'm sending you now, on the tips of my fingers.'

Didier touched her arm and awoke her from her daydream. He didn't talk much, indeed almost nothing, and made no comments; he absorbed those works of art in his own way. Maria didn't know what he was thinking, she didn't know him well enough, but they walked together, sometimes close, sometimes on the opposite sides of a room. They spent the whole afternoon in that way. They stopped to have a cup of tea in the museum's cafe and he told her that her face had changed since they had entered. "There's a light now that wasn't there before," he said.

"It's all these wonderful works of art, the energy of these artists who painted a hundred, a hundred fifty years ago, filling all these canvasses with the essence of their life. I'm absorbing the energy they have captured in these paintings, and we are so lucky to see them so close we can almost touch them."

"You 'feel' the paintings, don't you?" he asked, watching her closely.

"Yes, but it's the first time this has happened to me. I had never before perceived this deep connection, so strongly, from life to life, and I feel like there are no boundaries, no limits or age, it spans the centuries and reaches me directly, clear, without intermediaries."

"I had never thought of it that way," said Didier, thoughtful.

"Neither had I. Looking at Gauguin's paintings, for example, I felt the warmth of the sun he felt on his skin while sketching the first outlines of the women, and when he painted them, under the shade of a canopy, with his hat on, driving away the flies that buzzed around him. I seemed to be there with him, actually..." She stopped; a feeling was making its way into her heart, timid but certain.

"What are you thinking? Come on, say it! You can say anything you want," he encouraged her.

"I felt so identified with him, Gauguin, but also Van Gogh before him, that I felt I *was* them, as if I were in their skin, feeling the colours as they felt them at that very moment."

Didier smiled in amusement. "What? Both Gauguin *and* Van Gogh?"

"Not only the two of them, even though they were the strongest. I felt that way in front of all the paintings I've seen, I felt the flow of their lives into mine. I don't know if I am explaining myself well!"

"Maybe it's what we call inspiration...?" suggested Didier.

"I don't know, perhaps; it's a force of life... it's something I felt even in your garden."

He looked at her with surprise; he wanted to know what she had 'felt' in his garden. She told him how she felt connected to the trees, to the leaves moving in the breeze, to the birds, busy flying from branch to branch, chirping and hopping, to the flowers that opened with the sun's heat and closed to protect themselves from the night's cold. She told him she perceived those things while chanting her phrase, feeling connected to the whole universe. Didier was listening; there was no sarcasm in his eyes. He said only that he was glad to have met her and wanted her to write 'the' sentence on a restaurant's napkin, which he folded carefully and put in his pocket. "Before you go we'll chant it together; I want to see if I feel like you did, when I look at my garden. It will never be the same, now that you've described it this way."

That evening they all ate together in the large kitchen, then Didier wanted to chant the 'daimoku' and all the young friends joined in. For a few minutes they recited it slowly together, self conscious at first, then more and more focused, listening to that incredible sound that made their body vibrate, starting from the heart. They were minutes of pure magic, ten voices joined in, each one with its own tone, character, personality, and created a harmonious chorus that shook the walls of the house and soaked them with joy. When they finished, everyone remained in a suspended, enchanted silence, when they could just hear their breathing; and then they burst into a spontaneous applause, thanking Maria for sharing her 'secret'.

They went to bed very late. Didier woke her up at six o'clock with a cup of coffee. "After breakfast I'll take you to the Gare de Lyon," he said, and she knew that he was sad to see her go. With many hugs she said goodbye to Sylvan, Eve and Pierrot, and invited them all to come to Venice. They had given her hospitality and, more importantly, a friendship that would last forever. She climbed into the car with Didier, for the last time. At the station he hugged her: "Come back, Maria, whenever you want. We'll always be very happy to see you. And call when you get home. I want to be sure that you got back safe and sound!" She was moved by his affection.

It was already dark when she arrived in Venice and walked slowly toward her house with the bag over her shoulder, breathing deeply. She crossed the Bridge of Fists; the fruit seller on the boat was closing up and, recognizing her, greeted her cheerfully: "Travelling again?"

"I just got back from Paris," she said.

"Mamma mia! What an adventuress! Take this," he said, handing her a red apple, big and polished. Maria thanked him and bit into the fresh juicy fruit. She threw the core in a bin near her house and opened the front door. In the letter box she found an aerogramme from Franca, from Nepal. Anger swept over her at the thought of the risk she had put her through, but quickly her rage turned to relief, seeing herself in the entrance hall of her house, safe and free. She put it in her pocket and walked slowly up the two flights of stairs.

She opened the door; everything was as she left it, the same smell, the same cosy walls. She put her bag down and went straight to the bathroom. In the shower, under the hot water, she savoured the memories still fresh of Didier and her friends' kindness and friendship, Jean-Claude's voice, his face, his hands, his kisses. She took a cup of tea to bed; she wasn't yet ready to leave Paris behind. She saw Notre Dame and Jean-Claude arriving with his helmet in his hand, she went through the moments when they walked up to the tip of the island of St. Louis, the thrill of holding tight onto him on his bike, to shelter from the wind and to feel close. Those beautiful memories belonged to her forever. She was glad she went to Paris, saw him again and spent those precious hours together. She opened Franca's pale blue aerogramme; it had been posted from Pokhara.

28. Believe in yourself

Franca had received her letter telling her of the backpack's disappearance; she was very sorry, she wrote, with all those beautiful things she had bought! I bet you're sorry, thought Maria, her anger mounting inside, uncontrollable; if Franca had been there she would have hit her. She hoped the backpack would be found. Really? By whom, the police? Maria replied to the non-existent interlocutor. For the rest, she was pretty well; she was recovering from hepatitis and had gone to Pokhara for a period of convalescence. She was thinking of returning home at the end of October and was hoping to see her. Yes, so I can strangle you right away, thought Maria.

She folded the aerogramme; she had no desire to see Franca, either now or ever. She would talk with Ester and let her handle the situation. The sale of the things she had brought from India was going well, it had raised quite a lot of money, but if she wanted to return to India for six months, she was going to need a lot more. There was cash coming in from the sale of the charas and the opium, Ester said it belonged to her, but Maria didn't want it, it was 'ugly, dirty' money, which wouldn't bring her any joy, or luck. She remembered the story Patrizia had told them about her husband addicted to opium, of how he had ruined his life and had died young, a wasted life. She wasn't going to touch that money.

Instead, she went back to painting, making full use of the inspiration she had brought from Paris; it was nourishing her, day by day. She got up early, as if to go to work, recited 'daimoku', focusing on a fixed dot on the white wall, until she was ready to begin a new day. She remembered to set her determinations and one thing in particular had impressed her: Luna had told her that she imagined her life in ten years and twenty years time, in detail. Where did she want to be? With whom? Doing what? She told her that she chanted to understand the answer to these questions, by asking her heart. And she? Where did Maria want to be at the age of thirty-four? She didn't know yet. Who did she want to be with? To this question she already had an answer: she wanted to be with a man she loved and who loved her and to have a child. Doing what? Again, the answer was not clear yet, but she would like to paint, maybe write and use her knowledge of foreign languages, which she had studied for many years. Strangely, a phrase in English often came to her mind, when she was chanting or when she was about to fall asleep, and the phrase was 'I don't think so!' Who knew where it came from, but it made her smile: it showed a healthy contradictory spirit. With an open heart, a whole new life to be written, Maria lived one day at a time, with an eye on the future. She'd stand in front of the easel and let her hand draw what her heart dictated, choosing the colours as she went along. Her work was growing, painting after painting; she'd become very fond of them, but she had to let them go. The art gallery was selling her smaller works, Ester had sold almost all the things that had arrived in her backpack, but still she didn't have enough money to return to India.

One morning, in her letterbox, she found a postcard from England with a picture of Queen Elizabeth, from Sanya in London. It said she had a job that would take her to Cortina d'Ampezzo for three days; she would arrive at Venice airport and was asking if she had time to meet up with her. Maria checked the dates: it was Monday and Sanya would arrive on Tuesday, tomorrow. Excitedly, she ran up the two flights of stairs, jumping with joy.

The plane from London landed on time; Maria had been waiting eagerly for half an hour when Sanya walked through the sliding doors; she ran to her and they hugged tightly. Sanya looked beautiful in autumn clothes. Maria's heart was bursting with joy. She hadn't known whether she would ever see her again and certainly didn't expect their reunion to be so soon.

"How are you?" Sanya asked her, her hazel eyes lit by glowing specks of gold.

"Great, now that I see you," replied Maria. "I've made some important decisions. I quit my job and I'm going back to India in January!"

Sanya let out that laugh that came from her belly: "You have to tell me everything! How much time do you have?"

"I am free, what about you?"

"They're coming to pick me up at midday to take me to the mountains."

They had little more than an hour. Sanya was filming a commercial for a Swiss cheese. They laughed out loud, excited, happy to see each other again; it seemed a miracle to be together! Both she and Colin were fine; the trip to India had given him much material to work with and he was busy. She was working in television and theatre, in addition to these short and well paid advertising jobs. In front of two cappuccinos with a lot of cocoa-speckled froth, they rediscovered their precious friendship.

Maria told her of the decisions she had taken, and about Franca, who had sent her around the world with a backpack full of drugs; of her trip to Paris and Jean-Claude whom she had seen three times in twenty days; of Ugo, who took her and then left her, as he had done before she went to India. In Venice, she had few friends.

Her friend didn't say a word until she was sure that Maria had emptied her heavy load. Then, her eyes full of affection, she touched her hand: "First of all, I am happy that you are safe and well. Your life was hugely protected. Do you realize that? I don't even want to think what could have happened. And then, they even delivered the backpack to your door. Amazing!"

Maria nodded and said: "I'm so shocked by what Franca did! How could she?"

Sanya observed her carefully. After a pause, she asked: "Didn't you think it was strange that they asked to borrow your backpack? Didn't you feel uncomfortable giving it to them?"

Of course it had seemed a bit strange, but she didn't know how to refuse; after all Franca was a guest in Vale's house, and... she hadn't had the courage to say no.

Sanya was serious: "In this case, you haven't taken responsibility for your life. If you had even a tiny doubt, a little instinct telling you it was dangerous, you should have said no. In life we must have courage, Maria. We will never be happy if we don't have courage. Do you realize that you have to take responsibility for that story?"

"*Me?*" said Maria, pointing her finger at herself, involuntarily raising her voice, incredulous. "And what about them? Are *they* not responsible for what they've done?"

"Of course! And the law of cause and effect will take its course, but if you want to learn something from what happened and transform your life, you have to understand what *your* responsibility was."

She hadn't been expecting this! She was sure she had been the victim, but now that she thought about it, something was already telling her that Sanya was right.

"And what do I do?"

"Do you chant 'daimoku' sometimes?"

"Yes, every day, at least ten minutes."

"Chant with gratitude for the protection that you received, and to find the courage, from now on, to do the right thing in every situation."

Maria nodded. She already had a lot of gratitude. Develop the courage then, and take responsibility. She knew she was too afraid to say or do something that others might disapprove of. She would have to remember that. They had little time and she moved to another subject on which she wanted some advice. "And Jean-Claude?" she said. "He was very sweet, but I only saw him three times in all those days."

"Did you know he had a girlfriend?" asked Sanya.

"Yes... sure," replied Maria, hesitant; was she going to tell her that it was her responsibility, again?

"And you were expecting something more from him, right?" Sanya added, with kindness.

"I would have liked to have seen more of him, after the long journey I made; after all he wrote telling me that he missed me!"

Her dear friend didn't speak immediately, she was thinking. Finally she said: "When we expect something and it doesn't happen, we're disappointed, unhappy; often we don't even appreciate what we have received, because it is not as we had imagined it. That's the problem with expectations; they can be a trap."

"That's true. When we did meet it was beautiful; we really found each other again."

"So you're grateful for what you have received?"

Maria thought before answering. "I should be, shouldn't I? Grateful for what I received. You're right. I knew he had a girlfriend, so what did I expect? For him to drop everything to be with me?"

"You and Jean-Claude have a great relationship, but it's not an easy situation. Be patient, chant for your happiness, and his, *and* his girlfriend's, and see what the future brings."

"If they are roses they will bloom, my mother says. Thank you Sanya, I'll do just that."

The minutes flew by and she had another question: "And Ugo? We got back together for two days and then he started to behave like he used to, going from one woman to another. I felt so humiliated. I don't want him any longer or, to be honest, I would, but I don't think he will ever change. I don't know what to do." Sanya waited for her to continue. Maria added: "I feel as if I don't matter to anyone, as if I were insignificant. I need to find confidence in myself."

Her friend smiled and nodded: "You know, when we don't appreciate ourselves, the environment will reflect this lack of esteem; it is a mirror of how we feel inside. Do you appreciate yourself?"

Again, Sanya had hit the mark; Maria had never had a high opinion of herself. She laughed, thinking about what her father, her grandmother and her sisters used to say. "Not much," she replied. "At home they always used to say that I was the third wheel, so I grew up thinking I wasn't important. They pointed it out to me all the time; but it's not a problem, I've become stronger."

"To think that you are strong is one thing, another is to have no self-esteem," Sanya replied promptly. "You must reflect on this Maria, you *are* important, we all are. And you have the right to be happy. *Decide* to be happy." She looked at her, serious; she wanted to make her understand how important what she was saying was. "Furthermore, there is a concept that, for me, was a revelation, like removing a blindfold from my eyes," said her friend. "Have you ever heard of the principle of external cause and internal cause?"

Maria shook her head.

Sanya leaned toward her, her eyes full of enthusiasm: "Imagine a glass of water that, at the bottom, has some sediment. If you don't touch it, the sediment settles on the bottom and the water looks clear but, if you shake it, the water becomes cloudy." She observed her to see whether she was following. Maria was imagining the glass and nodded. Sanya continued: "So, let's take the example of Jean-Claude, whom you saw only three times, or Ugo, who makes you suffer because he is unfaithful. They represent the external cause, the action of shaking the glass; this is not something you can change. Then, there is the internal cause, and that is represented by the sediment; if there were no sediment, you could shake the glass for hours, but the water would remain clear. So, this is an image to explain that the cause of your suffering is inside you. This, fortunately, is the thing that you *can* change."

"And how?" asked Maria, hopeful.

"Chant to appreciate yourself, to begin with, then put into practice the concept of 'transforming poison into medicine' and you'll change the way you respond," said Sanya. "If you accept that the pain you feel at this moment has a very important role in your life, that it is an opportunity to transform yourself and become happier, everything changes!" She observed Maria, who was listening carefully, reacting with surprise and interest to her explanation.

"You're talking about karma, aren't you? It scares me a little, this concept of karma," she confessed.

"Why should it scare you? I see our past karma as the 'starting point' from which we can begin to create a great life and a better future." Sanya paused, thinking of something that made her giggle, her eyes shining with mirth.

"Why are you laughing?" asked Maria.

"Because I have this funny image of each of us arriving into this world, carrying an old, battered suitcase, with our past karma inside," she said. She stood up and mimed, between the tables, the dragging along of a large, heavy piece of luggage, attracting amused looks from the people sitting around them. They both laughed, and Sanya sat down again;

grinning, she continued: "A bit at a time, as we grow up and go through life, some beautiful 'clothes' appear out of the suitcase: they are the good qualities we possess, such as kindness, vitality, creativity and so on. Other times instead, a dirty, smelly, dress turns up. Those are the parts of our karma that make us suffer, but that we can change."

"That's interesting!" said Maria, still laughing. "So, basically, if I want to change a part of my karma that makes me suffer, I have to wash the 'smelly dress'?"

"Exactly! And it's simple, even if I'm not saying it's easy!" her friend confirmed. "Decide that you'll use the present suffering to change that particular tendency *forever*. It's your own personal revolution! You *challenge* yourself to transform your fear, or timidity, into courage, the lack of self-esteem into dignity and self-respect. When you do this you become stronger and, eventually you'll be able to encourage other people who find themselves in similar situations, thus transforming your karma even faster. When we turn on a light for another, this will brighten our path, too!" She paused, smiling and observing Maria, who was listening to her, her eyes attentive. Then, leaning toward her, she continued with warmth: "How do you want your life to be? Chant to understand this, listen to your heart and paint a vivid picture in your mind, adding details, one by one. That picture will determine your future. Your life is in *your* hands, can you see? It's up to you whether you're happy, no-one else!"

"Really simple!" Maria said jokingly.

Her friend nodded in understanding: "You know, I realized that, in the end, the answer is always the same: take responsibility for your life and become stronger inside; transform it, digging deeper when necessary, develop the 'treasures of the heart' and become absolutely happy!" she concluded, with passion.

Maria nodded. She knew this was her chance to make the most of her friend's wisdom. "So, if we go back to the glass with water and sediment, the internal cause of my problems is my lack of self-esteem and not enough courage, is that it?" she asked.

Sanya looked at her, smiling with empathy: "From what you told me about Ugo and the story with your backpack, it seems that way. Those tendencies drove you into situations that made you suffer… and could have been much worse. By transforming them you will transform your future. Be grateful for the things that have happened so far, because they have led you to this realization. What's important is what you do from now on, the new causes you make!"

Maria nodded, deep in thought, a sense of hope, a confidence, rising in her heart.

The time had flown; Sanya saw a man with a chauffeur's cap come in, carrying a sign with her name and looking around. She waved her arm at him and, as he approached, she stood up and hugged her, holding her tight, cuddling her. "I'll find out if there are other people who practice in this area and will let you know. It's much nicer to practice together and one grows much more quickly. You, too, ask around, I'm sure there will be someone!" she said before taking her leave. It had been a memorable hour. They didn't know when they would meet again. Maria felt stronger, inspired and grateful for what her friend had taught her. She had a lot to reflect on!

"Chant to believe in your Buddhahood, to develop your potential; you can't imagine how enormous it is. Believe in yourself, Maria. You can become really happy!" Sanya said with empathy.

She cared a lot about her; Maria could feel her concern and loved her for it. "Thank you, Sanya. I'll see you soon, I hope!" She followed her friend with her eyes while she walked away with the driver, her heart full of gratitude. Before walking through the glass doors Sanya turned and, with a smile, she sent her a kiss and then shouted: "I love you!"

That same evening Ester told her she that had sold six paintings that Maria had now to paint. "What do you mean?" she asked. With her typical loud laughter, Ester explained that a friend of hers was re-designing his restaurant and she had persuaded him to include some abstract paintings, made by Maria; she now had to go and talk with him and decide on the colours. The price had already been agreed and the income would be enough for Maria to go to India mid-January. If she was happy with that, she could begin right away. To complete a picture of that size she would have to work intensely for more than a week; she had at least six weeks' work ahead of her. Maria rolled up her sleeves and got started!

Ugo came to see her one afternoon while she was painting, unannounced as always. He sat on the bed drinking the coffee he had prepared, watching her. He wanted to know about her trip to Paris; he suspected that she had someone else and didn't like it. He didn't want her for himself; however, if there was a risk that someone else would take her away, well… that was different. But Maria was no longer blind. When he finished his coffee she told him she had to leave. He came up to her and put his arm around her waist.

"The Paris air has done you good! You're more beautiful than usual," he said. She read the desire in his eyes, but felt only irritation toward him and wanted to get away.

"I have to go out. Come on, let's go!" She pushed him out and closed the door behind them. Outside the front door, he asked where she was going. "In the opposite direction to wherever you go!" she replied. "Leave me alone, Ugo. It really is time to put an end to this. Don't ever come to my house again!" She moved away, without waiting for his reply; she wasn't interested. She walked for a long time, to shake off that feeling of always repeating the same mistake, of going around biting her own tail. Bridge after bridge, she walked, sometimes she ran, releasing herself from that past that had no future, free, free, free! In San Mark's Square, she walked to the water's edge where, in the summer, many artists spent the days painting and selling their works. There was almost no one now, it was too cold and the tourists were few. She walked up to St. Elena's gardens and sat on a bench. She was feeling stronger. Was she changing her karma? She probably was, because she was taking responsibility for her life. She was no longer dominated by his whims, but she knew she had to continue to remain strong. Did she appreciate herself? Definitely more than she did before.

Franca arrived in Rome; Gabriele went to fetch her at the airport with two other friends. She had returned triumphant, bringing some opium that she was now selling without any discretion. Maria saw her one evening in Campo Santo Stefano and, despite the hurt feelings, the anger that didn't seem to subside and the desire to blurt out that she knew the whole truth, she was glad to see that she had recovered. The colour of her skin had returned to normal and so had her personality, fast, frenetic, always on the lookout for more excitement; she hadn't changed at all. Franca approached her, as if nothing had happened, as if she had a clear conscience, so much so that, for a moment, Maria wondered whether she knew that she had sent her around the world with a backpack full of drugs. Franca said she was sorry that the backpack had been lost but, at the same time, Maria felt that she didn't completely believe it and suspected someone had taken her loot. Ester was nearby and noticed Maria glancing at her. She walked over and joined in the conversation.

"Yes, what a pity it got lost! I heard that it happens quite often, when you change planes. Who knows, maybe it was stolen in Moscow, or Delhi, or even Rome. We'll never know," Ester said, lighting a cigarette. "People tell me you brought some opium from India. And, apparently, it's good!" she added.

"Yes, it's very good and I am selling out fast," confirmed Franca.

"Yes, everyone knows that you're selling it; you're not making a secret of it! In a little while even the drug squad's detectives might come and ask you for some," said Ester, taking a puff on her cigarette.

"What do you mean?" asked Franca, defensively.

"I mean that you're taking risks in selling it so openly. You talk loudly, here in the Campo; everybody knows you've got it. You must be more discreet! You don't know if there is someone listening who might grass you up," said Ester, taking another puff on her cigarette.

"I don't need your advice! I manage perfectly well by myself, thank you," retorted Franca, aggressive, but surprised.

"Carry on as you like, then! By the way, would you sell me a little piece, since it's so good?" Ester dropped the butt on the floor and stamped it out with her foot.

Franca was uncertain as to what to do. She knew that she could trust Ester not to denounce her, but she was irritated by her approach. She put her hand in her pocket and pulled out a small package. "This is one gram," she said. "It's twenty thousand lire."

Ester took out her wallet, pulled out two ten thousand lire banknotes, handed them to Franca, took the opium and put it in her pocket: "Thank you very much, but this goes to prove what I said before. Not only are you reckless and risk getting caught, but you also put all of us at risk, you for selling and us for using it. You're looking for trouble selling so openly!"

"And who the hell are you to tell me what I should do?" Franca raised her voice. "As if you were a goody two-shoes. I know that recently there was some other opium around here; know anything about it, do you?"

"Who, me? Of course not!" replied Ester, moving slightly away from Franca. "And even if I did, I certainly wouldn't come and tell you. It would be like broadcasting it over the radio!"

Maria was watching the exchange between the two women; other friends had noticed the beginning of a fight and all the attention was focused on them.

"Why don't you stop being such a bitch?" cried Franca. "First you buy my opium and then you tell me off. What the fuck do you want from me?"

Gabriele came over; everyone had heard what she had said and he was worried. "Franca, calm down!" he said. "Keep your voice down."

"Fuck off! Who asked you? All of you, smoking my opium and then throwing shit at me behind my back. You're real *shit*, the lot of you!" cried Franca.

"I don't say anything behind your back," said Ester. "I have no problem telling you what I think to your face. And I'll say it again: you're irresponsible, and stupid, too!"

"But… what do you want? A punch in the face?" screamed Franca. She walked with her arm outstretched, violently wagging her fingertips together toward Ester's face, who seemed barely altered.

"You need to smoke a bit of your opium, dear. You're starting to have withdrawal symptoms, and it shows," she teased her.

Gabriele had to grab hold of Franca by her shoulders to prevent her from throwing herself against her. Enrico went over to Ester and told her to stop; he held her by the waist and pulled her away from the scene. Franca began to cry with rage.

Maria paused a few moments to observe her, along with other friends who had gathered in a small group; then she turned away and walked toward her house.

Ester called out to her and reached her while she was putting the key in the door: "So, what do you think?" she asked.

"Great quarrel, but I don't understand why!" Maria answered, confused.

"Because now Franca and I are not talking anymore. I wanted to distance myself openly. She won't be coming to ask about the backpack any longer, to you or to me."

"Do you think she suspects something?"

"She can't be sure, and obviously she can't say anything; now she won't be too keen to ask any more questions," said Ester with a satisfied smile.

"What an ugly experience. I want to stay out of it!" said Maria.

"Yes, sure! You keep well out of it, but Franca deserves this, and worse! What she did to you could have had terrible consequences; I'll never forget it. You got away with it, but only because you were ridiculously lucky. You must have an angel, or rather two or three, protecting you."

Maria smiled, but without joy: "Thank you Ester. I'm going to paint; I have a lot of work to do, thanks to you!"

One day in November a small packet arrived from Paris, it was a gift from Jean-Claude for her birthday. He had a beautiful opal stone, bought in Varanasi, set in a silver pendant. He wrote back in early December: he missed her very much and wanted to see her again. Maria was working intensely and, before Christmas, she bought a one-way plane ticket to Bombay. Later on, once the Art Gallery had sold more of her paintings, Ester would send her the return ticket. She was going to leave in mid-January, and wrote to Jean-Claude to let him know. Ten days later a telegram arrived from Paris: 'Possibilité venir à Venise pour trois jours.' He was coming to Venice for three days, one week before her departure. She didn't think he would do such a long trip to see her, but she was mistaken!

On a very cold January morning she waited on platform number seven as the train from Paris slowly stopped, coming to the end of its line. Maria felt a big smile surface and her heart danced with joy as she looked carefully among the people getting off. Finally, she saw him and realized that he was not only a man she loved, but also a great friend. She ran up to him and he took her in his arms, holding her close. He was here with her, and it seemed impossible. When they reached the station exit, Jean-Claude stood on the steps, watching Venice in the mist. Maria was telling him about the plans she had made for those three days, where she planned to go, what she thought of doing, but he seemed not to hear her. "You're not listening to anything I'm saying, are you?" she asked.

He was looking at the houses, the churches, the sky line and whispered: "I'm sorry Maria, it's true, I was only half listening. This is the first time I have seen Venice and it's so moving." He looked at her briefly, pressing her to his side, returning his gaze to the houses. "Do you realize what effect this city has on you when you see it for the first time? I'm an architect and for me this is a special moment. I will never again see these places through the eyes of someone who has just arrived. The first impact is unique, then you get used to things and they no longer touch you in the same way."

"Then, you look around and I'll direct you. You don't even have to worry about where you put your feet, I'll guide you!"

They walked in silence, their arms around each other. Most of Jean-Claude's comments were about the houses, the churches, steeples and squares. He was asking a lot of questions, but she didn't have many of the answers. She realized she didn't know much about her city; she simply lived here and loved it.

Before reaching Campo San Maurizio, Maria insisted he meet the Art Gallery's owners; she wanted him to know her friends, the people who encouraged and helped her, she wanted him to see her work, so he would understand her life better. She sensed his reluctance and, after a brief introduction, she led him home.

Jean-Claude took a shower and wanted to rest for a while. Maria made a tea and brought it to the room. He was lying on the bed, looking at her. It seemed impossible that he was here, on her big bed. She had spent so many nights alone and he had come from Paris to be with her. She lay down and he hugged her; calmly, without haste, he stroked her head, her arms, kissed her forehead, her eyes, her lips. He held her close with a confidence, a calm that he didn't have in Paris, feeling free to be with her, to be himself. It even seemed a little strange to her that he was here, but she let him lead her and they loved each other with a new passion, made of love, friendship and a touch of promise.

She wanted to take him along the water's edge she had seen in her dream, where he had taken her by the hand and entrusted her to Paul. She wanted to see whether that corner had a particular effect on him. It gave him a 'peculiar' feeling, he said, a sense of loss or abandonment. They were in Campo Santo Stefano at seven o'clock, time when everyone met. They sat on the statue's steps; Jean-Claude lit a Gauloise and offered one to her. Ester was among the first people to arrive and sat down with them, joined shortly after by Enrico. Franca was there and couldn't ignore Jean-Claude. She came up, with some embarrassment, exchanged a few words and then, with an excuse, hurried away, eager to avoid Ester.

Ugo was also there and kept his distance, but hovered close enough to look at her from time to time. Maria was aware of his presence, his glances; he was alone, serious. Jean-Claude laughed and joked with everyone, he was sociable, brilliant, charming, talking in that wonderful French that Maria translated, or in English, which he spoke with a strong French accent.

They went for pizza with Ester and Enrico and then they headed home. He told her that he wanted to be with her, not with all her friends; she would be leaving for six months, and who knew when he would see her again.

They spent the rest of the three days alone, and every day it was easier, more natural and more fun; they laughed a lot. He had with him his trusty camera and wanted to see everything, go everywhere. She took him to Murano and Torcello, and finally to Burano, where she knew he would love the colours and the atmosphere, and she was right. Jean-Claude took photographs from every angle, absorbed by his passion, while she observed him, not quite believing that he was there with her.

The bitter cold of January was offset by the warmth inside her apartment, where they spent the evenings drinking sparkling wine, cooking dinner, listening to music and making love.

They never mentioned Céline, but Maria visualized the face she had dreamed of, and she was always present. He would go back to her and, as much as she believed in his love, she knew she had to protect herself from pain. She kept a part of her heart sheltered, detached, ready to get used to being alone again. She looked at his eyes, she smiled, kissed him, adored him, but it was as if she were observing from the outside, imagining herself in a few days, without him. She didn't want to be unhappy any longer; if she didn't love him completely she wouldn't suffer as much, she reasoned. The day of his departure came, and the time to take him to his train.

On the steps leading to the station there was a black kitten with white paws, thin and sickly, shivering from cold and hunger. Maria picked it up and tried to warm it by holding it inside her coat. Jean-Claude held her close, his arm around her shoulders: "I guessed you'd pick it up. And now what are you going to do with it? Will you take it home?"

"He needs me, and I need him," said Maria.

"And what will you do when you leave?"

"I don't know; one thing at a time. For now he is with me; then I'll find someone who wants him." They had spent three days together, but it seemed a lot longer. Now that they were on the platform she didn't want him to leave. Tears slid down her cheeks and she couldn't stop them.

"Why are you crying?" he asked, holding her by the arms, the kitten between them.

"Because I don't want you to leave!"

"Who'll be going to India in a few days?" he asked, with that irony in his eyes, that she knew and loved.

"Me!" she replied, sniffling.

He gave her his handkerchief: "So don't cry. I'll miss you much more than you'll miss me. Just think, in a week's time you'll be in Goa, while I'll be in cold Paris, working."

She nodded, wiping her nose and tears with his handkerchief. There was nothing else to say. After the last kiss, the last embrace and a pat for the kitten, Jean-Claude walked to the train and turned around to say goodbye for the last time. Maria blew him a kiss and then walked away, before the train moved its wheels and departed without her. With red eyes she walked across the station, pausing on the steps, looking at Venice like Jean-Claude had looked at it upon his arrival, holding the thin and trembling kitten close to her heart: "Let's go home kitty, I'll give you some warm milk."

She fed him and he was good company. He made her laugh with his jumps, his games, the sudden ambushes, swinging on the back of the rocking chair; he climbed up the curtains and insisted on sleeping in bed with her. Who would take him in when she left for India? If only she could take him with her!

29. The stars and us

Ester took the kitten home and offered to accompany her to Milan airport. It was freezing, an incredible temperature of minus sixteen degrees centigrade. There were snow drifts one metre high on either side of the roads, the ice didn't melt and the cloudless nights perpetuated the extreme weather conditions.

Maria got out of the warm car in the bitter cold of the midday hours, said goodbye to her dear friend and embarked on the new adventure. She had no fear. In her luggage were paintbrushes and colours; she would buy the paper in India, so that her work would be truly 'made in India'. The flight with the Polish airline touched down in Warsaw for an eight-hour stop; it was the cheapest flight available and, because of this, it was full of young people travelling with a backpack and sleeping bag, like her.

She found herself sitting next to a girl. Rossana was nineteen years old, going to Goa to join her friends from Milan and very worried about travelling alone. Where was Maria going to stay, once in Bombay, and then in Goa? she asked, hopeful. Maria hadn't made up her mind yet, she had heard that there were people from Venice living in Colva, a long quiet beach in the south of Goa with a smell of dried fish, as the fishermen dried their catch in the sun. Although she didn't know this group of people well, it was reassuring to know there was someone she could lean on. Rossana begged her to come with her, at least until she found her friends; they had rented a big house and she was sure they would welcome her. She was so young, and the first time in India was a big challenge, Maria remembered it well. It wouldn't cost her anything to do a favour to this sweet girl, whom chance had put next to her. There was no problem, Maria assured her, she would accompany her to Vagator, on the north coast, and then she would think about what to do next.

In Warsaw the temperature was much lower than in Milan and they waited in the transit hall with all the other Italians travelling on the same plane. One had a guitar and began to play; someone began to sing, and soon all the others joined in. True to their reputation that all Italians knew how to sing, the transit hall was filled with cheerful music and songs. The police didn't object and, in that eight-hour wait, many friendships were formed.

They landed in Bombay at around eight o'clock in the evening and shared a taxi with another girl from Milan, who was wearing a fur coat, and a boy who was also travelling alone. It was winter here as well, but it was as warm as early summer in Italy. The girl with the fur coat had been to India many times, she was more confident than any of them and the only one who knew Bombay. They went to a cheap hotel where she always lodged and took a room with four beds. After a quick shower, they changed from winter to summer clothes and then the girl, who was going to leave her fur coat in the hotel until returning to Italy, announced that she and the boy were going to an 'opium den', to smoke a little opium; it was the best way to recover from jet lag, she assured them. Did they want to go, too? Maria said no, thank you, she didn't want to get into any more situations with drugs; she had already had her fair share. She wasn't obliged to smoke if she didn't want to, said the girl, but she advised her to go, if only for the experience. The government had decided to close all the 'opium dens' which, for now, were still semi-legal, and this could be her last chance to see one. Maria consulted with Rossana: "What do you think? Just to have a look!"

"All right!" agreed Rossana, "but I don't want to smoke opium."

"Neither do I!"

All together they got into another taxi and the girl gave the address to the taxi driver, who immediately understood and nodded. After a twenty-minute ride with the windows fully open, they got out in a dark back street. While the girl was paying him, the driver reminded her how to get to the opium den; she knew the way.

They followed her through a low door and then up some wooden stairs. It was so dark they couldn't see where to put their feet, the handrail on the staircase was loose and wobbly, and seemed as if it could break off and fall to the ground at any time. As they climbed higher it became darker and darker. Tentatively, Maria felt the next step with her foot before trusting to place on it the full weight of her body. Once again, she was in a dangerous situation, to say the least, with people she had only just met, she didn't even know their surnames, climbing invisible stairs in a pitch black Bombay alleyway, where anyone could do anything to them and no one would ever find out. Was she ever going to learn? If the four of them disappeared, who would ever find out, and when? But now it was too late to worry; she should have thought of that before. It had only been a few hours since she had left freezing Italy and now there she was, in another world! Finally they reached a landing. The girl knocked on a door. It opened within a few moments, illuminating a white-haired old man, who bowed with folded hands. He invited them to come in, polite, calm, greeting them one by one with a warm and relaxed smile, giving off a feeling of absolute peace. "He looks just like my grandfather!" exclaimed Rossana. Maria's fears and suspicions melted away, like snow in the sun.

The old man pointed to an area where they could leave their shoes and preceded them into the main room, barefoot and bow-legged, walking slowly, a sarong tied at the waist, white as his hair. The first thing that struck her was the feeling of well-being that filled the large room, dimly lit by soft lights, decorated only with colourful rugs scattered on the floor. They were invited to sit on a couple of rugs and asked if they would like a cup of chai. A chai! She hadn't drunk one for months.
Maria looked around: many people were lying on the rugs on their side, their head resting on a block of wood that served as a pillow, while a couple of helpers walked silently, assisting them. "Why do they put their heads on wooden blocks? It must hurt," she asked the girl.
"It's the traditional way to smoke opium. It's always been that way and it doesn't hurt; at least, you don't notice when you're under the influence of opium." She seemed perfectly at ease and both the old man and his assistants had recognized her.
'Rossana's grandfather' came over and invited them to sit on a rug where he had arranged the wooden pillows. The girl and the boy stood up, while Maria shook her head. "I don't smoke opium, I'm sorry," she said gently, but firmly. The old man hesitated for a moment, but then nodded, his head crowned with white hair. Smiling, he looked at Rossana, without speaking. She shook her head, saying: "No thanks!" He nodded and moved away, walking slowly on his bowed legs.

A while later came a young man who politely offered 'Chillum? Charas?' Maria shook her head, no thanks, she was too tired. Rossana instead, to Maria's surprise, said yes. The man prepared a big pipe and filled it with plenty of charas. Luckily for her, Rossana had never smoked from a chillum and inhaled very little, but it was enough to make her go very quiet. After that, no one came to offer them anything else and Maria was able to observe her surroundings with ease and absorb the atmosphere. Here I am, she thought, two hours after landing in India, in this place nothing short of amazing. She would never have gone there by herself; she realized that it was a unique experience and decided to appreciate it.
The assistants moved from one rug to another, filling the small opium pipes and waiting patiently for each person to smoke it. There were about thirty people smoking and the four of them were the only westerners. With the exception of the assistants' silent movements, everything else

was almost completely still. Maria waited patiently for the boy and the girl to finish smoking; then someone called a taxi and helped them get back on their feet. Rossana, who had fallen asleep, woke up and, in the ever darker night, they descended the steep and shaky staircases. At two in the morning they arrived back at their hotel, dived into bed and slept soundly.

The following day, rested and ready for their first real day in India, Maria and Rossana went to buy the boat tickets for Goa, following the advice of the fur coat girl. There were only two boats a week and the first one was leaving the next day. They booked two seats on the deck, the cheapest ones, and then, ready to explore, walked toward India Gate, the most famous part of the city.

They strolled on the wide sidewalk bordering the sea, in the vicinity of the city's most luxurious hotel, the Taj Mahal Palace, an imposing, beautiful, opulent hotel. But, no sooner had they crossed the road than they found themselves in a totally different world.

Bombay seemed poorer than Delhi, with extremes of misery that Maria had never seen before. The streets were populated by beggars and snake charmers; children three, four, five years old were wandering in groups and seemed to take care of themselves. The glorious city of Bombay had become grey and dirty, every surface was covered in layers of greasy dust; even the children's faces were covered with the same kind of grime, seemingly impossible to clean.

Despite this, and in stark contrast to the bleak appearance all around, there was an atmosphere of cheerfulness and friendship. Did it come from her, who was so glad to be back in India, this lightness and joy? Or did it really come from the environment? Rossana, instead, was shocked by her surroundings, visibly keeping well away from the walls, the beggars, the dirty children. It didn't last long: their large eyes, their dishevelled and dusty hair, their white teeth, but especially their bright smiles, began to break down her defences and win her over.

They sat down on a low wall, in a square without a name, to rest a little; it was hot and they were tired from the long journey. Four little girls approached, they must have been between four and six years of age, at most. Maria welcomed them with curiosity, expecting them to ask for money. The children spoke a little English and wanted to know their names and where they came from. They sat close by on the wall, smiling and confabulating between them, trying to come up with more questions. They had a natural grace that conquered Maria who, glad to have them near her, began to fiddle with their braids. She admired the plastic bracelets on their wrists and they stroked her hand. Then they asked her for a kiss and, having received one each, ran away.

"How sweet they are! I thought they wanted money," said Rossana.

"Yes, I thought so too... and instead they wanted a kiss! I've heard there are many orphans in Bombay; it may be that they are some of them. Who knows?"

A few minutes later the children returned, accompanied by three more little girls. The bravest of them came to stand in front of Maria; from behind her back, she produced an orange flower, a marigold, and handed it to her.

"Thank you, it's beautiful! You are very kind," said Maria, moved by her gesture. Proud of herself, the little girl sat on the wall, close to her. Another little girl, much more timid, came near. She handed Maria her closed fist.

"What do you have in your hand?" As the child didn't open it, she teased her: "You don't have anything. It's empty, right? You're just pretending!" The child turned her hand and opened it, showing a red plastic stone. "It's beautiful. Is it your gem?" asked Maria.

The little girl nodded and then said: "For you!"

"Oh, thank you, but I can't take it, you keep it!" How could she accept what seemed to be a real treasure from this little girl who had nothing? She took the child in her arms, stroked her dusty hair and asked her name. "Sunita!" she replied. Maria felt a strong desire to give something to these children, but to give them money seemed to ruin this exchange of innocent humanity. She sat Sunita next to her, put her hand in her handbag and began to feel for things inside. The seven little girls were all around her, their young faces full of curiosity and expectation, excited by the surprise they knew was coming. Understanding the spirit, Rossana, plunged her hand into her own bag and began to search. Maria found a scented towel from the flight, a pen, a booklet, a pack of chewing gum. Rossana pulled out some Italian sweets, a lipstick and a mirror. Each girl took what she was given, with grace. They didn't compare, didn't try to swap and didn't quarrel with each other; they were happy with their gifts. They touched the two young women, they wanted another kiss, that Maria and Rossana gave them with love.

And then, as they had come, they left all together, chatting happily, seven small, thin and dusty princesses, each one holding her own gift. Every two steps they turned to wave goodbye, leaving Maria and Rossana, who continued to watch them smiling, with the strong feeling of having given a little, but having received a lot. Those little hands had touched their hearts.

"That's why I had to come back to India," said Maria.

"Are the people always like this?" asked Rossana.

"The poor in particular; those who have the least are the ones who give you the most, they touch your life, you'll see. It happens to everyone; India changes you, it changes the things you want, the way you think. You won't regret having come."

"I'm already realizing that!" Then, looking at Maria, Rossana added: "I'm so glad you're coming with me until I find my friends. You can stay there the whole time, if you want. I would be very happy!" and she hugged her.

"You've been very brave to travel alone. I'm happy to accompany you," said Maria. "And you know, I left alone too, with an open heart, ready to accept what life has in store for me; if I met you, there must be a reason, I have no doubt about this!"

"Who knows, maybe coming to Vagator with me is just what you *need* to do," suggested Rossana, inspired.

"I'm sure it is!" replied Maria, laughing.

The ship to Goa was leaving from the main port; it was massive but the number of people waiting to board was unbelievable! How would they all fit? Wise from the experience gained catching Indian trains, Maria was ready to make her way just as soon as they unhooked the rope blocking the ship's entry. People began to crowd around the steps for boarding. "I'm going to take our places, you get on whenever you can," she said to Rossana. With her two bags hung over her shoulders, Maria pushed her way through the crowd and began to advance, head forward, determined to be among the first to get on the ship. As soon as she was on board, she walked quickly toward the bow and identified a sheltered niche, where she opened her sleeping bag, marking a nice place on the bridge for the two of them; from there they would have a spectacular view. The space around her filled quickly and, when Rossana arrived, she settled by her side. They were surrounded by young people who had come from all over the world and by Indians, all filled with excitement. The trip to Goa lasted twenty four hours and the ship was equipped with a restaurant and toilets. They didn't need anything else! Ahead of them were twenty four hours of pure magic during which the ship would never be very far from the coast.

It left Bombay behind and sailed past deserted shores: miles and miles of white sandy beaches, bordered by lush palm trees. For the passengers there was nothing to do, so the girls talked with the people next to them, ate the restaurant's curry rice for three rupees and admired the landscape. When evening came, they lay down on their sleeping bags, watching the starry sky. Neither of them had ever seen so many stars and the sky seemed to be upside down; the moon, and the stars too, were the other way up, or so said those who knew about stars. "The Milky Way, look, it's reversed, and the Chariot is upside down!" said Maria.

"Why?" asked Rossana.

"Because we are on the other side of the world!"

"Really?"

"Well, more or less."

"Ahhh!" Even without understanding anything about stars, the dark blue dome of the sky, interwoven with thousands of brilliant lights, spoke of eternity, of the universe, of being one with what surrounded them.

"Did you know that we are made of the same substance as the stars?" Maria said, looking up, her hands clasped under her head.

"Really? The stars and us, made of the same substance?"

"Yes, so I was told, and I trust it's true, because the people who told me knew about it! They were Buddhists." She paused, without taking her eyes off the sky. "It seems impossible, doesn't it? The stars up there, made of who knows what, and us down here, made of flesh and bones. And we're the same!"

"It seems impossible!" echoed Rossana.

"Indeed!" agreed Maria. "But if you believe that there is no separation between us and them, between us and the sea, and the palm trees, between us and other human beings, something fundamental changes here in the heart and here, in the head," she said, touching with her index finger her chest and head.

"If that really is so, and as it's you telling me I believe you, then we are connected, don't you think? All together. We don't need to feel lonely any longer. Am I right?" asked Rossana.

Maria smiled at the way with which she expressed herself: "I think so, I feel the same. Since looking at life like this I feel stronger, protected and… happier I must say!"

"You're right. Me too!" agreed Rossana, looking at the stars. Then she leant over and gave her a kiss on her cheek. "I'm so glad I met you!" she said.

"Me too. Very!"

"Where did you meet the Buddhist monks? In Nepal?"

Maria smiled. "They were not monks; they were normal people, like us! I met them around India. Two in Delhi, one in Jaipur, a girl my age, and another was a friend of hers, a young South African man who later became her boyfriend."

"And had they shaved all their hair off?"

Maria laughed out loud, remembering Sanya, Colin, Luna and Harry. "No! they had all their hair. It's people like us, only they chant a phrase that gives you goose bumps and makes you feel good; it changes your life!" She didn't know where to start.

"A sentence can do all these things? And don't you say it?"

"Yes, yes, almost every day, and it works, it makes you feel good, it gives you strength... and lots of other things!"

"What is this sentence? Will you tell me?"

"Of course. Nam-myoho-renge-kyo."

"What? Can you repeat it?" Rossana wanted to know everything; she wanted to chant the phrase, know what it meant, why it made you happy and gave you strength and how it changed your life. One thing at a time, Maria said, and besides she didn't know much. Tomorrow she would tell her everything she remembered but, in the meantime, they could chant the phrase, and then go to sleep.

She woke up early to the sound of voices, sensing a lot of activity nearby. The ship had stopped. Maria leaned over the railing and saw a rowboat approaching. It was packed with people standing, mostly women, being ferried from the nearby port, so that the ship didn't have to go into shallow waters. The women wore brightly coloured sari, in those red, yellow, blue colours that she would soon use in her paintings, and whose borders, embroidered with golden thread, reflected the sunlight and made them shine. Their glossy black hair, coated in coconut oil, was gathered in a big bun; in them the women had slipped fresh flowers of all colours: large red bells, white waxy flowers with five petals and a yellow centre, pink, purple and scarlet bougainvillea flowers that seemed to be made of coloured tissue paper. The women carried large wicker baskets covered with a white cloth, resting them on their hip. One by one, people climbed on board, helped by the sailor who held out his hand and supported them firmly below the elbow, pulling them up safely and nimbly. Every one thanked him with a big smile. They looked like healthy and happy people.

The ship departed, and after an hour or so, it stopped near another port to repeat the same operation and take on board more people. Around noon they reached Goa and docked at the port of Panjim, a town lined by tall palm trees. Not knowing another way to get to their destination, the girls caught a taxi to Vagator beach. With the windows open, the wind fluttering in their hair, they breathed in deeply; the clean air smelt of sea, salt and flowers. Goa was fertile and luxuriant. The rice fields were of a bright pea green and behind them stood dense trees, in all different shades of green.

"What are those trees?" Maria asked the driver.

"Tamarinds," he replied.

"And those?"

"Carobs."

"And these flowers?" They were hibiscus flowers, large red bells in tall thick bushes flanking the roadside, the same flowers they had seen decorating the Indian women's hair. Out of the forest, with the trees competing to be the tallest and thickest, emerged the tops of big white churches. "Are those *churches?*" Maria asked. Goa was a Christian state, said the driver; it had been a Portuguese colony, didn't she know? Yes, someone had told her that but, all the same, seeing churches with the cross on the top was a surprise. The houses too were different from the rest of India; these were built of stone and bricks, painted white, with red roofs and large covered porches. Almost all had spacious gardens at the front, with bushes and trees providing shade and coolness, where groups of pigs strolled around, the big ones heavy and lazy, the little ones cheerful and fast. The women they saw along the road wore blouses and skirts to the knee, only a few were wearing a sari. It was all very different from the India she knew.

Once they reached Vagator village, the taxi driver asked a passer-by where Angela De Souza's house was and, following his directions, stopped in front of a large villa surrounded by a garden. The girls got out and, in some awe, went through the gate. Timidly, Rossana climbed the steps leading to the veranda. "Anybody home?" she called.
"Who is it?" replied a female voice from inside. A young woman came out onto the porch, saw Rossana and let out a cry of surprise. Yes, it was the right house! They laughed, talked and hugged. Maria walked up the steps and Rossana introduced her to Betty, a tall, gentle girl with a kind, makeup-free face.
"Can Maria stay here too? She is wonderful! We did the whole trip together. Please, say yes!" she pleaded. Betty laughed and replied that Maria was welcome, the house was big and there was room for everyone. A few minutes later Margherita, shortened to Margo, arrived, carrying with difficulty two buckets full of water, and accompanied by her French boyfriend, also laden with water buckets. Their knees slightly bent to cushion the impact of the weight, they walked quickly up to the kitchen leaving a trail of droplets behind them. "Be careful not to slip!" cried Margo, small, fierce, sensual. Maria felt part of their group from that very first meeting. She chose a corner in one of the almost completely empty rooms, where she laid her sleeping bag and her two bags on the floor. She had arrived at last! Their hosts gave them just enough time to undress and put on their shorts and t-shirt. "Later we'll show you the well, but now let's go to the beach, come on, it's already late!" urged the blonde Margo.

They walked under the leafy branches of tamarind and carob trees, flanked by huge bushes of red hibiscus and bougainvillea of every colour, crossed an expanse of red earth and came to the top of a small cliff. Wearing only flimsy flip-flops, they climbed with great care down the steep flank of sharp rocks and soon reached Vagator beach.

It was large, semi-circular and covered in fine white sand, lapped by a crystal clear sea and surrounded by towering palm trees that sheltered it from the wind. In the shade of the coconut trees was a hut, whose main structure had been erected with wooden poles, while large palm leaves formed its roof and walls. A small but efficient restaurant was run from there, serving cheese omelettes, fresh fruit salad with yogurt, tea, coffee and biscuits.

The biggest surprise though was the people on the beach: they were all westerners and completely naked. Maria had sunbathed topless in Italy, and this had already broken many rules and taboos, but she had never been completely naked on the beach; that was a step far too daring and she wasn't ready or prepared to go down that route. She sat on her sarong with arms encircling her knees, and observed. She had never seen naked men walking around as if it were the most natural thing in the world, and here there were many.

Too embarrassed to watch them openly, Maria shifted her gaze to the girls; they were naked too, but this meant without clothes, certainly not without jewellery! There was a lavish display of large anklets, many from the Rajasthani tradition, made of silver pipes coiled around the ankles; of belts made of silver mesh; big necklaces with stones of turquoise, red coral, transparent amber, green jade, alternating with large chunks of silver and, of course, just as many bracelets, big, shiny, striking. These jewels adorned the bronzed bodies of the girls who were walking, playing tambourine, stretched out in the sun, and going in and out of the water like ancestral Venuses.

Maria watched silently, she was staring, to tell the truth, but no one else seemed to notice the nudity that populated the beach, apart from Rossana, who was just as shocked, and who, after a while, was told to close her mouth.

They took off their shorts, t-shirt and bra, up to this point there was no problem, but her knickers no… like that, in public, she couldn't, she simply could not. Rossana was equally certain. Betty and Margo insisted.

"Come on, sooner or later you'll have to take off those pants!"

"It's great to swim completely naked."

"You'll get used to it straight away!"

"What will you do, just the two of you with your big knickers on and everyone else naked? It's ridiculous!" They were pushing, poking, insisting, without a moment's respite.

"Okay, maybe I'll try, but not now!" said Maria.

"When then?" pressurized Margo.

"In a little while. I'm thinking about it!"

Maria looked at Rossana: "Shall we take them off together?"

"But I feel ashamed!"

"So do I! But sooner or later we will have to, won't we?"

"You're right. I'm thinking the same, too!"

Betty and Margo insisted, taking advantage of that wave of uncertainty: "Come on, nobody is watching you! What do you think? You'll suddenly be the centre of all the attention?"

"As if they had nothing better to do than watch you two. Come on! You're such a pain in the neck!"

Alright then! Without getting up from her sarong, Maria pulled one leg out of her pants and then, twisting and lifting her bottom the bare minimum, she pulled out the other leg, too. Rossana did the same, mimicking Maria, full of shame. The moment they were naked they heard a loud applause and male voices shouting:

"Good one!"

"Well done!"

"Hurrah!"

They looked in the direction of the voices; a group of five men were watching them, laughing heartily, commenting and joking. Maria bowed in their direction, thanking them. "It's a good job we weren't the centre of attention, huh?" she said.

But the girls were laughing and, finally, it was done! They sat in the sun for as long as they could stand it. It was scorching hot; they were sweating and getting over-heated.

"Now we must stand up and walk to the sea," said Rossana.

"This is the hardest part!" Maria agreed. "Together, come on, let's go!"

They got up and walked toward the sea, but this time there was no applause, they had already been forgotten, and the two girls arrived at the shore undisturbed.

The water was cool but not cold; they entered cautiously and finally dived in. It seemed like a dream, they were playing in the sea in mid-January, while people in Italy were sweeping piles of snow a metre high. It was liberating, exciting and it was true that nude swimming was a great feeling, at one with the sea that rocked them. Maria looked toward the beach, the view was magnificent! That wild and naturally perfect landscape, the wide beach, the tall and protective palm trees, the rocks behind and the deep blue sky above. She would come back to paint it, just as soon as she had tanned a little; with her olive complexion, a couple of days would be enough to change the colour of her skin. This place was beautiful! For the moment there was no reason to go anywhere else.

That afternoon they had to learn how the 'toilet' system in Goa worked. "There are two possibilities!" said Margo, with her straightforward and quick manner. From her fist she pulled out first her thumb and then her forefinger: "Option number one: you go into the woods with a small bucket of water and you do it there, but that's a bit dangerous. Option number two: you go to that closet over there," she pointed to a hut raised from the ground by a concrete platform, on the far corner of the garden, opposite the house, whose door could be reached by climbing three steps. "There too, you take your bucket, close the door and sit on an almost normal toilet bowl, just a little rougher than those we have in Italy. Is everything clear, so far?" Maria and Rossana nodded, amused, while Betty and the Frenchman started to laugh. "Now comes the best bit!" Margo announced, unable to hold back her mirth. "You *will notice*..." she enunciated in a louder voice, raising her index finger in the air, "that, as soon as you go out with your little bucket of water, the pretty pigs that you see around here, preceded by the mother *sow*..." they were already laughing so hard that Margo had to make an effort to continue, "... will follow you running, all excited, right behind your heels!"

"Why?" asked Rossana. The giggle from the three experts grew louder, uncontrollable.

"The reason *why* you'll understand in a moment!" They were now laughing even harder. It was so contagious that Rossana and Maria began to laugh without knowing why. "So, our pigs don't care for your pee, but..." Margo said, raising her finger and drawing a circle in the air, "... if you are preparing to do a *poo*, and they understand your intention from the famous bucket you are carrying with you, they get all excited because they love it, and get ready to *eat it*," she shouted. They were already crying with laughter but, when they saw the expression of disbelief on the newcomers' faces, they had to hold their belly, it hurt so much, and roared even harder.

"You're kidding," said Maria, disgusted.

"How revolting!" cried Rossana, "I don't believe it! Pigs don't eat shit!"

"*Pigs don't eat shit?*" Margo yelled. "*Rossana!* For them, shit is like the best pudding in the world, like... I don't know... tiramisu!"

"Or Christmas pudding!" prompted Betty, inspired.

"Or crème brûlée!" suggested the Frenchman.

The girls' expression of disgust only increased their enjoyment and they were howling. But it was not over! "Aaand... if you're going to do it in the jungle..." Margo couldn't continue from laughing too much.

Betty came to her aid: "You will see! The pigs can't even wait for you to get it all out, they push you with their nose from behind, trying to eat it... well, you understand, right?"

"*While it's still warm*!" yelled Margo, cracking up, until she couldn't get her breath back.

"It seems impossible! I can't believe it," said Maria.

Betty interjected: "Have you noticed that there is no smell of sewage, as there is in the rest of India?" It was true, no unpleasant smell around.

"Then it's better to go into the little cabin there?" asked Rossana, still in shock.

"You decide, honey! I would definitely say it is," advised Margo, with tears streaming down her cheeks, still reeling with laughter. Well, they were soon going to experience it!

Once the hilarity calmed down, the 'experts' took them behind the big house, where there was a wild garden full of tall leafy trees, low bushes and wild flowers. Following a winding path they arrived at the well from which the water needed for cooking and washing was pulled out. Above the well, supported by a wrought iron structure, was the pulley and, through this, they had to let down the long rope, that each group had to buy and take back to the house at night; thirty metres of rope were not cheap, and if left at the well, it tended to disappear, 'adopted' by someone. At one end of the rope a noose with a slip knot was made; this was hung around a ball-shaped plastic jar with a wide mouth, which had to be kept clean because it went into the water. They taught them how to get the pot down to the water surface where, of course, it floated. They had to move it a few times, pulling and letting go of the rope from above, until the mouth tilted just enough to touch the surface and let in the first few cups of water. At that point it became easier; they had to get a little more water into the container and then, thanks to the weight inside it, the bucket would sink and fill to the brim. Aided by the pulley, they hoisted the full container, emptied its content into their bucket and then began again, until they had enough water for the day.

It wasn't easy, but the first few times they would accompany the girls and then everyone could contribute to the running of the house, by taking it in turns to go to the well. It was such an ancient custom, and so fascinating, Maria thought she would be happy to do it. The peace of the 'jungle', as they called the wild forest, populated by tropical birds, was magical and timeless, while the action and effort required to pull the water out, made her acutely aware of where it came from. Her posture when bringing it back to the house, with the ball-shaped pot resting on her right hip and held in the curve of her forearm, the full and heavy bucket carried on her left, and the rope coiled around her shoulder, all made life more real, more *alive*. They explained that the wells dried up and that, toward the end of March, most were almost dry and the water no longer clean. Hence, they used only the water that was strictly necessary, always thinking of the hot and dry season, from April to June, before the monsoon, during which time it was more valuable than gold. Then, the rain would begin again in abundance and, during the summer months, it would fill the wells again. Or so one hoped!

That evening they went to eat at a restaurant near their house, called Julie Jolly Restaurant, which was the owner's name. They ate well: fish curry, potato chips and a good homemade cake with a strong taste of coconut. Betty and Margo said that all the people who came to Goa originally planned to stop about one week and then move on, but when the week was about to end, they didn't feel like leaving and decided to stay another week. It had happened to them, and they had been there two months, without any desire to pack up and go. In addition to the beautiful beaches and good food, there were a lot of parties, almost every night; the music began at about ten o'clock and went on till morning. Basically, leaving Goa was impossible. There was a party at the restaurant in two days' time, and they would go together, so they'd understand.

Maria decided that, for her, things would be different. She had come here with a clear plan: from Goa she would travel to the south of India, to the southernmost tip where the three seas met; from there she would travel north along the west coast, through Madurai, Puri, all the way to Calcutta, and then back to Nepal. She had six months' time and was determined to see as much as possible.

The second day was even better than the first. They went back to the beach and swam in the sea. Swimming naked really was different, she felt like a fish! They moved from the sun to the shade, from the sand to the sea, careful not to get burned. Sitting on the sea shore, with the waves lapping their legs, Maria and Rossana spent hours together. Rossana timidly mentioned sex; did she know much about it? A little, said Maria, laughing amused. When a stronger wave caught them by surprise and knocked them on their backs on the shoreline, Rossana confessed she wasn't sure she knew what an orgasm was. Maria decided to explain it in such a way that would clear any doubt. By drawing a picture on the wet sand she explained graphically their anatomy, and then she encouraged her friend to try on her own, hands on, until she saw the realization appear all over her face; she would be eternally grateful, said Rossana. They laughed to tears. "If you hadn't explained it to me, I wonder how long it would have taken me to understand this thing, which, in the end, is very simple!"

"Well, you took me to this beautiful place and I, in return, have enlightened you on this; it seems a good exchange to me!" laughed Maria.

On the third day, now rested from the long journey, Maria woke up early and went down to the beach shortly after eight o'clock. It was deserted, except for a naked man who was balancing on his head, in a perfect yoga position. The chai-shop man had just arrived and was heating the water for tea. Maria asked for a chai and, while she was waiting, she sat on a bench, quietly chanting her sentence and watching the sea. She saw a girl walking, carrying a red plastic bucket, a sarong tied above her breast, her straight hair of a coppery colour. For a moment she thought she recognized Karen, but it wasn't possible. She looked at her carefully, followed her with her eyes and... yes, it looked just like her. She didn't want to disturb the silence of the morning, but she had to know. She called her name quickly, loudly. The man in the yoga position didn't fall, as she had feared. The girl turned and Maria remembered that Karen was short-sighted. She began to wave at the same time as she walked toward her.

"Hi! Do you remember me? I'm Maria. We met that time of the landslide on the way to Manali!" she said, in one breath. Then, remembering other details, she added: "We were together in Mandi, at the guesthouse, and then we met at the baths in Vashist!"

Karen was finally able to focus on her and smiled: "Of course I remember you! And your friend? What's her name? Is she here, too?"

"Franca! No, she is still in Italy!" Maria told her that they had gone back to Italy and that she had only just returned to India. And how was she? And Paul?

Karen paused. "Paul is not very happy. He is at home; I'm going there right now. Why don't you come, too? He'll be delighted to see you!" she invited her.

"When? Now?" Maria hesitated.

"Yes. Come on, come with me! It's nearby, two minutes' walk; otherwise you'll never find the house. He'll be really glad to see you!" she insisted.

Maria thought for a moment, the decision was simple: sure, why not?

"Okay, I'll just grab my bag and come with you!"

30. I wanted you to be happy

As they walked on the sand Karen talked in her own peculiar way, quickly, quietly and chuckling to herself. Maria understood almost nothing, but there wasn't a second's break when she could ask her to repeat herself. When they had met in Manali, Paul had told her they would go to Goa, but Maria hadn't remembered which part and, after all, Goa was a big state not a provincial village; what a chance to have met her right here! And now Paul was close by; in a couple of minutes she would see him again. He had shaken her to her core; she could still feel on her skin his embrace in the temple, she recalled that silent look between them. Then she had met Jean-Claude, who had given her more than dreams and illusions and had won her over with his warmth and passion. He had made her feel she could be loved, that she was beautiful, and had helped her to put Ugo in the past. Without him she wouldn't be the woman she was today. She remembered the dream in which Jean-Claude had taken her to Paul. He had taken her hand and put it in his; then he was gone, and Paul had led her into the water of the canal. "How is Paul?" she asked, taking advantage of a brief moment in which Karen took a breath. She launched into another long whispered speech, out of which Maria caught a few words. Had they split up? It seemed impossible! "He's not your boyfriend?" she asked. From Karen's response, it looked as if she had understood correctly.

Soon they began to climb the rocky slope and leave the beach. She wanted to ask how far the house was, but was unable to stop Karen's flow of words. At last they came to a small house in the middle of a clearing, surrounded by a few trees, with a small covered porch and the traditional red-clay floor tiles. Karen went into the house and Maria followed her timidly, a strong emotion, a kind of embarrassment, filling her heart.

Paul was crouched in front of a kerosene stove, on which a kettle was placed, and was lighting it up. He wore only a sarong tied at the waist, his blond hair had been lightened in the sun and rolled up in ringlets where it touched his shoulders. He lifted his face to look at Karen, but didn't smile. She told him she had come with a friend, and at that point he looked at Maria.

"Hello, do you remember me?" Maria said.

He studied her carefully, the glare coming through the door was behind her and, with the figure against the light, he couldn't see clearly who it was; but then he recognized her, and his face broke into an expression of surprise, followed by a smile. He stood up and walked over to her, hugged her and kissed her firmly on the mouth. Well, she wasn't expecting this! And they said that the English were cold and reserved.

"How are you?" she asked, hiding the emotion that made her tremble inside.

"Okay," he replied, without conviction; he shot a serious look at Karen and then brought his gaze back to Maria. "What about you? You look beautiful! I remember those blue eyes," he said, looking openly at her face and her pink sarong, crossed over her breasts and tied around her neck; it suited her, she knew, and two days in the sunshine had already tanned her. He too was tanned and was even more handsome than she remembered. He looked at her closely with his beautiful green eyes; her legs were trembling and she wanted to kiss him.

"I'm making tea. Do you want some?" he offered, heading for the stove.

"Yes, please," she replied.

There was silence between him and Karen, a heavy silence. Maria improvised, telling them that she had just returned from Italy. Paul paid some attention, but every two or three seconds he gave Karen a withering glance. She was mumbling something unintelligible, moving with downcast eyes around the only room, pretending to focus on every little thing. Maria continued to fill those voids, talking about Varanasi and how it had struck her. Had they ever been? She told them about Nepal and Pokhara, the magic mushrooms, Franca's hepatitis, the job she had left. Paul put a tumbler full of hot tea in her hand, into which he poured a little milk. Maria had the distinct feeling he hadn't heard anything she had said. She felt in a hurry to leave the room and the couple who lived in it, with all their problems. She took a couple of hot sips, followed by: "I'm going to the beach!"

Paul looked at her, surprised that she wanted to leave so soon. "But you haven't drunk your tea!" he argued. Bringing his attention back on Maria, he told her there was a party at Julie Jolly Restaurant that evening; was she going? Yes, she lived just around the corner and the Italian girls said she couldn't miss it. He wanted to know where she lived and nodded when Maria described, more or less, where her house was. She drank half the hot tea and then stood up, approaching the door to prevent further protests. "I'll see you tonight, then!" she said, and took her leave; they needed to be alone.

Out in the sun she breathed a sigh of relief; the atmosphere in the house was so heavy, she wondered what had happened. She felt sorry for them, especially for Paul, who seemed much sadder than Karen. How could she no longer want a man like that? He was stunning and his spellbinding gaze made her forget what she was saying; her words came out all muddled and confused.

Her thoughts flew to Jean-Claude, in Paris; she wondered how he was, whether he was happy, if he was going through a difficult time. He had promised to write to her and perhaps he would do so, but she didn't count on it. If she didn't expect anything she wasn't going to be disappointed. Sanya had been clear about expectations, and it seemed a wise attitude. Living in the present was already quite demanding, with all these new people, different places and all the things she wanted to do: paint, travel and create.

She walked slowly toward the beach, enjoying the cool morning air and the warmth of the sun on her back, the chirping of birds, the tropical landscape in the middle of winter. Paying great attention, she descended the slope of jagged sharp stones. The beach was more crowded and the girls had already arrived. Maria removed her pink sarong, laid it next to Rossana on the fine sand and lay down on it, completely naked and comfortable with it. Where had she been? Maria told them about Paul and Karen from the moment she had met them, of the effect he had on her and of the tense situation into which Karen had taken her. From one thing to another, she also told them about Jean-Claude and their story. The girls were readily engrossed in Maria's romance, and couldn't wait to meet this Paul.

That evening they started to get ready way before time. They took a shower by throwing water over their head with a bucket, to rinse off soap and shampoo; a bucket each was enough for a good shower. Through many discussions, conflicting advice, experiments and changes they selected which clothes to wear.

Maria had very few items of clothing and her choice was easy: she wore her embroidered white silk shirt and her white pyjama trousers, which enhanced her tan. She clasped Jean-Claude's ankle bracelets, chose a necklace made of turquoise stones, and silver earrings with more small turquoise gems. For walking in the dark they had a home-made torch consisting of half a coconut shell, with a candle stump held within by its own wax. The candle, thus protected, gave a good light and wouldn't blow out in the wind. Finally, Margo gave her a stick: "Never go out at night without a stick!" she warned. "This is yours, don't lose it." Why the stick? Because of the dogs; she would soon understand.

As soon as they walked onto the dirt road, a pack of stray dogs sprang out of the darkness and started barking and growling, angry, aggressive and violent, like in Kathmandu. However this time the group of four girls and the Frenchman was well prepared and the dogs had to keep a good distance. They were barking, retreating and then advancing again, but with no chance to get to the calves of those foreigners who smelt so different. They were only a few minutes away from Julie Jolly Restaurant, which had been decked out for the party.

The whole area outside the restaurant gates was occupied by stalls on straw mats. The locals had organized small chai-shops with a kerosene stove, big teapots and all the necessary ingredients to make chai or instant coffee. Some prepared sweet omelettes filled with jam, and the more enterprising also sold biscuits, cigarettes, cigarette papers and matches.

"Do a lot of people come to these parties?" asked Maria.

"Hundreds, you'll see!" replied Betty.

People were coming from all directions, dressed in colourful, original ways. Maria found the only chair and sat down. She filled her eyes with those new, different young men and women, absorbing the atmosphere full of excitement, familiarity, music, and sensuality. Everyone else was seated on mats or on their sarong. Rossana was next to her, sitting on a mat, and looked around in awe.

Maria felt his presence before she even saw him; she just knew he was there, and looked in his direction. Paul was walking and scanning around; she had the feeling he was looking for her. She followed him with her eyes until he saw her; she noticed a light gasp, as if he had seen the person he was searching for, and smiled at her. She returned his smile and nodded her head, but didn't move.

Rossana had already figured it out: "Is he *that* one?"

"Yes."

"He is *gorgeous!*"

"Couldn't agree more!"

"Why don't you go and sit with him?" she asked, excitedly. Meanwhile Paul had found a friend and had placed his sarong on the ground, sitting down next to him.

"And how do I do that? I can't just go there and say 'now I sit here!'"

"No, you're right. So what are you going to do?"

"I haven't got the slightest idea! I'll wait, and later... we'll see. In any case, he's just a friend, don't get too excited. Where are the Frenchman, Betty and Margo?"

"Outside, drinking chai. But he looked at you; it seemed as if he was looking for you."

"I had the same feeling too. Let's go and find the others. We'll come back later." She stood up and, even though she was behind him, Paul turned immediately to look at her, and their eyes met. His eyes were saying 'where are you going'? Maria replied with a wave of her hand, as if to say 'I'll come back'. Paul nodded. They had understood each other perfectly. She was stirred within; she had to go out and give herself time to think.

After a long while looking for them, they spotted Margo and Betty sitting at one of the chai-shops. There were already a lot of people, the kerosene stoves were in full swing, giving off an unpleasant smell that no one seemed to notice.

"You should see this Paul!" Rossana blurted out immediately, unable to contain her excitement. "He's just arrived and he is *so handsome*. You're so lucky Maria!"

"Why lucky? He's not my boyfriend! I hardly know him," she said cautiously, but she could feel the same excitement. She ordered a chai. The girls were talking, but she couldn't follow anything they were saying; their voices were like a hum in the background, while her heart, her stomach, her breathing, were all in a whirl, and she was confused, agitated. The chai took a long time coming; she had almost given up waiting when she was finally handed a full glass of hot tea. She blew on it, but it was so hot she couldn't even hold it. She placed it on the mat, realizing she'd have to wait a lifetime before being able to drink it, but felt a strong sense of urgency to go back. "I can't sit here and wait for it to cool down, do you want it?" she said, offering it to Rossana.

"Are you going back inside?" her friend asked.

"Yes, I feel as if there was a huge magnet drawing me in that direction."

"Good luck!" said Rossana.

"Thank you!"

She had to control herself not to run, and slowed down just before crossing the threshold of the gate. The moment she walked through it, Paul turned and smiled at her. She had never seen him so handsome. He followed her with his eyes, every step she took, until she reached him. Quickly, he made room for her on his sarong and Maria sat down beside him; she smiled, but didn't feel the need to say anything. The music was very loud.

"Is this the first time you come to a Goan party?" he shouted in her ear.

"Yes!" she shouted and nodded.

Paul began to roll a joint. They smoked it together, passing it between each other. Their shoulders, their arms, their knees, their heads were touching; they were breathing in the same rhythm, in unison. Time had stopped, and it was beautiful. Paul sank the butt on the sandy floor and put his arm around her shoulders; it seemed the most natural thing in the world. He kissed her hair and she smiled. She turned toward him and he kissed her on the lips; then, looking into her eyes he kissed her again. Maria returned his kiss. She was feeling slightly lightheaded and everything was happening so fast, flowing effortlessly, without any resistance. He was the most beautiful man in the world and she felt from a place deep within herself that she could trust him. Completely relaxed next to him, comfortable, at ease in his embrace, she was happy to let things develop as they would and, trusting the present moment, which was taking her in an unknown direction, she let herself go, with abandon. They listened to the music, sitting ever closer, as if to merge one into the other, naturally.

"What do you want to do?" Paul had to shout to be heard.

"I don't like this music. It's too loud," she said, talking at the top of her voice: "Let's go to your house!" She wasn't rushing things, was she?

"Do you want to go through the village or the beach?" he asked.

She was surprised by his question and had no idea of the route to cover. The beach sounded more romantic: "Beach!" she shouted. When she stood up she met Rossana, Margo and Betty's eyes who, sitting nearby, had followed the developments. They smiled at her and Maria walked out with Paul holding her by the hand. She followed him out of the area of light created by the party and they walked down to the beach, in the dim light of his torch with weak batteries.

There was no moon to illuminate the path and the beach was shrouded in darkness. They walked holding hands. Paul would say something in his deep voice; Maria understood very little, but words were not necessary.

Every few steps they stopped, he held her tight and kissed her again, then walked a little further. The rising tide had taken up almost the whole beach and they had to climb the boulders and proceed carefully on the sharp rocks. Paul knew every inch of them while Maria didn't know where to put her feet and worried about cutting herself or twisting an ankle.

"Careful here," he'd say, "it's a bit dangerous!"

Yes, thank you, 'here' *where?* She couldn't see anything at all, put one foot in front of the other and trusted his instructions blindly. The decision to come through the beach wasn't at all romantic as she had imagined; quite the opposite, they were likely to break a leg! Paul helped her, taking advantage of every opportunity to hold her, kiss and touch her, learning to know her body in the dark.

Finally, to her great relief, they arrived at his house. He turned the switch on but the light wasn't working. "There is no electricity. I have candles, fortunately," he said. He lit the first candle and placed it carefully on the table. She observed him as he lit the second candle on the flame of the first one, this man she had dreamed of, who seemed unattainable, because of the distance between them, their culture, the language, his girlfriend, their completely different worlds, was there with her and wanted her. He stuck the second candle by dripping its own wax on the windowsill. As he lit the third candle Maria watched his blond hair curling up on his broad shoulders, his fine hands and the way he moved, at ease in the simple and cosy room.

He turned to her and took her hand. He sat on the mattress on the floor and pulled her down to sit on his lap. This was a dream, Maria thought, feeling as if she were watching the scene from the outside, a spectator that someone had pulled on the stage, and didn't know how to move, what to say, what to do, embarrassed and intimidated. Her mind insisted on asking her questions and giving explanations, while Paul caressed her, lifted her shirt, undid her pyjamas. He knelt on the bed and made her stand up, looking at her in the candlelight. She firmly pushed away all the competing, overlapping thoughts that were vying to disturb her. She looked at this beautiful man who desired her and, trusting his kind, charming eyes and the soft light of the candles, she let herself go to the present moment, his hands, his touch and the warmth of his body. She didn't ask anything else, didn't seek any answers and trusted her destiny, without fear. Something strong from deep inside was telling her to let go and be happy. It was a new skin, new smell, new gestures, another sensibility, another rhythm. They remained still after the love, her head resting on his shoulder, his arms holding her, his hands caressing her. She closed her eyes and lay on her side. Paul hugged her from behind, his arm around her waist, his knees bent behind hers, and buried his face in her hair. "You smell of salt and sun!" he whispered, with his beautiful voice. She smiled and, with her hand on his, she slipped into a light sleep, while the candles burned slowly, one by one.

When she woke up, he was busy with the kerosene stove, his sarong tied at the waist, his blond hair pushed behind his ears with those almost childish curls, and smiled. So it wasn't a dream, she was still here, with him. 'And now what?' asked her mind. Now it was a new day and she didn't know what it would bring but, for the moment, she was here and liked it. Paul turned to her and smiled. "I made you some tea. I'm going out for a minute," he said. He brought her a tumbler full of hot tea and caressed her, bending down to kiss her. "I won't be long!" he assured her.

She didn't ask where he was going or when he would come back. She'd take things as they came, without any questions. She leaned against the wall and began to sip the hot tea; she was thirsty. Her mind went back to the night before, to how things had developed; one emotion after the other, a look, a smile, a step, a hug, a kiss, holding hands, the feeling of being a precious, delicate thing to love and hold tight, like a treasure. The Treasure Tower! *You are the Treasure Tower, Maria!* Luna had said. She smiled, thinking about Luna. She felt just like that, a treasure tower, and would have liked to tell her, had she been here. I can send it to her, this moment of happiness; she will feel it with my 'daimoku', she thought. If it crossed the universe, boundlessly free, as radio waves did, then this is for you, Luna, Nam-myoho-renge-kyo, with all the joy I'm feeling, and I hope you are happy, too.

Her mind took her back to Jean-Claude and their last moments in Venice station, with the kitten between them. 'Don't cry!' he had said, giving her his handkerchief to wipe her tears. 'I'll miss you more than you'll miss me!' Only a week had gone by and here she was, in Paul's bed, in the Goan warm, tropical winter. She thought of the dream in which Jean-Claude had accompanied her along the canal and entrusted her to Paul. Had it been a premonition? In a way, he had been a bridge between the past, full of suffering, void of respect, and this present moment. Without his love that had helped her believe she *could* be loved, she wouldn't have had the quiet confidence to accept that Paul wanted her. Her heart clenched, thinking of Jean-Claude. Did he realize how much he had given her? She hoped he was happy.

Paul still wasn't back. He had probably gone to see Karen. They had a lot to sort out and maybe they were talking about it right now; five years together was a long time. Maria was happy to be here at this time and have the opportunity to console him in his sadness, even if it was only for a day or two. It was an auspicious beginning for her new trip in India!

Just then Paul came back; she saw his body silhouetted against the light coming in through the door. He approached, holding up his sarong in front of him, and let dozens of fragrant white flowers fall onto the bed and in her lap: a cascade of perfume!

Maria laughed, amused and touched: "They're beautiful! I've seen them before; are they real? They look like wax, or rubber!" The scent emanating from the flowers was so strong that her question didn't need an answer.

"Of course! They're frangipani," he replied. "There is a tree not far away. It has only flowers and no leaves; during the night they fall to the ground. I went to pick them up for you."

"How romantic!" she laughed, feeling happy. "I thought you had gone to see Karen," she added, "... to talk."

"No, not at all! I went to pick flowers for you," he said, kissing her on the lips, sitting on the bed and wrapping his arm around her waist. "What are you doing today?" he asked. She had to go home and remove her contact lenses, which she had left in overnight, and then she wanted to paint. He had to write three long articles for the travel magazine he worked for.

They went out into the sunshine together, Paul's arm around her shoulders. At that very moment Karen was approaching the house and, when she saw them, she slowed down abruptly; even without glasses she could see that Paul was happy. They saw her at the same time. Maria moved away from him, but Paul didn't let her go and instead brought her firmly to his side and held her close. "Shall we meet tonight?" he asked, looking into her eyes.

"Yes, okay...," replied Maria, uncertain. "Today I'll paint and then..." Karen had slowed down even more. "But... you two...?" she added hesitantly, looking at Karen out of the corner of her eye. Paul interrupted her: "There is no more 'us two'. She's made her choice," he said firmly, "and I know what I want: I want to be with you. I'll pick you up around seven o'clock. I'll introduce you to some people I love very much." He didn't seem to be in a hurry and Karen had almost stopped. "Where are you going to paint?" he asked.

"I don't know yet. Do you have any suggestions?"

"Yes! Carry on this way for a while," he said, indicating the path ahead, "until you are in line with the chai-shop, but stay on top of the escarpment; from there, there is a spectacular view. Many times I thought I'd like to paint that image."

"Do you paint, too?"

"No, but I like those who do!" he said, laughing. He hugged her and kissed her again on the lips. Then he broke his embrace and Maria turned away, looking at Karen; she smiled timidly at her. Karen returned her an unsure, confused smile.

As soon as she got home, Rossana, Margo, Betty and also the Frenchman, wanted to know everything, word for word, in fine detail, or at least as far as Maria was willing to tell them without feeling embarrassed.

"Just you look at this one!" said Margo. "She's only just arrived and has got herself the most handsome man in Goa!"

"How did you do it?" asked Rossana, who was happy for her.

"I did next to nothing; this time he did everything," replied Maria.

"See that there was a reason for you to come here with me, instead of going to Colva? If you had gone to Colva you wouldn't have met him, would you?" Rossana said triumphantly. She was right! Maria hadn't even thought of that.

That evening at seven o'clock Paul arrived at the house, causing a lot of excitement; they were all waiting for him, pretending to be busy with lots of things to do. The girls were fascinated by him and strove to say something interesting in English; even the Frenchman was excited to meet him. Paul sat on the porch, happy to get to know her friends. He wanted to see what she had painted and praised her work. He promised to accompany her every day to see different places where she could paint, he knew the area well. Then, he took her to a restaurant nestled in the forest behind Vagator, run by a Goan family that was almost 'his' family. Lily and Peter had five children, four girls and one boy, who was the youngest; they all worked in the restaurant and were very friendly. He told her that Karen had been at his house the whole day; she was confused, no longer sure that she wanted to separate from him. Maria wasn't surprised and told him that she had been in a similar situation with her first boyfriend; she understood how hard it was to make such a difficult decision. At that time she had felt awful, because she knew she was causing him pain, as he still loved her. "Five years is a long time," she said thoughtfully. "Would *you* like to get back with her?" she asked, expecting an honest answer.

"No, I don't! I know what I want; it is here now, and I'm looking at her!"

She didn't expect this response and felt she was blushing. He was paying her a huge compliment, but was also giving her a lot of responsibility for his happiness. "How can you be so sure? We hardly know each other," she said cautiously.

Paul looked at her in silence, at her eyes, her hair, her mouth, her throat, and then back to her eyes: "I have always known you, Maria, I've only just found you *again!* Can't you feel it?"

She was puzzled. "I don't know, I haven't thought about it. I thought... I'm not used to things like that," she mumbled.

"Neither am I! It's not the kind of thing I do every weekend," he said, amused. When he smiled, small wrinkles formed around his eyes, and made him even more fascinating. "I know I want to be with you tonight, tomorrow night, and the night after, and then again. This is all I know. Isn't it enough?"

She felt burning with emotion, and surprise. "Maybe you're right," she said, blushing. "But let's take it slowly, one day at a time, if you don't mind."

"That's fine by me, as long as you are with me," he said, touching her foot with his.

That evening, while she was in his arms, Maria, who hadn't stopped thinking about what he had said, asked him: "How can you say that you've always known me? What makes you think that?"

Paul removed the arm he was hugging her with and propped himself up on one elbow, his head resting on his hand, and looked at her: "Do you remember the first time we met?"

"On the bus to Manali?"

"Yes. And you were wearing that funny sari."

"How could I ever forget! Franca had persuaded me to wear a sari, so we didn't look like tourists!" They both laughed.

"The first time you looked at me I felt something very strong in here," Paul said, pointing to his chest. "And then, when you started to cry, climbing through the mud of the landslide, I felt there was a powerful bond, even though at that time I didn't do anything to help you, because I couldn't!"

Maria thought back to those moments, she had found his presence magnetic. "For me too, it was powerful. It seemed as if time had stopped and I kept thinking about you," she said, thinking back to that time.

"Then you came to smoke in our room and I watched you without being noticed," continued Paul. "I wanted to make love to you on that bed, and if I could have..."

Oh... *really?* And she thought it was all in her head. "You taught me to smoke from the chillum, with your hands around mine. It was a very strong emotion!"

"I wished I could have been alone with you just then," he said, looking into her eyes, kissing her on the lips.

"And then you gave me your address!"

"Yes, which I'd never given to anyone else. That was an excuse to make you sit next to me, and there was a small chance that you might visit. Why didn't you come to see me? After all, you were close by."

"Because I liked you too much. What could I do? I would have been unable to say a word, embarrassed by the way I felt. And there was Karen, I couldn't do that to her."

Paul nodded. He went on to confide: "Then we met again in Vashist; another 'coincidence'. I don't believe in coincidences. You were even more beautiful! After the restaurant, when we went to make charas and then inside the temple, I couldn't keep away from you, I was attracted to you like to a compelling magnet."

She remembered how alive she felt when he was close to her, when he embraced her and later, teaching her how to make charas. So, the feelings were mutual, while she had always driven those thoughts away as pure fantasy.

"I thought about you every day, wondering where you were, what you were doing, if I'd ever see you again," confessed Paul.

She was speechless with surprise. Then, her thoughts, her dream, were not just a figment of her imagination; they were coming from him, too, thousands of miles away.

"I chanted for you, many times," she recalled.

"What do you mean?"

"I repeated this phrase, a sort of mantra, many times, thinking of you, for your happiness, because I wanted you to be happy."

He wanted to know what the sentence was and Maria said it to him.

"And you chanted it because you wanted me to be happy?" He looked at her in surprise.

"Yes, when I was chanting, and you were coming to my mind, I would send you my wish, which flew on these words. I wanted your happiness, even if I wasn't going to be part of it… I just wanted you to be happy."

Paul hugged her tight. After a long pause he said: "I'm touched, Maria. You did well to chant that phrase. As you can see, it worked! You have to teach it to me, too."

All the time he could take out from his work they spent together. While he was writing during the day, Maria went to the beach with the girls or painted. Late in the afternoon Paul would come and pick her up from her house and he'd take her to see new places along the coast or inland, in the 'jungle'. They were places that could be a subject, or offer inspiration, for her paintings. She watched him as he talked with people: he was kind, friendly, treating everybody with respect, with calm and quiet confidence; everyone liked him, men, women, the young and the old. They spent every night together.

One morning she woke up early and decided to go to the beach; she wanted to chant while it was still deserted, so she could do it aloud. Then she would begin a new painting. She took with her some paper, colours and paintbrushes, and went out in the cool, damp early morning air. The chai-shop was still closed; she was the first to arrive. She sat on a bench and began to chant, watching the sea. When she felt energized and happy, she laid paper and colours on a table and began to paint. The chai-shop man arrived within half an hour. "Chai?" he asked with a smile. "Yes, please, I'd love some!"

Soon, more people arrived and they all came over to observe her work, exchanging a few words. Having to go for a pee, she walked into the forest behind the chai-shop and stopped near the small stream. As she was bending down, she noticed a long snake, of an unbelievably bright yellow colour, a few steps away from her. Instead of moving away, she thought that since she was born in the year of the snake, this creature would 'recognize' her; she stooped to pee, her eyes fixed on the big reptile. The snake reacted badly to her proximity and leapt toward her, almost flying. Maria darted to the side and moved several metres away, surprised by the snake's reaction and disturbed by her incredible naivety.

She returned to the chai-shop sweating, her legs trembling, and shared with everybody the experience she'd just had. She was finishing her story when she saw Paul approaching. He hadn't yet reached the chai-shop when he said: "I had the strangest dream, I dreamed of a snake." All the people present looked at Maria.

"What colour was it?" she asked.

"Bright yellow!" he replied.

That weekend they went to a distant shore, a very special place where, next to the sea, there was a fresh-water lake. They had walked for many hours to get there and decided to spend the night sleeping on the beach, returning to Vagator the next day. Later in the evening they settled their sleeping bags under a tall palm tree.

"The other day you told me it's not a good idea to stop under coconut trees," recalled Maria.

Paul pointed his flashlight upward and said: "There isn't a single coconut on this palm tree, look!" They had been lying down for a while when Maria felt Paul's breathing change; he had already fallen asleep. A strong feeling of uneasiness came over her, becoming more and more insistent; eventually she couldn't ignore it any longer. She shook him, called him and finally managed to wake him up.

"I was already asleep," he groaned.

"Yes, I know, I'm sorry, but can we swap places? Come and lie down here, I'll swap with you."

"Why? I'm sleeping!" Paul resisted.

"I know, I know, I'm sorry, but please, let's swap!"

Unwillingly, he exchanged places with her. In the middle of the night, she heard a thud next to her head, felt a rush of air and the earth shuddered; they both woke up. "What was that?" she asked, in the dark.

"I don't know," Paul replied, lighting his torch.

A coconut in its green and pointed bark, big as a football, had fallen from the top of the palm tree and had landed in the sand, one inch from Maria's head, where a few hours before Paul's blond head had been resting!

Day after day they were getting to know each other better, in a relationship where words were often unnecessary, and the idea of separating seemed inconceivable. Every day he told her that he loved her, nobody had ever said it so convincingly and so often; it was a new experience and she didn't know whether it was wise to get used to it. The need to protect herself from pain regularly raised its head and said: 'Be careful Maria, words are easy to say. Maybe this is just the way he is and, who knows, one day he could suddenly change.'

One evening, sitting on the wall of Lily and Peter's restaurant, waiting for the dinner they had ordered, Maria asked him if he had had some nice love stories. Thinking of her own, she could remember one, the one with Jean-Claude, and even that was only a half nice story, the other half was Céline's. And yes, her first relationship had been a good one, but habit had suffocated it. Paul didn't have to think about it long. He began to tell her about the relationship with Patricia, three wonderful years; then there had been Louise, a beautiful woman, two great years; then Valentina, ah she was amazing, tall, beautiful, interesting; and then the other... Maria listened, more and more serious, as he recounted, going on and on. The grilled fish with chips arrived but, meanwhile, she had lost her appetite. 'See that's what I warned you about?' her mind told her, putting her on guard. 'Although this with you is a beautiful story, it's just one more to add to the other great stories of his life. And what did you think, little romantic woman, to be the special one, different from all the others? That such a man would stay with you? He is handsome, romantic and clearly has good stories. You are but one of them, with a beginning and an end. Careful not to get hurt; don't get burned again!'

In her heart, she distanced herself, and began to think about leaving. How much longer could she stay in Goa? Everyone said they'd never leave. She had a six-month visa and when that ran out, what would she do? He lived in India, she lived in Italy. Her mind, always ready to help, said 'Better to suffer a little now than to suffer a lot later.'
A few days later, sitting on the same wall, she let him know that she was leaving.
"When? Why?" Paul asked, visibly shocked. Because she had come all this way to see India and had made plans. As much as Goa was beautiful and they were having a great time, she didn't want to end up like

everyone else and stay for months. And he, did he necessarily have to work from Goa?

"I've got another week's work," he said. "After that I could join you!"

'One week, the famous Goan week,' her mind pointed out. 'What did you expect?'

"I'm going to Hampi and I will stop there a week. Then I'll go down to Mysore, but that's a big city. If you come to Hampi you'll find me, otherwise it will be more difficult," she announced. She had no great hopes; there was the saying 'Out of sight, out of mind!' It had become famous for a reason, right?

That evening Paul held her tight, he told her he respected her decision although he didn't like it. After completing his work he had to leave his house; maybe in a week he could make it, but she wasn't giving him much time. He was thinking aloud, Maria was listening, but didn't want to have any expectations. The girls were just as surprised by her decision. Why was she doing that? She had found such a man, and she was leaving? Couldn't she at least wait for him? They didn't agree with her decision; Rossana was especially shocked.

And where would they see one another again? They made plans and decided to meet in Kathmandu at the end of spring. It was hard to leave Goa, it was true, and the only way to do so was to buy a ticket. Hampi was one and a half day's travel away, a place almost unknown outside India. It had once been the capital of one of the many kingdoms, where thousands of beautiful stone temples had been built in an imposing architecture.

Paul took her to the bus station; they had slept very little. He held her tight until she had to get on board: "I can't stand to see you go. I wish I could go with you."

"I'll be at Hampi's bus station in a week's time. If you decide to come, you'll find me there."

"I will come!" he assured her. She settled on a window seat. Paul held her hand from the outside. When the bus started to move he kissed her hand, then followed her with his eyes, as the bus drove away. He waved and smiled, but Maria could see his sadness; he was confused and worried.

31. Life is beautiful!

The bus was running and Maria was looking at the fertile Goan landscape, with its bright green fields. She wasn't so sure she had made the right decision; she could have waited another week, after all. Why had she left? To put him to the test? To put herself to the test? She could only send him Nam-myoho-renge-kyo, now that she knew it would reach him, and hope that he would come and join her. She looked around.

The young man next to her introduced himself, he was Swiss-French, travelling with a couple of friends sitting behind them and they were all going to Hampi. It was a consolation to know she had already found some fellow travellers.

As the bus drove further away from the coast and into central India, the lush tropical landscape was gradually becoming more barren and dry. She looked out of the window and pondered; as more and more miles separated her from Goa the more she missed Paul and her friends. Would she ever see them again? She focused on what was going on outside, but this time the children chasing their bicycle wheels, the women washing their pots, the white oxen with long horns, were not enough to dispel the heaviness she felt in her heart; everything seemed to be in black and white. The temperature rose and the dust came in through the open windows, hour after hour of a monotonous, endless journey.

It was already evening when they reached the town of Hospet, where the coach ended its run. With the Swiss friends she went up to a small guesthouse where they could spend the night; it was as squalid as the town. The next morning they covered on foot the few hundred yards that separated them from the coach station and caught a bus to Hampi. The Swiss couple had done some research and they told her that the city had been partly destroyed centuries ago; nevertheless there were two thousand temples still intact, some very big, others much smaller. It took only an hour to reach Hampi, and they were not disappointed.

The barren hills and rounded boulders created a lunar landscape against the deep blue sky. A stone's throw from the square where the bus stopped towered an extraordinary temple at least ten stories high, covered in exquisite sculptures. The Swiss girl read in her guide book that it was called Virupaksha Temple. There were no hotels, just a shabby boarding house on Hampi's only street. The few tourists who travelled here settled in one of the many stone temples, rich in statues and bas-reliefs, mainly images of people and elephants sculpted on the walls, and shared the space with the numerous monkeys. Maria had no desire to be alone and so, when the new friends invited her to stay with them, she gladly accepted. They were looking for a small temple in particular, which had been recommended by a friend and had an unforgettable name: Vishnu Temple Number Two, to distinguish it from Vishnu Temple Number One, obviously.

Their friend had drawn them a map, which they were now faithfully following. They came to the end of the dusty main road and, from there, took a side trail covered in dry vegetation, sprinkled with the same fine dust. A hundred yards below flowed a wide green river, which cut the lunar valley in two and made it look more alive, less unreal. With pea-green fields lining its banks, it brightened up the white and barren landscape, giving some movement and life to that place, seemingly motionless for hundreds of years. As they progressed, out of the dusty vegetation they were walking in, they began to notice an ever increasing number of stone temples, some in ruins, others in reasonable condition. They asked a local man where Vishnu Temple Number Two was. Without hesitation, he pointed north; it was up there, a small temple. They climbed the steep hillside, toward their 'new home'.

It was a lovely temple, decorated with beautiful bas-reliefs, partitioned by elegant stone columns and open to the landscape on the front side. It was deserted, except for a few monkeys roaming idly who climbed on the roof, watching the new arrivals with curiosity. The couple settled at the back of the temple, while Maria laid out her sleeping bag near the front, from where she could see the river. The young man travelling with them put his things next to hers, leaving the couple a little privacy. And now, what should they do with their luggage if they wanted to explore the area? Apparently, their map-drawing friend took his most important things to the chai-shop during the day, while leaving the remaining luggage at the temple, confident that no one would steal them. It was strange not to have a door to close behind them, nothing to cook with; what would they do for food?

She went down to the river to wash off the dust from the journey. As soon as she entered the shallow water she felt a strong current, while the sun was so hot it was like being inside a furnace. She undressed and looked around: there was no one in sight, so she removed all her clothes. She plunged naked into the water, keeping close to the shore, careful not to get carried away by the current. The warmth of the sun on her skin brought back memories of Goa and Paul. Everything would have been so much nicer, had he been there too. Sitting on the river bank's round rocks she washed her body with soap and her hair with shampoo, savouring the wonderful contrast between the cold water and the scorching sun. Clean and refreshed, she slowly climbed the hillside back to her temple. She felt lonely. She took out her colours, paintbrushes and a few sheets of paper. She could paint, there was no shortage of subjects and total peace all around her, but she had no enthusiasm.

They all had a rest in the shade, waiting for the midday heat to relent. As soon as it cooled a little, they ventured out to explore Hampi, taking money and passports with them. In a bag that could be left at the chai-shop, they put other important things, and left their sleeping bags at the temple, to show it was already 'rented'.

The chai-shop was full of westerners eating or drinking chai. They ordered a vegetarian dish and, whilst waiting, looked around. Maria noticed a young man with a guitar, strumming classical music; she thought she recognized him. She observed him a little longer before approaching him. "Fabio?" she asked shyly. He looked up and yes, it was him, a great friend of Ester.

"Mamma mia, what a surprise! What are you doing here?" he asked.

"I'm visiting Hampi. What about you?"

"I'm doing a yoga course. I've been here for weeks. I found a good teacher and I live in his ashram! Are you alone?"

"Yes, except for a small group of Swiss people with whom I travelled from Goa."

Italians liked to travel in groups and it was unusual to find someone travelling alone. In this, they were alike.

"Where are you staying?" he asked.

"At Vishnu Temple Number Two," she replied, and they laughed heartily.

That week Maria spent a lot of time with Fabio. In the mornings she would paint and he did yoga, but around lunch time she was sure to find him at the chai-shop near the ashram, with his beloved guitar. While the owner was preparing bhaji and chapatis, Fabio played; he played as he talked with her, as he looked around absently, and she noticed that he never paid.

"Do you ever pay for what you eat, or for the chai?"

"They don't want me to."

"How come?"

"Because they want me to come here and play. For them it's a good enough payment."

"What do you play to the Indians?" she asked.

"Bach, of course," he replied, making her smile.

She enjoyed his company. Fabio took her to see the ashram where he lived, immersed in an atmosphere of peace and surrounded by a garden full of flowers, unusual in such a dry climate. He took her to see parts of Hampi she would never have discovered on her own and insisted that she go to sleep in the main temple, the tallest building. "It's a unique experience!" he said. "There must be hundreds of pilgrims. You said you wanted to see the real India. In there you'll find it. You've got to go, at least once!"

Maria told him about Paul and of how she'd left Goa, agreeing to meet up here in Hampi. Now, however, she was beginning to have doubts about the wisdom of her decision. She realized that what she had found in him was more than special; and what if he wasn't able to come? What if he ran into problems? They had no way of communicating.

Fabio, who had adopted the Indian philosophy of life, told her not to worry: "If he is the right person he will come, otherwise, it means he's not the right person. Have faith in your life and enjoy Hampi, while you're here!"

She postponed day after day but, on the sixth day, she took his advice and went to the temple with her sleeping bag. She took her passport and money with her while the Swiss friends would keep an eye on her other luggage. She entered shyly, wondering whether people would want to know what she was doing there, but no one paid her any attention.

This temple was much larger than any other Hindu temple she had visited before and was as tall as a cathedral. Inside, hundreds of pilgrims had settled as well as they could, some were cooking on kerosene stoves, while others were eating or resting. Maria had had dinner with Fabio who, until the last minute, had encouraged her to come. And here she was! She found a small empty space on the floor where she laid her sleeping bag with her head pointing toward the wall; she was the only westerner there. She pushed her purse with money and passport toward the bottom end of her sleeping bag and slipped inside it. It was hot, but she felt more protected like that.

She closed her eyes and wondered what on earth she was doing there, alone, along with hundreds of Indians. She opened her eyes again and looked up, feeling as small as a grain of sand compared to the dizzying height of the temple. She was tired and tried to sleep, but the floor was hard and there was constant noise: people coughing, talking, snoring, always a new sound that kept her awake. Besides, if she fell asleep wouldn't someone cut her sleeping bag and steal her purse? While these thoughts were going through her mind, she felt a light, but firm, touch on her feet.

She lifted her head and saw an old man with white hair sitting on the floor, looking at her. He patted her feet once again and, moving his hand up and down, as if to say 'don't worry, I'm here', he let her know she could relax. To be even clearer, he brought his index finger to his eye and then pointed it at her feet: 'I'll keep an eye on your things', he was signalling. Then, moving his open hand up and down, he said: "Shanti, shanti!" She touched her forehead, in a sign of respect and gratitude, and smiled at this grandfather, who looked back at her, nodding calmly.

She closed her eyes, smiling. Fabio was right, she couldn't possibly miss such an experience. Her thoughts went to Paul, who should by now be on the road; if he had left Goa that morning he was probably in Hospet at that very moment. Tomorrow she would know. Nam-myoho-renge-kyo, she murmured; she'd have to trust her life, there wasn't anything else she could do.

She slept very little, and when she awoke, the white-haired old man was still there, next to her feet. She thanked him and, in the cool hours of the morning, her sleeping bag under her arm, she walked slowly back to her temple. She tried to rest, so the time would pass more quickly, but she couldn't sleep; those waiting hours were endless.

She decided to go to the river to bathe. With her soap, shampoo and towel she descended the steep hill leading to the river bank and noticed, further down on the same side, a couple of women washing clothes. They were beating them with a stick that looked like a baseball bat against a flat rock, absently turning them every now and then, whilst talking to each other, without haste. The women glanced curiously at Maria, who waved at them, smiling; they responded with one of their candid smiles. They kept looking at her and, not to offend them, she kept her knickers and bra on. She lathered and rinsed her body and, when she dipped her head in the river, she noticed once again how strong the current was. She shampooed her hair and decided to immerse herself completely in the shallow water to rinse it thoroughly.

Suddenly she lost her footing on the round slimy stones and slipped. She managed to break the fall by placing one hand on the riverbed but, in that brief moment, the strength of the current scooped her up and, holding her in its formidable grip, swept her away. She tried to find the bottom with her feet, but couldn't, and neither could she stop. The river was pulling her along, in an incomprehensible vortex. She was still close to the shore, but the current was dragging her further away. She looked toward the women, who had seen her fall, and shouted: "Ji! Ji!", while floundering in the ever deeper water, desperately trying not to sink, in the throes of a panic that made her feel faint. She tried to scream, but her voice died in her throat; she spat out the water that filled her mouth as she tried to breathe; she searched for the women with her eyes clouded by water, her arm raised, but her head disappeared ever more often under the overwhelming river. Her lungs were bursting and she wanted to cry. She couldn't die like this.

Like a film in slow motion, she saw one of the women stand up, take the sari she was washing and, holding one end in her hand, launch it into the water. The five yards of fabric came undone, slowly freeing their whole length along the river's flow. She shouted something that Maria didn't understand. The other woman stood up, too, and did the same with one of her saris. Maria glimpsed one coloured stripe, and then another, coming loose and floating above the green water, swelling with air bubbles here and there. She was approaching them, driven by the current. She couldn't miss the hold. And there were the saris, right in front of her face. She grabbed the first one, and straight after, the second one. While the river dragged her along by her legs, powerful, unforgiving, the two women began to pull the saris toward their rock and, with them, Maria.

She stopped floundering and clung to the cloth with trembling hands, afraid of losing her grip. She let herself be pulled, unable to help, all the way to the boulders. Through water and tears clouding her vision she saw the two women holding out their hands to her. They grabbed her, hoisted her out forcefully and sat her on their boulder. She was a dead weight, shaking, and exhausted. She clung to them, crying, coughing, struggling to recover her breath. They stroked her back and gave reassuring pats on her head, as one did with a child, to say 'it's over, don't worry'. And they laughed, they literally laughed. "Okay, okay!" they were saying.
"Dhanyavad, dhanyavad," thank you, thank you, murmured Maria, spitting water and retching. Streams of tears flowed uncontrollably down her cheeks, violent sobs shook her from inside, unable to stop crying, shaken up.

So close! It had been so close, and she would have gone forever. Those women had saved her life. They spoke in their language, repeating 'okay, okay', comforting her, stroking her forehead, wiping her tears, patting her back and laughing, with those perfect white teeth, as if nothing serious had happened. They wrapped one of their saris around her shoulders, to shelter her from the sun and to cover her semi-naked body, while continuing with the reassuring caresses, stroking her shoulders and head, laughing! They let her cry, and comforted her until she calmed down and was able to return their smile.

Still trembling, Maria stood up and bowed with folded hands to thank them, touching her forehead, many times. Finally she walked away, unstable, deeply shaken, aware of her almost nakedness, to the place where she had left her clothes, a hundred yards up the hill. The women followed her with their eyes, talking to each other. Maria got dressed, continuing to blow kisses on the tips of her hand toward the two women, who laughed.

With trembling knees, climbing with the help of her hands, she made her way up the dusty hill and reached Vishnu Temple Number Two which was, at that time, deserted. She sat cross-legged, looking at the blue sky over the green river and with her hands clasped in front of her heart, her voice still a faint breath, she whispered Nam-myoho-renge-kyo. She wept without restraint, vomiting on the dry grass the little food she had inside, and wept again, unable to control herself. Little by little, she began to calm down and wiped her tears, beginning to feel, at last, grateful. Gratitude swelled her heart to bursting point, and moved her. She was grateful for her life, so precious, fleeting, irreplaceable and, if her legs had been able to hold her, she would have danced. Thank you! This moment was a new beginning; she could feel it in her heart. If Paul was going to arrive, he would be on the bus from Hospet at that very moment, and she was alive, without a scratch. She lay down on the cool stone, closed her eyes and thought of Gemma, her mother. Nam-myoho-renge-kyo.

She had a stick of kajal in the bottom of her bag. With her fingers still trembling, she put on some light make up, while her long hair dried in the hot muggy air. She clasped Jean-Claude's silver anklets, put on her earrings and her turquoise necklace. Slowly, she made her way toward the square. There was still time before the bus was due to arrive and she walked past the chai-shop, hoping to find Fabio. He was there, with his guitar and his Bach.

"What happened?" he asked, as soon as he saw her.

She told him what had happened down at the river, but Fabio wasn't easily fazed; he listened in silence. "Thank goodness," he said only. Maria calmed down a little more and ordered a chai.

"Would you come with me to wait for the bus?"

"If you like!"

"Yes, very much."

They walked together in silence, and then sat down to wait, while Fabio played something sweet and relaxing. "Life is beautiful," said Maria. He smiled, without looking at her, and continued to play sweet arpeggios.

Preceded by the noise and the dust, the bus made its entrance and stopped in the middle of the square. Maria's heart didn't dare beat too strong. The people stood up, but she couldn't see him. The passengers began to get off and her mind was completely blank. Finally, at the back of the bus, she saw that blond distinctive head, taller than all the others. Paul looked out and their eyes met. Maria walked toward the bus, excited and, as in a dream, waited for him to get down. Without a word, he dropped his bag to the ground, pulled her to him and kissed her on the lips. Then he picked her up, lifting her off the ground, and kissed her again, laughing.

They spent a couple of days in Vishnu Temple Number Two, which was now their home. The Swiss friends had left and Paul and Maria found themselves within the absolute peace of that lunar landscape, ancient and magical. They started to *re-connect*, as Paul said, certain that Maria had always been his companion.

Together, they left for their journey, which first took them to the major cities of Mysore and Bangalore, where life was faster and better organized than in north India. Then they spent a few weeks in the mountains of Tamil Nadu, in Kodaikanal, a town six thousand feet above sea level, rich in lakes, waterfalls and green landscapes, impressive and wonderful. It had once housed the British colonists, who went there to spend the summer months when the heat in the cities was unbearable. The settlers had gone, but the beautiful homes they had built remained.

In one of these mansions Maria and Paul were able to stay for very little money and, with it, came also a waiter-cum-butler who was determined to serve them in every possible way. Maria nicknamed him 'Friday', like Robinson Crusoe's friend because, like him, he had appeared out of nowhere and didn't want to leave. His expression was calm, his pace slow. He taught her to appreciate the present, often recommending that she do things in a more relaxed fashion: "Go slowly, Madam, much better," he'd say, with a sweet smile. He'd turn up with local produce, seasonal vegetables and fruits, and refused to take the money they offered him. He'd call Paul 'sahib', which meant 'Sir', a term used in the days of colonialism by Indian people addressing the English settlers, and looked at him with an expression of admiration and affection. He'd appear at his side whenever there was damp wood to dry, the fireplace to light in the cool evenings, kerosene to find, potatoes to peel. They became accustomed to his presence, pampered by his loving gestures, grateful for his help, and 'Friday' became a beautiful part of those two weeks that seemed like a honeymoon. Maria observed how Paul behaved with local people; this man of courteous, thoughtful manners, awakened the desire to be close to him in everyone he met, and she liked him more every day.

They spent a few weeks in Kerala, exploring it far and wide. In this state full of contrasts, there were churches, crosses and lots of communists; it was normal to see protest marches led by banners and dotted with countless red flags. One day, in Cochin, they decided to take a tour of the canals crisscrossing the region. Boats sailed on a course covered in leaves and lotus flowers, effortlessly cutting through them in their advance, revealing the green water underneath.

While waiting for their boat, Maria noticed a little girl of about three years of age, who was playing with stones near the road. Behind her a stray dog was rummaging in the garbage, but it had no luck and didn't find anything to eat. It began to move toward the child; it was dirty, skinny and there was something sinister in the way it progressed, almost crawling.

Maria called Paul's attention: "Look at that dog, doesn't it look weird?"

Standing up, Paul watched it. "I don't like the way he moves; it's not normal," he said.

Just then the dog approached the little girl from behind while she, unaware of its presence, continued to play. It stood on its hind legs, put its front paws on her shoulders and began to lick her. The girl screamed with terror. Paul was already running. He reached the child and picked her up, holding her in his arms, pushing the dog away with his foot. The local people ran over, shouting. There was an exchange of cries in the local language, one of the men got hold of the dog, while others turned to Paul, saying 'rabies, rabies'. A few minutes later, the child's mother came running and took her crying daughter from Paul's arms, thanking him for saving her.

Travelling with Paul was quite a unique experience; his presence attracted the attention of men and women. He stood out as a very handsome man but, more remarkable still, was the charm he exuded, an alchemy of warmth, calmness and kindness, accompanied by a ready smile. He was growing a beard and looked more and more like the images of Jesus Christ that people kept in each store of Kerala. They'd look at Paul, then turn to the image hanging on the wall, of Jesus with a red heart drawn in the open chest, and turn back to look at him, saying 'same same', meaning that they looked alike, and laugh. Maria went unnoticed when they were together and she got used to the fact that Paul was the centre of attention. He had a good knowledge of India and Indian people and with him she began to understand their way of thinking.

A couple of weeks later they were in Kanyakumari, in the state of Tamil Nadu, the southernmost tip of India. It was a sacred place, where the waters of the Bay of Bengal, the Arabian Sea and the Indian Ocean met and blended, among conflicting waves, into a single expanse. It was a point of pilgrimage; many Hindus bathed in the sea, where an ancient temple on the furthest rock marked that important geographical and mystical point. The men wore very little, while the women entered the sea fully dressed in their saris, advancing with difficulty through the waves, where they submerged, doing 'puja', their prayers.

Maria and Paul were staying in one of the small hotels in the area and noticed how some men celebrated the pilgrimage by drinking generous quantities of beer and spirits. That evening they were returning to their hotel after a walk along the beach; it was almost dark and there was no one around, when they saw a man lying in the middle of the road. They approached and understood immediately that he was alive, but completely drunk.

"If he stays here he'll get hit by a car," said Paul, worried. "Give me a hand Maria; let's move him to a safer place." He lifted him under his arms, while Maria got hold of his legs.

"He's so heavy!" she gasped.

"We're doing him a great favour!" Paul said, panting. "Tomorrow, when he wakes up, we'll get him to buy us a drink." And they burst out laughing.

It was hard work moving him to the side of the road, but the man didn't seem to notice anything. They were walking away, when they saw him crawl and lie again in the middle of the road. They looked at each other, shocked, and laughed again.

"Look at that!" Maria said. "What do we do now?"

"We need to do something more drastic, otherwise the first car that goes past will make mush of him!" Paul said, looking around. "I thought I saw a ditch, a few feet from the road; let's put him in there, at least he won't be able to escape so easily," he said firmly.

They retraced their steps, grabbed hold of the man by his feet and armpits and, in the dim light of a half moon, carried him to the ditch, where a bed of dry leaves formed a soft base. Maria went down first, then helped Paul lower the man, who was sleeping soundly, and laid him on the bed of leaves. Paul climbed back out the ditch and held his hand out to Maria, hoisting her up. They stopped to observe him. "Stay there and sleep until tomorrow!" Paul ordered. As if to reassure them he wouldn't move, the man started to snore loudly, sounding like a motorcycle warming up its engine. They laughed for a third time, happy and satisfied to have helped another human being. Paul put his arm around her shoulders and kissed her. Slowly they walked toward their guesthouse.

They travelled up the west coast of India, stopping in a tiny lovely town. In Mahabalipuram there was a huge temple, a stone's throw from the sea, the only one remaining out of seven original temples. The whole town was decorated with bas-reliefs, sculpted everywhere, from the caves to the temples scattered in the surrounding fields. That too was a place of pilgrimage, but less touristy and more spiritual than Kanyakumari. The male population was dedicated to carving the stone and were skilled craftsmen. From morning till night you could hear the tick tick of chisels that, with patience and skill, gave shape to statues, large and small. Students were practicing under the eyes of the elders and carved all the rocks around, turning them into works of art. That background noise accompanied every action and every thought of the day, beating the same slow rhythm that Maria felt within herself; a constant feeling of exhaustion accompanied her from the moment she woke up and throughout the day, but she thought it would pass.

They continued up the coast and stopped in Madras. The city was huge, featuring dozens of high temples, composed of countless floors, each adorned with hundreds of statues of gods, painted in bright colours. They found a boarding house. Maria was not feeling well; maybe it was the April heat, but there was something else, the fatigue was becoming more and more difficult to ignore and was accompanied by twinges of pain in her lower abdomen.

The owner of the guesthouse, a man of about forty, friendly and cheerful, suggested she go to the hospital; they were good, he assured her. Accompanied by Paul, she asked to see a gynaecologist. After half an hour standing at reception she was made to sit in a waiting room; after one more hour, she was shown into a young doctor's surgery.

She explained her symptoms, feeling uncomfortable in front of this young woman who was listening with an openly critical expression. She asked Maria if she was married, if she had sexual intercourse, if she had had more than one partner, and was taking in Maria's answers with an ever more severe, almost hostile attitude. She ordered her to lie on the bed and examined her; then she went back to her desk and told Maria her verdict: she had a venereal disease.

"A venereal disease?" repeated Maria, in disbelief.

"Yes, you western people are very promiscuous," said the doctor. Then, looking straight into her eyes, she added: "Next time you'll take more care!" It seemed as if she was enjoying that moment, with a mixture of satisfaction and anger.

"Which one?" Maria whispered, dazed. "Which venereal disease? There are many!" she insisted.

The doctor took a long pause, staring at Maria, who, with red hot cheeks, was holding her gaze. Eventually, reluctantly, she replied: "Syphilis! You have syphilis."

"*What?*" she blurted out, shocked.

"Next time you'll be more careful," repeated the young woman with the white coat, standing up and shoving her hastily toward the door, without any advice, without a prescription, nothing.

Maria found herself out of the surgery, where Paul was waiting. Seeing her altered face he worried: "What did she say?"

She looked at him. "She said I have syphilis," she murmured, with a faint voice. After a short pause, she added: "If I have it, you have it, too."

She didn't expect Paul's reaction. He held her gently by her shoulders, pulled her close to him, and embraced her. With her head resting on his chest, she heard the sound of his words echoing inside her head: "If we have it, we'll treat it," he reassured her.

"But if we have it, it's my fault! You have been with the same woman for five years; I instead have been in several relationships," she said.

"I don't care Maria, we're together now," he replied, moving her away from him a little and looking into her eyes. "This is something that can be solved, and I love you."

In that moment she knew that this was the man she wanted to be with. 'I'm going to marry this one', she thought, her head leaning on his chest, the beating of his heart clear, comforting.

Unable to speak any further, her throat closed by a knot caused by the shock, they went out into the heat of the day and walked hand in hand. Maria was speechless, unable to emit any sound, despite Paul's attempts to get her to talk; she could only respond with a nod of her head. They found themselves outside the walls of Madras's largest temple. "Do you want to go inside?" he asked. She nodded. They entered the courtyard where a huge elephant, its head and trunk decorated with brightly coloured drawings, stood quietly. His keeper, wearing only a sarong wrapped around his waist, stood next to it. The man waved his arm, signalling them to come closer. "Blessing," he said, "blessing." And why not? It came just at the right time.

He told Maria to stand in front of the sacred elephant and remain still. The big animal lifted its trunk and slowly lowered it, resting it gently on her head; it felt like a very big hand, of considerable weight, covering her whole head. She laughed, excited, looking at her enormous friend's grey and wrinkly feet. The keeper said to Paul: "One rupee". Paul pulled out a one-rupee note and handed it to him, but the man shook his head, he had to give it to the elephant. Paul brought the bill next to the tip of the trunk, which the elephant bent slightly. With this, it grabbed the bill and, with a large swinging motion, swept its trunk to one side, lifted it into the air and lowered it again behind it, handing the note to its guardian. It was then Paul's turn, and the same ceremony was repeated. The open end of the trunk dropped carefully over Paul's blond head, covering it completely. Maria gave a rupee to the elephant, who took it gently from her hand.

They left the temple, in silence, smiling, holding hands. Vendors sat on their mats along the perimeter of the temple walls. They offered their wares, with a wave of their hand: "Madam stop, look Madam." Maria shook her head, still unable to speak. "Ishstones?" offered an old salesman with a white turban, pointing to the stones on display on his carpet. The notorious word, pronounced in the same way as the man who 'removed' the stones from people's ears in Delhi, had an overwhelming effect: Maria and Paul looked at each other and burst out laughing. She laughed to tears, finally letting out the trauma that had struck her dumb. Even the old salesman chuckled with them, infected by her irrepressible laughter.

Back at the guesthouse, they relayed the doctor's verdict to the owner, who had considerately asked them what had happened at the hospital. He reacted cheerfully, waving a hand in the air and saying: "Oh, syphilis! It's not a problem, I had it too! With penicillin it goes away." However, he reflected, how could this doctor be sure of it? Without a blood test it couldn't be diagnosed, and he advised them to go to a private clinic close to their hotel. They did so immediately and two days later, when they had their results, they discovered that neither of them had any syphilis. The lady doctor had vented on Maria her disapproval of western women's free culture! At the same time though, she had done her an unexpected favour: the way Paul had responded to the situation had convinced her that she couldn't possibly find a better man.

She wrote to Luna, she needed to open her heart and share what was going on in her life. She described the relationship with Paul, she was happy. In those months spent together she had become convinced, as he often told her, that they were made for each other, but she felt a great sadness at the thought of writing to Jean-Claude. She loved him, she knew he loved her and was sure she had created problems between him and his girlfriend. What could Luna tell her, was there a point of view in the Buddhist philosophy that could inspire her? She dropped the aerogramme with her sorrows and anxiety in a mailbox in Madras Post Office.

They continued their long journey that took them up the coast to Puri and then to Calcutta. Here Maria saw more poverty than in any other Indian city, but this was accompanied by a lightness of spirit and humour, unexpected in such extreme circumstances. They stopped only a few days, but she could easily have stayed longer; there was an intriguing atmosphere in this tough city where people were carried on rickshaws by skinny men running barefoot. They arrived in Varanasi in May. Paul had never been there and the temperature was so high it was impossible to walk in the sun for more than a few seconds; after that it seemed as if their brain might explode! They spent the hottest hours of the day resting in their guesthouse, lying under the ceiling fan that turned continuously, and going out only early in the morning and after six in the afternoon. They talked about everything, they laughed, they loved each other and, little by little, Maria's energy started to come back.

One day Paul returned carrying a tray with two chai and a plate of samosas that he had bought from a nearby restaurant. They were hungry and sat on the bed devouring them. Wiping the crumbs from her mouth, Maria said: "I almost almost marry you," translating literally into English an Italian phrase that one would tell a friend in a moment of harmony: 'quasi quasi ti sposo'. The English sentence sounded quite clumsy.
In the same awkward style, Paul replied: "I almost almost accept."
There was a moment of silence, in which they both digested what they had just said.
"Are you saying we get married?" enquired Maria.
"Yes, if you'd like. I *do want* to marry you. You were made for me… in Nirvana!" he said, grinning.
She laughed: "What a beautiful thing to say! And you for me. All right, then! I'll wear red, as Indian women do. How about you?"
"I'll wear creamy white! It's the colour that suits me best."
And so the decision was made! They continued to plan where they'd buy the fabric for the dress: in Jaipur, suggested Paul; where they'd get married: in Venice was Maria's first idea, with gondolas. They discussed the British passport that Maria could then request, giving them the possibility of living in India together, without visa problems, as British people didn't need one.

The next day, running from one shaded area to another, avoiding the scorching sun as much as possible, she went to the Post Office. She had given Luna that address and, to her delight, she found the answer she was longing for. She opened the letter in the nearest chai-shop, where she had rushed to sit down and ordered a chai.

"*Dearest Maria,*

Thank you for your beautiful letter, which I read many times. First of all, some news from London: I have just finished a television commercial and Harry is working in a theatre on a play about South Africa, just as he wanted. When we don't have acting jobs I work in a restaurant and he in a pub. The pay isn't brilliant but it gives us the flexibility we need. I have started a course on massage and want to eventually set up my own business, while Harry is still deciding between different options. We are both writing and are very happy. In a couple of months we'll be moving in together. I'm excited! It will be the first time I live with my partner.

We are delighted for you and Paul. From what you've told me you have a very deep relationship. I remember that, from the first time you met him, you felt there was a strong bond between you. I can't wait to meet him.

I understand you feeling sorry for Jean-Claude but I think that, if these two men have appeared in your life so closely one to the other, there must be a reason, and you shouldn't feel guilty. Jean-Claude helped you realize that you are beautiful and deserve to be loved. There must have been problems with his girlfriend before he met you; after all, he chose to come to Venice, didn't he? Don't forget that you gave him a lot, too. I think you should just accept that he was very important in your life. You've described him as a bridge between your past and your future; your dream of him in Venice taking you to Paul said it clearly. Was it a karmic relationship? I have no doubt about it, as was the meeting between us, as are all the important encounters that, in one way or another, change our lives.

We practice this philosophy of life to become stronger, learning to accept and use the suffering that life brings us. By the same token, we must also learn to accept happiness, when it comes. Jean-Claude has helped you find love with a man that's not him. Trust that what is right for your happiness, is also right for his. Thank him and help him become completely happy. How?

Buddhism teaches that we have nine levels of consciousness, the first five being our senses (sight, hearing, smell, touch and taste); the sixth consciousness processes what we perceive with the first five and helps us come to our own conclusions; for example if something is too hot, we realise quickly that we should stop touching it! The seventh is our sense of individual identity, of who we think we are; the eighth consciousness is the storehouse of our karma, which is connected to that of our families, country and environment. For this reason, any internal change we make, affects not only our life but also that of our family, society and ultimately, the whole of humanity.

But what I find incredibly exciting is the ninth consciousness, our deepest level, free from any 'karmic impurities'. It is the force of the universe itself, which we possess too and of which we are part, the world of Buddhahood. When we chant we nourish ourselves with this pure energy, extracting infinite life force, drawing it directly from the universe, becoming one with it and activating our inner Buddhahood. Then, the way we perceive everything around us is transformed; what before made us suffer becomes an opportunity, a springboard to become happier. It's not that our karma disappears but, as the light of the stars and the moon seems to fade when the sun has risen, so when our enlightened state rises it illuminates our lives and we are no longer controlled by our karmic tendencies. We can transform them in a positive way and create value from every situation.

We perceive how we are intimately interconnected with everyone and everything, with Life itself, of those who are alive and those who were. We sense how, fundamentally, we are all equal and every living entity is worthy of respect. It is much stronger than our karma. When we chant daimoku it's like entering the 'palace of Buddhahood' from which we can purify and enlighten the other eight consciousnesses in the light of our compassion, wisdom and courage. It's like putting on the right glasses and, all of a sudden, we see everything clearly.

I have this image of the ninth consciousness as being a sea, where there are no walls and no divisions. My Buddhahood and yours are like two drops of water in the same ocean. For this reason, when I chant for your happiness, my wish reaches you. That's why my chanting makes a difference to the collective energy and contributes to peace, because everything blends in the same great sea, and feeds it.

You can imagine how, from one heart to another, especially when there is love, we can feel this connection, even if the distance is immense. Let him know you'll be doing this, so that he can feel it clearly and recognize it. Isn't it amazing just how much we can do, and give?

Be happy Maria! Don't be afraid of deserving happiness. Continue to chant and learn more and more about this philosophy. It will give you so much, and you will be able to give ever more to others.

I can't wait to see you, and meet Paul. Harry keeps telling me to send you a big hug from him. He says that, without you, he'd still be waiting for the right time to kiss me!

A warm embrace from your dear friend Luna.

PS. I love you."

Before leaving India she wrote to Jean-Claude, posting her aerogramme from Varanasi, the very place they had met. She still felt as if a cloud was obscuring her heart's clear sky. She would have been completely happy, had she not felt so sad for him.

They spent a wonderful month in Nepal. In Kathmandu they were joined by Betty, Margo and Rossana for a week. Her friends were delighted to see her and Paul so strong and happy. Rossana kept reminding them that it was all thanks to her, and she was right. The five of them travelled to Pokhara and, after a few days and a magic mushroom omelette each, the girls took their leave. A few weeks later Paul and Maria went back to India. In a few weeks she would have to go back to Italy. Before leaving Nepal she had had to visit the Indian Embassy, where they had given her a new visa to re-enter India. All was well. They still had time.

32. Surprises

Considering the sweltering heat outside, the temperature inside New Delhi's police station was almost pleasant. Above her head the large fan hanging from the ceiling was moving its large blades at an irregular but steady pace. There was a point where the blades slowed down and then resumed with strength, a bit like an old lame man struggling to walk, one step right and one step lame, one right, one lame, hypnotic.

Unconsciously retaining their breath, not daring to get noticed, dozens of people were anxiously waiting for one of the three police officers to deal with their matter.

Indian men were dressed at their best, their hair brushed back, neatly coated with brilliantine. Maria wore a longer skirt; Paul had changed from Indian style pyjamas and kurta to western style trousers and a spotless white shirt, looking very handsome.

She only needed a stamp in her passport which, in itself wouldn't take more than two minutes, but the queue and the wait were interminable. Everyone kept their voices low to avoid getting scolded by the policemen, busy speaking seriously with the people who, one after the other, sat in their presence.

Of the three police officers they had been observing for a couple of hours, one was slow and slightly hesitant, the second one was more severe but efficient, and the third one, with the thickest moustache, seemed to find a problem with all those who, timidly, respectfully, sat down at his desk. They nicknamed him 'the bastard' and Maria was hoping she wouldn't have to deal with him. Instead, when her turn came, he was the one.

She smiled at him, uncertain, as she sat on the chair still warm from the previous person, but the cop wasn't looking at her and didn't see her smile. "Yes?" he said, absently.

"I have to get an extension to my visa for the last ten days," began Maria, handing her passport to him. Without taking his shoulders off the back of his chair, the moustachioed policeman reached out and took it. She went on to explain: "I have a six-month visa, but before leaving Nepal, the Indian embassy put that stamp that says 'fourteen days only'.

She was beginning to feel nervous while he flipped through her document, page after page. With some anxiety, she continued: "But, according to the visa they gave me in Rome, I still have ten days. That's why I came here to see you."

He wasn't looking at her and continued to study her passport. "I can't give you an extension," he declared. "You left India to go to Nepal. From there the visa is valid fourteen days only, and today is the last one. No extension!" He began to write her details on a log. Maria wasn't prepared for this response. She broke out in a cold sweat. She knew that arguing with a police officer wasn't a good idea, but… what else could she do?

"But... excuse me, if you look at the endorsement date from the Rome embassy, you will see that ..." her hands and her voice were shaking.

The policeman had finished writing her details in the register and was annoyed: "I cannot extend your visa, miss. You must leave India before midnight, otherwise we'll arrest you." He pushed her passport, sliding it across the desk with his manicured hands and nails.

"But... isn't there anything that can be done? I don't have a return ticket, I'm waiting for it from Italy. Can't I have a few more days... until it arrives?" she begged.

For the first time he looked at her. "Go to your embassy and see what they can do to help you. But you must leave!" he concluded. With a snap of his fingers he caught the usher's attention and ordered: "Next!"

She stood up, trembling, and looked at Paul, who understood immediately that something was wrong. She walked to him. "I have to leave by this evening," she said in a whisper, her throat closed by a knot of anxiety.

"Why? What about the last ten days?" Paul asked, incredulous.

"No, they won't give me the ten days," she murmured in a state of shock. They moved like sleepwalkers toward the exit, while she reported her conversation with the police officer.

"I can't believe it! You can't leave like this!" Paul protested. "Maybe you should have given him a 'bakshish', one thousand rupees." Maybe! But she hadn't offered him anything and, in any case, in public, it wouldn't have been possible. Now they had her passport's details, she couldn't risk being arrested, but she couldn't just leave either, she had many things to do, shopping in Paharganj for things to sell in Italy, and she couldn't leave Paul, not like that. Besides, she didn't even have a ticket!

"Maybe the embassy will give me those ten days; after all, I do have a visa. The Delhi Police can't take away what the Rome embassy gave me!" she mused aloud, and a ray of hope gave her the confidence she needed.

Paul said that the British Embassy was very good; was the Italian one good too? She hadn't the faintest idea, she had never been there.

They stopped the first scooter that drove past and, without haggling on the price, gave the driver their destination. They held hands, hoping the situation would change.

"If you leave tonight, you must promise me to write as soon as you arrive in Italy!" said Paul.

Maria didn't even want to consider the possibility of having to leave: "You'll see that there is a solution! In the end it doesn't do anyone any harm if I stay a while longer."

Paul held her close. Being English he didn't need a visa, but he knew people from other countries who, being without one, had had major problems. They looked at each other, mixed-up, confused.

The scooter stopped in front of the Italian Consulate, there wasn't an Embassy. Seeing the green, red and white flag waving gently in the midday sun, Maria took heart and felt an affection for her country that she didn't know she had. She wasn't completely alone, after all. They were surely going to help her find a solution. She smiled shyly as they pushed the glass door open. The air conditioning helped them calm the anxiety they felt; seeing the signs in Italian encouraged her even more; hearing her language, for the first time in weeks, was a great consolation. Hand in hand, they followed the signs to the waiting room.

She was received by an Indian employee who spoke Italian. She told him her name and the reason for her visit. Then, while Paul went to 'explore' the bathrooms, Maria entered the large waiting room. It was furnished with sofas, tables and chairs, and was very busy; there were at least a dozen people. She looked around, hoping to find somewhere to sit. A dirty hippy over there, a clean hippy near him, a young woman with a newborn baby, a pregnant one; the atmosphere was cheerful, lively, everyone was talking loudly. At last she saw an empty seat next to a woman she could only see from behind. A strange feeling took hold of her as she approached.

"Excuse me, is this seat free?" The woman ignored her, but... "*Franca?*" Maria exclaimed, stunned. "Is it *you?*" She sat down next to her and, without thinking, she hugged her. But Franca didn't respond and continued to ignore her. "How are you? What are you doing here?" she asked. Franca turned slowly and looked at her, but didn't recognize her, or perhaps she was joking. For a short while she stared at Maria with those pale blue eyes. She was limp, sitting like a sack of potatoes. She didn't move, didn't say a word, then turned around and went back to staring at the wall. Maria didn't know what to think! Maybe Franca was tired, but didn't she think it was an incredible coincidence? "How amazing meeting you here! How are you?" she asked. "If you knew who I am with... you'd never guess. We travelled all over India. Where have you been all this time?" The young woman turned slowly to look at her, but Maria had a feeling she couldn't see her.

"In the mountains," she replied and went back to looking ahead, staring at nothing.

"I bet it was beautiful," said Maria, trying to encourage her to talk. "Paul and I, in a moment you'll see him, he's just gone to the toilet, we've been everywhere. He came from Goa to Hampi, thankfully, where I'd gone earlier on, and from there we went to Kerala, which is wonderful, they're Christians, not Hindus... I didn't know. Besides they are communists and always marching with red flags, every day seems like the first of May! Then we went to the most southern point, it's called Kanyakumari, three seas merge there, a magical place, truly."

As she spoke, she observed Franca, looking for a spark of life or enthusiasm. The moment of resentment she had felt after she recognized her, had been replaced first by surprise and then by the feeling that something strange was happening. Or maybe she was joking? It wasn't like her, though. But, how well did she know her? She once thought she did, but had been mistaken.

She continued to speak, trying to get some reaction: "Then we travelled up the Madurai coast. It's incredible, there are some fantastic temples and a sacred elephant gave us his blessing, resting his trunk on our heads. Paul said 'You go first, Maria', not trying to be a gentleman, in my opinion, but because he was scared. It's a strange feeling, this huge thing on your head, it's like a heavy hand, as big as my head... and then, with the tip of his trunk he took the rupee that Paul gave him and passed it to his keeper."

Franca didn't laugh; instead she kept her lips tight. If she was joking, she was keeping it up for a long time. "And then we went to Calcutta. Mamma mia, what a place! Do you remember the feeling we had the first time we took a rickshaw? And ours was a bicycle. Well, Calcutta's rickshaws have two poles, the man picks them up and starts to run, and we, sitting there, are carried by him. Arghhh! I wanted to scream. How can people do this to other people? I wanted to get off and walk, but I knew that at least it was a job, no matter how exhausting, and we paid him double, poor man."

Maria thought she could see the beginning of a reaction; Franca was listening. She continued, watching her: "Then we returned to Nepal, because Paul had never been there. We went to the same hotel, and there I met the Italian girls I had been in Goa with, which was wonderful. And we also went to Pokhara. I thought of you while we were there!" Franca winced slightly, shuffling on her chair with a sense of unease.

"And then we went to Varanasi; it was stiflingly hot. And now we're here and it's possible that I have to leave earlier than I thought. And you Franca, are you leaving, too?" Slowly, Franca turned to look at her, still with that empty expression. This time, however, she continued to stare at her, and Maria felt a shiver run down her spine: "Don't you recognize me? It's me, Maria!" She touched her arm and stroked it gently.

"Yes, I know," Franca replied. She looked away and removed her arm, crossing her hands in her lap. Looking ahead she said: "I've been only to the mountains. Not good. I haven't seen anything. Did nothing. Very bad."

"What's bad, Franca? Are you okay? Are you tired?"

To her surprise, she sneered: "Yes, tired, very tired!" There wasn't even the shadow of a smile, no light in her eyes. She turned to Maria again, staring. Suddenly she smiled. "Is that you, Maria?" she asked, her eyes widening in surprise.

This time Maria was even more confused. But then, had Franca been joking before? She saw Paul come into the waiting room and beckoned him over. Then she turned to Franca: "Do you remember him? It's Paul; we met him in the mountains!"

Franca looked vaguely in Paul's direction and shook her head. Maria didn't know whether she had really seen him and insisted: "I'm sure you'll remember. You'll see he'll know you!"

Paul had approached and smiled when he saw the woman she was with, recognizing a familiar face, but then he shifted his gaze to Maria, quizzically, as if to say 'but isn't this the one who... ?' Maria nodded.

Franca observed him for a few seconds and then, without emphasis, said: "He's handsome."

Maria laughed. "Isn't he just? And so kind! I can't believe my luck! If you only knew how many things have happened, I'll tell you when I can. Is it your turn soon? I have a problem; I hope it's not too difficult. I wonder how long I'll have to wait! Have you been here long?"

This time Franca's answer was swift. "Yes, I've been here long, too long. They *sent* me. They *made* me come," she said, and then shut her lips tight. Under her apparent calm, Maria felt Franca was bursting with tension. She looked at Paul, who didn't understand what was happening but, seeing Maria's worried expression, began to pay more attention.

"Who made you come here? The consulate?" she asked.

"No! The voices," murmured Franca. "They are everywhere." She closed her mouth, pursing her lips even more, her jaw twitching uncontrollably.

Maria glanced at Paul, who was now watching carefully. Softly, she asked her: "What do the voices say, Franca?" The twitching became more frequent, more intense. Franca began to contort her hands, her breathing quickened.

"They say Kali, they call me Kali... destructive, evil!" She seemed very angry with the voices, and threatening. "I'll show them!" she said determinedly.

"Where do these voices come from?"

All of a sudden Franca turned to stare at her. She had lost a lot of weight. Maria noticed with dismay that she could make out the bones in her forehead, her cheekbones; her nose looked like a bird's beak.

"From all sides, even from the speakers in the bus station!" Getting angry at the memory, Franca raised her voice: "I've heard them, Kali, Kali. They want to send me away."

The expression of hatred suddenly froze, then, lowering her voice to a threatening whisper, staring at the wall in front of her, she declared: "But I'm not going!" She folded her arms and stomped her feet firmly on the ground. At that very moment, the usher called: "Franca Vianello." She didn't move.

"It's your turn Franca. Do you want me to come in with you?"

Franca didn't answer. She got up slowly. Maria glanced quickly at Paul and, gently holding Franca's elbow, she walked with her toward the consul's room.

The consul was much younger than Maria had expected. She had hoped to find a man with white hair, a wise man, and instead he was in his thirties, with dark hair and a friendly expression. Maria explained briefly that she was a friend and he didn't object to her staying in the room. He invited them to sit down, then turned his attention to Franca and, in a relaxed fashion, said: "Hello Franca, what can I do for you?"

She stared at him for a while, watching him, gathering her thoughts. In silence, they studied each other. Then, slowly, stiffly, using her words as darts, she hissed: "I want to know if there are any complaints against me... from the Indian Government... or the Italian Government!"

Maria felt a chill race from the base of her spine to the back of her neck, her hair stood on end all over her body. She looked at the consul, who seemed only mildly surprised. He recovered quickly and, in a pragmatic manner, replied: "Let's have a look. Franca... Vianello, right?"

She nodded solemnly and sat more upright, her lips tight, her hands clasped in her lap. The consul went to the filing cabinet, opened it, flipped through various folders and then closed it gently: "No, there's nothing against you, Franca." Unhurriedly, he went back to his chair. Settling comfortably, he said: "Why do you ask?"

Speaking slowly, accusingly, Franca said: "In that case... I want to know why they're persecuting me." The consul didn't interrupt and Maria felt another chill climb up her spine. "Why does everyone want me to leave India?"

"What makes you think they want you to leave?" asked the consul, kindly.

She seemed surprised by his question. It became clear she didn't like his style. She narrowed her eyes into slits and leaned across the table, as if she wanted to spit her words out: "That's what I'm asking *you*! Why are all these voices shouting at me Kali, Kali, go away, though I haven't done anything wrong? I'll tell you clearly. There is no way... that anything or anyone..." she raised her voice by three tones, "*You hear me?... Can make me go away! Is it clear?*"

"Maybe the voices know you're tired. How long have you been in India this time?" the consul asked, not at all fazed by her manners.

Franca withdrew defensively, leaning back in her chair, her arms crossed: "I still have one month's visa and sixty dollars. As you can see, I haven't spent a lot; in fact I spent very little. There is no problem, right? Why should I leave?"

"You don't have to leave, if you don't want to," he reassured her. "But a rest would do you good. How long is it since you last ate?"

This question caught her off guard: "I don't know, one day, maybe two. What's that got to do with it?"

For the first time she seemed bewildered. The reins of the conversation were now in the consul's hands. "It's got a lot to do with it. Do you remember when was the last time you had something to drink?" he pressed.

Franca felt uneasy; she shuffled in her chair, swallowing with difficulty: "Maybe yesterday... I don't remember." She ran her tongue over her lips, trying to moisten them, but her tongue was dry. She brought the back of her hand to her parched lips. The consul poured a glass of water, which Maria handed her. She took it with trembling hands and began to drink, a little sip at a time. It seemed as if swallowing hurt her throat. He remained silent until she emptied the glass and then, with no apparent interest, asked: "How many days is it since you last slept?"

The question hit home and Franca slumped in her chair. Suddenly she seemed exhausted. "Two, three nights, I don't remember," she replied. She was visibly struggling to keep her eyelids open and had lost all will to fight. When he spoke, she paid attention.

"The consulate has a nice place here in Delhi, it's friendly, clean and comfortable. There is also a garden with a lawn and flowers. There's a young man there just now." Both Franca and Maria were listening carefully. "He's only nineteen. During his trip he took 'datura'. Do you know what it is?" Maria shook her head, while Franca nodded, wary, but interested. The consul went on: "We don't know what he did under its influence, but we know that he was beaten up. After that, do you know what he did?" Both girls shook their heads. "He built a makeshift pyre with bundles of dry wood, in the centre of the village, sat on it and set himself on fire. You don't feel any pain under the influence of 'datura'." Maria felt nauseous, Franca was very interested. "Before people could pull him down and put out the fire, he was already burned. He will survive, but he'll never be able to have children." He paused, looking seriously at the girls sitting across his desk, then continued: "I want you to tell this story to your friends, when you go home. He's only nineteen. In a few days we will repatriate him to Italy, but in the meantime he is alone and has no one to talk to." He looked at Franca: "Why don't you go and keep him company? He'd be very happy and, meanwhile, we'll give you a clean comfortable bed, you'll eat Italian food, the cook is from Rome, and there'll be no voices bothering you. What do you say?"

He said it casually, as if he didn't care much, without taking his eyes off Franca's face. She averted his gaze and, staring at the floor, nodded.

He wrote an address on a piece of paper and handed it to her: "His name is Roberto. Get a scooter, it will cost about twenty rupees; have you got it?"

Franca nodded again. Maria looked at him with admiration and gratitude. She helped her friend stand up and took her to the office door. "It won't take me a moment, Franca. Meanwhile, please sit with Paul, then I'll help you, okay?" Franca nodded again, meekly.

Maria closed the door. Standing next to the window, the consul spoke before she could thank him: "She's not in a fit state to travel around India. Anything could happen to her, she could die; but I cannot force her to follow my advice. Can you make sure she gets in that scooter?"

"Of course," confirmed Maria. "We know each other well. And now what will happen?"

"We'll call her parents, ask them to pay for her return flight and we'll repatriate her, probably on the same plane as Roberto."

"But Franca already has a plane ticket," said Maria.

"She cannot travel alone, she'll be accompanied by an employee from the consulate and we fly with Alitalia."

"It'll be expensive!"

"For her parents it's more important that their daughter gets back alive. Are her parents poor?"

"No, quite the opposite," replied Maria.

He made a small movement with his head, as if to say 'then there is no problem.' They returned to sit at the desk.

"Now can I tell you my problem?"

He nodded and poured a glass of water for Maria and one for himself. He listened to what she told him, whilst looking at her passport. When she finished, he said: "The policeman was right. This visa doesn't allow any changes. No one can give you an extension. Unfortunately we can't do anything to help you. You have to leave by midnight. I understand your reluctance, but there is no alternative."

"But how is that possible?"

"You had a six-month visa, but it didn't allow you to leave India. Once you left, and before returning, you were given a fourteen days' transit visa, and this is the last day. That's why you have to leave," he explained.

"But I know people who go out of India and then come back without any problems. They go to Nepal, Sri Lanka, always with the same visa," contested Maria.

"It's a different visa, it's called 'triple entry' and allows three entries. But it's not the one you have."

Maria began to tremble, she wanted to cry. She explained the other problem: "I'm waiting for a plane ticket to arrive, they should bring it here. A friend of mine has bought it in Italy, but she thought I needed it in ten days' time."

"What's your name?"

"Maria Dal Fiore." How could she leave Paul like that?

The consul looked in the document tray on his desk and picked up an envelope: "Maria Dal Fiore. This is for you. It was delivered yesterday by a guy named Fulvio. Do you know him?"

Of course she knew him, he was a friend of Ester's. Despite the shock and the disappointment, when she opened the envelope, Maria felt a current of euphoria. There was her ticket, or rather two, with Aeroflot: Delhi-Moscow, Moscow-Milan.

"Is it okay?" asked the consul. She nodded, her heart full of mixed emotions: relief, sadness, gratitude, despair, worry, panic. "Go to the airline office immediately, they may be able to give you a seat for this evening. Otherwise come back here."

Maria looked at him, unable to believe how the situation was developing. Then she nodded again. It was true then, she was leaving, just like that.

"Thank you!" she said, "for everything!" She stood up when the consul did.

He accompanied her to the door; before opening it, he put his hand on her shoulder. "I leave to you the responsibility for your friend!" he said.

"Don't worry about it. Thank you!"

As soon as she stepped out of the office she saw Paul looking at her, as if to say 'What's happening?' His golden hair was like a ray of sunshine, his green eyes full of questions. She smiled faintly. First of all, she had to take care of Franca. "We have to find a scooter for her, then I'll tell you everything!" she said.

"Did they give you an extension?" Maria shook her head. "Does that mean ...?" he couldn't say the words.

"Yes, by tonight." She didn't want to look at him and see the shock in his eyes; she had to be practical and efficient now. "One thing at a time," she said, helping Franca to her feet. She was a dead weight. "Come on Franca, in a little while you'll be able to rest." She didn't resist when Maria held her by the arm and let Paul take her backpack.

As they pushed the glass doors open they were struck by a wave of sweltering heat, but they hardly noticed it. It was a quiet part of Delhi, with no cows, little traffic and trees lining the road, giving a little precious shade. Embassies and consulates had the privilege of being in an area away from the chaos of the capital; it seemed like another world. They waited a couple of minutes, without speaking, before an empty scooter drove up and stopped. Maria helped Franca settle in with her luggage; she was exhausted and unable to do anything for herself.

"Have you got the address?" she asked her. Franca gave her the piece of paper. Maria read the address to the driver, who nodded confidently. She gave him the twenty rupees he asked for and added an extra five rupees. She had plenty of money if she was to leave ten days early.

"When you get there, can you help this girl get inside the building with her luggage?"

"Of course, Madam, don't worry!"

"I entrust her to you."

"Don't worry," the driver reassured her.

Maria put her head inside the scooter cabin and gave Franca a kiss on her gaunt cheek. It seemed strange to kiss her, and she felt distant, but she was doing what she had to do. She was sorry to see her in that state, but also had the distinct feeling that the events taking place were inevitable. Franca had pulled the rope and that, at some point, had snapped. "Maybe I'll see you in Venice. I might be leaving tonight," she said. Franca looked at her; she was completely drained and didn't even have the strength to open her mouth. Maria stroked her cheek and waved her goodbye.

As soon as the scooter left, Paul embraced her. "Is it true, then? No visa?" Maria shook her head. It seemed impossible that this was their last day together. He had become so important to her, she couldn't conceive being without him, going back to Italy. Living in India with Paul had become her life. "I have a ticket, at least. I must go to the Aeroflot office and, if there is a seat, I'll leave tonight. I don't want problems with the police. At this point, I might as well go."

Paul understood; however she could see he was hurting. They hugged each other, unable to find any words to say.

There was no queue and it was cool in the Aeroflot office. Paul sat beside her, while Maria handed her tickets to the clerk: "I ought to leave tonight. Is it possible?"

The young man looked at the computer screen and said: "Yes! The plane leaves at two in the morning. Do you want me to book you a seat?"

The words refused to come out of her mouth, a sour lump in her throat. Maria nodded in silence. She saw Paul stand up, his eyes filled with tears. "I can't stand it," he said. "I'll wait outside!" and left the office, overwhelmed by his emotions.

Maria barely noticed the tears streaming down her cheeks; she wasn't ashamed of crying and didn't care what others thought. She felt she had the right to weep. The clerk looked concerned and shifted his gaze from the computer screen to Maria's face. "Everything okay?"

"It's a difficult day," she replied. "I didn't think I'd have to leave, but at least I have my ticket!" She wiped her eyes and blew her nose.

"You must check in at midnight, at the latest," he said, handing her the two tickets. Maria smiled and thanked him.

Outside the office, Paul couldn't stop crying. Both their faces wet with tears, they looked at each other and burst out laughing.

"All done?" he asked.

"Yes. Midnight at the airport!"

"We have a lot of things to do. What's next?"

"Post Office, then something to eat and then maybe shopping?"

He looked at her with irony: "Maybe we go back to our hotel, before the shopping, if that's okay with you." It was fine with her. A scooter driver who had been watching them approached. Did they want to go somewhere? Yes, to the Main Post Office.

There was a small queue at the Post Restante counter. Maria resigned herself to wait. Was it worth it? She didn't know whether anyone had written to her, perhaps it was better to go, but curiosity got the better of her. There was one letter only, from Jean-Claude. With Paul, she sat on the Post Office steps. She opened the envelope and began to read; it was the answer to the letter she had sent him from Varanasi. In it he told her that he had left Céline, to be free to be with her, that he loved her, but that, above all, he wanted her to be happy. She was a wonderful woman and he wished her all the happiness in the world. In a way, she had helped him make a decision that, sooner or later, would have been necessary. He hoped to find her again one day, indeed he was sure he would. He'd send his love across the universe, with the method they both knew. He loved her so much and hugged her tight.

Maria was weeping profusely, out of sadness, gratitude and love. Paul didn't understand and was worried: "Why are you crying? Has something happened?"

Through her tears, Maria explained the content of the letter: "Why is it that, before nobody wanted me, and now I found two men who love me, both wonderful, and one of them has to suffer?"

Paul put his arm around her shoulders. "I hope you don't have any doubts," he said, serious, watching her closely, "because I don't!"

How could she have any doubts? No one had ever loved her so completely, unconditionally. He wanted to spend the rest of his life with her and she couldn't bear to be parted from him, not even for a day. She shook her head: "I have no doubts. It's just that he was wonderful to me and I owe him much of the happiness I feel right now!"

Paul held her and kissed her hair: "Let's go get something to eat. We have so little time!" They stood up and he kissed her passionately on the steps of New Delhi Main Post Office, unaware of the embarrassed and amused looks from the people walking by.

33. Together

The afternoon sun flooded the covered balcony while the green river in the valley below muffled all noises with the sound of its rush. With uncertain steps, the little child walked toward Maria. She helped him with the last two steps and sat him on her crossed legs. Ashok was very fond of her and she knew he loved it when she scratched his small back. At the Post Office she had found a letter from Ester, which she was now going to read in peace. The child relaxed under the touch of her hand, while she massaged him slowly, absent-mindedly.

"Dear Maria,
By the time you read this letter you'll be back in those mountains while here autumn is approaching. I'm sure you'll be happy there; I know how much you adore that place and its people. A lot of things have happened since you left that I think you'll be interested to know. Franca: since she was repatriated, and after your visit, hardly anyone has seen her. Even Gabriele has little contact with her. He says she doesn't want to see her old friends because we are 'bad people'. No comment! But the most surprising thing for those who know her is that she's got a job outside of Venice. Her father bought her a car and she drives to work every day. The first problem is that she is a Venetian through and through, going back many generations, and drives like one, accustomed to boats and canals rather than roads. The second is that she's not herself any more. The one time I saw her, at first she didn't know who I was. She looked at me for a long while, then she suddenly recognized me and remembered our quarrel. After that she kept her distance, which is fine by me. Her reflexes have visibly slowed down. People ask her a question and she doesn't react, but then, ten minutes later, while they're talking about something else, she suddenly replies to what they had asked her earlier on. She has had at least two road accidents, quite serious, where she hit a couple of people; apparently she hadn't seen them. I don't know what has happened to her, but it's something radical; her personality is unrecognizable. She's gone back to living with her parents. Ironic, to say the least!
I don't know if you are interested in hearing about Ugo. He bought a share of a friend's shop, they sell sports equipment, and he's working

hard. He says he has no time to play guitar, much less the violin. He asked me about you and I told him you're happy. He doesn't let on what he thinks and doesn't say anything, but I have the distinct feeling that your decision to get married took him by surprise, and that he would have liked another chance.

The kitten has grown, he's now a big cat and makes us laugh a lot. I popped into the Art Gallery the other day and they told me they have sold almost all your paintings. I bet you like to paint in those mountains. I want to come and see you, with Enrico of course. Hopefully we can come in the spring for a couple of weeks; I'm already saving the money. I miss you very much. Write soon!

Big hugs to you and to handsome Paul, from your best friend Ester."

Slowly Maria folded the letter. How strange that Franca should have changed so radically. In a sense, she had achieved the exact opposite of what she wanted. When they had left for India, she had declared she wanted to 'get high', 'get out of it', and she had certainly done that, losing herself on the way. She had played with fire, to return to the starting point: work, routine and living at home with mum and dad. Maybe she was happy like that, Maria thought, with the same sad detachment she always felt when thinking of her.

She smiled at Ashok who was now lying on her crossed legs, happy and relaxed. He looked at her with those dark eyes enhanced by kajal and smiled back, showing his four teeth, two above and two below. She caressed his head and he closed his eyes. Ritu joined them, sitting as close as possible to her, and Maria stroked her back. The mountains in front of them were bathed in sunshine. She loved this place, she had loved it from the first day; it was full of peace. Shanti, Madam, shanti, she said to herself with a smile; local people said it all the time. She thought of Ester, in Venice, and of her family. She missed them. For everything there was a price to pay, but she'd see them at least once a year.

Paul came out onto the terrace and sat beside her. He observed Ashok dozing and patted Ritu on the head, then hugged Maria and buried his face in her hair. "I love your scent!" he said. "These children adore you. Good news from Italy?"

"Ester wrote about Franca. It seems that she's no longer the same, and has had two road accidents," she reported.

Paul mused, while stroking her back: "Unfortunately, this is the risk people run when they use certain drugs to excess; also, she may have had underlying problems that have flared up," he said. "I wonder what she took!"

Maria decided she'd chant with renewed determination for Franca's happiness. "Ester is putting money aside to come and visit us in the spring, with Enrico," she said.

Paul smiled: "That would be great. They'll love this place! Tell her we'll come back from Goa early April." He kissed Maria on her hair: "I've finished both articles; I need to stretch my legs and get down to some farming work. If you don't mind, I'll join Telsin in the fields. Later, I'll go and fetch water from the fountain."

She laughed, amused: "Great! You'll make all the women in the village very happy!"

"There's only one woman for me," he replied, grinning and putting on the traditional hat with the coloured stripes on the front. It suited him beautifully, with his blond curls. He bent down on his knees and kissed her again. "I love you!" he said, before going down the steep stairs. The hard work in the fields relaxed him. He liked the quiet company of Pushpa's husband and the other village men, and they were always happy when he joined them in the fields. Everyone liked him and he came home with the produce of the earth, of which he was very proud. Maria loved him more every day and he treated her as if she really was a Treasure Tower. She had finally let go of the insecurity of the past. She was a confident, loved woman, for the first time in her life.

She heard footsteps coming up the wooden staircase and Pushpa's smiling face appeared on the balcony. "Lakri?" she said, waving her hand in the air, as if to unscrew a light bulb. Shall we go and get firewood? She was smiling from ear to ear, with those white teeth and bright eyes.

"Baccha?" Maria said. And the baby?

"Mataji," replied Pushpa; grandmother will look after him.

At the sound of his mother's voice, Ashok began to fidget, looking at her with longing. Ritu ran to hug her and Pushpa stroked her with love. Then she picked up the little boy and kissed him all over, a few minutes of cuddles with her plump healthy child, before handing him over to his grandmother.

Granny came onto the porch, her aching legs crooked at the knees. She was dressed all in white, as was the custom for widows; she had aged a lot in those few months. She opened her arms, welcoming her grandson with her beautiful toothless smile, and kissed him profusely. With him, and followed by Ritu, she sat down cross-legged in front of the tandoori stove, where she was preparing dinner.

Holding on to the banister, they climbed down the stairs and Pushpa went to get the panniers, while Maria quickly gathered her long hair in a braid.

"Lara?" Your husband? Pushpa asked, as soon as she reappeared, with that movement of her hand, fingers up.

"Lara, kama kara, Telsin!" Her husband was working with Telsin.

"Tum, tike?" Pushpa asked, showing, as usual, concern for her.

"Ahan, Ji, tike. Dhanyavad." She was fine, thank you.

"Tum…?" Pushpa asked, miming a flow coming down from between her legs. Their cycle always came at the same time.

"Naih!" replied Maria. Hers hadn't started.

"Naih?" Pushpa said, looking at her, her eyes big with surprise. She stopped in the middle of the path. "Baccha?" she asked, a little boy? Then, leaning backwards, she mimed a huge penis in front of her.

Maria burst out laughing. "Naih!" she said, though she had been feeling 'different' the past couple of weeks. Jokingly, she pushed her hand on Pushpa's private parts and said: "Bacchee," a little girl.

They laughed out loud, happy and free. With this new possibility floating with them, they walked up the steep mountain side, Maria in her faithful jeans and a white t-shirt, Pushpa wrapped in the traditional grey blanket, a red scarf around her neck.

During the night a fierce wind had caused many branches to drop to the ground, making their job very easy. Pushpa stopped in a clearing to catch her breath, laid her pannier down and motioned to Maria to sit on the grass beside her, tapping the ground a couple of times with her hand. "Beto, beto, shanti!" she said.

Hot and sweaty, Maria removed her pannier and sat beside her, her heart pounding from the climb. Taking long deep breaths, she admired the Himalayan valley. She looked around; there was plenty of wood ready to be collected. "Bahut lakri hai!" she said. There's a lot of firewood.

"Ahan, bahut lakri hai!" Pushpa confirmed smiling, rocking her head from side to side, in that funny way. "Brahamanda acchah hai!" The Universe is good, she added.

Maria understood and nodded, smiling. "*Tum* acchah hai!" she said, touching Pushpa's arm with her index finger. *You* are good, great, nice, everything positive that the word 'acchah' could possibly mean.

Her local friend laughed, amused by Maria's Hindi, full of grammatical errors. She leaned toward her and playfully touched Maria's shoulder with hers. After a brief pause, she replied: "Tum *bahut* acchih hai... didi!" You are *very* good... sister.

Smiling happily, they held each other's hand and turned their gaze back to the mountains covered in trees. The honey-coloured light of the late afternoon sparkled on the branches, home to hundreds of busy birds. Maria never tired of the vast, majestic landscape; it was an inexhaustible source of hues, constantly providing new ideas for her paintings. She immersed herself in the simple, genuine life that provided endless inspiration for the stories she had started to write. Never before had she felt so free, so happy and full of gratitude. Out of the corner of her eye she glanced at her friend's profile and smiled, savouring the cool breeze that blew through their hair, tied back in similar braids; Pushpa's black and shiny, Maria's brown and coppery.

THE END

About the Author

Emanuela Cooper (maiden name: Taboga) was born in Treviso, Italy on 18th November 1953. She studied foreign languages in Venice and Political Science at the University of Padua. Following a difficult time in her life, she made her first visit to India in 1978, where she began to rediscover herself.

Over the following five years she travelled extensively throughout India, Sri Lanka and Nepal and spent longer periods of time in the mountains of Himachal Pradesh and near the beaches of Goa.

In 1983 she moved to England with her husband, settling in Nottingham until 2011. They are currently based in London, with frequent trips to Ibiza, where most of this novel was written. Since 1992 Emanuela has been practicing Buddhism and is a member of Soka Gakkai International (SGI), a lay Buddhist movement for the realization of peace through culture and education.

If you'd like further information on Buddhism see: www.sgi-uk.org, or www.sgi-usa.org

To contact the author you can write to: manucooper53@gmail.com

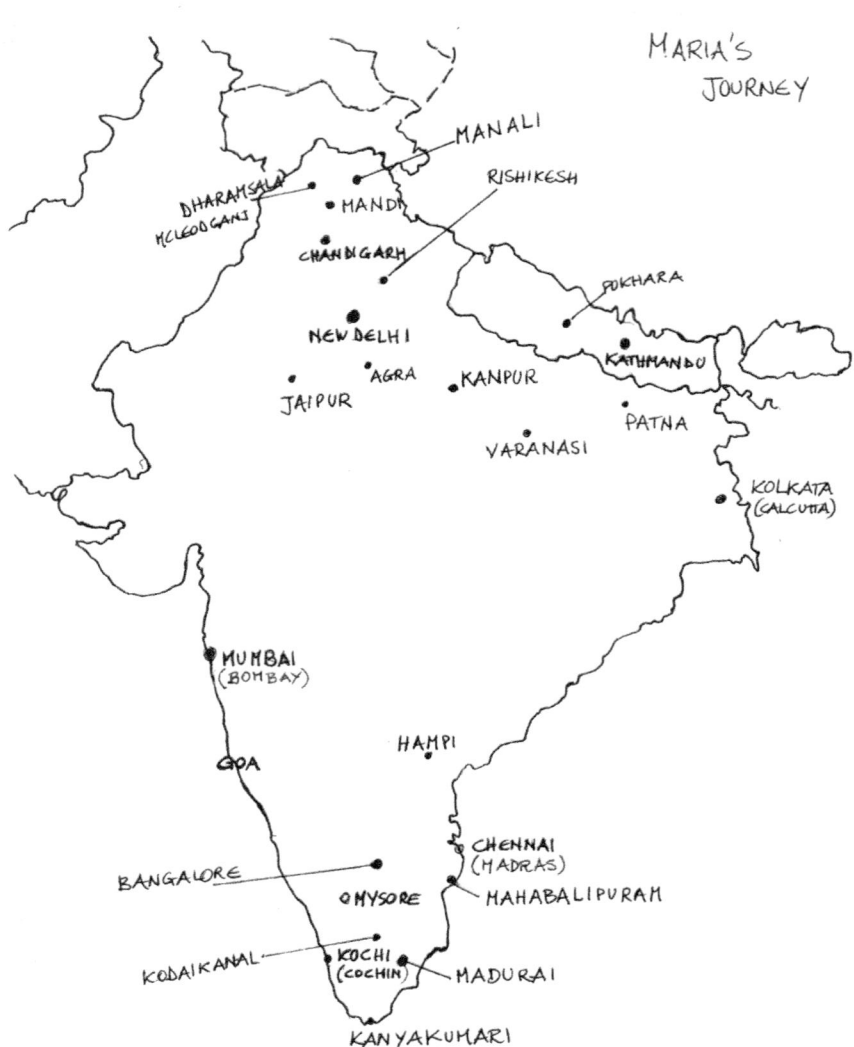

Printed in Great Britain
by Amazon